Praise for
A BLIGHT OF BLACKWINGS

"So strong it is very easy to become immersed . . . Kevin Hearne is continuing to prove how earned his reputation is as storyteller at the top of his game who is continuing to push his storytelling skills to new heights. *A Blight of Blackwings* is an immensely entertaining, rewarding, and powerful novel. The two books of the trilogy so far are proving that there are still new spins to be spun in the tried-and-true Fantasy genre and that through much of what may seem to be a dark time, human connection is still a potent assurance of hope."

—*SFFWorld*

"Elements mesh perfectly, presenting an inventive, eye-filling panorama; satisfying (and, where appropriate, well-resolved) plotlines . . . A charming and persuasive entry that will leave readers impatiently awaiting the concluding volume."

—*Kirkus Reviews*

T0112784

Praise for
A PLAGUE OF GIANTS

"A spectacular work of epic fantasy . . . *A Plague of Giants* is a roller coaster, a whirlwind and an absolute delight, and will leave fans of epic fantasy hungry for the next installment in the Seven Kennings series."

—*Shelf Awareness*

"If you're looking for some entertainment before *Game of Thrones* returns to television, this could be the series you need to read."

—*Newsday*

"There's a great deal of depth to this world, from its deep history, its magic, its characters and how they all come together rather organically. . . . The easiest and most apt comparison is to Patrick Rothfuss's Kingkiller Chronicle."

—*SFFWorld*

"A genuine page-turner . . . vividly described, moves briskly, and features a splendid climax."

—*Kirkus Reviews*

BY KEVIN HEARNE

INK & SIGIL

Ink & Sigil *Paper & Blood*

THE SEVEN KENNINGS

A Plague of Giants
A Blight of Blackwings
A Curse of Krakens

THE IRON DRUID CHRONICLES

Hounded *Hunted*
Hexed *Shattered*
Hammered *Staked*
Tricked *Besieged*
Trapped *Scourged*

THE IRON DRUID CHRONICLES NOVELLAS

Two Ravens and One Crow *A Prelude to War*
Grimoire of the Lamb *First Dangle and Other Stories*

OBERON'S MEATY MYSTERIES

The Purloined Poodle
The Squirrel on the Train
The Buzz Kill (in the anthology *Death & Honey*)

BY DELILAH S. DAWSON AND KEVIN HEARNE

THE TALES OF PELL

Kill the Farm Boy
No Country for Old Gnomes
The Princess Beard

A CURSE OF KRAKENS

A CURSE OF KRAKENS

BOOK THREE OF THE SEVEN KENNINGS

KEVIN HEARNE

NEW YORK

2024 Del Rey Mass Market Edition

Copyright © 2023 by Kevin Hearne

Published in the United States by Del Rey,
an imprint of Random House, a division of
Penguin Random House LLC, New York.

DEL REY and the CIRCLE colophon are registered trademarks of
Penguin Random House LLC.

Originally published in hardcover in the United States
by Del Rey, an imprint of Random House, a division of
Penguin Random House LLC, in 2023.

ISBN 9780345548665
Ebook ISBN 9780345548658

Printed in the United States of America on acid-free paper

randomhousebooks.com

2 4 6 8 9 7 5 3 1

Del Rey mass market edition: August 2024

*To Chuck & Delilah
and everyone who hopes to breathe peace*

Pogledajte ostrvske države, izolovane okeanima koji vrve od opasnih stvorenja. Iako krakeni nestaju na par meseci krajem leta, uvek postoje ajkule, jegulje i lavovski kitovi oko kojih treba brinuti.

"Behold the island nations, isolated by oceans teeming with dangerous creatures. Though the krakens disappear for a couple of months in late summer, there are always bladefins, eels, and lion whales to worry about."

Ajkule će napasti čamce u arhipelagu.

"Bladefins will attack boats in the archipelago."

PELES OKEAN

Brda

Ecula

AJKULA

Volá Vták

Konsky Trus

Baraní Roh

Vlnená Látka

Oveči Sen

Vlast

Sedam Záhrad

1.

Bokombrady

Drvo

Kotao

Slivovi

Tichá

Zeleno Kej

Siguran

Sveto Selo

Pustovna

2.

Zátva

Riba Oči

Mesto Kávy

Spása

Kôrovcovy Záliv

Brusnica

3.

Ustricové Lôžko

Lišajník Skalny

Obilia

Uska Luka

Kolíska Kostí

Žitnica

1. Školjka Zaliv
2. Jegulja Zaliv
3. Vidra Zaliv

Gondel's translations:
1. Clamshell Bay
2. Eel Bay
3. Otter Bay

Ecula je prokleta krakenima.

"Ecula is cursed with krakens."

Joabei

Poeshi

Godeuleum

Weidoeng

Chagaun Mul
Eomang
Gulbawi
Saeu Kobeu
Bada Jugeo

Yeonseong
Mugsang
Eosijang

Deungdae
Goyo
Ojingeo Meoli

Miseuteulal

Haddik

Tashind

Koesha says that means
Tortoise Islands; they
are populated by Joabeian
fishing villages.

Goebugi Seom

A R H I P E L A G

Bikkam

Vassur

Geffert

Mozend

According to Koesha, most
Omeshan cities are under-
ground. There is one port
city per island, but scattered
small villages too.

Safrett

Kashy

Omesh

LARIK OKEAN

"Beware the
cavern-jawed
eels."

Čuvajte se pećina-gubica jegulja.

Gondel says the words in the rose
translate to "abandon regret, seek joy."

UBILAČKI OKEAN

That is the same as Ocean

Bačiis

Sutrin

Želanie

Uporište
(Stronghold)

Odlazak
(Exodus)

Plashilo

Skloniše
(Refuge)

Pozharna

Daždivy

Sguriya

Vlažna

Map by Kevin Hearne

Dramatis Personae

FINTAN, BARD OF THE POET GODDESS KAELIN: Raelech bard assigned by the Triune Council to entertain Pelemyn until the allied counterattack.

DERVAN DU ALÖBAR: Brynt historian who writes down the Raelech bard's tales and assembles other sources into this chronicle of the Seven Kennings.

PEN YAS BEN MIN: Fornish greensleeve eager to escape the shadow of her famous cousin, Nel Kit ben Sah.

DARYCK DU LÖNGREN: Brynt leader of the Grynek Hunters, a mercenary company bent on vengeance for the destruction of their city.

GONDEL VEDD: Kaurian language scholar who is fond of mustard, Mugg's Chowder House, and old stories of the Rift.

HANIMA BHANDURY: Nentian hivemistress who led a revolution and now struggles to bear the adulation of the people of Khul Bashab.

ABHINAVA KHOSE: A plaguebringer of the Sixth Kenning traveling the world with his companions, Murr and Eep. Hopes to return home someday, where his heart resides.

NARA DU FESSET: Brynt gerstad, a trusted rapid in the pelenaut's service, and lifebond of the Mynstad du Möcher.

KOESHA GANSU: Joabeian zephyr and captain of the *Nentian Herald,* determined to complete her historic circumnavigation of the globe.

TALLYND DU BÖLL: Tidal mariner and second könstad of Brynlön's military, worried that her duties will push her to a final sacrifice and leave her boys orphaned.

HOLLIT PANEVIK: Hathrim firelord who is the head chef of the Roasted Sunchuck in Pelemyn, forced by circumstance to use her kenning for martial purposes.

FANJE: Eculan member of Šest, a resistance group dedicated to toppling the cult of Žalost in Ecula.

A CURSE OF KRAKENS

Day 40

SAGE AND SPROUT

Somewhat unusually, I had a morning meeting scheduled with the bard to record the previous day's tales. Fintan had heard about a place that was new to us both, an inn on the north side of town that the shingle proclaimed to be THE GASPING GILLS. That caused me to wonder what sort of air quality I might find inside, but as I saw no one staggering out, coughing or wheezing or, indeed, gasping, I figured I could risk it.

The interior proved to be much more pleasant than I expected, because I thought there'd be fish heads strewn about and vomit stains on the floor: That's the power of names. But the tables and floor were spotless, and there were small vases with wildflowers quivering in them from a gentle breeze wafting through the place. There was a large fire in the hearth for heat, but they'd designed the building with some Kaurian touches regarding the air circulation, which meant that it was probably the best possible place to spend time indoors when it was still chilly out in the mornings.

Fintan was at a table along the western wall, equidistant from the hearth and the door, and they had bench seating, which gave my bad knee a bit of trouble. Once I groaned and eased myself into place, Fintan apologized and said we'd not meet there again.

"There's no need for you to be inconvenienced, Dervan," he said. "There are plenty of places that have heard of chairs."

A young woman came out from the kitchen with tea and beamed at us as she put down the pot and cups and saucers. "Morning, men. Here for breakfast?"

"Sounds fabulous," I said. "What's on the menu?"

"Oh, I just told you the whole thing, love. We have breakfast. It's chef's choice these days, and we don't have a lot of choice, you know? We take what we can get."

"Fair enough. I think we'll have breakfast, then?"

Fintan nodded enthusiastically. "Can't wait. Thank you."

Her smile widened. "No complaints? Oh, I like you two. Coming right up."

"The shortages are becoming worrisome," Fintan said as she departed, "but I think the element of surprise is a bit fun. Breakfast could be brilliant."

"Or it could be a horrific sludge of porridge."

"True. But I find hopeful anticipation to be quite nourishing." He poured us each a cup of tea, the steam swirling attractively above them, and asked if I wanted to get right to work or to relax a bit.

"No, we can get started," I said. But I'd no sooner gotten out my pen and ink than we were interrupted by the arrival of a Raelech courier and another bard. I recognized the stones on her Jereh band and realized I'd never seen two bards together before.

She introduced herself as Eimear and said she'd come to share many developments in Ghurana Nent.

Fintan's eyes widened in delight. "You have updates on Hanima Bhandury and Tamhan Khatri?"

"Yes, but more important, Pen Yas ben Min."

"Pen? The cousin of Nel Kit ben Sah?"

"The very same. If I'm correct, she's going to be one of the most famous Fornish people in history."

"Seriously? She was just a kid, newly blessed."

"Aye, but blessed as a greensleeve. You're going to want to hear this."

"Absolutely." Fintan turned to me. "Dervan, my apologies, but this sounds like something I must hear sooner rather than later. We can catch up another time, right?"

"Of course, but I have a question. Why are you here?" I asked Eimear.

Somewhat taken aback, she extended an index finger toward her countryman. "To update Fintan."

"Yes, but why?"

"The Triune Council ordered it. I have spent some time in Talala Fouz, where much has been happening. When I returned recently to Rael and reported what I learned to them, they said Brynlön must know also, and I was to repeat everything to Fintan so he could include it in his tale of the Giant Wars."

"His . . . Wait—his tale is something the Triune Council is so concerned about that they'd send you here with a courier to update him?"

"It is."

"Again: Why? It seems like an extraordinary expenditure of your resources."

Fintan answered for her. "You and I haven't gotten to the part where the council ordered me here, but we will soon. Suffice to say that they feel this tale is important for both our nations and a key part of Rael's support for Brynlön."

Eimear nodded. "And of course they're aware that you are writing it down, Master du Alöbar, adding your own historical notes, and they are hopeful they'll get to read the completed version someday as a joint project between allied nations."

I wasn't so sure they'd be thrilled to read my additions where I was supposed to counter Fintan as a suspected spy, all while we'd had a Bone Giant operating as our master of spies for years, and he'd painted a target on Clodagh's back and pointed me at her like a weapon, assuming I'd want to avenge my wife's supposed assassination at her hands. I knew now that the Wraith had fed me lies, of course, but that didn't change the fact that much of what I'd written might be incredibly embarrassing to us. And to me personally.

Or it might bring a refreshing chance for honesty and dialogue and allow us to move forward together more productively. I couldn't know for sure. But one way or another, Pelenaut Röllend would eventually have to answer for some questionable choices he'd made. Answer to Rael, of course, but also answer to me.

"Very well. I assume you'll be occupied for some time?"

"Yes. There is much to share."

"I'll leave you to it, then, and I'll see you on the wall later, Fintan. You can have my breakfast, Eimear—I'll grab something elsewhere."

That freed up my morning, and I decided to spend it trying to hunt down either Rölly or his lung, Föstyr du Bertrum, to get some answers regarding the intelligence I'd received yesterday from Dame Nyssa du Valas—namely, that Sarena's assassination had come at the hands of the Nentian ambassador, Jasindur Torghala, whom Rölly had expelled, and that her poisoning had been ordered by none other than the shitsnake Melishev Lohmet, former viceroy of Hashan Khek and current monarch of Ghurana Nent. Rölly had known both of those facts and hadn't told me. He'd even sent a hygienist to Ghurana Nent recently who might wind up curing the loathsome murderer of his wasting disease.

Nyssa had explained that the ambassador had to be expelled for something else to keep her role in the embassy a secret, but that didn't explain why these secrets had been kept from me—especially when Rölly had a month's worth of opportunities to tell me and chose instead to let me believe the Wraith's lie that Clodagh had something to do with it.

Unless Dame Nyssa wasn't who she said she was at all and everything she told me was a fabrication. I supposed I'd need to confirm her identity and her story. But it had the ring of plausibility to it, whereas anything from the Wraith had to be suspect. I needed to see either the pelenaut or the lung to ascertain whether this was true.

My attempts to gain an audience, however, were curtly rebuffed at the palace. Both men were impossibly busy, and no matter how important I thought my news, they simply could not see me. I could leave a message with the mariner if I wanted.

That was some chum and shit right there. I just left word that I needed to see Rölly urgently and stalked away as best as I could on my tender knee to help at the refugee kitchen outside the city walls. It would allow me to wreak unholy vengeance upon some innocent vegetables, and besides, it seemed to be where I got my best information now.

Halfway through a rather small mountain of sad potatoes, I realized that if Eimear had been at Talala Fouz recently, she could have told me if Melishev Lohmet was still alive or not. I'd been so distracted I hadn't thought to ask.

The potatoes were finished long before I'd run out of anger, but it did make me wonder if the chef wanted a thin soup today or if our supplies were dwindling.

"Dwindling," Chef du Rödal confirmed. "I'm rationing what little we have left. I'm told there aren't any ships coming for a while, so we have to make things stretch. A lot."

That was disturbing. Tomorrow morning I would have my last toast from my current loaf of bread. It occurred to me to wonder whether it might also be my last loaf. A trip to the bakery confirmed that it was, for now.

"We're out of flour, sorry," the baker said. "We'll bake again as soon as we get some grain."

Ominous indeed.

I had plenty of reason to be frowning when I went to the wall that afternoon, and I am sure I wasn't the only one. By now, those who weren't already hungry knew that they would be soon. That sort of awareness tends to drown one's good spirits.

But Fintan did his best to cheer everyone up. Before the

day's tales, he introduced Eimear, who was going to perform a duet with him, and I must confess it was sublime to hear two trained voices in harmony. They performed a quick-tempo song in which we were supposed to grab a partner, clasp hands in front of us, and circle as quickly as possible, growing dizzy, until someone lost their balance and fell. This was not an activity I could participate in with my bad knee, but I was highly amused watching everyone else. The bards were essentially singing the same thing over and over with only small variations in lyrics but with great variations in their harmonies. It was magnificent.

Round and around and around we go,
Enjoying the dizziness ever so,
We don't know when we'll all fall down,
But we'll laugh and get off the ground
And thennnn . . .
We!
Will!
Go!
Round and around and around again,
We've been dizzy since way back when,
We don't know when we'll all fall down,
But we'll laugh and get off the ground!

"Friends, I've just received some remarkable updates from the west, thanks to Eimear, and I know many of you have been curious about what's been going on there. I have plenty to share, but it's going to require that I jump back in time for a while to catch us up. We're heading back to the month of Amber, in fact, and these tales will have some references to events I've already related, but from a new perspective, that of Pen Yas ben Min. Do you remember her? She's a Fornish greensleeve. On day two, I shared with you the story of her seeking. Her brother, Yar Tup Min, was killed by a Hathrim houndsman when the Fornish first discovered Gorin Mogen's illegal settlement of Baghra Khek."

Fintan threw down one of his black spheres—I saw that his bag of them had been resupplied by Eimear—and took on a new form: a young Fornish woman, pale-skinned, blond hair braided in multiple strands and pinned with blue and white flowers, which matched a waistcoat in blue and white rather than the browns and greens that greensleeves were often seen wearing. Her kinship to Nel was clear, but she had a visible independence.

Pen

Threaded throughout the tales of ancient Fornish heroes is the idea that the only thing capable of casting a greater shadow than the forest is one's own legacy. The famous riddle from *Leafsong*, by grassglider poet Nat Huf ben Zon, is a prime example. Sage and Sprout are walking through a hazel orchard, and Sage smiles gently and gestures around:

—*Tell me, Sprout: Without water, soil, or sun, what is always growing, always swelling?*

—*Legends, Sage, can grow ever larger with retelling.*

I have always loved that passage, because it's one of only four times that Sprout provides the correct answer on the first try. I used to think it was a warning against believing everything you hear or perhaps against elevating yourself above everyone else, but I see the bloom of literal truth in it now. My cousin, Nel Kit ben Sah, has grown far larger in death than she ever was in life.

When I first heard of her death—sacrificing herself to take down the hearthfire Gorin Mogen—I was of course wilted by grief that she was gone and burdened with guilt that I had not fought by her side, even though I'd been ordered to stay behind. She had taken me to my seeking, and when I was newly blessed as a greensleeve and writhing in pain, she took me up above the Canopy to bask in the sun for the first time. Nel was kind and fierce and honorable and an example to follow, in addition to being my most beloved cousin.

Later, I was grateful for the recognition she received for her service to the Canopy. It was (and is) well deserved: She immediately proved herself worthy when the First Tree named her Champion. I could not be more proud of her. And I was grateful, too, for the prestige and honor she conferred to the White Gossamer Clan.

But now—while all the rest is still true—I confess to feeling like the smallest shoot struggling underneath a silverbark. I am no longer Pen Yas ben Min so much as the cousin of Nel Kit ben Sah. People who meet me are awed and respectful and their eyes sparkle with dew, but not because of my wit or beauty or anything I have done. I am the blood relative of Forn's newest culture heroine, and that is all.

That has led to far more romantic overtures than I was used to before, but the reason for it is transparent and therefore unappealing. Is it petty or selfish to wish that I be appreciated for simply being Pen and not Nel's cousin? I feel like I am being both, even though no one has said or even implied as much. And on top of that, I also feel as if I cannot trust anyone outside my clan, because whatever favor or deference I'm given is unearned. Smiles are not for me but for her; the air I breathe is almost visibly choked with deceit, like pollen floating in springtime sunbeams.

To get out of a shadow grown larger than the Canopy itself, I realized I must first leave the Canopy. So when I joined the sway recently at the Second Tree in Pont, I asked for a mission that would allow me to leave Forn. Something that would serve the Canopy first, of course—perhaps a mission to expand the Canopy's influence north of the border. The idea was received well in general but there was no immediate notion of a specific mission, and I went back to patrolling Nel's old patch until a message came through root and stem a week later: I was to bid farewell to my family and meet Vet Mof ben Tam of the Gray Squirrel Clan in Pont. He would give me an assignment in the north.

My parents were tearful yet proud; my friends were happy for me but a little envious too. They wouldn't mind an escape from Nel's shadow either.

I was quivering like a wind-shook branch when I found ben Tam. He was in the Gray Squirrel tea treehouse on a private clan deck, alternately puffing on a hardwood pipe and sipping tea from a honey-laced porcelain cup. Coils of white smoke played about his head, and when I introduced myself, he gestured to a cushion next to him, inviting me to sit.

He was a culturist who specialized in remedies for crop blights, retired now, face weathered and tanned from years in the sun. He'd grown wealthy, judging by the iridescent silver and gold silk robe he wore over his tunic—some of it embroidered with spider silk from my clan. He liked to smirk around his pipe stem and waggle his bushy eyebrows about.

"Ahh, I can smell adventure in your future," he said. "Let's get you some tea and talk of pleasant nothings. Once we know we won't be interrupted, we can talk of knots and knurls."

"Pleasant nothings, eh? We can speak of poetry if you like, which is pleasant but not nothing."

The smirk intensified. "I've heard you like to quote ben Zon. Are you an aficionado of Sage and Sprout?" When I nodded, he chuckled a bit, and it turned into a gentle cough. He begged my pardon and reached for his teacup. He took a couple of long swallows before replacing it with a muted clink on the saucer. "Let's see if I can remember some. *Tell me, Sprout: How can a soft and blunted mind become keen?*"

I knew the answer and smiled. *"Leave the familiar, Sage, and seek the unseen."*

"Ahh, that's right. It's an apt reminder, especially as one ages. I should cast off my routine and get myself uncomfortable, to be honest. I am far too content and pampered these days." A server arrived on the deck with two fresh pots of tea and asked me how I took it. I said I took it like ben Tam, and she painted lines of honey from a jar in both our cups before pouring hot tea into them, and we thanked her. When she left us, the foliage around the deck shifted into an impenetrable thicket through which we could not be seen or even heard, so long as we kept our voices low.

"You see? Pampered," he said. We both drank from the fresh cups and, politeness being observed, got to business.

"Thank you, ben Tam, for this opportunity. You and all the Gray Squirrels," I said. "I'm ready to serve however I can."

"I see that you are, ben Min. But this assignment is neither my doing nor my clan's. I am merely the messenger. This assignment comes from the First Tree."

I just stared at him, dumbstruck, which he found amusing. He puffed on his pipe, and his grin partially disappeared in a cloud of smoke.

"Why don't you have some tea while you think of what to say?"

That wasn't needed. "I will of course do whatever the First Tree requires."

"Ha! Good answer. How long are you prepared to stay away from the Canopy?"

Shrugging my shoulders, I said, "As long as necessary."

"Another good answer. This may take anywhere from weeks to years." Ben Tam reached into a pocket of his silk robe and withdrew a small pouch tied with a strip of leather. Leaning forward, he placed it ever so gently on the table between us, as if it carried something rare and fragile.

"What's that?"

"Oh, I'm anxious to hear you guess. I can tell you now, I would never guess correctly if our positions were reversed."

"Is it a carved miniature, an art piece to be given to someone important in the north?"

"Not bad, but I would have guessed that myself. Try again."

"You're a culturist, so maybe this is a new hybrid seed of some crop the First Tree wants planted in the north?"

His brows shot up. "That's surprisingly close but only half right. The First Tree does want you to plant this in the north. But it's not a crop, my dear. No, what's in that bag is an acorn. A very rare, very special silverbark acorn."

My jaw dropped. "Not an acorn of the First Tree?"

"Exactly that. And the First Tree wants *you*, ben Min, to take this acorn north of the Canopy and plant it somewhere. Your assignment is nothing less than to plant the Fourth Tree."

"But . . . I'm barely an adult."

The old man waggled his head back and forth. "Eh, I think the First Tree is aware, having blessed you."

"Where am I supposed to plant it?"

"That's up to you, Sprout. Seek the unseen."

"You're joking. Something this important can't be my decision."

"Oh, it can. It most certainly is, because you can be sure the Gray Squirrels inquired on just that point. The First Tree said you would know where to plant it when the time comes."

"So you can give me no guidance whatsoever?"

"Sure I can. Head north."

"But where—Ghurana Nent, Rael, or Brynlön?" Forn spanned the continent, so *north* was an incredibly vague direction.

"As I said, that's entirely up to you."

"Why me? Why now?"

"Those are questions we also asked, but the First Tree did not answer them. You now know everything that I know, except that this is to be kept secret. Make up whatever excuse you want for your travels, but tell no one you are on any kind of errand for the First Tree."

A terror grew within me as I considered the small bag. "Ben Tam . . . what if I lose it?"

"Don't do that." He chuckled again, more heartily, and thankfully without coughing. "This is history, you know, happening right now. I'm sending a young woman off in secret to plant the Fourth Tree, and I won't be able to tell anyone about it until you've done the job."

"It's not much of a moment. I don't even know where to begin."

"There's a ship leaving in the morning for the north. You should be on it."

"How do I manage that?"

Ben Tam clenched his pipe with his teeth to free up a hand to slip into his other pocket, this time taking out a much heavier pouch. The kind that jingled with the music of coins. He took considerably less care putting that on the table.

"Money helps manage most things. The Red Pheasant Clan is shipping personnel up to Batana Mar Din and then Talala Fouz to staff some new tea treehouses they're building around the country. They should have a bunk for you. Disembark wherever you feel like it. You can even head upriver and across to Rael if you want."

Pointing to the purse, I said, "Is that a loan?"

"No, it's your traveling expenses and some pay from the government of Forn rather than your clan. Should you require more, you can replenish these funds—within reason— at our embassies. Word's going out to all the northern ambassadors that you're to be given whatever you need. Just show up and ask."

I didn't know what to say, so I reached for my tea, which earned some approval.

"It's wise to cultivate an open ear," ben Tam said. "That should serve you well. What other languages do you speak besides Fornish?"

"Nentian and some Hathrim, like many westerners."

He waved a hand dismissively. "Ah. You'll be fine, then. As long as you get some sleep. Boat leaves at dawn, but I'd head down to the docks now to arrange passage."

"I'll let that bloom in its own time," I said. "If this is indeed a historic moment, I'd like to pause and appreciate it." I leaned forward and refilled our teacups from the pots. *"Tell me, Sprout: What can never be held yet still must be taken?"*

Vet Mof ben Tam's features broadened in delight, then contracted in thought. "A challenge! I should know this, let me see—ah! *That would be time, Sage, lest our joy in life be shaken."*

I nodded in approval. "You know your ben Zon."

"It is not merely a masterpiece for the young. His words still resonate in elder years. They change, in fact, like autumn leaves, becoming richer as one's understanding and experience infuse the words with new notes."

And then we sat in silence for a half hour, enjoying our tea, meditating companionably as Sage and Sprout used to do in *Leafsong*. It was unlikely that ben Tam and I would meet again in this life—the fact that our branches entwined at all was remarkable—so the taking of time and tea was a custom I appreciated now, though I couldn't stand it as a child. I hadn't the perspective when I was younger to see how fleeting our lives could be, nor to appreciate the vast complexity of a living forest and its creatures, all striving to prosper under the Canopy. Taking the time to notice, to appreciate the importance of others and how we all contribute to life, makes perfect sense to me now. We all matter.

The smells of the treehouse—layers and layers of them,

pleated over the years—nestled deeply into my memory, for I understood that this truly was an important moment for me personally, if not in a broader historical sense. The likelihood that I would return to the Canopy soon—if at all—was very low. There was no chance of me planting the acorn of the First Tree and simply walking away, letting the Fourth Tree fend for itself. And though the Red Pheasant Clan might be growing tea treehouses in Ghurana Nent, they wouldn't be like this one, which had lived in the Canopy for centuries now. And regardless of how old a treehouse in Ghurana Nent might be, there wouldn't be kindly retired culturists from the Gray Squirrels willing to trade lines of my favorite poetry with me. I'd wished to live out of Nel's shadow, and my wish had been granted in a remarkably unexpected way.

The urge not to leave was strong, because the unknown and unseen are fearsome. But I'd already determined that I couldn't grow here anymore. It was time to find my place in the sun.

With a sigh, I signaled to ben Tam that I was ready to bid farewell. He opened his eyes, emerging from the quiet meditation, and gave me a tiny smile and a nod. I returned it, then took the two bags he'd deposited on the table.

"You have my eternal gratitude, ben Tam. May you and your clan always be blessed with an abundant harvest."

"Grow strong and stout, ben Min," he replied. "Thank you for enduring what lies ahead for the good of the Canopy."

I rose from the cushion and bowed deeply, as before an honored elder. He chuckled and said, "Go on, then, Sprout. Become a legend worth retelling, like your cousin."

My eyes blurred briefly with tears as I made my way to the exit. Reaching out with my kenning, I asked the wall of leaves to part, and they did. I gave thanks to all the teahouse staff as I exited, then made my way to my lodgings to pick up my

travel pack before heading to the docks. There was no way I'd
be able to sleep. Might as well be about it.

The Red Pheasant boat was easy enough to find with a
few queries, and there was plenty of activity on board even
though the hour was late. Enchanted firebowls played warm
light over dark wood. The captain had been warned I'd be
coming, and passage was easy to arrange. I dropped my travel
bag on my assigned bunk and pitched in where I could, once
I convinced everyone I wasn't just being polite but truly
wanted to help.

Most of the people on board were young like me, and
most of the cargo was tea for the teahouses. And most of us,
once we got under way, became violently ill before the day
was out.

Coming from a clan where no one ever sailed or had
much contact with sailors, I did not even know seasickness
was a thing. I learned as I joined a line of people along the
rails vomiting into the ocean that the Fornish were unusually
susceptible to it, and the experienced sailors gave us little pills
to help with the nausea. A few lucky ones didn't require any,
and the captain explained apologetically that, to conserve
supply, he needed to know who would get sick and who
wouldn't. He promised that after a few days we wouldn't
need the pills anymore, but we'd be fair-to-middling miserable in the meantime until our bodies adjusted.

My respect for sailors grew immeasurably during that
time, since merely existing on a ship at sea, let alone working
on one, was exhausting.

When we passed the site where Nel had died, I dug into
my pack for a special pouch of soil. I sprouted some poppy
seeds in a handful of it and let the wind take the flowers in
remembrance of her and all the Fornish who'd died there
protecting the Canopy. Since the Red Pheasants had some
clan members involved in that operation, I named them as
well.

We arrived at Batana Mar Din some days later, disgorging a few of the passengers and a good portion of tea, while taking on a single new passenger and some supplies for Talala Fouz, where most of the Red Pheasants were heading. I had to decide whether to disembark or carry on, and it was the new passenger who convinced me to keep going. He was a greensleeve for the Red Pheasants, Mak Fin ben Fos, who greeted me in a pub near the docks while the crew enjoyed some shore leave. He invited me to sit at his table, bought me an ale, and had much to tell me of the Sixth Kenning.

Mak was an astoundingly handsome man but clearly had no intention of flirting, which was a relief. He was enamored of Ambassador Mai Bet Ken, who had masterminded the idea of the tea treehouses that Mak was growing and his clan was staffing. This was Ambassador Ken's way of furthering the Canopy's interests in Ghurana Nent, because she believed the Canopy had serious stakes to pursue now.

"Economically, you mean?" I asked.

"Of course, of course. On both sides of the border. Combining the Fifth Kenning with the Sixth? Immense potential there. But we have security issues to address first, wouldn't you agree?"

I couldn't believe that he was speaking so frankly of such things with me, but then I remembered that I was a greensleeve of the newly prestigious White Gossamer Clan, and therefore my word would count for something in the sway, should he need an ally.

"I might agree," I said, "but I confess to being unschooled in the root system of Nentian politics. Please forgive my ignorance, ben Fos."

He waved it off. "Nonsense. I'm talking at you like you've been here and seen what I have seen. What brings you to the country, if I'm not prying? Is there some way I can help?"

"Clan business," I replied, mindful of ben Tam's admonition to keep my true purpose secret. "But nothing that would compete with yours," I hastened to add. "The White Gossamers are not into the tea industry at all. We only have our own clan teahouse in our lands, and I believe all of our teas are imported from your clan, now that I think of it." I didn't volunteer anything else, and he didn't pursue it. "I think it would be good to know more about our security interests here, if you feel like expanding on that."

"Happy to." He said that political upheaval would continue as the Sixth Kenning became more widespread, but it was difficult to know whether the current monarchy would remain in power or if something new would replace it. Regardless of who wound up in charge of Ghurana Nent, we wanted to make sure that they had no cause to threaten the Canopy, so we were dangling from fragile branches now.

"I've just come from Khul Bashab, where a decent-sized force was repelled by just a few of these beast callers. That gave me hope, because they have the people's interests at heart and a concern for the natural world. But there's a very large army on the way, and I don't know if they'll be able to hold against that."

"An army sent by the king?"

"That's right. King Kalaad the Unwell."

"And you're going to see him?"

"Not exactly. I'm heading to the capital—you heard it was burned down by Winthir Kanek?"

"Yes."

"We're rebuilding the Fornish embassy, and I still have to grow the teahouses upriver that all the workers on that ship are meant for. Plus, Ambassador Ken would like an update on what's happening in Khul Bashab, and I'm hoping I can explore a little bit of the Gravewood at some point."

"You've seen the Gravewood? What's it like?"

"Very different from the Canopy. Magnificent trees— more evergreens than leafy. Poisonous plants a far cry from what we're familiar with. And animals a good deal more vicious than what we're used to—I'd stay close to the river, just to get a taste of root and stem. But after you see so much of the plains around here, it's comforting to witness those stands of trees."

"I think I'd like to see that too."

"Excellent! It will be pleasant to have another greensleeve to talk to. Speaking of which: Since you're from the White Gossamer Clan, did you by any chance know Nel Kit ben Sah personally?"

I laughed in his face and immediately felt guilty for it, apologizing profusely. The truth was, I had been laughing at myself for thinking I could escape a legend.

Okay, she was delightful. And I would clearly need to get to the library to see if they had any copies of *Leafsong* lying about.

Anticipating my thoughts and no doubt those of many others, Fintan said as he returned to himself, "I believe the library has only two translated copies of *Leafsong* available, but if any private citizens have copies and would care to share, I'm sure you'd have no trouble finding someone who'd like to read it. But let's continue with one of your home-grown heroes, shall we?"

He changed his seeming to Gerstad Daryck du Löngren of the Grynek Hunters, and the people on Survivor Field roared a greeting.

Daryck

My request for a meeting with the quartermaster of Fornyd, Farlen du Cannym, was not immediately granted. I had to wait a couple of days, and I supposed it made sense: We weren't quite in the same military situation that we were before, and she had greater problems to worry about than what a group of broken hunters might want.

Still, it galled me somewhat. I recognized the need for cleanup—bodies upriver needed to be sent downriver if the cities were ever going to be habitable again—but emotionally I wanted something to do other than the logical, necessary thing.

The surviving members of the Grynek Hunters wanted it too. We were being confronted with our losses to the Bone Giants on a daily basis, and as a result we were sleeping poorly, having nightmares, and behaving extra politely to one another in that obvious pained way that suggested we'd much rather throttle our friends than speak to them. And we had lost our rapid and longtime friend, Sören du Hyller, to grief.

Before our last cleanup run to Grynek, he'd left me a note that he could not continue. The color and savor of life had all drained away since he'd discovered his family slain by the Bone Giants, and he was grateful for the joy I'd brought while he could still feel it, but now he was sorry, he was going home to the sea. I remembered that when we'd first discovered the aftermath of the invasion, we had wrapped up his family's remains together and taken them to the funeral barge, and he hadn't shed a tear. He'd assured me that he was grieving deeply in his own way, and I believed him. But I wished I'd been able to tell just how damaged he was. Perhaps I could have said or done something to make him stay.

Or, more simply: We could have done something other than return again and again to the source of our pain. So when one of the quartermaster's longshoremen issued a flat command to wait and we'd be summoned when she could see us, I nodded agreeably while gritting my teeth.

When I was eventually summoned a couple of days later, I was already two drinks into a meticulously planned blackout, and though I thought perhaps I shouldn't appear before the quartermaster even mildly impaired, I didn't want to waste the opportunity either, for who knew when she might next have a chance to see me?

I walked a straight line into the Wellspring. Or at least I hoped I did.

Farlen looked visibly older since last I'd seen her, and it had only been a month. There was a shock of gray at the temples and one on top of her head that hadn't been there before. Was that from stress and lack of sleep, or had she somehow overtaxed herself as a hygienist? They didn't tend to take on tasks that could trigger the aging penalty of a kenning, but if ever there was a time for it, this was it.

I wondered: Did I look older to her? I certainly felt it. The creaks and pops and various complaints from my joints and muscles when I woke up had grown in frequency and volume.

"Gerstad. I've kept you waiting, and I thank you for your patience while I dealt with some urgent matters. I also want to thank you for your work on cleanup efforts. Your crew has done Brynlön tremendous service."

Damn it. She was so nice I couldn't stay mad. And the calming waters of the Wellspring, their gentle chuckle and laugh, were most likely designed to dull the sharp edge of resentment.

"You're welcome, Quartermaster," I said, but then worried that I should have said something else. I am acquainted with good manners, but we are not best friends.

Her pause and small smile told me I was right to be worried, but she didn't call me out. "How may I help?" she asked.

"I wondered about the intelligence I provided last month when we raided the Bone Giant camp in the north. Did it provide any insight into their plans?"

"I sent it off for translation almost immediately but have yet to hear back. I don't know what the delay is—perhaps the translator is unavailable or word was sent but the courier never made it here. Regardless, I share your impatience and will try to follow up on that. I promise to relay what I learn as soon as it arrives."

"Thank you."

"Was there anything else?"

"Yes." I paused to stifle an inconvenient belch and then continued with my pitch. "Since we have no better intelligence, I suggest a scouting trip to the northern shore with several objectives: one, to make sure no Bone Giants are gathering nearby in the forest; two, to scout a location for a hunting lodge, which may serve as both a lodge and a sentinel station in case Bone Giants come south. You will simultaneously improve security and economic growth."

The quartermaster's lips twitched at the corners. "Look at you, singing sweetly to me of my most ardent desires."

I blinked, because that sounded like something I would do when I'd had one too many. "Did I . . . sing just now?"

"Only in the metaphorical sense. And I'm in a mood to grant this, since it does cohere with my wishes and you have served us so well. But I'm guessing your team is still a bit short, if memory serves."

"Yes. We'd need a new rapid and a new hygienist, as well as a sword arm or two."

"A new rapid? What happened to your old one?"

"He took himself home to the sea last week. Could not bear his grief anymore."

"I am so sorry. I had not heard."

"He was a good man who served with honor."

"Yes. Very well, Gerstad, return in the morning with your team and report to the barracks. I'll have a rapid and hygienist and two mariners assigned to the Grynek Hunters, and a voucher for provisions. You'll hunt and scout the northern woods and pick out a place for a lodge."

"Thank you."

"Don't thank me yet. I'm sending you into the Grave-wood."

"For which I am very grateful." Any assignment that wasn't cleanup duty would be perfect.

I left the Wellspring feeling better than I had in some while. There was plenty to do and no reason to drink myself into oblivion anymore—in fact, the first order of business was to catch the rest of my team and make sure they weren't sinking too quickly into their own cups. They might want some extra rest after hauling a particularly foul cargo of bodies downriver—which was true of every batch, as each got worse with more time to decompose—but they'd want something different even more. They'd want the chance, however slim, of getting some of their own back.

Gyrsön du Neddell, the cook, was easy enough to find. He was working as a guest chef in a restaurant that specialized in game meats. His eyes squinted above a cheerful smile at the news we'd have a proper expedition tomorrow, and his expansive mustache twitched in pleasure.

"You made sure to request provisions?" he asked.

"Didn't have to. Quartermaster said she'd have a voucher waiting for us."

"She did? Bryn's salty sword, that woman is good at what she does. Never met her, but I think I love her. Do you know if she's married?"

"I don't. She might be married to her job."

"Oh, gods, Daryck, stop," he moaned, clutching at his heart. "Extreme competence *and* an overweening dedication to service? I have no idea what she looks like, but she has to be hot."

"She's actually gone a bit gray in her hair from stress. Above the ears and a little streak starting at the top, just to the left of center."

"Hnngh. Wait, are you teasing me now?"

"No, she really has."

"Oh, gods. I want to cook for her."

"I'll let her know next time we speak."

"You promise?"

"I swear it. See you tomorrow."

The others were not so easy to find, nor to convince that they needed to be at the barracks in the morning, since I had promised them a week off before the next job, but they appeared, bags packed, horses brushed and fed. A longshoreman was there, along with a few others, to whom we were introduced.

"Gerstad du Löngren, this is Lörry du Bört, a new rapid assigned to Fornyd by the pelenaut and now detailed to the Grynek Hunters."

Lörry was nervous and trying not to look like it—a slim young man with thin lips and a narrow nose who thought that jumping into Bryn's Lung would be the end of him, and now he was blessed and expected to be of service. He had no idea how to behave, because he was dealing with the shock, from moment to moment, that this was his life now.

"Welcome," I said, nodding and smiling at him. "You'll fit right in."

Gesturing to a striking woman in soft blue and gray robes, the longshoreman said, "This is your new hygienist, Vera du Göslyn."

She nodded at me and said, "The quartermaster said you may or may not keep me safe. I hope you may."

"I surely hope to. But first I'd say we need to get you into something more protective than robes. The claws of the creatures out there can open long gashes that will have you bleeding out before we can do anything else. Perhaps you could visit the mynstad in charge of the armory here before we go?"

"As you wish. Excuse me."

We also met two new soldiers. I welcomed them briefly

and assigned them to Mynstad Luren, my master of horse, to look after.

"And I have a voucher here for provisions," the longshoreman finished, handing it over. I took it and promptly handed it to Gyrsön. He scanned it quickly and whispered, "I love her."

The rest of the morning was spent loading wagons and arranging for a ferry across the river to the northern shore. It gave me some time to talk to Lörry, as Gyrsön bossed everyone else around, telling them to pluck that bag of cornmeal or that bucket of lard. We walked a short distance away, talking in low tones.

"Any experience as a rapid in a company?" I asked him.

"No. I'm freshly blessed and newly trained. This is my first assignment."

"Okay. It won't be the easiest, but it won't be the roughest either. I'm going to need you to kill for me."

"What?"

"We can handle most things, but if we get attacked by gravemaws or fir apes or anything too big or deadly for spears, I'll need you to handle it instead."

"Okay. How?"

"What do you mean, 'How'? Whoever trained you didn't say?"

"No. Killing wasn't mentioned."

I stopped and rounded on him. "Are you fucking with me right now? We're in a war and nobody mentioned it?"

"No, I swear."

"How about dry direction? You were taught that?"

"Yes."

"Good. To kill a gravemaw—or anything else in this world—you target the water in its head and yank it in any direction you like. The blood ruptures the vessels in the brain, and it drops dead of a cerebral hemorrhage. It's that simple.

You're one of the most feared killing machines on the planet, kid. No other kenning can kill so fast or so absolutely."

The poor kid's eyes widened. "Oh," he said, almost a whisper. He must have led a sheltered existence.

"Don't worry about it now, and don't worry about it when we need you. Worry about it, if you want, after you've saved our asses. Because if you don't, we'll all be dead. A single gravemaw can take out our whole company if it wants."

"So just . . . big animals, then? That want to eat us?"

"It's the Gravewood, Lörry. Everything wants to eat us, big or small. But we can handle most of them, with a few exceptions. Gravemaws are the big one. And when one shows up—one almost always does—I need you to kill it before it kills us. If you hesitate, that's probably going to mean somebody dies."

"Oh . . . all right."

"And if we meet any Bone Giants, don't hesitate there either. You drop as many as you can; don't wait for my order. The order is given now."

"Okay."

I clapped him on the back. "Cheer up. It's not all bad. It's mostly good. Gyrsön there is one of the best cooks alive right now. And I'm a half-decent poet."

"You are?"

"I once wrote a popular volume of cock sonnets."

"That was *you*?"

"Ah, always nice to meet a fan."

"Are you going to write any more?"

"A hundred sixty-eight weren't enough? Sure, kid. If we ever get on the other side of this, I'll write another batch and dedicate it to you."

"You will? But why? Wouldn't people assume we were lovers or something?"

"That doesn't matter, and nobody will care. What's going to happen is that people are going to want to see the cock of the kid who got a book of cock sonnets dedicated to him. I'm doing you a favor."

"Whoa. Yeah."

"Attaboy. Enjoy that dream now and live it later. In the meantime, kill shit for me."

"Yes, Gerstad."

Ah, to be young and uncomplicated again.

The bard left us all laughing about that, which was a pleasant sound. The city's merriment came in two waves—once wryly at the bard's pronouncement, and then again when the younger generation took offense at being laughed at, and that was even funnier. Fintan dismissed his seeming and promised more of Pen and Daryck tomorrow. And then, turning from Survivor Field, he told me there was a chance we'd not be able to work tomorrow and apologized, because he might need to huddle up with Eimear some more.

"She really has a lot to share."

"Oh, understandable. Did she mention, by any chance, whether Melishev Lohmet is still alive?"

"He was alive during what she's shared so far—I haven't asked her if that's still true at the moment. Because we've been talking about events from last autumn, and we're now in Bloom."

"Ah, understood. Would you mind asking her for me, then? I'm keen to know."

"Oh, sure. Absolutely."

"Thanks very much. I'll see you for lunch tomorrow, whether we can work or not."

One more night to get an answer. Part of me wished Melishev dead, and part of me wished him alive and suffering. If there was a part of me that wished for forgiveness, it remained silent.

Day 41

THE MAN IN THE CABIN

I flared out my cane as I walked to meet Fintan for lunch, which would probably be a meager affair. Despite the looming prospect of hunger, I adopted a strut that was as close to a sashay as my knee would allow, because I was finally going to find out something that had been puzzling us for months. People smiled at me because my good mood was infectious, and I wished them a fantastic day. Though I couldn't be sure how I'd feel once I knew Melishev's fate, my gut told me that knowing had to be better than not knowing. The collapse of the Granite Tunnel and the subsequent revolution in Ghurana Nent had left us all wondering what was going on over there. The bard's tales formed the bulk of what we knew, since no information was coming voluntarily from the Nentians.

The last we'd heard, Melishev Lohmet had intended to kill the Fornish ambassador, Mai Bet Ken, but fainted from illness before he could do so. It occurred to me to wonder how Fintan had learned that story. Probably from the Fornish, who were keeping in very good touch with us. Which meant that, unless Fintan had been taking significant license, the ambassador survived.

The chowder house was becalmed, like a ship on a windless day. The chowder they served up with an apology only vaguely deserved the name, as it was briny and largely bereft of chunks. There was a small nibble of clam and one bite each of potato and carrot.

"So!" I said to him as I sat down. "Did you remember to ask Eimear about Melishev?"

"Of course I did. I never forget anything."

"Right, silly question. Sorry. What did she say? Does the shitsnake yet live?"

"I can't tell you."

"She doesn't know?"

"Oh, yes, she knows, and she told me. I simply can't tell you yet."

"Why not?"

"It's not my decision, okay? I want to be clear about that. I'm under orders not to tell you."

"Orders from whom?"

"From the pelenaut via the lung."

I blinked a few times to process this before clarifying. "The lung relayed an order from the pelenaut saying you were not to tell me whether Melishev Lohmet is alive or dead?"

"That is correct. I'm very sorry, but I feel I have to obey that order, as I am a guest here and can be forced to leave at any time."

"I understand that, yes, I totally understand. What I don't understand is why they would give you such an order."

The bard shrugged. "The lung did not offer to explain it."

"Of course he didn't. But can you guess? I mean, whatever happened to him, good or bad, will be a part of your tales in forthcoming days, am I right?"

Fintan nodded enthusiastically. "One hundred percent. You will find out at the same time everyone else does."

"So there must be some reason to keep it secret a few days longer. And I can't imagine what that would be. What difference would it make? It's not like I'm going to tell everyone and spoil the surprise."

"I wouldn't know," Fintan said.

"I see." The chowder in front of me looked as if it yearned to congeal like proper chowders in days of yore, but it sadly lacked enough fats to make that happen.

"Dervan?"

"Hmm? Yes?"

"Are you all right? You've been staring at your bowl for a while."

"Oh. Uh. Sorry, Fintan. My thoughts are swimming like a shad without a school. I think you mentioned we might not be able to work today, owing to your need to spend more time with Eimear. Do you know if that holds true?"

"It does, unfortunately."

"It's just as well. I don't think I'm up to work today. I know that it puts us even further behind, but there's no danger of it slipping out of your memory, is there?"

"No. We can resume later and make up for lost time."

"Excellent. My apologies, but my appetite has gone missing. If you'll excuse me?"

"Yes. I'll see you on the wall later?"

"I wouldn't miss it."

In front of the bard I'd managed to keep my temper, but it built and built in me as I walked to the palace and demanded to see the pelenaut and was once again denied. Röllend had me caged in a lobster trap in the abyss, and it hurt because I didn't know why.

The strut I enjoyed earlier had been tied to a boulder and tossed into the bay to drown. I probably should have eaten that chowder, thin and spare as it was, because the ill news had drained me mentally and was dragging me down physically as well; I felt as if I'd spent a full day watching young children play on a rocky, jagged shore, trying first to prevent injury and then trying to calm them when the injuries inevitably happened. I might as well be a wrung-out mop for all the life and juice I had left. Defeated, I trudged up the steps to the wall to witness the day's tales, and purchased a sad fish wrap of dubious provenance and a weak beer to fill the void.

Chewing mechanically, I mused that if Pen was heading in the direction of Talala Fouz, her next tale might offer me some clues. At least Fintan had assured me that I'd find out eventually. But I chafed at a wait that felt wholly unnecessary.

The bards performed an up-tempo instrumental song that day and got to it fairly quickly.

When we arrived in Talala Fouz, I couldn't stop staring at the Gravewood, which stood silent on the northern shore of the river. I wanted to plunge my silverbark shoots into the soil there and commune with the conifers. It wasn't until I walked down the gangplank that I really took a look at the capital of Ghurana Nent and realized what a horror it was. A fury and a firelord had torched the whole city, a stark example of what would happen if we didn't protect the Canopy from the Hathrim. There was an awful lot of rebuilding going on, and it looked like they had some Raelech stonecutters burying the ash in the soil and compacting it and so on, speeding the process, but the stink of burnt wood stung my nostrils.

"Ugh. They need to get a Kaurian cyclone here to blow this foul air away," I said.

"I agree," Mak said. "But I can do quite a bit to freshen things up once I'm finished growing the treehouses upriver. Listen, do you have a place to stay already? If not, I can take you to the embassy. Plenty of room. Most of the Red Pheasants plan on bunking there."

"Thank you, that would be great."

Mak had been expecting a warm welcome from Ambassador Ken and tea in her reception room but was dismayed to discover that she'd been arrested or abducted some time ago by the king's men and hadn't been seen since. Word had been sent to Forn about the incident, but it would be weeks before any response could arrive. Mak wanted something done now.

The embassy staff said they'd complained and made inquiries and been stonewalled by the king's underlings. Mak was convinced that he would get different results somehow and stalked off, prickly as a thornhand, to demand answers from the king.

I privately doubted he'd have much success and found a member of the staff who was willing to brief me about the situation. Del Mot Goh was a blond woman with a pert nose, who'd cropped her hair short the way cousin Nel had, and we had a chat around the back side of the tea treehouse, away from where the public entered the winding staircase around the trunk. Technically we could be overheard if someone above us wanted to cock an ear in our direction, so we kept our voices low.

"King Kalaad the Unwell is seriously unwell, physically and mentally," Del explained. "He kills people when he feels like it, and I fear the worst has happened to the ambassador."

"He kills them?"

Del nodded. "He takes them outside the city and chains them to a post, then he bleeds them a little bit, and their screams along with the scent of blood attract predators. They get eaten alive, and their bones get scattered around the area."

I made no comment on how cruel that was but stuck to whether it was likely. "He wouldn't do that to an ambassador, though, would he? That would start a war."

"Only if we can prove he did it. We'd have to find her bones among all the others and then prove that he chained her up there."

She had a point. That would be impossible, so the practical thing to do was to focus on something else.

"What does he do with people he's *not* going to execute? Is there a prison in the city?"

"There's a dungeon somewhere. Ambassador Ken told me about it. There's a Nentian prisoner in there who killed a

Fornish citizen, and she wanted to make sure he was locked up."

"Did she say anything about what it was like inside?"

"Damp and smelly."

"Moldy, perhaps?"

"Definitely."

"Then I might be able to find her, if he's holding her there."

"How?"

Shoots from the silverbark on my shin woke up and threaded their way into the soil beneath the Red Pheasant tea treehouse.

"The White Gossamer Clan specializes in finding animals using fungus."

"You do?"

I chuckled, because her voice was one part wonder and two parts revulsion, and I'd heard it before. "The giant spiders who live in our part of the forest like to spin their webs among large mushrooms. There are many species that work for them, and they tend to move on after a few days, so it's easier for us to find the spiders and harvest their silk if we ask the fungus where they are."

"The fungus is *aware* of the spiders?"

"Not exactly. *Awareness* is a bit strong for what's going on. But it responds, biologically, to stimulus, so in that sense it's aware of being walked on and having webs attached to it and the miniature exhalations of the spiders. The same principle should apply here, with some adjustments. First, I need to find a source of mold underground—oh! Got it."

"How can you sense that? Wouldn't the dungeon be enclosed?"

"Plants can crack stone given enough time and water. I imagine that it's probably an old dungeon, since this is the capital. There are plenty of small fissures through the rock—not large enough for a prisoner to escape, but plenty wide enough for water to seep in and fungus to line those fissures. That's my way to get a peek inside. And yes . . . it's quite moldy. Now it's a matter of determining whether any of the prisoners in there might be Ambassador Ken."

"How would fungus know the difference?"

"Through the difference in gases we exhale."

"I don't understand."

"The other prisoners are most likely Nentian or Raelech—which means they're bigger. At least a foot taller, and likely more. They're inhaling and exhaling more gases in those enclosed rooms, and the plant life in those rooms will notice."

"Oh! So if there's a prisoner in the dungeon who's less gassy, so to speak, then that could be Ambassador Ken!"

"Right. Or a child, I suppose. But this part will take a while."

"Of course. Can I get you anything, ben Min, while you work?"

"I'm fine for the moment, thank you. But if the ambassador is in the dungeon, we need to have a place for her to hide once I free her."

"You're going to break her out?"

"The Nentians are not abiding by the rules of diplomacy, so I don't see why we should allow her to suffer."

Del grinned at me. "Oh, I like you. You're right, they'd come search for her in the embassy rooms, but we can arrange a private clan deck up in the treehouse. . . . Okay, I am on it. Send word if you need anything."

"Can I stay in the treehouse too? They might be looking for a greensleeve after I'm finished."

"Yes, yes, absolutely. I'll move your things from the embassy to a clan deck now. Oh, I hope this seed will sprout."

She took her leave, and I threw myself into the slow work of surveying the dungeon through the limited senses of fungi. I could figure out the temperature and humidity and air quality of each cell, and from that I would have to make educated guesses about whether it was occupied and by whom.

There were ten cells, and two were unoccupied: number five, which was larger than the others and approaching a standard of cleanliness, and number ten, which was smallish and filthy. That room had a lot of dead somethings in it and maybe something living in it, perhaps a rodent or a cat or a very large spider. Of the eight occupied cells, seven of them were absolutely thriving on the exhalations of the occupants. And the eighth was doing very well but perhaps a petal or two shy of full bloom.

It was the actual eighth cell in the row; there were other prisoners on either side. Trying to determine the number of guards or the security arrangements was impossible, unfortunately. The guards weren't standing in moldy cells.

But the security boiled down to three things: locked doors, keys to unlock them, and armed guards who presumably had the keys. The variables at play were how many guards there would be and how skilled they were, but I wasn't terribly worried: Highly skilled fighters usually didn't pull dungeon duty. And how alert would the guard to a secret dungeon be, after all? It's unlikely that anyone would come by to challenge him if it was secret.

No time like the present. With Mak gone to see the king and making demands, the king might react poorly and move Ambassador Ken—or worse.

Withdrawing my shoots from the earth, I walked around to the treehouse entrance and told the greeter that I was a guest of Del Mot Goh. She descended in a few minutes to escort me to my room: a screened deck high up in the tree, with a cot and washbasin and my travel bag. Customers or other visitors would never know it was here; they would see only a dense cloud of leaves at the end of a thick branch.

"It's not much, I know—" Del began, but I raised a hand to stop her.

"It's perfect. May I make one more request? Hooded cloaks for myself and Ambassador Ken."

"Yes! I'll return shortly."

While she was gone, I opened my pack to withdraw a compartmentalized box full of seeds and spores, a small bag of soil, a tiny jar of resin, and a cheese knife I never used for cheese.

The deck was a living part of the silverbark and would respond to my requests. Squatting on my haunches, I let my shoots communicate with the tree and asked it to shape a part of its branches into a bowl. This took a few minutes, but it created a tight coil of wood, sort of like an upside-down beehive, which would serve me well. Into this I poured my bag of soil and moistened it with some water from the washbasin. Then I selected a seed of a gourd plant, pressed it into the soil, and accelerated its growth until I had five small gourds with thin shells. I sliced off the tops, scooped out the interior flesh, and set them aside to dry. Then I pulled out the plant and shook the soil from the roots back into the bowl. I had more work to do.

Using my cheese knife, I carefully lifted a tiny measure of spores from a sealed container, then wiped the blade off into the soil. I added more water and accelerated the growth. The resulting mushrooms were harmless if cooked and eaten while immature, but the spores were pesky. They absolutely loved to grow in lung tissue.

Cautiously, I brought the mushrooms to bloom and removed them one at a time. I was immune to the spores, but I still didn't want to breathe them in. I scraped the spores into the gourds, using three mushrooms per gourd, then I replaced the tops and sealed them with a smear of resin.

Five spore bombs. There couldn't be more than five dungeon guards, right?

Del Mot Goh called from outside the deck, and I opened the wall of branches and leaves to allow her entry.

"Sorry that took so long—" she said, holding two forest-green cloaks.

"Perfect timing. Is Mak Fin ben Fos back yet?"

"No."

"Let's go anyway."

"Wait, you want me to go with you?"

"Just to the site. So you can tell Mak where to look for me if something goes wrong."

Del's eyes widened. "What can go wrong?"

"So very much. I'm almost ready—I just need an excuse to get inside."

I put on the cloak, arranged the spore bombs on my belt, and made sure to pluck five small packets of powder wrapped in onionskin from my seed supply. I quickly grew another batch of mushrooms and simply picked them at the ideal stage for cooking. These I placed in a shallow basket that wove itself out of a living vine, which I cut off with my cheese knife when it was finished. I then encouraged that vine to thicken and continue growing. I had it trail down from the deck so that we could exit the tree without passing by the patrons of the teahouse. Once we shimmied down it—with me holding the basket in one hand and Del bringing the extra cloak—I had it break off and fall into a heap behind us.

"I hope she's really in there," Del said as we exited the Fornish compound and walked in the general direction of the palace construction project.

"Me too. Do you know much about the old palace layout?"

"Nothing. I've never had occasion to visit."

"But you've been around Nentian architecture, at least? I've lived in trees my whole life and wouldn't know where to begin."

"What are you looking for?"

"The kitchen."

"Oh, that's easy enough. It's one of the few parts of the palace that didn't burn down, since it was built of stone."

"They'd probably have a root cellar beneath it, right?"

"I imagine so."

"And since they excavated that space for a root cellar, they could have just continued excavating, and on the other side of the wall might be . . . ?"

"A dungeon!"

The palace grounds weren't all that far from the embassy grounds—perhaps three hundred lengths. We stopped well short of the gates, and Del pointed to the left side behind the walls. "The kitchen would be over there, and presumably the dungeon underneath. The king's residence and sky room would be on the far side of the compound, but I think it's all tents and construction at the moment. That's where Mak would be."

"Okay. Give me the cloak and head back to the embassy. Tell everyone that they should deny that I'm even here. Either I come back with Ambassador Ken inside an hour, or I'll be in trouble."

"Thank you, Pen. For trying."

"She represents the Canopy, and the Canopy comes first. I can't do anything else."

Del left me, and I walked up to the two bored guards at the gate.

"Name and business," said one, burping softly afterward but not begging my pardon.

I gestured to my basket of mushrooms. "I'm recently arrived and heard that King Kalaad is unwell. These mushrooms from Forn are renowned for their restorative and healing properties. I was hoping to give them to the palace chef and coach him or her in their preparation."

"They'll have to be tested," the other one said, and the first guard grunted.

"Name?" he asked.

"Yor Mah ben Dun of the Blue Piper Clan." Both name and clan were fabricated, but the guards were not sufficiently schooled in Fornish names to know that. They did, however, recognize that I was blessed—that was a little hard to miss, even if they didn't know the meaning of the *ben* honorific.

"You a greensleeve?" asked the second guard.

My eyes dropped down to the living wood growing on my forearms and then rose back to meet his, and I nodded twice, slowly.

He nodded back, but he wasn't impressed. "Welcome."

The guard who had belched turned to a small ledger on a desk and wrote down my professed name, then they waved me through, giving me directions to the back door of the palace kitchen. It seemed like lax security to me, but another guard greeted me at the back door, and he repeated the process of asking my name and business. He also asked which gate I'd used to enter the palace grounds, so that was at least a rudimentary tracking system. If I lied, they'd know. Once he wrote that down, he unlocked the door for me—which looked new.

"Chef is the one in the hat," he said, evidently assuming I would be unable to tell otherwise. I thanked him and stepped into the kitchen. A couple of prep cooks looked up at my entrance, but I ignored them. The chef in the hat had her back to the door because she was checking something cooking in an oven. Since she didn't look around, I didn't go straight to her. I walked like I knew where I was going, to an archway on the left, midway along a wall that was mostly covered in pantry cupboards. Once through, I discovered it was a hallway. It stretched away to the right before ending at an intersecting hallway. To the left, it dead-ended, because that led to the exterior wall. But along that very short stretch of hallway were two doors—hidden behind those pantry cupboards—and a guard lurking in front of one. Which meant those pantry cupboards were fake, built to conceal stairways leading down. The door nearest me was labeled in Nentian as the root cellar, and since I doubted they felt the carrots and potatoes needed guarding, the other door was most likely the entrance to the king's dungeon.

I smiled at the guard, tilted the basket so he could easily see I had produce in there, and headed for the door to the root cellar. It was unlocked. I held it open with my foot and, unhooking a spore bomb from my belt, asked him in his language if that was the dungeon.

"Who are you?" he demanded.

Instead of answering, I threw the spore bomb at his head. He ducked underneath it easily, and the gourd shattered on the stone wall behind him, releasing the spores directly into the space where he'd need to breathe. As he drew breath to shout at me and perhaps charge, he inhaled a lungful of spores. He knew something was wrong right away and gasped in shock—which only sucked more spores into his airway.

He wheezed and clutched at his throat, and I let the door to the root cellar close and put down my basket of mushrooms. As his eyes widened in alarm, I told him to try to be calm.

"If you panic, it'll get worse," I said. "Open the door for me and I'll give you the cure."

He didn't feel like doing that. He drew his sword instead, weakly, and I set myself defensively in case he charged. But he didn't have the strength, because he didn't have the breath. He swayed, tried to take a step, and fell to his knees, his face turning blue.

"You're running out of time, smart guy. Drop the sword and I'll give you the cure."

He really wasn't a smart guy. He kept struggling until he eventually slumped over, unconscious. I removed one of the small onionskin packets from my belt pouch, tore it open under his nose to let some of the fine powder inside get inhaled, then opened his mouth and shook the remainder in there. It was an antifungal that would kill the spores he'd inhaled, and he'd be fine in a few hours.

Using the large single key I removed from his belt, I opened the door to the dungeon and dragged the heavy stump of a man in there, leaving him at the top of a flight of stone steps. I locked the door again and took the key with me. I doubted he'd regain consciousness in time to pose a problem, but if he did, he wouldn't be getting out to raise the alarm, and his sword was in the hallway. One of the kitchen staff might come to investigate and raise an alarm, though, so I hurried down the curving flight of stairs. There was another guard at the bottom, and I dispatched him with another spore bomb, coolly waiting for him to fall unconscious before taking his weapons and his mess of keys.

"I don't have time to worry about these," I muttered. It was quite dark down there, just a small firebowl providing illumination, and I didn't want to fumble through a ring of keys looking for the right one. The faster I was out of there, the better. I administered the antifungal to the guard and then concentrated on my silverbark, sending a slim shoot into the keyhole. I let it grow and fill the space until it felt tight, and then I turned it, the tumblers obliging me.

Yes, I will admit that I grinned at that point. I'd known in theory that this was something greensleeves could do, but this was the first opportunity I'd had to do it.

Time to see if all this hassle was worth it. The air behind the door was definitely a festival of mold, and it was so dark that I went back for the small firebowl. I counted cell doors on my left as I went down the hall until I got to the eighth one. If I'd read the signs correctly, Ambassador Ken would be on the other side.

Straightening out the same shoot I'd used moments before, I slipped it into the keyhole and let it take the proper shape to turn the lock. Once it clicked, I hauled open the door and held the firebowl aloft.

"Mai Bet Ken? Ambassador?" I called. My voice, coupled with the noises I'd made, roused the occupants of the other cells to demand to know who was out there and cry for help. From the cell I'd opened—nothing. It was pitch black inside, the firebowl penetrating only a little way. I didn't mind stepping in, since even if the door closed behind me, I'd be able to unlock it anytime.

Squeaking noises alerted me that there were rats in there—big ones, as the firebowl soon revealed. As well as bugs of different kinds. And . . . a slumped form along the back wall.

"Oh, no."

I hurried over and set the firebowl down. It was indeed the ambassador—or if not her, some other Fornish woman in fine robes. They were filthy now, and her hair was slimed. She was breathing shallowly, and I opened an antifungal packet underneath her nose before feeding her the rest. In a moldy cell like this, she'd need it for sure.

She stirred as I struggled to lift her to a sitting position, eyes fluttering open and then squeezing shut.

"What—who's there?" she said.

"I'm here to get you out, Ambassador."

That got her to try again. "You're . . . you're Fornish."

"Yes. A greensleeve. We need to go. Can you get up?"

"Maybe? Ack. Did you give me something? What is in my mouth?"

"An antifungal powder."

"Oh. Thanks. It tastes terrible."

I helped her up and then gave her the cloak, telling her to hurry and put it on. The other prisoners were making more noise. That might wake the unconscious guards earlier than I would wish, and we could have company at any moment.

"Who are you?" she asked.

"A friend of Mak Fin ben Fos."

"He's here?"

She brightened considerably at his name. Hoping it would get her to move faster, I said, "We just got here a few hours ago and heard you'd been abducted. He's demanding an audience with the king while I'm breaking you out."

"Oh, no. He shouldn't do that. The king is mad and blames his illness on me. We need to get him out of there."

"Well, come on. Let's go. Are there any other prisoners down here you want freed?"

"Not unless freeing them helps us escape somehow."

It was possible they might distract the few guards we needed to pass on our way to escape. But then again, they might bring more guards running to contain the situation than we could handle. And they also might hurt those innocent people in the kitchen or even turn on us. "I think it would complicate things. So far this is a stealth mission."

"Lead the way, then."

"Grab the firebowl, please, and follow me."

She left the door open behind her—just as well. There would be little doubt that the Fornish greensleeve had come to free the Fornish ambassador.

I got another spore bomb ready just in case, but it wasn't needed; the two guards I'd taken out were still unconscious.

Ambassador Ken asked if they were dead, and I reassured her that they'd be okay soon enough.

"Good," she said, before succumbing to a coughing fit that racked her whole body. She wobbled unsteadily on the stairs, and I grabbed on to her robe to make sure she didn't tumble down them. She wound up ejecting some nasty stuff from her lungs and took a moment to catch her breath after that.

"Can you keep going?" I asked. "I kind of need you to."

"Yes. Sorry. That dungeon isn't good for your health."

"How long were you down there?"

"I've no idea. No sense of time when you never see the sun. But I wouldn't have lasted much longer, so thank you."

"Don't thank me yet. This escape is still springtime budding that might be cut short by a late frost."

Stepping over the guard in front of the door, I unlocked it and peeked out into the hallway. Sounds of pots banging in the kitchen reached my ears, but no sounds of alarm. The guard's sword was still lying where I'd left it. I placed it next to him, then waved Ambassador Ken through. Once the dungeon door was closed and locked, I deposited my mushroom basket and all the dungeon keys inside the door to the root cellar. After that, there was no helping it: We had to step into view.

"Lean on me and look as sick as you are," I said. "Our story will be that you're ill and I'm taking you to a Raelech herbalist in town."

We got some stares as we traveled through the kitchen, but once again the chef wasn't looking our way and no one else challenged us, since we were clearly heading for the exit and had no intention of interrupting their work. They must have been fairly used to people streaming past.

The guard outside the door, however, had questions.

"Hold on, now. You are . . ." He checked his notes. "Yor Mah ben Dun. Who's that?"

"A countrywoman of mine who fell ill in the palace. She entered on the other side of the compound. Her name is Jin Zoh Kel."

Ambassador Ken launched into a new coughing fit, and whether it was real or faked, the guard believed that she needed help.

"I'm taking her to a Raelech herbalist now."

"Right, good luck," he said, jotting down the fake name I'd given. The ambassador leaned heavily against me as I supported her on the way to the compound gate.

"Yor Mah ben Dun?" she whispered. "That is absolutely ridiculous."

"They bought it, though."

"When someone who knows Fornish sees that, those guards are going to get in trouble and hold a grudge against us."

"I don't plan on returning."

"I suppose I don't either. At least not for the short term. What's your real name?"

"Pen Yas ben Min of the White Gossamer Clan."

"White Gossamer?"

I clenched my jaw because I could almost hear her make the connection.

"Nel Kit ben Sah was my cousin," I said before she could ask.

"Well. In that case, I am grateful for you both."

"Time to be sick again," I said as we neared the gate. The same two guards stood sentry, but there was a small queue as they kept track of exits as well as entrances.

"That won't be a problem." As if the thought reminded her, her lungs convulsed in a fresh round of wet coughs, and it drew stares. The guards were not anxious to keep us waiting when I got to the front. I gave them the same name and story I'd given the kitchen guard, and they waved us through. She still leaned heavily on me afterward, so her weakness wasn't an act.

"Listen, Del Mot Goh is preparing a private deck for you in the treehouse. I think you should rest up there and stay out of sight."

"Agreed. And you too. But I don't think they'll be looking too hard."

"Why is that?"

"If they come looking for an escaped diplomat, they'll be admitting they imprisoned a diplomat."

We made it to the Fornish compound without incident,

but Ambassador Ken said we should keep our hoods and cloaks pulled close to conceal our identities. The Nentians would have spies in the public areas of the treehouse. We would need to reach the private clan sections of the tree without being seen.

That required some greensleeve work. Circling to the back side of the trunk, I connected my shoots to the treehouse and asked it to either move or grow enough leaf cover on that side to prevent any visitors from observing anything in that direction from the ground up. They'd notice that we were hiding something, but there was no helping that.

Once the leaves shielded us from view, we walked away from the trunk until we were almost directly underneath my private deck. There I had a thick root break the surface and coil horizontally to make a rough platform for us to stand upon. The ambassador and I stepped onto it, and then the root elevated us straight up until we could step through the leaf wall onto the deck. I let the root and the leaves return to normal when our privacy was assured.

Leading the ambassador to my cot, I said, "I'll go find Del and see about getting this deck plumbed so we can build you a living bathtub, but there's a washbasin with a pitcher of water to get you started."

A tear dribbled down Ambassador Ken's dirty cheek, leaving a clean trail through the grime. "You are wonderful, Pen. I wish to speak with you later at length and see if there is anything I can do to help you, though I'm sure it will be nothing compared to what you've done for me. You saved my life."

Maybe I did. I thought she'd require another dose of antifungals in the morning. But there was still plenty of work for me to do.

I left her to fetch Del Mot Goh and get permission to grow plumbing tubes that would pump hot water from the boiler platform and drain it as needed. When I returned, the ambassador had removed her cloak, washed her face, and made an attempt to de-slime her hair. She was still horrendously dirty and smelled foul, but we'd take care of that soon enough.

Del wept openly when she saw the ambassador and left almost as soon as she arrived, to fetch fresh robes and soap and such. I got to work instructing the tree to grow hollow plumbing branches up to the deck, which took perhaps twenty minutes with my encouragement. Once they arrived, I had a portion of the deck grow and shape itself into a bathtub, then connected the plumbing. Last, I grew a privacy screen around the bathtub for the ambassador. Soon she was sighing as she slipped into the hot water, and I stretched out on the cot, feeling like I needed a rest. I was about to nod off when Mak Fin ben Fos arrived, led there by Del.

I sat up and made room on the cot for him so he could sit, and he talked to the ambassador through the screen, mightily relieved that she was okay and grateful to me for busting her loose.

"They made me wait for hours," he said, and a sloshing sound told us that the ambassador was getting out of the bath. "When I finally got to see the king, he was in very poor shape, but he wanted to know what was happening in Khul Bashab before he would answer any of my questions. He wanted to know first why I hadn't killed the beast callers. I told him that I never even found them and that they'd overthrown the city watch and trapped the viceroy before I could get there. Then I told him that the beast callers had repelled an initial force when I left but that his main army was marching on the city when I caught the boat north. I had to answer dozens of questions about them before he'd let me ask where you were and who took you. He claimed he had nothing to do with your abduction and had no idea where you were or even if you were alive."

Ambassador Mai Bet Ken stepped out from behind the screen in a new clean robe in the colors of the Red Pheasant

Clan, her wet hair rolled up in a towel. She looked entirely different. Stunning, even.

"Those were all lies," she said. "Melishev Lohmet had his men bring me to him outside the city walls and intended to kill me himself, but he collapsed before he could do it. He ordered me thrown into that dungeon to rot instead, and I would have, if not for ben Min. I'm glad you're both here now. King Kalaad the Unwell has started something with Forn, but we are going to finish it."

For personal reasons, Pen and Mai instantly became my new favorites. I hoped they would finish their conflict with Melishev to my satisfaction.

Before changing his form, Fintan said, "And we continue with the newly reconstituted Grynek Hunters, now resupplied and scouting the Gravewood north of Fornyd."

Daryck

We made little progress inland at first. Once we were ferried across the Gravewater, we spent the bulk of the afternoon roaming the bank, looking for the best place to build a proper dock and also searching for any animal trails or paths that might indicate good hunting ahead. About midafternoon, Mynstad Luren called me to check out something downriver. I double-timed it back there with him, and he did indeed have something to show me: a small canoe hidden in the reeds, and the beginnings of a path heading north.

"Well, we weren't specifically looking for anything like this, but I think we've found the thing we're looking for. Let's camp here and follow that trail in the morning."

I left Luren to keep an eye on the area as I went to fetch

the others, wondering about what that canoe might mean. It wasn't built for heavy cargo. It was for single or maybe double occupancy, with room for a rucksack or two. So if it was a smuggling operation, what were they smuggling? And where on Teldwen were they smuggling it to?

They were certainly trying to keep their landing a secret. The canoe would be invisible from the opposite shore and maybe even on the river itself. Perhaps they were poachers of some kind? But that didn't make sense: The Gravewood wasn't protected land, and anyone who was willing to risk the dangers it posed was free to hunt there.

Regardless, we needed to check it out for security reasons. Someone had gone to the trouble of hiding a landing across from the city, and they'd traveled this route often enough to blaze a trail. Diligence required investigation.

Gyrsön cooked us something of a feast, since it would most likely be more of a famine as we started hunting in the morning. I set up a watch and slept first, planning to get the early-morning shift, but a small family of murder weasels woke us all shortly after midnight, trying to get either our provisions or our throats. Luren got one, Gyrsön got another using the cleaver he slept with under his pillow, and one of the new soldiers got a third.

The kid, Lörry, stared wide-eyed at the carnage, half his face hidden in the dark, the other half lit by the campfire.

"What's the matter? Never seen a murder weasel before?"

He just shook his head, his gaze fixed on the headless corpse that Gyrsön had expertly dispatched.

"They're no good to eat, but the furs will fetch some coin in town."

I wouldn't be getting back to sleep, so I busied myself with skinning them and preparing the hides for tanning.

"Watch yourself, now," Luren reminded the kid. "Since there's blood in the wind, more will come, looking for a meal."

"More weasels?"

"More everything. We don't really have to hunt things out here. They hunt us instead, and we just refuse to die."

Meat squirrels attacked. A horned spitting lizard. A dire owl swooped at Gyrsön's face, thinking his mustache was a small rodent, but the cook ducked, and the owl flew away with his hat in its talons. Nothing really huge, though, which was simultaneously a relief and a curious disappointment. Perhaps whoever was using the canoe had hunted the area extensively.

Lörry got only a few hours of fitful sleep and was dragging when we moved out after breakfast. Vera looked fine, however, largely untroubled by the evening's ruckus, and had kitted herself out nicely with some hardened-leather armor that should provide at least some resistance to the claws of smaller creatures.

A half hour into our journey along the trail, Gyrsön alerted me that he smelled something ahead. His nose was better than anyone's.

"What is it?"

"Woodsmoke. Enough for a campfire. Not a forest fire."

"All right, then, we should scout ahead. Remain here with the soldiers and guard the wagons. Luren, Lörry, Vera, come with me."

Another ten minutes on the trail brought us to a small lodge in a modest clearing. The woodsmoke was trailing out of a chimney.

"Damn it," I whispered.

"What?" Luren asked.

"Building a lodge was *my* idea."

"Well, to be fair, you didn't say we should build an ugly one. That's more like a pile of lumber that accidentally looks like a cabin, not a proper lodge."

"Somebody's obviously home, but I want to scout this place a bit first. Let's take a nice long look from the periphery and scope this operation. Watch for traps, hidden caches, anything unusual that might tell us who this is and what they're up to. We'll split up and meet on the other side. And keep it quiet. Lörry, you're with me."

Luren gestured at Vera, and they duckwalked off to the right as I led the rapid to the left. "Stay behind me," I said, "and I mean right behind me." Last thing I needed was for the kid to set off a trip wire or fall into a pit trap.

We took it slow. Couple of steps, check on the cabin. Couple of more steps, check again.

"Mind if I ask why we are being so careful here?" Lörry asked, but thankfully kept his voice low. "We have them outnumbered and we're armed and everything."

"I'm of the opinion that it's okay to be too careful in the Gravewood," I replied. "Whoever's in that cabin has managed to survive out here in secret for a long time. That tells you they have something to hide, so they won't be happy to welcome guests, and it also tells you they're pretty tough, or they wouldn't still be alive."

"Okay, that makes sense. Thanks."

I appreciated that the kid wanted to learn. He didn't know, so he asked.

The cabin hid an outhouse around the back and a woodshed to season fuel for the fire, but there was nothing special about it otherwise. No back porch with rocking chairs. No pots of flowers to liven up the place or the remnants of a vegetable garden. No snares or other traps that I could see, either, in the woods on this side. Which suggested to me that whoever was in that cabin, they weren't hunters. Hunters would have set something around the periphery as a rudimentary defense as much as in the hope of an easy kill.

Also hidden in the back: another trail, which continued north into the forest. Where in the world did it go?

Luren and Vera met up with us, and we huddled out of sight of the cabin on the trail, sharing what we'd found.

"No traps, no signs at all of this being a hunter's lodge," Luren said, mirroring my own thinking. "It's weird. Not sure what they're living on. If they're bringing in supplies, they are either bringing them overland from the north or they are making a lot of trips in that little canoe."

"I can't imagine them using the canoe that often and no one in Fornyd noticing," Vera said.

"Good point," I agreed. "Luren, you mind taking point on this? We'll move around to the side so we can watch the front door and the rear. You approach the rear door and call out. We'll have you covered."

"What do you want me to say?"

"You're a hunter who got separated from his party. You're wondering if they can spare any provisions. And of course you try to find out what they're doing out here."

"Got it. I'll wait five minutes for you to get into position."

Vera and Lörry came with me this time, and I situated us on the eastern side of the cabin behind an obliging bit of underbrush that concealed us while allowing us to observe.

"Be ready to do your thing, Lörry," I said in low tones. "If a bunch of guys pour out of there and go after Luren, you pull the water out of their heads."

The kid gulped. "Okay."

We had to wait for a tense minute before Luren called out to the cabin. We heard some shuffling inside, and after a few seconds a man opened the rear door, holding a sword. I half-expected it to be someone from another country, maybe even a Bone Giant, but it was a Brynt man whom no one would call handsome. He wasn't armored up but didn't seem to care.

"What do you want?" he growled. "I don't have any food."

"Perhaps some water, then?" Luren said.

"No."

"Come on. You have to have something to live on. Help me out. It's the Gravewood."

"You shouldn't be here." The man took his eyes off Luren and scanned the surroundings. I ducked down behind the underbrush, and Lörry and Vera had the good sense to do the same.

"Neither should you, but here we are. Please, friend. My party was attacked, and only I am left."

"You're alone?"

"Aye," Luren lied.

"Ha! That simplifies things, then."

Peeking over the tops of the foliage, I saw the stranger step past the threshold and advance on Luren, twirling his sword.

"What? Hold on, now, what are you doing?" Luren said. The man only laughed and kept coming. Luren backed up a few steps and drew his sword. I had full confidence that Luren could defeat him, but there was no reason to risk it.

"Drop him now," I told Lörry.

"Now?"

"Now! That's the order!"

He hesitated far longer than I would have liked, but he did it. Scrunched up his face, clenched his fist, and the man's full body spasmed once before he fell over. I thought that would be the end of it, but it was just the beginning.

"I could have taken him," Luren groused, and we all stood up. But something else stood too.

A silent, pale, yawning face of horror emerged from the dead man's head, and then a body flowed after it, deathly white and taller somehow than the Brynt man had been, and it lunged toward Luren, bony yet spectral arms outstretched.

"What in Bryn's blue sea—" Luren began, and he hacked through the apparition once before it dove right into his mouth and he seized up, shaking uncontrollably, eyes rolling back into his head.

It took me a couple of seconds to process what I had seen

and what was happening, but Vera figured it out as soon as I did, and together we exclaimed, "It's a wraith!"

"A wraith?" Lörry said. "Those things are real?"

Pointing at Luren, I shouted, "You just saw it!"

"What do we do?" Vera asked. That was an excellent question, and precious seconds ticked by as I realized that I had to answer it, and the answer was terrible, and even though there was no other viable answer I still didn't want to do it.

"Luren is already dead," I said. "The wraith is possessing him and will ultimately win. So we have to drown him."

"Drown him in what?" Lörry said.

"The contents of our canteens."

"Just so I understand," Vera said, "you want to drown your own mynstad."

"If we don't, the wraith will use him to do whatever evil shit it wants. And if we don't do it correctly, it will escape again and possess one of us instead. So do as I say while it's still fighting for control. Now's our best opportunity."

"This is dreadful."

"I know. Lörry, listen. You have to send water into his lungs but also maintain a globe of water around his head, so when he dies, the wraith will be trapped. The wraith can't pass through water."

"Can't he just rip the water out of his head while keeping containment?" Vera asked.

"No, that would be like trying to push and pull open a door at the same time," Lörry said. "Containment means pushing in from every direction, so pulling the water in his head in any direction would force me to drop containment. But even what you're suggesting is not simple waterwork. You need a tidal mariner for that kind of thing."

"You can do it. You have to," I said. "Once the wraith is trapped and looking to escape, you contract that globe. Fill every bit of space with water, and it will drown too."

"This . . . this isn't anything like what they said it would be. They said I'd be serving the country. I'm killing guys, and I don't want to do that."

"You *are* serving the country. The wraith who possessed that man," I said, pointing to the corpse, "was not a friend to Brynlön. He looked like a Bone Giant! And he won't be a friend when he has fully possessed Mynstad Luren either. He's an enemy, and we're going to find out what he was up to, but first we have to make sure he's defeated. So let's go. Get the job done and then, if you think I was wrong, bring charges to the quartermaster. I won't stop you and I'll take full responsibility."

Snatching my canteen from my belt, I strode out toward the convulsing Luren, expecting the others to follow. After a moment, I heard their footsteps behind me. Good enough.

"You need us to dump it out?" I asked.

"No, just removing the cap will be sufficient."

"Good. Because we're going to need to hold him upright, Vera, so the wraith can't break containment by smashing his head into the ground."

"What? There's no way I can prevent a man that size from doing whatever he wants. He's huge and I am not."

She had a point. Truth be told, I'd have trouble restraining Luren all by myself. But maybe . . .

"Okay, get him mostly drowned first. When he's nearly dead and starving for oxygen, I should be able to hold him."

We removed our caps and put our canteens on the ground, and Lörry was able to easily direct the contents of mine down Luren's mouth and nose to start filling up his lungs. That inspired plenty of coughing and spluttering, but the water kept coming, and Lörry applied all the pressure needed to simulate Luren being submerged in the ocean. He fell first to his knees and then toppled over to lie prone. That was going to be a problem. I'd have to lift him up to make sure Lörry could get containment around his head. But he was already weakening.

I knelt behind him and hooked some fingers inside his collar by his right shoulder to pull him into a sitting position. There I braced him as best as I could. He was still struggling but fading fast.

"Get a bubble around his head now, before he dies," I said. "If the wraith gets free again, it'll come after one of us."

Lörry directed more water from a canteen to circle Luren's head, and I said to my mynstad, "I'm so sorry, my friend. I didn't expect this to happen. But I can't imagine you'd want to live as a possessed man."

Luren couldn't respond, but I hoped he understood. His struggling subsided after another fifteen seconds, and then the wraith, denied a living host and therefore a way to hide, tried to escape. The inside of the water globe clouded, and Luren's head disappeared. Lörry looked like he was straining.

"You're doing great, kid, keep it up," I said. "In fact, I need you to contract the globe slowly, so it's tight around his head, and then bring up that water from the lungs to fill it. The wraith will have nowhere to go, because it can't reenter a dead brain, and you'll drown it too."

"How do you know all this?" Vera asked.

"Campfire stories. You hear some interesting ones if you've been around like I have. There's probably a better way to do this, something more efficient, but this is the best procedure I could think of under pressure."

"At least it's a procedure."

Lörry followed through on my instructions. The sphere of clouded water shrank and then bulged as the extra water from the lungs came up and filled the bubble. The clouding intensified and then, abruptly, cleared away. Luren's head could be seen again. The wraith was extinguished.

"Good job, kid. You did it. You can release it now."

With a grunt, the kid let go of the water and I got soaked. He fell to his knees, breathing heavily, and I gently allowed Luren to slump over and rest.

Vera knelt next to Lörry. "You okay?"

"Yeah . . ." he gasped, "but I'm older. I can feel that took a toll." He threw a resentful glare my way. "Didn't expect this assignment to spend my life so quickly."

"No, and Luren didn't expect to lose his," I replied. "None of this was expected. This cabin, or lodge, or whatever it is, wasn't supposed to be here. Join me when you feel like it. I'm going to check it out, try to see what he was doing."

What he was doing, it turned out, was spying for the Bone Giants. That became obvious once I saw the documents piled high on a desk, some of it in Brynt but much of it in the written language of the documents we'd taken from the Bone Giants earlier.

"Bone Giant wraiths are possessing us and walking around as spies," I said, hearing Vera and Lörry enter behind me. "You know what this means? When they invaded and came upriver, they didn't just know the locations of our cities. They had detailed intelligence on our numbers and defenses and everything."

"But who was he reporting to? Someone to the north?" Vera asked.

"Is there anything even up there?" Lörry added.

"Something's up there," I said, "because there's a path in that direction. We're going to have to follow it later."

"Why later?"

"Because Mynstad Luren needs to be taken home to the sea. And we need to take this intelligence back to Fornyd and let the quartermaster know the Bone Giants have been spying on us. We're going to need a new mynstad and maybe another rapid or a tidal mariner, if we're going to run into more of these spies." I frowned, looking over Lörry's face. He didn't seem visibly older. "How bad was it? I'm sorry you had to overextend yourself."

He shook his head and waved it off. "A stabbing headache and pain in my guts, but both of them passed. Probably aged a month or two. I think I can do it more efficiently next time. Anyway, it doesn't matter. I see what you were worried about now."

"Good. I need you and Vera to carry everything that has writing on it. Just throw it in a pack or something as quick as you can. We shouldn't linger. We need to get Luren out of here before scavengers show up."

"Right," Vera said, and started looking for something that would serve as a container for the papers.

While they got busy, I returned outside to defend the bodies until it was time to leave. Which gave me some time to think.

How many other cities had outposts like this? I knew that Grynek didn't have any—our band hunted all along the northern shore and never came across anything like this. But a cabin in the Gravewood wouldn't be necessary. Spies could live in the city easily.

Which implied a whole network of such spies. At least one or more in every one of our cities. The way I figured it, based on the intelligence the Bone Giants had before they ever set foot on our shores, the existence of that network was a near certainty.

I was aware that I should be grieving for Luren, but I also knew that grief rolled in on waves, and sometimes you could surf on them or dive underneath them, but eventually one of them would crash upon you and you'd be justified in thinking you might drown.

Right then I was fighting those waves with what felt like a bottomless well of fury. As they took from me, I wished to take from them—or, more properly, I wished to collect on a debt. The Bone Giants owed me an ocean of blood.

A small voice cried out in my mind, muted as if calling from a great distance, telling me that I wasn't in a healthy place and I needed to get out of there. But I didn't know where else to go, even if I wanted to.

———

A whole beetle could have flown into my mouth unimpeded after Daryck's final words. They so perfectly illustrated my own feelings regarding the loss of my wife and the vengeance I wished upon Melishev Lohmet. I should absolutely be in a better place mentally, but I don't think I wanted to be. The desire for a reckoning can sweep one's good sense away like a tide, and we are powerless to swim against such a force.

Day 42

ON THE TRAIL OF SPIES

I sang a tiny song in the morning to what might be my last toast.

"Laaaaaast toast!" I belted out. "You might be my final crunch! Tomorrow I must find something else to munch! But I will miss you the moooost, my tooooast."

Let those who may judge me remember that I was never blessed by the Poet Goddess Kaelin.

Upon one slice I heaped Kaurian orange marmalade, and on another I spooned a generous dollop of Fornish honey, both jars looking rather depleted. It was delicious and bittersweet. I supposed I still had some food available if I counted what remained in my jars, but without bread they seemed like sadness.

I went first to the bakery to see if some miracle worker had brought flour in the night, but the shop was closed entirely, with a promise to reopen when food returned.

Another man stopped next to me and read the sign, then waved at it and muttered, "We're so fucked."

The earliest winter-wheat harvest was still months away, and it would be meager, taking into account that the farmers surrounding many of our cities never got to plant a crop. I nodded sadly.

"I think sometimes that surviving the invasion was an illusion," he continued. "We were all killed back then, but some of us simply haven't dropped yet."

We parted ways, rumblings in our bellies and tremors in our hearts. I, for one, did not want to drop before I knew the

fate of Sarena's murderer. And since I was being redirected
into a whirlpool of futility every time I visited the palace, I
had a new idea on how to find out.

I visited the Kaurian embassy, inquiring if I might speak to
Kindin Ladd, the priest of the gale. He emerged after only a
short wait, dressed in oranges and browns, and welcomed me
with a smile.

"Master Dervan. What a pleasure. I hope you breathe
peace today."

"Thank you, Kindin. I'm not at peace at all, unfortunately,
which is why I came to see you."

"Oh? How may I help?"

"An inconsistency has built in my mind regarding the
bard's tale, and I'd like to have it resolved. I need to know
whether Melishev Lohmet is alive or dead, and I'm hopeful
that the Nentian citizens living here in Pelemyn might know
something about it. Unless you do?"

"No, I don't."

"Well, I wonder if you might agree to accompany me as I
ask some Nentians about it?"

"I might. Why would my presence be necessary?"

"In case they become violent, I'd like you to save me, since
I am no longer a very good fighter, despite my recent attempts at training."

The priest looked confused. "You feel that if you ask a
Nentian whether their current king is alive, they will attack
you?"

"I feel it's a possibility—an unlikely one, just to be clear.
But a possibility nonetheless, owing to the unflattering por-
trayal of him by the bard. Some Nentians have proven sensitive about that. I'm simply trying to anticipate it and hoping
you can prevent any permanent injuries."

"Are you asking this as a favor?"

"I would of course donate to a charity of your choice to
thank you for your time and effort."

"I see. And when would you like to do this?"

"Today, if your leisure serves."

"I'm afraid my schedule is filled for the rest of the day. You've caught me during a brief span of free time."

"Tomorrow, perhaps?"

"Yes. I'm free all morning."

"Excellent. Then I'll return tomorrow. I'm breathing easier already."

"I'm glad to hear it."

With a plan in mind, I was able to concentrate on work when I met Fintan for our daily scribe session, whereupon he informed me that he was just about caught up with everything that had happened elsewhere, except for recent events in Fornyd.

"We'll hear more from them soon, I feel certain," he said.

Upon the wall, Fintan welcomed Eimear and another Raelech singer to perform something they called a goddess chime.

"These are written in three parts to honor the triple goddess in Rael. They have no lyrics, just vowel sounds, and they are usually heard at religious services or public gatherings. The bass part, which I'll be singing, is supposed to represent Dinae; the tenor, sung today by Eimear, represents Raena; and the soprano part, which will be performed by our guest, Niamh, represents Kaelin."

They began, and I'm not sure I can describe it with mere words. It was beautiful, and sometimes they hit chords that made me shiver. It was music one could feel in the bones, and more than one person's eyes watered. I hoped I'd get to hear one of those chimes again.

When they finished, Eimear and Niamh left the wall, and Fintan took the stage alone after the break.

"We're going to return yet again to Pen Yas ben Min and Daryck du Löngren, with a bonus returning star in between," the bard said. "Pen's up first."

Pen

Securing the embassy at Talala Fouz technically wasn't my mission: I was supposed to be looking for a place to plant the Fourth Tree, and I knew I wouldn't be planting it in the city, so that meant I should be on my way. But at the same time, it really felt like the best way for me to put the Canopy first was to linger and make sure our interests were safe from a truly malicious man. The stories I'd heard about this Melishev Lohmet inspired the same horror as the creepy footfalls of some mystery insect crawling about on one's legs, and while he was currently very ill, we fully expected a difficult time upon his recuperation.

Ambassador Ken had been right: The Nentians didn't come storming into the embassy looking for her, because they couldn't afford to admit that they'd imprisoned her in the first place. What they did instead was flood the Red Pheasant tea treehouse with spies. More than one had to be stopped as they "got lost" in private clan areas of the tree-house. And one solicitous diplomat arrived at the embassy to ask, rather transparently, if the staff had heard any good news about Ambassador Ken.

Del Mot Goh lied and told him no, alas, we had heard nothing. Because while we did not consider the Nentian peo-ple to be our enemies, the current king and his minions were certainly no longer allies.

"Are there any other greensleeves in the city besides Mak Fin ben Fos?"

Del had been schooled to expect that question and to lie again. "Not that we're aware of. Why?"

"There have been rumors of sightings."

"Oh. Well, if a greensleeve passed through the city, we

would not know unless they specifically came here to tell us they were in town."

"Would they not stop here as a matter of course?"

"Not unless they had some business. There are many clans in Forn, and each has its own agenda to pursue; few of them, honestly, have any business with the embassy."

"I see. Speaking of clans: Can you confirm the existence of the Blue Piper Clan?"

"The Blue Moths are a powerful clan, if that's who you mean. But I can tell you with absolute certainty the Blue Pipers do not exist."

The diplomat found that interesting and took his leave.

In practical terms, the Nentian efforts to find both Ambassador Ken and me meant that we had to hide on our private clan decks during the day and come down only at night, when everyone was gone except for embassy staff. And that staff did not travel outside the embassy singly anymore but in large groups, to discourage abduction and interrogation attempts.

The necessity for this became clear when a group including Del was prevented from entering the Raelech embassy to speak to the diplomats there. They were searched for documents but weren't carrying any. The Nentian soldiers who stopped them wanted to know why they were going to the Raelech embassy.

"To conduct Fornish business."

"Some other time. Not now."

The Raelechs weren't oblivious to what was going on; their diplomats were likewise stopped from entering our embassy the next day. Which meant the king definitely thought Ambassador Ken was inside and wanted to make sure she couldn't get any help.

Fortunately, the Raelechs had a way around that. Or, rather, under it. The next day they had a stonecutter create a tunnel between their embassy and ours. There was a tense moment when the Raelechs first emerged, but some fast talking and the long trust between our nations established that they'd been worried about us and wanted to make sure we were okay. That allowed Ambassador Ken to tell them what had been done to her and that she—and we—needed help. They promised to send for some right away. They would dispatch messages upriver, and if a courier arrived in the meantime, they'd send a message through them as well. The Triune Council would be informed and help would arrive, though it would be weeks away.

Meanwhile, at Ambassador Ken's direction, Mak and I started growing a living wall of whipthorn hedges around the embassy compound. They were attractive plants with broad dark leaves, yellow flowers, and long, flexible branches that grew vertically, ideal for creating a wall six or seven feet high. Getting snagged by a thorn or two was no big deal unless you tried to yank away. You'd wind up causing a reaction where the other branches whipped down and snared you good. The more violence you offered it, the more you got in return. Especially if, say, a greensleeve was paying attention and helped the plants move.

In practice, this usually meant that the individual plant got destroyed in the snared creature's attempt to get away. But it also guaranteed that the creature would stay away from whipthorns after that.

The Nentians noticed and didn't like it, but they couldn't stop us. Every embassy had walls of some kind. Ours just grew faster than any that could be built.

A sort of gated entryway required some testing and tweaking. We wound up creating a single entrance to the compound with a greeting area, and from there visitors were directed to either the tea treehouse or the embassy building itself. We walled the paths to the treehouse and the embassy with whipthorns to prevent spies from "getting lost" on the grounds, and once that secured the rest of the compound, we were able to bring in that Raelech stonecutter from their embassy and have him dig a protected well for us.

The current water supply was courtesy of the Nentian government, filtered from the Gravewater. But since we had reason to doubt their courtesy, it would be better to have a filtered well designed by Brynt hygienists but built by a Raelech. And we kept the tunnel to the Raelech embassy open, not only for free flow of information between us but also in case we needed a food supply or, at the last extremity, an escape.

"Do you really believe that's necessary?" I asked Ambassador Ken when she shared her reasoning with Mak, Del, and me. "You think the king would attack the embassy or put it under siege?"

"If he feels sufficiently threatened or if he thinks it would work to his benefit, absolutely. I don't put anything past him. Let's be clear: He was going to have a cheek raptor tear off my face and leave me to be eaten by sedge pumas and wheat dogs because I couldn't get a Brynt hygienist to cure him of his disease. When that didn't work out, he wanted me to suffer in darkness until I perished. So, yes, I think he's capable of attacking us here. He is spiteful and murderous and, as far as I can tell, cares nothing for anyone but himself."

The four of us shuddered in revulsion at the thought of such selfishness. We had all been taught from sprouts to think of ourselves last.

"He will be so alone when he dies," Del said. "No one to mourn him. No one to testify how he helped them grow. I can't imagine."

That sent me to my private deck later, where I finally opened the small precious pouch that Vet Mof ben Tam had given me. After I'd picked apart the knot that tied it closed and upended it, a beautiful, lustrous acorn fell into my palm. The cap had a silvery sheen to it, and I had never seen anything so perfect and beautiful. I was weeping before I knew it.

"I know I should be moving on to find a place to plant you," I said, "but I feel that the interests of the Canopy require me to be here right now. It's hard to know what to do."

Before I could feel utterly ridiculous for talking to an acorn, a woman's deep voice spoke in my head, bypassing the ears. *Hello, Pen Yas ben Min. Tell me why you feel it's important to stay here.*

I couldn't reply at first. Had that really happened?

Yes, I am speaking to you.

"Oh, my—oh! Um. Ahhh . . ." So much for being heroic like my cousin Nel. She had always known what to say. At least, it seemed that way when I was around her.

Plenty of people get flustered the first time they hear my voice in their head. It's part of the reason why I don't speak often in the sway—I'd rather you make your own decisions. But as this decision bears directly on my fate, perhaps it's best to offer an opinion. Tell me the problem.

Okay, well, if everyone else had difficulty getting their thoughts together when hearing the First Tree, I could hardly continue to lose my mind, could I? The imperative here was to prove that I could be cool under pressure, not some fragile spirit who lost her composure every time she had a new experience. So I told them. (Whenever the First Tree spoke, greensleeves reported that the voice sounded different. Some identified it as male, some heard it as female, so the convention in our language was to use a genderless pronoun.)

And when I finished, the acorn of the Fourth Tree said, *Stay and help. When you feel an urge to move on—weeks or months or years from now—that will be the right time. I cannot speak much more until I am planted, but I am glad we spoke today. You have my trust and gratitude.*

"Thank you. I look forward to speaking again, wherever and whenever that is."

Likewise.

I put the acorn back in the bag and tied it up, feeling

strangely that it was so much bigger than me. There was a *consciousness* in there.

Feeling small and insignificant in the face of a vast world is something that Sprout often voices to Sage in *Leafsong*.

—*How can I know if I matter, Sage?* she asks. *I fear I am no different from the ant or the blade of grass, easily trod upon and forgotten.*

—*You bring comfort and warmth to all who know you, Sprout. You are like cotton, spun into threads and then woven into fabric. You are part of something large and wondrous, it is true, but without you it would not be so fine. Every thread in a tapestry is key to the whole's apparent mastery.*

I held on to that last line more than any other. It allowed me to sleep at night.

Ah, what lovely stuff. I really did need to get ahold of *Leafsong* someday and read the whole thing.

The bard delighted everyone by asking a leading question next: "Tell me, good people of Pelemyn, who would you say likes mustard more than anyone on the planet?"

"Gondel Vedd!" came the answer from Survivor Field, yelled by thousands of people.

Gondel

I have taken more sea voyages in the past year than I have in my life, and while there is much to recommend it, the drawbacks are fairly clear.

- The accommodations for relieving oneself are nightmarish. First, you're pretty much in full view of anyone who wants to watch. Not that anyone does—it's just that the potential for embarrassment is high. But in addition to a profound lack of privacy, dangling one's backside over an ocean full of hungry creatures is incredibly stressful.

- Reading is easy enough on a rocking boat, but writing is not.
- It is impossible to eat without spilling something, and I am already a low-skill eater.
- It's difficult to wash clothes, and nearly all of mine are stained because of the above.
- Sea shanties are difficult to tune out when you're trying to concentrate.

I therefore try to focus on what I enjoy. The salty air and the salty language; the extraordinary good manners, outside of the salty language, because we recognize that we are in cramped quarters and therefore in someone's way almost all the time; the creak of timbers and the snap of sails; the soft crush of waves against the hull and the whispers of wind. And this time, the company of my husband, Maron, with whom I am delighted to share close quarters.

He has been tremendously supportive, content to read poetry in his bunk, a mere arm's length away, as I try to translate the sheaf of Eculan documents given to me by Mistral Kira.

They had been in the possession of an officer slain by a party of hunters north of one of the river cities, and the pelenaut had sent them down in hopes that they might air out a foul room and provide insight into their plans.

They didn't do that, exactly—they were mostly reports of the aftermath of the invasion. But that gave breath to a much more urgent whisper: There were spies reporting on all Brynt cities, not just the previously identified Vjeko. There was a network of informers providing crucial intelligence.

"Brynlön is infested with spies," I murmured, mostly to

myself. But Maron heard me and thought I was talking to him.

"Better spies than dickskin mites."

"Pfff. You say that about everything."

"Yes, but only because it's true. Gondel, my love, I'll take twenty spies in the capital over a single mite nibbling on my dickskin all day, every day. Spies just aren't that bad in the relative scheme of things."

"No, no, listen. The man carrying these reports was found far from any of the Brynt cities. He was near the coast of the Northern Yawn, in fact, and had never been in any of the cities. So how did he come by this information?"

"I'm going to guess and say it was spies."

"Indeed. And the Brynts have no idea."

"Well, you can give them one," he said, returning to his poetry, and his dismissive tone annoyed me. I turned around to face him.

"Maron, what if we have a similar network of spies in Kauria?"

He looked up. "That would be bad, for sure, but I'd still rather have that than dickskin mites."

"I need you to forget about mites for just a minute."

"Why? It gives me the perspective I need to face life's challenges with equanimity."

I took a calming breath before replying. "This spy network has obviously been in place for a long time. It would explain the coordination of the invasion. If we have such a network in Kauria, they could be setting us up for invasion as well. Entire cities put to the sword."

That gave him pause. "So that Bone Giant—"

"Eculan!"

"—Eculan prisoner in the hold could be the first of many?"

"Yes. We have thought from day one that Saviič was a scout of some kind, and I discovered personally that more like Saviič landed in Brynlön prior to the invasion. So figuring out how that officer in the north got these reports should be a priority."

"You're not suggesting that there have been giants like Saviič hiding in Brynt cities all along and they never noticed?"

"No. Something else is going on. I just don't know what. But I'm fairly sure we should skip Pelemyn altogether and sail directly upriver to Fornyd."

"Skip the capital of Brynt civilization, where all the leadership is, and travel instead to a tiny, isolated hamlet?"

"I don't think it's that small or isolated. It might not have the tea culture you're used to—"

"That's what I'm afraid of, Gondel. That and the mites you told me to forget about."

"They'll have tea, don't worry. You'll be fine."

"Why do you think we need to skip Pelemyn? Shouldn't we at least stop and say hello?"

"No. Because I don't want to be intercepted or delayed. Logic says I need to go to Fornyd."

"Logic doesn't say that to me, so I am going to need you to explain, please."

"The hunters who found this intelligence are based out of Fornyd. All the other river cities were destroyed. Therefore, the only point of contact with the north that we know about is Fornyd, which means messages are most likely passing through there. Stopping at Pelemyn would introduce delays and the possibility that we would tip off the spies that no doubt remain there. I'd rather inform the quartermaster of Fornyd directly about this threat to eliminate middlemen and speak to the hunters if I can. What? Do I have new stains?"

Maron was looking at me with an amused expression.

"No, the old ones are holding fast. I simply think that you are adorable. The way you light up when someone asks you to explain."

I deflated. "Did you even hear me, or were you just enjoying your playtime?"

"I heard you and understand the decision," he assured me. "But will the captain go along with this scheme of yours?"

"Since she is supposed to take me where I want to go, by orders of Mistral Kira, I believe she will."

"Whoooa," Maron said in awe. "What does it feel like to have such raw power? Such potent puissance? Gondel Vedd, Scholar of Action!"

My husband loves to tease me. I adopted a look of smug satisfaction.

"It has its benefits. Some people are attracted to power, you know."

"And food stains?"

"In extraordinary cases, yes, one will find a person such as yourself who is attracted to both power and food stains. A rare overlapping of interests. You are incredibly lucky to have found me, a person blessed with an abundance of both, and I am lucky to have found you."

The captain was at first reluctant to change course, because she had messages to deliver to Pelemyn on behalf of the mistral, but I convinced her that my need took precedence and that she could stop by Pelemyn on the way back. She should further inform the pelenaut in person—dropping my name if necessary—that he should send only his most trusted member of the military to see me in Fornyd for information vital to Brynlön's security.

I am not sure what power I have except over language, but if it could help me save lives, then I would wield it to my utmost.

That tale told me that Pelenaut Röllend had definitely been keeping things from me. If this happened months ago, and he just recently sent Nara du Fesset to check on Gondel, then something had been going on there for a good while without the general public's knowledge. I needed to get the timeline nailed down solid with Fintan. Perhaps it would help shed light on the Nentian issues as well.

Fintan hefted a black sphere in his hand and said before dropping it, "While Gondel was journeying to Fornyd, the Grynek Hunters were about to begin their own journey north of the city."

He threw down the sphere and transformed into Gerstad du Löngren.

Daryck

We got no extra rapid or tidal mariner, but once Quartermaster du Cannym understood the gravity of our discovery, she assigned me a new mynstad, an extra provisions wagon, and an extra squad of archers.

Curiously, the Gravewood had very little problem with our presence—until we passed the cabin where Luren died.

Two wagons, a dozen people, all on edge because we were in the most hostile of environments headed toward unknown dangers rather than unknown safety, and we smelled delicious to everything in the forest with sharp teeth.

The path eventually got lost underneath a carpet of spruce needles, but that didn't cause as much dismay as the existence of the needles themselves. The chance of losing the trail was a minor danger compared to what lived among the trees.

Spruce marmosets are cute in isolation, perched upon a branch and making faces—and sometimes throwing feces, which I suppose makes them less cute. They are small and harmless on their own. The problem is that they are never, ever on their own. They cry out and relay information about targets, and eventually someone in your party will be assailed from the air—not by the marmosets but by spruce harriers, who live in symbiosis with them.

The harriers observe and listen from the tallest branches of the spruce, their plumage the same color as the blue-green needles of the trees. They're usually not seen until they're diving for your face, if at all—sometimes they dive for the back of your neck.

And the way to get picked as a target is to smell like fear and put up either a poor fight or no fight at all as the marmosets stalk you, jumping from the branches of trees and always watching, always noisily communicating information. Those who fire arrows—especially the ones who get close or even hit a target—are rarely chosen to be attacked. But the thing is, the marmosets *want* to be fired at. They are smart enough to know the ammunition is limited, and they want it exhausted.

Eventually a target is chosen, and then the harriers attack. Their talons are designed to slash open hide, so human skin is like tissue to them. They dive and either cut throats or cut through spinal cords and then ascend, assess, and wait. The marmosets reevaluate too. With other animals, the rest of the herd moves on, leaving the dead, and then the harriers eat first, while the marmosets clean up, taking whatever gobbets of meat are left. But humans are different: They'll defend the fallen up to a certain point. So additional targets get chosen, which is fine for all parties concerned, including any scavenging latecomers: It just means more to eat. The marmosets and harriers can be patient.

Fortunately, it's not a stealthy ambush. You know the danger when you're stepping into a stand of spruce. And you know there's more danger when the marmosets start talking.

So when we reached the spruce needles north of the spy cabin and I heard the first whooping yelps of the marmosets, I gave orders. The archers were to pick targets and fire two arrows at will. We draped chain mail over the necks of our horses. Like all the Grynek Hunters and me, Gyrsön wore a chain aventail underneath his helmet as a matter of course—it was basic protection against meat squirrels as well—but he added steel bracers to his forearms. He was to go ahead and be as afraid as he wanted, because he was the bait. The rest of us were to act aggressively.

And then we had to push forward through the forest and wait for the attack, shouting a warning to Gyrsön—or whoever was the target—if we could. Anyone targeted was to drop and cover their neck. When the harriers swooped up, the archers would try to take them out, because they were the true threat. The marmosets couldn't take down a kitten; their whole game was to help the harriers eat so they could enjoy the leftovers.

It was tense, walking through that stretch of forest. We were all soaked in sweat before long, and Gyrsön had to drop twice in response to attacks. We shot down three harriers; two had gone after Gyrsön, and another had attacked a horse.

But we made it through without any severe injuries—the horse got scratched. It did make me wonder, however, how the spies got through if they traveled this way. Were they traveling in covered wagons? Or did the marmosets and harriers sense somehow that those particular humans were possessed by wraiths and not safe to eat? When the needles cleared up and we had some grasses and leaves to look at instead, we spread out a bit to find the trail again, because we had indeed strayed somewhat. It turned out to be a few dozen lengths to the west.

The horse who'd suffered a scratch got attacked from the west by a pair of razor tusks, but the extra archers brought them down, and that meant we had dinner settled. Gyrsön was actually thrilled by this development and requested an early stop so we could slow-roast them, but I said that we had no time for slow-roasting and he'd have to adjust his culinary plans to whipping up something quick.

Another couple of hours on the trail brought us to another hut—this one empty of occupants but containing more records in the Bone Giant language, which we collected.

There was also a small barn—empty of animals but well stocked with tools and weapons, including arrows, as well as some extra wagon wheels, barrels of rainwater that Vera pronounced fit to drink, and oats for horses. That seemed to confirm that the path was often traveled by wagons. We camped there for the night, recognizing that we were looking at a waypoint shelter, a basic defense against nocturnal predators while one slept in the Gravewood.

The need for such shelter became clear before dawn, as the sky opened up and rained on us. A gravemaw showed up during my watch in the early-morning hours and ate one of our archers before we could wake Lörry to take it down. We spent an hour harvesting some of the gravemaw's natural armor, which would fetch a fine price, before breakfasting on pan-fried razor-tusk steaks and moving on in search of the next hut.

We suffered an average number of attacks from various animals on the way, but our armor held, and we kept calm and kept moving.

About midafternoon we got word from scouts that there was another waypoint ahead—a more expansive operation than the others and occupied by at least three people.

"Excellent. I want all the archers save one to come with me. Vera, I want you to stay with Gyrsön as well, plus two soldiers to protect the wagons. Everyone else is coming to shut down a spy operation."

The new mynstad, Söla du Högyn, raised her hand. She was shorter than Luren, certainly less muscular, but extremely quick and efficient in her movements and well respected. "Gerstad, can you remind us how we know these men are spies?"

"Sure. One, they're sitting on a trail used by spies we've already found. Two, no hunters for any Brynt cities would be established this deep into the Gravewood. Three, I imagine this waypoint is like the others—a cabin for the people, a barn for the animals, a woodshed, and an outhouse?" I looked to the scout to confirm, and he nodded.

"Yes, Gerstad."

"Did you see any skins drying? Hides to be tanned? Snares in the woods?"

"No, Gerstad."

"There you have it. They are not hunters. They are spies. Enemies of Brynlön, possessed by wraiths that will possess any one of us if they get a chance. So we're going to do this as planned."

And the plan was nothing like the other one, where we called out and hoped they'd expose themselves. That worked fine on a single spy but wouldn't work on three or more. At least one would hunker down inside the cabin, and then we'd have trouble getting to him before he destroyed evidence we needed. So it was going to be a very patient ambush.

If all else failed, we were going to wait for them to use the outhouse.

Chirping birds and chattering squirrels—the nicer kind, which liked seeds more than flesh—muffled the sound of our approach.

A gurgling creek passing nearby indicated why this was a good spot for a larger operation. They had cleared a bunch of trees to create a bit of a perimeter and had actually done some farming in the short growing season, which told me they'd been here for some years, plotting against us and planning an invasion that ultimately wiped out most of the people I knew and loved in the world.

The cabin was larger than the others, and its walls were dotted with murder holes through which to shoot arrows at attackers—or take shots at any unwitting herbivores that might stray too close. They might not be hunters, but they surely didn't mind some variation in their diet.

The outhouse sat to the right, and the creek ran to the left with perhaps thirty lengths of space between it and the house.

Also to the left, but past the house and barely visible from where we were, a barn squatted in the sun. We saw no one at the moment, but the scout maintained he'd spotted three men moving from the barn into the cabin. They might be in there now, or they could be in the barn or split up in any combination, since he'd returned to deliver his report.

"Okay, the barn's our way in. The far side of it will be a blind spot to the house."

We circled around to the west until we could see all the buildings—the cabin, outhouse, and barn. The outhouse was probably too far away to get an accurate shot, but I'd modified the plan a bit in any case. I stationed Mynstad du Högyn at our vantage point with three archers. I took Lörry and two more archers a bit farther north, until the barn hid the house from us. At that point, we changed course and headed straight for the barn, staying low and moving across open space as quickly as we could, making sure to keep the house out of sight. Once we got to the back of it—there was no rear exit, I noticed—I peeked around the corner on the side facing the creek. All clear, which was confirmed by the mynstad, who used hand signals from her cover to tell me to proceed.

The four of us, with myself in the lead, crept around the side. Once I reached the front, I dropped to the damp ground and risked a look at the house, hoping they weren't waiting with an arrow for just such a development. No cry of alarm. No sounds from the house either.

From the barn itself we heard a nicker. There was at least one horse inside, who probably smelled and heard us. There might even be a human inside who hadn't.

Pushing myself up, I spoke in low tones to one of the archers. "I want you to bang your bow on the side of the barn really loud, try to startle the horse inside. That might get a reaction."

The archer nodded, walked back a few steps to where we'd heard the nicker, and slammed the bottom of his bow into the wood as hard as he could. The horse whinnied in fear—precisely what I wanted. The alarm was raised.

Motion came from the trees a few seconds later. Mynstad du Högyn let me know via hand signal that we had one on the way.

"Arrows nocked," I said to the archers. "Lörry, be ready."

The rapid nodded and unscrewed the cap from his canteen.

Footsteps approached, the rustle and clink of leather and clasps, the dull thud of boots on the ground. Muttering in some language that wasn't Brynt. I counted several more steps, and when I judged he was about to the door, I signaled the two archers to do their thing.

They sprang forward around the corner, pulled, and fired at the target. He cried out and I moved fast, the archers joining me. We had a man who appeared to be a Brynt collapsed on the ground, with a couple of arrows sticking out of his left thigh. I hooked him under the armpit and an archer did the same on the other side, adding a hand over his mouth to muffle any shouts that might bring the others, and we quickly dragged him out of sight behind the barn, where we held him up. I told the other archer to be ready for the next one and to watch the mynstad for signals.

With time to take a look at the wounded man, I realized he was, in fact, a hunter I knew from Festwyf—though I hadn't seen him in many years. Could he really be here legitimately? Had I just ordered the shooting of an innocent man?

"Rynfyrd—is that you? Quietly, now." The archer removed his hand so the man could speak.

"What? Yes! Yes, it's me! Why have you done this?"

"If you're Rynfyrd, then who am I?"

"You're . . . you're my old friend! What is happening?"

"I'm going to need a name, Rynfyrd, if you truly are who you say you are."

"Auggh! I've got two arrows in my leg and can't think!"

"Huh. You're not Rynfyrd anymore, or you'd have no trouble remembering me. I'm not your old friend, you see. I slept with your mother *and* your sister and wrote a famous cock sonnet about them, and you challenged me to a duel. I accepted but then had you poisoned so that you were shitting yourself instead of attending the duel you had called for. There's no way you'd forget that." I caught Lörry's eye. "Begin. He's a wraith."

"What? No!" His visage changed from fear to wrath as he realized he'd been found out and that we'd obviously known in advance to expect a possessed man. He fought to break free, but we held fast, and soon he was struggling to breathe as Lörry started drowning him with the water in his canteen. I risked a glance at the archer standing sentinel.

"Are we still okay?"

He nodded. "Yeah."

The execution of the spy continued, and I told the archer not to lose his nerve when the wraith was freed from the brain and tried to escape containment.

The warning was well timed, because the archer flinched when the body died and the wraith clouded the globe of water, obscuring Rynfyrd's head.

"Ah! Bryn's black abyss, that's going to give me nightmares."

"You already have nightmares," I said. "We all do. And it's because of guys like this."

"True enough."

It surprised me that no one had emerged in response to Rynfyrd's initial cries. Were the other two napping? Or had they slipped out while the scout was reporting to us, and even now they were outflanking us in some maneuver in the forest?

"How are you feeling, Lörry? Did that go better this time?"

"Yes. No problem. I think I've got it down now. But I'm going to have nightmares too."

"Can't wait for the day when we give them some nightmares. Since those other two aren't very observant, let's throw this body out where they can see it. I mean when they get around to realizing he hasn't come back."

We first removed the arrows, then lugged the body out in full view of the cabin and left it there before retreating from sight. I used hand signals to let Mynstad du Högyn know she should wait and watch her back. She replied that she would.

It took a whole long hour before a voice called from the cabin, its tone querulous, clearly calling a name that wasn't Rynfyrd's.

We heard the cabin door creak open in protest, and the man bellowed the name once more. Then he cursed, evidently seeing the body, and called to someone else. Shortly thereafter, Mynstad du Högyn signaled that two targets were advancing. I waited until they had reached the body and started an animated conversation, trying to figure out what animal might have killed their colleague, before signaling to the mynstad that she should advance and then telling my archers to pop out as well.

I shouted to startle them, and the two men leapt from where they'd been crouching, one falling on his ass and the other turning tail and running back to the cabin.

"Get him first!" I shouted, pointing at the one in retreat, and he got an arrow in the left hamstring and another in the right cheek of his ass. He went down screaming, but nonfatally, which was key. The other one, seeing an opening, got up from the ground and charged one of my archers, drawing his sword. I stepped in front and parried, then was hard-pressed to defend myself, because he was actually quite skilled. Mynstad du Högyn ended it by coming up behind and slashing through the ligaments in the back of his knee. Off balance, his defense wavered, and I was able to slash at his sword hand and lop off his thumb, which meant he wasn't holding on to a sword anymore.

He collapsed to the ground and I backed off, shouting to Mynstad du Högyn, "Get in there and secure the cabin!" If any extra spies were hiding inside, I wanted them dealt with and the intelligence saved.

They ran right past the man who'd taken two arrows from the rear, letting him grunt and try to crawl, though the mynstad assigned an archer to keep an eye on him to make sure he didn't manage to slip away somehow.

I spoke to the archer who'd helped out before. "Ready for another nightmare? Same drill."

"Yeah."

I sheathed my sword, he set down his bow, and the other archer stood guard as Lörry did his work. I had no interest in interrogation, because all I would get were lies. My sole interest was in extracting their particular portion of the vast blood price the Bone Giants owed me.

Both were informed they were being executed for being wraiths and spies, which they denied before it became obvious that they were. We piled the bodies behind the barn so that any scavengers that came along would not threaten us in the cabin. I tasked the mynstad with taking Lörry and a couple of archers back to escort the wagons up to this site, where we'd camp for the night and maybe another, since it was safe now and we could use a rest.

The remainder of the journey contained smaller waystations a day's ride apart, but they were necessary shelters for warmth as we had entered tundra lands, where the snow melted only a few months out of the year, and it had already snowed a couple of times. The trail was marked with ribbons tied around tree trunks, well above the snow line. Eventually we reached the coast of the Northern Yawn, where there was a much bigger compound, with a building that qualified as more of a warehouse than a barn and a couple of docks with some small watercraft tied up. Were they fishing boats or cargo vessels? Coming and going from where? The sea might form an ice pack soon, but for the moment it sloshed coldly against the hulls.

The warehouse looked like it had plenty of room to stock dry goods and other sundries, so that answered where the spy outposts were getting their supplies if not from Brynt cities. The barn was larger too, expansive enough to house multiple wagons and horses.

They'd cleared a large number of trees, most likely for lumber and firewood. They didn't have a stockade or anything, but they had plenty of space to see us coming. We couldn't sneak up on them in the daylight.

I told the wagons to stay back and issued an order to make as little noise as possible—especially to Gyrsön. We didn't want his cooking to alert them that we were here. Quiet sandwiches would be a better idea for dinner than anything involving pots and pans.

Then we waited and watched, and I wondered: Was this the staging area for that Bone Giant army we'd seen to the west? There were signs of long-dead campfires around the compound, so I felt certain that they'd been here at some point—they had to have paid a visit on their way. But why here? What was the purpose of this place and the trail leading down to Fornyd? Was this the endpoint, and was the mastermind of the invasion in one of those buildings ahead? Or were messages and information brought here and then shipped to their final destination? Perhaps some interrogation would be worthwhile this time.

We observed and waited. Seabirds cried and curled in the air. Waves whispered promises of eternity against the shore. There were a few comings and goings to the barn, but no activity at the warehouse or dock. No fishing boats out there. When night fell, all the distant figures collected into what we decided were barracks. There were at least six people in there, by our count, if not more.

But they were six incredibly negligent—or confident—people. They felt so secure that nothing could threaten them that they didn't even set a watch.

That stung. Invaders to our own country, unafraid and behaving as if they were home in safety.

"Everyone's going in," I told the group. "Gyrsön should bring lengths of rope. Remember, we can't kill them outright. They need to be wounded first, then drowned. There are two blind spots, so potentially two entrances. I'm going to take a team around the left to breach the front door. Mynstad du Högyn, you take a team around the right to make sure there isn't another door. If there is, try to breach when you hear us go in. If you can't breach, just secure it in case someone tries to run. Come around to help if it sounds like we need it. And watch out for windows."

I never took my eyes off those barracks as we broke cover under a clouded sky. We padded softly across the powdery snow, using firebowls they'd set outside the barn, warehouse, and edge of the docks as guides. Out of sight to the front of the building was another firebowl, which backlit the barracks and guided us in the dark. My team, which included Lörry, broke off from the other, and we crawled under a window at the side and another at the front.

We had just set ourselves with three on either side of the door, arrows nocked, and my hand outstretched to try the handle, when we heard a startled cry around the side of the building. Then there were sounds of fighting—so I guess there was a door over there after all.

I yanked on the one in front of me and met the charge of a man barreling toward the door. He tried to pull up, but he got my dagger in his right thigh just above the knee, and he went down with a frustrated yell. He'd probably thought he was going to flank the mynstad's team and instead ran into mine.

"Get in and shoot legs!"

Two archers leapt in and went to work, shooting down the men trying to fight off the mynstad's forces at the side door. We had six traitors wounded and writhing on the floor in a few seconds, and then we had a longer operation of disarming them and trussing them to chairs, using the rope Gyrsön brought.

One of them—a snarling man with a scar on his jaw—tried to sell the idea that we were the traitors.

"We are here on orders of the pelenaut! You're committing treason!"

I could see that his words sowed some seeds of doubt in the squad, so I said, "Hold that thought," and went searching. The barracks were big enough to contain an office, and in plain view on the desk were plenty of documents in the Bone Giant language. I grabbed a handful and returned to the scar-jawed man, telling the Grynek Hunters to listen up.

"Funny thing is, we are also here on orders of the pelenaut," I said, and leaned forward, pointing to the documents. "We're hunting down spies for the Bone Giants, and we've rolled up your entire operation, down to that little cabin across the river from Fornyd. And the fact that you read and write the language of the invaders means you're not on our side. We know exactly what you are. You're all Bone Giant wraiths that have possessed Brynt bodies."

Scar Jaw didn't react to that, but some of the others did, and my people caught it. That reassured them that we had in fact caught spies and that Scar Jaw was lying.

"Ridiculous," he said.

"There's an army of Bone Giants camped on the coast to the west of us. What is their objective?"

"What army?"

"The one that camped here at some point. Surely you noticed that. They left signs of their campfires all around you, and it's mighty curious that they would leave you alive if you weren't on their side. Because they left no one alive in Grynek. I know because I've been disposing of the bodies. We all know what the Bone Giants do to Brynts, because we have all lost family and friends to your armies."

"I have no idea what you're talking about."

"Right." Whoever this guy was, he wasn't the mastermind, or he'd have a better answer than that. At minimum he would acknowledge that the invasion was a thing that had happened. I stood up straight, finished with this liar. "I've got good news for you, Lörry. I don't think we're going to need your kenning at all. We have the Northern Yawn all ready to do the job for us. May I have three volunteers for a detail to carry this wraith to the end of the dock and toss him into the sea?"

I was gratified to see everyone's hand go up. I picked three of the archers, since we probably wouldn't need their bows at this point.

"He's going to lie the entire way," I reminded them as they picked him up in his chair. "Don't listen. And even if he says he will talk, don't stop. He had his chance to talk and he didn't take it."

Scar Jaw didn't protest, but he did shout, "Tell them nothing!" as he was being carried out the door. Which only further confirmed that he had something to tell and he was, in fact, a spy. I covered my mouth with a hand and spoke in mock shock through my fingers to our prisoners, widening my eyes.

"Oh my stars and jellies, it would appear that your commanding officer is no longer your commanding officer!" I dropped the act and returned to deadly serious. "The penalty for being a spy and waging war against Brynlön is death by drowning, which will of course destroy you as wraiths as well as the bodies you're possessing. The only chance you have— the only one—is to cooperate. Tell me what I need to know and I will spare your life. Refuse and I'll toss you in the ocean.

It's that simple. Now. Which of you will tell me about that army to the west? What is it after?"

I was met with silence, so I turned to Söla du Högyn and changed the subject. Let them think on it for a second.

"Mynstad, I meant to ask, how did the breach get started on your side?"

"We didn't breach at all. There's an outhouse on this side. One of them opened the door to pay a visit and we surprised him."

Shaking my head, I clucked my tongue in disapproval. "Poor security from start to finish. No wall, no watch set, and a built-in weakness to your perimeter. You were so confident that we would never find you that you made it easy for us. But the easy part is over." I chose another traitor and pointed. "You. Time to decide. Do you want to continue living? Tell me what that army is doing."

When I got no response, just a stony glare, I asked for another volunteer detail, and he was carried out. That left four more, and I didn't want to send out another detail until the first returned.

I gave each one a chance to talk. In fact, I gave the last four a chance to tell me anything, anything at all, that I didn't know before. But they were determined to follow the last order of their leader. I had hopes that the final spy would break, but no luck, apart from the fact that I got to personally help carry him to the sea and throw him into the dark water.

Disappointing in a sense, yet fulfilling. We'd stomped out whatever they were doing, cut off their flow of information, and collected a vast amount of intelligence to be deciphered. We'd also gained a number of horses and had plenty of provisions for the return trip.

Mynstad du Högyn asked if we'd be putting the compound to the torch, which was a good question, and I thanked her for bringing it up.

"Listen, the temptation you may all be feeling now is to

burn this place to the ground. I am tempted as well, believe me. But if we do that, and some new spies come in by boat, they'll know for sure what happened. As it stands, the people they were expecting to be here just mysteriously disappeared. Could be anything. They might have gone hunting in the Gravewood and met their doom. Uncertainty is best. So we should leave nothing behind that would tell them definitively that we were here. In fact, Mynstad, I want a detail to clean up the cabin. Get all the blood mopped up as best you can, though I imagine there will be stains we can't do anything about. Another detail needs to collect the horses and all the supplies we can carry. And then, by Bryn, we are going back into the Gravewood and setting up a proper camp with a proper watch. We are not going to get caught unawares like them. We are going to get all the intelligence we've collected back to Fornyd, and maybe then we'll find an advantage to exploit against our enemy in the coming days. We've done well so far, but I don't want to give them a single certain thing to act upon because we were undisciplined when it mattered most. Understood?"

I got a chorus of "Aye, Gerstad," and they went to work.

I wish I knew what in the black abyss was going on, but since I couldn't read the documents, I'd have to be satisfied with pruning this seemingly important branch of their spy operation.

Perhaps I'd find occasion to prune more branches while we waited for the documents to be translated.

Having the benefit of knowing what else had happened in the Northern Yawn, some were quick to speculate that the compound had supplied the army in the north, and had even ferried messages to Lorson, the abominable lifeleech who'd been living on that island just off the coast of Malath Ashmali. The Grynek Hunters, therefore, had shut down one end of the spy network, while the ultimate recipient of all that intelligence had been burned to ashes by Olet Kanek, who knew not that in defending her people from the life-leech, she was also helping us.

Many mugs of Mistmaiden Ale were raised to honor Daryck du Löngren and the Grynek Hunters that night.

THE FACE OF CHANGE

A complete inventory of my food stores revealed that I would be able to dine on some questionable pickles, honey, marmalade, and assorted condiments. I had a few stale crackers as well. No meat. No bread or cheese. No vegetables or fruit either. I'd have to get in line down at the docks for something from the fishblade—I imagined anyone who had the coin to spare would be doing so. Fishermen would keep us alive, if not full. In Tömerhil, I supposed, they'd be depending on hunters to get by. But I was staring at the sharp end of hunger along with many others, even though I knew that Röllend had seen these issues coming long ago and had been exerting himself for months to keep imports coming and to get farmers out there producing crops for summer, fall, and winter.

He had also been exerting himself to keep me uninformed. Time to work around that obstacle.

It figured to be a long day of walking for me, questioning various Nentians scattered about the city, but first I had to pick up my escort.

Kindin Ladd was kneeling in the grass in the gardens outside the Kaurian embassy, meditating, when I arrived. He was still dressed in oranges and browns, but they were arranged differently. I waited patiently for him to open his eyes, and it wasn't long—he'd heard my uneven steps approaching.

"Master Dervan. Good morning."

"Good morning. Are we ready to go?"

"Unfortunately not."

"Oh. I'm sorry—I interrupted your meditation."

"No, that's not it. We can't go at all. I've been ordered not to help you."

"Ordered?" I blew out a puff of exasperated air. "Let me guess—by the lung, speaking on behalf of the pelenaut?"

"Yes. I am sorry."

"Did the lung say why?"

"I was told that it has to be this way for your safety and mine, and that there is no reason to imperil ourselves when all shall be resolved in a matter of days. That's the reason I was given. Whether or not there were other reasons, I cannot say."

"I can say. There are definitely other reasons."

"I imagine so. You know, I was visited and given these instructions not long after you left. Which means . . ." He lifted an eyebrow and waited for me to fill in the blank.

"I'm being followed. I am really terrible at this spy business."

"I shall not comment upon that, for fear of hurting your feelings."

"Ha. Well. I suppose we must assume we're being watched even now?"

"By someone who can read lips, yes."

"This stinks like fish left out in the sun. Not your fault, of course, but it's difficult not to feel angry and betrayed at this point."

"I understand. At least partially. You want to know whether Melishev Lohmet is still alive and the pelenaut does not want you to know, and both of you are going to some significant trouble to get your way. Do I have that right?"

"Yes."

"Then I am puzzled as to why that might be the case."

"I can tell you what I know easily enough. Melishev ordered my wife to be assassinated and was reputed to be very ill months ago. I would be pleased to hear of his death but also pleased to hear of his continued suffering. What I do not want to hear is that he has been cured by a hygienist."

"And that's a possibility?"

"It is. Röllend sent one not long ago, but I'm not sure if they've crossed the continent yet."

"Interesting. Do you have any idea why the pelenaut does not want you to know?"

"None."

"And asking him is impossible?"

"Yes, but not for lack of trying. I'm being shut out."

"If it makes you feel any better, I and many other members of embassy staffs are being shut out as well. He is consumed by something."

"Adroit word choice, since we are on the verge of starvation. Speaking of which, your promised charitable donation." I tossed him a small pouch of coins.

"But I haven't protected you from any angry Nentians."

"Doesn't matter. What am I going to spend the money on? There's no food unless you get fresh fish at the docks. Listen, I don't suppose you have any ideas about how I can let go of my anger here?"

The priest of the gale grinned. "I have plenty of ideas. But it seems to me you are grappling with issues of time and distance—you want to know what happened very recently on the other side of our continent, but our last communication with them was months ago. So. Traveling that distance is impractical. Is there anything you can do to close the gap of time?"

"I don't think so—the bard is supposed to be doing that, and I suppose he is, at his own maddening pace."

"I wonder if you have taken the trouble to place his tales in chronological order? Because he admitted himself that he's been jumping around in time lately, and I am fairly certain he's been doing it all along. If nothing else, it will distract you from dwelling on your anger, but it might also prove to be helpful."

"It would," I agreed. "And it's something I should be doing anyway, as a historian. We know that these tales have largely taken place in the last year, but future generations might be very unclear on the sequence of events. I should do that. Yes. That's good. Thank you, Kindin."

"My pleasure."

As a distraction, it helped tremendously. I had written up a framework for an appendix piece by the time I had to meet Fintan, and he was pleasantly surprised by the challenge of his perfect recall to assign dates to each of his tales. We didn't get through everything, because we still had some catching up to do with the tales themselves, but it was a productive day rather than one spent fuming and worrying about what I would eat (which was the marmalade and the honey).

Fintan confided that Eimear had finished updating him that morning on what had happened in the west and said I'd have my answer soon enough.

It would never be soon enough, but I held my tongue. And we were all treated to another duet from Eimear and Fintan on the wall that day, which they said would be the last, since Eimear would be returning to Rael tomorrow.

"This is a fairly famous song in Rael, intended as a duet," Fintan explained, "about a young couple who went to live in the mountains near Jeremech, where it can get mighty cold in the winters. So it's about that place but also about couples learning to listen to each other."

The two of them traded verses until they joined together at the end, so I'll note who was singing what.

(Fintan)
We moved up here to get away and do as we please
Breathe in that fresh air and commune with the trees
But now I don't know what we were thinking;
It's so cold that important parts of me are shrinking

(Eimear)
Why do I ever listen to a word you say
When every time you say how it'll be it goes another way?
Let's be clear on one point and speak true:
We didn't decide to move here, babe: It was all you

(Fintan)
Let's not lay blame and argue about the past
Because that's not how people make a love last
Let's think about moving to some warmer weather
And maybe that'll fix my freezing nethers

(Eimear)
If you got a problem down there, that's not my doing
And I can hardly believe the nonsense you're spewing
We won't last if you don't own your mistakes
And learn from them for both our sakes

(Fintan)
Well, I guess I need to swallow all my pride
And admit I was wrong if it'll keep you by my side
I'm sorry, babe, but I do think we need a plan,
So let me ask: What if we just ran?

(Eimear, spoken quickly)
I'll be packed in five minutes!

(Both)
You know this wind and snow ain't so great
Let's get out of here, babe, before it's too late

Yeah, this wind and snow, it ain't so great
Let's get out of here now, before it's too late

———

After the break, Fintan said, "If you have begun to think, based on the last few days, that nothing's been happening in Ghurana Nent but the adventures of Pen Yas ben Min, I wouldn't blame you. But it's time for us to revisit Hanima Bhandury in Khul Bashab, who has a little perspective at the beginning that we might all appreciate."

Hanima

I used to think that if I didn't have to worry about dying every day, life would be so easy. If I just had food security and a safe place to sleep at night, well, I'd be all good.

But once I got those things, I discovered that I was wrong. My old problems were replaced with new ones, and "all good" kept its distance, like the grass horizon. Even now, when I'm blessed with the Sixth Kenning and own a couple of businesses and am probably the most famous person in the city because of that time we repelled the monarchist army and threw cabbage at the viceroy, I'm just as stressed as I ever was. My new problems aren't life-threatening, but they sure do wear me down.

That might be because the problems show up as someone hollering at my face. Often many someones at the same time. Face hollering is the worst.

Well, no. Sleeping in the mud is definitely below that. And so is the backside of Khamen Chorous after he eats anything, anything at all. But face hollering is zero fun.

When I go out in public now, I'm pretty much mobbed as soon as people recognize me. They don't touch me, because I have a protective halo of hornets circling my body, but they want me to do stuff for them that I can't do, like solve all *their* problems, and it upsets me that they think I can.

I'm not an elected leader. And I'm not a prophet of a God

to be Named Later, though there are people actually saying that, and I'm not the only one who finds that idea really disturbing.

The eternally perspiring head of the church, Dhanush Bursenan, has taken to calling me a false prophet because people would rather follow me than the teachings of the Church of Kalaad. When I heard that, I went to Tamhan and actually demanded that he print up some of his posters to say what I wanted to say for once.

And he brought me into his office, sat me down, and told me no, he wasn't going to do that.

"Why? You had no problem plastering my face all over the city before."

Tamhan sighed and threw his hair behind his shoulders. "Those posters helped us achieve political goals. They shifted public attitudes so that people would accept new policies and join in this new economy and government. What you're suggesting is a fight with the church, and that's not going to work out well for you."

"You're talking like that's in the future, but it's already here and not working out well for me. Sweaty Cleric Man is just making stuff up. He says I'm a false prophet!"

"I've heard."

"Don't I need to be shouting a prophecy before I can get called a prophet? Or at least be out there preaching some fearful stuff about a god? I'm not doing anything like that."

"I know."

"All I'm doing, Tamhan, is saying that maybe we should try caring for one another for a change and see if that improves our lives."

"I know that too."

"So why won't you help me?"

"Because this isn't about your message. It's about you."

"How do you mean?"

"As far as I can tell, Dhanush is not upset about the idea

that compassion is the only moral use of power. He's upset that your message is so popular that you are becoming a powerful leader. And in his view, you are siphoning that power directly from the church—which means you're taking it from *him*."

"I'm not taking his power. I don't *want* his power."

"Again, I know. But he wants his power very much. And right now he believes that if you are winning, he's losing. So he thinks he has to knock you down, and this false-prophet business is how he's doing it. He doesn't care that it's a lie and makes no sense to anyone who's been paying attention. He knows that the lie will be repeated, and it will be believed by those who aren't paying attention."

"And you're suggesting that I do nothing in response? Let him continue to lie and let those lies go unchallenged?"

"If you address his charges, they're just going to circulate more. You'll be giving him your attention, which is what he wants."

"It sounds like your advice is to let him win."

"No. My advice is to let surrogates fight this for you. You deny him a broader platform by staying above the fray and saying absolutely nothing about religion. And then have your people counter his lies with the truth, while also labeling him as the liar he is. Eventually he will become irrelevant."

"Which people? My people are working in the greenhouses and kitchens."

"They will in fact be my people."

"Oh. And what will I owe you for this?"

"Continue to ignore him and refer people to their elected leaders when they ask you to solve problems."

"That's what I've been doing, and it's been getting worse."

"I haven't pushed back yet. That's going to change."

It didn't feel right to me, but I didn't know how to argue with him further. He's incredibly smart and I can see he's improving lives. Nobody is sleeping in the open now, and the dungeons are empty. We actually cleared them out, took the doors off the cells, and converted them to a mushroom farm. We sentence people who need sentencing to cabbage and exile and send them downriver to the monarchists.

The monarchists downriver in Batana Mar Din are one of the main things that people holler about in my face, though. Since we broke the king's army and sent Bhamet Senesh on a raft to his cousin, said cousin has issued a trade embargo and choked off nearly all river traffic. Now all we get are people who want to live in Khul Bashab—a really good number— and we send back people who don't want to live here, which is a smaller number. Which means our population is growing but we're not getting the goods we need to keep up with demand.

And I mean goods like lumber and steel and other important raw materials we can't produce in our area. We're absolutely fine on food and leather and textiles, but we depend on trade for things that the plains can't provide. Tamhan had thought about all of this in advance, and being able to survive was the part that made a rebellion possible, but he knew that we'd need to find a solution to the embargo soon if we wanted to be truly independent.

According to the face hollerers, I was somehow supposed to provide that solution. They weren't shy about sharing suggestions either.

"Go stomp them! We can't let the monarchists ruin our lives!"

"We need a port and that's it! Do what you need to do!"

We didn't need a port, though, except for seafood. What we needed were reliable land routes to Rael and Forn. We were supposed to get a Raelech embassy and, with that, the services of a stonecutter, who'd build roads to Rael and Forn for us. Once we had those and enough beast callers to protect caravans, we'd have a way to trade that the monarchists couldn't control. Part of that trade, no doubt, would be the services of some beast callers.

But that would take some time. We didn't have a Raelech embassy yet, and people were getting impatient. So I had to explain, over and over, that conquering Batana Mar Din would not be a compassionate or moral use of our power. It would in fact be the precise abuse of power we fought the monarchy to escape. I heard grousing that if I wouldn't do it, some other beast caller would, and I then had to make clear to the clave that anyone who used their kenning to attack a city would be expelled from the clave for life, and that was a sufficient threat to keep them in line for the moment. Because the beast callers were thriving with contracts already.

Suraji Adhikar, the spider queen, for example, was going to be incredibly wealthy, even under our new economic laws. She'd already set up a spider-silk production company, a pest-control service, and an import/export company to ship her spiders and silks around. She told me there was a clan in Forn that specialized in spider silks from giant spiders, and if she hired out her services to them, there was no telling what mutual profit could be spun out, so to speak.

I was going to be well off myself—already was. I had a greenhouse business, a pollination business that served farmers, a honey business, a wax business, and did sideline pest-control projects with Suraji by relocating ant hives and wasps. But people hollered at me in the streets, and nobody hollered at Suraji or the other members of the clave. Just me.

"How did I get here?" I said, eyes welling suddenly, and with the tears came a deep sense of embarrassment that this was happening in front of Tamhan. I tried to dash them away. "I'm sorry. Never mind."

"No, no, it's fine. Hey. I'm your friend. You can talk to me. What's wrong?"

So much. A fresh stream of tears came flooding out. "Lavi broke up with me last night."

"What? Why? Not because of this false-prophet nonsense?"

"That, and . . . everything. I mean, he said I'm so busy that I don't have time for him. But whenever I did make time for my super-cute moth man, he didn't want to do anything anyway. Which means he really broke up with me for some other reason."

"Honestly, I think he did you a favor. He couldn't keep up with you."

"I know that now, but *what was the reason?*"

"It doesn't matter, because you don't need to fix anything about yourself. It was his problem."

"No, it's my problem. Because he didn't want me the way I am."

"Which means it's his problem."

"No—you don't get it. The way I am is different from what people believe I am. I'm the girl on the posters now, the hivemistress who makes speeches and everything. So people look at me like I'm this person that I'm not, or they see only one small part of me and not the whole thing."

"Ah, I see. I can understand that, actually. I'm the city minister now, not the son of a wealthy chaktu butcher. I'm treated much differently than before."

"Exactly. So when someone says they're interested in you now, you can't trust it! They're interested in your power and your influence and *what* you are, rather than *who* you are." He nodded and I said, "Are you seeing someone, by the way?"

Tamhan shook his head in regret. "No one, unfortunately."

"So . . . how do we deal with this? Being something to people that we don't want to be?"

Tamhan sat back in his chair and sighed, contemplating.

"We are in different situations. A solution for you is not a solution for me."

"Different how?"

"You are, in spite of your unelected status, regarded as a leader. And you will probably remain one, unlike me. When my term is up, I'll no longer be minister and no longer be a leader. But you—you are this inspiring figure."

I pointed an angry finger at him. "A lot of that is your fault. You're the one with the posters and stuff."

"I accept the blame. But what you may have to accept here is that you inspire people to be uncomfortable."

"What?"

He blinked and waved that away. "Forgive my poor phrasing. Let me try again. You inspired a revolution. You made people see that the current state was unacceptable and then played a vital role in changing things for the better. That made you the face of change. So when people see you, they associate you with changing the current state. Whatever's bothering them now—even if it's better than it was before—they believe you can make it better still."

"Oh. I think that . . . is horribly, horribly true. And it makes sense of my life right now."

"I recognized it because of people going to you instead of me and then reporting back to me what you said, if anything. That's what I meant when I said you're regarded as a leader. And you should be aware that some of this pressure you're getting is in fact an attempt to put pressure on me. If I don't do what someone wants, they can go to you and hope you'll say something they like more, then come back at me with, 'Well, Hanima said *this*, so you're contradicting her wishes.' It's just people trying to press the levers of power to their benefit."

"Oh, no. I'm making things tough on you?"

"Not intentionally! I know that your influence as an unelected leader is by my own design. But yes. Maybe I could share some insights."

"Please."

"You will be plied with this and that, once people discover your preferences. People will try to get you to support one position or another on any given subject. They will make it seem like your backing will benefit everyone—and it might— but they will always be seeking your patronage for their personal benefit, because most people are not revolutionaries who want to look out for others but rather individuals looking out for themselves. And there will be others—like Dhanush Bursenan—who merely wish to ruin your credibility. He's doing it with lies. But others might try to sell you on an idea or a person to support and then later betray you, merely to demonstrate that you have poor judgment."

"Oh, Kalaad's sky-blue balls! This is a nightmare. I don't want to deal with this."

"You won't be given a choice. This is already happening and will only get worse."

"What do I do?"

"Reexamine everyone's motivations, including mine. But do not, under any circumstances, withdraw and isolate yourself. You only become easier to manipulate then. Collect facts and opinions from multiple sources. Make decisions that benefit the least among us, as you are already inclined to do. You are in the worst possible position, and I helped put you there, and I'm sorry."

"I can't trust anyone?"

"You can trust anyone you wish. But someone you trust today could become corrupted tomorrow. I can see I'm dumping a lot of worry on your shoulders, and I didn't mean to distress you. All I'm trying to accomplish here is to make you aware and careful—not frightened or paranoid or angry or anything else. And from now on I will ask for your approval on all posters with your likeness and words. I never should have done that, and I apologize. I'll understand if you don't want any more to go up. They wield enormous power."

We sat in silence for a while as I tried to process this. "It sounds like it would be best for everyone if I wasn't here," I said.

"No, that's not what I was suggesting."

"But it's a logical conclusion, isn't it? Sweaty Cleric Man will be happy if I leave. You'll have fewer problems as minister if I'm not around to accidentally contradict you or remind people that I can change things. And I . . . well. Maybe I can go someplace where I'm not a revolutionary figure, and people can like me for who I am instead of what I am."

"Hanima?"

"Yeah?"

"I like who you are. So does Adithi, and Khamen Chorous, and many others."

"Thanks, Tamhan. I like you too. But that doesn't change the logic or what would be best for everyone." The tears came back, and I pressed my palms to my eyes, then smeared them away to my temples. "Okay. I know what I have to do. It will take some time for me to settle my business affairs, but as soon as that's done, I'll go."

Oh, my. Hanima leaving Khul Bashab would probably cause all sorts of chaos—or, rather, already had. If she headed in the direction of Melishev Lohmet, I am sure it did not end well for him. I felt sorry that she had to leave, but it was probably the best thing for Ghurana Nent as a whole. My grin was wide as Fintan smirked at everyone with Hanima's face and held aloft a seeming sphere.

"And now, back to our regularly scheduled greensleeve."

Pen

Thornhands are really easy to spot, because there's no hiding the huge thorns growing out of their bodies. So when news came that there was a Fornish ship at the docks with a dozen thornhands on board to be smuggled into the embassy, we had to think a bit. If they simply walked down the gangplank and waved hello, there would be a fight before we wanted one, because the Nentians would definitely challenge their presence in the city. Thornhands didn't travel outside Forn unless it was for war; they couldn't make the excuse that they were on vacation or pursuing business, because their sole business was kicking ass, and they famously vacationed by the sea, because when they swam in open water, their thorns didn't snag on anything.

There was a grassglider on board too, but since her kenning didn't manifest in an obvious physical way, she was able to visit the embassy, along with a few others, to let us know that she was part of a force sent by a coalition of clans to help with the Ambassador Ken situation. They were the response to Mai's abduction.

I learned about this once Mak Fin ben Fos brought said grassglider up to the private clan decks to meet Ambassador Ken. She was dressed in bright Nentian fashion, eschewing the drab olives, greens, and browns that grassgliders usually favored, and had cut her brown hair short.

"Ambassador, I'm so glad you're well. I'm Rin Fel ben Sek, at your service, leading a small pod of fighters. We were sent to either free you or avenge you."

"Welcome. I'm so grateful you've come, but even more grateful that neither is necessary now. I would have been dead twice over were it not for the help of this quick-thinking greensleeve. May I introduce you to Pen Yas ben Min?"

Rin and I bowed and smiled at each other, and the four of us sat down to tea. There we decided that Rin's pod would not immediately return to Forn but rather would support us as the ambassador tried to hold King Kalaad to account for his actions. Proceeding from there would be a matter of bribes and distraction.

"I have some other news," Rin said, "that we heard on the way here and may not have reached the king's ears yet: Khul Bashab has defeated the Nentian army under the leadership of Royal Tactician Hennedigha. Hennedigha himself is reported to have fallen. The viceroy has been expelled, and the city is now under independent leadership."

Ambassador Ken sat up straighter. "When was this?"

"Mere days ago. We heard it at Batana Mar Din when we stopped to refresh our food and water. We were in port for only a couple of hours, and the news came in then."

"So they did it," Mak breathed in wonder. "They actually did it."

"Did you hear anything of the Sixth Kenning?" Ambassador Ken asked.

"Yes. They used stampedes of thunder yaks and ebon-armored rhinos and blights of blackwings, long before they could attack the city. The army never even threatened the walls. But what broke them was Hennedigha's death: They choked him to death with moths."

"*Moths?*"

"Tactical moths. Up his nose, down his throat—his officers witnessed it and shat their armor in their haste to escape, lest they be targeted next."

We all shuddered at the image. "And how are things in Khul Bashab?"

"We didn't hear that. All the news came from the broken army. The exiled viceroy is a cousin of the viceroy in Batana Mar Din, and supposedly he wants to go back with more men, but I don't think he'll find any volunteers. Nobody wants to mess with the Sixth Kenning."

Ambassador Ken sipped at her tea and then sighed happily. "You bring a most welcome bouquet of news. No doubt we will hear more details from Jes Dan Kuf in coming weeks. For now, let us plan how to get your pod inside the walls."

We waited until nightfall and spread some judicious bribes down at the docks. That got a covered cargo wagon—crammed full of the thornhands and a couple of barrels of tea leaves for show—out of there without inspection. The wagon rolled past the embassy a couple of blocks to the north, staying close to the riverbank. When it was time, we got an assist from the Raelech ambassador, who came in a very loud bother to summon Mak Fin ben Fos. That distracted and drew away the Nentian spies watching our embassy, because they wanted to know why the Raelechs needed our greensleeve in the middle of the night.

With most of the surveillance taken care of, the cargo wagon came around to the back of the embassy compound; the thornhands slipped out of it and darted through the hole in the whipthorn wall I created for them. They weren't unseen—the Nentians had someone on watch there too, but he had no power to stop them and no ability to summon help, because we'd siphoned it all away. A couple of the thornhands waved merrily at him as he shouted at us to stop.

Rin flashed a smile at him. "Make sure you report this, now. We'd be disappointed if you didn't."

Mak Fin ben Fos returned to the compound by way of the Raelech tunnel, so the Nentians wouldn't be able to stop him for any reason. That gave us some solid defenses for the morning, and we'd need them, because Ambassador Ken wasn't going to wait one minute longer than she had to.

She had handbills printed up and a formal letter ready to go at dawn. Del Mot Goh delivered the letter to a thin-faced

Nentian spy we'd observed outside our compound and said it was for the king from Ambassador Ken.

"Ambassador Ken? Where is she?"

"Her whereabouts are detailed in the letter, so I'd suggest you make sure the king sees it immediately."

The Raelech ambassador was delivering a formal letter as well, through proper channels, expressing Rael's outrage at Ambassador Ken's treatment and the violation of diplomatic law. He wanted an apology to Forn and reassurance that this behavior wouldn't be repeated against any diplomats and warned that the world was watching. There would be economic consequences for the king's actions too.

Ambassador Ken's letter promised economic retribution from Forn and demanded a public apology. But the true kick in the pants came from the flyers we posted around the city, as suggested by Mak Fin ben Fos, because he'd seen how effective they were in moving public sentiment in Khul Bashab. Rin Fel ben Sek led that effort, using her kenning to allow a small team to silently glue them all over town so that everyone woke to the same news:

King Kalaad the Unwell

Abducted and imprisoned the Fornish ambassador.
That's an act of war. Does Ghurana Nent need more of that?
Demand he apologize to Forn for his unprovoked aggression!

We closed down the tea treehouse for the foreseeable future and increased security at the compound entrance, stationing two thornhands in the greeting area and growing a portcullis of whincthorns over the gate. Nobody was coming in or going out.

That was the situation when a cadre of soldiers arrived with a Nentian diplomat soon after dawn, requesting to see

Ambassador Ken. Mak Fin ben Fos was standing in the greeting area with Del Mot Goh and the thornhands, and he relayed through root and stem what was being said. I relayed that in turn to the ambassador, so that she heard everything and could respond through me if she wished. But Del Mot Goh was well coached on what to do; the ambassador didn't say anything but did smile quietly at several points.

"Good morning. I am Arhan Saidhu of the Royal Diplomatic Office. I'd like to speak with Ambassador Ken."

"I am Del Mot Goh, her assistant. The ambassador will speak to no one but the king himself and only to hear his formal public apology and his proposed reparations for his criminal behavior."

Saidhu spluttered at that. "That is ridiculous."

"May the sun shine brightly on you, good fellow."

"What? This is nonsense. We have much to discuss with the ambassador."

"Nothing will be discussed until we receive a public apology from the king for the wrongful abduction and imprisonment of the ambassador."

"Open the gate and let's discuss this civilly."

"We are already discussing it civilly with the gate closed, though I don't know what more there is to say. Forn is on the brink of war with Ghurana Nent because of King Kalaad's actions. Only the king can restore calm."

"Did you say *war*?"

"Your hearing is excellent. Your ears are not only adorable but functional."

There was a pause while Saidhu grappled with how to respond to someone who had threatened unspeakable violence yet flirted with him. "*War* is an extraordinary word to speak out loud when you are a guest in our country."

"*Abduction* and *attempted murder* are also extraordinary words when applied to ambassadors, wouldn't you agree? If you were stationed in Forn and one of our clans abducted and tried to kill you—at which they would undoubtedly succeed—the least you would demand, if you miraculously survived, would be an apology, yes?" He ignored all of that.

"My point is that it is unwise to threaten war when you are surrounded by Nentian forces."

Del smiled sweetly. "Then you may wish to consider why we feel comfortable doing that. This is not the undefended compound of a few weeks ago when you abducted the ambassador. We now have greensleeves, grassgliders, and thornhands here. If we wished—and this is neither a threat nor our plan, just a statement of fact—we could abduct the king and assassinate him, and you could not stop us. Instead, we are merely asking for an apology and reparations."

"Yes, we heard you smuggled in some thornhands last night—twelve or thereabouts. That would be impressive against a garrison, perhaps. But we have an army of ten thousand."

"Are you referring to the force led by Tactician Hennedigha?"

"I see you're aware."

"I see you are unaware that Hennedigha is dead and his army broken, shattered by the beast callers of the Sixth Kenning. Khul Bashab is now independent of Ghurana Nent's monarchy, and you have no army. That being the case, perhaps you had better advise the king to apologize. He has plenty of weeds in his garden already, and he doesn't need to spread seeds to grow more."

There was another pause, then Saidhu simply replied, "We will speak more later." He left but told his military escort to remain and let no one leave the embassy. They wouldn't be able to stop even a single thornhand who wished to exit, but that was fine; we had no intention of leaving anyway, and if we did, we'd exit from an unguarded portion of the whipthorn wall, not the gate.

Ambassador Ken sighed happily. "I can just imagine the

impotent screaming that will ensue when the king hears that."

"Do you think he'll come to apologize?"

She shook her head. "Not a chance."

"So he'll attack us?"

"No, he won't do that either. He can't win now, and Melishev Lohmet is the kind of fighter who strikes only when he knows he'll win."

"Then what will he do?"

"He'll wait for something to change—or try to make things change himself—and hope that whatever it is erases our current advantage. That means we will have to wait too."

"Oh. Well, we can do that. I should probably grow some furniture out of living wood or something. I hear it's a thing greensleeves are supposed to be able to do, but I haven't learned how yet. Maybe Mak can teach me."

"If you grow a rocking chair, I volunteer to rock."

Gondel

Maron became quite excited when we were called up by the captain to see Fornyd before we docked. After weeks of cramped existence, he was ready to get off the ship.

But when he got to the deck and took a look at the city, his face fell in disgust and he turned to me, shrouded in opprobrium.

"What kind of tea," he said, "will a place like *that* have compared to Pelemyn?"

"I imagine it will be quite good. It's hot water poured over leaves, Maron, and the Brynts have the best water in the world."

"Fine, I'll grant that, but the *culture*, Gondel. Where's the culture?"

"You've brought it with you, my love." He groaned and covered his eyes. "Wait to pass judgment until you've walked around inside the walls, at least. You can't know what it's like from the docks and the, uh, soiled exterior."

"True, but I can make an educated guess."

Fornyd wasn't a glistening jewel of civilization, but what I saw was encouraging. It was busy. Plenty of activity meant a vibrant trade, and vibrant trade meant that the trappings of high society Maron longed for might well be inside. Thinking of my research, however, I crossed the deck to the starboard side to take in the northern shore of the Gravewater River.

Tall reeds masked much of the actual riverbank, ideal for hiding a sleek canoe, perhaps. Spies could easily take advantage of that. And a mix of deciduous and evergreen trees towered above the water's edge, obscuring any buildings that may or may not exist over there. But somehow, messages written in the south had traveled through Fornyd and reached an Eculan officer far north of here. It deserved attention.

No one thought it wise to bring Saviič out from the hold and parade him downtown, so we agreed that I would get a proper escort from the Wellspring, and once the prisoner transfer was complete, the captain could depart for Pelemyn.

Maron spoke only rudimentary Brynt—phrases I had taught him, such as *Where is the bathroom?* and *More tea, please*—so I did the talking once we disembarked. I asked directions to the city Wellspring and got lost a couple of times—perhaps the locals were messing with what they thought were tourists—but eventually was able to present myself at the gate to a bored-looking official and some armed mariners.

"How may I help you, gentlemen?" the official asked in a tone that communicated he had no desire to help us. He was youngish, perhaps the son of someone important, and clearly thought his voluminous talents were being wasted at the gate, clearing visitors.

"We'd like to see the quartermaster, please."

"She's busy."

"Indeed, I would be shocked to hear that she was not. However, I am the scholar Gondel Vedd from the University of Linlauen in Kauria, tasked by your pelenaut and my mistral to translate certain documents your quartermaster sent that were captured from an officer of the Bone Giants. I believe she will want to hear the information contained therein upon the instant. I have sailed directly from Kauria to deliver this important news to her. If you would be so good as to inquire if I might be squeezed into her busy schedule, I would greatly appreciate it."

I'd captured his attention, at least, and he no longer looked bored. He scanned me up and down, and I was grateful that Maron had insisted we keep one change of clothes pristine for just such occasions. I was never, under any circumstances, allowed to eat or drink while wearing them. I might be turned away for many reasons, but it would not be for mustard on my breast.

"Wait here," he said, and disappeared into the building, a blue-and-white affair with ceramic tiles on the floors and handsome murals of the ocean painted on the curved walls, with ships sailing under a blue sky dotted with cotton-ball clouds.

"Are these the kind of guards that never talk?" Maron asked me in Kaurian.

"No, I don't think so," I replied. "Why?"

"Ask them where's the best teahouse in the city."

"Really? That's all you think about?"

"If you want to start an argument about who is more single-minded, Gondel, I will win."

"You're right, you would. Hold on." I turned to two of the guards and asked them in Brynt their opinions of the city's teahouses. They immediately exchanged a glance of ferocity, then turned to me and answered simultaneously with two different teahouses. They spoke so rapidly with such venom that I didn't even catch the names, only that each one's favorite was far superior to the other guy's and, in fact, what the other guy's favorite teahouse served was little better than raw sewage. I was appalled, but when I looked at Maron, he was delighted by the argument, though he didn't understand a word.

"Look at that passion, Gondel. Such partisanship! These are my people. I feel much better now. I will find good tea here."

"They are each saying the other's teahouse is shit. Perhaps they both are."

"Nonsense. The mere fact that this argument is happening—and I can't believe it's still happening—means that people here care deeply about their tea, so a tea culture must exist, and I regret my hasty judgment earlier. Ask them if they would like an outsider's unbiased opinion."

"Is that wise?"

"Certainly not. But it will be entertaining."

I asked them, and it immediately turned into a wager. The loser would have to direct all tourist inquiries to the winner's teahouse for three months.

But after that quick agreement, the conditions of the tea service became an endless, tedious argument, because they wanted to make sure the kind of tea was the same, and each advocated for a different tea; plus, certain aspects of the teahouse could not be used in judgment, like the vaguely defined "ambience" or "culture." Rather than try to translate the argument for Maron, I told him they would like him to judge, but the conditions would take significant negotiation and I would let him know later.

That was necessary because the official returned and said the quartermaster would see us now. We promised the guards we'd return to hear the details of their wager.

The official was much more solicitous now that he knew

the quartermaster considered us to be capital-I Important. He remembered my name but inquired after my husband's.

"This is Maron Munn," I said proudly. "We have been married thirty-seven years."

"Ah? Congratulations."

The Wellspring of Fornyd was a smaller and more muted affair than the splendid one of the pelenaut, but it had that same blue light and wet air and the sound of running water from a series of fountains.

There were more armed mariners and some others in formal dress, which reminded me of my first audience with the mistral in Linlauen, except that the courtiers here favored a simple fashion that stressed quality over gaudiness. The official addressed a middle-aged woman in a white sheath, over which she had draped three diaphanous layers of material in progressively darker shades of blue. The first reached her knees, the second her hips, the third her breast, so that it looked like there were ripples originating from her collarbones. She had close-cropped hair, perhaps some gray at the temples, skin a few shades lighter than mine, and a string of pearls around her throat.

"Quartermaster Farlen du Cannym, I present the scholar Gondel Vedd and his husband, Maron Munn."

"Welcome, both," she said with a nod. She gestured to a man standing to her right, who had a full bushy beard and a shaved head. "This is my lung, Lans du Höwyll."

He gave us a tight nod and bid us welcome.

"It's an honor. My husband does not speak much Brynt, so please forgive him his silence. Before I begin, Quartermaster, I should warn you that the intelligence you provided shed light on some enemies of Brynlön working within Fornyd, so you may wish to hear it first alone and then decide who else can be trusted with it."

"I suspect I may already know, thanks to another source, but it's advice well taken. Will you all please give us the room? Lans, perhaps you could find someone who speaks Kaurian to entertain Maron Munn?"

"He loves tea," I said helpfully.

"I'll see to it," the lung said, and once I shared that with Maron, he cheerfully exited with him.

Once we were alone, I said, "Quartermaster, I believe you have enemy spies within Fornyd, and so do all Brynt cities."

"I was aware of the first, but not the second," she said. "The same group of hunters who got you that intelligence found a cabin hidden on the northern shore of the river, and it was full of more documents I'd be grateful to have you translate. There was a path leading to the north, and the Grynek Hunters are following it now to see what else they can learn. Our working theory is that the path was how messages got to that army in the north."

"That would make sense. Among the dispatches I translated, however, there are messages from spies in other cities besides this one. Tömerhil, Setyrön, Pelemyn—all of them are sending information through Fornyd to the north. There's a network of Eculan spies to discover."

"Perhaps the new information will help us find them, then."

"Indeed." I pulled out my translations and handed them to her. "For you, and the pelenaut, of course, to review at your leisure."

"Thank you, Scholar. May I invite you and your husband to be my personal guests while you work on the latest material? There will be a stipend as well. You should be compensated for your tremendous service to us."

"I would accept that gratefully. And perhaps your personal recommendation on the finest teahouse in the city."

"Oh, that would be my house," she said with a soft smile. "But if you mean a public house, then Lans can advise you better."

"Excellent. But there's another matter I wish to bring up.

We have brought with us an intelligence asset that requires some discretion."

"Yes?"

"He's an Eculan prisoner named Saviič. We need him transferred securely from the hold of the ship to an accommodation of your choosing."

The quartermaster's features drew down. "You brought a Bone Giant to my city?"

"Yes. But he's not one that attacked you—he was shipwrecked near Kauria before the invasion. He's been vital to my understanding of the modern Eculan language and a key reason why I'm able to translate effectively."

"He helps you translate?"

"Some unfamiliar words and passages, yes, though I need him less and less for that."

"Then why bring him?"

"He's one of the faithful sent to seek out the Seven-Year Ship. I was informed that you have actually found it now and have it docked somewhere."

"That is true."

"Well, I thought perhaps he would provide us more information if he were to visit it. He can be evasive under direct questioning, but when the subject turns to his religion, he talks freely and reveals more than he probably intends. He wants to see the Seven-Year Ship more than anything. Even the chance that he might see it has made him very cooperative. I know that you may not be able to authorize his visit yourself, but perhaps you could consult the pelenaut on the matter."

"Hmm. Tell me about your ship."

"The captain has messages for the pelenaut from Mistral Kira and will be sailing back to Pelemyn as soon as the prisoner transfer is complete."

"So she could take my message as well."

"Yes."

"Very well. I have much to do, and you will have much to do tomorrow. For now, please rest. I'll have you reunited with your husband and leave instructions to get you settled. We'll sequester the prisoner and allow you access to him whenever needed. Is he violent?"

"He can be if given cause. But treat him politely and he should be docile. Mention that he'll see the Seven-Year Ship soon and he'll do anything. I'll provide you a note to give to him, and he should come along willingly."

"Thank you, Scholar Vedd. Welcome again, and I look forward to speaking with you more casually soon."

She led me to a different exit and asked someone on the other side of the door to take me to wherever Maron was. That turned out to be a courtyard patio with a fountain in the center, ringed by small bistro tables. He had a pot of tea and a biscuit and looked immensely pleased, but I was thinking about the trove of new intelligence I'd need to translate soon.

"Gondel? Gondel!"

"Hmm? Yes?"

"Whatever you're thinking of can wait until tomorrow. You're missing the moment."

He was right. We had the evening to spend together without any work to do, and I was so grateful that he was there with me, or else I would have found something to work on anyway. Sometimes I needed the reminder that I didn't work for the sake of it; I worked for the sake of those I loved.

When brief opportunities to breathe peace arrive, we must inhale deeply and be fortified.

Preach, Gondel, preach.

Day 44

THE ARMY IN THE NORTH

I had no choice but to scrunch up my face and wolf down the Pickles of Questionable Provenance for breakfast. My stomach immediately complained, perhaps wondering what it had done to deserve such abuse. I could not remember where the pickles came from—a gift basket, most likely—and I don't know how long they lurked in my pantry before I was forced to eat them. If I were a better steward of my supplies, I most likely would have tossed them out long ago. But now, though they might be dodgy, I was grateful for them.

There was a smidgen of good news delivered by the lung before I met with Fintan—he had Fintan use his kenning to broadcast it to the entire city, but obviously from a place where I could not ask him why they'd kept Sarena's murderer a secret from me.

"The Raelech army will arrive tomorrow and set up camp on the outskirts of Survivor Field. They bring with them a wealth of dry goods, grain, and root vegetables—so food is coming. We ask—politely, but backed up with force if necessary—that you do not mob them. The food will be rationed and distributed in an orderly fashion, and a list of where you will be able to pick up necessaries and baked goods follows."

He then spent a long while listing locations and items that would be available. Highly organized, and I could see the mind of Rölly behind it. The lung finished by saying that the Fornish and Kaurians would also be bringing food with them, and if we rationed ourselves and farmed like mad, we would get through this lean time and have full bellies again.

I was obviously not privy to current thinking, but I assumed that at some point Röllend had ceased to worry about the Raelechs coming to conquer us softly, since I'd heard no further paranoia on that score for some while. I was truly out of the loop and had not realized to what extent I'd been pushed out.

The incident with the Wraith deceiving me into dropping a letter destined to travel north through their spy network had something to do with it, no doubt.

Work was the best thing to keep me from dwelling on the rumbling of my belly. I drank plenty of water and tea, though I knew that wouldn't fool my system for long, and met Fintan at the fishblade's.

We stood in line for a long time to get a few sautéed scallops and three raw oysters on the half shell with hot sauce, and the fishblade, Gellart du Tyllen, was apologetic that he didn't have anything else or enough. He had a mustache that normally appeared brisk and bushy but now seemed to droop in dolor. I assured him that everyone knew he was doing his best. The meal didn't fill the void, but it was delicious.

Later, the bard smiled fondly at Survivor Field. "We're going to have a tale from Gondel Vedd today, and someone shared a Brynt farmer's song with me that I think he'd find amusing, since he is often taxed by the requirement to look presentable in public."

It's really quite alarming
How many fops think they're charming
I tell you they'd be better off farming
Because at least that is real

If you're a man concerned with brocade
Or with running out of pomade

Then your priorities, I'm afraid
Are less than ideal

Oh, your stitching is not nearly so bewitching
As you might assume
You're daft if you think that needlecraft
Is admired in this room

If that finery palls, grab some coveralls
Or a tunic off the loom
Do some proper work, don't shirk
And get rid of that dandy costume

When we resumed after the break, Fintan informed us that it was time to catch up with events in the north, as we had last left the Joabeian zephyr Koesha Gansu departing Malath Ashmali with Abhi and Fintan as passengers.

Koesha

The crunch of ice underneath the hull of the *Nentian Herald* is loud and relentless, but you get used to it and it can even be soothing, as it represents a marker of progress. It's to the point now where I think we might actually be alarmed when the sound disappears and we're in clear seas. The crew is smiling and enjoying the journey, knowing that every moment is a length closer to home, a length closer to history as the first crew to sail around the world and navigate the Northern Yawn.

But while we are fairly accustomed to the cold, as our islands experience harsh winters, Abhi and Fintan are struggling, our Nentian friends are trying and failing to pretend they're not bothered by it, and Abhi's animal companions are constantly shivering and miserable. They stay huddled in the cabin by the enchanted firebowl, and Abhi has convinced them to wrap up in blankets, which is at once adorable and sad. As far as Murr and Eep are concerned, we cannot escape the north fast enough.

About six days after we left Malath Ashmali, on a misty morning under a gray marbled sky, the unbroken coastline of trees was interrupted by campfires and the stink of human settlement. We saw them and they saw us, because an ice-breaker ship is not a stealthy vessel, but what alarmed me was that they did not wave and beckon us to stop by for a visit. No, the shadowy figures of men started shouting and scrambling around as if we represented a threat, waking up anyone who slept. And they were armed.

I instructed Haesha to put some more distance between us and the coast, heading into deeper waters, and then I asked Fintan if he knew of any settlement up here besides Malath Ashmali.

"No, I don't. It's not marked on any of the maps I've seen in the atlas I took from Lorson. And I don't think that's a settlement so much as a camp. I think those are tents, not permanent housing."

"Why would anyone camp here for the winter?"

The Raelech bard shrugged.

"I'm going to take a closer look."

And then I summoned wind and flew up into the mist to conduct a threat assessment, wafting high enough that I'd be out of bowshot range. If anyone shot arrows at me, I'd be able to blow them off target, provided I saw them in time—but there was no guarantee of that until I had a better idea of who these people might be.

I noticed right away that a significant amount of timber had been cut down, both to clear space for their tents and to provide fuel for fires; large stacks of it were distributed around the camp. They were getting their fresh water from a river that emptied into the sea; they had built a platform that allowed them to punch through any ice that formed and that secured their supply.

Fintan had been correct—they were living in tents. And they'd arrived by boat during the thaw, albeit in flat-bottomed ones that were now frozen in the ice and dotting the coastline a bit farther down. These were winter quarters, and they planned on moving again when the ice pack broke up. But who were they?

I was at a sufficient height that I couldn't really recognize them, though one characteristic seemed strange: They appeared to be pale-skinned individuals, and I'd been given to understand by Fintan that we were sailing past a country called Brynlön, where the population largely had dark-brown skin.

Some of them were pointing up at me, and that was fine. Let them understand that they were dealing with someone of the Second Kenning; let them have time to shoot at me if they wished. That would tell me something of their intent.

But it was becoming clear, as I surveyed the camp, that this was a military operation. Tents staked out in a grid, no place for kids to play, no women or children at all, in fact. And there were thousands of them. This was an army bivouacked for the winter.

For what purpose, I could hardly imagine. What was their target? Surely not Malath Ashmali—how would they even know it existed, since it didn't until a few months ago, and only the governments of Ghurana Nent and Rael were aware of it? I could tell that these people were neither Nentians nor Raelechs in any case, and they didn't match the description of Brynts that I had heard thus far. Was there some other target to pursue up here? I'd have to ask Fintan to consult his atlas and come up with a list of possibilities.

In the meantime, I needed a closer look at these men. Easing the updraft pressure and angling into a dive, I swooped

down toward a fire, partially to glean more details and partially to see if that provoked an attack.

That provided me with two crucial facts: First, these pale-
skinned people looked just like that monster Lorson, who
had killed the priestess of the flame in Malath Ashmali. They
were very tall and thin and wore bone armor, which matched
the description of invaders that Fintan had spoken of called
Bone Giants. From my own knowledge—which I had not had
the language to communicate to the Nentians when we met
Lorson—they most likely hailed from a nation of five large
islands called Ecula, with which Joabei had very little contact
and, apart from a longing for certain trade goods, liked it that
way.

The second fact was that they had no bows, but they had
spears and did not hesitate to throw them at me once I got
low enough to make a strike feasible. That instant hostility
was a hallmark of Ecula and a large reason why Joabei made
no effort to trade with them. One made efforts for friends.

An Eculan with his beard tied into five braids and trained
to start out from his jaw in angles caught my eye. He offered
no violence except the thoughts behind his hateful glare.

Once I'd directed the winds to whirl about me and lift me
up again, the spears had no chance of completing their intended trajectories and landed elsewhere—perhaps harm-
lessly, but perhaps not, considering how many targets there
were underneath me. If someone suffered from friendly fire,
I was not going to worry overmuch. They were not going to
be our friends.

Having seen enough, I propelled myself back to the ship.
We definitely wanted to keep our distance from these men.

Once back on board, I reaffirmed that we needed to steer
around that camp as much as possible and ordered an all-
hands-on-deck to receive a briefing, which I delivered in the
Nentian language for the benefit of our guests.

"That is a hostile army encamped on the coast—Bone Giants, I believe, or Eculans, which Fintan says have caused much death and ruin for Brynlön and Rael. There are thousands of them, and they attacked me without any warning or attempt to talk. Depending on how eager they are to keep their presence here a secret, we may be facing an attack across the ice pack. They have swords and spears and the advantage of reach. But we have bows. I want every available archer and all arrows on deck. Everyone should be armed and ready to repel boarders. Hopefully it won't come to that and we'll sail on past without bloodshed. Best to be prepared. Let's go."

Everyone sprang into action, but I called Abhi and Fintan over for a chat.

"Fintan, I'd like you to consult your atlas and any information you took from Lorson that might indicate why this army is here. What possible targets exist? And, Abhi, I'd like to know what you can do to help with your kenning if the army decides to attack."

Fintan nodded and replied almost immediately. He had perfect recall, as a bard of the Third Kenning, so he didn't truly need to look at the atlas again to tell me what was there. "There are no listed targets in the atlas, and I haven't translated the other documents sufficiently to know what they might contain."

That was frustrating. The frown on Abhi's face hinted that I might be met with more of the same.

"There are very few insects I can call up here. They either don't exist or are dormant for the winter. There are some birds and meat squirrels somewhat close by but not in sufficient numbers to make a difference, and they don't like these targets. The best I could do would be a pair of gravemaws, but I'd need to call them to the area, and it would take them some time to arrive."

"Gravemaws?"

"Large ambulatory mouths with lots of teeth, a gigantic muscular tongue, and armor."

"Oh, my goddess, I have seen one of those." One had latched on to the prow of our landing craft and tried to pull us back to shore, and almost succeeded. "They are terrifying."

The plaguebringer shrugged. "They are if you can't talk to them, yeah. I think they're kind of sweet in their own way, but they're certainly easier to talk to when they're not hungry."

"Are the two you can call hungry?"

"Not sure."

"Call them anyway, please, in case they're needed. What about the ocean? Anything in the deeps that can help us out?"

Another shrug. "I'd need to be in contact with the water to discover that."

My eyes flicked back to the small dinghy we had available aft. Abhi sighed.

"You want me to find out."

"Yes, please."

I corralled a few sailors to help lower the dinghy into the ocean behind the ship and watched as Abhi descended a rope ladder to climb in. Once he was settled, we gave him a little bit of slack to let the dinghy trail behind without bumping up against the hull, and he dipped his hand into the freezing waters. He sucked a sharp breath past his teeth at first contact but kept it in there with his eyes closed for perhaps half a minute before he yanked it out and looked up at us.

"No krakens," he called. "But I might be able to call in something else to help if needed."

"Quickly, or with delay?" I asked.

"A delay for sure. I'm guessing twenty minutes to a half hour."

Haesha spoke up. "Captain? The Bone Giants are forming and moving this way. They're coming across the ice."

"Thank you." That made the decision easy, and I called

down my reply. "Bring whatever you can as fast as you can, Abhi. The gravemaws too. We're under attack."

He nodded and plunged his hand back into the water. Realizing that I could do absolutely nothing to help him and had only a small hope that he could help us, I turned my attention to the Bone Giants.

A scrambled force of twenty-one was advancing—not exactly running, more of a quick shuffle across the ice, keeping their weight centered over their feet to minimize the chance of slipping. They carried no spears, I noticed, but had rather nasty-looking swords. Experimentally, I sent a quick gust at their faces. Almost all of them recoiled, leaning back from it, and that made them lose their balance and fall on their asses. Their shoes—if they could be called that—were not designed to grip the ice. They were smooth-soled and slipped easily, and while the ice pack wasn't a glassy nightmare, it was still treacherous.

Knocking them down was a good delaying tactic, perhaps, which might help us escape, and escaping was the goal.

It would take them a few minutes to muster a more organized charge—we'd caught them by surprise and unready to fight. They were getting ready as quickly as possible.

The vanguard regained their feet and formed up this time in three ranks, seven across and three deep, and began their shuffling march toward us. Interesting.

"Seven archers, please, lined up to take out that front row. Do we have seven? Good. When you shoot, I want a straight shot—no arc for distance. I'm going to help with a little wind. Nock. Take aim. Draw." I gathered a powerful, focused gust of wind and pushed it behind the arrows as I said, "Fire!"

Normally, arrows would lose altitude with distance, but the wind and I weren't going to let them do that. They sliced through the air at height and gained speed, so much that when they shot into the torsos of the first rank of enemies, the arrows passed entirely through them and pierced the second rank. Both first and second ranks tumbled down, and the third also fell, but mostly because of the wind and stumbling over their fallen comrades. The seven survivors, however, had little chance of achieving a victory on their own, and they knew it. They turned to the shore and threw up their arms in frustration.

I hoped such a demonstration would make them rethink attacking us and they'd simply let us go, because they would pay a heavy price to take us out. We didn't have thousands of arrows, only hundreds, but I'd make sure every one of them found a home in an enemy's heart. Would they continue to throw themselves at us in such numbers for an uncertain prize?

The answer, apparently, was yes.

Cubes of soldiers, seven by seven, began to run east along the coast, using the surer footing to gain some ground and try to get ahead of us. They'd take an angle across the ice and be waiting for us while others came at us broadside, providing a more immediate threat that we couldn't ignore, and then we'd sail into their ambush. Someone on their side had a head for strategy. It made me wonder what the army would do if that particular person no longer had a head.

"Fintan. Anything you've heard about the Eculans that suggests they give up without leadership?"

"No, but I know almost nothing about them. I've been in the west up to this point and can tell you the Hathrim will pause without leadership, but everything I've heard about these Eculans suggests that they don't stop."

"Yeah, that's what I've heard too."

Back in Joabei, I never paid much attention to the stories about the Eculans, because I figured I'd live my entire life without meeting them. My plan was to sail around the north and never tack in their direction. The people in Omesh saw them more frequently and never had a kind word for them; the Eculans used to be agreeable enough in generations past but at some point had become religious fanatics and made everyone miserable. The god in question supposedly knew the Seventh Kenning, but if Lorson was an example of that god's gifts and favor, I could not abide it. Cruelty in the name of a god is still cruelty.

I heard some whispers in Nentian about whether killing those men had been necessary, and I turned to confront them. It was two men who'd paired up with my sailors.

"Again, friends, they attacked me first. They are approaching us with swords instead of a flag for parley. They are thousands, and we are fewer than a hundred. We cannot let them reach us."

The two men nodded their understanding, and one of them said, "I . . . understand. I've just never seen or heard of the Second Kenning used in a military manner."

"You are referring to the Kaurians, who practice a religion of peace? Do they never defend themselves?"

"They do. Just . . . nonlethally."

I smiled at him. "I guarantee you they have been lethal at some point. But they have an excellent myth-building apparatus to make you think they haven't. Do you know how a Kaurian would peacefully dissuade this army of thousands from attacking us?"

"No," he admitted.

"We will have to ask them if we ever meet them. For now," I said, and turned back to the archers, "nock and aim. That formation coming straight at us. Yes. Draw. Fire."

It was a grim few minutes, sending volley after volley and littering the ice with bodies. It created something of an obstacle course for the Eculans and definitely slowed them down, but they kept coming, either stepping over or around, and soon enough we were out of arrows and facing an overwhelming opponent. There were still thousands of them, and we hadn't put enough distance between us to keep them from continuing the onslaught. In the end it wasn't a strategy so much as a numbers game.

I sent powerful gusts at the soldiers running ahead on an intercept course. The wind caught them on the side and was much more effective at knocking them down. They all fell over, sometimes on their swords and sometimes accidentally wounding a comrade as they fell. More effective than a flight of arrows, honestly, at taking down a formation. But a headache built at the base of my skull and wrapped around until it pinched, painfully, right between my eyes. I was using too much power and aging myself.

But what use would I have for my youth when I could be cut down in the next few minutes—or, worse, lose my crew? I didn't want a single one of them to die. Too many had already fallen like leaves in the wind. So I would spend myself regardless of the cost.

I sent gust after gust to topple the giants, especially the ones ahead, since we were now technically past the camp by a small margin, and every new sortie would need to run a bit farther to catch up to us. But they could still run faster than we could crunch through the ice, and they'd be upon us soon.

Haesha reported the smallest glimmer of hope: Two gravemaws had emerged from the forest and begun to wreak havoc on the camp.

"That's good, but what can two do against thousands?"

"Two invincible death dealers can do quite a lot."

"Invincible?"

"Abhi said he told them to keep their mouths shut, which is their only vulnerability. You have to pierce through the top of their mouth and into their brain to kill them. Their armor stops everything else, so they are simply smashing through the Bone Giant camp and can't be stopped."

"Can they forget the camp and come out here and escort us to safety?"

"I'll check."

While she was gone, I kept sending gusts to knock the pursuers back, but I could see it wouldn't be enough. There were too many of them closing on us, and I didn't have the strength of a tempest to pick up groups of them and drop them again. I could manage one, as I managed myself, but . . . well. It was worth a try. I focused on a single Eculan in the front and gathered enough wind underneath him to lift him up and blow over a few others in the process. Then I changed the wind violently to hurl him at an entirely different block of soldiers, bowling them over and killing several, including the Eculan projectile. It would have been satisfying if the effort didn't temporarily blind me with pain, causing me to crash to the deck. Haesha was there immediately.

"Captain! Are you okay? Say something."

Everything hurt, but I couldn't admit that. "What did Abhi say?" I asked, choosing not to answer.

"The gravemaws won't step on the ice, no matter what."

"Okay. I think I'm tapped out for the moment. Time to repel boarders."

She helped me to my feet and to the rail, where I could assess the threat. It was . . . puzzling. On the one hand, we were still vastly outnumbered. On the other, I wasn't sure how they expected to board us. Because we were a moving target, the rails were over their heads, and they had only one hand to grab on if they took a running leap and held on to their swords. They had no ladders or grappling hooks. A few of them demonstrated the futility of this—some of them leaping, outright missing the rail, and sliding down into the icy water. A couple slipped when they tried to jump and wound up crashing headfirst into the side of the boat and then into the water.

And a few made it onto the rail, only to have their hands or heads struck off by our blades before they could bring theirs to bear.

Seeing that they weren't even getting close, they paused their attempts but kept pace with us and shouted ideas to one another. When I saw two ahead plant themselves and cup their hands, I shouted, "They're going to try throwing someone on! Be ready!"

The first attempt was an abject failure: The would-be boarder slipped on his plant leg and skidded face-first across the ice, taking out the two guys who would have thrown him. But others were pairing up and gesturing to their fellows to get launched, and one or more of them would eventually succeed and do their best to lay waste to as many of us as possible, making it easier for others to follow.

A couple of them successfully got airborne, but they discovered that once there, I had little difficulty batting them down out of the air with my kenning. Apart from the splitting headache and my struggle to remain conscious, that is.

There were soon too many for me to handle, and one of them successfully got onto the boat. He landed less than gracefully, however, and Haesha split him open with her Buran.

The second one to make it on, however, brought his sword down overhead onto the skull of one of our Nentian guests, and had it not gotten stuck, he might have killed others. He was quickly gutted from three directions by my crew.

But that success was enough to encourage the Eculans to keep going. Their whole game was attrition. Take out ten or fifteen more of us, and our defenses would crumble when we could no longer guard the rails.

I saw a line of them at our side and, waiting ahead, ten or more pairs willing to give others a lift, one by one, to break us.

Despair clutched my heart then. No matter what carnage the gravemaws were inflicting onshore, it was too little to help us. My eyes welled to think of surviving both the krakens and Lorson and building a ship to complete our journey, only to be cut down by this inexplicable army in the coldest stretch of winter.

A shout from aft warned us to hold on, because a wave was incoming.

"A wave?" I said, sure I couldn't have heard correctly. Why would there be a wave on a frozen sea?

Turned out I had indeed misheard, and I wasn't holding on to anything when it hit, so I and many others toppled to the deck as a behemoth of the deep breached the surface right next to our ship, sending chunks of ice and men flying into the air.

It was a whale, not a wave. A lion whale, to be exact, its mottled yellow and gray skin shining in what weak sunlight had made it through the cloud cover, and it broke even more ice for us when it fell back into the Northern Yawn, rocking us harder. But its breach had effectively created a moat of freezing ocean between the edge of the ice and our boat, making any attempts at jumping impossible for the short term.

"Abhi, you have saved us all again," I said, even though he couldn't hear me. I would kiss that kid if it wouldn't absolutely horrify him.

The Eculans would have to travel around and get ahead of us to try any further boarding operations, and they gamely did so, only to be taken out by another breach.

They gave up after that, finally, watching us crunch through the ice, knowing that we were silently guarded by an unseen leviathan.

I worried about Abhi and what those waves might have done to him in his dinghy, but he was safe. He was trailing behind our left side, which meant the span of water was too wide for them to jump across, and he had kept low so as to not attract attention.

I called down to him. "I think we're safe now, Abhi. You

can tell the gravemaws to back off. But maybe the lion whale can stick around in case they try again."

"He will. I'm not positive, but I think he believes that was fun."

"Come on up. But be advised that you will have to submit to a hug from a grateful friend."

"All right," he groused.

I don't know if I'll ever be able to repay him for saving us twice. Was he a little older-looking than when he went down to the boat? Had the summoning taxed him at all? I knew I must appear older, but I wasn't going to look in a glass anytime soon.

A half hour later, the Eculan army was out of sight, their numbers reduced, and the sound of the *Nentian Herald* crumping through ice was a comfort again. If it weren't for the deceased and my poor aching head, it would be a lovely morning.

We still had no idea why that army was camped there.

My stain-free clothes safely stowed for the next special occasion, I got to work in the quartermaster's library wearing something only mildly grubby.

Maron was joyfully headed to a neutral location to conduct a blind taste test of tea and settle the wager between the two guards.

I had a cup on some fine service dropped off for me by a longshoreman, and I took one delicious sip but then forgot it existed until long after it had cooled.

The papers arrayed before me had been collected from a cabin on the northern shore with a single spy inside, and he'd hidden a canoe among the reeds. When I asked if I could question him, I was told that he died.

Pity. I'd been hoping to extract from him the identity of the mysterious L, to whom many of the dispatches were written. It was not only Vjeko who wrote to him. But unlike Vjeko's letters, these dispatches were signed with locations, as in *Setyrön,* rather than by any individuals, so there were few clues as to who the spies might be.

I hadn't heard if the Brynts ever discovered the identity of Vjeko—I'd left after informing them of his existence and then wound up in Fornyd rather than Pelemyn, so I'd have to wait longer to hear, most likely.

Of much greater interest to me was how these messages were delivered. There were no addresses, so they couldn't be using the regular post.

A message I translated in late afternoon provided the answer: They were using dead drops. The message in front of me noted that the location of the dead drop in Tömerhil needed to change due to the recent compromise of the first, and this was the last message to be left at the old one. The new one was behind a loose stone in the wall of an alley between a bathhouse and a pub.

So the author of the message left a note somewhere in the city, and someone else—perhaps the dead man, perhaps more than one person—made sure it got to the spy shack across the river from Fornyd.

The location of a dead drop in Tömerhil was a solid piece of intelligence and worthy of a day's work. It might lead to the capture of an actual spy, and if he spoke the language of the Eculans, there was no telling what we might learn.

I collected everything to be returned to my room and informed the mariner outside the door that I had something to report to the quartermaster when she had a free moment. I'd be dining with Maron shortly, but nothing was on my schedule after that.

My husband gleefully shared that he had chosen the winner of the finest cup of tea and brought much glory to them, while doing his best to salve the feelings of the loser by declaring that they had the finest biscuits. "It's a distinct pleasure to be a tastemaker, even in a small space," he told me.

"If I had not been dressed in my finest clothes, they may not have thought you so tasteful."

Maron laughed. "Perhaps not. They would come around and see how discerning I was later, as everyone does eventually."

The quartermaster called for me after dinner, and I immediately changed into the stain-free garb.

"I'm very proud of you, Gondel," Maron said. "Dressing responsibly twice in a row. She has no idea what an honor you are doing her."

"It's such a tremendous burden, thinking about appearances," I replied. "Now she probably has this expectation of me dressing respectably. It feels like a lie."

"It's not a lie."

"Skulduggery, then. I am wearing a mask, a tidy disguise."

"Think of it as courtesy. You like to be courteous."

"When convenient, yes, and that means I'm courteous in conversation. Nothing about clothing oneself is convenient. Think about it: No one *wants* to wear pants. It's just an oppressive social custom."

"Dressing well can open doors that might otherwise be shut. That's convenient. Think about that."

I grudgingly admitted that he may have a point. On more than one occasion my expertise had been questioned because of my slovenly appearance, whereas the festively ornamented, such as Elten Maff, were given credit far beyond their intellect.

Gathering my translations and giving my husband a quick, delicious kiss goodbye, I followed the longshoreman to the

Wellspring, where Quartermaster Farlen du Cannym was finishing a conversation with the Raelech ambassador, a stout man with a full but neatly trimmed beard. She introduced him—though I promptly forgot his name—and said he would stay to hear what I'd learned as well.

"These new documents confirm what the earlier ones told us: Eculans have spies in each of your remaining cities," I told her. "They're using dead drops to relay messages here and then presumably across the river to the cabin where your men discovered them. The new information is that a dead drop in Tömerhil is specifically mentioned, the location of which we can probably determine. If we can use that information to catch a spy and bring them here, I might be able to learn more. I can speak Eculan to them, pretend to be a part of their network."

"That's a sound idea. Did you learn any more about why they are so interested in the north?"

"The spies are all writing to someone with the initial *L*, who lives somewhere in that direction. Your city is a stepping stone on the path to him, wherever he may be—"

"Begging your pardon, if I may ask," the ambassador interrupted, "were any of these messages from spies in Raelech cities?"

"Not that I have seen so far. I might come across some if we receive more documents. But I also saw no messages from any Brynt city that had been destroyed. If there was—or is—a spy in Fandlin, for example, it's possible their relay in Bennelin was eliminated."

"That is certainly worth investigation."

"Please continue, Scholar," the quartermaster said.

Waving the translations, I said, "I'll let you peruse these at your leisure, and of course I will happily work on anything further you bring to me. I'm sure it's too soon to hope for an answer regarding a visit to the Seven-Year Ship, but I wished to remind you that it's a priority. There's no telling what we might learn."

"Yes. I sent a message to the pelenaut with your ship captain, asking permission."

"Excellent. In the meantime, perhaps I could visit Saviič, tend to his needs, and ask about the mysterious L?"

"Certainly. I'll have my lung take you to him. Thank you, Scholar."

Given to the care of Lans du Höwyll, I was escorted out of the Wellspring and through a maze of corridors. The lung slipped me a pouch of Brynt currency on the way. "Your promised stipend," he explained. "And I'm given to understand you could use one or two extra outfits?"

"How did you come to understand that?"

He chuckled softly but didn't bother to answer. Instead, he gave me the name and address of his personal tailor, who was expecting me, and said that if I would pay him a visit, the cost of two changes of clothing would be taken care of by the quartermaster.

The place where they were housing Saviič was behind a heavy iron door and down a slick flight of stone stairs. It was—like all dungeons, I suppose—a dank affair, but colder and darker than the one in Linlauen. It possessed rough stone walls and a ceiling low enough that Saviič might have difficulty standing at his full height. The lung introduced me to a mariner on duty, gave instructions that my requests were to be fulfilled, and left me with him. Said mariner was an aging man with gray hairs on his chin and his temples, who perhaps had imagined a more glorious ending to his military service than a dungeon posting. He farted robustly as soon as the lung closed the door, but rather than apologize he pretended nothing had happened. It was a comment, perhaps, on how his day was going, and as such, he would let it stand. To add an afterthought, he hawked up a glob of snot and spat to the side before accompanying me to Saviič's cell.

The Eculan was well, but he complained immediately of the cold and damp and cramped quarters. I asked the mariner if we could get him some blankets, an extra firebowl or two, and a nicer pillow.

"Why pamper him?" he said. "He's a Bone Giant."

"This one did not participate in the invasion," I said, which was technically true. My doubts about his motivations aside, it would be best to cast his behavior in a positive light. "He's more of a religious pilgrim. Think of him as a resource rather than a prisoner. He's helping me break their spy network, and a little bit of comfort goes a long way to secure his cooperation."

The mariner grunted. "All right. I'll cozy up his cell after you've left. I'll be up the hall when you need me." He shuffled away in a dungeon keeper's dirge, an ominous tone poem of jangling keys, snorting sinuses, and creaking leather.

"This place is not like the other," Saviič said. "I don't like it."

"I am very sorry. I just now asked him to improve your conditions, and I'm sure he will. I've come to share some good news: I confirmed that the Seven-Year Ship is somewhere downriver—closer than I originally thought—and we have requested permission to pay a visit."

He rushed to the cell bars and gripped them, eyes bulging in excitement.

"When do we go? Is it soon?"

"I hope it's soon. It may be days or weeks until we hear back, but certainly not a month."

His face fell. "I have to wait in this place for weeks?"

"We can't have you visible in the city. This place was invaded by Ecula, and the people here would slay you on sight. I will do what I can to make improvements. How is the food?"

"Terrible. No fish. Some kind of bird meat."

Probably swamp duck, which was divine if prepared well

but could be fairly tough and tasteless if handled carelessly. I doubted the dungeon chef cared very much.

"I'll see if I can improve that too. Fish might be in short supply here, since we are inland. May I ask you a question about Ecula?"

"Ask."

"Did you know of any great leaders, military or spiritual, who had the first initial of *L*?"

The giant frowned. "That is a question about a person, not Ecula."

"Apologies. But does anyone come to mind?"

Saviič shook his head. "I do not know anyone in military. Only leaders I know are of the church, and none has a name like that."

A defeated sigh. "Someday soon, Saviič, may we both know the truths we seek."

"Yes. This is a good prayer. You to your god and me to mine."

"If you remember a name later, please let me know."

"I will."

"And I will see to improving your cell."

It occurred to me that in translating all those notes in a single day, I no longer had any pressing work for tomorrow. I could catch up on something else. Or maybe even take a day off. What would *that* be like?

"I remember days off," Fintan said wistfully as he dispelled his seeming. "Not that I don't enjoy this work of a lifetime, telling you this tale. We are approaching its end in the coming days. But let's return our focus to the west now." He took on the seeming of my new favorite greensleeve.

en

After Sage and Sprout walk the entire Leaf Road from Pont to Keft in *Leafsong*, the teacher points out to the student that even though they have traversed the breadth of Forn and seen so much, they have seen only a fraction of what the Canopy shields from the sun. From a treetop in the east, Sage points to the west.

—*Think back on all the new life you have seen, Sprout, and you can imagine the new life that lies ahead. There are wonders waiting down every unfamiliar road.*

—*Are there not dangers also?*

—*Sometimes. You can avoid them if you wish and confine your-self to the familiar, but that which is safe is rarely wondrous.*

—*But don't we need to be safe?*

—*We need a measure of it for stability. But we need a measure of danger too. Safety allows us to grow; danger encourages us to grow. Too much of either prevents us from achieving our potential. We need the proper mix to become our best selves.*

—*How do we achieve the proper mix?*

—*Discovering that is why we live.*

I still pore over that passage and wonder if I have found the proper mix yet. I suspect I'm getting closer, since I'm en-joying my stay in Talala Fouz and feel excited every day about what will happen next and whom I might meet. I have my measure of safety in the tea treehouse, where I've been hid-ing since freeing the ambassador, but the danger is that my presence could be discovered or reported at any time. Mean-while, I'm encountering many new people, thanks to sharing so much time with Ambassador Ken.

People like the Raelech bard and the courier who arrived in company with the Raelech ambassador through the secret tunnel linking our embassies. I'd never met anyone blessed by the huntress or the poet goddess before, and since this road was bringing me so many wonders, I felt I should continue to walk it.

The courier and I exchanged smiles as we checked each other out. She was perhaps a third taller than me, her frame slim and taut and encased in red leather armor marred by an assortment of colorful stains. Her hair was glossy black like a Nentian's, but she had pulled it back and twisted it into braids for convenience. Her large brown eyes traveled up and down, lingering on my forearms and shins where the silverbark grew. Unexpectedly, her voice was pitched fairly high, but she spoke Fornish flawlessly.

"Forgive me, my duties have never sent me to Forn, so this is my first chance to meet a greensleeve. You are extraordinary."

"As are you." How fast could she run? Judging by the magnificent splatters of insect guts on her armor, *very* fast.

"I am Seelagh, master courier of the Huntress Raena."

"Bright sun to you, Seelagh. I am Pen Yas ben Min of the White Gossamer Clan."

The bard, whose brown skin had slightly cooler undertones to it than Seelagh's, introduced herself as Eimear. She had a small harp strapped to her back and a lower, mellower voice that was probably outstanding in song.

Seelagh had brought Eimear as Rael's initial response to the news of Ambassador Ken's harrowing brush with death. They wanted a full account of her abduction and escape, which Seelagh would take back with her perfect memory; Eimear would remain to witness any further developments.

Relating those events somehow made them unreal to me—I had difficulty believing that had actually been me who'd arrived in a foreign capital and immediately set about engineering a jailbreak. And while our stories riveted the Raelechs, they were nothing next to the news we'd received

of the independence of Khul Bashab. Seelagh and Eimear reacted visibly to that and thanked us for the news. Seelagh said
she'd need to leave in the morning to report to the Triune
Council.

But then they told us something that made us react in the
same way—as in, it was the most significant thing said so far.
"Have you heard of the new city established in the Gravewood by the Nentians and Hathrim?"

"What? No. Where is this?"

"It's called Malath Ashmali. Walk due north of Ghuli Rakhan until you reach the coast of the Northern Yawn and
you're there. They have a road made by one of our stonecutters and fully expect to trade come spring, provided they survive the winter."

"What about the animals?" Ambassador Ken asked.

"They have a beast caller controlling them. The first one,
in fact—the plaguebringer Abhinava Khose. We've heard he's
figured out how to enchant stakes that repel predators.
They're going to plant them along the road so anyone can
travel it. We wanted you to know because the stonecutter is
staying on. They've set aside land for every nation to build an
embassy, and he would build one for you should you wish to
send someone up there."

It was all I could do not to erupt that the ambassador
should send me. I was not, however, a member of the diplomatic service. But a new city in the north surrounded by a
vast forest? That interested me greatly.

"So this is a Nentian city?" Ambassador Ken pressed.

"Technically, yes. But not like any of the others. There is
no viceroy. There's a Hathrim executive and a council made
up of elected Nentians and Hathrim."

"Who's the executive?"

"A firelord named Olet Kanek."

Ambassador Ken sat up straighter. "Daughter of Winthir
Kanek? The reason he came here and burned down the city?"

"The very same. She's nothing like him, though. Here's the earthshaking part: They met some people from across the ocean. An all-women crew from a country they call Joabei."

"What were they doing up there?"

"Searching for a northern passage. Their ship was attacked by a kraken right in front of the plaguebringer. He somehow got the kraken to stop and saved their lives. Turns out they are people of the Second Kenning."

We all gasped. The ambassador leaned forward. "They have a place to seek a kenning in their country across the ocean?"

"Yes."

There was more, but I had already heard enough to make up my mind. There was an unfamiliar road leading into the Gravewood and many wonders waiting at the end of it. It might be a place where a certain acorn would like to be planted. It was clearly a place where legends could be made, far from the Canopy.

Come spring, I would walk that road.

Day 45

A BONE-COLLARED DREADMOOSE

The long-expected Raelech army arrived around mid-morning, but that arrival kept happening and stretched into afternoon. It was a slow accretion on the outskirts of Survivor Field, and many people, including myself, went to the wall to watch them file in, pitch tents, and make camp. It was a significant force with significant resources, the trailing supplies for them and for our city taking up far more space than the people who were supposed to fight.

"Look at all those fighters, though," a man about my age said as he joined me at the parapet. "If they had a notion to come in here, what could we do, eh? Throw a bucket of fish heads at them?"

I chuckled politely before saying, "They don't have a juggernaut in the lot, and we have tidal mariners and rapids, so I think we'd hold our own. Not that we need to worry."

"Aw, naw, naw. I don't really think they'd come for us. Raelechs are all right."

"Yeah?" I replied, wondering who, by implication, wasn't all right, and whether he was the sort to actually say it out loud. Turned out he was.

"Hathrim are terrible, though," he said.

"Oh? Is that based on personal experience? You've met some and were treated poorly?"

"Well, no, but, you know . . . they burn people."

"Some do, that's true," I admitted. "But there's a Hathrim couple who have been living here for years—both of them lavaborn—and they haven't burned anyone in all that time."

"Hathrim are here? In Pelemyn?"

"Two of them, aye. They used to run a very popular restaurant until recently. It had to close down because of the shortages, you know."

"But they're still here?"

"Yes. And very friendly."

"Huh. Didn't know that." He snorted. "Pelemyn's a big city."

"Indeed it is. Have you lived here long?"

"Naw, I'm from Göfyrd originally. Was here on business when the Bone Giants came, and then I didn't have a home or a business to go back to."

"I'm sorry."

"Aw, well, I'm swimming in the same ocean as everybody else. Good to see the Raelechs are here to help us." He nodded at this conclusion, figuring that was a good line to make his exit, and left me there. Someone else promptly took his place to get a good look at the army: a younger woman, cradling a toddler against her hip.

"See there, sweetie? That's the Raelech army."

"Ah-mee," the toddler said, pointing.

"That's right. Some of them are fighters, but most of them are people who support the fighters. They bring along food for the soldiers, and they brought food for us too."

"Food!" the child said.

"Yes. We'll get to have some soon. I hope."

She glanced my way, and I gave her a friendly nod and a tight-lipped grin. She nodded back, returned her gaze to the army, and pointed at wagons and knots of soldiers setting up camp. Eventually she caught my gaze again, a small furrow of concern between her eyes.

"Pardon me, but do you know how many soldiers they have?"

"I've heard it's in the neighborhood of ten thousand."

"Ten thousand. And how many mariners are in our garrison?"

"Perhaps four thousand. Most of them will be joining the counterattack, leaving the city quite vulnerable while they're gone."

"It sounds like we're vulnerable now. I didn't really think of it until I saw them, but . . . if they decided to lay siege to us right now, with plenty of food on their side and none on ours . . ."

"We wouldn't last long, you're right," I said. "But I wouldn't worry."

"Why not?"

That was an excellent question. If I name-dropped the pelenaut and said he wasn't worried, she probably wouldn't believe me. She might even think I was trying to impress her and had amorous intentions. So I gestured along the length of the wall.

"If there was any reason to worry, we wouldn't be standing here right now. The parapets would be lined with archers. They'd be telling everyone on Survivor Field to get inside the walls."

"Oh. I guess that's right. I can't stop feeling nervous, though."

"That's entirely understandable. But look. Some of those wagons are queueing up to get into the city. And the mariners are coming out to escort them in."

"Food!" the child cried again.

"Yes, food," his mother agreed. "Hard to believe something might go well for us for a change."

I wished them both full bellies very soon and descended from the wall, making my way to the refugee kitchen to inquire whether I would be needed tomorrow. Chef du Rödal nodded her head enthusiastically. "I've nothing for today, as the supplies won't likely arrive until this evening, but tomorrow will be a full day. Come down for breakfast, and I'll put you to work through lunch."

"Will do. Have you heard if there will be enough food for restaurants to reopen?"

"I don't believe so. These are all dry goods, roots, and tubers. But my understanding is that the bakeries should reopen. There might even be some loaves by this evening."

"Toast!" I cried. "Yes!"

The line at Gellart du Tyllen's fishblade hut was even longer and the portions even smaller that day, and a few angry voices were raised and a fistfight broke out at one point, everyone's temper shortened by hunger. But the bard and I were able to bear the growling of our systems, knowing that tomorrow we should be able to quiet them. And professionally speaking, we were finally able to catch up and the manuscript was current once more.

The bard beamed at Survivor Field once he took his place on the makeshift stage on the wall. "We'll all eat well tomorrow, eh? Welcome to the Raelech army, especially your supply wagons! I am Fintan of the Poet Goddess Kaelin, and you have joined us for day forty-five of an ongoing recounting of the war. I have two tales to share today, but first we will have a song, a short break for necessaries, and then we'll get into it. Today I'll sing a popular miner's tune from Rael and hope the Raelechs will join me so that our Brynt allies can all hear you in the city. Raise your voices, friends!"

The response was the same until the end, and everyone quickly caught on, so that the whole city was shouting it. Apparently, there were infinite variations on the call, but the song always ended with a different response for the last two lines.

> Poke your finger in the foreman's eye—
> Take a shot of that Aelinmech rye!
> It's got that taste you can't deny,

Take a shot of that Aelinmech rye!
My sweetheart left me so I'll cry,
Take a shot of that Aelinmech rye!
Shake your fist at a cloudy sky,
Take a shot of that Aelinmech rye!
Order a slice of butternut pie,
Take a shot of that Aelinmech rye!
Last thing I'll do before I die:
Take a shot of that Aelinmech rye!
This cheap whiskey just ain't doing it,
Give me a shot of the real Good Shit!

"We begin today with Abhinava Khose, the plaguebringer of the Sixth Kenning, who will hopefully join us here soon. But this takes us back a few months into winter, when he was sailing from Malath Ashmali with the Joabeians in the Northern Yawn."

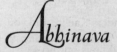

Abhinava

I am pretty sure I remember what it was like to be warm. Or I would if it wasn't so cold.

Murr and Eep may have entirely forgotten warmth, but they remember very well that I'm the reason they're freezing. They spend all their time in the ship's cabin, wrapped in blankets and huddled by the firebowl, glaring at me whenever I'm in there. I feed them, but they won't eat in front of me. Murr snarls at me, and Eep screeches. They are miserable and it's all my fault.

I've told them repeatedly that we will head south as soon as we can. We just have to traverse the Northern Yawn first, and it's slow going because we have to break through ice.

They have not been receptive or forgiving when I apologize, and I worry that they'll take off as soon as we touch land and I'll never see them again.

Eep could, of course, fly away whenever she wants. Maybe she's just waiting for a day that's slightly less bone-shuddering cold than the others.

After we had that terrifying encounter with the Bone Giants, I started to think about the problem of feeding that many people throughout the winter. They weren't going to get the necessary fuel from the Gravewood—I knew exactly what was available, and it wasn't enough. They weren't ice fishing. So they had come with supplies in those smaller boats we saw frozen in the ice, which didn't have cargo holds.

There was no way they had crossed the Peles Ocean and then continued to the spot we found them without resupply. So where, I asked Koesha, was the resupply point?

"You expect me to know that?" she said.

"No, I'm just saying it's likely ahead, so we should be on the lookout. It's either a great opportunity for us or a great danger."

"Okay. That is good thinking. Thank you."

Eventually we found it: docks and buildings but no signs of activity. Koesha summoned wind to lift her from the deck and scouted the site from the air but returned to report that she saw no one.

"It's abandoned as far as I can tell. Is this place marked on any of Lorson's maps, Fintan?"

The bard shook his head sadly.

"Would you mind if we took a look inside the buildings?" I asked. "Just to satisfy my curiosity. And if they have some dry goods in storage, well, we could use them, right?"

"We're not pirates. We would leave payment."

"Of course. Didn't mean to suggest otherwise. But I'd really like to go take a look."

Koesha thought for a few seconds and said, "We'll set you

down on the ice, do a circle in the sea, and come back. You need to be ready to go by then."

"Okay."

Except she didn't just set me down. She sent Haesha and Fintan with me, and Murr and Eep as well. It was a clear, still day, the least cold we'd felt in weeks, if not actually warm, so my animal friends were willing to leave the firebowl to get some exercise.

What we found confirmed my theory: It was a supply depot. One of the buildings was a warehouse stocked with dried food and assorted supplies—there was even a box of enchanted firebowls and sparking stones, which I just had to take with us when we left.

There was a stable with no animals inside but plenty of wagons and carriages. And there was a bunkhouse with bunks and . . . blood on the floor.

"Oh," I said, staring at the stains. "I guess whoever was here didn't abandon the place so much as die."

"Now I'm wondering if this was a Brynt outpost that the Eculans plundered or if it was an Eculan depot that the Brynts discovered," Fintan said.

"It's the second one," I said. "All the papers are gone."

"What papers?"

"All of it. Inventory, orders, shipments, you name it— there are no records. Someone took them all."

"The Eculans might have been interested in Brynt documents, you can't know for sure."

"Okay, granted, but why would the Brynts even have such a depot? Supplying what? That's a huge question. But on the other hand, we have evidence that an Eculan army received resupply here."

"You're saying the Eculans took the trouble to build and supply this well in advance of the army's arrival."

"Yes. That fits with everything else we know about them— they have plans and they act on them."

"All right, then, but why here?"

"That is an excellent question. Maybe . . . maybe it's the end of a line."

"What line?"

"Let's check. Murr, Eep, stay here out of the freezing air; we won't go far or be gone long."

"We're going back out?" Fintan did not appear anxious to leave. Even without an active heat source, the bunkhouse was noticeably warmer than the outdoors, and there was a still hearth, which practically begged to have a fire built in it. There were logs and kindling neatly stacked off to one side, and Fintan's gaze pointedly drifted there. Haesha did not say anything, but her eyes darted back and forth, following the conversation.

"That's where the information is. Just for a bit."

Fintan's shoulders slumped in defeat and he sighed, but made no other complaint. The three of us pushed into the cold, squinting at the light bouncing off the snow, and circled around the bunkhouse, where we found what I sought.

It was snow-covered and there was no way to tell how far it went, but there was a definite trail leading south into the trees. Two small pillars of stacked rocks peeked above the snow to mark its boundary, and there were some ribbons tied around the trunks of trees past that.

"Fintan, where are we, would you guess, in relation to Brynt cities? I mean, I know we're north of everything, but . . ."

"We're probably north of Fornyd."

"You think that trail leads there?"

The bard shrugged. "Maybe."

"One way or another, though, if I head south, I should run into the Gravewater River eventually, and that will lead me to a city. And, more important, it'll get warmer every day I travel."

Haesha spoke up for the first time. "What, you mean . . . abandon ship?"

The plan, vague as it was, seemed good to me. "There are wagons and supplies and firebowls."

"But no horses to pull the wagon and supplies," she pointed out.

"Yes, but I can find something else nearby that will do the job."

We turned back to the bunkhouse and Fintan waved in the general direction of the ship. "You'd leave this historic journey?"

I broke into a smile. "Hey, I thought *mine* was the historic journey."

"It is, but . . . it's simply convenient for me to have all the history in one place, where I can see it."

I chuckled at that. "You're welcome to come with me if you want. And I've made up my mind: I *am* going. Because Murr and Eep need to get warm soon, and the ocean voyage won't be heading south for days or weeks yet. I can tell you right now, they'd rather walk south to the warmth than get on that boat again."

"Where are you going, besides south? What's the goal?"

"No specific plan beyond getting warm again. Once we achieve that, we'll look around and see who needs a beast caller."

"Well, I need to get back to Rael and report what I've seen, get this atlas looked at by scholars, and so on. Any chance I could talk you into going with me?"

"There's a chance, sure. Depends on the temperature."

"Excellent! The winters are milder. But will everyone on the *Herald* be safe if you're not on board?"

"Safe from krakens, yeah. The hull's still enchanted. Safe from the world? Never."

Fintan waggled his head. "Fair point."

Haesha shook her head. "Captain will not be happy." She

tensed and a flash of anger crossed her face, perhaps interpreting my decision as a betrayal, but then she deflated, looking hurt. "*I* will not be happy."

"No, and I'm sorry about that. It's been an honor, and I hope we will meet again, but we must part here for now."

"Tell you what," Fintan said. "Build a fire in the bunkhouse hearth, get the animals warm, maybe get a wagon or whatever all ready to go, and we will return to the ship to get my things—and all those trunks full of documents we took from Lorson's study."

I agreed to that, and my friends were quite excited to lie next to an actual fireplace, which threw off some real heat, rather than a firebowl. Fintan and Haesha departed for the ice pack, and I got busy warming up Murr and Eep and finding suitable transport for us. I loaded a wagon with boxes of food, the firebowls, a couple of extra wheels, and some tools. There was a sled attachment for the winter, which basically operated by rolling the wagon onto it and locking the wheels down with some rope tied to anchor points. There were cooking supplies and canned vegetables, everything we'd need to hit the trail, so it all went in. I also stretched out with my kenning to find some animals willing to help pull the wagon in exchange for the protection of a beast caller.

I finished all that before the *Nentian Herald* circled back around, so I was sitting in the bunkhouse and warming myself with Murr and Eep when Koesha burst in, her face a storm.

"You're leaving us?"

"Yes. Sorry, it's just too cold. It's why we left Malath Ashmali, remember? I wanted to get warm again."

"We promised to take you south. It can't be long now before the end of the Yawn."

"I know, and I appreciate that." I clambered to my feet to be respectful. "But Murr and Eep are more comfortable on land, and we'll be warmer sooner. It's the best decision for them and for me."

Koesha blinked a lot, trying to process it. She clearly didn't want me to go but was having difficulty raising a valid objection. Rather than wait, I took the opportunity to say what was in my heart.

"I am so grateful to you, Koesha, and meeting you and your crew has been—and will always be—a highlight of my life. As I told Haesha, I hope we will meet again. I wish you a safe journey home and a very long and happy life."

A tear spilled down her cheek and her lip quivered. "You saved our lives twice. Once from the krakens and once from the Eculans. And this enchanted ship is going to take us home. I owe you a debt I can never repay."

"I didn't do any of it to place you in my debt, so please don't feel like you owe me. Your friendship is all I've ever wanted."

"You will always have it."

"And you mine."

She sniffled, then sobbed, then hiccuped and sniffled again, her eyes watering even more.

"What is it?"

She clenched her fists at her sides and shouted, "I require a hug!"

So I hugged her, and she clutched me fiercely for about three seconds before pushing me away, sniffling and wiping at her eyes.

"Thank you. In our language we have words for different kinds of love, which Nentian does not have. So when I say I love you—and I do love you—I do not mean it as a romantic couple. I feel that I lost my sister forever on this journey, but I gained a brother. That is the love I feel."

Her words reminded me of my own lost family, and abruptly I felt tears welling too. Could we who have lost so much find love like that again—not the same, but similar—

and perhaps hurt less, if not heal? I did not know for certain, but I knew what I felt for Koesha.

"I feel the same love for you. And it will not fade with time or distance."

We smiled and laughed in relief, shoulders relaxing, putting our hands over our hearts.

"Okay, I am really glad I said that," she breathed. "I feel so much better."

"Me also."

"Okay. Okay." She wiped at her eyes and nose and tried to compose herself. "The others will be here soon. Please don't tell Haesha, you know, that I, uh . . . lost my composure."

I promised I wouldn't.

There were plenty more emotional farewells, because some other Joabeians wished to say goodbye, but eventually Fintan and I were left that night with a loaded wagon and a warm place to sleep that didn't buck and dip and undulate with the waves. It was the best sleep we'd had in weeks.

In the morning, Fintan asked what would be pulling the wagon for us.

"He should be outside. Let's go meet him."

I bundled up, resigned to feeling cold again, and told Murr and Eep they could stay inside until the moment we left. Fintan and I stepped out quickly into the snow and closed the door. The bard was looking directly at the stables when he emerged and failed to see the magnificent beast standing to his right.

"Good morning," I said to him. Fintan turned his head, wondering whom I was talking to, and then he saw it.

"Gah, Kaelin preserve us! Oh, my—what is that?"

"That is a bone-collared dreadmoose." I had seen a couple of them during a scouting trip on the way to Malath Ashmali. They were huge animals, like regular moose, but these had massive racks of sharp-bladed antlers. Their necks also had segmented plates of bone, growing out of their spines and circling their throats, to protect them from the bites of meat squirrels and other small predators that thought a gushing jugular would bring down anything. This one had a reddish-brown coat that would keep it camouflaged among many trees.

"My name is Abhi and this is my friend Fintan. What's your name?"

"Ohhwuh," the dreadmoose said, in a sonorous bass that vibrated in my skull.

"Excellent. Ohhwuh, thank you so much for agreeing to help us. Are you hungry? We have some high-quality oats in the stable if those sound good. Nod your head like this for yes; shake your head from side to side for no."

Ohhwuh shook his head, and it took some more questions to determine that he had never had any interest in oats and there was plenty of food in nature for him to eat, even in winter.

When he pronounced himself ready, we hooked him up to the sledwagon, and I let him know that a bloodcat and a stalk hawk would be joining us.

"Don't worry about either of them. They're my friends, and they won't ever try to eat you. Nor will anything else."

Ohhwuh snorted. He wouldn't have been concerned anyway. The only thing he really feared was a gravemaw.

Murr and Eep did not want to leave the warm bunkhouse, but I got a firebowl going in the back of the sledwagon for them and plenty of blankets snuggled around it. They'd be as toasty as possible.

Ohhwuh was incredibly strong and his hooves were adapted for the snow, so we had a quick and smooth ride across the powder. We found a shelter along the path before the day was out and immediately decided to take advantage of it. Since the trail continued past it, I was willing to bet it kept going all the way down to Fornyd, with similar shelters along the way to give travelers a safe place to rest each night—and a chance to sleep in a warm enclosure.

Murr and Eep were still annoyed with me but grudgingly agreed that this was better than freezing on the *Nentian Herald* and never getting a moment's rest.

Fintan was great entertainment, of course, so those few days on the trail wound up being some of the most peaceful and stress-free of my life since leaving Khul Bashab. He kept me from thinking too much about Tamhan and worrying about Hanima, Adithi, and Sudhi. I hoped they were all okay.

We both had many questions about who had built these waystations and where they might be, since the shelters appeared to have been recently occupied, but we assumed that we'd find out eventually if we just kept going.

Fintan dispelled the plaguebringer and smiled wryly. "I'm going to pick up where Abhi left off, because he would have entirely skipped the manner of his coming to Fornyd as the first member of the Sixth Kenning to ever visit a Brynt city."

Fintan

Though I'd woken in the night a couple of times with nightmares of burning flesh, I was in generally high spirits with Abhi as we traveled south, largely because I knew I was currently safe and heading toward home and all its comforts and securities. And I was aware that the people I'd met and the horrors and victories I'd seen would make excellent stories, so I was feeling optimistic about my future.

When we reached the shore of the Gravewater River, we faced a significant obstacle, for there was no bridge across and no established ferry. A boat would need to be hired to take us and our cargo across into Fornyd, but first we needed to get to where a boat could be hired. I didn't feel especially confident about swimming across; I could tread water, but swimming against a current might be a challenge. Abhi couldn't swim at all.

One of the benefits of being a bard, however, is that you can call for help pretty effectively. I projected my voice into the city.

"Good afternoon, Fornyd. I am Fintan of the Poet Goddess Kaelin, and I stand on the northern bank of the Gravewater with my companions. We need a ride across to the city. We have intelligence about a Bone Giant army to the north and are anxious to share it with your quartermaster, if someone would be so kind as to collect us."

That got a response. Just as a barge unmoored itself from the docks, a rapid named Lörry du Bört emerged from the river to greet us—or eye us suspiciously.

"Is that . . . a bone-collared dreadmoose?"

"Well spotted," I said. "He's harmless. As are the bloodcat and the stalk hawk from the Nentian plains. They are companions of Abhinava Khose here, who is a plaguebringer of the Sixth Kenning."

"The Sixth?"

"Yes. It provides an affinity with animals, the source of which is in Ghurana Nent. He's the reason we were able to walk through the Gravewood without harm."

"I didn't know that was even a thing."

"It's fairly new. He's the first one to be blessed."

"Are the animals coming with you?"

"The bloodcat and stalk hawk for sure," Abhi replied as he unhooked Ohhwuh from his harness. "I haven't talked to the dreadmoose about it yet."

"Talk to the dreadmoose. Yeah." Lörry was having a little trouble assimilating the new information.

"Anyway, my good rapid, I have much information to

share with your quartermaster about a Bone Giant army camped on the coast of the Northern Yawn north of Grynek, a whole new civilization of people we met from across the ocean, and questions about a curious series of cabins that we encountered on our way down."

The glaze in Lörry's eyes as he stared at Abhi and the dreadmoose abruptly cleared and his expression sharpened. "Those are spy outposts," he said.

"Spies for whom?"

"The Bone Giants. We just came back from clearing those places out. Bunch of stuff in their language we couldn't read. But there's a scholar who's working on it now."

I lit up at that. "You have someone who can read their language?"

"Yeah. He's an old Kaurian guy."

I pointed to the wagon. "That's full of documents I can't read. We brought trunks full of them from an island in the Northern Yawn, where a man had been receiving messages for many years."

"Okay. That barge you see coming will take you across. Go straight to the Wellspring. The quartermaster will be expecting you."

Abhi had a conversation with Ohhwuh. It turned out he wouldn't mind seeing the city but had no desire to get on a barge. He'd just walk or swim across the river, as needed.

The plaguebringer looked worried. "I've never really walked into a city with my friends before," he said. "I mean besides Malath Ashmali, where everyone knew me already."

I solved that problem by making another announcement to the city: A bloodcat and stalk hawk from Ghurana Nent would be accompanying a Nentian man into the city, as would a bone-collared dreadmoose. They would be harmless so long as they weren't approached or threatened, so please, good citizens, do not attempt to harm or pet the wild animals, and maybe it would be best to keep the children away.

Loading up the barge took some time since there was a single ferryman, but several longshoremen were waiting for us at the docks, and they promptly took everything to the Wellspring and said we should follow them.

We didn't follow closely, however, because we couldn't. Despite my announcement—or because of it—Abhi attracted quite a crowd by walking down the street with three animals the people of Fornyd had never seen before. They were a bit slack-jawed at the spectacle, and though they kept a respectful distance, there were still quite a few of them to wade through, and the throng kept growing and the babble of excited voices increased in volume.

"I think we need to get them to a place where they can eat and rest in safety," Abhi told me. "This curiosity isn't going to help them do either."

"Yes, I can see that."

"Why don't you go into the Wellspring and make my apologies? I'd love to meet the quartermaster, but I need to see to my friends' needs first."

"Of course. Where will I be able to find you?"

Abhi paused and closed his eyes for a few seconds, then opened them. "I'm going to take them to some farmland to the southwest of the city. It has an orange barn."

"How do you know that?"

"I searched for horses as a way to pinpoint farmland, and I got a tiny visual flash from them. They're in the barn," he said, grinning. "Murr and Eep will find something to hunt there, and there's probably some wooded area in which Ohh-wuh can eat the bark or whatever he likes. Maybe I can arrange to stay at the house. I'm sure the farmer could use a guy who can talk to animals and assess what's happening regarding pests and so on."

We clasped hands and parted, and Abhi took the crowd with him. Some mariners had helpfully shown up to keep folks away and remind them not to approach, and they would guide Abhi and his companions out of the city to the south.

What followed was a sequence of revelations, for I got to meet Quartermaster Farlen du Cannym, Gerstad Daryck du Löngren and the Grynek Hunters, and Scholar Gondel Vedd. They were every bit as surprised at the stories I had to tell as I was to hear of theirs. And with the benefit of their aid, I could see that the warehouse and series of cabins Abhi and I had used to travel south were part of a spy network that shuttled messages back and forth from Brynlön to a certain individual living on an island in sight of Malath Ashmali. They, in turn, understood that Lorson had been the mastermind of the invasion and were gratified to hear that he was dead, slain by Olet Kanek. We were each providing pieces to solve the other's puzzle.

But we still didn't know why that army was camped up there in the cold. Daryck was very pleased to hear that Koesha and her crew had dealt them many casualties and that the total had been increased by a pair of gravemaws summoned by Abhi. Gondel shared that, based on prior intelligence, the army may have been looking for something called the Kraken's Nest, and I told all assembled that the coast off Malath Ashmali—and probably a good distance east and west of it too—would fit that particular description. The Northern Yawn was where the krakens spawned.

All of the intelligence from Lorson's mansion was wheeled into the quartermaster's library for Gondel's translation. Since he'd finished working through everything Daryck had brought him from the spy outposts, he smiled at the infusion of new documents. Any insight into Ecula's plans— especially the purpose of that army—would be welcome. If they were looking for the Kraken's Nest, for example: Why was it so important as to merit an army needing to be provisioned through the winter?

While Gondel busied himself with that, Daryck escorted

the quartermaster and me out to the farm with the orange barn, where Abhi had indeed ingratiated himself with the farmer and secured food and lodging.

Ohhwuh the dreadmoose was happy with whatever he foraged in the snowy woods surrounding the fields, and Murr had hunted down a troublesome boar that had been periodically ruining portions of the farmer's crop. Eep was well fed on rodents around the farm, and they were all living very well and staying warm. It was still cold but not breathtakingly so as it had been up north, and Murr and Eep seemed happier now.

The farmer and his family were overwhelmed to have the quartermaster visit their place, but she shed all her formality and gave them hugs and told them to relax, for what they did was far more important than what she did. As a hygienist, she insisted on checking their well water and purified it of the tiniest traces of pollutants.

We built a fire in a pit outside, bundled in some quilts, and sat around it with mugs of warm mulled cider after the sun went down.

"The bard will no doubt entertain us soon," Farlen said, dropping me a rather large hint, "but before he does, Abhi— I'm going to have Fintan translate for me—have I been informed correctly that you have a beast callers clave?"

"Yes."

"Well, the city of Fornyd would welcome any beast caller, and I hope you'll let them know that they are welcome here. We don't have a Nentian embassy, but I will leave word with my garrison that any beast callers who present themselves should be granted an audience."

"Thank you. I'm not sure when I will return home, but I will let them know."

"What's keeping you from home?"

"A couple of very powerful men want me dead because they see my kenning as a threat to them. I thought it better to leave than begin a bloodbath. I am curious what's happened since I've been gone, though. Perhaps I can return in the spring. Have you heard anything from Ghurana Nent?"

The quartermaster shook her head. "Not since the tunnel to Rael collapsed. We're the last to hear anything now. If you'd like to finish up your winter here, I'm sure we can arrange a contract."

The plaguebringer nodded in contemplation. "That might not be bad. There are some interesting animals here I'd like to document. Do you know of something that's like a marmot but pointy?"

"Sounds like a sunchuck."

"A sunchuck? Oh, because the spines radiate like rays from the sun. Got it. I could sense them but didn't know what they were called."

"They're poisonous. Best tell your bloodcat and hawk to stay away from them."

"Thanks, I will. Let me think on a contract and get back to you."

Since Abhi was well pleased to explore the area, I left him there for a couple of days and collected stories from Daryck and Gondel. Daryck left with the Grynek Hunters to pursue a spy that Gondel thought might be in Tömerhil, and I helped Gondel where I could in organizing the notes according to subject or sender. It was late in the afternoon, near dinnertime, when I saw his body tense up as he read something.

"What is it?"

"Where is this from?" he asked me, shaking the piece of paper in his hand. I peered at it to see if it dislodged a memory, and it did.

"From Lorson's desk. It was some of the stuff I couldn't read."

"So we may reasonably conclude that it was his most recent reading?"

"I believe so. We didn't find any other material in his house besides what we brought from his office. Why?"

"It says there will be another invasion in late spring or possibly early summer. Overwhelming attacks on Pelemyn and colonization forces for the rest. The boats are being built now."

When Fintan dispersed the seeming of his past self, he immediately deferred to Könstad du Lallend, who spoke to all assembled for the first time. He was the modest military type, the son of a military family, bathed in washes of honor and duty since birth. He exuded a soft glow of gravitas from the blades of his cheekbones and possessed a posture that reminded me not to slouch. His logistical prowess and command of figures was a vital reason we'd done as well as we had, a perfect match to Rölly's desire for data to aid his flow studies. Hearing from him at that moment was an instance of the perfect time to speak, because few commanded more respect, and the news of a second invasion had already stirred up some cries of alarm and despair in the populace.

"Good evening. Before you worry too much about the revelation of this invasion, let me point something out: This counterattack we are planning with our Raelech, Fornish, and Kaurian allies is not simply revenge. It is in fact intended to prevent this second invasion you just learned of—because we heard about it a couple of months ago and set in motion these waves that are about to break upon our shores.

"The Fornish army will join us in a couple of days, and hopefully the Kaurian fleet will arrive soon after that. Once we are all assembled—certainly by the end of Bloom—we will load the boats and launch in the first week of Rainfall. We can do that because of the maps that Fintan brought in Lorson's atlas, and we will arrive in Ecula before late spring, thereby foiling their plans. I am sure you may have other questions, but my understanding is that the bard's tale will be finished by then, and you will know all that we know before the launch."

"That is true," Fintan confirmed.

"Thank you for your patience during these lean times. Thank you again to our Raelech allies for their aid. Eat well tomorrow, friends."

The könstad's speech did much to quell panic, but the city certainly had plenty to talk about, and talk they did. I could hear the excited babble from the wall: Near me, the discussion was about how we'd actually cross the ocean, since we didn't have access to the kraken blood that Eculans used to stain their hulls, and we didn't have a fleet of enchanted ships blessed by the plaguebringer either.

"And what if they launch earlier—or if they're already on the way?" one man asked another, both of whom were sloshed on ale and slurring their speech a little bit. "Huh? What then? What if our fleet and theirs—*urrrrp*—pass each other on the ocean? It's big enough. Because, you know, it's an ocean."

The man's friend wrapped an arm around his shoulders. "Tell me something, Pösnan."

"What?"

"Are you *trying* to shit yourself right now? Because that's what it sounds like."

"Naw, I'm just trying to be realistic here. It could happen."

"That's about as likely as you spending the night with my sister. Stop looking at her, by the way."

"It could happen!" Pösnan insisted.

"You better be talking about the fleets right now."

"Yes, that's what I mean."

"It took you all of three seconds to worry about that stuff. *You.* So don't you think Könstad du Lallend would have thought of that too? And that he's got an answer?"

"Sure, of course, yeah. But what is it?"

Pösnan's friend farted audibly. "That's all the information I have, sorry. You'll just have to wait for the bard to catch us up."

I sighed. *Join the club, Pösnan.*

A VERY IMPORTANT CLOAK

Pancakes. With syrup. A side of fennel-spiced sausage, and a hot cup of tea. What absolute bliss!

Chef du Rödal put me to work after that, peeling a righteous mountain of potatoes and carrots of a quality we had not seen for some time. I went to it cheerfully. There is nothing quite like feeling full again after going without.

With an hour to go, a visitor appeared: Dame Nyssa du Valas, the Brynt spy who supposedly knew my wife and overheard that her poisoning had been ordered by Melishev Lohmet and carried out by Jasindur Torghala.

"Hello. And where have you been?" I asked.

"Working. Trying to find out what is happening in the west."

"And have you had any success?"

"None except for listening to the bard."

"We are swimming the same currents, then."

"The tales are remarkable, though. I get so focused on my own small piece of the world that I forget sometimes how wide it is. It's good that the bard is here to remind us."

"Agreed. But remind me: Were you authorized to reveal to me what you reported to the lung about Sarena's poisoning?"

Her eyes dropped. "No. I'm in a bit of trouble over that."

"Why did you tell me?"

"I mistakenly believed you were in the same security pool as me."

"But it was all true? Lohmet ordered it, then Torghala did it and was expelled for that reason?"

"I'm not supposed to answer that now."

"Ha!" I barked. "Then why have you come, if not to tell me anything?"

"I was rather hoping you could tell me something."

"Doubtful. My days of having a clue were all too brief. And even if I do know something, I am not sure I'm authorized to tell you."

"You absolutely are. I'm collecting intelligence for the lung, after all."

"What do you think I might know that he doesn't already?"

"You are in daily conversation with the bard."

"I imagine the lung could be as well. While I spend my mornings here, I'm sure the bard is in discussions with our leadership regarding what he knows."

"I believe that's correct. We're just checking up on him to see if he's telling the same story to different ears or if there are discrepancies. Has he shared anything more with you regarding what Gondel Vedd discovered in those documents?"

"Master Dervan du Alöbar!" a voice rang out. I turned to see four armed mariners marching in my direction. A whole lot of heads were focused on me, clearly wondering, as was I, what sort of trouble I might be in.

"Yes?"

"Do not say another word!"

That was easy enough. I went very still except for putting down my paring knife. I wouldn't want the mariners to think I had any intention of using it on something besides a potato.

Resigning myself to another stint in the dungeon and questioning by humorless lackeys, I raised my hands in surrender. And then the mariners marched right past me and seized Dame Nyssa du Valas.

"You're under arrest," they informed her, and some very confused protesting ensued, not least from myself.

"Hold on a moment, she works for us! She reports to the lung!"

"True enough," the mariner admitted. "But she may also be reporting to someone else."

"What? Who?"

"We'd like an answer to that as well. You may carry on. Thanks for putting down that knife, though. Very kind of you."

I didn't think it was kind so much as self-preservation—my sense of which was apparently quick to manifest itself when visible weapons were involved but utterly asleep when it came to spycraft. They hauled Dame Nyssa away and left me there feeling deeply, deeply embarrassed and wondering if anything she had told me was true. I should have checked her credentials first thing; instead, I got distracted by what she told me.

"I'm still swimming with fucking bladefins. I hate this!"

Chef du Rödal had come to see what the fuss was and overheard that last bit. "You're not required to be here, Dervan. You can leave anytime if you hate it."

"No, no—sorry. I wasn't talking about my work here. I actually love this, because I feel that I'm being helpful somehow. I don't suppose you have any garlic I could smash? Smashing sounds fantastic at the moment."

"No, the potatoes and carrots are all I need. What was all that business with the mariners?"

"An object lesson in my own gullibility. Nothing for you to worry about. I'll get back to this. Sorry, Chef."

She held my gaze for another moment, but then shrugged. "Whatever. I have work to do."

Once she turned away and left me alone, I picked up the paring knife and stabbed an innocent tuber until the worst of my anger had been exorcised. It was inedible after that, and I tossed it into the refuse pile, where my own self-respect was.

Up on the wall later, Fintan was joined by a group of

drummers. The drums were of different sizes, and he let them do a thrumming, pounding song on their own before he told us that one of the day's tales reminded him of a Hathrim song, so he'd brought the drummers in to help him perform it.

"In Hathrir, it's fairly common slang to say that something good is smoke. Did you just win a contest? That's smoke. Create a beautiful glass sculpture? That's smoke too. And from what I understand, this song was written as a bit of a fashion statement, part of a backlash to the privileged wearing ice-howler furs as status symbols about twenty years ago. It was very popular, sung everywhere in the country, and remains popular today. Typically it's sung while wearing a cloak and stomping about, so that's what I'm going to do."

He donned a cloak and began to step around, raising his knees high; he also shrugged his shoulders or raised his elbows to make the cloak billow and waft. He did not sing so much as speak, and that was more of an angry growl, spat out in short bursts along with the pounding of drums. But after the first time through, his dancing became more violent, and he repeated the last line several times while the drumming got louder and faster, until he was howling it in long, throat-shredding screams.

> *My cloak. Is. Smoke.*
> *Fluffy. And. Fine.*
> *I wear it all the tiiiime.*
> *You can keep your ice-howler fur—*
> *Of this point, I'm very sure:*
> *My cloak. Is. Smoke.*

Fintan needed a mug of ale to cool down after that, because he'd worked up a sweat with his exertions. The drummers cleared away, all smiles, because that had been fun for them.

Once recovered after the break, the bard said, "Today we will hear from someone new. Or, rather, new as a narrator: She has been featured in many other tales up to this point, but we have not as yet heard anything from her own lips. That changes now. Please welcome Pelemyn's own Gerstad Nara du Fesset."

Before the Bone Giant invasion, life was simpler—as it was for everyone, no doubt. The tide came in, the tide went out, every day was spent serving Brynlön, and I was . . . content. Happy. I had a commission as a gerstad and had met the pelenaut a couple of times. I had a side business where I brought nautilus shells and other castoffs from the deep to artists and home decorators who liked to place such things in niches or on top of mantelpieces. I fell in love with an extremely deadly and beautiful woman, and she became my lifebond.

But since the invasion, my contentment has been sunk and pulled away by riptides. I lost family and many friends to the Bone Giants and every day wondered if there was something I could have done to prevent it. Had I not been vigilant enough? Had there been some sign I missed?

Long underwater meditations near the pelenaut's coral reefs taught me how to cope. Coral grows on the blood and carnage of the past, thrives in the present, and promises an abundant future. Likewise, we live in the present because of our past, and abundance lies ahead if we live in our present now. These truths keep me functioning when I would rather stay on the reefs with an old longarm who's become used to me and sits nearby whenever I come to visit. I lie in repose and offer my hand, and she wraps a tentacle around my finger, and together we watch the fish paddle by and the anemones quiver in the current and acknowledge that we are sad and grieving for different reasons, but together we can let the ocean wash it away—or at least wear down its sharper edges.

I still go to visit her, though duties have kept me away for longer stretches, and she always welcomes the time. If we could speak, I think we would be friends.

After one such meditation in late Frost, I was summoned to the Wellspring by a mariner. When I arrived, the lung and the pelenaut were there, dressed in warm colors, in a visual attempt to beat back the cold, perhaps, or to help us remember the sun. They cleared the Wellspring of all personnel except for the mariner posted at the Lung's Locks, and we circled around to the other side of the pelenaut's waterfalls so that we could not be heard over its noise. There were four carved silverbark chairs there—a gift from Forn, no doubt—arranged just so to have quiet conversations like this.

"Gerstad du Fesset," the lung began after reintroductions were made, "we are interested in offering you a special assignment but want to be frank that it could be dangerous in ways we can't begin to predict. Your duty has been light thus far and perhaps you'd prefer it to stay that way. We know someone else who would, and we like to keep her happy."

It took me a second to process what they were saying. "Do you mean the mynstad?"

"We do," the lung confirmed. "But I wish to stress that she has never specifically said we shouldn't offer you something more dangerous. She has merely remarked, from time to time, that she is glad you're not often in danger or that you're safe on duty. And that she didn't like that time you went to get the Seven-Year Ship with Tallynd du Böll. Innocuous. Loving. But clear."

"Have you refrained from giving me dangerous assignments in the past because of it?"

"No," the pelenaut said. "But normally we assign such things to a tidal mariner if we can. The problem is, we cannot spare Tallynd for this. And we require extreme discretion, which normally rules out all but a few. You have managed to recommend yourself on that score without knowing it."

"I have?"

"Yes. In addition to your discretion regarding that episode with the ship, you've never revealed the mynstad's first name, as far as we know."

"That presupposes that she has a first name other than *Mynstad*," I said, and the pelenaut laughed.

"You see? Perfect discretion. That's what we need."

My lifebond, Mynstad du Möcher, does have a first name, but it's not for the public to know. She knows she is beautiful, because people won't stop telling her, and since she cannot keep that beauty specially for me, she keeps her first name a secret. Speaking it is a gift given only to me, one that I enjoy when we are alone, when she is the warm soft spring and not the icy hard mynstad. When she came to the armory seeking the position of the pelenaut's mynstad, the mariners on duty demanded her full name. She said she'd freely give it as soon as someone beat her in combat, and no one ever has. She pays her taxes as *Mynstad du Möcher*, and it's a point of pride.

"I'm ready to accept any mission you require, Pelenaut Röllend."

"Good. You will tell no one, not even your lifebond, where you are going."

"Understood and agreed."

"As you have prior knowledge of the Seven-Year Ship and its whereabouts, you are to travel to Fornyd as quickly as possible without triggering a penalty with your kenning and deliver a message regarding it. You may give it only to Quartermaster Farlen du Cannym and a Kaurian scholar named Gondel Vedd. A Kaurian ship arrived here yesterday with a question from them, and you're taking the answer. You're going to present this seal to anyone who asks—even the lung—and insist that none but they are to hear your words."

He handed over a square of paper sealed with a circle of blue wax imprinted with the pelenaut's sign, a detailed long-arm head. "Aye."

"The message is: 'Permission granted to visit the Seven-Year Ship in secret, with military escort to guard the prisoner. Keep us informed, and relay any new information you have through this rapid.'"

And then they laid a whole lot of information down on me, much of which they had just learned from another rapid who'd been stationed in Fornyd: the existence of that Bone Giant prisoner, the army in the north, the spy network, this whole other seafaring civilization from across the ocean, the kid named Abhinava Khose with the Sixth Kenning, that Lorson guy who had the Seventh Kenning, and the second invasion planned for the spring—none of which are secrets now but were mind-blowing at the time. They said I needed to know all that in case a situation developed that required me to make decisions on my own without waiting to hear from them.

"A situation like what?"

"We have no idea," the lung replied. "The only thing we know for certain is that it's impossible to know what to expect when it comes to the Bone Giants. They have been swimming ahead of us in the current all along, and we're trying to catch up. But we might be gaining a length or two. That scholar has plenty more to translate and may have more to share when you get there." He paused to pick up an empty waterproof satchel near his feet and gave it to me. "Take that in case he has something for us to read."

"We'd like you to leave now," the pelenaut said. "We'll tell the mynstad you're on special assignment and not to expect you home for a few days."

"She's going to be angry that I didn't take time to say goodbye."

"We'll tell her you wanted to. We can't have her guessing where you're going. It has to be this way. There's a place to rest and eat in Festwyf. Föstyr will give you the details. Stay the night there and continue your journey in the morning. Thank you, Gerstad du Fesset."

And so I was ushered around the Wellspring's waterfalls to the departure pool, where I would sleeve myself all the way to Fornyd.

"There are no lives at stake that we know of," Föstyr said as I lowered myself into the pool leading to the Lung's Locks. "Your best reasonable speed will suffice."

I wasn't so sure. The enormity of what they'd shared pressed on me like the darkness of the abyss. Mustn't we do everything possible to prevent another invasion? It felt as if the only reasonable response was to move faster, and then somehow it might be avoided.

It was the perfect time to remember serenity, but panic kept intruding. That swim was more exhausting than it should have been. I'd thought that I wouldn't need a rest, but by the time I got to Festwyf, I admitted that I sorely needed one. It was enormously difficult to ignore the idea that resting might result in an advantage to the enemy, but I was beat; emotional turmoil can be draining. There are few burdens so heavy as grief and secrets, and I had a surplus of both. Only by telling myself that I'd be little good to anyone if I wasn't functional could I manage to get some sleep. But I was sleeving upriver at dawn and arrived at Festwyf around noon.

The pelenaut's seal got me quickly past a series of mariners to the quartermaster's lung, Lans du Höwyll, and he took me to meet Farlen du Cannym right away. When I said my message was for her ears and Gondel Vedd's only, she had me follow her through some hallways until we entered double doors into a wonderful library. An older Kaurian man sat surrounded by papers and ink, a forgotten cup of tea, and a board of cheese and mustard that had been absently picked over and partially smeared upon his person. He was so absorbed in his work that he didn't notice our entrance.

"Scholar Vedd," the quartermaster said, to which she received a mere grunt. She repeated herself, this time with a firmer tone, and that got him to look up.

"Hmm? What? Oh. Quartermaster."

"This is a rapid in the pelenaut's service, Gerstad Nara du Fesset. She has a message that only you and I may hear."

"Ah, excellent. Welcome, Gerstad. May you breathe peace."

He beamed at me, and maybe I did breathe in a little peace. He was such a friendly sort and working so hard to help us, and I felt reassured somehow. If the finest mind of Kauria was on our side, why, it couldn't all end badly, could it? I knew that he had been showered with gift baskets already for his aid to our country, but I wanted to give him another one for being so effortlessly soothing. I delivered my message, and the two of them consulted briefly. While Gondel was very curious about the ship, he thought it best to delay visiting for a few more days, since he had so much to translate, and he could work faster in the library than in a ship's cabin.

"Your timing is fortuitous, for I have just found something here mentioning the ship and its relationship to the Seventh Kenning," he said.

"In Lorson's papers?" the quartermaster inquired.

"Lorson," I said, recognizing the name from my briefing. "That was the man with the Seventh Kenning?"

"Yes, yes," Gondel said. "These are his documents, brought to us by Fintan, the Raelech bard, with the help of that handsome beast-caller lad. Now, the source of the Seventh Kenning is in the Mistmaiden Isles, where you found the ship, correct?" he asked me.

"I'm not sure. We never set foot on the actual island, because it was infested with wraiths."

"Exactly! That's the place. Did you ever get a chance to look around on the ship?"

"Yes, once we got it to Dead Man's Point."

"And did you find anything in it? Anything at all?"

"It was largely empty. Some nice books and maps in the cabin that you would love, I'm sure, and some nautical instruments. Down below, there were a lot of empty bunks and an unusual cloak."

"Ah!" He waggled a finger at me. "That, yes, that. Describe it."

"The cloak? It was black but embroidered in gold thread with designs I hadn't seen before. The wool felt a little different from the wool I'm used to."

"And where is it now?"

Another shrug. "I don't know. Still on the ship, I imagine, unless someone took it."

"According to what I've been reading here," he explained, "that cloak is supposed to be enchanted. It protects the wearer from the wraiths! In other words, it is the key to seeking the Seventh Kenning! Only with that cloak can the Eculans reach the kenning site and have a chance at gaining the power they desire. This is why they are obsessed with finding the ship."

"Bryn preserve us," the quartermaster said.

"Speaking of the ship," the scholar continued, "you need to move it back."

"What? Why?"

"We—or, I should say, Mistral Kira—sent a tempest to Ecula with the message that the Seven-Year Ship could be found in the Mistmaiden Isles. Which was true at the time— all I was told was that you'd found it, not that you'd moved it. We thought if the Eculans got what they wanted, that might end the war, and as followers of Reinei we could do no less."

"You should have told us earlier," I said. "When was this?"

"I left Kauria at the end of Amber. We are now at the end of Frost, so two months ago. And we've heard nothing. The tempest Ponder Tann is either lost or dead. Or I suppose it's possible he returned to Kauria and we simply haven't heard the news here yet. It may be that he never delivered his message and so the point is moot, but in case he did, the ship should be returned to the place you found it."

All those secrets that I thought had been a burden were actually helpful now. "But if we go back to the isles with the cloak—if it's still on the ship—and take your Eculan prisoner, who wants more than anything to be a seeker, he'll actually be able to seek the Seventh Kenning."

"I suppose so."

"And there's a chance that he might then become something like Lorson if he does. Do we really want that?"

"I don't," Farlen du Cannym said, "but the pelenaut might feel differently. This is obviously information he needs to have."

"Agreed. But it might be best to learn whether that cloak is still there. We had no idea it was so important. Let's have you continue your work for now, Scholar Vedd, while I run to the ship and see about the cloak, then to Pelemyn to confer with the pelenaut. I should be back in a few days. Is there anything at all I can get you from the big city, Scholar? A favorite cheese or mustard you've been missing?"

The old man laughed. "Thank you. I lack for nothing. The quartermaster is well supplied, and you Brynts are nothing if not gracious hosts."

"Do you have any new documents that the pelenaut should see?"

"Ah, yes. Take these." He rummaged around his desk until he found a sheaf tied with string. I placed it in my waterproof satchel and bid them farewell.

I sleeved myself downriver, pausing briefly at the boardinghouse in Festwyf to wolf down a meal before carrying on to Dead Man's Point, which I hoped to reach before nightfall. Judging there was an hour's worth of daylight left when the lighthouse hove into view, I smiled in relief. Perhaps there would be a cot I could sleep on and something warm to drink.

But the smile melted as I drew closer and realized that, in addition to the small fishing craft, there was a very strange vessel docked next to the Seven-Year Ship, which was itself rather strange. The new one had a rounded prow and unfamiliar design. There were people milling about on its deck and also on the dock. And these people, when I got close enough, proved to be women in uniform, with swords at their belts. Some Nentian men were with them, and indeed the name of the ship was the *Nentian Herald*.

"Kraken cocks," I muttered. They must be the civilization from across the ocean that the pelenaut had told me about.

Fintan used a green sphere to return to himself and told us we'd need to rewind the clock just a little bit.

"I'm switching to Koesha Gansu now and bringing you up to the moment where she and Nara first meet. It was perhaps a little more tense than either side would like, owing to a circumstance that will become clear soon."

The ice seemed to go on and on, the bottlebrush trees of the Gravewood on our right witnessing our passage, until a week after we'd left Abhi and the Raelech bard behind, the trees disappeared in the night, and we turned south, and then west, backtracking, to find them again. In the early-morning hours we saw them, a line of trees marching south, sentinels of a new coast and a different ocean, and we knew that we had finally accomplished what no other crew had done before: We had traversed the Northern Yawn. It had taken two ships, of course, one of them enchanted, and it required the aid of the Sixth Kenning, an entire village of remarkable people, and a mountain of good fortune, but it illustrated perfectly how we are all leaves on the wind of Shoawei.

We would be historical figures in Joabei for this, our names echoing through generations. We gave thanks to Shoawei for this honor, and we honored our fallen sisters too, and we blessed Abhi, wherever he was, for making it possible.

I missed him; we all did. I hoped he and his companions were doing well.

After midday, we broke through the last of the ice, and our pace increased. According to maps that we had discovered at Lorson's, we would soon reach a thin strip of land aptly called Tentacle Peninsula. If we sailed directly south from its point, we'd run into the Mistmaiden Isles, which we did not want to do. Previous Joabeian settlers had attempted to live there and had disappeared. We did not want to suffer that fate but rather to meet the people of Brynlön, who were supposed to possess the Fourth Kenning.

How strange it was that our people had found the Mistmaiden Isles time and again but never sailed past to find the continent beyond. Or perhaps they had, but their window of opportunity had closed, and the krakens returned to end such exploration.

Fintan told us that if we hugged the coast and followed the peninsula back around, eventually we would come to another, smaller peninsula that marked the southern edge of the Gravewood; at the tip of that was a lighthouse and small fishing village called Dead Man's Point, where we should be able to refresh our supplies. South of there we would find the settled lands of Brynlön and the mouth of the East Gravewater River, which he cautioned us not to drink from.

We followed that plan, and when we spied the lighthouse and the smattering of houses, the docks with seabirds whirling above, crying for fish, we cheered and sang and danced the way sailors do, just moving the upper body around, for here was our first encounter with a long-established settlement and our first contact with the Brynts.

Naturally they saw us coming, did not recognize our sail or our boat, and a fair-sized party of them awaited us, including some infantry and archers, but only twenty altogether. I made sure to line the rails with our Nentian men along with some of my sailors and ordered them to wave and smile so they'd know we were friendly. I kept an eye on the archers: If any arrows were launched our way, I could blow them off course.

The Brynts were a darker-skinned people than the Nentians, their hair often worn short and curly but sometimes grown long and gathered into braids. Their uniforms were dark blue edged in light blue, with gold pips denoting rank, if I didn't miss my guess. One man with a few more of these pips gave an order to the others to rest at attention, which meant they lowered their weapons and allowed us to dock. There followed a frustrating time where we tried to figure out how to speak to them.

No one on board spoke the Brynt language, and apparently no one on the dock spoke Nentian. Eventually we discovered that the man with the pips spoke Raelech, and one of our men knew that language too, so we used him to translate.

We first declared that we were peaceful and interested in trade and hailed from a land across the sea. I introduced myself as captain of the *Nentian Herald* and told him that we had traversed the Northern Yawn in our icebreaker boat.

The Brynt man welcomed us, pronounced his village to

be peaceful, and introduced himself as Mynstad Ülf du Nylsen. The translator explained that the rank of mynstad was
something like a master soldier in Ghurana Nent, and he
wasn't quite sure how that translated to our military, but it
was a rank beneath that of captain.

I asked permission for us to come ashore in groups, bathe
if possible, and trade for food and water. It was granted so
long as we entered the village unarmed, and I negotiated that
I might retain my weapons as captain.

The mynstad and two escorts came aboard first to inspect
our ship, and we gave him a tour, explaining that this ship was
built in Malath Ashmali with the help of Hathrim and its hull
enchanted to keep us safe from krakens. We had some of
Abhi's enchanted stakes to trade, plus firebowls enchanted by
Olet, but little else. Fortunately, the stakes were tremendously valuable, as the village was still technically in the
Gravewood and occasionally subject to attacks.

Haesha took a squad into the village for baths, and we rotated through our crew in shifts while we negotiated and
brought on barrels of fresh water, fruit, and dried meats.
When it was my turn—I went with the last batch—a smiling
grandmother welcomed me into her home, which smelled of
honey and pine. I was given a fresh cake of lemon-scented
soap, my uniform was taken to be washed, and a fresh woven
tunic and pair of pants were folded on top of a small wooden
dresser. I'd been informed in advance that the village was
used to serving ships like this and that we could either spend
the night ashore or on our boat, and our uniforms would be
returned to us the next day.

I sank into the tub gratefully, alone and with no responsibilities for a half hour but to take care of myself. I spent half
of it weeping and the other half smiling and sighing in contentment.

When I emerged, I bowed deeply to my hostess in thanks
and stepped outside to rejoin my crew, buffeted by breaths of

goodwill. Mynstad du Nylsen was still on the docks, and I asked through our translator about the other large ship moored there. He said it was a foreign ship that the pelenaut wanted stored for some reason; he wasn't too clear on why. A couple of superior officers dropped it off and told him to keep it there until further notice. Having an interest in ship design, I asked if I might have a tour of it. He shrugged and said he didn't see why not.

The interior of the cabin was absolutely exquisite. Hand-carved wooden finishes from a master craftsman, leather upholstery, a chart table with thick glass over a map, cubbies filled with more maps, and narrow shelves of books kept in place with clever brackets.

"Have you examined these maps, Mynstad?" I asked.

"No," he replied. "But I'm not much of a sailor."

"Might I be able to make copies?"

"I don't think I can authorize that," he replied. "Sorry."

I nodded and gave him a tight grin. I'd expected that answer, and it was fine.

Down below, there was a smallish cargo area—I imagined largely for food and water—and an extensive bunking operation for a much larger number of people than would be required to crew the ship. It was almost like a passenger vessel, just without much in the way of amenities. There was very little to see except for a black cloak hanging on a hook, somewhat tattered but fetchingly embroidered in gold thread with patterns I'd never seen before.

"May I take a closer look at this?" I asked.

The mynstad shrugged and gestured that I could go ahead. I fingered the fabric—a fine wool that I could swear was the sort Joabei imported on very rare occasions from Ecula, through Omesh. If it was the wool I believed it was, then it was fantastically expensive stuff, which meant only the incredibly wealthy could afford it.

"Is this an Eculan ship?"

Mynstad du Nylsen was bemused. He had never heard of Eculans.

"Whose cloak is this?"

"I have no idea. It was here when my superiors left the ship at dock."

"May I try it on?"

He nodded, and I removed the cloak from the hook. It disturbed a layer of dust and I sneezed, somewhat to my embarrassment. The mynstad smiled.

When it settled about my shoulders, I discovered that it fit perfectly and had a comforting weight. Everything about it, in fact, was perfect: a found treasure on a strange ship in a new land. And I simply felt protected, somehow, like I wore armor rather than a layer of wool.

"I rather like this. Since it's obviously been abandoned, may I keep it?"

"Ah . . . I don't think it's mine to give away."

"Purchase, then. Trade."

That got his attention. I saw an eyebrow twitch. "Trade what? We have already arranged for all the firebowls and enchanted stakes we need. And you don't have Brynt money."

That was a valid point. What few goods we had to trade from Joabei went down with our original ship.

Feeling a mite foolish, I tapped the hilt of my Buran, a fine weapon but with no sentimental value to me, easily replaced with an identical one when I got home. I would still have my Bora, which was more important in battle. The Buran would be one of a kind to him, however, as the cloak was one of a kind to me. The truth was I would never be able to find a cloak like this in Joabei at any price.

"The short sword?" he said, pointing. "The sword for the cloak?"

I nodded and he readily agreed, and his wide grin indicated that he clearly thought he had made the trade of the century and I was a world-class gull. I offered my hand to shake to seal the deal, and he understood the gesture and pumped my hand up and down four times. Then I removed my Buran and its scabbard and handed it over.

Mynstad du Nylsen was properly awed when he withdrew it from its sheath. "Magnificent," he said, or something similar. The Nentian translator gave me several related words. "You probably have a different martial art than we do. If you have time, I would love to see a demonstration."

"That might be possible later," I said. I wouldn't mind seeing how Brynts fought either. "But for now, I should probably return to my ship and make sure the needs of my crew are met. Thank you for the tour."

Both of us tremendously happy with the trade, we exited the ship and parted. Haesha remarked on the cloak instantly upon my return to the *Nentian Herald* and confirmed my suspicion that it was Eculan wool.

"Captain, this must be worth *thousands*. Where did you get it?"

"On that ship."

"Are there more?"

"No, just the one. I traded the mynstad for it. Gave him my Buran."

Haesha snorted. "Seriously? A short sword in exchange for a priceless cloak? He must be a fool."

"He thinks I'm the fool and that he got the better of me. Let's allow him to continue to believe that."

The crew was in general high spirits after having bathed and facing the prospect of a dinner made with fresh food instead of something pulled out of a barrel in the hold. We were going to stay on our own ship out of an excess of caution, but it was going to be something of a party boat. We'd bought a keg of Mistmaiden Ale brewed in Pelemyn, and I was considering having a pint as the sun neared the horizon, but a new arrival killed the mood.

She was a military rank above the mynstad, for she had

more pips on her uniform, and she came directly out of the sea onto the dock next to the strange ship, whereupon all the water from her soaked uniform leapt out of the fabric and fell back into the ocean. She was one of Bryn's blessed, and it was our first encounter with such a one.

The guards stationed at the gangplank to the strange ship let her aboard, and one of them hurried off to inform the mynstad of her arrival. Soon enough, Ülf du Nylsen was hurrying out to the docks in the company of the guard, and he got to the ship just as she was disembarking. She shouted something at him in Brynt and he froze. His eyes drifted in our direction, and he pointed with his chin. The woman's face turned to us for the first time and rested on me for a few seconds, then she unleashed an absolute torrent of anger at the mynstad. He dropped his head and returned to the village. I got the feeling that he may have just been relieved of duty.

She consulted the guards on the ship for a moment, gave very clear orders that earned a salute from them, and then stalked toward our ship. I ordered the revelry to end and called for our translator. If this woman spoke Nentian or Raelech, we'd be fine. If not, she'd need to call the mynstad back, and I could only imagine how much she did not want to do that right now.

It turned out she spoke Raelech, and her name was Gerstad Nara du Fesset. Her hair was long and tightly woven into many braids, gathered with a single brass ringlet at the back of her neck. My translator indicated that her military rank was equal to mine.

"She says welcome to Brynlön," the translator conveyed. "Due to a terrible error in judgment, the mynstad allowed your cloak to leave the Seven-Year Ship. She requests that it be returned."

"It didn't leave the ship on its own. I traded for it, and it's now mine."

"She says that it wasn't the mynstad's to trade."

"Then seek compensation from the mynstad, not me. I made a trade fairly and legally."

The gerstad pointed at the strange ship and then at the docks as she spoke. The translator said, "That ship and all its contents are the property of Brynlön, not the mynstad."

"That's a Brynt ship? The one that looks nothing like all the other Brynt ships here?"

"It is by right of salvage."

"Why are you so worried about a salvaged cloak?"

"It's a unique item, in many ways more valuable than the entire ship. She demands its return."

"That is not believable. If it were so valuable, it wouldn't have been left hanging and unguarded and traded so easily."

The gerstad seethed visibly and clenched her fists at this, looking on the verge of violence. As I'd already witnessed her ability with her kenning—absolute control in manipulating water—I knew she could kill me instantly. Push or pull the water in my blood out of its arteries, and I'd be done.

"Tell her I want to remain peaceful," I said. "I have made friends with Raelechs and Nentians and Hathrim. I want our countries to have a friendly relationship."

That calmed her down somewhat, reminding her that I represented an entire nation.

"It would be friendly of you to return our property," she said.

"Except it is my property now, and a friend would not try to take it from me. Is there some absolute emergency preventing you from explaining why this cloak is so valuable?"

The gerstad deflated. "No. But there is some secrecy, and the need to reacquire that cloak is dire."

"We can discuss it in peace as friends."

The gerstad suddenly seemed to become aware that I had a crew and they were all staring at her. "Did I interrupt a celebration?" she asked.

"We were celebrating the fact that we have met Brynts for the first time and also had a bath for the first time in weeks."

"Do you have a kenning?" came next, which seemed like an abrupt change in the direction of the wind. But perhaps it was an assessment of our defenses after first determining that we might be a little drunk.

"The Second Kenning, yes. I have been blessed by Shoawei." I didn't know if our translator would be able to handle the difference in terms, but he said that the differing words for my title both existed in the Raelech language. "In your language I am a cyclone. In my country I am called a zephyr."

"A zephyr? Interesting. That's the highest military rank in Kauria. Speaking of which—Kaurians are the people we know of who possess the Second Kenning, and they follow a religion of peace. Their god is named Reinei. And it was a Kaurian scholar, in fact, who sent me in search of that cloak, which may be the key to forging a peace with the Bone Giants."

I thought back to that army of Eculans in the north who had attacked us and would have killed us all if it weren't for Abhi. I doubted very much that I could have stopped them with this cloak.

"Kauria is far to the south, right?" I asked the translator, and he confirmed that it was. He translated my next question: "How does a scholar from the south know anything special about a single cloak in the north?"

"The scholar is in Fornyd, and he translated some documents brought from the north by a Raelech bard named . . . Finlan, Finman, something like that."

"Fintan? Fintan was in this place called Fornyd? Was there anyone else with him?"

"Yes, I believe he arrived with a Nentian named Abhinava Khose, but they had already left the city when I arrived. They were going to Rael."

"I am glad to hear they're well. They are good friends."

"Zephyr—Captain! May I invite you and your crew to be our guests in Fornyd? There you can meet the Kaurian scholar, who can explain the importance of that cloak, and we can come to an agreement as friends."

. That sounded tempting. The documents Fintan brought were from Lorson, and I was very curious about his writings. "Those documents," I said, "have something to say about that ship?" I pointed.

"Yes."

My cloak was Eculan wool taken from what was probably an Eculan ship, written about by a monster of a man who had most likely been Eculan.

"Tell me more about Fornyd. Where is it, and how big is it?"

Nara du Fesset said it was an actual city, not a village like this, with plenty of lodging and amenities and accustomed to larger vessels like ours that sailed upriver from the ocean. It was on the south bank of the Gravewater, so all the dangerous animals were across the river, and it was otherwise surrounded by settled farmland.

"And we will be guests, not prisoners?"

She blinked, perhaps shocked that I required clarification, and said, "Of course. There is no question of that. You've committed no crimes."

I was wary of a trap but did not think she could have fabricated the names of Fintan and Abhinava unless they had actually been there.

"My primary concern is for my crew. I want us all to make it home."

"I want that too."

"Did this scholar find anything to explain why there's an army of Bone Giants camped on the coast of the Northern Yawn?"

"He was looking for that when I left. Fintan brought many documents."

That earned a laugh. "I know. They were in my hold for a while."

Abhi had no doubt demonstrated the effectiveness of his enchanted stakes when he went through town, so in a sense, he'd prepared a market for us to trade the ones we still had. It would be nice to establish actual transactions and return home with something in our hold besides the promise that trade was possible. And scouting a Brynt city would let us know what they had and what they needed. "How far is it to this Fornyd?" I asked.

"From here? Takes most ships four to five days. Depends on how much you want to fill those sails."

"And who rules there? Will they abide by the word of a gerstad and welcome us as guests?"

"Quartermaster Farlen du Cannym is the administrator there, and she answers to the pelenaut in our capital, Pelemyn. I guarantee she will welcome you. I'll give you a letter."

"You won't be coming?"

"I will guide you to the river mouth and then make a detour to Pelemyn. I'm going to fetch a translator who speaks Nentian and give your man a break."

No doubt she would summon some other reinforcements too. But that was all right: The amount of effort and expense she was willing to go through to get this cloak back had piqued my curiosity, and I would find out what made it so valuable. If Joabei could either profit or be protected, I needed to follow through.

"May we resume our celebration, then, and depart in the morning?"

"By all means."

The gerstad placed a hand over her heart and bowed as a farewell, then turned on her heel to stalk into the village, presumably to give Mynstad du Nylsen a further scolding. I told everyone on the boat to resume emptying that keg we'd bought, but I called Haesha over to fill her in and note that we really needed to set a decent watch tonight. And I'd be sleeping on top of my cloak in a locked cabin.

There was much speculation after those tales about what sort of kenning site would be guarded by wraiths and whether the wraiths were in fact the products of unsuccessful seekings.

A couple of scholars I recognized from my days at the university were up on the wall that night—being near the bard as he performed had become a privilege won through lottery—and they were absolutely certain the connection existed. I'd seen them together at holiday gatherings for faculty staff. They were the sort who exuded a sort of crusty salt-and-pepper pomposity with every breath.

"I know that correlation is not causation," the maths professor said to his sciences colleague, anticipating his objection, "but where else are wraiths found in such concentration? Nowhere else except the source of this Seventh Kenning."

"I'd agree that the link is impossible to dismiss," the sciences fellow replied on his way to the stairs leading down into the city, "but the squid ink in my eye here is what kind of kenning site could create wraiths instead of simple dead bodies."

"Oh, absolutely. And what other blessings does the Seventh Kenning offer besides that of lifeleech? Would any blessing be worth the risk of such an unnatural husk of existence?"

I didn't get to hear the answer, as they took the steps much quicker than I could manage with my poor knee. As I made my slow, painful journey down, Fintan caught up behind me.

I congratulated him on a fine day of tales and asked if he knew already what was on the island, the way he already knew what had happened in Ghurana Nent.

"I don't, actually," he said. "If I don't get an update from Fornyd soon, we'll all be left to wonder. But I think it would be safe for me to say . . . things are *happening* up there."

Day 47

THE REVELATION
OF SERVICE

After a quick breakfast at the refugee kitchen, I asked the chef if I could conduct a personal errand before getting to work.

"You're volunteering, so I don't see why not," she said. "But I do appreciate the help, in spite of your occasional waste of a good potato."

"You *saw* that?"

"Mm-hmm."

"I thought you'd left. Bryn drown me now, I'm so mortified."

"Don't worry about it, Dervan. It's therapeutic. The day after my ex broke up with me, I took a meat-tenderizing mallet to a swamp duck and hammered it into paste. Felt a whole lot better afterward—all that negative energy worked itself out—so I get it. Go do your thing and get back here."

Promising to return as soon as I could, I made my way to the Nentian embassy and asked to see Dame Nyssa du Valas, a member of the cleaning staff. The steward of the building regretted to inform me that she was on leave at the moment.

"Not to worry," I said, and thanked him. I'd learned everything I needed: She *had* worked at the embassy, and so her story about Sarena's poisoning was at least plausible. Whether it was probable was less certain, and whether it was true might be shaky now, considering that she'd been hauled away for questioning and she had clearly been fishing for information yesterday. On one side of the scale, there was my desire for it all to be true because Melishev Lohmet was an easy man to hate and to blame for almost anything despicable in the world, but on the other side was the very real possibility that I had been a target in someone else's spy game and everything she'd told me was manipulative, like the Wraith's assertion that Clodagh had arranged Sarena's death.

I peeled potatoes thoughtfully that day, but it was little more than treading water in shallow seas. I kept getting stung by unseen jellyfish, and there was little I could do about it except keep swimming.

The Fornish army arrived while I was working, bringing even more food with them as they added to the tents on Survivor Field. Their wagons provided a greater variety and quantity of food, though it was announced that this too would be rationed to guard against lean times ahead. It wouldn't allow restaurants to reopen, but there would certainly be enough basics to fill larders and pantries until more cargo could be brought in by sea.

My mood was improved by the thought that I might reasonably expect to score a loaf of bread at the bakery on my way home. I may be no closer to answers than before, but tomorrow, by Bryn, there would be toast.

After our recording session, Fintan sang a Fornish song to welcome our allies to Pelemyn.

"When the Raelech army arrived a couple of days ago, we did a call-and-response song about Aelinmech rye to welcome them. The Fornish have their own song in that milieu, so join in as soon as you have the response down."

Run the Leaf Road from sea to sea,
Bright sun shine down on you and me!
Dollop of honey in my tea,
Bright sun shine down on you and me!
Blossoms for every wasp and bee,
Bright sun shine down on you and me!
I sleep at night in a silverbark tree,

Love to my clan and Canopy,
Bright sun shine down on you and me!

"We haven't heard from your favorite tidal mariner in a while," Fintan said after the break. "Time to fix that, eh?"

The gases that enveloped him dissipated to reveal the second könstad.

Tallynd

The pelenaut has been kind and attempted to give me duties that would keep me in the city near my boys, since my priority is to spend as much time with them as I can. The extent to which I've spent my youth on my kenning is obvious to all; I'm visibly gray and wrinkling, and I don't move like I used to. Part of that is due to taking a spear through the top of my foot, but part of it is the low-level pain of aging joints, which never bothered my youthful body. My respect for those who have aged the traditional way has never been higher: They seem to me now as boulders in the river of time, slowly worn down but determined to remain despite what the river does to them.

People are gentle and kind to me, and the boys have been so sweet, understanding that I cannot move the way I used to. But I caught my oldest, Nyls, crying once as he watched me struggle to reach something high up in a cupboard. I can't lift onto my tiptoes anymore, and his voice broke as he said, "It isn't fair!"

"What isn't fair, baby?"

"That you're old already! And all my friends' mothers are still young."

"Oh, no, come here, sweetie. Come on." I wrapped him in a hug and said, "I'm still thirty-two. It's just that my body is keeping a different tally. And I think it's fair because it's the price I paid to make sure you were safe. You and all your friends too. I'd pay that price again, and I thank Bryn every day that I was able to do it. Now, will you help me and climb up on a stool to get those spices I wanted?"

"No, see, this is what I mean!"

I drew back. "You won't help me?"

"No, I'll help. I mean I shouldn't *have* to. You shouldn't need my help."

"Well, I think it's time we gave you a different spyglass than the one you're using to see the world. Get out of your own head now, Nyls, and think about all those people who shouldn't have died the night the Bone Giants attacked. Think about how the Bone Giants never should've been sent here by whoever sent them. And their mothers, who probably don't think it's fair that they ran into a tidal mariner here and died when most of the others had an easy time invading us. Think about the fish out of shelter on the reefs when the bladefin swims by. None of it is fair, Nyls. It's all what the currents wash our way, and everybody's swimming in them. You can pout and complain about the currents, but it never helps. You know what helps?"

"What?"

"Help! Help everyone you can, even if that's just smiling at them and wishing them well. Because they have had something unfair happen to them too—or they will soon enough, because that's the way currents work. And people who help give the rest of us hope. Your other option is to be angry and bitter about the unfairness, and you'll be pulling people down like a kraken tentacle with your sourness. So try looking through that spyglass for a while and see if you aren't happier."

"Okay, Mama."

I kissed his forehead. "I love you. Will you get me those spices now?"

He palmed away the tears from his cheeks and sniffled. "Yes. I want to help."

One thing I've learned is how to treasure every moment, since I'm going to have fewer of them. I hope I'll be able to see my boys grown and settled before I pass, but the war isn't over and I might not be granted such a blessing, since my blessing as a tidal mariner demands so much.

Gerstad Nara du Fesset, recently sent to Fornyd on a mission to spare me a trip away from home, returned with intelligence that required my absence anyway. It was an alarming series of events regarding the Seven-Year Ship and the moldering cloak in the hold we thought was unimportant, a planned second invasion, plus an entire new civilization that had crossed the seas, which we would rather keep as friends than harbor as enemies. Their native language was impenetrable, but they had picked up Nentian on their way to us, so if we brought a translator we trusted, we could be assured of communicating our goodwill and perhaps avoid any unpleasantries.

We did our best to prepare the translator for a long swim—during which she would need to do nothing but breathe inside the bubble we created for her—but she didn't appear to enjoy the journey very much. We stayed overnight at Festwyf and in the morning caught up to an unusual ship called the *Nentian Herald,* making good progress against the current thanks to the efforts of the captain, who was a cyclone. We hailed them, asked if they wouldn't mind taking our translator aboard, and received permission. As soon as she was climbing the rope ladder lowered for her benefit, I wicked all the water out of her clothes so that she'd be dry and would warm up quickly. Then Nara and I added our kenning to the captain's, the Second and Fourth working together, and we made truly excellent time sailing upriver to Fornyd after that.

Once there, Nara swam up to the docks to personally welcome the Joabeians and Nentians to Fornyd and usher the captain and any entourage she wished to the Wellspring, while I used the Lung's Locks to go ahead to the quartermaster and prepare her for a rather sensitive meeting.

As with my previous visits, Quartermaster Farlen du Cannym didn't keep me waiting, which I deeply appreciated. I technically outranked her now, but she had been just as quick to see me when I was a gerstad. She tried to mask her surprise at the signs of age in my visage, but I caught it. She smiled immediately afterward.

"Bryn bless you, Second Könstad. It is so good to see you again."

"And you as well, Quartermaster."

"Do you mind if my lung remains?" she said, gesturing to a man on her right. "This is Lans du Höwyll." He bowed and I nodded back to him.

"Of course, my pleasure. I've been sent by the pelenaut because we have an unexpected diplomatic situation that needs a deft touch here. There is a crew of people from across the ocean at your docks right now. Their country is called Joabei, and they are Joabeians. They speak Nentian, and their captain, Koesha Gansu, has something we dearly want. We've brought a translator from the capital to assist. If we can arrange our best possible hospitality for the crew and welcome Captain Gansu here for talks with Gondel Vedd, that would serve the country's interests right now."

"Of course." She turned to her lung. "Lans, I need you to find rooms and meals for them all and get me a suitable gift basket to give the captain."

"Yes, Quartermaster. Do we know how many?"

"I estimate forty to fifty altogether," I said, and he departed. "Please tell me Scholar Vedd is still here and available."

"He is."

"We will need him. It's my understanding that the documents he's translating were transported at least part of the way on this captain's ship. She'll be interested to hear what he's discovered, and if she understands the threat that the Bone Giants represent to us, she's more likely to give us the cloak we need."

"Wait—the cloak from the Seven-Year Ship? Scholar Vedd told me about it."

"Yes. Captain Gansu has it because some fish head of a mynstad at Dead Man's Point traded it to her for a short sword."

The quartermaster scowled. "I hope he's been decommissioned."

"He has."

There was some scurrying and calling for longshoremen after that, instructions to be given to the Wellspring guards to allow the captain to pass with whomever she wished to bring, and their weapons would be fine. I did not think them hostile, and they surely must know that both Nara and I could kill anyone instantly if we wished.

I was grinning at the hustle to get all in order. So much hurrying about before we all sat calmly, to project the appearance that we knew what we were doing and absolutely, unequivocally, had our shit together. We weren't some village in the Gravewood, easily gulled into a disastrous trade.

A harried Gondel Vedd entered perhaps a minute before our guests. I'd been warned that he might appear unfit for polite company but was astounded by the understatement. His hair was an unkempt mess around his temples, and his tunic, which looked to be somewhat new, was stained with mustard and other smears of food. Eating must be a game of percentages for him: So long as a goodly percentage made it to his stomach, he didn't care where the rest of it landed.

"Hello, Scholar Vedd, remember me? I'm Tallynd," I said, summoning some water from the Wellspring's many waterfalls to clean him up.

"Of course! The tidal mariner. You were in Pelemyn."

"That's right. Forgive me, but I'm going to get you wet for just a few seconds and then you'll be dry again. Just to tidy you up before our guests arrive."

"Oh. Am I untidy again?" He looked down and sounded resigned.

I didn't answer but rather concentrated on removing the stains as best I could by penetrating the fabric of his tunic with jets of water and then pulling them out, bringing the soil with it in solution. I also wet his hair so that it laid flat, and when I removed the moisture, it looked neatly poufed rather than haphazard.

"Reinei preserve me, you're better than ten launderers! That kind of tickled."

I sent the water back into the Wellspring's falls and informed him of our goal. The chamber doors opened grandly a few seconds later, a longshoreman announcing Captain Koesha Gansu and some others, along with Gerstad Nara du Fesset and Bela du Köflund, the translator.

The captain was wearing the cloak in question, and it concealed much of her uniform, which was a dark blue; she also wore a hat with some embroidered wavy lines near the base, and the top of it was mesh, which allowed one to see through to her hair piled on top of her head. I'd never seen such a hat before. The hilt of her longsword could be seen poking through the cloak, her hands invisible.

Some painful time was spent on introductions and smiling before the quartermaster could present the welcome and an impressive gift basket that the lung had summoned from somewhere. It may have been my imagination, but I think that Scholar Vedd envied her the cheese and mustard in it—or maybe it was the small jar of swamp-duck liverwurst. The captain thanked us graciously and apologized for having nothing so fine to give us, but she did present a map of her country, Joabei, with its densely populated southern island and sparsely populated northern one.

Once seated, Farlen asked Captain Gansu how they came to us, and we heard the tale of the krakens in the Northern Yawn, and how Abhinava Khose saved them and eventually enchanted their ship's hull, and their intention to continue sailing east to become the first crew to circumnavigate the globe. There was a good deal of horror in the captain's voice as she described the encounter with Lorson, the lifeleech. She'd apparently run him through with the sword at her waist and it hardly bothered him. Luckily, Olet Kanek was able to defeat him, and they recovered many documents that she heard Fintan and Abhi had brought to us.

"Indeed they did," Farlen said. "And it's because of those documents that we learned the cloak you're wearing is much more than protection against the elements. It's key to seeking the Seventh Kenning. I will let the scholar explain." She gestured to Gondel, and he nodded once.

"We have an Eculan prisoner, and from him we learned that the Seven-Year Ship you saw at Dead Man's Point was the object of a search more than a year ago. The ship was supposed to return to Ecula and take away a load of seekers, and when it didn't arrive on schedule, that was the pretext for sending scouts to cross the ocean—our prisoner is one such. The scouts didn't find the ship but determined we must have it somewhere. We found it docked on an island we've named Blight, one of the Mistmaiden Isles. Gerstad du Fesset and Second Könstad du Böll report that this island is infested with wraiths."

I raised my hand to signal that I wanted to add something. "And the scholar has found mention in those documents of a second invasion coming soon."

"That's right," he agreed. "We believe that the key to defeating the Eculans—or at least understanding them—is on that island at the source of the Seventh Kenning. We need that cloak to reach it. It's the key to unlocking a room full of answers."

"We are therefore very anxious to have the cloak back," I said. "We understand that you traded fairly for it. We wish to trade for it again, and seeing as you understand now how valuable it is to us—our national security being at risk—you can negotiate a very profitable deal. So what may we give you in return for that cloak?"

The captain took this in, held up a hand to beg for our patience, and turned to her first mate to have a quick conversation in their own language. I believe the first mate's name was Haesha. Her hat was similar to the captain's but lacked the embroidered symbol in the center; there were two golden pips there instead, perhaps to denote her rank. Her face was marked by multiple scars, but they looked recent rather than the faded marks one would see from a childhood accident. Perhaps something had attacked her in the Gravewood.

The tone that the captain used when she spoke to the translator did not give me hope that she was listing a tidy series of demands in return for the cloak. Scholar Vedd, who could speak Nentian and did not need to wait for the translation, confirmed it with his expression.

"I deeply appreciate your position and wish to help you as an ally against the Eculans—without giving up the cloak. It already has profound sentimental value to me, as it represents my people's first contact with yours, and Eculan cloaks are rare and valuable in Joabei. I propose that I use my kenning to fly over the island of Blight to see if I can spot the source of the Seventh Kenning."

Nara began shaking her head no as soon as I did. "The island is covered in trees," she said. "If the source is sitting in a clearing, you might be able to see it, but otherwise you won't. Besides that, we don't even know what to look for. It's a kind offer but insufficient. What will convince you to trade the cloak?"

"I believe a flyover is worth a try," Captain Gansu said, refusing to budge on her stance. "And please believe me when I say Joabei is interested in defeating the Eculans. An army of them attacked our ship on our journey here—perhaps you heard of that episode—and we wish not only to see them defeated but to put an end to Eculan ideas of conquering others. Our islands, after all, are much closer to them than you are, and if they are crossing oceans now, it is only a matter of time before they focus on us."

That was disappointing, but I supposed we could not expect an easy resolution. She at least appeared willing to wash ashore on our stretch of coastline rather than Ecula's.

"And if the flyover doesn't work?" I asked. "Will you continue to refuse us the cloak and thereby prevent us from seeking a solution to the coming second invasion?"

"Should the flyover not work, I think we can profitably negotiate further at that point."

"Very well. I must consult with the pelenaut in our capital, and that will take a while. Will you remain here as honored guests until I return? I have no doubt that the quartermaster has made arrangements for your crew to enjoy some time ashore."

Farlen du Cannym flicked her gaze to her lung, who nodded, and she confirmed it.

"Yes, Captain, we have accommodations ready for your crew and hope you will enjoy our hospitality."

Captain Gansu smiled and bowed at the waist briefly. "You honor us, and we would be delighted to accept. We have not had time to rest for many weeks. In truth we would like to stay longer, learn a bit of your language, earn our keep and some supplies for our journey home across the ocean."

I pounced. "We will fully supply your trip home in return for the cloak."

She chuckled softly at that. "Perhaps that could be a starting point in our negotiations should it prove necessary. But we would like to stay for the remainder of winter and become friends, with the aim of forging a lasting relationship."

Ah, well. It was worth a try. Anything more aggressive risked too much; it would be unwise to alienate a potential ally when we desperately needed all the help we could get. And since they were in no hurry to leave, there was no need for us to pressure them further. Let them stay here and come to like us. The captain might feel like doing us a favor later.

The necessity of talking this over with the pelenaut meant I'd get to see my boys again soon, but I could see the currents pushing me, right back to that unholy island where wraiths yawned with their unhinged jaws, hungry for a taste of the living.

When Fintan dissipated her seeming, he said, "That's the last I've heard regarding events up in Fornyd. We are getting very close to our current time. Hopefully I'll have some more to relay on that front soon. For now, let me share Abhinava Khose's first visit to Rael."

He took on the seeming of the plaguebringer in coils of black smoke.

Abhinava

While crossing the Poet's Range, we spent most of one day paced by a pack of what Fintan claimed were "sonnet wolves." Carnage was their poetry, according to him. They were slightly smaller than regular wolves, with a slimmer snout, entirely black coats, and they vocalized in a series of rolling, jerky howls rather than barks.

Beautiful creatures. They were very interested in Murr, who did not like them at all, and even more interested in Ohhwuh, who thought they were kind of cute. They would not be able to bring him down; he knew it and they knew it too, but under different circumstances they might be willing to try. We paused for a short while so I could sketch a couple of them, and we left behind some meat for them and wished them good hunting elsewhere.

When we got to the first Raelech city—Kintael, I believe—we stopped well outside it, at a border inspection station where I was given a Jereh band to wear on my arm and informed that I must keep it on at all times within the country.

Left to right, the three stones they assigned me were malachite, obsidian, and turquoise. Fintan explained their significance.

"Malachite means you're foreign national; obsidian means you either have a foreign skill or no recognized professional status, and you might get questions about that as a result; and turquoise means that you're blessed, so everyone is going to know that you have a kenning but not which one. Normally we'd clarify with some little pinned badges attached to your tunic, but there aren't any available yet for the Sixth Kenning."

"So it's real?" the border official said. Fintan gestured to Murr, Eep, and Ohhwuh.

"Profoundly so. None of these animals is in its natural habitat."

"Right. Uh. About that." He waggled a finger around at them. "I'm not sure they're allowed into the city under regulations."

"Gentle friend, there are laws regarding pets and livestock entering our borders, but there are currently no laws against the animal companions of plaguebringers. We're going to visit the Triune Council, which will be able to make such laws if they're needed."

"Plaguebringer? He's got a plague?"

"No, but he can summon plagues if he wishes. Plagues of insects or toads, things like that. Not diseases."

After some additional negotiation and assurances, we were allowed to approach the city, with Fintan broadcasting an announcement that the stalk hawk, bloodcat, and dread-moose were not wild and not to be shot but also not to be petted. They were my companions as a beast caller of the Sixth Kenning. This earned us a few naked stares as we passed through town and sought lodging for the evening on the far side of it, near the rural outskirts, but nothing perplexing.

I did some of my own naked staring as we neared Kintael, because I'd never seen a Raelech city before. Its walls were lower than I expected, perhaps only three lengths high, and rising easily above them were the buildings of the city itself, the tallest in the center, all with large windows facing us. But most stunning were the towers surrounding the city, each made of a different rock and with broad stone platforms or balconies jutting out from them.

"That is not what I expected," I said to Fintan. "I thought you'd have much higher walls, and . . . what are those tow-ers?"

"Those are ready materials for a higher wall if we need them. A stonecutter or a juggernaut can easily take those down and add the material to our walls. But since we don't require high walls at the moment and we prefer a nice view, those are currently public balcony spaces. We're into outdoor parties when weather permits."

"You just . . . go there and party?"

"You make reservations for certain balconies, but yes."

I struggled to think of a Nentian equivalent but couldn't. Public spaces tended to be marketplaces or small parks or amphitheatres, with a statue of some king or other promi-nently displayed. Eep gave me a quick goodbye chirp and flew off to check out the view from one of those towers.

As we walked through the streets of Kintael and passed the citizenry, I noted that eye contact happened only after people checked out the stones I'd been given at the border.

"When did the Raelechs start doing this whole Jereh thing?" I asked Fintan. The band felt strange and constricted on my arm.

"Originally it was a reaction to the Fornish system, where it often seems that an individual's standing in society has more to do with their family and clan than their actual accomplishments. So we have no surnames, and we identify by our chosen profession and level of skill."

"I see. And this somehow prevents wealthy families from securing privileges for their spawn?"

"Spawn? Ha! Well, I wouldn't say they're entirely unable to do so," Fintan replied, "but their influence is reduced through the Colaiste."

"That's the national boarding school you all go to?"

"Correct. The parents can't determine course of study or make decisions for their children. The kids have to go through the entire curriculum and make their own choices. And when it's time to assign apprentices to masters, that's done by lottery to prevent corruption in the process."

"So your parents can't pressure you to be anything other than what you want?" I asked.

"Oh, they try to apply pressure, of course. Before they send their kids off to the Colaiste, they often make clear what they're hoping for or even expecting. But the kids have no obligation to fulfill those expectations. I certainly didn't. My parents wanted me to be some kind of smith, to practice a trade and never seek a kenning. They most definitely did not want me to be a bard."

"Have they changed their minds now?"

"I doubt it very much. I haven't spoken to them since shortly after I was blessed, when they made their disappointment plain."

"But they're—forgive me for asking—alive and well?"

"I believe so. I have a younger brother who's apprenticed to an armorer, so he's making them very proud."

"It's an interesting system. I wonder if I'd be here now if Ghurana Nent had something similar."

In truth, I did not need to wonder: I'd most definitely not be here. The fact that I'd been tied to my family's occupation and expectations inspired my revolt and ultimately their untimely, accidental deaths. Had they been supportive rather than coercive, they'd be alive and I'd be doing something entirely mundane, because I never would have entered that nughobe grove. Had Fintan's parents been supportive, they'd still have a relationship with their son.

The more I encounter examples of it, the more I am unsure that conditional love is actually love. It should be easier to walk away from it once identified, but choking down that reality can be harder than choking down a sour bowl of borchatta soup. Because walking away means facing the possibility that you were never loved the way you should have been, and every step is creating space you may never be able to fill.

But every step is also potentially closer to someone who will cherish you unconditionally. Conditional love wrecks lives—sometimes outright, more often by stunting them. And I know that most every love has conditions—it *is* a condition—but most conditions are reasonable things, like, "Do not physically abuse me." When love comes with limits on your growth as a person—"go to *this* school" and "get *that* job or else"—it's like a set of shackles on your spirit. We often don't have the keys to those shackles when we're young, and sometimes we don't realize we have them as adults, or we're unwilling to use them. It means an awful lot of people are being prevented from realizing their potential.

As I traveled with Fintan and learned more about the Raelech political system, I came to admire it more than the Nentian and Fornish systems—certainly much more than Hathrir's system—but less than the interesting experiment at Malath Ashmali. And far, far less than the ideas of Tamhan

Khatri; memories of him were my dawn, my noonday sun, and my starry nighttime sky.

I wondered—truly wondered, for I had no idea—if he was well and hoped his ideas had the chance to come to fruition someday. He might not know it—nor ever know it—but I loved him unconditionally.

And Hanima Bhandury too, though not in any romantic sense. She was someone I wished every happiness, having suffered so much.

Since Murr, Eep, and Ohhwuh seemed perfectly content with the warmer weather and food supply, I could see myself staying in Rael until Ghurana Nent was ready to welcome me again. Or in Brynlön; it had been very pleasant there, and the lands surrounding Tömerhil had improved the mood of Murr and Eep considerably.

And mine as well. There were so many new and different animals to meet. But the human animal—that one continued to surprise me. I was beginning to notice how a culture's kenning manifested itself in the daily life of a country, and it made me wonder how the Sixth Kenning would manifest itself in Ghurana Nent.

Granted, I'd had limited experience so far, but in Brynlön there was great emphasis on clean water and general hygiene, owing to the Fourth Kenning. The public baths were luxurious, for example, and I'd been told they weren't even considered fancy by Brynt standards. In Rael, the Third Kenning meant that everyone had a sturdy place to live. Literally rock-solid shelter was a given, provided by stonecutters in the Triune's employ. But beyond that wonder, Raelech cities were works of art, with tremendous layering of colored stone and mosaics on the walls, sculptures everywhere, and parks that featured plenty of cooling grasses but always had three obelisk fountains somewhere in a meditative rock garden, surrounded by colored sands and pebbles arranged in pleasing patterns.

The contrast of color and texture became a theme some days later when I was introduced to Killae, the capital of Rael. Smooth and rough stone of varying colors faced the buildings, and thin-slate tiled roofs topped them. The streets were paved with stone, but not with the rough cobbles I was used to seeing in Khul Bashab. These were flat and expertly fitted. There was drainage, too, and fantastic sewers, owing to the input of Brynlön. When it came to infrastructure, no one did it so well or beautifully as the Raelechs.

I had to absorb this peripherally, however, as I became a person of great interest upon my entrance to the city. That was because Fintan announced our presence, of course, using his kenning to broadcast it as he had in Kintael. Unlike the smaller city, however, it seemed that everyone in the capital wanted to see the world's first plaguebringer with his bloodcat, stalk hawk, and bone-collared dreadmoose, and the streets became choked with the curious. We quickly acquired an escort of master couriers, who warned folks away from approaching too close as they took us to the Triune Council. Eyes widened and hands clasped to mouths as the people witnessed our passage, and they commented excitedly to one another, and I didn't understand a word.

"What are they saying?" I asked Fintan.

"That Ohhwuh is awesome, that Eep is beautiful, that Murr looks ferocious, and that you are an incredibly pretty man."

"Shut up."

"You asked. If it makes you feel any better, a few have commented that my nose is too big and I could use a sandwich or two. I'm really not faring well here."

Our progress was slowed by the crush of people in the streets, and my companions were growing visibly agitated.

"Can you remind everyone not to crowd us? I would hate to see them provoke a defensive response."

Fintan broadcast that reminder and it helped, and I reminded my companions that they should try to restrain themselves. Ohhwuh in particular could kill instantly with a swoop of his bladed antlers or a kick to the side—moose were capable of doing that.

We made it to the gates of the Triune compound with only a few irritated snarls, bellows, and screeches.

My shoulders relaxed as soon as the crowds were behind us. My companions relaxed too, and Murr sneezed. That was no doubt from a wealth of scents filling his nose, some of them unpleasant.

"Was all that really necessary?" I asked.

"It got us here quickly. We have a lot of information to share with the Triune, and the curiosity of meeting you is our ticket to a fast audience."

I looked up at the Triune, the seat of Raelech power, and felt suitably awed. Three towers rose from the base of a large central building, atop which flew bright flags that probably inspired patriotism. But the towers themselves were works of art, composed of a rose stone inlaid with quartz that softly reflected moonbeams at night and glinted in the sun. It was breathtaking to me and demonstrated the fullness of all that the people of the Third Kenning had accomplished with their blessings. What legacy could the people of the Sixth Kenning build?

There were some wooded park areas within the compound, which the Raelechs agreed Ohhwuh could enjoy while we went inside, and they promised he'd be unmolested. I asked Murr and Eep if they would like to stay with him, but they insisted that they remain by my side, so we all entered the Triune together.

The central meeting place was a triangular room with seating areas at each corner and a circular space in the middle for visitors. The Triune could seat themselves at any single corner, which had significance depending on which of the triple goddesses that corner represented, or they could spread themselves among them, forcing the visitor to turn to divide attention between council members. Fintan warned me that might be the case when I entered, since my status was unclear and no decisions had been made.

He gave me quick rundowns on the council members as the courier led us through marbled halls to the Triune chamber.

"Clodagh is now the senior member, since Dechtira's three-year term has ended. She is widely reputed to be militant. Carrig, now in his second year, seems a neutral sort, who sometimes voted with Clodagh and sometimes with Dechtira. The newest member is named Brádach, and little is known yet about his governing style, beyond his campaign promise of 'strong, sober judgment,' which implies that the judgment of others is weak and possibly inebriated, I guess? Anyway, I'll introduce you and translate as needed. I don't believe any of them speak Nentian."

When we entered on one side of the triangle, I noticed that the council members were indeed at the corners and that doors also occupied the other two sides of the triangle. Perhaps those led to private offices or accessed the towers.

"Please watch my back, friends," I said to Murr and Eep. Eep hopped around on my shoulder to face the rear, and her tail feathers fell down the front of my right side while my hair fell on my left.

"Murr," the bloodcat said, and paced around to glare behind me as I turned. Fintan introduced each council member to me, rotating clockwise. He started with Clodagh, who was in her mid-forties, I guessed, glossy hair intricately braided, tied, and piled about her head like fortifications. She gave me the barest nod and never blinked. Then we spun to meet Carrig, who appeared affable and curious, likewise middle-aged but perhaps younger than Clodagh by a few years. His hair had been cut short, but as if to compensate, he kept a mustache the size of a squirrel on his upper lip.

The new council member, Brádach, was a much older man, perhaps in his sixties, with a curly gray mane and a long salt-and-pepper beard. He was clearly vain about the latter: He'd oiled and braided it, and you could tell he thought it gave him all the gravitas available in the room—nobody else could have a smidgen of gravitas until they grew a better beard. His tiny eyes glinted with suspicion, if not hostility, underneath bushy black brows.

Still, I did not detect a whiff of malevolence from any of them, the way I had from Melishev Lohmet; at first glance, they seemed merely to be people interested in protecting their country, and if they had any selfish agendas, they were hidden for now.

"From here on out, I will translate simultaneously between you and them. Say whatever you want to say," Fintan explained. I pivoted to address them all as I spoke, Murr circling with me, and the bard spoke in Raelech a few seconds behind me.

"Honored Triune, I am Abhinava Khose, a beast caller of the Sixth Kenning—a plaguebringer, in fact, which I believe to be the most powerful blessing. These are my friends, Murr and Eep, a bloodcat and stalk hawk from the Nentian plains. Outside I have another friend, a bone-collared dreadmoose from the Gravewood. All creatures can understand my speech and often come when I call."

"Often?" Clodagh said.

"Always, in my experience thus far, but I would not wish to assume."

"We welcome you but wonder why you are here," said Brádach, so I faced him to reply.

"Primarily, I am here to give my friends a bit more warmth, as they were too cold where we were. But of more interest to you, I am sure, would be the services that beast callers can provide, such as safe passage through dangerous territory. I escorted Fintan here over kraken-infested waters, through the Gravewood, and over the Poet's Range to bring you intelligence from an architect of the Bone Giant invasion."

There was silence for a few seconds after Fintan finished translating, and then Brádach's face scrunched up as he said, "What?" in Raelech, but I knew that much at least and had to suppress a chuckle. Fintan turned to me and said this might go a bit faster if he explained, and I grinned at him.

"You've probably been waiting for this, haven't you? I bet you have a speech all prepared."

"I do."

"I wouldn't dream of denying you the pleasure." I waved at him to proceed, and he launched into it. There really was an awful lot for them to digest. Minutes passed as Fintan spoke and shocked them with revelation upon revelation, but eventually a question was directed my way.

"Do you wish to return to Ghurana Nent?" Clodagh asked.

"Eventually," I said, "but not at present. King Kalaad the Unwell wishes me dead for embarrassing him while he was still a viceroy."

"We have heard very little from him," Carrig said. "Rumors are that he is truly unwell and there might be some rebellion in Khul Bashab."

"I have no doubt of either," I said. If Hanima Bhandury *hadn't* started something, I would be shocked.

"What *do* you wish, then?" Brádach asked.

"Oh. I suppose I'd appreciate room and board for my friends and myself. I should probably add that if any Nentian officials ask for me to be handed over, please do not agree, as I will not surrender myself to the nonexistent mercy or justice of King Kalaad. And . . . maybe send a message to a couple of friends in Khul Bashab?"

The tiny eyes flicked to the other corners of the room. A couple of quick nods, and Brádach mirrored it. "Done. You are a favored guest of the Triune, and we will have you stay in the compound with every luxury afforded. A courier will take your messages in the morning, and should you require anything at all, you need only ask the staff."

"You must be tired, Plaguebringer," Carrig added. "You are welcome to take your ease now, as we have much more to discuss with the bard, and it may take a good long while."

"Ah. Well. Lovely. My thanks."

Murr, Eep, and I were delivered into the keeping of a matronly woman who spoke Nentian and introduced herself as Majella, master of service of the Poet Goddess Kaelin. Her Jereh stones were citrine, amethyst, and amethyst again.

"Forgive my ignorance, but what is a master of service?"

"It's hospitality, in whatever form that may take. It's admittedly a broad category, so in addition to the stone, we have badges that specify our profession." She tapped a few shining golden brooches pinned above her left breast. "These indicate that I'm the steward for the Triune. I manage the staff here on the compound and see to the few guests we have."

She inquired after the needs of my companions, and I told her I'd have to take Murr hunting somewhere. Eep was easy—she'd find what she needed without too much trouble, since rodents were plentiful in cities, and I'd already confirmed that there were squirrels in the compound's park— but Murr was another matter. And Ohhwuh might not find much to eat in the park after a day.

"Would you like to visit a temple of the Huntress? Not to worship, I mean, but to meet up with a hunter who might be able to direct you to suitable game?"

I could find suitable game on my own, but visiting hunters that weren't my own family might be instructive. "That sounds perfect."

"I'll arrange it, then. These are your rooms." We had come to a pair of carved double doors, which she threw open to reveal a vision of wealth I'd never before seen. I stopped at the threshold to marvel at it—furnishings from Forn upholstered in khernhide, a Hathrim glass sculpture of a lava dragon above an enchanted hearth, and a bar stocked with so many different distilled spirits I'd not know where to begin.

"Rooms, plural?"

"Oh, yes, there's much more; this is just the conversation room. Please, let me show you."

"You hear that, Murr? This is a whole room just for conversations."

"Murr."

"We could talk about anything here, just like we could talk about anything anywhere else, but if you do it here, then it's fancy."

"Murr-urr-ur."

"Forgive my curiosity," Majella said, "but is he saying something back to you?"

"He is, but I'm not able to understand him. I can guess, however, that he's probably expressing his disdain for human comforts."

The bloodcat nodded enthusiastically.

"Yeah, see? That was a good guess."

Majella laughed. "He will have plenty more to disdain, then. Let's go to the kitchen in case you're hungry."

It was very well stocked. "We have most basics here, but if you'd like to eat something specific, we can certainly arrange it. If you'd like to leave me a list of your preferred dishes, we'll have a chef come in and fix them for you."

"And a mixologist to fix me drinks?"

"Of course."

"Oh. I was kidding, but . . . wow."

"It's advisable, really. Some of the Hathrim liquors can explode if you're not careful."

"So don't touch the bar, got it. I am a bit hungry—perhaps something vegetarian that isn't a salad. And to drink, some of the Good Shit. Fintan wouldn't stop talking about how he was going to have some when he finally got home."

"We can do that. Let's go to the other side."

The other side contained a decadent hygiene room followed by a washroom that boasted a thermal hot-spring pool sunk into stone, which one entered via an incredibly tiny beach, next to a smaller pool Majella described as an "icy plunge," fed by a chilly waterfall. The actual plunging was accomplished by climbing some flagstone steps to the top of a slick waterslide that curved around and looked pretty fun. Towels, soaps, perfumes, and robes awaited nearby, and the steward made sure to point out that there was an assortment of brushes and combs and hair ties available for use, all new. Next to the beach, a coarse woolly mat was provided to remove wet sand from one's feet.

That wasn't all, of course. Past these luxuries was another set of double doors, faced in a stone bas-relief depicting the triple goddess. I paused before it and Majella did too.

"It's lovely, isn't it?"

"Yes, it is."

"Shall we?"

"Please."

She hauled open the doors and I beheld the bedchamber, which boasted a carved Fornish bedframe, another enchanted hearth on one side, and an upholstered chair and ottoman next to a floor-to-ceiling bookcase.

"Should you not find anything to your liking on the shelves, you of course may request anything you want from the national library, and it will be brought to you."

"Truly?" I strode to the bookcase, my interest immediately piqued. "Do you know if you have anything here regarding Raelech wildlife?"

"I don't believe so. It's mostly poetry and political discourses, since our guests are often diplomats and the like."

"Fair enough. May I request anything the library might

have regarding wildlife, then? Raelech or otherwise. I'm particularly interested in species identification and would prefer illustrated volumes, if any exist, since I can't read Raelech."

"Of course. I should have anticipated your interest. Apologies."

"I've only just arrived. You couldn't possibly have anticipated me. I know you are a master of service, Majella, but I'm unaccustomed to being served. May we be friends?"

She beamed at me. "Of course. I'll see to the books and ask if we have any nature volumes in Nentian. I'll also send a chef and mixologist and inquire about a hunt for your friends. I have just a couple of more questions."

"Okay."

"May we launder your clothing and send a master tailor to see to a new set or two for you?"

"Oh. Sure."

"And understand that I do not ask out of any wish to give offense, since people have different feelings on the subject, but can I arrange for a sexitrist to visit you?"

"Ah . . . no. Thank you. Very kind of you to offer. But perhaps you can send the chef, mixologist, and tailor in an hour, and after I eat, I'll go out with my friends to see to their needs? The books can wait until after my return."

"Absolutely. I'll give you some privacy until then."

"Thank you so much."

"Abhi. Murr. Eep. It's been a pleasure." She departed, all smiles, and I could not have felt more welcome. After a moment I realized how incredibly rare it was for me to feel that way—this kind of accommodation simply didn't exist in my experience. I realized with a whuff of breath that Nentians could learn a good deal from Raelech masters of service. All they had to do was feed me, give me a bath, and send over all the books I wanted, and I'd do most anything in return.

"Well," I said, clapping my hands together and then rubbing them in anticipation, "shall we try out the baths? You might have missed it, but the sandy one is hot and the one that looks cold is actually cold."

Both of my friends shook their heads.

"Ah. Well. I'm going to indulge in a little bit of luxury while I have the chance, and once I'm finished, we'll go outside and see to you, all right? Unless you'd like to go outside right now and join Ohhwuh in the park until I'm ready."

They both said no again, indicating that they'd wait, and I thanked them for their patience. I stripped and they padded along next to me, curious to witness what I thought was the height of opulence. They watched me sigh as I sank into the hot spring, which relaxed my tired muscles, and Murr went so far as to dip a paw into the water to test it, since I seemed to be enjoying it so much. He yanked it out quickly and shook it, letting loose an annoyed yowl.

"Probably not your thing," I said. "But this is heavenly for me."

The waterslide turned out to be every bit as fun as I expected, and the icy plunge lived up to its name. I leapt out of it as quickly as I could and shrugged into a robe, then spent some time drying and brushing my hair, while Murr and Eep both groomed themselves in their own fashion.

The master chef, mixologist, and tailor arrived together, along with a tailor's journeyman, who quickly took my measurements and departed to fetch "fitting garments" plus a loaner outfit to hunt in while my old clothes were cleaned and new sets made. All of them spoke flawless Nentian, and for a fraction of a second I wondered if the Triune kept multilingual staff purposely to cater to their guests, before concluding that of course they did.

The mixologist was a woman named Dedra, who was in fact a master brewer of the Earth Goddess Dinae, according to the stones on her Jereh band. But the pins on her breast identified her as a mixologist by trade.

"So you are a master brewer, but instead of brewing beer you mix cocktails?" I asked.

"I do both," she said. "I distill spirits more than brew these days. The bartending is more of an enjoyable side gig for me. The mastery allows me to speak knowledgeably about the craft and pair drinks well to different dishes."

"I see. So could you craft something to pair with whatever the chef will make?"

"Certainly."

The chef, Oran, spoke up at that point. He was a younger man with a clean-shaven jaw and all his hair tidily pinned underneath a chef's beret. His tunic was a spotless bright white that nearly made me squint. "What are you in the mood for?"

"Whatever you wish to cook, provided that all its ingredients come from plants or with the indifference of animals, if not their full-throated consent."

"Eggs and dairy are permissible, then?"

"Yes."

The two of them consulted and got to work, while master tailor Dallin took more measurements and spoke to me about different outfits and materials I might wish to wear. The Raelechs loved their leathers, but I requested entirely plant-based materials, which seemed to present him with a pleasant challenge.

"I requested only room and board, Master Dallin, so I assume your services are outside that, and I want you to know I am prepared to pay for them."

"Oh, no. My services are considered part of your board. I'm compensated fully by the Triune. Think nothing of it."

Once he took his leave, Master Oran informed me that the first course was ready.

"The first . . . course?"

"Of three, yes."

Kalaad in the sky, it was the most incredible meal of my life.

First, a chilled pickled cucumber and onion medley on top of sesame crackers paired with a spicy gin and tonic garnished with a Hathrim magma pepper. A study in heat and cold, much like the baths I'd enjoyed earlier.

The main course, Master Oran informed me, was a brandied Raelech mushroom sonata with a Fornish wild rice pilaf, which Master Dedra paired with a whiskey cocktail made with the Good Shit, a muddled sugar cube, and sour cherry bitters, finished with three brandied cherries.

Dessert was raspberry mousse and a rich chocolate rum livened with lime juice and ginger beer.

The sumptuousness of this meal was not something that Murr or Eep could appreciate, but, regardless, once Master Dallin returned with a set of hunting clothes for me, I was able to stagger forth in high spirits to a temple of Raena on the western outskirts of the city, there to follow a huntress into a wilderness where Murr and Eep could hunt without fear of offending some nearby farmer or rancher.

I felt guilty at indulging in such excess in a time when so many must be suffering through privation—especially in Brynlön, where much of their agriculture had collapsed. But I also understood that this was merely a pleasant interlude in the midst of a continental tragedy. There was a long and unpleasant road ahead of me, and all of it would be bereft of such joys.

But it was all the more reason to savor such joy while it was in front of me. We are allowed so few moments of perfection in our lives that it would be a shame to let them pass us by, unnoticed and unremarked.

What could Nentian cities be like, I wondered, if the Sixth Kenning flourished and we somehow won free of an oppressive monarchy? Would such bliss become possible for our people?

The way I saw it, the matter was not to be left to hopes and wishes; I must work to make it a reality, and that work meant acknowledging that humans are not a species apart from the others. We are brethren, at best.

So I accompanied a huntress into the wilderness as Murr and Eep sought out their supper. It was a silent business, as stealth was required, so I passed the time composing messages to Hanima Bhandury and Tamhan Khatri.

I slept better than I had in ages, and in the morning a master courier named Numa arrived to memorize my words and convey them to my friends.

Only when I met with Fintan after breakfast did I learn that Numa was his lifebond.

"What? You could have enjoyed a happy reunion with her! Surely some other courier could have done it?"

"We *did* enjoy our reunion, and it's true that someone else could have ferried a message to Ghurana Nent. But no one else could find out what I want to know."

"Which is?"

"Where your blessed friends have been and where they are going. Numa will have the truth of it, and an answer for you in the bargain. I guarantee it."

A COURIER AT THE FERRY

The resumption of toast was glorious. I'd been able to score a loaf at the bakery, as I'd hoped, and a new jar of strawberry preserves, so I would have a week of breakfast as a result.

And this modest repast, for which I was very grateful, was in stark contrast to what Abhi had enjoyed in Rael not so long ago. It was much on the minds of the citizenry, so far as I could tell. Everyone in line at the bakery was talking about it.

Some were resentful of the excess and a tad annoyed with the bard for sharing it.

"He didn't need to rub salt in that wound," a man groused.

"But he remembered us and that we are not so fortunate now," a woman pointed out. "He was aware that it was a rare experience. I'm happy for him. And if this second invasion can be prevented, then we will return to having plenty someday."

"I suppose that could prove true," the man admitted. "It's just difficult to imagine when one is living on rations and there's nothing but sludge coming downriver."

"I can imagine it," the woman replied. "Those food descriptions gave me new reasons to live. I want to try all of that someday. And I didn't know Hathrim liquors could explode."

"Emberfruit, yes," I volunteered. "If it ever reopens and you get the opportunity, try the Roasted Sunchuck. They have it there. Hathrim proprietors."

"Oh, yes, I've heard of that place, and I think I saw one of them walking around the city once. They're tough to miss."

Chef du Rödal was in high spirits at the refugee kitchen, since she felt like she'd be able to finally prepare a proper meal for everyone.

"It's not going to be a fancy Raelech mushroom sonata," she said, "but it'll be buckets better than the thin chowder we've had to live on for weeks."

Once I hooked up with Fintan and brought my timeline up to date, I noticed something upon review that I hadn't before: Gerstad Nara du Fesset had been extraordinarily busy but only recently given a voice in the stories. Even now she was intimately involved in whatever was happening in Fornyd. This despite the fact that she had made the same recent mistake that I had: trusting the Wraith. She'd been detained and questioned like me, but unlike me, she had not been shut out of continuing developments. Why was that?

Fintan could see that I was bothered by something and asked me about it, but I could hardly bring up such matters to him. He'd not have a solution. He was content to simply work, though he admitted that unless he received some updates soon, he was nearly finished. Which was just as well, since he was supposed to entertain until the armies arrived, which they had.

"Are we going to hear about that? I thought you said we hadn't gotten to the point where you were assigned to us. We have to be getting to it soon."

"Tomorrow, in fact."

"And the fate of Melishev Lohmet? Is that tomorrow as well?"

"Day after tomorrow. I know it's been frustrating for you, but the answer is coming."

"Good." I had no further comment.

Once on the wall, Fintan said he had another song from Kauria. "It's a five-line structure with lots of internal rhyme called a trail tune, and these are sung around campfires by merchant caravans as they travel around the country." He plucked a rolling rhythm on his harp and sang over it.

> Teapot whistling on the fire, hands clasped around a warming cup
> As I think of you the comfort's steeping, I'm laughing, grinning, drinking you up
> You're a gentle tempest in my mind, the soft, considerate, cozy kind
> Inclined to blow away my troubles and keep our hearts entwined
> Alone on the trail I'm not alone; these thoughts of you are my home.

"Back to the west," Fintan said after the break, "where we catch up with the hivemistress."

Hanima

Deciding to leave the city and actually leaving it, I discovered, were two very different things. There was the small matter of deciding where to go, for example, and what I would do when I got there.

It excited and terrified me at the same time, because I'd never left Khul Bashab's walls before, except for the time I went to seek my kenning and when I went to scout Hennedigha's army. Since both those trips had been rather life-changing, I had good reason to wonder what awaited me out there.

I talked it over with Adithi, who remained my best friend. We had both come from literally dirt-poor circumstances and trusted each other, and she agreed that leaving might be the best option for me, even though she didn't want me to go.

"You could come with me," I said.

"What? No, I can't. I have the stables to worry about."

"Do you seriously need to worry? The horses are happy now, and you have people to run things your way while you're gone. They'll be fine. And think of all the new horses you can make happy. That's the way I'm looking at it. My people know how to take care of the hives and greenhouses without me."

"There are some things only I can do, though."

"True. The same applies to me. Some services will have to be discontinued until we return. But we *will* return, and in the meantime, our businesses will keep going and our people will be paid, and we can maybe expand into another city."

"Which city? The monarchists aren't going to welcome the way we do things."

"I've been thinking maybe we should address that. Go to the monarch himself. We know the Senesh cousins aren't going to be rational. But maybe the king will be more reasonable."

"Or less," Adithi replied. "He's the guy who thought the Senesh cousins would be good viceroys. He sent that army to subdue us."

"True. But maybe he'll be more willing to talk now that we broke his army. Or maybe we'll have to foment a rebellion like we did here."

Adithi laughed at me. "Without Tamhan pulling strings behind the scenes? We're not political geniuses. We're just cute beast callers."

"So let's go find the political geniuses hiding in the shadows there. Maybe they'll be cute too."

Her eyes narrowed at me. "Hold on. Is this really about finding a new boyfriend?"

"No! Well. Okay, maybe it's five percent that. But it's ninety-five percent running from being famous and bringing down the monarchy."

Adithi sighed. "I'll go with you. All you had to say was that I could make new horses happy. But I need a few days to prepare."

"Me too. But yay! This is going to be the best."

We both spent time recruiting a few other beast callers to come with us and making sure things wouldn't fall apart in our absence. We had to clear our roster with Tamhan so that the city wouldn't be defenseless. Most of the beast callers would be staying: Talika, the bat woman; my ex, Lavi, the moth man; Manu, the lord of creepy-crawlies; and Vibodh, who could summon ebon-armored rhinos. The sedge puma lady was staying too, so the defenses would be solid even if all the rest were lords of gnats and suckerfish.

Besides Adithi, Jahi was going to come along, and he'd ask the blackwings what dangers might lie ahead for us and scout the best route to take across the plains. Charvi was the thunder-yak and wart-oxen fella, so he would provide the muscle if we needed it. And Suraji the spider queen decided to come along too, which surprised me a little bit, but she said she had family in Talala Fouz and wanted to see them again.

Word got around that I was leaving, because I had to tell my people and of course the others told their people that they were leaving with me, so the face hollering got worse, because everyone wanted me to stay and fix things, or at least fix *their* thing before I left.

Tamhan asked me to make one last speech before I departed, something to reassure everyone that he and the elected councils would take care of everything. I could tell it hurt him to ask. He announced a time that I would address the city in the South Side Market, where the revolution had started, and for a stage I stood in the back of a hunter wagon. The place was packed full.

I looked out at the faces staring at me and smiled, then tried to project my voice as far as I could. "I lost my parents, but I found you, Khul Bashab. You are my family now, and I love you. And because I love you, I need to leave for a while to do what's best for you."

That earned me a chorus of nos and boos, and I had to get shouty for a bit until they quieted.

"We will remain threatened by the monarchists until they agree to let us live as a clave republic, so I want to make our case in Talala Fouz. My greatest hope is that the entire nation, not just our city, will become a clave republic, but failing that, I want the trade embargo ended and for us to live unmolested by the monarchy."

I pointed at the building that loomed over us all. "While I'm gone, I'd like you to take a look at the Tower of Kalaad every day as a reminder of why our family is different. In every other Nentian city, the tower is where the viceroy sits above the people he rules, looking down on them. But on the day we expelled Viceroy Senesh, we filled that tower with the poorest of the poor, who had no homes and few possessions besides the rags they wore. It is no longer a tower that represents a monarchy's power over us; it is a tower that embodies the moral use of power. It is a tower of compassion—and perhaps, if the councils and city minister see fit, they will officially rename it as such. When I look at the Tower of Compassion, I see the people who need our help—our family members—and I am motivated to work hard to give them that help. Because what happens when we do—what has already happened—is that those family members get better, and they get jobs and homes, and then they work hard to lift up someone else. In just a few weeks we have put roofs over everyone's head and no one is starving, because we decided together that was important.

"So will you continue to do that for me while I'm gone? Lift up the least of us in that Tower of Compassion so that we can see what work needs to be done. We will all prosper together as a family.

"I am all love and honey for you, Khul Bashab. Farewell until we meet again."

And that was the last poster that Tamhan printed of me and pasted around the city: LIFT UP THE LEAST OF US. He promised he'd change the name of the tower to the Tower of Compassion too: ninety-five percent because it reinforced the ethos of the government, but five percent because it would annoy Dhanush Bursenan. Or maybe it was the other way around.

What made me sad, though, was that Tamhan was clearly relieved I was leaving. He was convinced things would be easier with me gone, and he was looking forward to it.

In the morning, however—the middle of it, really, after breakfast, when we'd had time to assemble our small train of horses and wagons down by the docks—we got a very happy surprise: A Raelech courier debarked from the same ferry we were preparing to board, with a message for the hivemistress. I instantly forgot all about my sadness at leaving, because there was a message! For me! By courier!

It seemed all the more important because the courier was a stunning woman named Numa with a semi-splattered moth on her armor, which struck me as a metaphor for my relationship with Lavi. When she asked if I might be Hanima the hivemistress and I said yes—the hornets probably gave me away—she said she had some words to relay from the plaguebringer Abhinava Khose. I gasped and looked at Tamhan, who also gasped and looked at me. We jumped up and down and held hands and hugged.

"He's alive!" I said.

"Yes, he's alive!" Tamhan agreed.

"Where is he?" I asked Numa.

"He's in Killae, or at least he was when I left. He's with my husband, in fact. The two of them have had some interesting travels. But your message, word for word from his mouth: *Hanima, do you know what you are? You're the best! I hope you have not forgotten the joy you felt at being blessed. I am well, as are Murr and Eep, and thinking of you.* Message ends."

I was hoping for more but was still happy he'd thought of me. "Aww! What a sweet kid! I wonder how he got all the way up there? When I saw him last, he was heading south-west to Hashan Khek."

"Did you have any other messages?" Tamhan asked.

"Yes, for the son of a chaktu butcher named Tamhan Khatri."

"That's me. I'm Tamhan Khatri, City Minister."

Numa blinked a few times. I guess he wasn't what she was expecting—or perhaps she wasn't expecting to meet him at the gate down by the docks.

"Very well. Here is your message: *Every day under Kalaad's blue sky I think of you and your safety and happiness. There will not ever be a day in which I do not think of you. I hope you have been well. I have had many adventures since we parted—too many to list—and I fear we will remain parted for some while longer. I have no doubt that you have had adventures as well. I look forward to the day when we can sit together and trade stories.* Message ends."

Tamhan looked stricken by these words, which didn't make much sense to me at first. His mouth was open a little bit, and a tear welled up and ran down his cheek, which startled him out of his thoughts. He dashed the tear away and sniffed and thanked Numa.

"I can take back a reply to him, but only with the understanding that there won't be any follow-up. No other couriers will return to carry on a conversation."

"Right, right. Give me a moment to collect my thoughts," Tamhan said. "And as city minister for the free city of Khul Bashab, I have a message for the Triune Council."

"I can give you my reply now," I said to Numa.

"Okay, I'm recording. Go ahead."

"No, silly boy, *you* are the best! I am sort of a holy woman running from my own holiness. I am going to Talala Fouz now with Adithi and some other new beast callers, so find me there if you want me."

"Got it. Thank you. Are you leaving for Talala Fouz now?"

"Yes. We were about to board the ferry."

"You're cutting across country, no roads?"

"Yes. We have nothing to fear from the animals, since we're all beast callers."

"Interesting. May I join you for a short distance to hear details of what happened here? My husband would be interested. He's a bard."

I shrugged. "Sure."

"Thank you. But don't let me keep you. I'll catch up easily."

"Okay. Tamhan, are you going to reply?"

"Yes, yes. I was just overwhelmed; I feared that Abhi might have died out there. So, are you ready, Numa?"

"Yes. Go ahead."

"Adventures indeed! I am now the elected city minister of the free city of Khul Bashab. The viceroy is banished. My father despises me because I am more powerful than he now and immune to his corruption. I have you to thank for it—and I do. Thank you, Abhi. Your friendship—our friendship—has already changed for the better many lives beyond our own. I can only dream of what more can be accomplished when we are reunited. Above all will be the joy of seeing you again. Please be safe and well, do good deeds, and return home when you can to a city that loves you."

When he nodded to indicate he'd finished, Numa assured him that she had it. And me? I was smiling so hard my face hurt. Because that message unlocked so much of Tamhan for me. I wished I had known how he felt before this. If I had been paying attention, I probably would have noticed on our way back to Khul Bashab, but I'd just been newly blessed and my boob still hurt from where the bloodcats bit off my nipple and I could talk to bees and simply talk again, period. There had been legitimate distractions.

"Will you stay the night as a guest of the city minister?" Tamhan asked Numa. "We were hoping someone from Rael would visit us. I have much business to share with the Triune Council."

Numa darted her eyes to me, obviously worried about how far out of her way she'd need to go the next day. I tried to reassure her.

"We're going to leave very clear tracks through the grass, and Jahi will have some blackwings circling above us to help you pinpoint our position tomorrow."

She followed my gesture to take in Jahi, who was still looking malnourished even though he'd been eating well for weeks now. I wasn't much better. He gave her a tight-lipped grin.

"I'm a beast caller attuned to blackwings," he said, "but I don't have a cool name for it like *hivemistress* or *plaguebringer*. *Birdboy* is fairly accurate, but it doesn't sound very cool compared to everything else, and I have to admit I'm struggling with that a little bit."

One corner of Numa's mouth twitched upward for just a second, and I was going to tell Jahi later I was pretty sure that meant she thought he was hilarious. The way I sized her up, she was the sort who laughed loudly and easily when comfortable with friends, but when she was on the job, she was professional and focused.

"Perhaps inspiration will strike during your travels," she said, her voice carefully even.

"We'll work on it," I said. "I'm sure we won't get terribly far today and you can catch up easily. And then you can take all the time you want, because animals won't ever attack us."

"I'll look forward to it."

Then it was truly time for us to say goodbye. I told my hornets to give us some room, and I hugged Tamhan hard.

"Love is the best," I said into his ear. "And it's good to re-member that, Tamhan, because sometimes we forget. You are my friend and I love you. And I think it's clear that others love you too. Please do not ever make us regret it." He clutched me close and spoke softly at my temple.

"I won't. Love is the reason I do what I do, and I will never betray it."

"Compassion is the only moral use of power."

"And you are the reason I believe that to my core. Please be safe, my friend."

I squeezed him once more and withdrew, tears sheeting down my cheeks, worrying that fortune could not be so be-nevolent as to let us both live for long.

"And you as well."

I could not take a proper breath until we were on the other side of the river. Goodbyes are such a complicated mess of worry and love.

That tale was nothing but good news for me. Hanima head-ing to Talala Fouz would not end well for Melishev Lohmet.

"We're going to stay in the west and catch up with the Fornish in Talala Fouz," the bard said, switching up his seem-ings.

It's difficult to train yourself to relax while waiting for a fight, yet that is the attitude one must cultivate under siege. There was little likelihood of the Nentians trying to take our com-pound by force, but we needed to be alert and constantly pre-pared for an attempt.

Normally I would entertain myself with an appropriate

passage from *Leafsong* and wonder if the wisdom of ben Zon still bloomed or wilted in the face of contemporary circumstances. For situations like this, Sage famously tells Sprout to sit with him on the edge of a field to watch the grass grow. The section has been mowed at the border of a clan member's garden, and before them is wild uncut grass—a meadow, really, possessing a medley of species. Sprout complies, but when some time passes and nothing of significance happens, she begins to have doubts.

—*I know there must be a lesson here, Sage, but what it is I cannot guess.*

—*Then you must take some time, Sprout, to assess.*

—*Am I to notice that, like people, some grass is neglected and some is cared for?*

—*That is an excellent observation, but I was hoping for more.*

—*Perhaps instead we are to mourn the grass cut down in its youth?*

—*We may, but I am hoping you will accept a simpler truth.*

Sprout keeps offering theories as to the purpose of the exercise and is always applauded, but never does she offer the answer that Sage seeks. Finally, she confesses that she cannot fathom the reason for it, and Sage judges it is time to ask a leading question.

—*All this while, what has the grass been doing while you thought things through?*

—*It's been growing, as grass tends to do.*

—*And you have done the same. So I hope you will remember that even in the midst of a waiting game, there is no doom but rather a quiet time to bloom.*

I would have done my best to grow on my own if I had no other choice. But these were not normal times, because I had Eimear, the Raelech bard, to keep me occupied with endless stories, and in return I told her what I could of Forn and what it was like to be a greensleeve. At one point she looked at the mushrooms growing on my shin bark and asked if I knew how to make a mushroom sour; a few Raelechs had enjoyed the drink down near Aelinmech from an obliging greensleeve and had bragged that it was the finest drink in the world. There were, she claimed, a total of seven Raelechs who had tasted it, and she would give almost anything to be the eighth.

"I am so sorry," I said. "I don't even drink spirits and wouldn't know the first thing about how to make such a wondrous beverage." She looked so disappointed I nearly wept. Clearly, she had built up a mighty store of hope and I had spoiled it all. I would have to learn how to craft this drink, starting with the mushroom whiskey, if it was so important to Raelechs.

Eimear tried to recover. "It's a silly thing, please forgive me."

"No, no, I understand. It's not silly at all when you look forward to a thing and are so sure it's at hand and then suddenly it isn't."

I would need a hobby outside the duties of a greensleeve. Distilling might fill that void very well. I'd need to make inquiries.

No one had come to offer apologies for Mai's imprisonment, and I took the trouble to confirm that all this had been over Mai's inability to do something she could not do: supply a Brynt hygienist. How many others had he imprisoned or killed because he couldn't be healed? Mai suspected it was in the double digits at the very least.

"When is he going to try the obvious thing," I said, "and ask the Brynts?"

Word reached us the next day that there was a caravan departing the city to do just that. They were going to conduct some trade, of course, to pay for the cost of the trip and make some profit, and would reestablish some vital contact with Brynlön after the collapse of the Granite Tunnel, but the primary purpose was to ask for a hygienist to save the life of the king. Word was out that they were looking for muscle to accompany them.

"They're going to attempt to cross the Poet's Range?" I asked. My understanding was that those forested mountain-tops were nearly as dangerous as the Gravewood itself. There weren't any gravemaws, but there were plenty of other carni-vores that would look upon a caravan as a buffet.

"That's the plan," Mai confirmed.

"Why don't they ship everything to Brynlön from a Rael-ech port? That would be safer."

"The Nentians have no shipping on that side of the conti-nent. They've been entirely dependent on the tunnels for trade with Rael and beyond. If they load everything into a Raelech ship, their profit disappears, and they have to worry about stabling their horses and so on."

That interested me, because traveling in a group who knew where they were going would be preferable to wander-ing a strange land alone. I had no intention of accompanying them all the way to Pelemyn, but this might be an excellent opportunity to cross Ghurana Nent and see if anyplace up-river or in Rael would prove suitable for my mission. I'd get closer to that new city in the north, for example, that had sounded so enticing to me earlier. Perhaps it was time for me to go. Or perhaps it was best for me to stay? It was difficult to know.

"Who is leading this caravan?" I asked.

"A meat merchant named Subodh Ramala," Mai said. "I'm told he's joining with others in Ar Balesh. Are you thinking you might join them?"

"I might. I'm not sure if I should."

"Why? What's keeping you here—or urging you on?"

Recalling the admonition of Vet Mof ben Tam to keep my mission secret, I lowered my eyes. "Forgive me, Ambassador, but it's clan business I must keep close."

"Oh! No, please forgive me for prying. My curiosity got

the better of me. I am eternally grateful that your clan business brought you here and allowed you to help me—and all of us. Your welcome here is in full bloom and shall remain so, ben Min."

"Thank you. My business is not particularly time-sensitive, so I am torn between the desire to take advantage of a traveling opportunity and the desire to stay here and defend you and this compound from a terrible king."

Mai Bet Ken was in the midst of protesting that there was no need to worry about that when an embassy staff member burst in and said part of the whipthorn wall had been set on fire, so we definitely needed to worry about that.

"Does ben Fos know?" I asked, springing from my seat and summoning a vine to descend to the ground.

"Someone is telling him."

"Which portion of the wall?"

"South side."

"Then I'm going north, in case that's a distraction from the true attack. Send a thornhand to meet me there."

I was already sliding down the vine while the ambassador was just getting to her feet, speaking about protecting her documents in the embassy.

Once on the ground, I sprinted for the northern wall and knelt by it, sending out shoots to communicate with the whipthorn roots. I felt the alert of a fire to the south but nothing else. As a defensive measure, to prevent further mischief, I asked the non-burning parts of the wall to lash out once at maximum strength. Anyone near enough to cause harm would be struck—and I knew there was a risk of hitting someone innocent, but we'd apologize if so. I thought it wise to teach everyone the lesson that our wall should not be approached.

I heard a couple of high-pitched cries off to the left, so I disengaged my shoots and shuffled over there to see. I peered through the wall and saw two young boys entangled with the thorns, their arms and shoulders bloodied. Jars of volatile liquid had broken on the ground underneath their feet—I could smell the fumes. They'd been planning to set another fire.

Given those facts, I thought it fine to let them struggle and bleed some more. But I doubted they'd done this of their own volition. Someone had set them a task. I looked past them at the other people on the street. Most were shocked. A woman with a basket full of vegetables from the market dropped it and ran to help the boys. But standing in the shadows, a Nentian man with a hat pulled low over his eyes observed dispassionately, his head moving minutely as he scanned the wall for movement. And off to my right, on a rooftop, an archer with a nocked arrow was likewise scanning for targets. They wanted to draw us out, then.

Shoots dove back into the ground to communicate through root and stem with ben Fos.

Don't go outside the walls, I said. *Archers in wait.*

Thank you, the reply came a moment later.

Communicating to the whipthorn, I had the branches snared on the boys snap, high up where they could easily regrow. The boys would be able to untangle now without much more trouble.

A thornhand arrived and I caught her up on the situation, told her to patrol but not to attack anything unless it got inside the wall.

"Do you need an archer to take out one of theirs?" she asked. "I'm proficient and I have a bowstring."

That hadn't occurred to me as a possibility. But though she would readily take my orders, I didn't feel like I should make the decision. That would be something for the ambassador to decide, since it would be an escalation she would have to deal with.

"What's your name?"

"Lee Ros ben Bar."

"Thank you, ben Bar. Just patrol for now and report anything that happens."

I jogged toward the west wall to check on things there and reported my intention through root and stem. Ben Fos said the fire would be out momentarily and he'd check on the east.

Once I got to the west wall and turned south to patrol along its length, an arrow sliced through the air in front of me. It had made it through the hedge somehow. Had I been seen or was it just a random shot to test our defenses?

That was probably what this was—a test of our defenses more than a concerted effort to attack. I dove to the ground and told ben Fos we'd been fired upon. I thought we should fire back if the ambassador agreed. And I also had the whipthorn thicken to hamper any further shots.

While I was at it, I grew some armor around my torso, employing the whipthorn roots to snake about me in an impenetrable mass of wood that should stop any sword or arrow from puncturing something vital. When I stood, I was robed in roots.

Orders came from ben Fos through root and stem: *Ambassador says fire upon the archers. Nonlethally if possible.*

I sent an acknowledgment back to him and a request to the roots of the silverbark tree: We needed a bow and five arrows. I set my legs to pumping toward the treehouse, and by the time I reached its canopy I saw a perfectly curved bow growing from the ground and five arrows growing like flowers, fletched with paper-thin wood instead of feathers, heads with four sharp barbs. I plucked them up with thanks and ran them over to ben Bar on the north wall.

The thornhand knew what was up when she saw me coming with fresh-grown weapons for her. She turned to the wall to find a good angle on the archer. She parted the whipthorns manually, having no ability to communicate with them, but their thorns did her no harm. Satisfied, she pointed to a spot in front of her as I arrived and handed over the bow and arrows.

"Porthole there, please," she said, taking out her bowstring to complete the weapon while I spoke to the wall and created a space for her to take a clear shot.

"The ambassador would prefer them to be wounded instead of killed," I informed her.

"Well, we'll see what I can do. I might miss entirely. It's been a while."

"I think that's fine. They simply need to know we'll resist if they attack us."

The wood-fletched arrows weren't as good as feathered ones, but they would certainly do in a pinch like this, and it was preferable for thornhands to travel with bowstrings and have a greensleeve grow a bow for them as needed rather than carrying one around.

Ben Bar nocked an arrow, targeted the archer through the small port I'd created in the living wall, and let fly. The archer shifted slightly and thereby escaped death: The arrow sheared off the top of their ear and grazed their temple rather than sinking into their eye socket. They cried out, dropped their bow, and disappeared from view on the rooftop.

"That was perfect, ben Bar," I said, "even if it's not what you intended."

Some additional arrows were shot through the wall, and one sank into the thigh of an embassy staff member, but we shot right back, wounded at least two more archers, and put out the fire while preventing any more from being started. The Nentians made no further attempts to harass us, having failed to draw us out into an ambush, and so we let it go. If they had shot fire arrows, however, at the tea treehouse or had concentrated their fire in hopes of killing someone, I am sure the ambassador would have authorized deadly force.

It did clarify whether I should stay or go; I absolutely

needed to stay. I was still needed to defend the embassy, so the caravan would have to head east without me.

Ben Fos and I worked on a secondary inner wall of brambles to reduce the penetration of arrows if they tried that again, and we reviewed fire-control procedures for both the wall and the tea treehouse if they decided to escalate. The ambassador, together with her Raelech colleagues, sent furious messages to the palace about the attack.

A week later I visited the Raelech embassy, using the tunnel between us, and asked to speak to Eimear in private. She took me out to a small sculpture garden on the embassy grounds that featured Raelech heroines shaped out of Nentian stone. There, once I secured an oath from her not to share it with others until she returned to Rael's borders, I told her of my purpose, just in case something dire were to happen to me. Because the establishment of the Fourth Tree *was* historic, and I thought someone besides the Gray Squirrel Clan should know that the world was changing.

And I admit there was some vanity in it too. Defending an embassy and thwarting a mad king served the Canopy and was noble, but it wasn't the sort of thing that would allow me to step out of the shadow of Nel Kit ben Sah. But maybe it indicated that I was worthy of the honor bestowed upon me by the First Tree, which was a thing I was still struggling with. Did I deserve to be the greensleeve who planted the Fourth Tree?

Perhaps the decision was unwise of me, but I didn't think it could hurt. I had no intention of remaining in this part of Ghurana Nent much longer. As soon as I could, I would head north into the Gravewood, far from the scheming of King Kalaad the Unwell.

That tale was one I'd need to fit into my chronological timeline. Pen had mentioned that the merchant caravan we'd met here a couple of weeks ago was just leaving Ghurana Nent. That had ended with Jahm Joumeloh Jeikhs choking to death on a swamp duck and ultimately the pelenaut's decision to send some hygienists back there. If I knew how long it took them to get here, perhaps that would give me an idea of when the hygienist would arrive.

Maybe the hygienist had arrived and saved him already, and they knew I'd be upset.

THE SPIDER QUEEN

The Kaurian fleet arrived and filled our harbor with ships and sails. They brought more food for the city, but once that was unloaded, they had to reload for the journey across the Peles Ocean, taking on different supplies. That was a process that would take days at the least but likely a week or more. An expert in logistics, like the Mynstad du Möcher, would be able to provide a better estimate. But the bard obviously visited with the pelenaut somewhere, because as I worked in the refugee kitchen, his voice carried over the city.

"Pelemyn welcomes the Kaurian fleet under command of Zephyr Bernaud Goss. We are grateful for your aid and that of our Raelech and Fornish allies. We hope you will enjoy our hospitality and breathe peace before it is time to secure it for the sake of all our nations."

"So what news?" I asked Fintan when I saw him after lunch. "Surely with a visit to the palace this morning, you have heard something about goings-on in the north?"

"I have. Incomplete fragments, and not enough for me to weave them together into a narrative, but I have assurances that I will get entire stories soon."

"How so?"

"You've rightly pointed out that we haven't heard from Fornyd in a while. Turns out there have been *very* good reasons for that. The good news is that Daryck du Löngren is coming to Pelemyn tomorrow—perhaps others as well—and I'll have the opportunity to catch up, which means I'll be able to catch everyone else up immediately afterward."

"We'll hear from Gondel Vedd?"

"I'm assuming so. Big day tomorrow. You'll get to hear about Melishev and I'll get to hear what's been happening in Fornyd."

When Fintan took the stage on the wall, he was accompanied by musicians wielding large stringed instruments and a single large drum.

"In Hathrir they have a genre of song called a living dirge. It's pretty grim, as you might imagine, and is basically a death threat set to music. They are ritualistically played before duels between firelords competing for the title of hearthfire. The one I'm going to perform is more than three hundred years old, and it's not because there are any Hathrim in today's stories, but one of the lines does directly relate to something that happens in one of our tales."

The music from the bass drum immediately set a dire tone. He spoke the first verse with pauses before the last word in each line and then sang most of the next verse with a building menace until he screamed the last line.

I'm telling you now just get out of my . . . face
Your prideful strut lacks style and . . . grace
Gonna have to put you in your . . . place
Cave your skull in with my . . . mace

I'm mustering your suffering
It should come as no surprise
When I've shattered all your fragile bones
And your broken body dies

I've curated all my hatred
And cursed your soul and name
Today you've seen your last sunrise:
I'll set your heart aflame!

"Whew! Pretty dark, eh? Let's all give one another a reassuring hug during the break."

Upon his return to the wall, Fintan said, "We're going to head west first and then pull back just a wee bit to Rael," before taking on the seeming of Hanima Bhandury.

Hanima

I don't know what I expected when we entered the walls of Talala Fouz, but it didn't match my expectations.

Well, that's probably not true. I expected fancy people in fancy clothes slurping down marinated eels and chuckling to themselves about luxuries they were going to indulge in later. They would take one look at our plain tunics and shabby boots and know instantly we were poor folks from the backward backwater city of Khul Bashab.

So I chided myself for making such assumptions when we realized that the people in the capital were, if anything, worse off than we had been in our much smaller city.

That had much to do with Talala Fouz being burned down, I supposed, and only partially rebuilt so far.

The guards at the Hunter Gate were pretty suspicious of us since we weren't hunters, and entering the city from the plains rather than the river just wasn't done. Had Numa still been with us, we could have gone right in, because they wouldn't have messed with a Raelech courier, but she had returned to Rael after spending only a day with us on our journey, collecting our stories. Remembering too well what happened the last time we approached the Hunter Gate at Khul Bashab, I warned everyone to firmly control all the beasts of their kenning before we hailed the guards. If they made us afraid or angry, we could not afford to have our creatures kill them in an effort to defend us. One of them had a dimpled chin that looked like a rear end, and the other had a mustache that twirled and curled up at the edges, so I mentally dubbed them Buttjaw and Curly.

"Where's the meat and hides?" Curly asked, inspecting our wagon.

"We're not hunters," Adithi explained.

"What are you, then?"

"Business people."

"Where did you come from?" Buttjaw asked.

We didn't dare tell them we were from Khul Bashab, because Adithi had made the astute observation on the way that we were technically at war with their king, so we lied and said we'd risked an overland crossing from upriver.

"Why?"

"We smelled an opportunity," I said. "The city needs fresh food, and we're going to start a greenhouse. I even brought a hive of bees for pollination." I pointed to a box hive we'd loaded in one of the wagons. There really was a hive in there, but it wasn't the one I'd left behind in Khul Bashab. It was a feral hive I'd found on the way and convinced to swarm into the box with the promise of a steady supply of nectar. I asked two whole bees to come out and then return so the guards would know the hive was real, but reminded the rest of the bees to stay inside otherwise no matter what.

"A greenhouse?" Curly snorted incredulously. "With what glass are you gonna build a greenhouse?"

"We'll no doubt have to negotiate that with local tradesmen."

"Ha! Good luck."

"Might you know a good inn where we could stay for the evening?" I asked, not because I wanted to stay there but because I wanted to know where not to stay. Curly and Buttjaw were not the helpful kind of guards who were interested in actually guarding the populace from misfortune or terror. Those were rare and easy to spot. No, from long experience, I knew they were the kind who delighted in harassing citizens and administering small cruelties.

Buttjaw rattled off the name of an inn and gave directions that I promptly forgot, but I told him it sounded fabulous and thanked him.

We had left a small bag of coins in the back of one of the wagons for them to steal, and Curly took care of that and nodded at Buttjaw. We were cleared to proceed. Nobody had to die for us to enter the city, and nobody would be looking for us. That was so much better than before. I felt like I'd grown.

Of course, back when we'd first been blessed, we didn't expect to return to Khul Bashab and had no coins to offer up to smooth our passage. We'd gone to seek a kenning with Abhi with no expectation of surviving, and we had literally nothing but our bloody clothes on, our starving bones poking at the insides of our skins. And the mindset of the corrupt guards who'd died had been the same as that of Buttjaw and Curly: If they couldn't profit, they would be entertained or enriched some other way. They'd chosen to entertain themselves by threatening us, and it got them skyboned when our animal friends reacted.

I was fairly certain Commander Dhawan was doing his best to weed out such fellows from the new city watch of Khul Bashab, but I'd have to remind him next time I saw him that shakedowns shouldn't be a thing our citizens experienced anymore.

We decided to keep going straight down the main road from the Hunter Gate, since we had no idea of a destination. We figured we'd see what developed. Something very interesting did.

The city was rebuilding, but a very tall tree, distinctly unburnt and looking extremely healthy, towered over all other structures except the city's Tower of Kalaad.

"Hey, doesn't that look like the tea treehouse in Khul Bashab?" I asked Adithi, pointing.

"Yeah! I wonder if that handsome greensleeve is there. He probably grew that tree just like he did the one back home."

"Either way, I think we should go there. We know the Fornish are friendly to us, and they would welcome this hive of honeybees."

We started to head that way but noticed that Suraji had tranced out and was not paying attention.

"Suraji? Are you okay?"

She blinked a few times and refocused on us. "Hmm? Oh. Yes, thanks. I did a search for spiders in town, and there are some *really* interesting ones. Where are we going?"

"To the Fornish tea treehouse."

"Oh! Lovely. Maybe they'd like some garden spiders for their compound."

"I'm sure they would."

It took us a while to get there, and I noticed that we were drawing some stares. I wondered what made us stand out. Our clothes weren't expensive. We didn't have anything flashy except . . . oh. The horses. Those could be considered as a marker of wealth, and I guess they would be if we'd had to buy them. It was easier to come by horses when they just wanted to hang out with Adithi.

When we arrived at the Fornish compound, it was visibly different from the one in Khul Bashab. It was surrounded by a wall of some thorny bushes that looked pretty threatening. We had to circle around it to find an entrance, and a woman named Del Mot Goh told us that the tea treehouse was closed until further notice due to some dispute with the crown.

"What?" I looked around and saw some hired-muscle types watching us from across the street. There were a couple of actual soldiers in the area too, and they were all eyeballing us. Past the Fornish guard at the gate was someone who had to be a thornhand, with spikes growing out of his forearms. Those guys were kind of heavy infantry. Something might be up. "Oh. Well, look, we're not here for tea so much as to see Mak Fin ben Fos. Might he be around? I think he'd want to speak to me."

"I can check. If I find him, who should I say is calling?"

"Hanima Bhandury, a hivemistress from the beast callers clave in Khul Bashab. I'm here with some other beast callers, and we're friends of Ambassador Jes Dan Kuf."

Del's eyebrows shot up. "Interesting. Look, you should know that you're going to be questioned by the king's people no matter what happens next. If you leave, you'll be questioned. If you come in and then leave, you will definitely be questioned."

I waved a hand to dismiss it. "We're not scared of them. We ran off a whole army of those guys. We'd like to come in if that's okay. Maybe you've heard, we're no friends of the king."

Del grinned. "We have. Welcome. But come in quickly before they try to arrest you." She turned and said something in Fornish to the thornhand, who came up closer to the gate to provide protection—or maybe to make sure we didn't try anything aggressive, I don't know. Then she unlocked the gate and swung it open wide. As soon as she did, we darted in there, and Adithi had the horses provide a sort of rear guard— because the Nentians who were watching shouted at us to stop and probably would have arrested us if they could. But they were unable to get past the horses and then the wagons to get to us, so we made it in to a sort of greeting area surrounded by those thorny hedges. One of the hired-muscle guys thought it would be smart to try to take something out of our wagon to . . . I don't know. Make us sad? Make us come back out to get it because it was so valuable? It was a burlap sack full of Suraji's personal items. But it was in the

wagon that had my hive in it, and I told the bees they were
under attack by that man, so he was shortly under attack
himself. He dropped the sack, and when he did, I called off
the bees, though the man had been stung multiple times in
the face and neck. Hopefully it wasn't enough to kill him,
but, regardless, I knew we were going to have some more
unpleasantness after that.

There would be some investigation, no doubt—where
had we come from? I wondered if Curly and Buttjaw would
admit to letting us into the city. In the short term we could
say the man had tried to steal from our wagon and inadvertently disturbed a hive of bees, and that was it. Del Mot Goh
said exactly that to the soldiers who came to the gate and
demanded we be surrendered, suggesting further that he got
what he deserved and that these guests of the Fornish embassy had done nothing wrong. After that she went to fetch
Mak Fin ben Fos, leaving the Nentian soldiers to shout at the
thornhands, which would profit them as much as talking to
the mud down by the riverbank. We were supposed to stay in
the little waiting area until the greensleeve arrived to confirm
our identities.

It didn't take terribly long. He emerged from a gate that
led to the treehouse and smiled broadly when he recognized
us. Adithi took a deep breath and sighed happily with a tiny
shiver.

"Oh, that pretty man makes me tingly," she said under her
breath.

"Me too," I whispered, and then we had to be good because he was drawing near.

"What a pleasant surprise!" he said. "Welcome, Hanima
and Adithi!"

He greeted everyone and invited us into the treehouse,
where we were taken to their largest platform and treated
like honored guests. We met a Raelech bard named Eimear,
who was visiting, a greensleeve named Pen Yas ben Min, and

Ambassador Mai Bet Ken, the woman that Mak loved and who had secretly supported us from afar.

I could see why he was in love with her. Not only was she beautiful, but she was incredibly smart and vibrant and smelled like flowers. We talked the day away, sharing details of what had happened in Khul Bashab. We found out that it was lucky we came to the Fornish first, because the king was a vile man who'd almost sent a cheek raptor to eat Mai's face but threw her into a dungeon to rot instead. She would have died there if Pen hadn't saved her and cured the fungal infection in her lungs.

That explained why the compound was surrounded and well defended; the king had taken a step over the line toward a war with Forn. But since he had no army, he couldn't take another step and "make them disappear" in a supposed accident.

"If you had gone to him, he may have tried to punish you for the rebellion in Khul Bashab. But I think it more likely he would have offered forgiveness if you attacked us," Mai said, "and then he would have betrayed you once we were no longer a threat."

"Ew," Adithi and I said in unison.

"Yes. But comforting in a way to know that he is so predictable. He will always use his power to remove or neutralize any threat to it."

That observation certainly fit the pattern of monarchists we'd seen so far.

"You may not know the answer to this," I said, "but is that the way all the viceroys operate? It seems like you give one man power over others and he stops thinking about anything except how to keep it."

"Most of them do, with a couple of exceptions. The viceroys upriver at Ghuli Rakhan and Ar Balesh try to govern well, perhaps because of their proximity to Rael and the Raelech influence there."

It's such a warm feeling when you meet people you know will be friends. Mai set us up in guest rooms in the embassy and enthusiastically agreed to have my hive relocate in the compound, where they'd pollinate all the things that the greensleeves could think to grow. Suraji agreed to summon some spiders to control pests in the gardens, and we went to our beds happy and full and feeling safe, and it was just the best.

We even had two whole hours of awesome time after breakfast before word came that something dreadful was happening.

Del brought news of reports from the docks: A fleet of boats was landing, and it carried the remnants of Hennedigha's army, now led by none other than our exiled viceroy, Bhamet Senesh. They were acting casual, not marching in ranks or anything, but they weren't dispersing and going home either. They were milling about the city center in clusters.

Most of the Fornish were worried immediately that the army would be used against them as soon as orders were given and that we all needed to prepare for an assault, but Mai Bet Ken held up a finger to keep us from shouting while she lowered her head and thought it through. When she looked up, she was alarmed. "He's not here to bend the knee, and he doesn't care about us. He's here to take over. He has the manpower, and the king doesn't."

"You mean he wants to make himself king?"

"That's the solution to his problem—he's a man out of power and he wants back in, and he's got a few thousand men who will do what he says. This is his chance and he's taking it."

I immediately saw the truth of that. He'd been willing to burn down Khul Bashab to prevent the loss of his power. He'd certainly burn down Talala Fouz again to get it back. "Well, no, we can't let him do that," I said. "He absolutely hates us, and he likes to torture people."

"The king is no better," Mai pointed out.

"Right, except that he's weak at the moment and can't hurt us. Senesh can. So as much as I hate to say it, we need to protect King Kalaad the Unwell from Senesh."

"How?"

I gestured to my friends. "Thunder yaks and blackwings. Adithi will take their horses, if they have any. Suraji might find a few useful spiders, and I can throw bees at their faces." Suraji's dark expression suggested she would go further than that: She looked like she would use a knife if she had one and access to his throat.

"Will that be enough?"

"These guys already broke once. We just need to get someplace where we can see and maybe not be seen. Charvi needs to be able to direct the herd."

Mai looked to Mak. "Can you grow an observation platform for them?"

"No need," Charvi said, waving his hand. "I can't get thunder yaks into the city walls anytime soon, and right now there are only three wart oxen available. It won't make a difference."

"Okay. We need to be strategic, then, and stop this before it really starts. What won the battle before was taking out Hennedigha. That scared the survivors so much that they ran, and it was the best because they all stayed alive. I still want them to live, because some of them, at least, if not most of them, are just trying to earn a living."

"So we need to find Senesh?" Jahi asked.

"Yes."

"And then what?" Suraji asked.

"We convince him to stand down. Somehow."

"You need to talk to him to do that. We can't talk to him from here."

"Well—yes, we can, technically," Mai said, and pointed to the Raelech bard. "Eimear can use her kenning to project anyone's voice throughout the city. They would hear it, in-doors or outdoors. So it wouldn't be a private message, but Senesh would be sure to hear it."

"As would the rest of the army—and the king?"

"Yes."

"Sorry—sorry," Eimear said, holding up her hands. "I'm not really allowed to use my kenning like that. I'm supposed to entertain. Inserting myself into Nentian politics would create no end of trouble for me and for my country."

"Okay, I understand that," I began, "but if you don't insert yourself you might create no end of death for the people in-side the palace walls."

"I wouldn't *create* it—that's absurd," she said.

"No, you just wouldn't prevent it when you had the chance." I pulled a hair from my head and flung it at her, which was kind of silly because hairs don't fly all that well, but I was mad and not thinking about how it looked. "Split that for me, will you, and tell me what's the difference."

She appeared offended, and I was probably in fact being offensive, but I have little patience when lives are at stake, and I had no doubt they were. Talking to Senesh and everyone else would ruin the surprise he was planning, for one thing. The palace would be on alert, for another.

"Look, you do what you need to do as Fornish and Rael-echs, even if that's nothing, but we have already lived our whole lives under Senesh's rule, and the last thing we want is to be under it again. We can't do nothing. So please excuse us while we go somewhere and do something. Can we sit in a different room or platform or . . . ?"

"Of course," Mai said. She gestured to the stairway around the tree trunk. "Feel free to head up to the next platform. I'll send someone with tea presently."

"Thank you."

Adithi, Suraji, Jahi, and Charvi followed me up to the next platform, which was slightly littered with leaves from disuse the past few days. We chose a table and brushed it off before sitting down.

"You have a plan?" Jahi asked.

"Find Senesh first and confirm he's really going to do what we think he's going to do. That's Jahi and me, looking through the eyes of our beasts, and maybe Adithi if he's on or near a horse. Suraji and Charvi, see what forces you can muster if we need them. If there are thunder yaks that can get here in the next hour or so, that might be worth the effort."

Everyone nodded and we got to work, stretching out the senses of our kennings for the animals to which we were attuned. I had the hive I'd brought with me, of course, but there were wasps and hornets and sweat bees and others that I called on to scour the city center and the docks.

Some of them got alarmed by Jahi's blackwings flying over—the sudden shadow of wings tends to freak out insects, I've learned. But I reassured them that the birds weren't out to eat them and were in fact looking for the same guy they were.

It took perhaps ten minutes before Jahi found Bhamet Senesh, surrounded by a few military types who were no doubt his newly promoted tacticians.

"Got him. He's right on the border of the dock district, staying away from the palace. There are men around him and he has some guys running up, saying a few words, then running away."

"They're reporting deployments," Charvi said.

"How do you know where the border of the dock district is?" Suraji asked. "Have you been here before?"

"No. There's a gated archway with a sign over it that says DOCK DISTRICT. He's standing outside it to one side."

"Oh. That makes sense, then."

"Sending some bees over there to confirm . . ." I said. It was disorienting to view the world through compound eyes, but I was getting better at it. Before the minute was out, I saw him. He was richly dressed, like he expected to be holding court soon, and he was moving onto the shaded front porch of a bathhouse and brothel that catered to sailors. Women smiled at him and his companions and made some offers, but he turned them down. Maybe later, he seemed to say, but right now he was busy plotting to usurp the crown.

"What do we do now?" Jahi said. "When he gets his men in position, he'll probably move on the palace, right? The attack can come at any moment."

"Well, we have to wait until he does something. We can't just attack him for no reason."

Adithi spoke quietly. "He gave us many reasons. Pick any day he was in power."

"Our assumptions could be wrong. He might not attack, and then we would be attacking someone innocent."

"He is not an innocent man. He had Sudhi killed. He shot fire arrows into the city from the tower."

"I know, but we exiled him for that. We can't decide that wasn't good enough and now he needs to be assassinated."

"He killed my mother," Suraji said, her eyes unfocused.

"He did? When?"

"Years ago. She worked in a bathhouse, much like the one he's standing outside now. And I don't understand why you're telling us to wait when a few minutes earlier you told the Fornish we needed to do something, and you scolded that bard for refusing to help."

"We *are* doing something. We're in position to thwart him if he tries anything."

"We're also in position to thwart him *before* he tries anything."

"But that would be murder. There has to be a better solution. Jahi, can your blackwings harass the soldiers gathering around the palace? No serious effort to hurt them, just scare them so maybe they'll decide not to follow through on any orders."

"Demoralize them. Sure, I can do that," he replied.

"They're not using horses at all," Adithi reported. "They didn't bring any with them, and all the others are accounted for."

"Bad luck for us. Charvi, what's the status on thunder yaks?"

"I can get some outside the walls in about a half hour, but they'll be tired if I make them move that fast."

"Okay, but—wait." Something shifted in the vision of the two bees I had watching Senesh. Weird movement. What was it? I focused on what they were seeing, trying to locate the source. Under the covered porch of the bathhouse there was some deep shadow, and something in that shadow behind Senesh rippled and moved. Was that . . . ? "Suraji! No!"

An absolutely huge spider leapt from the shadows onto the shoulder of Bhamet Senesh and bit him on the back of the neck before jumping away to avoid the reflexive slap of his right hand. As he grunted in pain, the men on either side of him tried to identify the threat and shouted when they saw the spider, pointing at it and drawing their daggers. It scurried away on the ceiling of the covered porch until it reached the edge, and then it crawled onto the shingled rooftop and disappeared from the men's view.

By that time Senesh was convulsing violently. He fell to his knees and then onto his side, gurgling and crying out, obviously suffering from a fast-acting poison. He died seconds later.

I stood up, horrified. "What was that?" I demanded of Suraji. Her eyes cleared and focused on me coolly.

"A kind of spider that people call a face jumper. She knows Abhi."

"What?"

"He called her Cutie Pie. And he had her kill Hearthfire Winthir Kanek in response to him murdering the king and burning down this city. I had her kill Bhamet Senesh in response to him murdering my mother—a crime, by the way, that was not accounted for in his exile."

"You assassinated him when you just heard me say we couldn't do that."

"What I did was avenge my mother's death. Which I had planned on doing in Khul Bashab, but you exiled him before I could. Coincidentally, I also prevented a bloodbath from unfolding. Because there's not going to be an attempt on the king's life now, is there, Jahi?"

"I don't think so. The blackwings are scattering the soldiers pretty well, and it looks like they won't be getting any orders to attack."

"You see?" Suraji grinned. "We saved a monstrous king from a monster."

"No, what you did was abuse your kenning to kill someone."

"Abhi did it."

"That was different. Winthir Kanek had actually killed the king."

Suraji snorted. "And Senesh had killed my mother. And he was going to order the king killed in a few moments. Now who's splitting hairs?"

"We can't have a murderer in the clave, Suraji. The clave can't pretend what you did was okay. People won't be able to trust us to do the right thing."

The spider queen stood up. "Fine. Expel me from the clave for avenging my mother. I am *not* sorry, and I *would* do it again. I used the exact same spider as Abhi to kill a man who had killed someone else—which, again, is what Abhi did. Are you going to expel him from the clave too? Because your moral code isn't worth a damn if you're not consistent."

"The difference is that Winthir Kanek had just committed an act of war. Senesh was standing outside a bathhouse."

Suraji pointed a finger first at me, then swept it around to include the others. "You committed acts of war. Everyone at this table has. Senesh waged war on poor people for years and was about to take the throne so he could continue that war."

"You don't know the second part for sure, and we made him pay for the first already."

"Made him pay? You threw some vegetables at him and sent him downriver to his cousin. And what did he do there, Hanima? He recruited the remainder of Hennedigha's army and put himself in a position to take over the whole country. You didn't punish him; you practically promoted him!"

"My conscience is clear."

She threw up her hands. "So is mine. How about that?"

"We'll see what the clave says."

"I guess we will, though I imagine the clave will say whatever you want. But I'm not sorry and won't ever be. If the clave needs me to cut ties, so be it. Forn or Rael would love to employ my talents, I'm sure, regardless of my clave status."

At that moment a Fornish teahouse server arrived with a tray full of tea, and Suraji took advantage of the interruption to exit. We thanked the server, and when she left, I spoke to the others. "First, I want to say that my voice is only one of many in the clave, and what I say does not matter more. Your voices are equally important. So I would like to know what you think, and know that if you disagree with me, I will still love you."

Adithi answered first. "I see merit in both arguments, and I will need to think on it awhile. It is not so clear to me as it is to you."

"Okay."

"I'm with Suraji," Charvi said. "If someone killed my mother and I had a chance to take him out, I absolutely would, whether I had a kenning or not."

"Understood."

"I think it matters what his intentions were," Jahi said. "If he was merely here to see the king as a loyal subject, then yes, that was murder. If he was here intending to murder the king and usurp the throne, then Suraji may have saved a whole lot of lives just now by ending his."

"Do you still have blackwings in the area?" I asked, looking through the eyes of my bees again to check on Senesh. He was definitely dead, and a crowd was growing to see what all the fuss was about. "We should follow the two men who were close to him and question them when we can."

"How are we going to do that when the Fornish are stuck in here and us with them?"

"Oh, I'm sure the Raelechs would be delighted to find out for us. Eimear would probably be happy to assist."

When Fintan dissolved his seeming, my interest in the case of the spider queen was piqued, as was that of many others. What happened to her after that? Did the beast callers clave judge her? Was she reported to Nentian authorities for murder? And would her actions have been justified if Senesh really did plan to usurp the throne? No one was suggesting that the death of Bhamet Senesh was a tragedy, but the morality of it was interesting, since both sides were absolutely convinced they were correct.

In Brynlön, there hadn't been a documented case of the blessed killing someone (outside of war) for decades. I'd honestly need to look it up. There were laws against it, as there were in most countries with a kenning—though I wasn't sure what penalties existed in Hathrir. Their laws tended to be counterintuitive to most others. But in Ghurana Nent, they probably didn't have any laws regarding the use of kennings against civilians, since they didn't have a kenning until recently.

"Next up will be my past self," Fintan said, "though it's a version from only a couple of months ago. After that, if you think about it, there will be very little else to tell you, because we will have caught up to the moment that I arrived here. But I will have a couple more tales tomorrow to finish up what happened in Ghurana Nent. For now, we shall go to Rael, and I won't bother spending a seeming sphere on this, since I look almost identical." He passed his hand quickly in front of his face a few times to simulate a seeming. "Here we go."

For a while, I thought that I would not need to travel again, and that grounded me in the most pleasant way. I'd been away from Rael for so long, traveling throughout Ghurana Nent and then Brynlön, seeing things no other Raelech had seen, and I had so much intelligence locked in my memory that I felt sure I'd be needed for frequent consultations, and I had borne witness to such amazing events—the battle of the Godsteeth, the razing of Talala Fouz, the founding of Malath Ashmali, and more—that I could profitably entertain small crowds in pubs for a long time.

But the Triune Council saw things differently. They took in the vast trove of intelligence I'd brought with me and thought I should go out again to get more, since it seemed to find me wherever I went. And if there was a second invasion coming, they wanted someone there to witness it. This did not fall on welcoming ears.

"You want to send me to Pelemyn, the city where the Bone Giants are likely to deploy their most overwhelming forces?"

"Yes," Clodagh said. "But you're leaving now, well in advance of the invasion. Couriers have been flying fast between the various countries of late, and you and Master Courier Numa will be traveling together to inform the pelenaut that we're sending aid and an army to strike back at the Eculans before the invasion is launched. The Fornish and even the Kaurians are joining this effort."

"The Kaurians are getting involved?"

"They have an impressive navy, and I understand they have a new type of barge designed to help feed larger fleets. Intended for their merchant fleets, of course, but easily adapted to a military expedition."

"Forgive me, Clodagh, but I don't understand why my presence is necessary. Numa can inform the pelenaut on her own."

"True, but she can't remain and collect information on developments there. We are assuming a lot of information will be flowing through Pelemyn in the coming months. You're to be part of that. You're going to give and take."

"What will I give?"

"We'd like you to perform for the people of Pelemyn. A true demonstration of what a Raelech bard can do outside our borders. They need to know what's been happening elsewhere, to help them understand why we are *all* invested in defeating this threat from across the ocean. You are uniquely qualified to weave a tale unlike any other. You're a living copy of every bit of intelligence you've brought us, so the pelenaut will feel well informed and assured of our good intentions when we send soldiers into their borders."

"And what do you want me to take?"

"Only what drops in front of you. You're just a passive observer. But a Raelech one."

There were innumerable small details to look after when I was dismissed, but those orders were what landed me here, telling you this story for forty-nine days. I came knowing much but learned so much more once I arrived, and recent revelations will be shared with you very soon. The Raelech and Fornish armies are of course here now, and since the Kaurian fleet arrived this morning under command of Zephyr Bernaud Goss, I imagine that the allied counterattack against the Bone Giants will be launching as soon as logistics are straightened out.

One of the details I had to see to was to ask Abhinava Khose if he wished to accompany Numa and me across the Poet's Range.

"Thanks, Fintan," he replied, "but that's not going to work with my plans."

"Heading home, eh?"

"Oh, no. I don't think I can yet. Melishev Lohmet is still king, and you remember that journal where he made a note to kill me later—what am I saying? Of course you do, you're a bard! Well, I imagine he can still get to me if he finds out I'm back, so I'm going to stay away awhile longer."

"Understandable. What are these plans you have, if I may ask?"

"There's a Nentian trade caravan in town looking for passage over the range, and I think I've convinced them to let me guide them."

"Oh, so you *are* going back to Brynlön, but doing it slowly."

The plaguebringer nodded. "Ohhwuh has eaten most everything available in the compound and doesn't like the sounds of the city very much. He'd like to return to the Gravewood, but neither he nor I think it would be a good idea for him to just head north through Rael. He wants to go back to his territory the same way he came down, through Fornyd. Maybe I'll come to Pelemyn after I see Ohhwuh off. I imagine it's a pretty big city, though. Any idea where I'll be able to find you?"

"Shouldn't be difficult, since I'm to make a very public spectacle of myself. Just ask anyone where you can find the Raelech bard. If that doesn't work, drop by the Raelech embassy and ask for me there. I'll let them know you might show up at some point."

"Good enough," he said, and then looked down uncertainly at his khernhide boots. It was time to say farewell and he was unsure of what to say, so I jumped in.

"It's been an honor, Abhinava Khose. I've never met anyone like you, and you've certainly made my life more exciting. Thank you for letting me tag along."

"I'm grateful you came with me. You've been a really good friend, Fintan. I'm not sure I would be here if you hadn't helped me get out of Talala Fouz and smooth things over with Olet. I hope we see each other again someday, but if we don't . . . thanks for seeing so much of the world with me."

We embraced and then went our separate ways. I couldn't say if he shed a tear afterward, but I can tell you that I sure did. Just like Koesha, I miss that kid.

Once Fintan signaled that was the end of the tale, he added some personal notes. "And I can tell you, Pelemyn, that while I was initially reluctant to leave my comforts behind in Rael, I am so glad I did and am now grateful for this assignment. For I have met the most wonderful friends here and witnessed the strength and resilience of the Brynt people as they mourn and rebuild and help one another recover from a tragedy unlike any in history. I believe you have successfully weathered your nadir, and now that you are resupplied, there is nothing but prosperity and security ahead, provided our mission to prevent the second invasion succeeds.

"And how can it not, with such armies and navies assembled?

"Tomorrow we'll have momentous tales from Hanima and Pen! Sleep well tonight, you allied peoples of Teldwen!"

Day 50

THE FATE OF
MELISHEV LOHMET

According to my calculations—and the aid of Fintan—it had taken the caravan of Nentian merchants thirty-two days to travel from Talala Fouz to Pelemyn, after being guided over the Poet's Range by Abhinava Khose. They had begun their trip—or, at least, Pen Yas ben Min had reported they were leaving—on Snowfall 18, according to Fintan, and arrived on Thaw 18. Their return trip should take nearly as much time, and since Röllend dispatched a hygienist around Thaw 19 and it was now Bloom 30, they might have arrived in Talala Fouz a few days ago. And if they traveled on horseback, without having to adopt the slow pace of wart oxen pulling wagons, that would have sped their arrival. So I genuinely had no idea what to expect. Melishev could be alive and on the mend and plotting further vile murders. He could be wallowing in sweat and vomit and pus. Or he could be dead.

Beyond knowing which of those was true, what I truly wished to know was if he had been the one to actually order Sarena's assassination. It was infuriating to have only partial answers; I'd heard nothing else regarding Dame Nysaa du Valas and whether her story could be independently verified. But I hoped for a large wave of resolution to roll in today.

"When Master Eimear was here, she shared with me a couple of chants that she heard the people shouting in the main market square of Talala Fouz. In lieu of a song today, I thought you might enjoy hearing them, perhaps even trying them on for size. Shall we shout them in solidarity?"

Fintan then led us in a couple of rally cries.

Proclaim it, blame it, say it out loud:
Monarchy shouldn't be allowed!

The voice of freedom sings:
Let this be the end of kings!

"The events that I'm going to share with you today took place in Ghurana Nent on Snowfall Thirty-two, and I arrived in Pelemyn the very next day on Thaw One, having no idea what was happening there. I only learned about these events eleven days ago from Eimear, and this is the reason we needed to go back in time and share the journey of Pen Yas ben Min. Let's check in with the world's biggest fan of Nat Huf ben Zon."

Pen

If it seemed like an army floated into the docks at Talala Fouz every week, that's because it did. One week after the disgraced Bhamet Senesh tried to leverage his way onto the throne with the remains of a defeated army, Viceroy Naren Khusharas from upriver landed with the bulk of his garrison in an attempt to dislodge or repel Senesh's forces. He'd reacted immediately to a report from one of his spies in the capital that a coup was intended, and he never heard that Senesh had been killed by a face jumper before he could make a move. So Khusharas landed with a force that met no resistance, a populace at relative peace, and some questions about where all these guys were going to stay and what food they'd be eating, since food and shelter were somewhat scarce. Most people didn't know how close they had come to a usurper taking the throne.

We knew only because Eimear the Raelech bard confirmed it. A quarter hour after the Nentians from Khul Bashab had gone upstairs to "do something," the spider queen stormed down and out, saying nothing to us, and soon afterward the rest of the beast callers descended to inform us that Senesh was dead. But what they really wanted to know was whether or not he had intended to take over. They knew of two men close to Senesh that they could ask—if they could get safely out of the compound and make those men believe they were someone entitled to an answer.

The bard volunteered to get the information without having to be asked. She and Hanima exited our compound via the tunnel to the Raelech embassy; from there they entered the city and went to find one of Senesh's men—formerly Hennedigha's men—near the palace. It wasn't too difficult, as they were waiting for orders that had yet to arrive and never would. Eimear flirted with one, touched him briefly on the shoulder, and then she and Hanima continued on toward the docks. Halfway to their destination, she pulled a dark sphere from a pouch tied to her belt, threw it on the ground to shatter it, and a gas billowed up and enveloped her form to make her resemble the soldier she'd flirted with, right down to the voice. In this disguise she approached a man on the front porch of a bathhouse that Hanima pointed out.

"Hey," she said, because she didn't know his name, "are we still taking the palace?"

The man flashed a look of annoyance at her—or, rather, at the soldier—and replied, "No. Senesh is dead." He pointed at the body lying on the deck.

"So? Why does that matter?"

"Because he was going to pay us once he was king, you fool."

"So let's make someone else king instead and they'll pay us. Why not you?"

The man gave a short bark of laughter. "I don't want to be king. I'd have guys like you planning to kill me all the time."

"Then what do we do now?"

"Go home and pretend that was the plan all along. There was never any other plan."

The bard left without another word and dispersed her disguise with another sphere of gas once she was out of sight. The old army gradually dispersed too, melting into the populace, catching boats upriver or staying as they wished, but no longer wearing weapons or armor.

That didn't mean we had a reprieve at the Fornish compound—we were still very much under guard until Khusharas arrived with his garrison, and then everything changed.

Eimear immediately went to visit him and asked if she might accompany him as a witness into the palace.

"Why? You think there will be something to witness?"

"I do. The king, if nothing else."

"Make you a deal, there, uh . . ."

"Eimear, master bard of the Poet Goddess Kaelin."

"Right. You sing to me for an hour, Eimear, while I'm in town—songs I've never heard before—and I'll let you come along."

She readily agreed and joined his small escort to the palace, where he was welcomed in, and a soft, breathy chamberlain informed him rather delicately that he couldn't be granted an audience with the king, because, well, the king was dead.

"Beg your pardon?" Khusharas said.

"He died miserably—"

"How?"

"—of his illness—"

"When?"

"—three nights ago, whimpering impotently in his bed, beyond all help."

"Why didn't I hear about this as soon as I stepped off the boat?"

"We kept it a secret because we needed time to inform his chosen successor."

"Oh, great, I'm glad you've got a plan there, that's perfect, very sensible of you. But can I ask—who is this chosen successor?"

"It's you, Viceroy."

"Ha! Good one. No, but seriously, who is it?"

"It really is you."

"What? Come on, now, quit joshing, or back it up. You have that on a piece of paper he signed in front of witnesses?"

"I do." The chamberlain pulled a scroll right out of his sleeve. "I and two others witnessed it."

"Whoa, you were prepared," Khusharas said, taking it from him. "Nothing pleases me like basic competence, my good man, so now I must know your name."

"My name is long and awkward, so I go by Moh, Viceroy."

"Moh. Okay, let's see what you witnessed here." Khusharas unsealed the scroll and read aloud: *"Whereas my body is failing and I have no heir; whereas the kingdom of Ghurana Nent needs stalwart leadership in a time of war; whereas I would seek to prevent a power struggle upon my death: I name Viceroy Naren Khusharas to be my heir and become king in the event of my demise.*

"Signed *King Kalaad the Unwell, Melishev Lohmet,* witnessed by you, Moh, and a couple of others. Huh."

He chewed his lip and read it again in silence, then slapped it with his fingers. "This makes no sense. He hated me."

"Yes, Viceroy."

"Yes? Do you mean yes, he hated me, or yes, this makes no sense?"

"He hated you. I believe I can quote him on this issue, if you'll forgive me: 'I despise that skinny fast-talking horse-faced bastard. I hear he powders his balls.' I could go on at length, because he often did, but I believe the general tone has been established."

"Yes it has, quite well, thank you, Moh. Did he say I powdered my balls like it was a *bad* thing? Never mind, don't answer that. So now we come to the part where it makes no sense. Why did he do it if he hated me? Why didn't he name one of his corrupt cronies to be king?"

"I believe he thought it would cause the most chaos, and when you consider his generally malevolent nature, the decision makes perfect sense. I've been considering it for three days. He did not wish to prevent a power struggle but rather to create one. He knew that his cronies would object to you taking the throne and also that you would object to *them* taking the throne. However, he judged that you would not plunge the nation into civil war over it, but they just might, or else they'd send multiple assassins to remove you. Also, you never displayed any ambition for the job and seemed quite content in Ghuli Rakhan, so he thought he could get his revenge by thrusting the job upon you and thereby ruining your life and perhaps the lives of countless others by depriving Ghuli Rakhan of your leadership."

"Revenge? Revenge for what?"

"I think he envied your contentment, Viceroy."

"Contentment? Ha! I don't think I can remember the last time I felt contented—no, wait. I can. It was just a couple of minutes ago, in fact. Did I hear you say he died miserably?"

"Yes, you did indeed. He died miserably, in tremendous pain."

Khusharas went still and smiled. "I have to admit, that was a pretty good moment. Even on repeat it feels very fine."

"For me also, Viceroy."

The viceroy sprang into motion again. "Ha! Well, that was a petty moment of contentment and that's all I get, because now there's work to be done, am I right?"

"That is correct."

"Are you up to date on how the transfer-of-power thing happens? Because I gotta confess here, I never expected to have it transferred to me, you know, and I imagine I should be giving all sorts of orders right now, but I don't know what sorts they might be. Can you help me out, Moh?"

"I believe so. We must notify the public and the other nations of King Kalaad's death and inform them that you're his successor."

"Ah, see there? Competence. I like that. You should beware, however, because I'm going to add you to the list of people who can get things done, and that means I'll make you work. But from time to time I try to reward my competent people with nifty bonuses of things they like. What do you like, Moh? Boots? Books? Marinated eels?"

"I am rather fond of the Raelech rye they distill in Aelinmech."

"Oh! You're talking about the Good Shit?"

"Yes, indeed: the Good Shit."

And this is where Eimear cleared her throat and spoke up. "Begging your pardon, Viceroy, but the late king has the Fornish embassy under surveillance and locked down because of a disagreement with the ambassador. That relationship might need to be repaired quickly. I can save you the trouble of informing Rael's ambassador, however."

"Whoa, hold on there, Eimear. What's the nature of this disagreement?"

"He had her abducted and thrown in the dungeon because she couldn't get a Brynt hygienist to see him."

"Aw, Kalaad's thundering ass! She's not in there now, is she?"

"No, she escaped."

"Oh. Well, I'm glad she's out, but I guess that means it's not much of a dungeon, is it, Moh?"

"It's horrifically efficient at killing prisoners slowly, Viceroy," Moh explained, "but it isn't hardened against jailbreak attempts by the blessed."

"It was a jailbreak?"

"An unknown greensleeve freed her."

"Okay, well, I obviously need to go deal with that now. But look, Moh, I want you to get me a list of everyone in that dungeon and why they were put there. If they're moldering in the dark just because Melishev didn't like them, then we should let them see the sun again, you know?"

"Of course, I will see to it. What about your accommodations for this evening?"

"Not a priority. Whatever they are, they're gonna be better than a dungeon, so we're going to deal with the prisoners first. And, hey, keep on keeping that secret until I get back, all right? And maybe make me a list of urgent matters you think I should attend to when I'm finished with this."

"I have just such a list already drawn up."

"Wow. I like you, Moh. We're gonna work through that as fast as we can, because this bard here has promised to sing to me for an hour, and that will be an hour of contentment, but I'm gonna earn it. Okay. Eimear. You can guide me to the Fornish?"

"Yes, Viceroy."

"You think they have tea there? I can feel myself starting to slow down, and I gotta ramp back up if I'm gonna start a new job today."

And that is how I came to meet Viceroy Naren Khusharas, who talked faster than anyone I'd ever met even *before* we gave him tea, and then he found another level; I wondered if he thought the rest of the world moved in slow motion. I caught myself speaking more quickly than usual just so I wouldn't waste his time. He'd come to visit Ambassador Ken and me in company with Eimear and several other Nentians, and we gladly invited him in since he relayed through Del Mot Goh that he had come with "joyful tidings of Melishev's miserable demise."

We sat down on the largest platform, together with most of the beast callers—the spider queen who had stormed out the week before never returned. Introductions were made and Khusharas said he was delighted to meet everyone.

"Hey, I gotta say up front, I know I talk fast, but I tend to operate on the principle that good leadership is all about very short meetings. Apologies if I'm skipping twenty to fifty steps of diplomatic etiquette here; it's just that I have a lot to do, and if I don't do it, someone who has a terrible life has to endure it a bit longer.

"So I have two big news items to share with you, and the first one is that King Kalaad the Unwell actually died from being unwell, and because he died three days ago, I'm really glad for the excuse to visit you and get out of the palace because, wow, that is not where you wanna be right now if you're looking to show your nose a good time."

When he paused, there was some stunned silence, partly to process what he was saying and partly to process how he said it. There was no diplomatic playbook for dealing with someone who talked so quickly and casually about their leader's death. Khusharas was fine with the silence—he was even used to it. He busied himself by picking up his hot cup of tea and dashing the whole thing down in three gulps.

"Oh, that's good, that's good right there," he said, setting his cup down with a clink. "Top-shelf stuff, you have my thanks, but can I get maybe a whole pot of that? Yeah, I think maybe a whole pot would set me right."

"He's really dead?" Ambassador Ken said. "Melishev Lohmet died from his disease?"

"Yes and yes."

All the tension sloughed away from the ambassador's shoulders, and she exhaled sharply, then sat up straight and grinned.

"By the First Tree, I'm so relieved," she said. "You may have known him better, Viceroy, but in my sight he had no redeeming qualities. He was a loathsome person. Dying from a wasting disease is precisely the fate he deserved."

"I would not argue with that assessment. So his death brings up a rather obvious question—would you like to ask it?"

"Who will be king now?"

"The answer is: me. He left an official document saying it should be me, witnessed by three people. Eimear here saw me getting the news, probably took a peek and memorized the whole thing, eh? Yeah, she did! Look at her, she's smug about it. I would be too, remembering stuff I saw only once for a few seconds. But, look, you don't know me and I don't know you, but the upside is that I want to be the kind of leader where people in the future won't smile when they hear I'm dead. So to that end: I don't know what Melishev did to you. I'd like to hear what happened, and if I can do something to patch things up between us and restart our relationship, I'd love to do that."

"Oh. Well—do you have time?"

"As long as you have tea. And if you don't mind me getting up to pace a little bit. Helps me think."

So he got a full pot and drank it bit by bit as he paced around the platform and Ambassador Ken provided details of her abduction and imprisonment and, yes, her escape. His eyes swung to me at that last part, and it was unnerving to suddenly be the focus of such an intense person.

"Do I need to be worried, ben Min, about further incursions into the palace grounds?"

"Not so long as you avoid imprisoning our ambassador."

"Ha. I should be safe, then. Good."

Though his constant motion suggested he was impatient, I noticed that he didn't interrupt the ambassador and instead waited until she'd stopped talking, then raised an eyebrow at her until she said, "And that's all."

"Thank you for telling me all that. I'm appalled and very sorry. Those men around your compound—they'll be gone and you'll be free to move about as you wish. Let's start there. I have absolutely no problems with you or with Forn, and I am glad you're here to help both of our countries grow. What sun can Ghurana Nent shine on Forn right now?"

Ambassador Ken blinked and gave a tiny laugh. The change in tone—even couching his language in Fornish terms—was so wildly different that she was taken by surprise. She took a sip of tea while she marshaled her thoughts, then replied.

"We'd like immigration access to the city built by Gorin Mogen on the border with Forn and some input into the forest management on the hills." That first part, I learned later, had already been agreed to by Lohmet, but the ambassador had no confidence he had documented it anywhere or even named a viceroy for the city yet. It was best to ask the new leader to reaffirm it.

"Done. Let me send over someone to hammer out details."

"We'd also like some sort of arrangement where we are able to contract the services of the beast callers clave."

"Okay, that's interesting and something I'll have to come back to, because I haven't had a chance to talk with the beast callers myself, but I'm happy to have that discussion later." Khusharas turned his gaze to Hanima and the others. "I have an awful lot to do today, and this meeting is about Forn, but I would love to talk to you at length. I want to say first you have nothing to fear from me and I seek a mutually beneficial acquaintance. Would you all join me for breakfast tomorrow morning? I promise I won't make you wait."

Hanima beamed at him. "We'd be delighted."

"Excellent. Well, then, I have much else to do, so I hope you all will excuse me. Thanks so much for your hospitality. We'll make amends and I look forward to a prosperous relationship."

Ambassador Ken rose and thanked him and said all was

forgiven and we parted amicably. Everyone felt somewhat giddy after that.

"By the First Tree, what a difference!" Del said. "I think he's right about short meetings being the root of good leadership. I already feel that he'll be good."

Ambassador Ken ordered some celebratory drinks, and I was about two or three cups in before I realized that with this resolution, I no longer had any reason to stay in Talala Fouz. It was time for me to move on and find a place to plant the Fourth Tree.

Yes! Thank Bryn and all the gods that despicable man had exited the world. It felt better to be alive already. But had he been responsible for Sarena?

And furthermore: Why had this needed to be kept a secret from me? Why had Fintan been ordered to keep this knowledge in reserve and Kindin Ladd ordered not to help me find out via other means? What possible calamity had been avoided?

Perhaps Röllend would stop being "impossibly busy" and answer my questions soon.

Fintan left me little time for further rumination.

"So let's skip to the next day's breakfast on Thaw One, a very important meeting happening in Talala Fouz even as I was arriving at the Wellspring here in Pelemyn."

He broke a seeming sphere and transformed into Hanima Bhandury.

Hanima

When I was preparing to leave for the capital, Tamhan insisted that I take a bunch of documents that explained the workings of the clave republic, how we eradicated homelessness, and how the wealthy would still be well off but not obscenely so. He took special pride in a case study that laid bare the accounts of his father, who had become grotesquely rich as a crony of Bhamet Senesh. The clave republic temporarily seized his assets, reorganized his business, paid his employees profit shares for the past five years, then returned the balance—still a sizable sum—to him and let him proceed on the employee-owned profit-sharing model. He remained very wealthy, still the primary owner of Khatri Meats, but his employees' lives were immeasurably improved, and their production soared because they knew that they'd be fairly compensated and continue to share in the profits going forward.

Tamhan did all that publicly to show how it should be done (which alienated his father forever), then gave all business owners in Khul Bashab the option to voluntarily reorganize and share three years' profits; if they waited for the government to do it, they'd be forced to share five.

There was a general rush to reorganize voluntarily. The wealthy merchants' complaints stopped once they realized that it didn't look good to object to treating their employees fairly, but they also saw that their employees worked much better when they weren't being exploited.

Still, I didn't see how that bundle of documents would be helpful in persuading a king who'd sent an army to destroy us. He would never look at them, and even if he did, he'd never consent to giving up his power.

But now that king was dead, and his anointed replacement, a viceroy from Ghuli Rakhan, seemed to be an entirely different sort than Bhamet Senesh or Melishev Lohmet. He might actually read that stuff—or at least make one of his people read it and report back. So I dug it out and cradled it under my arm when we went to the palace.

Adithi, Jahi, and Charvi came along, as did Eimear, the

Raelech bard. Suraji hadn't been seen since she stomped off in anger, and I hoped she was okay. I didn't know where she was or what she planned, but at some point the clave would have to make a decision about her status.

When we arrived at the gate leading to the palace grounds, the guards were expecting us and directed us to the kitchen entrance. There another guard announced us, and the head chef welcomed us and led us into the dining room, asking if we had any dietary preferences.

"We tend not to eat animals," I said, and she gasped.

"Oh, I'm so glad I asked," she said. "I'll make sure there are plenty of options. We have tea and muffins to start. I'm fairly certain the viceroy has already started on the tea, because I've already learned he gulps it down like water—yes! Here we are. Viceroy Khusharas, your guests have arrived."

He had indeed started on the tea. He was holding a cup as he paced around the long dining room table, rattling off some directions to a man I supposed must be a chamberlain. But he stopped midsentence, set the cup down on the table, and threw his arms open wide when he saw us. I noted that he wasn't dressed super fancy. No khernhide boots for him! In fact . . . he was dressed like us—quality woven material for his tunic and pants; even his belt and boots were plant-based rather than leather. I wondered if this was his preference or merely a costume he was wearing for our benefit.

"Ah! Welcome! Thanks for coming. Please sit wherever you like."

Once we'd arranged ourselves and poured tea and put muffins on tiny plates and made introductions, he asked about the Sixth Kenning and the beast callers clave. He utterly ignored his muffin but almost immediately drained his cup and poured more.

"The seeking site changes locations and animals every few weeks," I said, "but the success rate has thus far held steady at twelve percent."

"Only twelve? That's the lowest of any of the kennings, isn't it?"

"Yes. But you do get remarkable benefits. You're attuned to certain animals, become physically stronger, faster, and healthier, and, best of all, you become immune to predation. You can go anywhere without fear of animals eating you."

"Oh, that's fantastic. Can you imagine casually petting a sedge puma? And I hear you already have a clave."

"Yes. But, more important, we have a clave republic."

"You mean Khul Bashab?"

"Yes. I represent the elected city minister, Tamhan Khatri, as well as the beast callers clave. We'd like to be friends."

"Yeah? You sure? Kinda killed a lot of people, didn't you?"

"Only so we weren't killed in turn. Once the monarchist army attacking Khul Bashab broke, we did not pursue, and we're not here to threaten you. We want to live in peace, just not under a king."

The viceroy's lip curled up in a half-grin. "You want to run the show?"

"Not at all. What I want is for you to give serious consideration to the incredible opportunity before you."

"What's that?"

We were interrupted by the arrival of food. Oatmeal and pastries and lots of fresh fruits for us, some fried chaktu patties and eggs for the viceroy. He was quick to spot the difference.

"Whoa, you guys don't eat meat? Okay, that makes sense. I should have thought of that." He turned to the member of the kitchen staff who'd served him. "So, hey, could I please have what my guests are having? Take this back and feed it to whoever's hungry, please. And I want to stress that I'm not annoyed, not even a little bit! This is new for all of us, so just as a standing order going forward, I'd like to be eating whatever my guests are. Great. Thank you so much."

Once the plates were taken away, he pushed back from the

table and stood, immediately telling us to stay seated as he reached for the tea and poured himself yet another cup.

"You probably noticed yesterday, I have this thing where I think best on my feet. You said you want me to consider something seriously, Hanima, so that's how I have to do it. I'll be pacing back here and listening, and whenever you're ready, you tell me about this incredible opportunity."

Well, I wasn't going to eat when he wasn't eating, no matter how hungry I was. But I poured myself a fresh cup of tea and sweetened it with honey. I took a small sip for courage and then held it in front of me, letting the porcelain warm my fingers, and I spoke over the rim.

"Thank you, first of all, for listening. It's more than we expected, and it gives us hope. So the situation is this: You can be the next King Kalaad. You could announce it today and it would happen, and I would understand that decision because it's tradition, and tradition tends to run things. Plus, you know—you'd be king. But the Sixth Kenning is here now, so this is no longer the same country with the same traditional needs. The discovery of the Sixth Kenning was, in my opinion, a revolutionary event, so it's no wonder we had a revolution in Khul Bashab. You can easily see that it's going to come to the whole country soon enough, so the smart play is to get ahead of that. We have a chance to try something new—I'd argue we really *need* to try something new—and we have many alternatives to monarchy. Alternatives where poor people don't have to be poor, and the rich won't be as rich but won't really suffer either. It's the best, and we're doing it successfully in Khul Bashab."

"Who's *we*, Hanima?"

"The people. We held elections and elected a minister to govern us, together with elected councils that represent the city wards and claves. So we have representatives of the populace and businesses plus an executive, and they all work together to make sure everyone prospers, instead of one guy making decisions with his buddies to exploit everyone else for maximum profit. I think, because of your record of leadership and your willingness to listen, that you could be elected minister of the country. Which would have a lot more legitimacy to it than a letter from Melishev Lohmet saying you're the boss now. And if you run for election, I can practically guarantee that you would have the support of the beast callers clave."

"And if I just go ahead and be king, as I'm allowed to do, thanks to that letter?"

"Sure, you could do that. But you'd be the king of a country that wants to be rid of kings. Terrible job security."

He waggled a finger at me as he continued to pace. "Does the whole country truly want that, though? Or just your friends in Khul Bashab?"

"I think everyone wants security, Viceroy. And in Khul Bashab, the beast callers are using their power in such a way as to provide security without oppressing the people they're securing. Because they have accepted the simple fact that compassion is the only moral use of power."

Khusharas blinked rapidly. "Compassion is . . . the only moral use of power?"

"Correct."

He paced back and forth even faster and began to speak several times, never getting out more than a word or two. I sneaked a quick spoonful of oatmeal while he thought about it, his brows furrowing as if the weight of the idea was compacting his skull. He abruptly stopped and turned to look at me. "I never thought of it that way, but that . . . might be accurate."

He realized his teacup was empty and went to refill it, only to discover he'd managed to drain a whole pot already. He eyed our fairly full pot speculatively but then called for more, pretty please, before sitting down in a chair, frowning for two whole seconds, and then springing back up to resume his pacing.

"I am intrigued. So intrigued that you got me to sit down. You have a facility for shifting paradigms, Hanima. So tell me, for the sake of intellectual exercise, what would you have me do?"

"Turn Ghurana Nent into a clave republic. I have plenty of papers on how it works and case studies of our transformed economy. We have no homeless people and almost full employment. To begin, call all the viceroys here. When they arrive, ask them if they could win an election in their city because they have governed well and earned the respect of their citizens. If they say yes, tell them to go back and run for city minister against anyone who might oppose them. If they say no, keep them here."

"Keep them? And do what with them? Throw them in the dungeon?"

"No. Show them how it's done. Win your election. Govern kindly. Give them jobs where they can learn to do the same, and when they're ready, send them to some other city to run for office."

"That's not nearly as easy as you make it sound."

"Oh, no. Governing with compassion will never be easy. The easy thing to do is to be mean and back it up with swords and crossbows, which is what Nentians have done for far too long. We have done that for, I don't know, forty-five kings now? People aren't better off. We have evidence as wide as the plains and high as the sky that this monarchy business doesn't work well for most Nentians. So it's time to try the difficult thing. Which also happens to be the right thing."

"And if I don't do the right thing?"

"Well, if you want to be king, I won't stop you. I'm not here to abuse my power as a hivemistress. But I will be watching. And if you crown yourself king and then use your power to hurt people instead of help them, I will lovingly, with compassion for all Nentians, use my power to throw bees at your face. And I don't care if the bees are asleep for the winter. I'll wake them up."

"Ha! The gentlest and most serious of threats."

More tea arrived for him, and no one said anything until the server departed and the viceroy had poured himself a cup. Once he had and sampled the brew, sighing in satisfaction, he sat down. Did that mean his mind was made up?

"I only asked out of curiosity. The truth is, Hanima, I want to do the right thing. I was doing the best I could in Ghuli Rakhan under the current system."

"I know. I've heard good things. But despite your efforts, you still have a lot of people there living in the mud while others are living in ridiculous luxury. Which isn't your personal failing so much as a failing of the system. Monarchy is designed to grind up people to feed a few at the top, so anything you do to help people is just mending the hem of some pant legs that will always be raggedy as soon as you put down your needle and thread. Like all these charities that the church likes to talk about—every single charity that tries to alleviate a humanitarian crisis is a systemic failure, because there should be no humanitarian crises. So think about what you could accomplish as a leader if you adopted a system that is designed instead to help as many people as possible. A system, I might add, that has the backing of the beast callers clave."

"You think it could work for the entire country?"

"I do. It's working in Khul Bashab and it's the best. Which doesn't mean it's flawless. Someone will try to find ways to exploit it and introduce corruption, and when they are successful, we'll have to improve the system. But it is definitely a better system to begin with than monarchy, and we should not refuse to make the attempt to improve our lives and our country just because it's our tradition to be terrible at it."

"Can you explain how the clave republic works? Get into details, I mean. If you're comfortable with that."

"I think the papers I brought from Minister Tamhan Khatri would explain it better—he has a mind for politics and economics. It's his special genius." I pointed at the bundle resting in the middle of the table. "Please review them at your leisure. The essence is that everyone deserves to profit from their labor, not merely business owners. You begin by lifting up the least of us."

"Huh. I would definitely like to dive into those papers."

A server arrived with a bowl of oats and fruit for the viceroy, and with a twitch of startlement, he realized none of us had touched our food. "Maybe we should begin by lifting up a spoon to our soup holes. This was supposed to be a breakfast. Sorry. I just got so absorbed and wrapped up in possibilities there."

I smiled at him and took a bite. I had no illusions that he was perfect—no one was, certainly not me—but at least he was capable of thinking of someone else besides himself. It occurred to me that worlds can change for the better when the right people are in the right place at the right time, but it very rarely happens. Most often the wrong people are in the right place at the right time to inflict untold suffering on the rest of us. That's probably because it's the wrong people who crave and grasp power to dominate others, then cling to it with everything they have. We need more people who seek power for moral purposes—for compassion.

"Hey, what if I do this?" Viceroy Khusharas, apparently unable to sit still for an entire minute, put down his spoon and took to his feet again, talking rapidly and pacing. "Bear with me now, because I'm doing a bit of thinking aloud, and—hey, you know what? I need Moh in here. He's my new chamberlain guy, has this sense of humor that's dry as the Glass Desert and this soft voice that flutters in your ears like moth wings. He's absolutely hilarious but super competent.

I'm telling you, you're going to love him. Moh! You in shouting distance? Moh, get in here!"

A middle-aged man we had seen Khusharas talking to earlier entered from the kitchen, dressed well but not gaudily. He had apparently been waiting just out of sight in case the viceroy hollered for him. He did not hurry to the viceroy's side, but neither did he tarry. He oozed confidence and dignity, and his voice was fluffy somehow, like pillows.

"You summoned me with some urgency, Viceroy?"

"Yeah, Moh! And like a thunderbolt from the fingers of Kalaad, kaboom! You arrived. You are sky-blue magic, my man. I just want you to be present and offer feedback if I say something that won't work or might backfire in a way I'm not seeing."

"You want my advice . . . on an idea?"

"That's exactly it. Like, if I am metaphorically going to step in a pile of thunder yak shit, I want you to warn me, and I will be so grateful, so, so, so grateful, okay? I also want you to warn me if I'm *literally* going to step in a pile of thunder yak shit, just to make that clear, but I think we're safe in that regard at the moment. The point is, I need good information and advice to make what I hope will be good decisions, so I have to trust you to tell me things and you have to trust me when I say it's okay to tell me. Like right now I'm going to shut up so you can say something, so, yeah, go ahead."

"I stand ready to advise you."

The viceroy's face split into a grin and he looked at us, pointing at Moh. "Eh? What'd I tell you? Isn't he great?" He didn't wait for us to answer but immediately began pacing again, waving his hands around as he spoke. "So my idea is that if we want to transition to a new system of government, that's great, but that also requires a lot of time and uncertainty and attention to detail, and we definitely need to look at those details under a clear sky, which means we need a clear authority in the meantime or people might get unsavory ideas. The simplest solution is that I have to go ahead and *temporarily* be king. The problem is if I take on the title of king, some people might not believe I'll ever give it up, right? Yeah, Hanima, I'm looking at you there, getting ready to throw bees at my face. You'll think, oh, great, it's another knob in a crown telling us what to do, nothing ever changes. So what I'm wondering is, what if we can kind of make a big deal of my nickname at the coronation tomorrow and say that I'm not King Kalaad the Manic or King Kalaad the Teabrained but King Kalaad the Last? As in, this is all there is, folks, there won't be any more kings, and I'm not planning on holding on to this circular hat for long. Like, what if I promise there will be something else coming soon, and that I'm only going to be king until we can elect some leaders? But warn people too—I'm thinking of people like the Senesh brothers—that they better not get any ideas of usurping the crown during the transition or the beast callers will have something to say. Not that I want to speak for you, you understand. I'm not sure what you'd be comfortable with. I don't know—see, this is where I need you to jump in, Moh, and tell me what you think, so yeah, go, I'll be silent and maybe have some more oatmeal, because I hear food works better if you eat it."

He sat down and I looked to Moh, who blinked twice before speaking.

"Provided the beast callers clave will support your brief transitional regime," he said, "and we circulate a date immediately for national elections, with details to come a bit later, I think that would work—if you have a plan, that is, to deal with the remaining Viceroy Senesh in Batana Mar Din. Because he will not meekly submit to an election that he will obviously lose."

Khusharas only winked at him and smiled around his spoon. Then he looked to me and made a tiny gesture of his hand to indicate that he'd wait for me to add something.

"As you said, Viceroy, we will need a clear sky under which to examine details. But in general principle, I believe the clave would support a transitional monarch and protect him should it become necessary. But I must emphasize we will act in a defensive role only. If Viceroy Senesh refuses to give up his power willingly, we will not do anything to force him. The kinds of employment the clave will accept are open to negotiation, but in general we are not to be used to achieve victory in conflict—except in defense, as we fought for Khul Bashab against the former king's army."

"Okay, okay. That's fine. My plans for him didn't involve you anyway, so I think we're looking at the same sunset here. Why don't we pick a date for Ghurana Nent's national election and then work through as many other details as we can until Moh here tells me it's time to move on to some other pressing business? Then we can keep meeting to work out more details after I have a chance to digest the wisdom of Tamhan Khatri."

I wanted to ask him what plans he had for Senesh but figured I should focus on what he asked me. "We are the nation of the Sixth Kenning now, so how about six months after your temporary coronation?"

The viceroy shot a quizzical glance at Moh and received a spare nod in return. He slammed a fist down on the table, grinning wolfishly.

"Yes! Kalaad in the sky, we're efficient! This is a good team. I like this. We're going to get so much done." He suddenly went still, closed his eyes, and shuddered. "But maybe after I visit a lavatory, because, you know. I've had some tea. Excuse me."

It was too soon to know whether Viceroy Khusharas would follow through on his promises, but his willingness to take steps in the right direction gave me so much hope. And you know what? Hope is the best.

———

Fintan dissolved his seeming in a cloud of green smoke. "So that was almost two months ago," he said. "And I haven't heard any more than that, except that Ghurana Nent will be having its elections about four months from now and will transition from a monarchy to a clave republic. If I'm lucky, tonight I'll hear about what happened in the north, and I'll be able to share that with you over the next few days. Have a wonderful evening!"

It *was* going to be a wonderful evening—that is, if I could find something to pour into a glass and raise it to honor my wife's memory and celebrate the painful, pathetic death of the man who ordered her assassination.

People near me on the wall were wondering if the Khul Bashab reforms had a chance of working on a large scale and maybe of taking hold worldwide.

"I'd like to read that stack of papers Hanima gave to Khusharas," said one man, whom I recognized after a moment as a longshoreman who had served me breakfast once in the palace. He was speaking to a mariner stationed there for security. "The idea that employees should share in the profits of a business is a sound one, but what about government workers like us? The government isn't a for-profit enterprise. There's no opportunity for us to get a big payday. If the government gets a budget surplus, they don't share it with us, eh?"

The mariner nodded and gave the longshoreman a side-eye. "It's the source of corruption. Greedy lads figuring out how to steal from the public they're supposed to be serving."

"Aye," the longshoreman said, apparently unconscious that the comment might be directed at him.

As I joined the general crush heading for the stairs, I heard others talking in admiring tones about the ethos of the clave republic.

"Lift up the least of us," a woman said, as if trying on the phrase to see how it fit. She was middle-aged and speaking to a peer. "I think that's what the pelenaut's been trying to do with the refugees, you know, but I like hearing that put into words."

"Mm-hmm," her companion agreed. "That's a pure way to live for sure."

I smiled wryly. While the events in Ghurana Nent might bring some economic headaches our way, Röllend didn't have to worry about a revolution or winning his next election. Whatever personal resentment I felt at the moment, it was abundantly clear that he and his government had been trying to help people and they appreciated it.

As the crowd inched forward, I saw the bard a few folks away, moving toward the stairs as well.

I was about to thank Fintan for sharing those stories, finally, but someone else called out and beat me to it.

"Those were the finest stories I've ever heard!" a young man said, and when Fintan located the source of the voice, his face lit up.

"Abhi! You made it!"

They rushed to embrace like old friends, and my jaw dropped. Abhinava Khose, in person! Fintan had spoken just the day before of leaving him behind in Rael, but obviously the plaguebringer had managed to catch up in the last couple of months. I wondered where his animal companions were but assumed he must have them tucked safely away nearby. I was so enraptured with their reunion and heedless of my surroundings that I didn't see the pelenaut coming until he cleared his throat next to me.

"Dervan," he said.

Blinking, trying to gather my thoughts and adjust to a very different situation, I managed to say his name back to him by way of greeting, but my voice was cold as the Northern Yawn. "Pelenaut Röllend."

"This might be a good time to have that conversation you've been wanting," he said.

He was alone, no mariners or lung hovering about, but he didn't look like he was trying to blend in with the common man. He sort of had that "behold, I am a world leader" look going on, with a twisted sash in blues and whites mimicking rapids streaming across his chest; on his breast was a shell with mother-of-pearl, gold, and gems nestled in its center. People around us went a bit starry-eyed and slack-jawed to be suddenly in his presence, and peripherally it looked as if a few of them might say something to him, but they decided against it once they assessed the intensity of our regard. Rölly appeared tired, but he was focused in a way I'd seen before: He had a problem to solve. And I was the problem.

"I don't think I'm fancy enough for such a conversation," I said, gesturing to his tailoring.

"I just came from the Wellspring. It's been quite the day. Quite the last few weeks, actually."

"That's your excuse for avoiding me? You've just been too busy to talk to me?"

"No, I have a much better excuse than that. But why don't we go to your place? I'm certain as the tide you want to yell at me, right?"

"You are absolutely correct."

"Good. I want to let you do that properly without interference. And then I'm going to yell back."

"Yell back? What have I done, except get shut out?"

"Let's save it for your place. Too many ears up here."

That was true enough. We descended from the wall and walked in tense silence back to my house, though the pelenaut got hailed many times along the way; he waved and smiled and protested that he couldn't stop to chat. The only minor pause was when a longshoreman caught up with us, apparently by prearrangement, to hand over a bottle of the Good Shit.

"To fortify us," Rölly said, waggling it a couple of times as we continued.

I was finally a priority. Why now?

Once we entered my home, I fetched two glasses and Röllend uncorked the bottle. He poured us a couple of shots—doubles, I noticed—and we clinked silently before tossing down the lot. The burn traveled up to my sinuses and we both coughed a bit, but I was glad for the warmth.

"Okay, my friend," the pelenaut said. "Open that sluice and flush out your anger."

"You've lodged a crab claw in my anus, so it's going to be rough," I said. "You haven't been treating me like a friend at all. Apparently, you've known for more than a month that Melishev Lohmet ordered Sarena's death, and you didn't tell me."

"And you found this out from Dame Nyssa du Valas."

"Yes. Whom your mariners arrested a few days ago with no explanation. Was it true? He ordered it, and Jasindur Torghala carried it out?"

"Yes, as far as we're able to confirm, that was true."

"So then you not only didn't tell me, but you sent a hygienist to Ghurana Nent to heal him!"

"She obviously did not heal him. By the time we sent her, he was already dead."

"But you didn't know that when you gave the order. The potential was there—the intent to heal a man who ordered the murder of one of your citizens. One of your spies!"

"The potential was not, in fact, there at all. I was trying to help the merchants whose families were at risk. I think that tomorrow the bard will be sharing more about their journey here. You remember meeting them—they were desperate for help. My hope was that if Lohmet received news in advance that a hygienist was on the way, the merchants' families would be spared. But we suggested to the hygienist that she take her time arriving, and that part worked out."

"Fine. But Torghala—the man who actually poisoned Sarena—was escorted to a ship and sent home."

"Expelling him was the best we could do at the time, because he had diplomatic protections. But, as you heard today, there will be a new administration in Ghurana Nent in a few months, and communication between us will resume. When it does, you may be sure I will be bringing up the issue of Torghala first thing. His punishment—I solemnly promise you this, Dervan—will be at the top of my list, before we even begin talks on resuming trade. And you heard how quick this Khusharas was to address grievances when the Fornish brought theirs to him."

"Good. So why couldn't I know any of this earlier? Why did I have to wait? You could have told me all this before."

Röllend sighed and briefly pinched the bridge of his nose, as if I was giving him a tremendous headache. "Because, Dervan, you are a terrible spy."

"I know!" I exploded, throwing my arms wide. "I told you that on the day you recruited me for this assignment! I am not cut out for deception and skulduggery and whatever. By training and inclination, I am predisposed to telling the truth—the worst spy possible! And you recruited me anyway. So don't you dare let that flotsam wash up on my shores!"

"I'm not laying blame—Bryn drown me if I am. I'm explaining why you had to wait. These present-day additions you've been making to the bard's tales—which I know I encouraged you to write—made you a target. The Wraith read them. His people read them. And from that he figured out how to manipulate you. He cooked up that fake story about Clodagh arranging Sarena's death, put you in his debt, and then used you as a courier to deliver a dead-drop note to Lorson. But"—he raised a hand to forestall my protest—"that's not all. He had more people than just the woman you called Approval Smile. The network was larger than that. You were a possible source of intelligence, and your point of vulnerability was known: your wife's murder."

"What are you saying?"

"I'm saying I kept you in the dark regarding Melishev because anyone who worked closely with the Wraith and knew of your writings might try to use them as leverage to turn you. And eventually that's exactly what happened. Nyssa du Valas told you what she'd told us earlier, creating a sense of obligation. That by itself was a tip-off, but there was a chance she simply suffered a terrible lapse in judgment. When she approached you again and tried to get you to reveal something about what was happening in Fornyd, however, that was a clear sign she was working for someone else."

"So you used me as bait. Chum to attract a bladefin."

"You mean to catch an enemy spy? Yes! And I had to prioritize that, Dervan. It's my literal job and sworn duty to defeat our enemies."

"Leaving aside how incredibly hurtful it was to use me like that, what master do you imagine she has? Lorson's dead. And you have the Wraith imprisoned with Approval Smile."

"No, they're both dead now, as is Nyssa du Valas. I put her in there with them to see if they might say something useful, and instead Approval Smile killed her."

"Why?"

"An excellent question. Maybe they don't suffer failure. But Dame du Valas had a wraith in her—it came out when she died. I drowned them all then. But to your point: I imagine there are plenty of masters left in Ecula, and there might be a way to contact them. And even if that's simply to warn them we are launching our own fleet, we don't want that. And we didn't want you inadvertently letting slip any information about the goings-on in Fornyd, so all of that was embargoed too."

It was breathtaking, how I'd been pushed around like an urchin piece in a game of Otter Colony. "Okay, Rölly, I'm no longer leaving it aside—I have to circle back and repeat: That was an incredibly hurtful thing to do to me."

"For which I apologize and hope you can forgive me. But

you ironically turned out to be an asset by being incompetent."

"That doesn't make me feel any better."

"Maybe this will." He ticked off points on his fingers. "Melishev is dead. Torghala will be punished. And because you made such a tempting target, you helped us catch the Wraith, Approval Smile, and Nyssa du Valas."

"It would be one thing if I had done any of that intentionally. But you manipulated me every step of the way. There's not a lot of difference between what you did and what the Wraith did."

"There's a huge difference, Dervan. The Wraith was trying to destroy us. I did what I did to protect our people."

"You still used me, and you didn't have to do it that way."

"You know what? It worked."

That provoked me to raise my voice. "So that's your defense? You'd do it again?"

"Absolutely!" he roared back.

"I think you'd better go." Reaching out, I pulled the bottle closer to me. "This stays here."

Rölly deflated. "I'm sorry I didn't think of a better way, Dervan. But exposing those spies in our government was a victory for us."

He waited for me to respond, but all he got was a stony glare. That metaphorical crab claw was still lodged in my anus.

"You're doing well with your work," he said, backing away to the door. "Keep it up. Governing is messy, and I'm glad you're recording that. Because all our lives are messy. People are messy. Friendships are messy. Any order we impose on the world is just making the bed until it's undone again. But we have to make the bed."

I let him exit without making a comment, and then I poured myself another drink. First I'd need to cycle back through the argument and think of all the things I should have said but didn't. *Sometimes people shit the bed too,* for example, might have been a nice parting shot. But then I'd need to figure out if either of us actually won, and if that mattered.

That was going to take a while. I poured myself another shot.

Day 51

THE ISLE OF BLIGHT

My hangover was magnificent in the morning and a fitting punishment for my navel-gazing and inebriated excess. If there was any swell to the trough I was in, it was that my anger was spent. Some resentment might linger, but that was a fish of a different scale.

The truth was that if I swam out past the reef for some perspective, Rölly was right. Exposing the spies and securing our national safety had to be the priority, however much I might wish for other things—like, to appear as if I had a clue about my surroundings, if I couldn't be a fiendishly clever master of espionage. I was glad for the final score in his game, in other words, but ashamed that my own shortcomings had allowed me to be used with such facility. My pride was battered and wounded and probably had some weeping sores and other metaphorical ailments.

But the same distance from the reef allowed me to see that at least my suffering had a point to it, whereas many of my fellow citizens suffered—and died—without any clear reason why. Perhaps this chronicle, once published and distributed, would help someone appreciate the scale of what happened and allow them to place their own experiences in a larger context.

I skipped working at the refugee kitchen that day and hoped the chef wouldn't be too incensed by my absence, using the morning instead to recover so that I was nominally functional by the time I went to meet the bard. He was simply agog.

"Dervan. I spent all night and this morning hearing what's been going on in Fornyd."

"From Abhinava Khose?"

"Yes, but also the second könstad, and Daryck du Löngren, and Koesha Gansu. Let me tell you: It will liquefy your brain."

"I think I may have already done that last night," I muttered.

"What?"

"Never mind. You were saying?"

"I'm just astounded. Four more days, I think, and we'll be finished. Which should bring us fairly close to the departure of the fleet."

"Excellent," I said, and he frowned at me.

"Is something wrong? You're not even interested in what this mind-melting stuff might be?"

"Of course I am. But I shall wait. Far be it from me to know something before I'm supposed to. That would be dangerous."

"What are you talking about?"

"It doesn't matter. I am bitter about old fish, and you shouldn't mind me. We'll get to each tale when its moment arrives. For now, it's time to record yesterday's."

"Yes, I suppose it is."

Fintan had a much easier time getting the crowd fired up for the day's tale. First he told them they had four days of stories left, all of them happening fairly recently and very close by. That caused some excited babble to swell from the city. But, for reasons Fintan assumed would become clear, he was going to start them out with a sung sonnet about sonnet wolves, written by a Raelech bard about a hundred years ago.

What you hear at night in the Poet's Range
Are conversations of carnage and woe
As the black sonnet wolves warble their strange
Language and softly stalk you from shadow.

> No one can parse the meter of their rhyme
> Except that when they speak from forest gloom
> One feels the quickening shortness of time
> And prepares to meet their imminent doom.
> Beautiful sound of death, a set of chords
> Fulsome and sweet, a fell chorus blending,
> Swelling, coming ever closer toward
> Your position, until your life's ending.
> In the Poet's Range the weak and the strong
> Alike hear the wolves sing their mortal song.

After the break Fintan said, "We're going to begin today with Abhinava Khose, who is not only back in Brynlön, he's here in Pelemyn, and he'll be joining us as we launch the counterattack! He told me this story last night. But I'm going to remind you all that in terms of timing, he was leaving Rael soon after King Kalaad the Unwell died, except he had no way of knowing that."

Abhinava

Shortly after Fintan departed for Pelemyn in the company of his spouse, Numa, I was hired by a Nentian caravan to escort them safely across the Poet's Range, since they had urgent business in Brynlön and the Granite Tunnel was still collapsed. They'd been trying to find a company of Raelech mercenaries willing to do the job and were wincing at the cost. I said I'd do it for a third of the price, guaranteeing their safety from animals, and I was a whole lot cheaper to feed than a squad of fighters. They tried to haggle me down to a quarter, but I held firm. It was a great deal and they knew it, and they liked the idea of paying a Nentian instead of a Raelech anyway. And they appeared to be in a hurry.

Once we were under way, I found out that they were not only a trade caravan but also a diplomatic one. They were to appeal directly to the pelenaut himself, if possible, on behalf of King Kalaad the Unwell, which rang a chorus of unwelcome bells in my head. Had they engaged my services in order to capture or kill me? I'd be making my own meals and sleeping apart and under watchful guard, thanks to Murr and Eep and Ohhwuh, just in case. But they did not present themselves as the sort of men accustomed to skulduggery, and they'd shown little curiosity in my kenning or why I was in Killae except so far as it could help them.

The leader of the group was an older, jowly man from Talala Fouz named Subodh Ramala. He had an entire wagon full of dried cured meats and wheels of cheese that kept well in the winter months. He looked tired and irritable, however, so I asked gently if he traveled often; the road didn't seem to agree with his constitution.

"We wouldn't be making the trip at all if it weren't for the king," he said, and the others grunted assent. "We would prefer to sell our products locally and remain at home with our families. But he removed our families from the equation, so we had no choice."

My sharp intake of breath startled Eep, and she screeched. "What? He killed them?"

"No. They're his 'guests,' in the sense that they're politely held hostages. Should we fail, then we won't have families anymore."

"That is utterly skyboned. Why you?"

The old man snorted derisively. "Because he doesn't trust any of his diplomats. Thinks they're all out to get him, and maybe they are."

"How would they get him?"

"By not relaying his most urgent request for help," Poudresh Marekh said. He was a fiber merchant—cotton, hemp, and the wools of llama, alpaca, and sheep—and walked next to a wagonload of blankets and clothing made from these. He'd made the interesting decision to grow patchy sideburns that connected to his wispy mustache but left his chin shaven clean, but it wasn't a chin that especially begged to be shown off. It was a shy chin and looked like it might prefer to hide behind a curtain of whiskers. "He claims some Fornish ambassador promised to apply pressure on his behalf but broke that promise, thinking she would suffer no consequences."

"Forgive me if I'm being naïve here, but why doesn't he use Nentian diplomats? Surely they'd be more loyal?"

The leathers merchant, Ghurang Bokh, smiled wryly. "Diplomats can be more loyal to systems of power rather than to a person, and they have access to leverage outside his control."

"Like what?"

"Contacts with powerful people—some of whom are safely beyond his reach. We do not have that leverage. He has all the leverage against us, so to him, we are trustworthy."

"And he is . . ." I trailed off, letting the obvious conclusion about his character go unspoken. But the last of the merchants, a bootmonger named Jahm Joumeloh Jeikhs, responded over his shoulder from the front of the column as if I'd said it.

"Yes, he is." He horked up something green from a lung and spat to the side. "An absolute shitsnake. May he lie down with flesh eels and never wake again."

There was much in that vein I could say, but out of an excess of caution—in case this was entirely fictitious and a ploy to draw out a treasonous exclamation by making one of their own—I confined myself to saying, "I'm sorry. It's a terrible situation to be in. I'm glad I can help you get through the trial."

They all grunted an acknowledgment of the sentiment, but they weren't particularly comforted. They fell into silence, lost in their thoughts, and I took the opportunity to

send Murr off to hunt while I spoke with the wart oxen pulling the wagons, asking them how they felt and if they'd be up
to walking a bit faster if I could get them a treat or see to
anything bothering them. They were in pretty good shape,
but one had an itch she wanted scratched, and I took care of
it. They moved faster after that, and the merchants were very
pleased. It may have been a tactical error, however, because
this practical demonstration of my kenning—besides the fact
that I had three animal companions—finally pulled their
thoughts away from their own troubles and stirred their curiosity.

"Why are you escorting merchants to Brynlön when you
could be lord of the plains in Ghurana Nent?" the bootmonger asked. He was the youngest of the lot and paid enough
attention to fashion that his tunic matched his khernhide
boots. Both were gray and embroidered with teal thread, and
his black breeches and belt, echoing his hair, kept things
classy rather than gaudy.

"Lord of the plains? I don't even know what that means."

"Come on. If you can have animals do anything you want,
you could seize power and run the country."

"You're right. But I have no desire to be king or to do the
bidding of anyone who wants the job. I've removed myself
from the sphere of ambitious men."

"Do you not have any ambitions of your own?"

"Of course. I want to see the world, and I'm pursuing that
right now."

"That's it? See the world?"

"Very few have seen it. And since I have the freedom to
travel where I wish, it would be a shame to waste the opportunity by staying in one place."

"Don't you want a family?"

Shrugging, I said, "Perhaps someday, sure. I'm in no
hurry."

That quieted them for a while as they digested it, thinking

perhaps what they would do if they had been blessed as I was, at my age. Maybe they'd do the same and explore: If nothing would eat you and you had no family ties, why not? But some hearts—I may go so far as to say most hearts—are not fulfilled by wonder. Many require a deep personal relationship with someone to feel whole. But some gather whatever power they can and twist like funnel clouds, consuming yet never satisfied, spreading ruin wherever they go. The king was one such, and many more like him were out there, hiding in plain sight because they lacked the power to do as they wished, avatars of woe waiting for their moment. So I figured it was only a matter of time before one of them circled back to the subject. Statistically, there was a decent chance at least one of them dreamt of power.

Murr's return some while later with a bloody muzzle made Eep squawk.

"What, are you hungry now?" She nodded her head. "Go on, then. Find something delicious. I think there's a nest of voles in the meadow that way, past where Ohhwuh is trying to find leaves in the snow." I pointed to the southeast. She chirped and launched herself in that direction, and Ohhwuh bugled a hello as she flew over.

And that is when Jahm Joumeloh Jeikhs spoke up.

"You could free our families," he said. "Why don't we do that instead of walking all the way to Pelemyn to try to get a hygienist for him and then hoping that the king will keep his word?"

"That's what he wants? A hygienist?"

"To cure him, yes. He actually is unwell, you know. It's not just an epithet."

"And what happens if he dies?"

"Our families die. He's given orders."

"You heard him give the orders, or he just said he did?"

"What's the difference?"

"I've heard he lies a lot."

"We can't take the chance."

"Trying to free them would also be taking a chance."

"I think the odds would be skewed heavily in your favor," Jeikhs replied.

"Maybe so. But it's not the kind of work I'd be interested in. I hire myself out for protection."

"If it was your family held hostage, you wouldn't hesitate."

"You're right. That would be deeply personal, just as it is to you. But professionally, I now only accept contracts where violence is a mere possibility rather than a certainty."

"Now?"

"Yes. My first contract was basically assassination, though it was also supposedly to defend the country against the Hathrim invasion down by the Godsteeth. I'll regret what I did for the rest of my life."

"You were there?" Subodh said. "But the Hathrim were defeated, so you did defend the country."

"Yes, but—"

"Hold on, hold on," Poudresh interrupted, frowning at me. "Who hired you to do that?"

"Viceroy Melishev Lohmet."

"You mean the king?"

"He was viceroy of Hashan Khek at the time."

"I don't care about that! You've worked for the man who has our families, and now you're going to let him keep our families hostage!"

"No. I accepted a contract to escort you safely across the Poet's Range to Tömerhil, and that's what I'm going to do. I did not know about the situation with your families when I agreed to the contract, so you can't accuse me of secretly working on the king's behalf. I'm working for you under the original terms. I guarantee you'll get to Tömerhil safely."

Poudresh argued that I had a moral responsibility to directly intervene to save lives if I could.

"But would I be saving the lives of the people guarding them? No, I'd most likely have to kill them. Attempting a rescue would almost certainly result in someone's death, perhaps many someones, and there's no guarantee I'd be successful in saving your families. Plus you'd permanently become fugitives from the king afterward. The best course is the one we're on—get you to Pelemyn and secure a hygienist so your families can be freed."

They grumbled and had nothing kind to say after that, and I walked a bit ahead of them with Murr and Eep, since my company was not wanted. Ohhwuh continued to keep pace with us and graze as he walked.

We spoke very little in the coming days and had little reason to do so until we were traversing the pass in the Poet's Range. The merchants had seen and heard sonnet wolves and meat squirrels investigating the caravan but noticed that they never attacked, so my word was good as per the contract, until we met with an obstacle that wasn't animal in the general sense.

Murr and Eep tried to warn me, making noises that I couldn't interpret properly, but I don't think I could have done much even if I'd been able to understand them, because a dozen Raelechs stepped out from behind cover all at once, shouting and brandishing weapons. The swords I wasn't too worried about, but the bows could be problematic. I immediately told Eep to stay on my shoulder and Murr not to move. If Murr looked like he was going to attack, they'd put an arrow in him for sure. Ohhwuh was off in the woods somewhere—in earshot, probably, but he wouldn't understand a word anyone but me said.

I didn't understand what they were saying, but they were obviously bandits and intended to rob us. They weren't wearing any Jereh bands, and that in itself was a crime in Rael. Whether they intended to kill us was unclear, but since they hadn't perforated us already with arrows, my guess was that they planned to simply take everything and leave us stranded in the woods.

Reaching out with my kenning, I searched for something nearby that could help us. I told the merchants not to resist, everything would be fine.

"Fine?" Ghurang Bokh said, outrage in his tone. "This is the part where you're supposed to protect us!"

"And I will. Nothing will be lost. Just give me a little bit of time."

"Time for what?" one of the Raelechs said in Nentian. Whoops. That was a tactical error. I shouldn't have assumed that because I couldn't understand them, they couldn't understand me.

"Time for reinforcements to arrive," I explained. "I'm Abhi. What's your name?"

He was a thickly bearded man, stocky and hairy all over, his red leather armor scuffed and scored but clean. He held one of the Raelech oak cudgels inlaid with stone. Instead of answering me, he stepped back and his eyes darted to the sides, looking for threats. He shouted something in Raelech to his companions and they immediately spun, checking the flanks to make sure that the ambushers weren't about to be ambushed. That was all good. It gave me time to mutter under my breath and summon reinforcements—not the kind they expected—and, most important to me, without sacrificing my own life at the expenditure of power. The Raelech man returned his attention to me.

"There are no reinforcements out there. You're alone, a fat and unprotected caravan in the wilderness. Normally a caravan like this would have a dozen mercenaries protecting it, but you've got nothing. How could we resist?"

"That's a pretty good point. We didn't think there were bandits prowling along this pass."

"Well, there didn't used to be, because everyone used the Granite Tunnel and it was secure. And it's damn cold up here.

But this road is ripe for the plucking, so as I said, how could we resist?"

"I've always found it easy to resist thievery myself, but I won't judge you. Are you the leader?"

"I am. And are you the former leader of what is now my caravan?"

"No, that would be the old guy at the back who's offering no resistance. I'm the protection."

He snorted, his eyes flicking to Eep on my shoulder and Murr at my side. "Nentians don't have a kenning, so what are you, some kind of animal trainer?"

"Not exactly. You might not be up to date on current events regarding kennings, but that's understandable."

"Your hawk and cat won't give us any trouble. If they move, we'll shoot them full of arrows."

"Oh, I know. That's why my hawk and cat haven't moved, and they won't move, I assure you, uh . . . You never told me your name."

"You don't need to know it."

"Oh, but I do. I would like for this to end peacefully, but if it doesn't, I will inform your next of kin what happened to you, so they won't spend their lives wondering."

He scowled at me and spat at my feet. "I tire of this." He gestured to an archer behind him, flicking a finger in my direction and uttering an obvious command in Raelech. How strange, I thought, to be in such a position again, where a man pointed a weapon at me and decided, after a brief conversation, that my life should end. Reassuring, too, in another sense, because not only Nentians thought that a weapon gave them the right to dominate others. But this time there wasn't a boy to leap in front of me, and I knew very well what I could do.

The archer pulled, aimed, and let fly, but I was already twisting out of the way as he did so, Eep taking flight to my left. I snatched the arrow out of the air, spun, and pressed the tip of the arrowhead to the flesh of the bandit leader's neck in what must have appeared as a blur to him. Eep lit in the branches of an evergreen, screening herself from view.

"Your name, please, right now. So your loved ones will know."

His eyes widened as he realized he had made a spectacularly mortal blunder. "I am Calvagh. My mother is Rhienne, master farmer of the Earth Goddess Dinae. She lives south of Naelin."

"Thank you," I said, as I stepped away from him. "I swear to Kalaad in the sky that I will send word."

There were some general shouts of alarm from the bandits as they realized something had gone terribly awry, and the archer who'd tried to shoot me was nocking another arrow for a second attempt, but it was too late for them, as my reinforcements arrived.

I had summoned a colony of saw-legged juniper beetles, large and dark-brown specimens that had been huddled inside a hollow log for warmth during the winter months. Their rear legs were long and serrated, more than capable of slicing open jugulars when drawn across the flesh at speed. Not all of them successfully hit their targets on the first pass, but Calvagh was cut deeply and he dropped his weapon, clutching his throat. The archer had suffered a scratch but not enough to take him out. Still, he was distracted and worried about something finishing him off, as he should be.

"Murr, please take down the man with the bow."

While the bloodcat roared and sprang at the archer, I checked to make sure Eep was all right. She blinked at me from between the pine branches and chirped querulously.

"Stay there," I told her, and turned to assess what remained to be done. Of the ten bandits who'd been behind me and surrounding the wagons, six, including the leader, were bleeding out, vainly trying to stanch the flow pumping between their fingers. Four at the rear had escaped somehow—

perhaps they'd seen what happened to the others and had time to duck—and they were now clustered together behind the train, batting at beetles in the air.

"Just fly in circles above their heads, out of reach, and keep their attention," I said with the force of my kenning, and the beetles obeyed. The bandits cursed and kept their eyes trained on the sky, so that they never saw Ohhwuh coming at them with his head lowered until it was far too late to get out of the way.

The raw force a charging bone-collared dreadmoose can deliver will pulp muscle tissue and shatter skeletons. Ohhwuh's wide rack of antlers encompassed them all, and if the four of them weren't killed on impact, they were killed a second later when their backs broke against the trunks of trees on the other side of the path after a brief, high-velocity flight through the air. One man's head exploded into mist when his skull hit the tree but his body missed it.

Ohhwuh sneezed afterward, his breath steaming in the air, and Subodh Ramala, crouched down by his wagon wheel, said softly, "Kalaad, I think I just shat my pants."

I confirmed with a quick jog around the wagons that it was all over except for some gurgling and wheezing as the bandits stained the snow red. I thanked the saw-legged juniper beetles for their help and told them they could return to their log to get warm again.

"Thanks, Ohhwuh. You were very helpful. Eep, it's safe to come down now, unless you'd like to stay up there."

"Eep!" she said, gliding down to resume her perch on my shoulder. I was a lot warmer than a tree branch. Murr was spitting and licking his chops to get the archer's blood out of his mouth. Humans didn't taste all that great to him, which was probably a good thing.

"Are you gentlemen all well? Any injuries?" I stopped in front of Ghurang Bokh, who'd loudly pointed out that I was supposed to be protecting them.

"Uh, no. I'm fine." The leathers merchant adjusted his clothing and slapped at some imaginary soil on his thighs, as if he'd had an especially rough fight, when in truth he'd done nothing but stand there.

"Do you feel adequately protected now?"

"Yes, well, uh. That was . . ."

I cocked an eyebrow at him and crossed my arms, waiting for him to finish the thought, and Eep added a piercing yellow-eyed glare. He wasn't going to get an easy pass from either of us on this one.

". . . That was outstanding," he finally admitted.

"Thank you. I agree."

My fiercest critic, Poudresh Marekh, stalked over to be contrary. "Yes, yes, incredibly efficient you are, ten bandits dead in a matter of seconds, and no hesitation either. You called the beasts and they came. But it's all unnecessary. You could have just as easily done this to the guards holding our families hostage in Ghurana Nent."

"No, I could never do that."

"Why not? What's the difference?"

"The difference is, I did not come to this pass seeking these men's deaths. They came here and found their own. Judge me as you wish, gentlemen, but you cannot deny that I keep my contracts. You are safe and so are your wagons full of material goods. Let's move on."

"You're just going to leave them here? Raelechs like to be buried."

"That's true, but we don't have shovels, and even if we did, the ground is frozen. They attacked Nentians, so they have earned a Nentian burial under Kalaad's wide blue sky. In the end, we are nothing but meat. There will be scavengers coming soon for a meal, and we shouldn't be here when they arrive."

The same pack of sonnet wolves that I'd met with Fintan on our trip into Rael was coming. They'd most likely go straight to luncheon, but if they showed up near our train, I'd direct them to a rapidly cooling but still-warm repast.

The remainder of the journey to Tömerhil was uneventful; I received my payment once we got there, and I wished them all good health and that their mission would prove successful. The road to Pelemyn from there was well traveled and patrolled, and escorts were easy to come by, but I warned them that they'd need robust protection going back because of the sonnet wolves and others that had a taste for humans.

With apologies to Murr and Eep, I headed back north to Fornyd, because Ohhwuh was ready to return to the Gravewood, and I was hoping to see Koesha and my other Joabeian friends again before they returned to their home. But since there was no terrible hurry, I didn't take the roads and actually backtracked somewhat toward the Poet's Range, though I headed northwest rather than strictly west. I used some of my money to buy proper provisions and explored the Brynt wetlands in the foothills, taking extensive notes in my journal and drawing what I could. There were so many creatures living there, even in winter, that I'd never see in the Nentian plains. For whatever reason, Brynlön and Kauria (or so I'd been told) had the fewest deadly creatures—but that didn't mean they lacked variety or beauty.

Brynt marsh foxes had a mottled pattern of dark gray and reddish-brown fur that broke up their silhouettes when they hunted underneath the canopy of trees. There were rodents of a startling number and variety that both Murr and Eep enjoyed hunting. Sunchucks were among them, and I warned against hunting those, but they found plenty else. Murr discovered a colony of bog bunnies, for example, that had built an impressive warren into the foothills. Eep caught one of those as well, but she preferred to dine on slough hyraxes, which were more her size and not especially fast.

There were plenty of other birds of prey wintering there too, hunting the same things. Snow-hooded owls and ghost kites were so beautiful, and I talked to one of each until Eep screeched, apparently a bit jealous. But as we reached the end of Thaw, I figured I should get moving in case Koesha decided to leave in Bloom, so I struck out due east, figuring I'd eventually run into the road from Tömerhil to Fornyd and take that. And that army in the north was really bothering me—I mused aloud as I jogged through the undergrowth with Murr and Ohhwuh keeping pace alongside, Eep gliding overhead.

"That army of Eculans could move at any time. They might decide to come south, in fact, to escape the worst of the cold. They could be on the march now. And then Fornyd would be at their mercy, if they wished to move east to attack. And it's likely they would wish that, because attacking seems to be their favorite thing to do. I'm thinking I should go scout them again. How would you feel about that, Murr?"

He stopped abruptly, growled in annoyance, and very clearly, very deliberately, shook his head.

"No, huh? What do you think, Eep?"

She spiraled down and landed right next to Murr and shook her head too.

"Wow. A united front against me. Okay, I hear you, so we won't go. You're going to have to listen to me worry, though."

After losing my parents, which would normally be the worst thing ever, I never really got to settle into a cynical fatalism and say, *What's the worst that could happen now?* because the world kept presenting me with viable scenarios in which something worse could happen, like entire civilizations being wiped out.

Eventually we found the road and made much faster progress. Whenever we saw someone coming, Ohhwuh and Murr veered off into the trees until well after we'd passed them. They were Brynts and I didn't speak the language, so I couldn't answer the questions they hollered at me. One group of merchant wagons, however, spotted Ohhwuh an

Murr trotting next to me as we came around a bend, and then they witnessed my friends change course into the trees. This excited them and they stood up in their wagons, pointing and shouting, and I simply smiled and waved, replied in Nentian, and kept going. They had a couple of mercenary guards accompanying them who tried to stop me, but they were laughably slow and didn't have bows, so I dodged around them and kept going.

It occurred to me a bit later that maybe they were trying to warn me that something terrible had happened in Fornyd, that all my fears had come true, and my guts twisted in dread. My blessing apparently came with the curse of a worried mind. There was nothing to do but keep going and find out.

Once I arrived, I learned that there was nothing immediately wrong, and the excitement of the travelers had probably just been curiosity about the Nentian guy running with strange animals.

If anything, something was immediately right: When I got to the ferry to arrange passage across the river for Ohhwuh, I saw the *Nentian Herald* docked there. Baejan was on duty and came down to hug me. She said that Koesha had left a couple of days earlier on an important errand with Scholar Gondel Vedd and a Bone Giant prisoner, together with someone named Second Könstad Tallynd du Böll. She wasn't sure what a könstad was, let alone a second one, but guessed from the tone of reverence surrounding her name that she was a pretty big deal.

I asked her to tell Haesha and the rest of the crew that I was back in town and that I'd love to see them if they wished to see me, then I boarded the ferry with my animal companions and asked Ohhwuh if I could display some human affection and pet the top of his muzzle. He did an uncertain shuffle away from me, a little step toward the edge of the ferry, and his eyes widened in alarm. He was probably thinking that if he had swum across the river like he had before, he wouldn't be getting these awkward offers. "You might like it. You won't know until you try. If you don't like it, I promise I'll stop."

He thought about it for a few more seconds, saw that Murr was shaking his head no to advise him against it, then nodded his assent anyway, because Ohhwuh was a daring dreadmoose. I asked him to lower his head so I could reach. Moose are really tall, and dreadmoose even more so. Once that great red-brown head dipped down to my level, I gently ran my hand down from just below his eyes to just above his nostrils.

"There. That's not so bad, is it?"

"Ohhwuh!"

He let me keep going, and I told him true things. "You have been so helpful to us, and I wish there was something more I could give you than this. You shaved many days off our journey by pulling that sled, and I think you might have helped save the world. You are so strong. You are smart and handsome and loyal and kind. You are the best bone-collared dreadmoose in the Gravewood, Ohhwuh. I'm going to miss you. But you go and have a long and wonderful life now. If all goes well, you'll never see or even smell a human again. If you do, run—they won't see you as a friend like I do. Can you do that for me?"

"Ohhwuh." He nodded, then flipped his muzzle under my hand so I'd pet him some more.

"You see, Murr? This is good. If you'd just let me give you a belly rub, you'd understand." The bloodcat hissed and shook his head. "Okay. You don't know what you're missing."

We got to the other bank, and I gave Ohhwuh the best and quickest hug I could. "Be safe, my friend. I will think of you every day. No matter where you are, remember that you are loved."

He stepped off the ferry onto the distant shore and looked back at us as the ferryman poled us away. I waved at him. "Goodbye, Ohhwuh."

He threw his head back as far as he could and bugled loudly, "Ohhhhwuh!" Then he walked into the tall evergreens until he disappeared from view, finally home again.

Someday, I will get to go home too.

With some small annoyance, I rubbed at the corners of my eyes. Why was I getting emotional about a dreadmoose I'd never met? Maybe it wasn't him so much as the idea of going home. For those of us who want to go, it's sometimes impossible, either because the place no longer exists or the people who made it a home are absent. Home is a magical place we've lost somehow, and whenever we see someone find their way back, we feel that stab of longing to cross that wondrous threshold and be whole once more.

Fintan dispelled his seeming and said, "We're backtracking now a few days from Abhi's arrival in Fornyd. You heard Baejan tell him he'd just missed Koesha and Gondel Vedd and the second könstad, who went off on a mission. That mission was historic, and you won't want to miss a bit of it, so let's hear it from the beginning."

He took on the form of Tallynd du Böll.

Tallynd

There is a satisfying moment when you perform a chore well—like filleting a fish quickly and lifting up the bones by the spine so they all come out in one piece—and you know that because you've done it properly, you get to enjoy a net full of contentment later. Meetings with the pelenaut and the

Könstad du Lallend were like that. Necessary, but short and efficient and pregnant with purpose.

We knew that the wraiths on Blight were obviously an enormous threat to us—the spy network headed up by none other than our own ironically named Wraith, Vjeko himself, proved as much—so if there was anything we could do to defeat them, we needed to do it. We'd let the Joabeians spend all of Snowfall and Thaw in Fornyd while we dealt with local issues, but with Vjeko finally found, it was time for us to focus on the source of our wraith problem. The pelenaut granted me broad authority and permission to do whatever was necessary to get the island of Blight explored and to secure some usable intelligence about the Seventh Kenning.

"Do what is required, Tallynd. And I need you to accompany them on the mission."

The pelenaut must have seen something in my face to make him blink and hold up a placating hand.

"I know it's asking a lot of you, and we have already asked so much. But who else can I trust to get this done properly? Who else would you send?"

Who, indeed? If he sent someone else, I would wind up volunteering to go as backup anyway.

And how could I say no, when those monsters had already taken so much from us and wished to take more?

The meeting was quick and easy; preparing myself to confront wraiths again was not.

I returned to the archives and sought out the master archivist this time rather than the master of charts. It was an errand to slake my curiosity but also to give myself time to think of how to say goodbye again to my boys without alarming them.

The master archivist, a delightful elderly woman named Fönna du Henspyll, moved slowly but spoke quickly, peering at me through a gold-rimmed monocle and smiling.

"How can I help you, Second Könstad?"

"I am hoping to find something about how one can defeat a wraith, or shield oneself from becoming possessed, or even free someone who's been possessed from the possession."

Her smile faded into lines of worry. "Oh, I'm afraid I won't be able to help you with those questions."

"There's nothing in the archives at all?"

"There used to be, but the Wraith's assistant took everything we had a couple of years ago and never returned it."

I sighed in exasperation. "Of course she did."

"You're not the first to ask."

"Oh? Who else asked?"

"The pelenaut's lung. He was quite determined to find something, and, well, you already know what he found—all that business with the old scouting expedition a hundred-something years ago."

"Yes. I don't suppose you've ever read any of that material and remember anything that might be useful?"

"Nothing you probably don't already know. Water confounds them and can kill them."

I remembered breaking the lure of a wraith with water but hadn't thought to try to kill one with a directed stream of water. My only thought then had been escape. Had I not broken the lure, would it have taken over my mind? Their ability to possess us still made no sense to me.

"We're mostly made of water, though, so how can they take over our bodies if it's so deadly to them?"

The archivist shrugged. "Not to be flip, but I expect they're latching on to whatever isn't water. I don't know what precisely that is or how they're doing it, but I expect someone like you could find a way to disrupt them."

"Okay, thank you."

"Sorry I couldn't be more helpful."

Here is what absolutely terrified me about possession: that I might still be conscious and aware of what was being done with my body. Would I still love my children and be helpless to save them as the wraith directed my body to kill them and everyone I knew? I would rather be dead.

If the meeting with the pelenaut and the könstad was a successfully filleted fish, the trip to the archives was so catastrophic that I had turned something edible into little more than a briny fish slurry. It occurred to me that I should probably quit trying to equate my activities with food preparation. But the shortages affected us all.

The boys were overjoyed to see me when I came home, and that was a current in which I was content to swim. I hugged them hard and told them how happy I was and announced that I thought it might be time to break out that one special gift basket I'd been saving. I'd donated all but this last one a few days ago. It included some dried sausage that I didn't think existed anymore; its like wouldn't be seen again for many years, if at all. It was a cylinder of what's known as the Triple M sausage—the Möllerud Midsummer Mushroom. It was a pork sausage mixed with mushrooms that grew only on a specific farmer's land, and he and his family were no doubt dead now. There were rare Nentian cheeses and dried fruits in there too, which would also be impossible to find again for years. A fitting last meal with my family, if it turned out to be such. If I didn't make it home, they'd remember it and understand that I was trying to say goodbye. And I decided that they'd remember a conversation about their father too, because I started one.

"I wish your father was here to enjoy this."

"Me too," Nyls said.

My youngest boy, Turyn, considering his wedge of Nentian thunder yak cheese, had a question. "Did he love food like this?"

"Yes, he did. He liked to nibble on it and savor the taste. And he nibbled on you when you were a baby, because he loved you too."

Wide eyes and outrage. "He did not nibble on me!"

"He absolutely did. He would nibble on your neck and say, 'Nom nom nom!' and you would laugh so hard."

Turyn clapped his hand to his neck and giggled as if it were happening to him at that instant. Had he remembered somehow? If so, how precious that was!

"He still loves you, wherever his spirit is. His body may have gone home to sea, but his spirit wishes he could be with us now. Love endures even when our bodies do not. I hope you'll remember that."

That strayed too close to the idea that my body might not endure much longer, and Nyls was quick to seize on it.

"Mom? Why are you talking about this? Are you okay?"

"I'm fine. It just needs to be talked about sometimes," I said, shrugging. "I don't want you to forget that your father loved you and still does. He can't tell you himself, so I have to do it for him. That's all."

We played games until it was time for bed, and I didn't tell them I was leaving again until the morning. I said only that I was going to Fornyd and left out the probable trip to the Mistmaiden Isles afterward. I tried not to hug them too hard and make them worry; I smiled a lot, and they told me to be safe and hurry back. I promised to do my best, and then, after they left for school, took one last look around the house and cried a little bit before locking the door behind me and calmly walking into the ocean, all business now.

Upon my arrival in Fornyd, the same assembly of people gathered again in the quartermaster's Wellspring, but somehow the air did not seem so heavily misted with tension and desperation. Perhaps that was only my own perception, since I was confident that I could make decisions and had the pelenaut's support, but I think that Captain Gansu and her crew were also feeling less on edge. They'd had a restorative stay and had picked up some simple Brynt phrases.

The captain did not reveal even a trickle of willingness to trade for the cloak, however. She continued to insist that she would like to scout the island of Blight with us, and that being the case, I steered negotiations toward how exactly it would be worked out.

She wanted her crew to remain safe on the *Nentian Herald* and a guarantee that they were free to leave should we not return. I hesitated, wondering why she would even ask for such a guarantee and worrying that I might be missing something crucial, but that very hesitation made her feel like she was right to ask for it. I assured her they were free, but mostly I was surprised that she didn't want any of her crew to go on this mission.

"You don't want some bodyguards, at least?"

"What good would bodyguards do?" she asked. "If you wanted to kill us, you could do so before we'd be able to draw swords. And besides, if I am asking you to trust me with this cloak that is so important to you, then I feel I should trust you with my life, which is very important to me. I merely want my crew to make it home, no matter what happens."

"They will."

Gondel Vedd wanted to make sure that the Eculan prisoner, Saviič, would be able to come along and perhaps even conduct a seeking, if he still wished to do so.

"I've made great progress with the Eculan holy scripture, *Zanata Sedam,* but its vague language requires some interpretation itself, and there are granular details and practices outside the text that he tends to reveal in fits of religious ecstasy. I think we'll learn as much from him as anything else."

Once aboard a boat that would carry us to Dead Man's Point and the Seven-Year Ship—crewed entirely by our mariners, as the *Nentian Herald* would remain in Fornyd—Saviič informed us through Scholar Vedd's translation that the cloak Captain Gansu wore was in fact called a *wraith cloak,* and he was worried that the captain intended to seek the Seventh Kenning before he could.

"I'm already blessed," she assured him. "I don't need to seek another."

He smiled a horrible smile but looked genuinely happy. "It has been so long. I was supposed to go on the Seven-Year Ship when it came to Ecula. And then I sought it out and landed far away in Kauria." He lifted his shackled limbs. "Since then I have been in chains or a cell. But of all the faithful, all the seekers, I am the one who will board the Seven-Year Ship to seek the Seventh Kenning. Žalost has seen my suffering and heard my prayers. This has all been a test, and I have passed."

Once we docked at Dead Man's Point, Saviič danced and giggled his way onto the Seven-Year Ship. The prospect of sailing to an island seething with wraiths filled him with glee, and he felt none of the horror the rest of us did.

He was looking forward to visiting an island of monsters like he was coming home, and that told me he was dangerous despite his good mood and seeming cooperation. I made sure our mariners kept a close eye on him during our journey.

That was an unexpected development. For some reason, I never thought Saviič would do anything but help Gondel with his language acquisition. The idea that he might become blessed was deeply uncomfortable.

"I'm going to warn you now," Fintan said, dispelling Tallynd's seeming, "that a lot happens on that island. So much that I won't be able to share it all today, and tomorrow's tales will be long and—I promise—revelatory. But we'll begin with the Joabeian zephyr, Captain Koesha Gansu."

When he took on her seeming this time, she was wearing the wraith cloak draped over her uniform.

Koesha

Here's a curious thing: Nobody knows if wraiths can fly. Maybe not even the wraiths.

I mean, they supposedly float, not really touching the ground. They apparently can float up to the height of an Eculan—about eight feet—but no records exist of them flying any higher than that. So nobody knows for sure what they're capable of. And if I'm going to do some aerial reconnaissance of the island of Blight, I would really like to be sure. Once I get over the land, will they swarm and gobble up my life? If I direct winds against them, will they be blown away or will the wind pass through them?

And if they can float at least eight feet aboveground, why can't they float over the water and escape the island? Why aren't they wreaking havoc on the mainland?

"Those are excellent questions," Gondel Vedd told me. "Should you get an opportunity to ask a wraith—you know, if it comes up in polite conversation—please do find out."

It took a few seconds to realize he was joking with me.

Saviič was physically quivering in his excitement to debark from the Seven-Year Ship and seek the Seventh Kenning. He explained the process to Gondel, who translated it to us.

"I wear the cloak and go to the temple—"

"Which temple?"

"There is only one on the island."

This was news to everyone. He'd kept that particular detail of the seeking to himself until now. "Is the temple dedicated to Žalost, your god?"

"Yes. But his brothers and sisters are also recognized. I go to the temple, get more cloaks, and bring them to the ship so others may wear them and seek a kenning."

"Wait—there are more cloaks, just like this one?" I asked.

"Yes. Many more."

"Oh! Well, then, this can easily be replaced."

"That would have been nice to know earlier," Tallynd said, her voice bone dry as desert wind.

I smiled at her. "Yes. Now no trading will be necessary, so long as I get to keep one. So what happens then?" I prompted Saviič.

"Then I return to the temple and become blessed by the Seventh Kenning."

"Or die, right?" Tallynd asked.

"Or die. But I will be blessed. I have endured much with patience—months of imprisonment—and yet remained faithful. Žalost will see this."

"But what is the process of the seeking itself?" I pressed him. "For the First Kenning you jump into a lake of lava. For the Third you walk into quicksand. For the Seventh, you do . . . what?"

"I pray to Žalost."

"Pray? You can do that anywhere."

"Yes. But here it is different. When I pray at the temple, that is the seeking."

That did not seem anything like the other seekings. Where was the obvious dance with death? Besides the wraiths, that is, for which there was the solution of an enchanted cloak?

"What if he *does* get blessed, Gondel?" I asked the scholar. "What if he becomes a lifeleech like Lorson, or something worse, and uses his blessing to come back and kill us all?"

The scholar shrugged. "The counters to the kenning appear to be water breathers and lavaborn. That was what Lorson feared, correct?" When I confirmed, he pointed to Tallynd and said, "We have a tidal mariner. If he threatens us, she can defeat him. And, honestly, this is our best chance to solve the mystery. We've come too far to turn back now, though I suppose we can if you feel strongly about it."

I felt pretty strongly that this was not the reason I had left home. I'd wanted to find my sister and circumnavigate the globe. Maesi was long dead, though, and I wouldn't be able to see the remainder of my crew home if I died here.

Tallynd du Böll was perceptive and saw I had doubts. She had Gondel translate her words: "You don't need to do anything now, Koesha. Saviič can take all the risk. We can wait for him to return with more cloaks and then we can send volunteers to investigate later as needed. I know you have a responsibility to your crew."

I did. But I also had a responsibility to Shoawei and to the wider world. If I am a leaf on the wind of Shoawei, should I not appreciate that her wind had brought me here?

I replied, "Thank you. But neither I nor my crew would be here today if someone who had no need to do anything simply stood by and did nothing. I wish to help. But should anything happen to me, please make Haesha captain and tell her to sail for Joabei immediately."

"I will."

The sailors tied us up to the dock, and Tallynd kept it clear of wraiths by using her kenning to pull water out of the bay and over the surface of the dock in an arch, creating a continuous fountain. The wraiths wouldn't pass the moving water.

"Pretty, but unnecessary," Saviič declared. "Wraiths would not get on the boat. The space between dock and boat is still water, and they can't cross it."

"Not even with a gangplank lowered to the dock?" Tallynd asked.

"Oh, yes, well, they might in that case. Don't do that."

"How do seekers safely get to shore, then?"

"Wear the cloak and jump onto the dock. First one brings more cloaks, like I will. Then it proceeds."

"When I found the ship, this bay was full of dead bodies. Hundreds of Eculans like you. They were piled up as if they'd drowned in one spot, and their boats were abandoned." She pointed to flotsam on the shore and some still-intact boats in the bay. "How did wraiths manage to do that?"

Saviič shrugged. "That does not sound like something wraiths could do. So it must be something else."

"That something else could still be on the island."

He flashed a careless grin. "I will seek it out. Ha ha."

Tallynd shook her head. "Okay, then. Koesha, you ready?"

I nodded and gave the cloak to Saviič. He received it with an awed breath and donned it reverently, with the wonder of a little boy given his heart's desire. A cloud that had been blocking the sun took its cue and moved out of the way. Sunlight bathed him and he turned his face up to it, closing his eyes and basking. I could see he chose to interpret it as a benediction rather than a coincidence of complex weather patterns. "Žalost, the time has come. Finally I will know the truth."

That was some suitable drama, and I hoped he would be as happy an hour from now.

He hopped easily from the deck to the dock and faced the seething boil of wraiths that waited beyond Tallynd's improvised water barrier. We watched as he strode confidently toward them, stepped over the barrier, and the misty wraiths parted before him, somehow repelled by his cloak. So at least we knew that worked. Who, I wondered, had enchanted it?

It was time for me to take to the sky. I walked to the prow and leapt off the side. The summoned winds caught and lifted me in a chimney of air so that I was far above the surface of the water, and then I redirected them to fly me over the island. We would see if the wraiths would pursue me or not.

Happily, they did not. Saviič disappeared into the forest, and the treetops stretched like a verdant green carpet for a short distance, undulating in the wake of my passage, until they stopped at the edge of a space paved with flat white stones.

Grass grew between the stones, but it was . . . maintained. Mowed. From above, it was a green-veined mosaic.

A white copper-domed temple, now graced with a pale-green patina from decades of weathering, looked like it could hold about a hundred people, if they were friendly with one another. Seven marble statues of seated people faced the entrance to the temple. They were unusual first in the sense that they were life-sized rather than larger-than-life, and while their seats or thrones were identical, they looked like very different people. Each statue sat on a dais with two steps down to the stone courtyard, so it was still above anyone who came to visit, except perhaps a Hathrim.

But beyond the first oddity of creation, a raft of questions floated in my mind: Who had sculpted them, and where? I doubted the marble had been quarried here, so were blocks of marble imported to be sculpted on site, or were the completed works shipped here and installed? Who would build such a monument where it would be seen by no one but wraiths—except the occasional seekers, who supposedly arrived only every seven years?

As I circled above the site, I realized I'd been wrong: The wraiths weren't milling about the area. They didn't set so much as a spectral tendril on the white pavestones.

Perhaps it would be safe to descend and take a closer look at the statues.

I lowered myself to the top of the dome, checked the perimeters of the clearing to make sure that no wraiths would rush me, and took out my captain's spyglass when I felt safe. I extended it and peered through the eyepiece to examine the statues.

The one on the far left was a dour, bearded man with a plaque on his plinth that identified him as Jarost.

Never heard of him.

The second was an interesting figure: I could not tell if

they were male or female, which may have been intentional. They wore robes and exuded serenity. The sign said Mir.

Next to them was a definite woman of generous proportions, a kind mother figure whose name was Kamen.

The center statue, which one would assume to be most important, bore the name of Žalost. Finally, a name I recognized: It was the god of the Seventh Kenning, whom Saviič worshipped. He was fairly thin, with sharply bladed cheekbones, straight hair pulled back into a queue, and a singular beard tied into seven braids that stuck out from his jaw like the rays of a sun.

I remembered seeing that one individual on the coast of the Northern Yawn—an officer, perhaps, of their army. He had worn only five braids. Perhaps that was to represent rank, or perhaps it represented the five islands of Ecula, or maybe he simply couldn't grow a beard sufficient to braid seven times.

If this figure was the god of the Seventh Kenning, then the other statues must represent his siblings, and the unfamiliar names were the Eculan designations for them. Looking back to the first one, I could easily believe that Jarost was the god of the First Kenning, fire. But would that mean the second one, Mir, was supposed to represent Shoawei? Or Reinei? I found it fascinating, because Gondel's people thought the god of the Second Kenning was male, while we in Joabei thought of her as female. And here was a representation of that deity that could be interpreted as either.

Kamen looked like an earth goddess, so in theory the sequence was proceeding from one to six, with seven placed in the middle. On the other side of Žalost was a figure named Talas. The tight curls on his head and the structure of his face were reminiscent of the Brynts, so hello there, god of the sea. He had a growth on his left hand—no. It was the head of a longarm, perched on the back of his hand, its tentacles intertwined with his fingers. Had I missed clues on the others? Yes.

Jarost had a hammer and tongs leaning against the front of
the chair, next to his right leg, signifying his relationship to
the forge. Mir's hair looked a bit windblown.

The representation of the goddess of the Fifth Kenning
had flowers in her hair, which was piled and braided in a fashion I'd never seen before, and her name was Razvoj.

Last on the right, therefore, would be the goddess of the
Sixth Kenning, who supposedly blessed Abhinava Khose:
Meso. Her hand rested on the head of a marble likeness beside her throne—a bloodcat, the very creature that walked
around with Abhi.

You could have blown me away like a puffball. I could
hardly wait to get back to tell Gondel and ask him what he
thought it all meant.

But then Saviič emerged from the trees, entering the
plaza, and I watched him run straight to the statue of Žalost
and prostrate himself. He spent some time mumbling things
in his own language, his voice choked with sobs because he
was so overwhelmed to arrive at his most holy place after
many trials. When he finally stood and turned, he saw me
standing on top of the dome. I waved to him, and he waved
back. He pointed at the temple and said something I didn't
understand. I just smiled and waved again.

He jogged into the temple and I settled in to wait, but he
emerged after only a few seconds with a handcart piled high
with those impressive Eculan cloaks. It must have been waiting for him just inside the entrance.

"Who prepared that for you, Saviič?" I asked under my
breath. "Do you not ever feel that you're being set up, when
things have been so clearly set up for you?"

Looking around, I saw nothing that resembled a kenning
site. There was no natural wonder here; everything was
crafted by people, somehow, on an island populated by
wraiths. I summoned wind to take me back to the ship. Tallynd's water barrier was still in effect, keeping the wraiths

away from the dock, and everyone gathered around as soon as I touched down.

"There's a temple and seven statues of the gods in front of it. I think they're all named by the Eculans. Žalost is in the center. Saviič is on the way here with cloaks, but I didn't see anything that looked like a kenning site. Maybe it's inside the temple."

Gondel wanted to know the names of the gods and I told him, sharing the descriptions of the statues as best I could.

"But here's the disturbing part—besides its very existence, of course: If we're to believe the Eculans, this site shouldn't have been visited in, what, eight years? Because the Seven-Year Ship didn't come last year, right? Well, it looked like the whole place had been cleaned recently. The statues were spotless. The grass between the courtyard stones was trimmed, nothing overgrown, no weeds." Saviič emerged from the forested path and called out, hauling the handcart. "And that pile of cloaks was all ready for him. So who's maintaining all this and living among the wraiths?"

Tallynd was shaking her head. "Uh-uh. We need to go and find someone with a death wish to figure this out."

"Wait. What is he doing? No, Saviič—wait!" Gondel cried out.

The Eculan had pushed the handcart of cloaks past Tallynd's water barrier, where we could easily reach them and the wraiths couldn't, but evidently he figured that was good enough and we didn't need any fond farewells from him. He was running back into the woods to seek the Seventh Kenning.

"If the kenning site is inside the temple, I'm not following him in," I said. "But I'll go see what I can see."

I returned to the roof of the temple and waited for Saviič to appear. When he finally did, his breathing labored, he bent over and rested his hands on his knees, trying to regain his wind. After he'd recovered somewhat, he walked over to the statue of Žalost again. Presumably he was going to offer up another prayer before entering the temple.

But this time he didn't prostrate himself. He unclasped the cloak and let it fall from his shoulders into a puddle of fabric behind him. He stood tall, threw his hands out wide, and cried, "Žalost!" and then a bunch of words I didn't know, except that they probably had something to do with asking to be blessed. It didn't sound like a prayer but rather like a child demanding attention from a parent.

And then he made a strange noise in his throat and collapsed onto his cloak.

"Op! What? Did he just—"

He wasn't moving. There was no rise and fall to his chest. Did he die of happiness? Or had that truly been the seeking and he simply died?

I called out his name a couple of times and got no response. I waited awhile to see if some villainous murderer showed up. Nothing.

Part of me wanted to fly away and be done with it. But another wanted to check on him, because I knew that if I didn't, I would always wonder, and I didn't want to spend the rest of my life thinking about him.

A gust and a twister carried me down to the courtyard, where I kept looking all around to see if any attacks were imminent. I'd be out of there instantly if I saw a hint of a wraith.

The temple doors were open, but nothing could be seen inside. It was unlit by torches and apparently lacked windows, so all I saw was shadow. Something or someone could be hiding in there, watching me. I wouldn't be turning my back to it, so I approached Saviič from the side, keeping an eye on the temple as I knelt next to him to check for a pulse.

He didn't have one, and his bowels had loosened. Saviič was unequivocally dead.

Rising to my feet and believing I was alone, I wondered aloud in my own language, "How did he die?"

A male voice answered in my own tongue, "You're different."

I leapt back and drew my Bora, searching for who had spoken. No one at the temple door. No one peering out from behind the statues. "Who's there?" I demanded, continuing to back away from Saviič toward the goddesses of the Fifth and Sixth Kennings. "Who spoke?"

The head of Žalost's marble statue turned and smiled. "I did."

I screamed then, not only out of instinct but because that seemed an entirely appropriate response, and summoned wind to fly me out of there.

"Come back when you want to talk!" he called after me, and I could hear him chuckling creepily long after I should have been out of earshot.

Fintan dispelled his seeming to loud protests, and he snickered a bit.

I was on the crowd's side. "Hey, you can't stop there," I said, not particularly shouting it and sure Fintan couldn't hear me above all the general noise. Everyone wanted to know what happened next, and no one was particularly pleased with where he chose to stop.

"I warned you I'd be splitting up the story! It's honestly the best place to pause. For those of you Raelechs, Fornish, and Kaurians who have recently joined us, the names of the gods on those statues are the Eculan names for the same sons and daughters of Teldwen that we worship. That was discovered by Gondel Vedd, and we'll be hearing from both him and Koesha tomorrow. We'll find out why Eculans have been seeking the Seventh Kenning at a site not far from Bryn's Lung—what the nature of the seeking is—and plenty more besides. It will be a long day, so make sure you have snacks tomorrow."

Anyone who wasn't here was missing out, I thought. All those people who left to repopulate Festwyf and Göfyrd and Möllerud would have no idea about these revelations on the Mistmaiden Isles.

And then I remembered that I was going to write it all down, so they'd hear about it eventually.

THE RIFT REVEALED

To say that Fintan's story caused some lively discussion would be an understatement. The stories generally did, but this was exceptional. Why had the Eculans built a temple to their gods less than a full day's sail from Festwyf? Did all of the statues talk or just Žalost? Could we go there and speak to Talas, the Eculan equivalent of Bryn, and be spoken to in return? That last question was raised quite a bit, and evidently someone—or several someones—must have decided to act upon it, because an hour later, Könstad du Lallend announced to the city via the bard that travel to Blight for any reason was absolutely prohibited.

"After you hear what the bard has to tell you tomorrow, you won't want to go, I guarantee it. And even if you still do, you will not find what you seek. Blight is a place of death and sorrow. For your safety and the safety of everyone here: Stay away. Our cultural taboo against the place is well founded."

That sent commentary in new directions:

"Death and sorrow tend to drag down property values. I'm thinking I should really move to the interior."

"Do we even have marble on this side of the continent? The creepiest part is that the raw material for the entire site had to be imported."

"Hearing that is about as welcome as a questing kraken cock in the abyss."

I heard all that and more at the Siren's Call, recently re-opened after closing due to shortages, but unfortunately didn't get to question Fintan personally. He wisely ducked away to his lodging, since he'd be hounded for answers if he showed his face in public. But that was okay: I'd get to question him in private the next day.

I met Fintan at noon at the Steam Spire Loose Leaf Tea Emporium, which we hadn't visited in some time. Thanks to the influx of foodstuffs from the various armies, they had managed to get enough flour and sugar to start making pastries again and opened for business on a reservation basis only. He smiled when he saw me walk in.

"Ah, you look a bit more enthusiastic today."

"Yes, well, I'm looking forward to having my brain liquefied as you promised. I am sure everyone's excited to learn what happened next. It's all anyone can talk about."

Fintan hummed in pleasure. "This is probably my peak as a storyteller. The anticipation of thousands for my next performance."

"The anticipation is the peak?"

"Oh, absolutely. Because the reviews after the performance are always mixed. But the anticipation is pure."

"Ah. Well, then, congratulations."

"Thank you." He looked supremely content for a moment as he sipped from a cup of some rare Kaurian tea and gazed over the ocean from our table near the top of the spire. But after five seconds of that, his expression clouded.

"What is it?" I asked, worried that he saw sails on the horizon.

"There's a chance that things could get ugly after today's tales."

"Ugly? In what sense?"

He shrugged. "Some people might not take it well. Or . . . maybe a lot of people. It's difficult to predict, because this is going to be unprecedented. But you should know we're going to have a security detail of mariners escorting us off the wall when it's over."

"What in the abyss are you going to say that will require that?"

"It might turn out to be unnecessary. We're just trying to anticipate some issues since there's the potential for . . . unrest. There are some uncomfortable revelations ahead. What Koesha and Gondel Vedd discovered on that island is—"

"Gondel Vedd? Is he here too, finally?"

"His story is, but I haven't seen him personally yet."

"What happened to him?"

"Maaaaaany things, if you'll allow me to be cryptic. Interwoven with the stories of others. If I try to tell you out of order it'll mess you up, and there's no quick way through it."

"But whatever happened is the reason Nara's been gone?"

Fintan nodded, eyes widened. "Very much so. And it's darker than batshit in a mine shaft."

"Have you heard any of the questions people had after your tales yesterday?"

"Yes." He nodded sheepishly. "I got an earful."

"Will today's tales answer them?"

"Most of them. They will also answer questions people didn't know to ask. And there will be new questions too. For reasons that will become clear, Gondel and Koesha didn't feel safe sticking around to learn absolutely everything we might want to know. But that is an important way in which stories imitate reality: We are often not given satisfactory explanations for why things are the way they are. A certain amount of mystery is built into the structure of the world."

I waved a hand dismissively. "Okay, let's get to work, then. But if you get to the end of your tales and I still have questions, I'm going to try to pin you down so we can record things for posterity."

"Fair enough."

Once we finished and it was time to go to the wall, Fintan had a rapt city and several armies waiting for him. He was incredibly short with his musical intro, playing only eight bars before stopping and saying, "That's it. We have such a long tale today I think we should get started as soon as possible. So that's your warning! Get ready!"

And after the break, he told everyone he was going to pick up just a couple of minutes after he left off, with Koesha Gansu returning to the Seven-Year Ship after a panicked flight away from the animated statue of Žalost.

Koesha

The others were alarmed when I landed on the deck of the Seven-Year Ship, sword in hand. It might also have had something to do with the fear I felt—I could only imagine what it must look like on my face. They asked me what happened and I told them that Saviič was dead.

"How did he die?" Gondel asked.

"I don't know," I said, remembering to speak Nentian. "I watched him fall, but I don't know what caused it. No arrows. If I'm honest, it looked like it was an execution the way Tallynd would do it: a brain hemorrhage."

Gondel translated this for the others and then asked, "Was he seeking at the time?"

"Maybe. He took off his cloak, spoke to the statue of Žalost, and dropped dead. I went down to confirm it and then . . . I'm not sure this really happened. The statue of Žalost came alive and spoke to me."

I had to recount the brief conversation exactly then, word for word, including the scream and the creepy laugh.

"I would have soiled my pants," Gondel admitted. "I'm glad you're okay."

"Thanks."

"I have so many questions now. Was the statue animated

by someone of the Third Kenning, who perhaps hid behind it?"

I hadn't thought of that. Technically it would be possible, though it would be a marvelous feat of control. Plus, that would mean there was an earth shaper who could speak Joabeian living there.

"And if not," Gondel continued, "can the other statues talk as well? Is the temple dedicated to all the gods or only to Žalost?"

Tallynd said something to him in Brynt and he translated for me. "The second könstad still wants to know who was responsible for killing all the Eculans she found underneath the Seven-Year Ship."

I looked around at their expectant faces and realized what they wanted.

"You think I should go back and talk to the statue."

"You were expressly invited. Saviič was not, and he died."

That was a good point. While incredibly menacing by virtue of existing, the animated statue did invite conversation and made no threats. "All right. If I don't come back, sail away from here and live curious. Don't risk yourselves."

I sheathed my sword, nodded a farewell, and flew on the wind back to the temple and the talking statue, muttering prayers to Shoawei the whole time.

Saviič's body had disappeared, and the cloak was now draped over the shoulders of the statue of Žalost. There was no one hiding behind the statue, so the suggestion that an earth shaper was manipulating the stone was incorrect— unless the person was buried underground. Theoretically possible for them, but unlikely that someone would do that to play an elaborate prank.

Besides, the statue was now partially sitting on the cloak and posed differently. So the statue had moved out of the chair, and it was not truly a statue.

"Hello," I said. "I would like to talk."

Žalost remained still for several seconds, and I was about to repeat myself when the head turned ever so slightly and he replied. "Ah. You've returned already. A welcome surprise. It has been a long time since I have spoken your language. It may sound a little archaic to you now."

It did. He was using the sort of diction and vocabulary we read in our oldest stories.

"Are you the god of the Seventh Kenning?"

"I am."

I gulped. "And these are the other gods?"

"Ha! No, these are just statues."

"But you look like a statue."

"I am often very close to being one. Slowing down my body helps pass the time. Would you be more comfortable if I looked less like stone?"

"I honestly don't anticipate feeling comfortable at any point in this conversation."

"Fair enough. I will return fully to flesh in hopes that it will ease your mind a little bit."

As I watched, the likeness of stone all over his body cracked but did not crumble, changed tones somewhat, and then smoothed out into pale skin. The same process held true for the fabric of his robe, which turned out to be spotlessly white, as were his boots. His hair and braided beard were dark, his eyes a deep brown.

"There. Better, yes? To whom do I have the honor of speaking?"

"Koesha Gansu, a zephyr and captain of the *Nentian Herald*. And you are Žalost?"

He scoffed. "Žalost is what the Eculans call me, but it is not my name. The people of the continent nearby do not even know me, for I have purposely been erased from their tales. And in the stories of your people I am a minor figure who annoyed Shoawei: Vo Lai the White Demon."

I tried to stifle a shudder and am not sure I pulled it off. "*You* are Vo Lai?"

"I was. But please call me Sedam. That is my name—it would translate merely to 'Seven' if you wished to ascribe a meaning to it."

"Seven. Because you are the seventh child of Teldwen and Kalaad?"

"Precisely."

I took a few deep breaths to process that I was standing in front of an actual deity, many thousands of years old, and coincidentally one of the great villains of our culture. Vo Lai was *not* a minor figure in our stories but rather a primary reason why our people settled in Joabei. His sobriquet was a reference to his preferred clothing, which was always white, but also to his character: He always had plenty of dirty work to do, but he had others do it for him so that he could remain pristine. He was content to let me work through it and he remained silent, studying me. Finally I asked, "Did you kill Saviič, who was here to seek a kenning?"

"Oh, was that his name? Yes."

Such a casual confession! I had to blink and take a couple more breaths before following up. "Where is his body?"

"Why does it matter? Was he a friend that you wish to honor with a howling tube?"

"No. But why did you kill him?"

Sedam shrugged. "He was a seeker."

"You kill all your seekers?"

"No, just a certain proportion of them. Those whom I do not kill, I bless. It's no different than what my siblings do. You're saying it like I've done something wrong."

"Haven't you? The situation was vastly different. You murdered him."

His eyes narrowed, and he cocked his head to one side. "You are blessed with the Second Kenning." Pointing to his right past the statue of Kamen, he said, "By the goddess Shoawei, correct?"

"Yes. Is that what she really looks like?"

"It is. In Kauria they are known as Reinei and thought of as male, but in truth they have no gender. That's not the issue—the issue is you think I have committed some crime when Saviič came to me for a kenning, knowing full well he might die. You did the same thing when you were a seeker."

"I did not present myself to Shoawei and receive her—or their—personal blessing."

"You absolutely did. Even if you did not realize that was what you were doing."

"I threw myself into the wind tunnel on Weidoeng and passed through. I didn't kneel down before them as Saviič did to you."

"You are focusing on details and ignoring the core action: You offered yourself as a sacrifice. Every seeker does this, whether they dive into Bryn's Lung or Thurik's Flame or submit to the roots of the First Tree. Some are blessed and some are slain, out of necessity."

"Necessity?"

"Yes. Of course."

"I don't understand. Why did Saviič need to die?"

"Because . . . oh." His eyebrows climbed up his face. "You truly do not understand how blessings are achieved?"

"No, I thought it was random chance."

"There's an element of randomness, to be sure, because we do not know who will be next when we have sufficient energy to bless someone, but there is absolutely will and intent behind it too. Which blessings we bestow varies according to our whim, and we can store energy enough for multiple blessings if we choose. But what it comes down to is energy— we must consume many souls to bless one."

"What? Did you say *consume?*"

"Perhaps my vocabulary is limited. *Burn* might be a better

word. A blessing is essentially an enchantment on a person that takes tremendous energy to bestow. That energy has to come from somewhere, and with the possible exception of the very first one, it's not coming from us."

"So when people seek a kenning and die . . ."

"Their spirits are saved and used to bless others, yes."

Horror crept into my voice. "You're saying my blessing was made possible by the souls of those who died before me?"

"Yes. You and every other blessed person. The gods do not benefit from your sacrifices; you do."

"No. No, that's—" Saliva flooded my mouth, and my forehead broke out in sweat, harbingers of being ill. I had heard that you could become ill from mental revulsion but had never experienced it until now.

"You're not going to be sick, are you?"

I was very, very sick.

"I have clearly been out of touch too long," Sedam said. "What did you think was happening when people died during a seeking?"

"I thought their souls moved on to the next world. I didn't think they were being *consumed*."

"That is a fundamental misunderstanding of the gods, then," he said. "We are all harvesters of souls."

"No. These are lies. There is a reason we call you the White Demon."

"I am portrayed as the villain in the stories of most cultures, it's true," he admitted. "At least where stories of me still exist. But I am not lying. The children of Teldwen and Kalaad, regardless of what name you call them, consume the souls of many to bestow kennings on the few."

I heaved once more, though my stomach was empty. He waited, and when I'd wiped off my mouth and caught my breath again, I said, "And what is the Seventh Kenning? There's considerable confusion surrounding that."

"It is life itself."

"Ha! I met one of your blessed. He was a monster."

"You did?"

"His name was Lorson."

Interest suddenly piqued, Sedam leaned forward. "Lorson? You met Lorson?"

"Yes. I watched him drain the life from someone else and grow young. It was evil. If that's your blessing, I think it's more of a curse. Thank the winds he's dead now."

"Dead?" That was the first time his smug expression wavered. "How?"

"The person he drained was the best friend of a firelord. And that firelord charred him to cinders."

Some real emotion finally showed through. A snarl through clenched teeth. A pounded fist on the arm of his marble throne.

"When was this?" he demanded.

"A few weeks ago."

"Where?"

"My guess is that you know very well where he was. An island in the north."

"Yes, I did know that. But why were you anywhere near him?"

"I was trying to navigate the Northern Yawn."

"By ship? I'm surprised the krakens didn't have something to say about that."

"They did. I lost a third of my crew." I decided there was no need to inform him of Abhi and the Sixth Kenning. "But I am here nonetheless."

"And did you see a party of Eculans on your way across the Northern Yawn?"

I paused before answering. "From a distance," I said, which was technically true. I didn't want to say much else, because if he knew about the army that attacked us, he probably was part of the reason they were up there. "It was strange. Why were they so far from home?"

"Exploring, the same as you."

He was being coy. Fine. I knew enough: He was upset at Lorson's death and knew the Eculans who attacked us were up there. If he kept company with those who wished us harm, then I did not need to know the details of his plans to know that he was not on our side. He was indeed a villain.

"It would seem they also do not have to fear krakens. So does the Seventh Kenning manifest itself in other ways besides the ability to grow young at the expense of another's life?"

"Oh, yes. Most of those ways are the reason I'm here."

"Why *are* you here, on this island that nobody visits?"

"The Rift, Captain Gansu. The Rift."

I could feel my face scrunch in confusion, trying to attach the name to something familiar. I'd seen it on maps of the six nations. "You mean the sea south of Forn?"

"That too. I mean the series of events that led to the creation of that sea. And the Hathrim, and the mountain ranges surrounding Rael, the Eculans, the krakens, the kenning sites . . . the Rift, in all of its varied meanings, is why the world is the way it is today."

"That sounds like a fascinating story."

The god snorted. "*Fascinating* is one word you could use for it, sure."

"I want to hear it—I have no doubt I *need* to hear it—but I think maybe someone else should as well. Would you mind if I brought a friend to listen?"

Sedam's eyes narrowed into thin slits of suspicion. "That depends on who it is."

"His name is Gondel Vedd. He's a scholar from Kauria, a follower of Reinei, or . . . Mir." I gestured at the second statue. "Them."

"Ah, Kauria! How interesting. I never learned their language, however. Does he speak any others?"

"Many. But I only speak this tongue and Nentian."

He immediately switched. "I know Nentian. Does Gondel Vedd speak it?" When I confirmed that he did, Sedam nodded. "Then he is welcome. But not the water breather you have on that boat. I can sense her. If she steps foot on the island, I will turn her into a wraith."

I gasped. "You're the one who made the wraiths?"

"You saw me do it. Saviič is one of them now."

"No, I just saw him collapse."

"His spirit exited his body, I assure you. They're difficult to see in the sunlight sometimes."

And it finally clicked. "All the wraiths on this island are former seekers who arrived in boatloads on the Seven-Year Ship?"

"Yes. I am a harvester of souls." He smiled sardonically and gestured around. "Witness my bounty."

"So you're just keeping them here instead of using their energy for a blessing?"

"They have other uses."

I remembered that Tallynd wanted a question answered. "I'm supposed to ask if you're the one who killed the Eculans who were found in the bay underneath the Seven-Year Ship."

"Regrettable, but necessary. Because of the Rift."

Necessary murders? That was a defense I hadn't heard before. "Right. The Rift. Okay. I'll go get Gondel. You won't . . . harvest my soul, will you?"

"I wouldn't dream of it. That would indeed be murder because you are not a seeker offering yourself as a sacrifice. And you are blessed by my sibling, and all they have ever wanted is peace. I would not trouble them, for they alone among my family have never troubled me. Even when I was Vo Lai, I was only mildly perturbing, never a genuine threat."

I doubted that very much. In the old stories, our people inhabited a rich and bountiful land. We would not have migrated across oceans and abandoned a paradise over someone who was only mildly perturbing. It was true that we had come to Joabei partially to escape fire demons, but it was also because it was beyond the reach of Vo Lai, who was always scheming to bring ruin to his enemies via trickery and subterfuge. While he may never have caused any direct harm to Shoawei or Joabeians—probably the basis for claiming he was never a genuine threat—that was only because she'd denied him the opportunity. And *because* of him we wore the Bora and the Buran—one blade to face a frontal assault and one to protect against the sneak attack that we may not see but must assume is coming. I wondered if he knew about the story in which the first Bora and Buran were forged to fight him but wound up being used against his followers who attacked a village at night and then claimed in the daylight that it had all been "an accident." He was a dissembler who would say one thing and seem to keep his word but meanwhile would do something else to undermine the promise he made. And his assurance that he wouldn't kill me because I hadn't offered myself as a sacrifice was hardly reassuring when he had confessed to murdering all the Eculans that Tallynd had asked about. It was highly doubtful they had all come to offer themselves as sacrifices.

"And Gondel will be safe if he walks here wearing a cloak?" I asked.

"He will. But follow the path and you won't see wraiths at all. I will clear them away."

"Very well. We shall do as you say. But before I go get him, can you tell me why wraiths cannot fly?"

"They are souls of beings who walked the earth and as such are tied to it. Fly too high and they dissipate into the wind. And because of their tie to the earth, they cannot move across or through water."

"That's good to know. I'll return soon."

———

Once Fintan dispelled Koesha's seeming, a swell of conversation picked up, largely devoted at first to exclamations and curses. I was absolutely a part of that, because I felt, as Koesha had, a bit nauseous at the idea that blessings were fueled by the souls of others. I thought especially of that period after the invasion when the line for Bryn's Lung was long and Culland du Raffert was part of that line. The woman he'd described in his tale who'd died in front of him: Had her death been the final one required to bless him as a tidal mariner? I could only imagine how ill the blessed in the city must feel—how Fintan himself must feel, knowing that the seekers who perished in the quicksands of the earth goddess allowed him to be blessed as a bard. And I wondered what "other uses" the spirits might provide to the gods. If they were energy, then that meant . . . food, right? But mostly I wondered where the other gods were, if they weren't on that island with Žalost, or Sedam. Where was Bryn? Was he hiding somewhere in the underwater cavern we called his lung? Did Thurik dwell in the lake of lava at the base of Mount Olenik? And I hoped we would hear more of what Koesha knew about him—the Joabeians apparently had a deep mistrust of this god that we'd somehow never heard of until recently.

Fintan held up his hands in an attempt to quiet us and said, "I know that was difficult to hear. And what comes next is even more difficult, and it will take some time to wrestle it into something we can accept. But I think reporting it is necessary, and if it helps, please consider the source. The interests of this god of the Seventh Kenning are not ours. As you will find out, he is motivated to destroy this city, and as such, he will not hesitate to mix lies with the truth. Our job, as allied peoples, is to make sure he is defeated and not let him defeat us with a few words.

"Let's allow the Kaurian scholar, Gondel Vedd, to reveal the rest of it."

Gondel

Tallynd du Böll noticed the wraiths moving away from the end of the dock and pointed it out moments before Captain Gansu returned to inform us that Saviič was dead and that the source of the Seventh Kenning was in fact the god of the Seventh Kenning, Žalost, who was waiting by the temple and preferred the name Sedam.

"His name is the number seven in the old language?" I asked.

"I don't know the old language," Koesha reminded me. "But, listen, he is responsible for the wraiths, he knows Lorson—he *created* Lorson—and he also knows about the army in the Northern Yawn. I'm pretty sure he's the reason behind everything bad that's happened, but of course he's not taking responsibility. He claims that it all goes back to the Rift."

"The Rift? What does he know about the Rift?"

"He is willing to share everything he knows." She waggled a finger between the two of us. "I mean with you and me, Scholar. He hates all his siblings except for the second, who is either Shoawei or Reinei, so he will talk to us specifically since we worship them."

"Them?"

"Yes. It turns out the god of the Second Kenning originally had no gender. Who knew?"

"Certainly not the priests of the gale. Some of them are going to be surprised."

"And, Second Könstad—Scholar, translate for me, please—he said you should not set foot on the island or he will turn you into a wraith."

Tallynd blinked and asked, "Why?"

"I'm not sure, except that he seems to have a special hatred for Bryn and his followers. I think that's part of the Rift thing. But he says he can sense you from where he's at, and it must be true because I didn't tell him you were here. So I wouldn't test him on that point. I think it's good that Brynts avoid this place."

I donned a cloak and so did Koesha, even though the wraiths had withdrawn to the trees and stayed clear of the path. I took a sheaf of papers along with a pen and inkpot to scribble down some notes, in case I got the chance, my mind whirling like a torus. If this god preferred the name Sedam, then the title of *Zanata Sedam* could be translated to *Sedam's Kenning* just as easily as it could be *The Seventh Kenning*.

The island was mostly silent, except for the whispering of leaves in the wind. I wondered if Reinei was trying to tell me something.

When we got to the temple site, I imagined that whispering might be telling me I should get back to the ship as fast as I could. Because the mere existence of the site was impossible. The stone on display suggested a quarry nearby, but I was fairly certain marble was not part of these islands. If it had been shipped here, then that was across kraken-infested oceans hundreds of years ago, and someone—I couldn't imagine who—built it all.

The statues facing the temple, just as Captain Gansu described, were remarkable, though the pale, thin god sitting on the center throne with his legs crossed and his hands clasped across his knee was singular. "You are the Kaurian scholar who speaks Nentian?" he asked when my eyes fell on him. No greetings or welcome.

"Gondel Vedd, yes. And you are Sedam, the god of the Seventh Kenning?"

"I am."

"May we breathe peace. Who built this place?"

"Some followers of mine, a few hundred years ago."

"Would that include an individual named Lorson?"

"It would indeed. Have you met him?"

"No, I've only heard of him. I'm also told you want to tell me the story of the Rift. That's a keen interest of my personal studies."

"Is it? I'm curious what you've learned. Do you already know the origins of the Hathrim?"

"All I've been able to discover are some claims that they used to be Fornish, but no explanation of precisely when or how that happened. I think many records have been lost."

Sedam chuckled wryly and shook his head. "They weren't lost. They were purposefully erased. This is precisely why you need to hear this story: It hasn't been told in a very long time. If my siblings are going to thwart me at every turn, I think the rest of the world should know what they've done. I'm counting on you to spread the word."

"I will do my best. I've brought writing materials. Might there be somewhere I can take notes?"

"Of course. If you'll wait here a moment." He rose and strode into the temple, presumably to fetch something, and that gave me time to examine the statues of the other six deities.

I of course took particular interest in the second, and Captain Gansu joined me.

"What do you think, Scholar?" she said.

"Call me Gondel, please. What do I think about what, Captain?"

"Call me Koesha. Do you think their name was really Mir all this time?"

"I don't think so. No more than Žalost was the correct name for Sedam. It is merely the Eculan name for them. I think the name doesn't matter so much as the essence of the being. Looking at that expression, I think we got that right, no matter if they are called Reinei or Shoawei or something else. We worship a deity of peace."

"Shoawei is more focused on exploration and trade and

does not prohibit warfare the way I've heard Reinei does, but we tend to favor peace because it allows us the freedom to explore and profit."

"I'd be fascinated to read your sacred texts, if ever I get a chance."

"And I yours."

Sedam returned with a stone pedestal that had to weigh more than he did, but he carried it with little apparent effort. He set it down, made no mention of whatever had been resting upon it before, and gestured to it grandly.

"A makeshift desk. I haven't any chairs, unfortunately, besides my own." He crossed to it and seated himself as I thanked him and put my papers and pen on the pedestal. I couldn't budge it—a casual demonstration of his strength.

"Are you aware of the Eculan invasion of the continent, Gondel Vedd?" he asked.

"I am."

"No doubt it has caused tremendous grief and suffering and continues to do so. But I was forced to engineer it, together with Lorson and others, because I felt it was my best chance at freeing myself from my exile. I have been alone on this island—imprisoned, really—for thousands of years. I long for a change of scenery."

Koesha and I exchanged a glance, openmouthed, to see if the other had heard the same thing. "You launched a genocidal war because . . . you wanted a change of scenery?"

"Don't sound so surprised. Most wars, I think you'll find, are fought over scenery. Or land, which is the same thing. And again: *thousands* of years. Here, on this pathetic collection of crags and trees, with no end in sight. What other options did I have—just wait longer? No. My desire for change is well beyond your comprehension, and there was no other path available to me than the one I took."

"Go on," I said, and reminded myself that it would be better to interrupt less if I wanted the story. I wrote: *Genocide for scenery. Simply no other choice!*

"I am trapped here by my brother, whom I believe you know as Bryn, together with the krakens, and they monitor the island to make sure I don't escape. My powers are remarkable, but I cannot summon winds to fly me away from here, and if I try to swim or take a ship, I am soon thwarted by the efforts of my siblings. I have been physically borne back to shore on waves many times, at all hours of the day. I have had krakens destroy multiple ships and then pluck me from the deeps and toss me onto the beach. Once, in my desperation, I killed a kraken, and I was handled rather roughly after that and nearly drowned. It became clear that the only solution to my problem would be a long-term campaign to weaken Brynlön—ideally taking over the site of the Fourth Kenning—while simultaneously seeking the elimination of krakens. But I couldn't achieve such goals alone: No, indeed, to make that happen I would need a large army willing to commit atrocities. The simplest way to get one of those, if you have the time, is to start a religion, because people will happily do terrible things to one another if they can tell themselves they're doing it to please a god."

He paused while I jotted down a few notes, and when I looked up and nodded, trying to keep my expression neutral, he continued.

"We came to this state of affairs because long ago, when we seven were worshipped together and humans made sacrifices to us all, I blessed some humans to become harvesters, lifeleeches, balms, and—most important—metamorphs. Two of the humans I happened to bless as metamorphs were Fornish, who are, as you're no doubt aware, somewhat diminutive. They often wished they were taller, and as metamorphs, they had the ability to do something about it."

"I'm not familiar with all of those terms," I said, scribbling furiously.

He waved a hand dismissively. "Come back to it later. Focus on metamorphs for now. The Seventh Kenning, as I was telling Captain Gansu, concerns itself with life. Every creature is built according to a code embedded in its blood, and that code determines what it looks like—its health, appearance, everything physical about it. Metamorphs could see that code, manipulate it, and force a change. So a Fornish person who wished to be taller—say, like me—could make it happen by rewriting the code. One particular metamorph on the eastern coast altered himself, his family, and his friends into taller Fornish people. When others in their village saw this and wished to become taller as well, he obliged them, and likewise for others of his tribe in other villages. When the Rift happened, this tribe was cast out of Forn, migrated across the ocean, and became the Eculans you know today.

"But these people had done nothing wrong; they simply grew taller and passed that trait down to their children. It was the work of two other metamorphs in the west that caused the Rift. One was named Fil Ben Suf—and that second name was an actual Fornish name at the time, not an honorific to signify the blessed, as it is used today. The honorific originated with Fil Ben Suf, to denote someone who had been changed from their original nature.

"He experimented with plants as well as animals and had a much broader imagination than the fellow who wished merely to be taller. Fil Ben Suf created the bantil plant, exploding gas gourds, whipthorns, strange fungi, giant spiders, and so much more. Some of his experiments were not viable and did not survive. But the success of some giant spiders inspired him to work in a similar vein—making larger, more vicious versions of creatures that already existed. Thus we got sand badgers and lava dragons, glass scorpions and all the extraordinary creatures of Hathrir, and some of the plants, like emberfruit.

"But then, like his counterpart in the east but at the same

time unlike him, he made taller Fornish. Much, much taller, and more muscular, and prone to grow lots of hair of differing colors. From a group of volunteers, he created the Hathrim—and, soon afterward, the Hathrim hounds."

"Reinei bless me, all of that from one metamorph?" My research that claimed the Hathrim used to be Fornish had never suggested origins like this.

"Correct. The Hathrim were incredibly pleased with themselves at first, and in their elation encouraged others to become like them, until there was a fair number. But then several things happened almost at once: They realized that the amount of food they needed to consume to fuel their larger bodies was absolutely enormous and not sustainable using Fornish methods. They realized that they could fairly easily take what they needed from the smaller Fornish. And then, when some of them realized where this was headed and didn't like it, they discovered that Fil Ben Suf couldn't change them back."

"He couldn't?"

"No. Metamorphosis by its very nature occurs in only one direction. The butterfly cannot return to being a caterpillar. He attempted to change a couple of them back, and they died rather horrifically in the attempt. When you have an enlarged heart and skeleton and everything, there is no way to safely size them down to their former dimensions. There was a lot of howling after that, and Fil Ben Suf was summarily executed by one of the enraged Hathrim, ending his experiments.

"But, meanwhile, there was another metamorph of the people you now call Nentians, who crossed the Godsteeth and traveled the plains, creating the many dangerous animals that plague the land today: flesh eels, cheek raptors, kherns, bloodcats, and more."

"May I have his name?"

"Bharat Vellala. He traveled north and kept experimenting, creating both the ravenous creatures of the Gravewood and interesting prey animals to feed their appetites. Like Fil Ben Suf, he often tweaked existing animals to make them more dangerous. Regular squirrels became meat squirrels, common weasels became murder weasels, and so on. When he got to the Northern Yawn, he made even more wondrous beasts. Most significant, a common longarm was swollen and warped to become a kraken.

"That particular metamorph's life ended when he decided to create the first tripod of gravemaws and they wound up eating him. We wouldn't know what happened except that his family witnessed the entire thing from the safety of a ship in the Northern Yawn. They sailed back south and reported it."

"Amazing. So there were only three metamorphs, then?"

"Yes. I hadn't blessed that many. The first one, which created the Eculans, avoided changing animals after that and focused on food plants, primarily tea, wheat, things of that nature. The Fornish and Kaurian teas the six nations enjoy today were mostly his doing."

I was writing as fast as I could, but luckily Koesha asked one of the many questions in my own head. "And did the other gods bless people with kennings at the same time?"

"They weren't called kennings yet, but yes. We were all experimenting with different blessings."

"Why?"

Sedam shrugged a shoulder. "Partly out of curiosity. Because we wanted to see what people would do with them. Or encourage them to use them in certain ways."

"And this was all happening in Forn?"

"Not Forn as it is today. This was everything south of the Godsteeth, which was, I must stress, a natural mountain range created by great plates of earth crashing together and pushing upward. Hathrir and Kauria were both still connected to the main continent at the time. All the various peoples of the world were in that area, but after the Rift, all tribes save the Fornish spread across the globe, following their patron god or goddess."

"And so we have finally come to the Rift?"

"Essentially, yes, though it was a layered event that unfolded over time. The first rift was between me and my siblings—they began by demanding that I make no more metamorphs, and I obliged, seeing how much uncertainty and chaos could be sown by so few. But then they also demanded that I stop blessing people altogether, and that annoyed me. My other blessings were gifts of extended life—though someone always had to pay the price for it. I thought it fascinating to see what choices would be made. The others found it abominable.

"The second rift was between the Hathrim and all the other tribes. The latter did their best to kill the animals created by Fil Ben Suf whenever they saw them, and they included the Hathrim in that classification. Tensions—a polite term for violent clashes—rose over a period of decades, until there was a general belief that all the Hathrim were murderers and raiders and needed to be wiped out. The other tribes began to gear up for war and prayed to my siblings and me for aid. That is when blessings began to get specialized and sorted themselves into the Seven Kennings."

"You could all perform the same blessings?"

"No, but there was some overlap here and there. I have no powers whatsoever regarding water or wind but some skill with the earth. My siblings also have some of my abilities, but not to the extent I do."

"So you are a metamorph yourself?"

"Oh, yes."

"Have you tried creating a creature capable of taking you away from here, one that could defend itself against krakens?"

"I have. I did create a couple of such creatures and attempted my escape. And as soon as I did, my youngest sister took control of them and thwarted me, for her abilities regarding animals are unmatched."

"I see. Thank you. You were speaking of how the kennings became sorted."

"Yes. My oldest brother, whom you know as Thurik, took the part of the Hathrim, seeing them as unfairly persecuted, and while he was a god of the forge and encouraged his blessed to use it in craft, flames obviously had a martial application as well. He began granting his blessings exclusively to Hathrim and sought their worship through some teachings he dictated. A culture and religion coalesced around this and became known as the First Kenning."

"But just to clarify, these blessings were granted in person—seekers coming directly to the gods, who walked the earth at the time?" I asked.

"Yes. As Saviič so recently came to me."

"And they knew that the gods might simply kill them to bless someone else?"

"They did. It was always a willing sacrifice. We did not demand them. Humans actively sought our blessings. And the Hathrim, newly organized and powerful due to Thurik's favor, became even more of a threat that needed to be countered. My other siblings reacted to this in different ways: The god you worship, whether under the name of Reinei or Shoawei, wished for peace and to simply live far away, where the fighting could not reach them or those who chose to worship them. They harnessed the power of air, the absence of which would render the firelords powerless, and blessed their followers with it, creating the Second Kenning and its attendant religions. And it is at this point that the world physically changed, for they went to my eldest sister, whom you know as Dinae, and begged her to give them a land far from the war and to put an end to the war by separating the Hathrim from the rest."

"So Dinae is a goddess of the earth?"

"No, our mother Teldwen is the goddess of the earth. I think it is more accurate to think of Dinae as governing stone and memory, but the earth, of course, is a convenient catchall term. In any case, out of love for her sibling, and during a rather epic battle where a tremendous number of people of all tribes died and the Glass Desert was formed, she was moved to grant their wish. In a literally seismic display of power, she split Hathrir and Kauria off from Forn, creating the physical Rift. That ended the battle—the entire war, in fact—and began a massive migration around the world. Most of the tribes left Forn and settled in the countries you find them in today, because my brothers and sisters consciously focused their blessings on chosen tribes and created the specific kennings, all out of a fear that the others would become aggressive, like the Hathrim had. They were making an effort, in other words, not to counter just my blessings but Thurik's and every other, to create a rough sort of stability by giving each people a kenning that would help them thrive and defend themselves but would make it difficult to dominate the others. The Joabeians, fearful of not only the Hathrim but what else may arise from the followers of Vo Lai the White Demon—that's what they called me—left the continent entirely and settled as far away as possible in some islands in the northeast."

I checked in briefly with Koesha and she gave a curt nod, indicating that her people did in fact call him that.

"Since Dinae wished to protect her favored tribe, the Raelechs, from the rest of the world, she settled her people in a bowl north of the Godsteeth that she created by raising up the two mountain ranges known as the Huntress and Poet's, and she filled those ranges with mineral riches that guaranteed the Raelechs would prosper. Another tribe who worshipped her migrated across the ocean to Omesh—you would know of them, Koesha.

"Bryn's people settled far from Hathrir, wanting nothing to do with them, though of course they are very close to these islands and have a strong cultural taboo against visiting them. My second-eldest sister, whom the Raelechs call Kaelin, remained with the Fornish. The Nentians followed my third sister northwest to occupy the vast plains, but curiously, unlike the others, she didn't bestow any blessings or create a religion, despite the pleading of her people. She claimed she never wanted to accept sacrifices."

"Absolutely fascinating," I said, again neglecting to mention that she accepted them now. "But that doesn't address the kenning sites."

"No. Because that came a bit later, after the physical creation of the Rift and the mass migrations began. The Eculan tribe had not done anyone harm and lived in peace, but since they were my favored people, a lot of ire was directed at them. I was to blame for metamorphs, you see, and therefore all the misery and war that followed, which caused the Rift. Eculans became a target. There were lifeleeches among them, and a harvester too. They hadn't left Forn like the other tribes, but the Fornish wanted them out and began to starve them by killing their crops, encouraging the growth of poisonous plants nearby, and with innumerable harassments using the Fifth Kenning, never raising a blade.

"I warned my sister that this was provocation to war and asked her to intervene. She refused and suggested that I solve the problem by asking my tribe to migrate instead—there were large islands across the sea, waiting to be settled, and the Eculans could move there and have plenty of room to grow without harassment.

"The unfairness of it still galls me today. The Eculans had done no wrong, offered no arms. Threatened with starvation and worse for no crime other than worshipping me—why were they supposed to leave? I told them to fight. I showed them how.

"A harvester of souls can pluck a person's spirit out of their body and then command the wraith to possess someone else and fight for him. A lifeleech can drain someone's life and use the energy to reverse their own aging process, regenerate tissue, increase their physical strength, or all three. I watched a leech take a sword to the heart, grab the arm of the soldier who had dealt what would normally be a fatal blow, and drain their life away to heal up their heart and keep fighting.

"Still, when we had some success at fighting back the Fornish, the other tribes allied against the Eculans, forcing them to flee after all, and I went with them to ensure they prospered.

"The great irony is that the Fornish at that time did not have thornhands or greensleeves. They had culturists and grassgliders, the lower-level blessings only. But Kaelin—and, indeed, the rest of my siblings—eventually tampered with life's coding the same way that my metamorphs had, and they did this to create their most powerful blessings, like greensleeves and furies and juggernauts. Yet even though they were behaving the same way, I was in the wrong somehow. They saw me as a long-term threat, even after decades had passed and I was living peacefully in Ecula, offering them no problems. Still they joined together to isolate me and render me powerless."

I held up a finger as I scribbled madly, signaling that I had a question. I had many questions, in fact, like how much of this were we honestly supposed to believe? Because his siblings wouldn't plot to isolate him even more after decades of living in peace. But what I asked was, "Do you know where they crafted this plot?"

"Yes. They did it in Rael—Killae, to be precise. My sisters crafted the scrolls that the Raelechs consider their sacred texts and devised a long-term strategy. My other siblings were there too, even my eldest brother, and they decided in concert that they would remove themselves from their physical forms and take on a new, distributed existence as the sources of kennings, while simultaneously propagating religions and cultures built around those sites."

"But why?" I asked. "That's an extraordinary decision. Why did they decide to bind themselves to sites?"

"Convenience, as far as I can tell."

"How so?"

"They couldn't be in two or more places at once otherwise. Their peoples were scattered across the world. Dinae's people in Rael, for example, would have the benefit of her blessings for a while, and Omesh would languish in the meantime. When she departed to help Omesh, Rael would suffer. That seemed unsustainable and unfair to them. But more important, I think, binding themselves to geographical features also removed the eye contact."

"I'm sorry—the eye contact?"

"Yes. The direct pleading, the bowing and prostration, the prayers, and always, always, the moist, weeping eyes. It's deeply uncomfortable to be assailed with them even once per day. Imagine a nonstop parade of it and you'll have a glimpse into the horror of being a god. If you're a lake of lava at the base of Mount Olenik, you don't have to look at supplicants or listen to prayers or anything. You simply deal with the sacrifices when they jump in to offer themselves. And if you're a twirling tempest off the coast of Kauria or a gale gusting through a tunnel in Joabei, it's the same thing. There are no eyes."

"I see," Koesha said, and I shot a sharp look at her to determine whether she was interjecting with a joke. Sedam took no notice, however, and continued.

"Dinae split herself between the quicksands of Rael and Omesh. Kaelin transformed into the First Tree in Forn and eventually split into the Second and Third Trees as well.

"The deity you both worship obviously split into Reinei in

Kauria and Shoawei in Joabei. Thurik also divided himself, between the volcanoes at Olenik and Odlazak. But Bryn and Raena—they were different. Purposely so. Bryn has only the one source of the Fourth Kenning, at Pelemyn, and otherwise diffused himself in the actual oceans. And Raena, well— for some reason, she decided to inhabit the consciousness of that kraken created by one of my metamorphs but otherwise bestow no blessing, leaving the poor Nentians to fend for themselves on the plains."

I very carefully did not look at Koesha and merely accepted that as true. I saw no reason to correct him and point out that at least one man had been blessed with the Sixth Kenning now, and Koesha likewise kept silent about that.

And I also tried to hide my shock as earlier intelligence finally made sense. The Eculan army headed to the north and looking for "the Kraken's Nest" was most likely looking for a very specific kraken: the first one created by a metamorph, now hosting the goddess Raena. I wasn't sure what they thought they'd be able to do if they found her, but presumably they had a plan.

Sedam continued, "The two of them are most directly responsible for imprisoning me here. One day, thousands of years ago, as I was walking along the coast near Sveto Selo, a kraken's tentacle emerged from the ocean and grabbed me from behind, then threw me unceremoniously into the ocean. That was Raena. She didn't touch me except for those two seconds, before I could target her and rip her spirit from the flesh. Once I plunged into the sea, Bryn took over, and he had no bodily form for me to target. I was completely at his mercy. He bore me on waves and, later, on a chunk of ice, all the way to this island. I washed up on this shore, coughing and spluttering, and a tentacle tossed a sealed container onto the beach with a scroll in it, explaining what had been done and that my actions had left my siblings 'no choice' but to exile me here for eternity, supposedly for the benefit of all humanity.

"And so I ask you: If they can create religions to manipulate populations for their own purposes, why can't I?"

With almighty restraint, I did not point out to him that the other faiths of the world frowned upon genocide. "Why indeed," is what I said instead.

"And if they had no choice but to exile me, then I have no choice but to escape, however I may."

I made a noncommittal sound. He had rationalized his behavior quite neatly. "Forgive me, Sedam, but might you know why Raena chose to bind herself to a kraken?"

"To prevent me from getting any help. The krakens keep the nations isolated and allow only a brief annual window of unfettered sailing. It's not enough to find me and set me free, and this location, you'll note, is far away from Kauria and Joabei, where fliers such as Koesha might find me."

"But Lorson obviously found you."

"That he did. That was a good piece of luck. I was very tempted to try sailing away with him when he landed, since the krakens were absent at the time. But I knew that Bryn would be watching, so I conceived a different plan. Together we have accomplished rather a lot—some holy writ; a famous ship to bring me a fresh cargo of beseeching eyes every seven years; armies pointed at Brynlön and searching for my tentacled sister. It's not been enough, of course, because I'm still here, but despite Lorson's demise, our efforts may yet bear fruit."

"Even still?"

"Of course. The kraken may yet be found. Brynlön may yet fall."

"Forgive me, but . . . how would that help?"

A hint of impatience crept into his tone. "Have you not paid attention? My siblings derive their powers from souls, just as I do. If people stopped throwing themselves into

Bryn's Lung, then my brother would be weakened, perhaps enough for me to win free of the ocean's pull. Taking over Pelemyn, therefore, has long been the answer to my problem."

"Which the Eculans failed to do," I said, "so what might be your answer now?"

Before Sedam could respond, Koesha asked, "Why don't you have me fly you out of here?" I thought that was a terrible idea that just might work. But Sedam barked in laughter.

"Ha! Think about why I might hesitate."

"Because . . . I could drop you from a very great height and you can't recover from a shattered skull?"

"Precisely. I am sure you are an honorable person, Koesha Gansu, but forgive me for being unable to trust my long life to a new acquaintance whose culture literally demonizes me. The fault is mine."

"No, no, I understand completely," she said.

Sedam smirked and leaned back as a thought occurred to him. "Perhaps we could build a bit of trust now, however. Would you permit me to grant you a blessing?"

"What? No, thank you. I've seen a lifeleech, and that sort of thing is not for me."

I noticed he did not ask me if I wanted a blessing, but I was not particularly put out, since I would have provided the same answer. While I hadn't met a lifeleech, it didn't sound like a savory business.

Sedam leaned forward again, interested. "I wasn't thinking of making you a lifeleech but rather its opposite: a balm."

"What's a balm?"

"Balms can give others youth and vitality at the expense of their own. They also heal any wounds in the process."

"Oh. So it really is the opposite of a lifeleech."

"Yes. And there is no risk to you, no sacrifice that must be offered, because I am offering it to you as a gift."

"Without expectation of anything in return?"

"Without obligation, yes. That's what a gift is."

"That's kind, but . . . why me? Why not Saviič, who dropped to his knees and begged you for a blessing?"

"He did not want to be a balm. You should have heard him. He wanted the power to destroy, not heal. He wished to take rather than give." Sedam gestured widely to the east, apparently referring to the wraiths. "All of these seekers from Ecula wanted power to dominate others. So I have not blessed any in a very long time, and now there will be no more. The Seven-Year Ship isn't returning to Ecula again."

"I don't understand—are you offering that up as evidence that you have benign intentions?" Koesha crossed her arms in front of her and cocked a skeptical eyebrow at him. "Because you've also admitted to creating the very religion that made Eculans want to come here and discover a way to dominate others. If they're doing exactly what you prompted them to do, it's a bit cheeky to judge them for it."

The god smiled. "I am not offering any defenses or rationalizations. I am merely saying that there is more than enough energy available for me to give you a blessing—energy that would go to waste otherwise—and I believe you would use that blessing for good."

"This would do nothing to my current blessing from Shoawei?"

"Correct. You will still be a zephyr. But you will also be a balm. People can be blessed more than once, but it's extremely rare, because you would have to offer yourself for sacrifice each time."

Koesha stared at him, thinking, and tapped the toe of her boot on the ground a couple of times. She blew air in exasperation through her nose, which reminded me that I should probably breathe.

Finally, she said, "I admit I am suspicious of your motives. I suppose the trust isn't there."

Sedam nodded his understanding. "Ah. You think I'm a monster."

I could not speak for Koesha, but I absolutely thought he was a monster. He could pull my spirit out of my body with a thought and leave me to roam the island with the other wraiths, silently screaming until he decided one day to consume me. He was unassailable and he knew it, and his siblings had been very clever to exile him the way they did. Part of me wanted to ask him for more details about the old wars and the formation of the Glass Desert and the Rift, cataclysmic events that he skipped over in a few sentences, but the larger part of me wanted to flee at this point, far away from this god who casually plotted to murder and manipulate civilizations and claim he had no choice. It would be best not to provoke him, but Koesha flirted with the tempest anyway.

"I think you're more of a puppet master," she replied. "This whole world's been dancing on the end of your strings, and they never knew you were here."

Sedam snorted. "That's a bit unfair, don't you think? Surely my siblings are keeping the world dancing every bit as much, if not more, than I am."

"That might be too big for me to judge."

"So you don't want the blessing?"

"I didn't say that. I'm trying to peer through the wind you're blowing in my eyes to see what's coming behind it. I must have a believable reason why. Because your other actions do not point to a soul inclined to goodwill. We did not label you as a demon for nothing."

He nodded thoughtfully. "Ah, okay, thank you for explaining. But the reason is simple enough: I am motivated by guilt to do something unequivocally good. Making you a balm would in fact be a balm to my troubled conscience."

"Oh, I see. This is for your own redemption."

"Yes."

"That makes sense to me. But uncounted thousands have died—"

"Hundreds of thousands," I jumped in.

"Hundreds of thousands have died because of your actions. Making me a healer will not balance the ledger."

"I'm well aware. But the world should know I am capable of doing good things when I am no longer unjustly imprisoned. You know those cloaks made of Eculan wool? I helped the Eculans develop those sheep. Best wool in the world. I could have done so much more if . . . I wasn't here."

"You've done plenty. I don't wish to rehabilitate your image, but neither do I wish to pass up the opportunity to heal someone when they need it. I feel that if I refuse this blessing, I'll find myself in a situation where I really wish I'd said yes, and, anyway, this small thing cannot possibly make up for the war you've started. So go ahead. Make me a balm if that is your desire."

Sedam grinned like a schoolboy given permission to go outside and play. He scooted himself forward so that he sat on the edge of his seat with an erect posture. He stretched out his right hand.

"The blessing has temporary side effects. You will feel hot for a few seconds, then cold for a few more, but after that your body will stabilize."

He closed his eyes and said something in a language I did not recognize, and shortly thereafter Koesha widened her eyes. Sweat stood out abruptly from the pores of her forehead.

"Op!" she cried, which was an exclamation of surprise I'd heard from other members of her crew. I really must begin to learn their language, but Koesha's jaw dropped and she clutched herself, suddenly freezing. In a rare moment of situational awareness, it occurred to me that now might not be the best time to ask her about language lessons. She sucked in a couple of heavy, shuddering breaths, and then it was over.

"There," Sedam said. "Now you are a balm. Practice on Gondel Vedd."

"What?" Koesha said at nearly the same time as I did.

"Simply take his hand and concentrate on granting him a year of youth."

"Which means I'll age a year?"

"Yes. But I will replenish you, never fear. This is a free exercise."

Koesha and I stared at each other uncertainly for a while, but then she took my hand and said, "Ready?"

"Not in the slightest. Aging backward is not something I've ever done."

She grinned at me. "You deserve a much longer life, Gondel. I wish I could give you more."

"You can," Sedam said. "Give him five years, or ten or twenty. I'll replenish you."

"No," I said. "No. Just a year, Koesha, to feel what it's like. It wouldn't be fair to Maron to do any more than that. We wanted to grow old together, and that's still what I intend to do."

"Aw. You are the sweetest man," she said. She took a deep breath, closed her eyes, and squeezed my hand. It flooded with a warmth that traveled throughout my body, after which I felt incredibly refreshed and my aches were all gone.

"Reinei's sweet breath, I feel amazing! Did you heal me?"

Koesha nodded, her eyes half shut and looking drowsy. "I think I fixed up your joints a bit."

"Do I look any different?"

"Yes. It's subtle, because it's only a year, but you look better."

"It's wondrous. But what about you?"

"I can reliably report that I do not feel better."

"Oh, no. I don't want that—can you reverse it? Take it back?"

"No. That would make me a lifeleech."

Sedam spoke up. "I promised I would take care of it, and I keep my word." His hand flicked carelessly toward Koesha, and she gasped and shuddered briefly before standing a bit straighter; she obviously felt invigorated.

"I've read *Zanata Sedam,* by the way," I said, changing the subject before either of us could get carried away with gratitude. "May I ask you about a passage?"

"Of course."

"It's about the first few lines: *In the beginning there were seven, and in the end there shall be one.* Seven and one of what?"

The god laughed. "You have hit upon the delight of vague language in religion. The most toxic interpretation that serves the interests of authorities at the time will always take hold. It refers to my siblings, of course, but I am sure it's thought to refer to the kennings and that the Seventh Kenning will ultimately triumph over the other six, which means that Ecula would eventually dominate all other nations."

That was precisely what Teela Parr and I had feared when I first translated it, and I could see now that it may not only be responsible for driving Ecula to be expansionist but that it had been intended to do so from the beginning.

"I initially had trouble translating what follows. Even though I think I have the words right now, it still escapes me. Could you help me with this? It said, *Only when there is one shall the Rift be healed and ideation return to the world. Then those who were shunned and exiled will thrive, and the selfish and rapacious will perish.* Is that correct?"

"Not sure about the word *ideation*—it might not have a satisfactory analogue. The original word stands for the ability to realize your full potential as a being."

"Understood," I said. "But how can the Rift be healed if you're the only one of the seven siblings left? Will all their powers be absorbed by you somehow and you'll be able to control the waters as Bryn does?"

Sedam chuckled. "Not at all. You're so concerned about

the literal specifics that you're missing what it accomplishes metaphorically. That passage suggests that when my siblings are defeated, good things will happen for Eculans, while bad things will happen to their enemies. It reflects the basic concept at the core of all religious manipulation: Behave in certain ways to please a deity, and you will be rewarded while others outside your group will suffer—or at least not prosper so well as you. Yes, that's at the heart of the faith of Reinei and Shoawei too. And I see by your faces you're horrified by this idea, and you're probably making lists in your head of all the pure and good things that your religion promotes or inspires. I will grant you all of it. The faiths of the world do produce people who are genuinely good and inspire the wretched to be better. They do that while also furthering the corrupt agendas and desires of people in power. My siblings created religions that accomplish many things, but primarily they have accomplished keeping me in exile for thousands of years.

"So you can ask me all day, Scholar Vedd, about what this line or that line means in *Zanata Sedam*, but the truth is I don't care, because it's already served its purpose, which is to get Eculans to act in my interests while thinking they are acting in theirs."

"And you are telling me all this because . . . you plan on killing me shortly?"

"No! I already said that I want you to tell the story of the Rift. Tell your people everything, because they know nothing. Let them judge me if they wish. But they should judge their own gods first."

"But if you are judged harshly, won't that simply ensure that you remain here?"

"It might, if human judgment had any power to affect my fate." Sedam settled back on his throne and crossed one leg over the other, bobbing a foot gently as if he were having friends over for a spot of tea and a natter. "Events are in motion now that I cannot stop, even if I wished to."

"But you don't wish to," Koesha said.

"No. I very much wish to get off this blasted island. But what holds true for me holds true for you as well: These events cannot be stopped. Their success is rather more uncertain, but I imagine the odds are even, and there is nothing that you or I can do to make them better or worse. Should you still live at the end of the summer, Koesha, come by and let me know what happened, won't you? I give you my solemn vow to do you no harm, even if events do not play out the way I hope."

Koesha gave him a tiny bow. "I promise to visit if, as you say, I still live."

How she could say that so calmly was beyond me. I wanted nothing more than to leave while he was still of a mind to let us. I had additional questions, for sure, but no desire to ask them anymore when he had admitted so frankly to evils and thought himself a virtuous victim.

"Thank you, Sedam." Normally, manners would dictate that I say how pleasant it had been to visit him and wish him peace, but it had grown steadily more terrifying as I learned he'd been engineering a genocide for decades at the very least, so peace was not high on his personal wish list. Instead, I said, "I appreciate you taking time to speak with us."

He knew, unfortunately, exactly what I had failed to say. Steepling his fingers, he said with a soulful expression, "Farewell, Gondel Vedd. May you breathe peace. And, Koesha, may the winds of Shoawei steer you to prosperity."

The zephyr nodded and summoned a wind to fly us out of there, all my notes trailing behind us. When we landed on the deck of the Seven-Year Ship, she started barking orders for an immediate departure, after first ordering that the wheelbarrow full of wraith cloaks be brought on board. The second könstad understandably wanted to know what had happened, but Koesha convinced her that we needed to make all possible haste back to Fornyd. I scrambled to snatch my notes out of the air and retired to the cabin to write down as coherent a narrative as I could while it was still fresh in my mind.

I didn't know how much—if any—of what Sedam had told us was true, but I wanted it preserved so that other minds could pore over it and determine what was truth and what was lies.

"And that was all we learned from the island," Fintan said, dispelling Gondel's seeming. "It was a *lot*."

I agreed. I remembered that Gondel Vedd's earliest tales had been focused on the Rift and I'd thought it was kind of endearing, because becoming briefly obsessed with the Rift was a thing most history buffs did at one point or another, before running aground on a sharp reef of want—a want of primary sources. The records available were scant, and most everything one could read now summarized the same few scraps and then speculated endlessly. I mean, you could go visit the Glass Desert—that was an undeniable record that something absolutely heinous had happened a long time ago, with what had to be multiple furies and firelords—but the shining surface kept its secrets. To have the tiniest glimpse of an actual narrative of that time—from someone who had been there and yet was not exactly trustworthy—was maddening.

I expected that, after this, every history buff would revisit their Rift phase. We would be cross-referencing every detail of Gondel's narrative with what we knew to determine what might be true and what couldn't be confirmed. And I'd be asking Fintan to share any detail, however small, that he might have elided for the purposes of pacing in his storytelling.

Did I want to go the island and ask Sedam a few questions?

Sure, sure. But it was a desire subordinate to the wish for his immediate destruction, because he was the reason so many of our friends, relatives, and fellow citizens had been murdered. I wanted a fury to raze the surface, the pelenaut himself to send a tidal wave after that to drown everything, and then a juggernaut to drop the whole island into the ocean. How's *that* for a change of scenery, Sedam? Even as I thought this and a swell of rage was building in the city and on Survivor Field, I saw Fintan look back over his left shoulder. Following his gaze, I spied the pelenaut standing there. Fintan beckoned him forward and then he said, "Pelenaut Röllend would like a word."

"Friends," Rölly said, "I know what you just heard was immensely disturbing. It's going to take a lot of time to evaluate and there will no doubt be some vigorous debate over how to respond. But I'd like to fish a few options out of the ocean right now. First, no one is going to Blight for any reason. Bryn and his sister have Sedam contained, and as you heard, he thinks events still might work out for him. One of those events is the second invasion, which we are going to prevent. And the other is finding the kraken in the north, which is going to prove more difficult than he hopes. The way for us to prevail, therefore, is to go forward with the plans we've made. That has to be our priority. After we stop the second invasion, then we can think about dealing with Sedam. He will wait because he has no choice.

"Second, at the urging of some monks from Bryn's Lighthouse, we are temporarily—and I stress the word *temporarily*—closing Bryn's Lung to seekers, until the church has had some time to discuss these revelations and form a new policy going forward. It may not change at all, or it may change quite a bit. I think that will be determined by conversations we all need to have. And I am sure similar conversations will take place in Rael, Forn, and Kauria.

"Third: Anyone thinking this is a great excuse for violence

or rioting or looting of any kind should stop thinking that right now. Security has been increased throughout the city. Let's not be fish heads about this. Bryn has done his best to keep us safe for a very long time. Only by scheming tirelessly for centuries has Sedam been able to create a vulnerability. But we will remedy that very soon, together! You have my love, and tomorrow you shall hear more."

The tenor of the crowd noise shifted slightly after his speech—maybe it was not quite so angry—but there was still a lot of emotion to work through and the volume remained high. It would be a tense evening, and I wanted to get to the Siren's Call to hear what people were saying and talk things over.

But my plans were thwarted because we were surrounded by a group of mariners, led by Mynstad du Möcher, and escorted off the wall. Apparently both the bard and I were to stay the night in the palace as a precaution.

People did seem to be riled up and shouted at us as we traveled, but no one attempted to get at us, thanks to the armed escort.

"Plug Bryn's Lung!" was heard more than once, which made me worry that a mob would try to damage it and perhaps do Sedam's work for him. Others advocated the opposite, that we needed even more seekers to sacrifice themselves so that Bryn would be more powerful. And some loudly urged the pelenaut to send all our tidal mariners to Blight to drown the island's wraiths and rob Sedam of his store of souls, despite the warning that he could sense tidal mariners from a distance and add them to his army of wraiths. My heart agreed with that suggestion in principle: The tidal wave could be started from afar. It might exact a fatal price, however, on the person who summoned it, and while others might blithely say the sacrifice would be worth it, I wouldn't want to ask that of anyone when we could come up with a better solution if we took some time to plan. I was curious, though: Would Bryn allow it to happen if we tried it? My gut told me no, because Bryn could have done it at any time in the last few thousand years. Exile had clearly been the choice of Sedam's six siblings.

Kill him! some part of my mind demanded, intruding on my rational musings.

"Yeah," I said to Fintan, "I think that one liquefied some brains."

Day 53

THE DEAD DROP

One benefit of spending the night in the palace was the expectation of breakfast in the morning. Fintan and I dined alone, however, for which I was grateful. Something was off about the toast—perhaps it was my own disquiet about what lurked on the Mistmaiden Isles and not inherently the fault of the innocent slice of bread. The sausage looked abnormally greasy, and the eggs weren't cooked to my satisfaction. Maybe the chef was hungover. Maybe *I* was hungover, wrung out both by emotions and the depredations of the alcohol we drank the night before.

To quiet the pounding in my skull, I asked for a Kraken Dawn, an unholy breakfast cocktail made with clam juice, tomato juice, a vile fermented anchovy vinegar called Nubbins Sauce, and potato gin, the rim garnished with lime juice and spicy chili salt, the whole thing presided over by a pickled baby squid perched on a golden cherry tomato, impaled by a toothpick. It was a terrible idea from its inception, and I am fairly certain the rest of the world thought us unwell for continuing to drink them, but somehow it had become the only socially acceptable drink one could have in the morning.

I didn't think I was ready to make small talk with Röllend yet, and he'd not paused to speak with us the previous night other than to wish us a restful sleep. He was probably already in the Wellspring, working. We had to get our news from the longshoreman serving us in the dining room.

"Have you heard if anything alarming happened last night?" I asked.

"Some folks tried to mess with Bryn's Lung but ran into the mariners stationed there. Other than that, a few brawls broke out, but no major mob of fish heads doing damage to anything but their own skulls."

That was good to hear. Once he left us, I had a question for Fintan.

"Tell me, would you seek a kenning now, knowing that your spirit might simply be used to power a blessing for someone else?" I never would have sought a kenning regardless, but I imagined that if I had ever entertained the notion, recent news might cause me to reconsider.

Fintan smiled. "That didn't take long at all. I expect that's a question all the blessed are going to be asked, and it's going to be something mentioned to everyone who considers seeking. And I think the answer will vary according to who you're asking, but for me, the answer is yes, maybe even more so."

That cleared away some of my fog with a bright stab of surprise. "Interesting. Why is that?"

"The question is whether you're willing to sacrifice yourself or not. Before we knew this, the sacrifice was almost a waste. You were chucking your life away in the hope that it might work out well for you. But now, even if you're not blessed, you're still helping others and indirectly helping your country prosper and defend itself from threats. It's a trade-off. I think you'll see a dip in seekings in the short term, but ultimately they'll resume. Any country that ceases to allow them will eventually suffer from lacking the benefits that the blessed provide. What would Brynlön—and, indeed, the world—do without hygienists? How would Forn be able to defend the Canopy against the timber raids of the Hathrim without thornhands? How would Rael build and maintain its infrastructure without stonecutters? I think we're going to have some very interesting discussions about the various faiths and how the children of Teldwen have been irresponsible in sweeping all of humanity into the dust of their family squabble, but the kennings will survive. We can't afford to lose them, economically or defensively."

"Good point. Or set of points. That tale certainly provided a different lens through which to examine history. I think there's going to be a lot of renewed interest in the Rift."

"What little I've read about it is tremendously spotty. A lot has been lost—or, as Sedam claims, purposely erased. But perhaps a worldwide interest in it may unearth some hidden records."

We never left the dining room except for short breaks, working through the morning on those tales until it was time for lunch. We took that there as well and finally left the palace in the early afternoon, having a few hours to ourselves before it was time for the day's tales.

I used my time to replenish my stores of jam and honey and some other staples; I also scored another precious loaf of bread.

"Our narrators today will be all-Brynt!" Fintan said when he arrived at the wall later. "But first, the day's music. How about a shanty from the Brynt merchant fleet?"

Fintan welcomed onto the small stage a crew of men that did frequent supply runs to Rael. They were going to sing a work song called "Bonny Little Shot." They stood packed in three ranks: One man in the front sang a line, and then the others joined in on the response, while all sang the chorus.

> Beware, beware, the lion-whale glare, she'll breach your
>   hull if you stop to stare,
> Singing hey, lads, keep your heads down now and let's go,
>   haul away, ho!
> Navigate by the sun and moon and soon we will make our
>   women swoon,
> Singing hey, mate, got a date with fate, now let's go, haul
>   away, ho!

(Chorus)
We free sailors be many leagues from home on a shining sea,
We don't smell good but we have our tea and a bonny little
*   shot or two of rum!*

If near the shore we carefully keep we won't be a-wrack in
*   the kraken's deep,*
Singing hey, wheel, 'ware the mast and keel, now let's go,
*   haul away, ho!*
I hope we all get home unscathed and I can't recall when
*   last I bathed,*
Singing hey, bub, give yourself a scrub, now let's go, haul
*   away, ho!*

(Chorus repeats)

"Okay, rewind the clock just a bit," Fintan said when we returned from break. "Before the momentous events in Fornyd and the Mistmaiden Isles unfolded, Gerstad Daryck du Löngren and the Grynek Hunters were still on the trail of Eculan spies."

Daryck

The Kaurian translator that the pelenaut had been depending on finally came through and deciphered all that intelligence. He had come straight to Fornyd because some of the stuff we'd previously gathered—from that star-bearded Bone Giant officer—indicated the presence of spies in Fornyd. When we came back from our trip to the Northern Yawn, I got to meet him, briefly. An aging gentleman with disheveled clothing, Gondel Vedd had a mind like the keenest blade—there was a clarity to his brown eyes that spoke of vast knowledge—but to balance out these intellectual gifts, he was cursed with an inability to feed himself without making a mess. He'd get distracted by something he was reading and completely miss his soup hole. We had a lunch meeting to talk over the spy network my team had found, and I watched him open his mouth, raise his hand with a sandwich in it while looking at documents I'd brought from the main compound up north, and press the sandwich to his cheek while biting down on nothing at all. He pulled it away in confusion and then in disapproval, glaring at the sandwich as if it had done that on purpose, leaving a smear of mustard and tomato snot clinging to the gray stubble of his jaw.

"Damn messy food," he complained, neatly absolving himself of any responsibility for the tragedy.

I absolutely adored him.

Especially since he taught me how to say something in the language of the Bone Giants that I asked him for: *Don't worry, I'll take care of you.*

"Why do you want to know that?"

"If I meet someone I suspect is possessed, I can say that to reassure him that I am like him. If he responds in the same language, or even nods his understanding, I'll know he's a spy."

I also got to meet a Raelech bard named Fintan and the world's first beast caller, a young Nentian man named Abhinava Khose, who traveled with a bloodcat on one side, a bone-collared dreadmoose on the other, and a stalk hawk on his shoulder. We were practically on our way out of the city when they entered it, but we stayed an extra couple of days to talk with them and get a better understanding of the scope of things, because they'd run into that army up north.

Since then we'd been camped in Tömerhil, keeping an eye on a dead drop that Gondel was able to identify in the documents. The hope was that the spy would not have heard we'd eliminated everyone to the north and would eventually use it again. The dread was that he *had* heard that we'd cleared the board and we were wasting our time watching this spot around the clock.

We were not well suited for such duty. As hunters, we liked being outdoors, but we had to watch the drop site from a basement window that looked upon an alley—an alley between a pub and a bathhouse, which stank of garbage and urine and the hurried sex that one particular couple liked to have there twice a week in the small hours before dawn.

Being hunters, we liked to actively seek our prey rather than passively wait. We were familiar with the sort of hunting conducted in stands and blinds—and that's how we had to approach it, mentally—but it wasn't our favored way to stalk. It felt like lurking and ambushing more than hunting.

The novelty paled quickly, and we loathed the duty after a couple of days. But we endured it for weeks, noting who came and went on a semi-regular basis and doing our best to keep quiet so that no one would know we were in that basement, let alone actually using the window.

A bizarre consequence of rotating shifts through a cramped workspace with little to do was that the hunters became obsessed with leaving the space cleaner for the next shift than they'd found it. None of us was particularly good at it except for Gyrsön, who was sought out for cleaning tips and tricks by the end of the third day.

A small argument escalated into demanding a ruling from me on whether we should clean the exterior of the window we were using for our surveillance. I came down on the side of the men who argued that cleaning it would draw attention and create suspicion, which was more important than improved visibility of the target.

Said target was a loose stone in the masonry of the bathhouse; we were camped in the basement of the pub. The stone could be removed entirely, a message placed in the hollow, and then it could be replaced without anyone being the wiser. It did require a deserted alleyway to use it effectively, however, so we kept track of repeat visitors who appeared to have no business there when others were around. There were a few odd ones, and we started a pool. I put my money on the matronly woman who looked like she should be teaching school instead of traversing dank alleyways. She appeared at different times of the day, always traveling north to south, and my feeling was that she was trying to happen upon the place unoccupied.

Mynstad du Högyn was convinced it was the thin bespectacled fellow in a waistcoat and clean boots who often appeared lost, even though he knew his way around enough to use the alley every other day.

"What is he doing there?" she demanded. "He's the sort you *do* want to meet in a dark alley, because he appears totally harmless! Which means he can't be. He has hidden weapons and knows how to use them."

Lörry placed his bet on an obvious choice: a thickly built bruiser with a scowling visage who looked like he might simply take your purse and dare you to ask for it back. He came through twice a day, albeit at different times, using the alleyway as a regular route between whatever point A and point B were.

When my matron paused in front of the dead drop during my daytime shift and checked to see if she was alone, I held my breath. When her hand dipped into her cleavage to fetch something hidden there, I felt a tug of hope on my heart. It was a note! I was going to win!

But then she pulled out a small tin of something snortable and inhaled, sighing happily before closing it up and returning it to its hiding place.

I got some teasing about my ruined hopes, and I envied her that moment of plump satisfaction, even if it denied me any.

But less than an hour later, Burly Swole Man entered the

alley, looking no different than usual, except that this time he stopped, looked behind him to check that it was all clear, and quickly removed the loose stone from the bathhouse wall. He slipped a folded piece of paper in there and replaced the stone, then moved on. The whole operation had taken less than ten seconds.

"You win," I said to Lörry.

"I do? I was right?"

"At least in one sense. He might not be the actual spy, just a convenient messenger, so we need to follow him. Gyrsön, you keep an eye on the drop to make sure no one takes the message. Follow anyone who does." I pointed to an archer on our shift as I was already heading for the stairs. "Get Mynstad du Högyn to round up everyone else. I need at least two down here with Gyrsön to watch for the pickup. I need everyone else with me to follow the messenger. Lörry, stay with me. Let's go, we can't lose him!"

We ran out of the basement, pushed our way through the throng of bodies looking for a pint and a basket of grease, and burst out onto the street, looking for Mr. Burly.

He was tall, fortunately, and easy to spot, his broad back to us as he headed east toward the neighborhood where rich merchants tended to live. I pointed him out to Lörry.

"Follow on the other side of the street. Hopefully between us we can keep him in sight until we get backup."

Mr. Burly seemed unconcerned by the possibility of a tail. Either he was supremely confident or very calm under pressure.

A right onto a slightly less busy street. A left onto an even less populated one, still headed east. Another right, and we were walking among fancy houses. Alone. As in, there was our mark and us. And, of course, the row of towering city estates, the sort that had narrow street footprints but stretched like caterpillars behind their front doors, long and multistoried affairs where the wealthy drank cocktails and laughed with soft contempt at the lower classes. If anyone was watching from their dark glazed windows, we could not tell.

We were a good dozen lengths behind him and walking softly, and he didn't turn around. What he did instead was bring his left hand up to chest height for a moment, curl his fingers into a fist, and pump once to signal success.

What in the black abyss was that for? A reaction to his private thoughts? Or was it a signal to someone on the street? If so—who? Because there was no one else on the street.

If it was a signal, it had to be to someone watching from a window on the opposite side of the street, where Lörry was walking. Mr. Burly would not raise his left hand to signal the right side of the street.

It could be nothing. But if it was something . . . then it was a tip-off to someone that the drop had been made. Our spy was in one of the houses on the left side of the street. Probably the one directly opposite, or one ahead of, where Mr. Burly had been walking when he made the signal.

Abruptly deciding to try something different, I crossed the street to Lörry, hailing him like an old friend I hadn't seen in a while.

"Hey heyyy, Lörry, is that you? How have you been, my friend?" I held up my hand as if to grasp arms with him and smiled broadly. Lörry was confused for a second but recovered admirably.

"Hey, Daryck! Very well, thank you, and yourself?" We grasped arms and then pounded each other on the back.

"Keep smiling," I said in lower tones. "We're most likely being watched by the real spy from one of these houses, so we are ending the tail here. We can pick him up later if he follows his pattern."

Lörry said through a grin, "How do you know the real spy is in one of these houses?"

"That fist pump was a signal that he made the drop."

"How can you be sure?"

"I can't. It's a gamble. We're going to find out who lives in these houses, get the rest of our crew together except for those watching the drop, and conduct some interrogations."

"How are we going to find out?"

"The local constabulary. Come on, let's go, looking like buddies off to get a drink together." I put my arm around him, clapping him on the shoulder a couple more times, and we turned around the way we had come, presumably to a pub somewhere to catch up. That was the impression I hoped we were giving, anyway. Regardless, we certainly weren't tailing Mr. Burly anymore, and the spy shouldn't be worried.

Once we got back to a populated street and asked a local where to find the constabulary, we lost an hour finding it and showing a scroll of our official capacity, signed by Quartermaster Farlen du Cannym, to progressively higher-ranked officers until one of them consented to divulge who lived in the houses along that street. We'd used that same scroll to secure our lodging and surveillance at the pub.

It took us another hour to round up the rest of our crew, then we went to those fancy houses in the company of three constables and began with the house directly opposite where Mr. Burly had flashed his signal.

The home was impressive, with expert woodwork on the front porch pickets and around the doorjamb and gardens full of spring flowers. It took a suspiciously long time for anyone to answer the door, and I was about to declare we should break in when it finally opened. An elderly woman peered out at us—the owner, according to the constables—and she was extremely confused by our appearance.

"Yes?"

The constable accompanying us introduced himself and said we were there on a security matter. "Are you all right, ma'am?" I asked. "It took a long time for you to answer."

"I was gardening in the back."

So the gardens were her doing and not that of some company hired to do it for her. That sounded like something an actual old woman rather than an enemy spy would do.

"Is there anyone else in the home currently staying with you?"

"No," she said. "I'm alone. My husband passed years ago, and I lost my children in the invasion. They were in Möllerud at the time."

"I'm sorry. You'll still need to come with us for questioning."

"Questioning? About what? You can ask me anything right here."

It seemed unlikely that she was the culprit—but, then again, an old woman's body might be the perfect disguise for a wraith. No one would suspect her of being an agent of the Bone Giants. Perhaps the next house—not strictly across from where Mr. Burly had signaled, but very close—would yield a better prospect. I asked her to remain with the constables while my crew and I checked next door.

The man who answered was one Henning du Ludvöll, a jowly middle-aged merchant who'd made his money in specialty foods, like sunchucks and swamp ducks. If he'd been in Grynek before the invasion, he would have been a convenient middleman for us, buying portions of what we brought home and sending our kills to restaurants so we only had to deal with a single person.

Dressed in a finely woven white tunic with embroidered blue waves, he shifted his eyes nervously among us, as I supposed anyone would. But he seemed much more tense than the elderly woman had.

I sent the others to the next house in the row, even though I didn't really think it was a legit target, so that I could be left alone with him. Once they were out of earshot, I gripped him by the arm and whispered the phrase Gondel Vedd had taught me: *"Ne brini, pobrinuću se za tebe."*

The tension in the merchant's shoulders relaxed and he sighed in relief, replying with something that sounded like *"Hvala ti, brate."* Which told me that he was definitely a wraith and the man we were looking for.

He started to say something else in that language, but of course I couldn't understand a word of it and I didn't want him to know yet that I'd gulled him, so I cut him off.

"No more of that," I said, and pointed to the constables talking with his neighbor to the left and my crew with his neighbor to the right. "They might hear you. Wait until we get to Fornyd. There's one of us there who can explain everything in a safe environment."

"We're going to Fornyd?"

"Aye. It's for the best. Play the bewildered citizen until we get there."

He simply nodded, and I called to the others to leave off the other houses. We had our man, and he was going to come along willingly.

"What's all this about?" he asked, sounding convincingly bewildered.

"Theater for the locals," I replied in low tones. "An excuse to move you publicly. Here we go." The others rejoined me, and we took him away in a wagon down to the constabulary. He was placed in a holding cell, which gave me the opportunity to send word to Gyrsön and the others that they should just take the note from the dead drop and get ready to leave. Whoever was supposed to pick it up could wonder what happened, but they'd probably just be a messenger like Mr. Burly. Though we'd be safe and pick him up too, I knew the real prize was Henning du Ludvöll.

I'd take him to Gondel Vedd in Fornyd and would bet five beers and a buffet that my favorite sloppy Kaurian genius could get him to talk freely about what the wraiths were plotting.

Fintan dispelled his seeming and grinned. "Next up is Nara du Fesset. I am going to apologize in advance for the entirely justified profanity you'll be hearing, and beyond that I'll just say, hold on to your nether regions. This is a ride."

Nara

When the Grynek Hunters arrived in Fornyd with a prisoner in tow that Daryck du Löngren claimed was a spy for the Bone Giants, I was momentarily elated. But then I joined him in frustration at the timing, because he'd arrived counting on Scholar Gondel Vedd to be able to speak the Eculan language to draw the prisoner out, but the scholar had gone to the Mistmaiden Isles with Second Könstad du Böll, Captain Gansu, and the Bone Giant captive known as Saviič to seek the source of the Seventh Kenning. We had no idea when they'd be back, and in the meantime this prisoner, Henning du Ludvöll, was expecting someone like him—someone able to speak Eculan—to "take care of him," as Daryck had promised.

It was like being given a pearl only to be told you must toss it into the abyss.

Daryck knew only the one Eculan phrase Gondel had taught him, so he didn't want to be alone with the prisoner, who might then speak to him and figure out that we were playing him. I accompanied Daryck at all times, therefore, and played things severely while Daryck winked at him behind my back.

"You're being held on suspicion of treason and espionage," I told him, and he spluttered and demanded to know on what grounds we suspected him of that, which forced me to improvise.

"I don't know the details of your case, and frankly I'm not interested. The man who typically handles cases like this is currently out of town, so we need to wait for his return before we can even begin to ask you questions. That means we're going to hold you in a secure location with every convenience afforded, and should you prove to be innocent, we'll of course release you with our apologies. We have to ask for your patience in the meantime."

He declared this to be an outrage and a mistake and all the things people say when taken into custody, and we ushered him into a dungeon cell and told the guards to treat him politely and asked if we could get him any books to read or any other small things to make him more comfortable. He asked for extra pillows and a towel and for a series of lurid adventures featuring a crime-fighting rapid in Setyrön. I'd read them, and they were utter trash that bore no resemblance to my life as a rapid, so I ordered him some books on sea slugs, snails, and other mollusks found near Setyrön. They at least had a chance of reflecting reality.

That gave us some time to brief the quartermaster and her lung—much more time than we needed, because the scholar didn't return the next day but he did the day after that. He and Captain Gansu had much to tell us—revelatory things, they assured us, which they had shared with the second könstad on the way; she had returned to Pelemyn to brief the pelenaut. But it sounded like it was going to take some time to fill us in, and the quartermaster and I worried that the information the spy had might be time-sensitive, so we wondered if Gondel would consent to questioning him for a few minutes in case we could learn something actionable.

The scholar looked surprised for a moment, then nodded. "Yes. Let's do that. After I tell you what's been going on in the Mistmaiden Isles, you'll forget about everything else, so we should get this smaller matter out of the way."

He and the lung, Lans du Höwyll, went to get paper and ink and set up in a secure room, while Daryck and I went to fetch the prisoner. Captain Gansu departed to bring most of her crew back to the Wellspring and update them on what had happened and also to find the plaguebringer Abhinava Khose, since she'd heard he was back in town.

Henning du Ludvöll was not pleased to see me. I'd left him waiting too long and had sent him the wrong books.

"Apologies for the clerical error. But we have in fact come to fetch you as soon as possible. The man who can help with your case has just returned to the city. Let's go."

He came along willingly enough, his hands shackled at the wrists in front of him. When we got to the appointed room, Gondel and the lung were already there. It was bare except for a long wooden dining table with a chair at either end of it. Gondel sat at one end, paper and ink and a pitcher of water beside him, a glass half full, and the lung stood behind his right shoulder. The prisoner took the hint and went to the other end. I poured him a glass of water from the pitcher waiting there, because everyone was to be fully hydrated in Brynlön. He picked it up and drank most of it in one go. Daryck and I stepped back and stationed ourselves behind him on either side.

"So, who are you?" the spy demanded. "You look Kaurian, not Brynt."

"Excellent observation. I am Scholar Gondel Vedd from Kauria, but I've been stationed here on a temporary basis for very good reasons. You are, ah . . . Henning du Ludvöll, is that correct?"

"Yes."

"Very good. My records say you're a procurer and supplier of game meats to markets and restaurants."

"That's right."

"As such, might I assume you have picked up an extra language or two?"

The spy hesitated, then shrugged and said, "A couple."

"I'm a language enthusiast myself. It's why I'm here." And then he spoke some words in the Eculan language, which I didn't understand. It sounded like a simple sentence followed by a question. Henning du Ludvöll didn't reply, but he tensed visibly, which made me think he understood those words just fine. When someone says something you don't understand, your body doesn't do that. You simply say, *What?* or something along those lines. Too late, the spy realized this. He made an effort to relax before responding.

"I beg your pardon?" he said in Brynt. Gondel chuckled and spoke again in the Eculan language. He gestured to the lung and then to Gerstad du Löngren and me, smiling and giving a tiny shake of his head—reassuring the spy that we didn't speak that language and he could say anything he wanted in front of us, I guessed. He asked a short question and the spy remained mute, but I noticed he tensed up again. That made me nervous.

His hands were shackled, but his feet were not. Could he threaten the scholar? I judged the distance he'd have to travel around the table and was just concluding that either I or the gerstad would be able to stop him when the scholar said something more and Henning du Ludvöll launched himself *over* the table, hands outstretched for the scholar's throat. The gerstad and I lunged forward simultaneously as Gondel and Lans flinched, but I could see that the spy would get to Gondel before we could. He could snap the scholar's neck before we had a chance to defend him. There was no way I would let that happen, so I ripped the water out of the spy's head and he went limp, though his momentum still carried him into Gondel. The scholar was toppled over, the body of Henning du Ludvöll falling on top of him.

"No! Gerstad, what did you do?" cried Daryck.

"What does it look like? I saved the scholar."

"No, you set the wraith free! Quick, contain it! Surround his head with water!"

"What? Whose head?"

"The spy's! Oh, shit, it's too late, it's coming out! Lans, run and get the quartermaster!"

"What are you talking about?" I asked.

"Get the water around Gondel's head to protect him, hurry! Lans, run!"

"Kraken cocks," Lans muttered, his eyes wide with fear as he dashed out.

I stepped forward to see what the gerstad meant. A white spectral mist was flowing out of the spy's head and into the scholar's mouth and nose. Gondel's eyes rolled up, showing only the whites, as he began to twitch underneath the dead-weight of du Ludvöll's body.

"The water, Nara, now!" the gerstad shouted. "Surround Gondel's head with it!"

"Okay, but tell me what's happening!" I upended the pitcher of drinking water and caught it with my kenning, directing it to surround the scholar's head. Gerstad du Löngren talked fast and at high volume.

"The spy was possessed with a wraith, and now it's trying to possess Gondel! Water is its only weakness, so you have to fill every orifice with water right now before it takes the scholar over completely!"

"Oh, shrimp shit! Oh, no!"

"You have to drown the wraith without drowning Gondel!"

"How am I supposed to do that?"

"I don't know, you're the rapid here!"

Gondel was twitching all over now, as if having a seizure. He was also choking a bit as he breathed in some of the water I'd sent into his mouth and nose, chasing the wraith. I tried to concentrate on keeping the water in his nose and the top of his sinuses and throat while leaving a passage where he could breathe through his mouth. Concentrating was difficult, however, as Gerstad du Löngren wouldn't stop yelling at me.

"If the wraith takes him, we will lose our number-one intelligence asset! You have to save him or we're fucked!"

"I know the fucking stakes, fucking shut up and let me fucking work! Help me prop him up—his tongue is getting in the way!"

The two of us struggled to get the scholar sitting up, wrestling the body of Henning du Ludvöll off his torso, but once we managed, I was able to stabilize his breathing if not his muscle spasms. I could maintain the globe of water around his head, filling his ears and nose and sinuses, but while it was obviously giving the wraith some difficulty in completing its possession, it wasn't halting the process or easing the scholar's seizure.

"Now what?" I said. "I think I'm doing all I can."

Gerstad du Löngren nodded, his voice much calmer. "You're right. This is the best we can do for the moment. Keep it up."

"Just keep it up? This is unsustainable! Look at him! He's in extreme distress right now!"

"We all are, believe me. Just keep him like that until the quartermaster gets here."

"Why? What can she do?"

"Maybe nothing. Maybe everything."

"What aren't you telling me?"

"The shaking is good in a way. It means the wraith doesn't have full control yet. We still have hope."

"Hope for what?"

"Hope that the quartermaster will have a better idea of what to do."

Farlen du Cannym arrived at that point and froze in the doorway, frowning down at us on the floor. Lans was behind her, peering over her shoulder. "Status?" she demanded. I admired her economy of words in an emergency. Gerstad du Löngren answered.

"A wraith is trying to take over the scholar. Nara has it contained and may have injured it as it was entering, but she can't do any more except kill the scholar and the wraith together."

"Okay, Nara, keep doing what you're doing." The quartermaster gestured to the body of Henning du Ludvöll, still partially draped over Gondel's legs. "Lans, help me get that body out of the way first, then we'll see what can be done."

A half minute of grunting and cursing got the body out of the way, but then the scholar's legs were free to flail around, which made it more difficult to keep him still. The lung sat on them, while the quartermaster took a knee next to me and grasped the scholar's left hand with one of hers, then covered the top with her other. She closed her eyes in concentration, the spheres moving around under her eyelids, while the scholar continued to thrash about.

"Ahh. That is . . . awful. Okay, Nara, maintain containment, especially around the orifices, even the eyes. It might try to bolt when I do this."

"Do what? You can do something?"

"I didn't know until I began, but, yes, a hygienist is blessed with the ability to see and remove impurities from any liquid medium. The human body is mostly liquid, and the wraith is an impurity."

It took some time, perhaps two full minutes, but Gondel eventually quieted and slumped in our arms. I maintained the containment, because I wasn't going to be lulled into complacence. Both the gerstad and I looked at the quartermaster, but she was obviously still working on something, a snarl on her features as she attacked whatever it was that she saw in his blood, so we said nothing. The silence stretched, and after another minute the quartermaster's features smoothed out, but she didn't let go of the scholar's hand. That took another minute, then she gently let go of his hand and opened her eyes, taking a deep breath and exhaling slowly.

"It's finished. The wraith is dissolved. You can release containment."

I directed all the water I'd been holding around his head back into the pitcher.

"So it *can* be done," Gerstad du Löngren said. "A hygienist can end a possession."

"Well, I can definitely kill the wraith. But that doesn't mean the host will recover. I don't know if the scholar will return to himself or not."

"What? Why not?" I gave the scholar a gentle shake. "Scholar Vedd? Gondel? Come back to us. We have some mustard you've never tried before."

We waited for a response, and I gently patted his cheek, hoping he'd feel it and startle awake, but he remained unconscious.

"It was damaging his brain while trying to possess him," the quartermaster said into the quiet.

"How?"

"What I just learned in the process is that the wraiths behave like soap. They're hydrophobic."

"Oh, no."

"What? Hold on, what does that mean?" Gerstad du Löngren asked.

"The reason soap works is that it's made of hydrophobic material," the quartermaster explained. "It really hates water, all the way down to the smallest possible unit of it. So when you put it on your skin with water, those tiny bits of soap do one of two things: They either bind themselves to oil and grease and dirt and then the water washes them away, removing them from your skin, or else they try to find a place to hide, which is the interior of disease-causing agents. Their cells."

"Cells."

"Yes. The soap breaks into a cell, thinking it will be a nice place to get away from the water, but in the process it kills the cell. That's what the wraith was doing in the scholar's head. Breaking into the cells of his brain to get away from water and eventually to control enough of them that the possession would be complete."

"That sounds extremely bad."

"Indeed it is. So I can remove the wraith, but I can't fix whatever the wraith did to his head. Let's get him to the infirmary and looked after. Let his husband know, Lans."

"I will."

Farlen du Cannym caught our gaze. "Did you learn anything from the spy?"

"The scholar may have. He was speaking to him in the Bone Giant language, and the spy reacted to something the scholar said, which might be a clue. But we didn't understand a word of it."

"Regrettable. I'm going to retire to a private a room to say some incredibly rude words about this, but then I need to get back to the Wellspring. Apparently the scholar and Captain Gansu learned something remarkable on the Mistmaiden Isles, and I need to hear what it is. Join me there," she told us, "when you've made personally sure that he is being cared for and monitored for improvements."

The quartermaster and the lung left the room, and at that point I didn't sob, but I couldn't help the tear running down my cheek. The gerstad saw it, and his lips pressed tightly together before he spoke.

"You did nothing wrong. You acted to save the scholar every step of the way. I should have had du Ludvöll's feet in chains. I should have warned you what happens if you kill the possessed."

"No," I said, shaking my head. "I'm not looking back at my wake to see how I could have steered differently—or at yours. I'm looking at the ripples and worrying what else will be capsized because of this wrack. Without him, how will we prevail?"

He didn't have an answer. "Let's get him to the infirmary."

Like many others, I was absolutely horrified at the turn of events. No wonder Nara had been absent the last few weeks. Keeping watch, no doubt, over an irreplaceable friend to us all.

"I hope to have an update for you tomorrow," Fintan said, dispelling Nara's seeming. "But regardless of whether I hear anything on Gondel's condition, tomorrow will be our last day of tales. I'll see you then, Pelemyn."

"Fintan. Fintan!" I said, as he turned away from Survivor Field. "Gondel is okay, isn't he? Tell me he's recovered."

"I honestly don't know," he replied. "His story that I shared a couple of days ago was written down for me—he wrote it on the Seven-Year Ship right after they left the island, and Koesha brought it here with her. And Nara's tale was also delivered to me in writing from Daryck du Löngren."

"She wrote it down for you?"

"No, it was more of a report. A debriefing intended for the pelenaut but shared with me."

"Does that mean she's not here?"

"Not that I'm aware. But I think she's on her way. Fairly certain she's supposed to be shipping out with the fleet, and that's obviously going to happen soon."

"Ugh. I am not going to sleep well."

"Me neither."

We arranged a lunchtime meeting for tomorrow, since I'd been absent from the kitchen and had other errands to run in the morning and wished to remedy both.

THE KRAKEN
IN THE NORTH

There is a certain stress to rations but a certain security too. A worry that you won't be able to secure what you want, but some assurance that you'll receive what's needed, that supplies won't be hoarded by anyone. It does mean more-frequent shopping and longer queues, but it also means more opportunities to get out and chat with people. No one stood in line silently anymore; the queues had become chances to socialize, especially the ones that flowed like streams curving back on themselves. As I was passing the bakery on the way to the refugee kitchen, one such snakelike queue held a surprise, for a couple of young voices called my name.

"Dervaaaaaan!" It was Tamöd and Pyrella, and with them, of course, was their mother, Elynea. Seeing them happy and well instantly made my morning spectacular. It had been only a few weeks since I saw them last, but they seemed taller somehow. Or perhaps it was just good spirits, which tend to make one seem larger than one's actual self.

They greeted me with hugs, and Elynea with an unforced smile.

"What an absolute pleasure. You all look well."

"We are!" Tamöd said, then added, "I mean, we're a bit hungry, but who isn't? Mom says we're going to be fine."

"Yes, you will."

Pyrella and Elynea both said quiet hellos, and then I asked how the apprenticeship was going.

"I love it," Elynea said, grinning unreservedly at just the mention of it. "The Fornish are excellent teachers and very patient with me. I'm learning so much, and I can see my work improving already. When I'm finished, I think we'll be in a good place. How have you been?"

"Busy with the bard most afternoons. But lately, since I haven't had to watch these two," I said, gesturing to the kids, "I've been spending my mornings volunteering at the refugee kitchen, and that's where I was headed."

"Oh, we shouldn't keep you. But I do have a question, if you don't mind."

"Of course. How can I help?"

"The Fornish have been extremely interested in the tales of Pen Yas ben Min, as you can probably imagine."

"Oh, yes, I'm sure."

"My master, Bel Tes Wey, won't stop talking about her. Simply loves her. Well, the bard sort of ended her tale by saying that she'd go to Malath Ashmali in the spring, and now it's spring. We're in the second month of it already! So she must have left by now. Have you or the bard heard anything new? Did Pen make it there and plant the Fourth Tree?"

"No, we haven't heard, but I am so glad you asked. I'm going to pursue that and see if we can get an answer from the Raelechs sooner rather than later. I'm quite interested too. And I want to read *Leafsong* now."

"Oh, it's wonderful," Pyrella said, and I gaped at her.

"You've read it?"

"Well, when the bard first started the tales about Pen, Tamöd and I both said we'd like to hear more about Sage and Sprout, and since Mother works with the Fornish, they had a copy and started translating it into Brynt for us. They said it's difficult, and what the bard is doing is really skillful, taking the meanings and making things that rhyme in Fornish also rhyme in Brynt. They're huge fans. I bet if he came by the workshop, they would just give him a finished rocking chair or something."

"I'll let him know." To Elynea I said, "If I hear anything, would it be all right if I came by the shop?"

"Of course. You're always welcome."

"Thank you. Wonderful to see you all."

It truly was. Elynea and her kids gave me hope, because they had lost so much, like many of us, but were proving their resilience. Their lives were forever changed by the invasion, and their destinies now would be far different than if it had never happened, yet they were crafting a way to thrive. The wheels of war rolled over so many and they were still turning, but I needed the reminder that some of us escaped, and even the damaged could return to the road and find their way to prosperity again.

I left them in high spirits, and the currents of my thoughts flowed toward what the narrative would look like after this last day of tales—for it had to continue, did it not? The Giant Wars were only half over, if we considered the western front to be concluded with the Battle of the Godsteeth and the revolution in Khul Bashab. The Eculans still had to be dealt with and that had to be recorded, so how to do that? It would need to be written, of course, but I hoped we could continue to have it told by the individuals involved, rather than a dry report from me. Perhaps I could enlist Fintan in my scheme.

When I got to the kitchen, I apologized profusely to Chef du Rödal for missing a few days. "I've had some tumultuous mornings of late, and I hope my absence did not burden you overmuch."

"Aw, don't you worry, Master Dervan. The course of this stream is ever-changing, and I just go with the flow."

I let her know it would be my last day, since I'd be going overseas with the allied fleet. That stopped her.

"Okay. But you come back and see me when you get home. It doesn't matter if it's here or if it's in my restaurant when it reopens. I'll cook you something special." She gave me a quick hug with a stained apron, smelling of sweat and broth and greens and love, then pushed me toward a mountain of potatoes. "I saved you some, sweetie."

"I'm grateful to you, Chef." We locked eyes for a few seconds, because she thought I had something more to say—like maybe *why* I was grateful—and I did, except that I couldn't put it into words. "I . . ." Felt like helping at the kitchen was helping me. Volunteering gave me a concrete thing to do that wasn't simply wishing things were better. Plus, I was able to take out my anger and frustration on potatoes instead of picking fights with Mynstad du Möcher. Potatoes have no martial skills and never hit back. But I didn't want to make it about me, so I nodded and finished, "Well, I'm just grateful. I should keep it simple."

She smiled and nodded back, and then turned to her work.

When I joined Fintan on the wall, I asked if he'd heard anything about Gondel Vedd.

"I have!" he said, but I couldn't tell by his expression if it was good news or not.

"Well, what is it?"

"You'll hear about it after Abhi's tale today," he replied, then he turned and waved at Survivor Field. "Good afternoon, Pelemyn! So here we are. The last day of my tales, which should finally catch you up on all you need to know before the armies depart for Ecula. The latest word I've had is that the ships are being provisioned and soon we'll start moving troops into place, with departure in just a few days. So it's time for me to sing you my last song, a triple verse thrice, and then we'll begin with Abhinava Khose."

The magic of verse and rhyme
Transcends space and time
As it lands upon the ear.

It can mend an eternal soul,
Make what was broken whole,
And banish every fear.

I'm grateful that I could practice my art,
And grateful for your open hearts;
We made magic together here.

He got an extended ovation for that, and he raised a mug of Mistmaiden Ale to everyone as the last break began before his final tales. When he returned to the stage, it was his largest audience ever, for there were two armies and a navy out there in addition to everyone who had already been in Pelemyn. I took a moment to marvel at it and try to store the sight in my long-term memory. I would not see such a crowd again.

"This is going to build directly upon what we learned a couple of days ago about the Rift," Fintan said. "Prepare yourselves."

A sphere of gas broke open at his feet, and out of the black smoke stepped the plaguebringer.

Abhinava

My feeling that something significant would happen in Fornyd came true a couple of days after I bid farewell to Ohhwuh and wished him a long and happy life in the Gravewood. It was afternoon, and I was just about to leave the city to go hunting mushrooms for dinner while Murr and Eep hunted for something else. A mariner stopped me as I was heading out the gates and summoned me with some urgency to the Wellspring.

"The zephyr Koesha Gansu has returned with Gondel Vedd from the isle of Blight, and she has information she needs to share. Everyone is waiting on you."

"Everyone? Is that a literal thing or do you mean a smaller set of people?"

"The quartermaster, gerstads Daryck du Löngren and Nara du Fesset, and more besides. But the zephyr insisted that you be there once she heard you were in town, because some of what she has to share involves the krakens."

I asked Murr and Eep if they would be all right hunting without me, and they said they would, so I pointed them in the direction of the nearest swamp ducks and wished them good hunting before returning with the mariner.

When I got to the Wellspring, the mist from the quartermaster's waterfalls hung in the air like a manifestation of wet anxiety. I had missed their eventful return, but Scholar Gondel Vedd was in a coma after being attacked by a wraith that had possessed a spy caught by Gerstad du Löngren, so Koesha was the only one who knew what really happened on the isle of Blight with the wraiths and the source of the Seventh Kenning. The second könstad had gone to Pelemyn to brief the pelenaut, so she would not be attending. The Brynts had a Nentian translator from the capital working hard to keep up as Koesha relayed that an actual god had been imprisoned on Blight for centuries by his siblings, who no longer had physical bodies but had bound themselves to kenning sites in the hopes of keeping their peoples safe from one another but mostly safe from this god, who called himself Sedam.

"He tries to come across as this reasonable guy who could simply do nothing else but engineer a genocide, but I'm sure he's leaving out quite a lot, and he just glossed over the war that created the Glass Desert in a single sentence. I'm not sure how much of his story we should believe, but I think he's telling the truth about a couple of things: He really wants to destroy Pelemyn to get at his brother Bryn, and he also wants to destroy the krakens—one in particular." She searched for my eyes and locked on. "He says his sister—the one that blessed you, Abhi—has bound her spirit to the oldest kraken in the sea. I think that's why that army is up there, and I think that's why Lorson was living on that island. They're trying to find her and kill her."

"Why?" Gerstad du Löngren wondered aloud.

"The krakens choke off shipping and exploration, meaning very few can reach Sedam and give him aid. They're effectively his jailers, and, until recently, they kept Ecula isolated."

"She needs to know," I said. "She probably doesn't know they're coming, so I have to tell her."

"Tell who?" the quartermaster said.

"The old kraken. I know where she is. We can't allow that army to find her—or kill all the other krakens when they come back to spawn, which they might settle for, and which might accomplish Sedam's goal just as well."

"How do they even do it?" Gerstad du Fesset asked.

"I don't know that, but they've obviously figured out an efficient method, or else they wouldn't have enough blood to stain the hulls of their fleet. I'll leave in the morning."

There were plenty more revelations, no doubt, but I'd heard all I needed to. I had to find Murr and Eep and let them know I'd be traveling back into the cold, and if they didn't want to come that was all right; they could stay at the farm with the orange barn.

They opted for that, and I got them settled in and made sure the farmer and all the neighbors were aware that the bloodcat and stalk hawk were not to be touched while they hunted in the area.

In the morning, I boarded the *Nentian Herald* with the full crew present and accounted for, and we sailed upriver to Grynek. The crew would dock there and work on cleaning up the city, while Koesha and I continued on over land to Malath Ashmali.

It was a rough and cold stretch of days but not without its wonders. We got rides from different large beasts along the way, all of which had been created long ago, according to

Koesha, by a Nentian metamorph named Bharat Vellala. We rode on the backs of fir apes and dreadmoose and white-furred snow deer, for example, and sometimes Koesha lifted us into the air and we flew for short distances, until we couldn't take the cold anymore. During nights we slept back-to-back underneath warm down blankets that constituted the bulk of what we carried, and we ate what I could forage along with some bowls of thin mushroom soup that thankfully cooked quickly.

Olet Kanek was mightily surprised to see us again so soon—it had been only a couple of months since she bade us farewell—but she was grateful we'd come with the news of that army. She hastily convened a meeting with the city council so Koesha could share again all that she'd learned on Blight, especially a full understanding of who Lorson was and what he'd been doing out on that island: studying the kraken migration patterns and trying to figure out where the oldest one was. I'm not sure what kind of success he expected to have without diving underwater and exposing himself to danger, but he obviously must have valued the isolation as well. Had we not found his island accidentally by settling in Malath Ashmali—and scouting it thanks to Eep—he'd still be there, silently running the spy network for Sedam, because Gerstad Daryck du Löngren and the Grynek Hunters never would have found him.

I began to wonder how much of it was accidental, however. If that kraken knew Lorson was there and she was the goddess who blessed me, had I been pushed and nudged along, perhaps, to a place where I could thwart the plans of her little brother, Sedam?

Maybe I'd have a chance to ask her. I wanted a decent meal and a good night's sleep first, and the Nentians on the council were happy to provide this. They'd had the Raelech stonecutter Curragh build a formal Joabeian embassy while we were gone, and Koesha and I were able to spend the night there in our own rooms.

In the morning, we breakfasted with Curragh and the master courier Tuala, and I shared with them my appreciation of their country, since I'd visited it recently, and that Fintan was now in Pelemyn perfoming an epic retelling of the Giant Wars.

It was a small soft time of contentment with friends, perhaps unworthy of comment for many people, but my eyes welled somewhat at the wonder of having friends. All too soon, it was time for me to do what I'd come to do, and I had no idea if I'd be successful or not.

Bundled up tightly against the cold in a borrowed heavy jacket and gloves, I was escorted across the ice pack by a Nentian fisherman to a fishing hole he had drilled and used regularly. The bottom of it had frozen overnight, but he'd brought his drill and punched through the ice, revealing the cold water underneath. I sprawled on my belly, removed the glove from my right hand, and plunged my arm down the hole until I could get my fingers into the water. Then I reached out with my kenning to locate the old kraken I'd sensed when Koesha and her crew first arrived. It was still there—the only kraken around now.

"Raena. Meso. Sixth child of Teldwen and Kalaad. I am Abhinava Khose, blessed by your Sixth Kenning, and I have news of your brother Sedam."

I got no response, so I repeated myself a couple of times. Maybe she was napping or hibernating or something.

"Sedam is trying to escape his prison. He knows you are in this sea. He has sent an army to find and kill you, and he sent more armies to kill the people of the Fourth Kenning so that your brother will be weakened."

That elicited a reaction. The kraken moved.

"I don't know how much of what I'm saying you understand or if you can answer, but I will happily explain the situation. You may not be aware of everything that Sedam has been planning."

The cold numbed my hand, but I could tell what the kraken was doing. It was surfacing, albeit slowly, and farther out from shore than where I was. Eventually the ice pack shuddered and thundered until it burst apart, great chunks of heavy ice flying, and thick black tentacles rose from the sea. That was all I was expecting, but then a massive oblong head emerged, pulsating, with orange and yellow eyes cresting just above the surface. The tentacles very clearly gestured that I should approach, so I removed my hand from the freezing water and gingerly walked across the ice toward the kraken, telling the Nentian fisherman he should stay where he was. He nodded enthusiastically at this instruction, never so willing as now to comply with an order.

Looking back briefly to the cliffside of Malath Ashmali, I saw a line of Nentians and Hathrim there, watching and gesturing, though I could not hear anything spoken. Koesha had come down to the shore with me but remained near the wind tube that memorialized her fallen crew, drowned or consumed by another kraken. She looked like she might be reliving that horror, and I felt ashamed that I hadn't thought of how this meeting might hurt her. Best to make sure this didn't play out like that. I returned my gaze to the kraken.

"When I speak to creatures," I called out, "they understand me but cannot speak back in any language I understand. But they do nod their head to indicate yes, or shake their head to say no. Could you maybe do that with one of your tentacles?"

The kraken flattened most of the tentacles on the ice but left one up, curled at the tip as if to represent a human head, and waggled it up and down in imitation of a nod. But then she gestured again that I should come closer.

Why, I wondered? She could obviously understand me

from where she was. Did she want to eat me, the annoying man who'd woken her with bad news?

It turned out that was not what she wished at all. Before I got to the edge of the broken ice—perhaps six lengths away—she straightened her tentacles up together in a wall, telling me to stop. Once I did, a single tentacle advanced toward me at eye level, slowly, perhaps so as not to alarm me. It was too late for that; the smallest tip of it was still as big as my head, and I was acutely aware of how insignificant and vulnerable I was. It halted in front of me, easily within reach, dripping on the ice—though I imagined that would start freezing soon. When I did nothing, uncertain of what to do, the other tentacles twirled rapidly, as if I was supposed to proceed.

"You want me to . . . touch it?"

The tentacles all curled and nodded. So I kept my freezing right hand in its glove and removed the glove from my left hand before reaching out to touch the tip of the kraken's tentacle. It was cold and wet, which should not have surprised me, but I gasped anyway, because I was touching a kraken with its full consent. Or maybe the gasp was because I heard a voice in my head.

Hello, Abhinava Khose.

"Oh! Hi. Uh . . . what should I call you?"

I have many names. But I like Raena, the one that the Raelechs gave me. I am a huntress. And the first person I blessed was a son of hunters who no longer wished to hunt.

"Yeah . . . I know. But why me?"

You are kind. And you are willing to act according to what you believe is right, even when it will surely earn the disapproval of those around you.

My mind raced to catch up to the implications. "So you were aware of me deciding to leave my family? Did you . . . did you send that boil of kherns their way?"

No. The kherns were stampeded naturally by a pack of hunting sedge pumas, just as you saw. I learned of your motivations later, through the pack of bloodcats that blessed you. They hosted a fragment of my will at that time, as this kraken does.

"Why didn't you bless anyone before?"

It was strategically better to wait. I knew that someday my brother would make another escape attempt. I did not want him to be able to anticipate the Sixth Kenning and plan countermeasures for it. Now tell me what he has planned.

"Using a religion he created, he has turned Ecula into a culture that will go to war for his purposes. He wanted to wipe out Brynlön and take control of the Fourth Kenning, and possibly Rael and the Third Kenning as well. Eculan ship hulls are stained with the blood of krakens, and that has allowed them to cross the seas unmolested."

Clever. I knew that many krakens have died recently, but I did not know why or who was killing them. Did he succeed in wiping out Brynlön?

"No, but he nearly did. They are going to try again. A second invasion is scheduled soon."

And you have plans to stop it?

"I think others have the plans. I'm going to help if I can."

Good. How did you learn that Sedam was behind all of this?

"A scholar from Kauria and a sailor from Joabei spoke to him on his island."

That was dangerous. I do not recommend repeating that. Whatever crimes he admitted to committing, I assure you they were far worse. He will give you a leaf and tell you it is the whole truth when there's an entire tree—not to mention a forest—behind it.

"I will relay that to my Brynt friends. You should also know that there is an army of Eculans camped for the winter to the east of here on the shore, next to a river. We believe they are hunting you or, failing that, trying to kill as many krakens as possible. Either will serve Sedam's purposes. Once the ice pack melts and the kraken come back here to spawn, they will be ready."

That is excellent information. Leave them to me. The creatures of the Gravewood will fall upon them and they will never see the spring. Who are these people living nearby?

"A community of Nentians and Hathrim and a couple of Raelechs. There were some Joabeians too. They mean you no harm."

Perhaps not directly, but they have been fishing here.

"Yes. I used my kenning to enchant some of their hulls to repel krakens so they would be safe."

Also very clever. If I knew Sedam was dead, I could tell the krakens to stop pursuing ships, and you would not have to fear them anymore. Your solution will suffice in the meantime. Tell them I am pleased to see Nentians and Hathrim living in peace, but they must keep these waters pristine and not overfish or I will be ignoring that enchantment and destroying their ships myself. And if that doesn't stop them from polluting my home, I will destroy their homes and many of them in the process.

"I will tell them. Forgive me for asking, Raena, but can Sedam be killed?"

One of Bryn's blessed could do it, if they could get close enough. But he will never allow that. Keeping him neutralized is the best we can hope for.

"Why didn't Bryn do it ages ago? Or the rest of you? Why let him live to visit so much ruin upon the world?"

Because he is our brother. And we hoped that someday he would be better. Instead, his poisonous mind has grown more toxic.

"I understand. May I ask you something about your parents?"

Bubbles rose to the surface around the kraken's head, the eyes squinted a little bit, and her voice in my head changed. I think she was amused.

Go ahead.

"Like most Nentians, I was raised to worship Kalaad in the sky. Is he . . . still around? And does he care about us?"

He's alive but exists in a perpetual dream state. Obsessed with sunrises and sunsets, clouds and shadows. Praying to him does no harm but does no good either. Which is pretty much true for all of us. We simply administer the kennings and let you make your own decisions.

"Why didn't you ever start a faith, like your siblings did?"

I contributed to the Raelech faith; the scrolls of Raena are mine, as Kaelin's and Dinae's are theirs. But to start something in Ghurana Nent would have created an expectation of blessings, and I did not want to bestow them until now.

"What made you start with me?"

Hathrim hounds hunting north of the Godsteeth. That was an imbalance of power that needed to be addressed. And I thought, erroneously, that Sedam must be behind it somehow, because the Hathrim had not dared to try such an invasion for centuries. Inciting them to act seemed like the sort of thing he would arrange.

"So you didn't intend me to counter the Eculan invasion of Brynlön and Rael, which he actually did arrange?"

No. I didn't know about that until you told me just now. I am aware of events in Ghurana Nent only. Part of me is here, and the other part travels among animals, blessing a few.

"That reminds me—why do you bless such a small percentage?"

Inhabiting the animals and traveling from place to place takes tremendous energy. It leaves less available for blessings. Still, there are many more blessed now than before.

"I see. Raena . . . did you have anything to do with bringing me here to find the lifeleech?"

I don't know what lifeleech you mean. But even if I did, the answer is no. We never control humans directly; if anything, you are controlled indirectly through religion, which is what you said Sedam used to weaponize the Eculans against you. And if I wish to be fair, it is what the rest of us used to keep an uneasy peace among humans for a very long time. In response to the Hathrim invasion, all I did was bless you and hope you would be disruptive, and you were. But you always made your own choices, and you always will.

"Oh. Well . . . what should I do now?"

What you are already doing: Be Abhinava Khose. It has worked out well for the world so far. I have no further wisdom to impart, but I hope you will manage to live long and well.

The tentacle withdrew, and understanding that my audience was over, I said, "Farewell, Raena. Thanks for talking to me, and . . . everything. Kalaad in the sky, that sounds so inadequate."

Another flood of bubbles as she sank back into the Northern Yawn, the soft laughter of a kraken goddess.

"Oh! I just swore by your dad, and that was incredibly rude. I'm sorry! I just—oh, balls. Incredibly uncool. So embarrassing. Shutting up now."

Well, I'd be replaying *that* in my head for the rest of my life, thinking of ten thousand better ways I could have said goodbye to a goddess.

The last tentacle sank out of sight, leaving me to shuffle back across the ice to the shore. I shared everything that was said with the people of Malath Ashmali, emphasizing that Raena was clear that they must be careful not to pollute the waters or overfish or she'd destroy their fishing boats and then the city itself. They should make sure to craft such laws and customs that future generations would never dare to stray from them.

Curragh and Tuala were rather shaken to discover that an avatar of the triple goddess had been dwelling offshore all this time—the author of the scrolls of Raena. Tuala, especially, was overcome, since she was so devout and lived ascetically, as the scrolls of Raena suggested, pursuing service and duty and craft. Curragh was also devout, though he honored Dinae. They stayed on the cliff's edge until sunset, their shining eyes staring at the hole in the ice the kraken had made, and it was obvious that they would never choose to live anywhere else.

Koesha and I left the next morning in the company of

Tuala, who needed to tell the Triune Council of these developments anyway, and she'd get us back to Fornyd much faster and more comfortably than we'd managed on the way up.

I asked Tuala if she'd share some of the scrolls of Raena with us, since I knew only a little of them, and she happily recited them from memory.

Fintan took a deep breath and exhaled upon dispelling the seeming. "I wish I had been there to witness that. A daughter of Teldwen and Kalaad still lives among us—and unlike her younger brother, she wishes us well! The scrolls of Raena take on additional shadings of meaning for me now that I know what she has done with her own life. She preaches service and duty in her scrolls and has made it her duty to serve the world by protecting it from her brother. She waited for millennia in the deep for the right time to bless someone to counter him. Together with Bryn, they worked to keep calamity from washing up on our shores, and, until recently, they were successful for thousands of years."

"Makes you think of krakens differently," I said, and Fintan heard me.

"Yes! Someone here on the wall just mentioned that we have long thought of krakens as a great evil, holding us back from exploring, but now we know from painful experience they were intended to protect us from a much worse fate than losing a ship here and there."

Conversations bubbled up, and Fintan let it go for a little bit because he understood people needed to process things. Near me, one man was dismayed to hear that his prayers didn't matter. And his companion—I don't know if she was related or a romantic partner or what—clapped him on the back.

"Cheer up. It means you're free to do what you like and always have been. But you're not free of responsibility for your own actions. You'll have to recognize that and reckon with it. We all will. Might be the only part of life that's fair."

Another couple was talking in relieved tones about Raena's plan to take care of that army in the north, and I felt sure that the pelenaut and many others had also been relieved to hear that.

Fintan resumed. "Much as I wish I could have been there, I was here, with you, and that was a gift also, and it continues to be. We all have much more to talk about, eh? Now let's return to who we were talking about yesterday."

When he took on a seeming this time, it was the disheveled and very welcome form of Gondel Vedd.

Gondel

"Mmf. Bleaggh. Urrgh."

I didn't know whether the headache I felt woke me up or if it appeared suddenly to punish me for doing so. Either way, it hurt. As did the cries of Maron and Nara du Fesset.

"Oh! Gondel! My sweet husband. Thank Reinei you're back. Thank Reinei."

He was cradling my hand against his cheek and had tears streaming down his face. Nara was saying something too, but it was unintelligible.

"What . . . happened?"

Nara gushed a stream of words that made no sense, and I just blinked, looking to Maron with a question forming in my eyebrows.

"You were possessed by a wraith," he said. "Or at least partially. Do you remember? You had just come back from the Mistmaiden Isles with Captain Koesha Gansu."

"Oh . . . yes, I remember that."

"They had you talk to an Eculan spy, and he attacked you.

Nara killed him, then the wraith that was possessing him tried to possess you. The quartermaster was able to purge the wraith from your brain, but you've been in a coma for almost two weeks."

"Eculan spy? I don't remember that at all. My head hurts, Maron. Have to pee. Thirsty."

"We can take care of that. Tell Nara you need food and drink, and she'll leave to give you some privacy."

"Why don't you tell her?"

"Because I don't speak Brynt, and you do."

"Ah. Right." I turned my gaze to Nara and said, "Food and drink, please."

"No, Gondel, tell her in Brynt."

"I did—oh." Had I just spoken in Kaurian? I supposed I had, because Nara obviously did not understand me. I wished the pounding in my head would stop. It felt like howling winds slamming a door inside my skull. How did one ask for food in Brynt? Why was this so hard? I was a scholar of languages. I spoke all the languages of the six nations plus Eculan. This should not be a problem.

I returned my gaze to Nara, and she waited patiently as I searched for the words.

"Food, please," I finally managed. Not much of a sentence at all, just two basic words that children and beginners knew.

"Aha! Yes!" she said, suddenly lighting up. "Food!" She said something else I didn't catch and then departed, leaving me with Maron.

"Something is wrong. But I really need to pee."

I felt weak and stiff, but Maron helped me out of bed to take care of nature's call, and by the time I'd finished, I wasn't so unsteady on my feet. But I didn't want to get back in bed.

"May I sit? I think that would be better."

"Of course, of course. Now, what's wrong?"

"I have the worst headache ever. And I am having trouble remembering how to speak Brynt."

"Just Brynt? Or any other language besides Kaurian?"

"That is . . . a very good question. Let's see. Shall I try saying something basic yet profound in every language?"

"I think that would be good," Maron allowed.

"I require cheese and crackers with mustard, a cup of tea, and a good book," I said, then repeated it flawlessly in Fornish, Hathrim, Nentian, Raelech, and . . . that was it.

"Cheese . . . and mustard," I said in Brynt, then looked pleadingly at Maron as I sat in a chair. "It's gone, Maron. Where did it go?"

"It's not *entirely* gone. You can still remember some words. And you can relearn the rest."

"But why have I forgotten?"

"The quartermaster told me that the wraith might have damaged your brain while it was trying to possess you. Since the spy was Brynt and you were thinking in Brynt at the time, those portions of your brain were active and firing—perhaps that had something to do with it?"

"Perhaps. Reinei's peace, Maron, what if I've lost it?"

"Then we'll fix it. However long it takes. I'm just so glad you're back. I was terrified I'd lost you, Gondel. I love you."

"And I love you. Thank you for being here when I woke up."

"Of course."

"Do you think I might actually be able to get that tea and some books? Brynt ones. Maybe I can read them and it will come back to me."

"Absolutely. Nara will be back soon, and I imagine you'll have other visitors too. We were all very worried."

The prospect of speaking with a bunch of people with whom I really couldn't converse terrified me. "Could we . . . maybe delay visitors, perhaps? No one except Nara until I have a chance to assess the damage and maybe get rid of this headache?"

"I think that's wise. Yes. I'll see to it. We'll get you everything you need, and you can rest and recover. There's no hurry."

"Well, maybe there is."

"There isn't."

"There's the situation with the Eculans—blow me down, the Eculans! Can I still read and speak their language? That's what I need to know."

"No, you need to recuperate."

"You're right, I do need a skull that doesn't hurt. But could you have someone bring me some Eculan documents or maybe that holy text of theirs with my notes in it?"

"I can do that later. Let's get you fed and hydrated first."

Nara returned with a tray of cheese, crackers, mustard, and tea—precisely what I would have wished. There were benefits, I supposed, to being predictable and easy to please.

Maron knew very little Brynt—though perhaps more than I did at this point—and somehow communicated that I needed Brynt books and time to recover. Nara tried talking to me, but I had to shake my head and shrug helplessly. Apart from a word here and there, it was all babble. Maron pointed at his head and explained in Kaurian that we couldn't understand her and needed a translator. She looked confused for a while, but I think she may have gotten it eventually, as she nodded and departed again after saying something reassuring.

The tea and cheese tray helped considerably, and the pounding in my skull eased somewhat. When Nara next returned, she came with the Nentian translator who'd been helping communicate with Captain Gansu. Since I had no trouble remembering my Nentian, I asked her to relay my issues to Nara and requested Brynt and Eculan literature in an effort to restore my faculty with those languages.

Nara looked shocked when the translator spoke, but then she nodded and spoke rapidly in Brynt, of which I caught maybe one word in ten.

The translator said, "The gerstad will get you the documents right away and begs your forgiveness for allowing you to come to harm. She will never forgive herself."

The poor woman looked genuinely distressed, and I could see that her eyes were filling with tears. I waved a hand to banish them.

"Nara, my dear, you are forgiven. Go now, and do forgive yourself. The world heaps enough burdens on our back without us adding to them. We must move forward at speed, for there is peace ahead of us, and if we are slowed by regrets, we might never reach it."

She bowed and exited with thanks, and Maron pulled up a chair next to mine so that he could sit and hold my hand. I smiled at him fondly.

"You are the best husband. I may have forgotten a language or two, but I am so glad I haven't forgotten that."

He smiled back and squeezed my hand, and together we took a deep breath of peace.

A roar of relieved approval from the audience only intensified when Fintan dismissed the seeming and invited the real live Gondel Vedd to join him on the wall! I'd been so intent on the tale that I hadn't seen the scholar arrive. Maron was with him—a handsome older man, who still had most of his hair, only some of it gone gray, and a very neat, trim beard that hugged his jaw.

"Hello, Pelemyn," Gondel said, his voice carrying across the peninsula, and the response he got was far more than I think anyone expected—a sustained standing ovation and an outpouring of love for the man who'd been working so hard to help us.

When he finally got everyone to stop, he said in less-than-fluent Brynt, "I am most better, because last weeks—in these last weeks—I practice. I talk much with Gerstad du Fesset and others. Verbs still difficult. But every day: better. Holes filling. What? No, Maron. Not those holes." He switched to Kaurian to chide his husband for interrupting him with a risqué joke but then started giggling. And since it was all being broadcast by the bard, that got everyone giggling. There is nothing quite like an entire city and three guest armies laughing at the same time.

"Anyway. I continue to improve," he said when the laughter had died down. "In Eculan also, because I translated the holy book to Kaurian, and it helps much. Also: Thank you all for the mustard and cheese. That is all I want to say now. May we all breathe peace together soon."

He got another sustained ovation as he withdrew, laughing some more with Maron, and then Fintan surprised us all with his last tale.

"This ending will also be a beginning. For we are not at the end, are we, so much as the opening curtain of the final act. I have a new story from someone who has lived here in Pelemyn for many years. Some of you already know of her and her husband. But it's unlikely that you really *know* her, or why she came to live here, or why she will travel with us to Ecula. And, of course, the armies of Raël, Forn, and the navy of Kauria might not even know she's here. So please welcome the chef and co-owner of one of Pelemyn's finest dining establishments, the Roasted Sunchuck, who also happens to be a Hathrim firelord hailing from Sardrik: Hollit Panevik."

The immensely tall form of Hollit Panevik grew out of the mist, but unlike the other Hathrim narrators we'd witnessed, she was dressed in an apron and a chef's beret. Not a scrap of armor. No hint of martial ambitions. Instead of a sword, she held a wooden spoon.

Hollit

At its most basic level, eating is an act of survival. It is fuel for the fire within us. But once elevated above that, it can become an affirmation that life is good, and one can forget for an hour about the struggle and worry of existence. There is nothing like a full belly to make one believe that we are doing something right and living well.

Among the Hathrim, my husband and I are "daffy sand badgers" because we are blessed and do not use our kenning in the service of a hearthfire. When I climbed out of the lava of Mount Olenik and discovered that I was a firelord, I was immediately offered fireproof clothing and positions in the crucibles of every hearthfire in the land. There were permanent recruiters, sweating at the base of the volcano. I could have lived anywhere in Hathrir in relative luxury, so long as I pledged loyalty to the hearthfire there and did what he said.

I put them off. "Let me think about it. This is unexpected," I said. And it was, because I had not expected or particularly wanted to live. My vague attraction to the kenning had been more about the craft of the forge than anything else; I certainly did not jump into the lava dreaming of becoming muscle for a strongman.

That response was apparently not new, and they were willing to let me go home and adjust, but they wanted to know my name and where I lived—a bizarre request that I granted to get them to leave me alone. They wanted to pay for my lodging in town and my passage south to my home in Sardrik, give me food money or just money for whatever I wanted. Anything to create a sense of debt, though they assured me I wasn't expected to pay anything back; they only wanted to make sure the blessed were taken care of. But I knew it wasn't true generosity. That money was a long coil of rope to bind me into service.

Still, I took some, because I had nothing. I stayed at an inn down by the docks, having no intention of going home, and saw immediately how I was treated differently by people because they recognized I was wearing clothes given to me by recruiters. I was newly blessed and was advertising it by simply walking around.

Attached to the inn was a bar of wide renown called the First Kenning Taproom. They had ales and beers from all over Hathrir as well as imported Fornish, Raelech, and Nentian kegs. After securing a room, I sat at the bar and stared at the list of choices without really seeing it, because my mind was trying to latch on to this new reality but having trouble finding purchase.

A voice interrupted me. "Any ideas about what you want?"

I looked up to see a friendly man behind the bar with a full dark beard; his mouth, stretched wide in a smile, was hidden by his mustache.

"Uh," I said.

"Overwhelming, isn't it?" He gestured at the beer menu. "So many choices and still, none of them might be perfect for how you're feeling right now."

"That's apt," I agreed. It summed up my life pretty well. My room was paid for courtesy of the hearthfire Gorin Mogen in Harthrad. My food and drink were being covered by the hearthfire Winthir Kanek in Narvik. Living in either city would be preferable to returning home, but I wasn't especially keen on getting involved in their power games.

"If you're in the mood for something besides a beer, I can do that too."

"Like what?"

Encouraged, he raised a thick eyebrow. "You like emberfruit?"

"Sure. Who doesn't? It's delicious, nutritious, and incendiary. You can't ask much more of a fruit."

Similar in taste to a plum but larger in size, emberfruits were native to Hathrir and needed to be served chilled, because they tended to ignite easily. More than one house had burned down in the summer because the owners hadn't stored their emberfruit safely. Squirt some of the juice on a fire and it would flare up.

"Okay. Let me whip up something for you," he said.

Out of an icebox, he pulled a frozen emberfruit and plopped it onto a cutting board. He drew a gorgeous hand-smithed knife from a scabbard on his belt and sliced the frozen fruit easily into cubes. These he placed into a shallow drinking bowl.

From a chiller, he pulled another emberfruit, which was cold but not frozen. This he juiced into a glass and then mixed with carefully measured portions of soda and several spirits that I missed entirely because I was staring at his face and how serene and happy he was at practicing his craft. Once he stirred that concoction together with a long-stemmed spoon, he poured the whole purple potion over the frozen cubed emberfruit in the bowl, filling it near to the brim, and then dropped a pellet of dry ice into an inedible steel-mesh cage, which he lowered into the drink. The potion began to bubble and smoke.

He pushed it gently to me, pointed a finger at it, and the surface ignited with a blue-orange flame, which elicited a startled "Oh!" from my lips.

"I call that a Firelord Fizz," he said. "Invented it myself. If you weren't blessed, I'd say blow out the flame first, but you can put that right up to your face as is with no problem."

"You're blessed too?"

"Just a sparker, but yes."

"But you're not contracted into the service of a hearth-fire?"

He shrugged and shook his head. "Sparkers can get away with that. I've got immunity to flames and the ability to start them but no control. Hearthfires are all about control, aren't they? So sparkers can escape service if they want."

"And you wanted to? You like doing this?"

"I love this," he said, nodding enthusiastically. "What I do helps people celebrate their good fortune or forget their misfortune. Sometimes people let me make drinks like I did for you instead of just pulling tankards of ale. Give it a try. If you don't like it, we can try something else."

A smile played at the corners of my lips. This was something new. I'd never seen a drink like that before. And when I brought it to my lips, the heat from the flames a pleasant warmth instead of a dangerous burn, I sipped and it was the most delicious thing I'd ever tasted up to that point.

"That is flaming good," I told him, and smiled. He smiled back through his beard and bowed slightly in thanks. "What's your name?"

"Orden."

"Thank you, Orden. I'm Hollit. You've made me feel better."

"Glad to hear it. But sorry to hear of your troubles. Happily, a good drink and a good meal can often help to reset one's perspective."

"Yeah," I said, the sentence hitting me with the force of revelation. Because I did feel hopeful, of a sudden, that my fate didn't have to be tied to a hearthfire. A pause to eat and drink and converse with someone new, and a reset was possible. Orden moved away to help some other customers, and I wondered if I might be able to pull off something like he had—living a life of craft with his kenning that didn't involve politics.

The next time he came back to check on me, I asked him to make me something different, whatever he liked.

"Are you on a recruiter's tab?"

"Yes. You know about them?"

"You're not the first new firelord to sit in that chair. And I was recruited too, but I came here and realized I never wanted to leave. Okay, hold on. I'm going to make you something really special, since someone else is paying for it."

He had a supremely rare bottle of Fornish mushroom whiskey back there, which he used to make a mushroom firelime sour. He wedged a pink glass flower between two firelimes on the rim so that they looked like leaves on the stem, then placed a sugar cube in the bowl formed by the petals. He piped two drops of emberfruit juice onto it, then sparked it and served it to me aflame, a gorgeous drink that I had to simply marvel at and store in my memory before touching it.

And it was exquisite, earthy and bitter but also tart and sweetened by firelime syrup, made by reducing the juice and sugar until it thickened and browned.

"Is this your invention also?" I asked.

"It is. Mushroom sours made by the Fornish typically use common lemons and honey rather than firelime juice and syrup. I can't supply the mushroom garnish grown on the bark of a greensleeve's limb, but they don't have access to firelimes either."

"You must be pleasing Thurik as a craftsman."

"I hope so," he said.

"How can I do that? I don't want to fight and burn."

"Plenty of firelords go into forging, either glass or steel. Mogen's good for either." He tapped his sheathed knife. "I use Mogen steel."

That endorsement almost swayed me into signing on with Gorin Mogen, which I can see now would have been a disastrous choice. I almost certainly would not be alive today if I had, because his firelords either died in the eruption of Mount Thayil, were skewered by Fornish thornhands under command of Nel Kit ben Sah, or were crushed by a boil of kherns sent by the plaguebringer Abhinava Khose. But the more I thought of it—crafting something exquisite, and then never seeing it used or appreciated in the world—the more I believed it wouldn't satisfy me. There were people who could feel satisfied, even fulfilled, by the act of creation itself, but I knew myself well enough to realize I would need to do something with immediate positive feedback.

After lingering at the bar and talking to Orden longer than strictly necessary—because I liked that he just wanted to make me happy with tasty drinks—I got a fitful night's sleep and returned to the taproom the next day, to find the recruiters waiting for me there.

I asked them what jobs I could do for their hearthfires that guaranteed no fighting. Smithing was immediately mentioned. Hunting lava dragons was another, since they basically charred anyone who wasn't fireproof, and then there was harvesting emberfruits, which were essentially unstable firebombs until they chilled. The enchantment of firebowls was steady work that the world relied on. These were all guarantees of comfortable living that would either repulse or bore me. I asked them to give me more time to think about it, and they were visibly disappointed for a second before plastering on accommodating smiles.

Once they left, Orden made me a new drink and said, "I have a very small job if you're interested—would take about fifteen minutes and the chef would be so happy he'd make you something special for free."

"What is it?"

Orden took me into the kitchen and introduced me to the chef, Ullin Berinok, who was delighted at the prospect that he might get some help. His red hair and beard were netted, his apron spotless.

"I have to make a delicate custard but heat it at a steady temperature," he said. "Too much heat and it burns; too little and the ingredients won't mix properly. It's difficult to get right and requires my undivided attention, but as a chef my attention is often divided. In theory, you should be able to keep the temperature constant."

"In theory?"

"You should have a sense of the heat if you focus on it. I'm told firelords can do this. Come here. I have a filet on the grill that is supposed to be medium rare in the center. Can you tell?"

He pointed to the filet—it looked and smelled delicious. But I couldn't tell its internal temperature until I focused on it with my kenning. Once I did, I could feel the gradients of temperature within the steak, hottest on the outside and cooler in the middle.

"It's there now. If you keep it on much longer, it'll be medium."

"Oh! Thank you." He grabbed a pair of tongs and removed it from the fire, plating it on top of a flare of green sauce expertly spread with a spoon, then adding side dishes. It looked like art. He called out, "Order up!" for the server and then smiled at me. "Help me get a few batches of custard right and I'll make you anything you want."

Chef Berinok talked me through the process and . . . I loved it. He was happy and grateful, and I felt like I'd done something worthwhile.

"Do firelords ever become chefs?" I asked him. He snorted.

"I've never heard of it."

"Why not? Wouldn't they be great at it?"

"They'd be great at cooking things properly, yes, but there's more to it than that. The knife work, the sharp mind required to keep track of multiple orders, the business acumen—none of that comes with a blessing. And besides, every hearthfire I've heard of would consider it a waste."

"A waste? Was that custard a waste?"

"Of course not. I don't agree with the hearthfires, Hollit. I'm just saying that those recruiters are not paying for your food and lodging and clothes in hopes that you'll come to their city and prepare a perfect sauce for a scorpion tail."

"Ha! I guess not."

The chef thanked me again and said he'd whip up a special brunch for me soon and have Orden deliver it at the bar.

It was remarkable to me how much I instantly loved using my kenning that way and how rewarding the experience was. Back in Sardrik, I'd been nothing but an extra mouth to feed. My existence was not valued but resented as a drain of resources. If I returned now, I'd be valued for sure, so long as I fulfilled the role a hearthfire assigned me. I wouldn't be Hollit, who had her own wishes and dreams, but rather a firelord in the hearthfire's employ. *What* I was would matter more than *who* I was.

Over yet another fabulous drink, I asked Orden, "Can't I just work in the kitchen somewhere?"

"Not openly as a firelord. Hearthfires won't let you."

"Why?"

He regarded me evenly for a few seconds, trying to gauge whether I was joking with him or seriously didn't know. Evidently he decided on the latter and replied, "Because if you're not loyal to one of them, you're a threat to them. They'll think you plan to challenge them as soon as you have full control of your powers, and they'll want to snuff you out before you can become a problem. You'll be in a fight whether you want it or not."

"That is a poisonous mindset."

"No argument here."

I spoke with Orden in snatches throughout the day, worrying over my fate, and later that afternoon Chef Berinok invited me back into the kitchen and asked if I'd like to help out.

"I'll pay you for your time, of course," he said. It was such an unusual request that my eyes darted to the door leading to the bar.

"Yes, Orden might have mentioned you would like to work in the kitchen."

"I would, thanks." He set me to chopping and slicing and dicing vegetables with a Mogen-forged blade. He showed me some techniques and I copied them, albeit at a much slower speed. Time passed quickly, and eventually there was nothing left to prepare.

"Can I work here some more tomorrow?" I asked the chef.

"I wouldn't mind, but I think the recruiters might."

"It would require lying, for sure. I'll check out of the inn and find someplace else to stay. I'll be back here, never showing my face in the taproom, and they'll never know."

"Don't check out. The hotel staff will tell the recruiters immediately. And you're probably being watched. You need to simply disappear for a few days. Do you have someplace to stay?"

My shoulders drooped. "Not yet. That was always going to be the difficult part of escaping, especially since I have no money to speak of."

"Hmm. Hold on."

Chef Berinok arranged for me to stay with Orden. They smuggled me out the back entrance at night, my fireproof clothing concealed by a cloak, and no one accosted us.

Orden had a spare bedroom, full of junk, which he cleared away enough for me to lay down some ice howler furs and giant sponge pillows. I had to stay there for two days while recruiters searched for me in town and complained loudly to the management of the inn and questioned Orden about the last time he'd seen me.

I cut and dyed my hair and got new clothes, courtesy of the chef, then began my apprenticeship on the third day. For months I did nothing that required me to use my kenning, except for the odd batch of custard. People were looking for me everywhere, hearthfires worried about the rogue firelord with an unknown agenda.

My agenda was to serve hungry people, not hearthfires.

Once my knife skills were built up, I spent additional months learning to cook and grill and even bake. And falling in love with Orden.

But during that time, I lived as a fugitive. I didn't go out much—there was only work and sleep—because if I was discovered, I'd be pressed into service or a hearthfire would have me killed. There would be no more wooing; there would be demands, and then blades.

"Let's get away from here, Orden," I said one night.

"And go where?"

"Someplace where the hearthfires won't worry about me. Where we can live in the open and in peace."

"Are you suggesting Kauria?"

"There, or anywhere that isn't Hathrir. I don't know where I want to be so much as where I don't."

He wanted nothing in the world so much as to see me happy. So he bid farewell to his friends, wrote letters to his family, and we bought berths on a Nentian ship to Talala Fouz. I had no family I wished to tell of my travels. They said goodbye to me when I went for my seeking, and unless someone told them otherwise, they must have assumed I was dead. That was fine by me.

I enchanted firebowls in exchange for most everything we needed on our travels. I even crafted a few glass blades, seeing as they were prized along the river, since they would never rust.

We spent some time in Ghurana Nent, more in Rael, but truly loved Brynlön. We settled in Pelemyn, worked in local restaurants, and saved until we could open our own, the Roasted Sunchuck.

Here we are immigrants, and giants, and in some ways little has changed from my situation in Hathrir—people see what I am rather than who I am. Every day, Orden and I must work to be seen as people rather than as lavaborn.

But our restaurant is a place where Brynts and others come to have some of the most memorable moments of their lives. And there is no pressure here for me to swear allegiance to a hearthfire or do anything I don't wish to do.

Except for lately.

The pressure doesn't come from the Brynts. No one asked us to do anything. But supply chains have broken down because of the war, and we've had to close our doors. There's little hope of reestablishing dependable trade until the issue of the Bone Giants is resolved, so if we can help resolve it, we only help ourselves. And we also help the land we've come to love and think of as our home.

I've listened to the bard's story with wonder and horror, grateful that I was spared the violent end of Gorin Mogen, and thankful to Thurik that I have been allowed to use my kenning in craft rather than war.

But perhaps this had been Thurik's plan all along—years of peace, paid for with fire in the end. I don't want to employ the destructive side of the First Kenning, but I see little choice now. I will sail across the ocean with the armies and burn what needs to be burned. My hope is that we can all rebuild from the ashes.

"And that, my friends, is the end," Fintan said, "of me telling you stories, anyway. You'll doubtless hear my voice in the coming days as I relay orders to this army or that while we load up ships to sail across the ocean. But I have done my duty and practiced my art as a master bard of the Poet Goddess Kaelin, and I thank you all so much for allowing me to give the performance of my life."

Was he kidding, thanking *us*? All of Pelemyn stood and applauded him until our hands were raw. And I mean *all*—

I learned later that people were standing in their homes or at their workplaces, on the decks of ships in the harbor, or wheresoever they were, even though he couldn't see any but the crowd on Survivor Field. Because that *had* been the performance of a lifetime. Fifty-four days of tales piecing together events we would have never otherwise known: When would we experience its like again?

And Fintan was overcome, understanding that this ovation would not be ending soon. Because the greatest performance required the greatest applause, and Brynts are culturally trained to thank someone properly when they have done us a good turn. I mean, yes, the gift baskets would obviously come later, but the moment demanded an epic ovation, so it went on in waves, became rhythmic at times, inspired brief bouts of dancing and chanting, and celebrated the power of stories to bring us together. For we were allied peoples who cherished our friends and the sweetness of life, determined to thwart the will of those who would destroy us, and his tales had played no small part in helping us to realize that.

After twenty minutes of uninterrupted and unflagging applause, Fintan bowed his head and his shoulders shook, tension long held there finally releasing. Perhaps he was wishing his parents could be there and understand that he had become the greatest bard of our time.

DERVAN

A Grim Fleet

At the beginning, Fintan told us that his tales might take up to sixty days, and I'd thought that was a pretty decent guess, considering how much he didn't know when he began and what new information would be coming his way. The fifty-four days it actually took filled us in admirably on what had come before, but I worried that what came next—a necessary inclusion for any decent history of these times—might not be recorded so well. Some of the major figures would be scattered across the fleet with very different missions, and the bard might not be able to collect all the stories in a timely manner. And what's more, we were heading into an extremely uncertain situation; some of us—perhaps many or all of us—might not live to tell any of it.

Fintan and I had discussed how to proceed, however, and he came to breakfast on our last day in Pelemyn with a surprise. It was a gift basket of sorts, though the gifts weren't really for me.

"These should help," he said.

I plucked a small leather-bound chapbook out of the basket. Its pages were blank.

"They're diaries," the bard explained. "Tidier than loose paper. Give them to the people you think will provide you the narratives you require. If they're at least somewhat diligent about recording what they see and hear and feel, you'll have a decent set of tales to work with, whensoever you're able to assemble them in their final form."

"Oh, that's very thoughtful of you."

"Not at all. I'm so glad that a written copy of this experience will exist. My perfect memory will last only so long as I do, so it's best to have something left behind for future generations. And I'll be shipping out with you anyway, right?"

"Right," I confirmed. Our berths had been assigned by Rölly himself, and we had to go down to the docks around lunchtime, as we were launching with the afternoon tide. So we worked diligently until it was time to board the rowboat that would take us out to the Seven-Year Ship anchored in the harbor, and I hurried as much as my knee would allow to give diaries to those from whom I most wished to hear.

Hollit Panevik recognized me as that Brynt friend of Fintan's, so she happily took one, as did Captain Koesha Gansu. They were sailing together on the *Nentian Herald,* and when I asked whether the ship was built to accommodate Hathrim, the firelord smiled and shook her head. "I'm going to remain above deck in a tent the captain has kindly rigged for me."

"Surely there is a ship that would be more comfortable?"

"There might be, but I wanted to be on this one. I want to hear more about Olet Kanek from this crew." Then she put a hand up to the side of her mouth as if to shield it from lip-readers and said in a mock whisper, "And maybe pick up some pointers on their cuisine, because it has to be different from what we're used to, right?" I laughed and she grinned back. "I confess I may have some selfish professional motives here."

"Orden's not coming?"

"No, he's staying behind. He has even less interest in fighting than I do, and he can't do very much with his blessing. Besides that, it was pointed out to me that he'd just eat a lot and be a huge target, so it wouldn't be practical to bring him."

Farther down, on one of the Brynt ships that was being filled with our mariners, I found Gerstad Daryck du Löngren and the Grynek Hunters. He agreed to take a diary but warned that he might simply fill it with cock sonnets.

"I'd be honored to receive whatever you see fit to write," I assured him. He was sailing on one of the ships that Abhinava Khose had been able to enchant to repel krakens. Since the entire fleet could not possibly be enchanted in time, the strategy to cross the ocean would be twofold: Ships would sail in clusters around a central enchanted ship, trusting that it would shield the others close by from attack; and Abhi would spend the entire journey in a low-slung boat so that he could periodically dip his hand in the water and check for approaching krakens. The greatest risk to the fleet, therefore, would be during the hours he slept. The hope was that even if an attack did occur, he would be able to stop it before too many ships were lost.

The boat was a pleasure craft confiscated from the holdings of a merchant who'd been hoarding food shipments during our incipient famine, and one of Abhi's Joabeian friends—Leisuen, the bosun—was accompanying him, along with his bloodcat and stalk hawk. He sailed in front of the fleet so as not to be tossed about by various wakes, and he of course had a diary with him.

I likewise gave diaries to Tallynd du Böll, Fintan, Nara du Fesset, and Gondel Vedd, all of whom were sailing on the Seven-Year Ship with me. And I told Fintan that we needed to find out what happened to Pen Yas ben Min, if we could, so he put in a request at the Raelech embassy to inquire at Malath Ashmali if she had safely arrived and to ask for an account of her travels.

There remained a few diaries left over, held in reserve in case someone distinguished themselves in the coming weeks. Word was that Temblor Priyit was on one of the ships, unaware that she'd become somewhat famous in Pelemyn because of her appearances in the tales of the stonecutter Meara and the courier Tuala.

The Eculan fleet that invaded Brynlön and Rael had sent ten thousand troops to each of the coastal cities; we were sending a fleet that was about half their original total, three hundred forty-seven ships in all, most of them Kaurian, and mostly carrying Raelech and Fornish armies that were each about ten thousand strong.

Since the fleet was so spread out and the leader of it, the Kaurian zephyr Bernaud Goss, was well offshore by the time we had to leave, our departure was somewhat anticlimactic and made a celebratory leave-taking impractical. But Pelenaut Röllend sleeved himself out to our ship, where he asked Fintan to broadcast him, and he was at least able to say a few words to both the fleet and the city of Pelemyn. He'd taken the trouble to wear his dress military uniform, which he almost never did because it was elaborate and impractical, with polished shells and decorative netting and so on, but I supposed the occasion called for it.

I remembered how he and I used to laugh at military dress uniforms when we were a couple of poor hungry fish heads and how we groaned at the inconvenience of them during our own years of service. But now, removed from both eras and looking at it from a civilian perspective, maybe I could see a point to dress uniforms. Perhaps they inspired confidence in our leadership, because if they could manage to wear all that stuff and look good in it, then surely they could manage a war?

"My friends," he said, "today you sail both to protect Brynlön and to avenge it. You all have our gratitude for putting yourselves at risk and our best wishes for a speedy victory. Pelemyn will be defended by three tidal mariners, including myself, while you are gone, and we will be waiting for your return. May the gods of six kennings keep you safe from the seventh. I know we all look forward to the day when we can live together in peace again. You have our love and support and hope, so farewell!"

From the city, people cheered and waved, pennants and flags flying. Rölly spent some time distributing handshakes and smiles to us, then dove gracefully off the side to sleeve himself back to the Wellspring. The command to sail was given, and gradually the sounds and sights of the city faded, to be replaced by the glare of sun on the sea and snap of wind in the sails.

We were well supplied at first, full up on breads and fruits and vegetables, which would be consumed in the first days of travel. We were hoping to cut down travel time by two or more days because Kaurian cyclones, plus Captain Koesha Gansu, were providing fair winds to fill our sails.

The cyclones were also performing other functions. Most ship-to-ship communication was done by semaphore, but for longer messages, one could write a note, seal it, and have a cyclone float it on the wind to another ship. One such arrived on our ship from Zephyr Bernaud Goss the day after our departure, requesting the presence of Fintan on his ship. He wanted to make an announcement to the fleet if the bard would be so kind as to join him briefly.

It would have made sense for Fintan to simply be assigned to the zephyr's ship for that reason, but he'd insisted on remaining with us and volunteered to be flown over as needed for such occasions. A cyclone flew him there, and I went belowdecks into the cabin to see what Scholar Gondel Vedd was working on. He was chatting amiably with Maron about something in their own language and did not appear to be busy or worried, which I found reassuring. They both smiled at me, and Gondel asked if he could help me with anything.

"Yes, I was going to ask you what the Kaurian fleet is and is not allowed to do, since I'm a little unclear on the finer details of Reinei's prohibitions. Not sure if you would know but thought it worthwhile to inquire."

"Strictly speaking, we're allowed to do whatever the zephyr says at this point."

"You are?"

The scholar spread his hands wide in resignation, though he also looked gently amused. He paused frequently and flubbed a few verb conjugations but said in Brynt, "The stretching of the text has already been done. Once engaged in a defensive action, anything goes. Though there's some hedging in saying Kauria is simply providing the transport and won't actually fight except in defense, in truth we can make war like anyone else by sending the fleet into situations where they will be required to defend themselves. But sending this fleet to defend Kauria when Kauria has yet to be attacked—that, my friend, is the part that makes you scratch your head."

"Oh! What was the justification?"

"I wasn't there when the arguments were made, but I can imagine they leaned heavily on our erstwhile Eculan prisoner, Saviič, and his implication that Kauria would have been targeted if they thought the Seven-Year Ship was in Kauria. We now know that Kauria was never a target and never would have been, but the zephyr didn't know that then, and it won't matter to him now."

"Why not? Is he so eager for conflict as the earlier tales of him made it seem?"

Fintan's voice interrupted us, projected via his kenning to the entire fleet. "Your attention please, especially ship captains. A message from Zephyr Bernaud Goss follows. Zephyr, please, go ahead."

"Ahem. Yes. Thank you. I have a rather important update to share from the plaguebringer: Thus far he has warded off three separate kraken attacks. He foresees that there will be more every day. However, the current configuration of the fleet is straining him, and he requests that we tighten up so that he doesn't have to protect such a large area. It is so ordered. We must reconfigure into a circular formation, with my ship and the Seven-Year Ship in the vanguard behind Abhi himself. That should enable him to monitor and protect us more efficiently. I understand that this will take some time and a lot of coordination and signaling and adjustment of winds, and I thank you all in advance for the pains you will take. But again, this is to make sure our plaguebringer isn't overly taxed and can continue to protect us from krakens. May we sail safely to victory. Zephyr Bernaud Goss, out."

Gondel raised an eyebrow at me afterward. "Does that answer your question?"

"Not really. He didn't say anything particularly militant."

"True, but neither did he say anything about his hope for peace. To a Kaurian ear, that is a glaring omission."

"Ah, excellent. That was the sort of insight I was hoping you could provide."

"Glad I could help. Are you peckish at all? I have some cheese and crackers."

"No mustard?"

"Of course I have mustard. That's a given. I was merely offering some things to put mustard on, you see."

"I'd like to learn more about the delights of mustard. I'm not very well schooled."

"You have come to the right man, then. What food do you typically enjoy?"

"Toast. There is likely to be very little of that on this journey, as we are running low on fresh bread and there's no galley on this ship to make any. This is a grim fleet so far as my gustatory preferences are concerned, so I might as well steer my tastes in a more crackerish direction."

The scholar and his husband eagerly set about arranging a tasting for me, and that was a singular experience. But hearing later how forlorn I was about a toast-free life, Fintan arranged a remarkable gift for me in the morning. He had Hollit Panevik use her kenning on the *Nentian Herald* to make me four slices of toast with the last of the bread, and then Captain Koesha Gansu wafted it on thermal winds to me on the Seven-Year Ship.

I had Magic Toast for breakfast. It tasted like love and friendship.

FANJE

The Reckoning Sky

In all the hills and roads and villages and oceans of the world, there are few people I can trust, and it is exhausting. From my family, and most of my friends, and every stranger I meet, I must hide who I am not.

I am not a cultist of Žalost. And it claws at my spirit to say that I know who I am *not* better than who I *am*.

If my parents knew my secret, they would cast me out and deny I ever sprang from their seed.

And if my brother knew, he would report me to the isposniks, and I would disappear into a cold stone dungeon and die screaming for the pleasure of men who say they are only doing the work of Žalost in Ecula.

If anyone knew, really, it would be much the same thing: a time of white-hot pain before an early death.

And so I live saturated in fear, a sour sickly feeling, trapped on an island populated by diseased minds, and I must pretend to be one of them to survive. Perhaps my family is pretending too, but I cannot risk raising the question. Because I am not sure that their love for me is greater than their fear of the cult.

It's slightly better where we are on the southwestern island of Drvo, where for long stretches it is just you and the road, and no one is around to witness you cursing the isposniks and Žalost himself. You can have moments of solitude, and in those moments there is freedom. In the capital of Sveto Selo, it's easier to get a cup of kafa, but it's also easier to get reported for sacrilege. There are eyes and ears everywhere.

I will admit to exactly one benefit of the cult launching a massive invasion force and preparing another: There are no more bandits prowling in the timbers and I can travel with a single companion, which is next to being alone. Almost every miserable bastard who dreamt of violence signed up for the armies of Žalost to commit righteous murders across the ocean, plunder vast riches, and secure Ecula's future. Miserable bastards became our number-one export.

Which does not mean there is a shortage of miserable bastards now. We just lack the massive surplus we used to have.

The young man seated next to me in the front of a wagon loaded with kafa beans is fortunately of my mind: Žalost is a sweaty, unkempt ballsack of a god, and those who spread his faith have turned our once-peaceful nation into a seething cauldron of hate and resentment.

Radič and I have been friends since childhood, and he is more of a brother to me than my actual brother. He has a mop of brown hair that falls over his eyes so you're never quite sure where he's looking, whereas I always keep mine tucked behind my ears. He tends to speak in a monotone and then, if he makes a joke, he'll laugh about it anywhere from ten to twenty seconds too late. You will have already moved on when he says, "Ha! That thing I said. Pretty funny." He doesn't grow a beard and he likes to eat, which disqualifies him from becoming an isposnik or even one of the svećenici. And that pleases him.

Our families are part of a farming co-op that sells kafa beans and other crops to the big city across Eel Bay—some of which, I'm told, actually gets exported to Omesh, which cannot grow kafa trees. Perhaps because of our relative isolation in the countryside, we have been able to hold on to some old scrolls of the past. Or, at least, some of those scrolls have escaped the periodic purges conducted by the svećenici at the behest of the isposniks.

I found them tucked away in the darkness of my root cellar but never dared ask my parents how they got there, and I definitely never told my brother about them. He might be pretending like I am, but I suspect he might be a true believer in Žalost.

To get the scrolls out where I could read them, I constructed a drawer to hang underneath the back end of a workbench in our barn. No one looked under there. You don't work on a farm of any kind without learning some basic carpentry.

One by one, I smuggled the scrolls underneath baskets of carrots and apples intended for the horses and read them at my leisure. They were histories of the nation and scriptures of the old faith, before *Zanata Sedam* poisoned everything.

Had my parents left them in there for me to find? I hoped so. It was the sort of thing you had to do if you wanted to communicate—leave clues and a wide window of deniability.

The last entries of the histories told of a mass migration to Bačiiš once the cult began taking hold and acquiring power, changing laws. They were heading for the largest island, Odlazak. That was nearly a century ago, and I am of a generation that largely knows of no other way to live than under the cultists' rule. I don't want further generations to grow up mouthing venomous lies.

There are a few of us who have read forbidden texts and understand that governments rise and fall, and the cult leadership is vulnerable right now, with much of its muscle and economic power sent overseas and the remainder bound up with financing a second invasion. We have heard that the initial invasion met with mixed success: Many of the target cities fell but not the main one with the source of the Fourth Kenning, Pelemyn. So the leadership asked for more bodies to throw at that problem, and when they didn't get enough, they announced conscription. Radič will be forced to go very soon if something isn't done.

There's a meeting of like-minded people in Sveto Selo to

discuss a course of action, and Radič and I plan on making it. The kafa beans provide our excuse to travel—though we should not need one, and it grinds my mind that our people have accepted these shackles willingly.

"I have been thinking," Radič says after looking around our cart and seeing no one but the oxen pulling it, "that if this second invasion goes forward, I will not be going."

"They're not going to give you a choice," I tell him.

"I'm not going to give them one either. I would rather die, Fanje, than board a ship to take me far away to murder some stranger who never did me harm."

The thought of him harming himself brings a tear to my eye, because it seems inevitable now. We are so close to launching, and it means Radič has little time left. I sniffle and say, "I understand."

"You're not going to try to talk me out of it?"

"No. I would do the same. It is the right thing to do." The rattle and crunch of the wheels turning fills our ears for a time as we let that settle. The oxen snort and chuff and pull us forward, or else we would remain motionless.

"We are told," I say, "that these people across the ocean mean us harm. For years they have schemed against us, and every misfortune we suffer is because of them, and somehow it is they who hold us back from greatness. Yet not a single one of them has ever been here. The chasm between those claims and what is plainly true is so deep and wide that I fail to see how anyone could believe them. We are told that these people are shorter than us, darker skinned, and well fed— I doubt that even that much is true."

"I bet that *is* what they look like," Radič replies. "A single set of facts will anchor a ship full of falsehoods. So when our warriors get there and see that the people are just as described, they will believe all the lies told about them."

That sounded accurate: the cult using a skeleton of truth on which to hang the flesh of deception.

"Do you have any hope we can stop this?" I ask him after another pause.

"It is a guttering candle in the dark, but yes. I have that small amount of hope."

Sveto Selo is on the island of Vlast, so we take a ferry across Eel Bay into the city, keeping to ourselves and making no eye contact, and arrive in the smelly crush and noise in late afternoon. The beans are easily unloaded to a distributor in the Fishskinning district, and after that we find a stable for the oxen and wagon.

Once on our own without a visible loincloth of trade, it's a matter of avoiding secular and religious authorities without seeming to avoid them. We can tell the truth—we're staying the night after selling our kafa beans—but we'd rather be lost in the bustle of the city and never lodge in anyone's memory. Our southwestern rural accent tends to linger in the heads of city dwellers.

We skirt the edge of the Featherdown district, where there are far more guards, and head east into Baitbucket. Since we know we'll have to pass some sentinels to get into the Hammerside district, we stop at a kiosk and spend a few coins to buy cartons of mutton rice and horns of ale, partially because we're hungry and partially for the camouflage they provide. We're just citizens enjoying some street food, nothing suspicious here, like empty hands would be.

I'm looking at Radič as we pass the sentinels loitering in the street to Hammerside, listing things we need to buy tomorrow, hoping we won't be interrupted when we're so clearly intending to contribute to the economy, and it very nearly works. We're past them when one calls out to our backs.

"Hey. Hold on a moment," he growls.

We turn, eyebrows raised in innocent query. He's an older fellow, cheeks sallow and sunken, skin sagging under his jaw, with small mean eyes, and as he draws closer, I get a faint

whiff of sweat and shit. One hand rests casually on the hilt of
his sword.

"Haven't seen you before. You live in Hammerside?"

Oh, gods, an observant one. "No, we're from Drvo," I say
brightly. "Came up to sell a load of kafa beans, and we stabled
our oxen for the night. We're going to stay at the Loafing
Haywain." It's a perfectly average inn we've stayed in before,
the epitome of mediocrity. It has a nonzero number of
roaches, but they're very polite.

The sentinel seems disappointed that we have plans and
know where we are going. "Names?" he grunts.

"I'm Fanje, and this is Radič."

The sentinel squints at my friend. "You joining the second
invasion?"

"Of course," Radič replies.

"Volunteer or conscripted?"

That question is the latest test of loyalty among men. If
you had to be conscripted, then maybe you weren't fervent
enough in your faith.

"Conscripted," Radič admits. If he said he'd volunteered,
they'd demand to see his volunteer card. If he didn't have it,
they could look it up and catch him in the lie. And, of course,
holding on to him while they looked it up was a convenient
way to harass him.

"Why didn't you volunteer?"

Radič shrugs. "My older brothers already joined the first
invasion. My parents need me on the farm. I'm going anyway."

It's a perfectly valid answer and the sentinel knows it, but
he's looking for a reason to detain us. He turns back to me.

"What of your brothers, Fanje?" He says my name with a
bite, letting me know he'd been paying attention.

"I only have one. He wasn't old enough to volunteer for
the first invasion, but he's volunteered for the second."

"And what of you? Will you be going to colonize?"

"No, my parents also need me on the farm, since my brother is leaving. The country will still need its kafa."

Frustrated, the sentinel snaps his fingers at us. "Let me see your bill of sale for the beans."

Radič produces it for him, and he takes his time looking it over. Unable to find anything suspicious about it, he hands it back, defeated. "Enjoy your visit to Sveto Selo," he says in a tone that hoped we wouldn't.

"Zalost's blessing upon you," we say in unison, and continue on our way. Our mutton and ale don't taste so good anymore, robbed of their savor by a shitty, sweaty bastard who enjoys limiting the freedom of people to simply walk around in the city.

We enter the Loafing Haywain and pay for a single room for the evening, because Radič has a bedroll and pillow that he uses to sleep on the floor. He likes to make a show of it and circle around, delivering a stern warning to the polite roaches that he should be left alone while he sleeps. We have to wait an hour before leaving for our meeting, but when it's time, Radič waggles an eyebrow at me, which I can just barely make out through his curtain of hair.

"I pray you, young lady, do you not think it a fine evening to engage in some light skulduggery?"

"It is a beautiful night indeed, gentle friend, to speak of sabotage and treason."

"Let's be about it, then."

A couple of blocks away from the Loafing Haywain, down an alley filled with garbage and rats and decidedly impolite roaches, a set of stairs leads down to a low door with the number 6 carved crudely into the top left corner of the frame. Checking to make sure we're unobserved—even looking up at the rooftops—we dart down, deliver a secret knock, and gain admittance. It's damp and close inside but warm. We greet our fellows and take seats on some wooden packing crates.

Pavle, the leader of the group, tells us we're waiting for two more to arrive. He's in his thirties and walks with a limp—the legacy of a broken hip he suffered in shearing season. It prevents him from joining the armies, though lately he's been forced to carry a healer's declaration to that effect, since the svećenici periodically come to believe that he's faking it. He lives outside the walls in the Woolens but has cause to enter the city frequently.

We call ourselves Šest. The focus on *six* does not necessarily mean we follow the old religion of all the gods minus Žalost, though it can mean that. It means we remember a time when the cult was not in power, when the number seven meant nothing special, and we can excise the teachings of that pernicious seventh god and live in such a society again.

The stragglers arrive—Gojko, a sinewy man in his forties, and Milenka, a young woman about my age with braids flowing back from her temples and twining at the base of her skull—and they offer their apologies for being late.

Pavle gets the meeting started. "I'll make this quick so you can avoid suspicion. We need people to sabotage the lumber mill in Riba Oči, where they're racing to build the last ships needed for the second invasion. Fanje, Radič, Gojko, Milenka—you're all from Drvo, so we are tapping you for this assignment. The mill is taking on extra workers to supply the demand, and at least one but preferably all of you need to get on staff and figure out how to destroy it."

Gojko shakes his head, raising his hand. "I can't get away from the farm, and I'm on the other side of the island from Riba Oči. They'd be suspicious about me even applying for such a job."

"What about the rest of you?"

"I can try," I say, and the others say the same.

"Good. There are another two pods working to destroy the fleet. If we gum up the lumber supply, the invasion will be delayed for months—or sent ahead with reduced strength.

It will stress the armies across the ocean and sow doubt among the people that the invasion is part of the divine plan."

"It will also enrage the soldiers and the svećenici," Milenka points out. "We will be scrutinized for working there. We could die, and our families too. Saving lives is admirable, but I hope you have a more solid plan in mind to bring down the regime than sowing doubt. Because doubt won't do a thing to remove the kraljic or the isposniks from power, and that's not worth risking our lives."

"There are three additional pods of us working on that. I can't tell you exactly what they're planning, but I feel certain they need to cast the cult as illegitimate and encourage people to revolt. We know that there is significant sentiment against the invasion and therefore against the cult because of the numbers of conscripted. All we need to do is to show the cult *can* be defeated. So if we do our part, that will be the spark the others need."

"Just to be clear," Milenka presses, "if we provide a spark, there are concrete plans to take down the Citadel and the Cloister?"

"Not by direct assault. But rendering them impotent and making way for a new government, yes."

"There are plans for a new government?"

"Of course!" Pavle accidentally spits as he speaks, so annoyed is he by the question. "Otherwise, what are we doing? Infiltrate the lumber mill, figure out how to destroy it, and wait for orders to do so. That's all. Get home safely."

"How do we know the new government will be better than the current one?"

Pavle glowers at her. "Because you won't have to account for your whereabouts and activities like you do now. You'll have freedom and privacy, and your friends won't be conscripted to fight across the ocean. Are you inquiring on behalf of the kraljic, Milenka?"

"Of course not."

"Good. Get home safely."

We leave in pairs, and as we return to the street, I ask Radič if he knows anything about working in a lumber mill.

"I don't know the first thing about it, except maybe that it involves trees."

"Same here. Well, it's time to pretend, I guess."

ABHINAVA

Teeth in the Abyss

If it were not for Leisuen, I think we all would have gone mad by day three. Neither Murr nor Eep was particularly fond of sea voyages, and I wasn't much of a fan either, but I understood how necessary it was for us to be doing this duty. Especially once it became clear that if I didn't pay attention, the fleet would be obliterated.

I told the Kaurian zephyr that I'd fended off three "kraken attacks" but let him assume that these were single krakens, when in fact they were groups of krakens that could have methodically taken apart the majority of the fleet. I'd enchanted a mere ten ships out of more than three hundred, and these afforded only a modicum of protection outside a certain radius; in each case, the krakens had been converging on stragglers and outliers, of which there were many. So many that I was having trouble making sure they were all safe. The farther I had to search for threats, the more effort it took, and it began to wear on me, since the fleet was strangely spread out in a wide front. And I couldn't really just leave things be for a half hour, or even a quarter of an hour, because the krakens could come into range and target ships in a matter of minutes. It meant I wasn't able to relax when I was awake; if I wasn't dunking my hand into the water, checking for krakens, I was thinking about how I needed to check for krakens again soon. And while I slept, I dreamt of krakens, and they told me my skin was wrinkled like a prune.

It was the sort of situation where I imagined myself becoming haggard, which for some reason conjured a likeness of me slumping with half-closed eyes and some unruly stubble on my jaw, as if I was even capable of growing whiskers like that.

"What if I had a beard?" I mused aloud on day two, not really thinking who else might hear, but I got outraged cries from Murr, Eep, and Leisuen in response.

"Don't you dare!" Leisuen said. "No beard!"

"Why? Don't men in Joabei grow beards?"

"Only old men. It's a hobby when they retire."

That made me laugh. "Okay. Maybe when I retire someday, I'll grow a hobby beard." If I was able to live that long.

After I communicated my issues to Zephyr Bernaud Goss, he ordered something a bit more manageable, and though it took most of a day to get everyone in position, it was worth it. I could keep track without trouble after that—apart from the need to sleep, that is, or do anything else for more than a few minutes at a time.

But the night after the fleet had tightened up, three krakens attacked while I slept. They emerged off the port side and destroyed three ships before I could be wakened to tell them to back off. I did not only that but asked them to help recover crew. They obliged, plucking mariners out of the sea and depositing them on other ships, while Tallynd and the other rapids rushed to help and keep as many alive as possible.

Still, the ships were reduced to kindling, and many died. I knew Koesha and the other Joabeians must be reliving the horror of their experience, and I cried because no one would have perished if I had been awake.

Leisuen tried to console me, and I appreciated it—she herself had been rescued from the sea by the same kraken that had destroyed her ship and killed many of her crewmates—but it only emphasized how everyone's life depended on my vigilance.

"I need to learn how to take quick naps instead of sleeping for hours," I said.

"That's impractical and you know it," she replied. "And everyone understands that you will do everything you can to save lives if it happens again. This is how it is and how it must be. There is no reason to curse yourself with blame."

The blame settled around my shoulders anyway, and I slept very little for the next couple of days. But strangely, after that attack, I didn't detect even a single kraken out there. We sailed safely over the abyss, and it made me realize that over the truly deep part of the ocean, far from shore, there would be no need for krakens to patrol. They lurked closer to the shorelines, where they might find ships more easily. Once I confirmed with the zephyr that we were truly in the deepest part of the ocean, far from any land, I relaxed and slept for twelve glorious hours.

Murr and Eep woke me, requiring breakfast. They needed feeding since they couldn't hunt on a boat in the middle of the ocean. Feeling refreshed if somewhat apologetic, I tried to make myself look presentable before climbing up to the deck.

"You know, Leisuen would be happy to feed you in the future if I'm not available," I told my friends. "As in, if I'm getting some much-needed sleep. Would you allow her to feed you under my supervision this morning so that she understands what to do?"

They consented and we had a pleasant interlude there, where I felt rested and happy and unstressed. I dipped a hand in the waters and checked for krakens: nothing. I waved to the lookout on the zephyr's ship sailing behind us, and he waved back. The zephyr himself was standing on the prow but didn't see me, as he had a glass held up to his eye and was scanning the horizon. But when the lookout shouted to him that I was up and about, he glanced down and we exchanged distant hellos, he in Kaurian and I in Nentian, our voices carrying across the waves.

The sounds of sailing on a sunny day like this were perhaps my favorite part of being at sea. The wind, of course, filling the sails, would ripple and snap the canvas at times. The creak of boards weathering, the crush and hiss of the hulls plowing through the water, the sounds of many sailors' voices floating in the air—some of them singing shanties as they worked, some laughing at a bawdy joke, others cursing the general stink and discomfort of being in close quarters with so many others—it was charming and companionable, especially since I liked my companions. Very different from the sounds of the plains I used to hear while hunting with my family, but a similar experience too in that we were small creatures carving a path across a flat expanse of the world, and our petty complaints and dramas meant nothing to Teldwen or Kalaad in the sky.

Eep didn't mind cuts of raw fish, even though she didn't normally eat it; fish had been only an occasional meal for her, if she caught something in the shallows of a river. Her normal diet of rodents or smaller birds wasn't available, though, and we had plenty of fish, so she delicately speared chunks of it from Leisuen's hand.

Murr wasn't a fish eater, however, and required the raw meat of mammals. We had plenty of that too, since the fleet had a butcher barge; that was a Kaurian invention that they'd rolled out in their merchant fleets a few years before the Bone Giant invasion, though it depended on having cyclones and tempests around. Small sailboats delivered paper-wrapped packages of various cuts to ships' cooks on a rotating schedule. It wasn't enough to keep everyone in chaktu and ox steaks, but it meant that each boat got their fish-and-rice diet interrupted with goat stew or something like that once a week. They sent over something for Murr every couple of days, and Baejan's responsibility was basically to unpack it from ice and put it on the deck where we could easily scrub it clean after Murr was finished. The idea wasn't just that meat would provide variety, but the blood and offal, once dumped in the ocean behind the barge, would attract blade-fins and more, and that made for bountiful fishing from aft. It meant the fleet could sustain itself with fresh food much longer without having to resort to dried rations.

The sun was shining, and we were all happy and full. Leisuen had taken to telling me about Joabei and how different it was from the land on our continent. I told her my home was a sea of green for half the year, a sea of yellow and brown for the other half, but just like the Peles Ocean, it hid things with lots of teeth. She told me about the lizards and many crawling things that lived in the wind tunnels, always hungry, always ready to take a bite of whatever got close enough to taste.

I was about to ask her for more details of a six-legged rodent of extraordinary girth that lived only on their northern island when the tenor of the fleet's collective voice changed. Something alarming had happened at the rear of the fleet, and, worried that I'd missed something, I ran to the side and plunged my hand into the water to check for krakens. Nothing.

But something was causing an uproar back there. It would be some time before anything intelligible made its way to us, but there were very clearly some shouted warnings as well as orders being bellowed by captains—the happy shanties had all died.

We couldn't see very well past a few ranks of boats—the massed sails were just a blur of cotton balls resting on the surface of the blue. But then whatever it was struck again, much closer to us, somewhere in the middle of the fleet, off to our left but to the right of everyone else facing forward. I knew it was something huge because, through hulls and canvas sails, I could see hints of a large spume of water as a creature rose from the sea and crashed back down into it. And the sounds of panic and shouting grew much louder. What could it be? A lion whale, perhaps? I hadn't been searching for them, because while massive and potentially dangerous, they weren't typically aggressive. But searching for them with my kenning, I got nothing. So it wasn't a lion whale.

A sailor rushed to the front of the flagship with news and told the zephyr what was going on, which was good because that meant I might get to hear next. He did in fact turn to shout something urgently at me in Kaurian, but of course I didn't understand a word, and neither did Leisuen. We shrugged in confusion, and he clenched his fists and stomped in frustration and yelled for the translator we'd been using.

She was a tiny Kaurian woman named Hondi Rett, who'd spent much of her childhood in Ghurana Nent and claimed to actually like borchatta soup. I never believed her, because she always said it with a huge smile, which I thought meant she was teasing me.

Hondi wasn't smiling now. She looked worried. "Abhi, it's an eel! You have to stop it!"

"An eel? The kind we marinate and eat?" I asked.

"No, a cavern-jawed eel. They're huge!"

It was clear that she was talking about a deep-sea creature I'd never seen or even heard of—which meant that it was a blind spot in my kenning. I couldn't search for creatures I'd never seen before, and I certainly couldn't communicate with them until they made themselves plain.

But maybe I could get a sense of it if I searched for a large eel, the way I'd been able to get a vague sense of a kraken by imagining a huge longarm.

"What do they—" I began, thinking Hondi could tell me what they looked like, but the request died in my throat as their appearance became extremely clear. I saw the wide-open mouth first, rising from the ocean behind the flagship, cresting over the deck with so many rows of teeth in it. Then it kept rising behind them, a slick blue-gray tower, but with tentacles beneath the gills that reached out, wrapped themselves around Hondi Rett and Zephyr Bernaud Goss, and yanked them right off the ship into the air, where they had time to scream in surprise and terror before they were fed into that yawning mouth. They disappeared even before the leviathan fell back into the waves near us, its lambent yellow eye watching me as it plunged beneath the surface.

"No!" I said, and that was echoed by Leisuen as I launched myself over the side of the boat into the icy waters, forgetting that I wasn't much of a swimmer.

The shock of the cold disoriented me for a second, and I realized this might turn out to be a fatal error, but I had jumped in with a purpose and bent to it: I reached out to the cavern-jawed eel and felt its presence almost click into place in my head, the kenning recognizing it for the first time. Connection established, I kicked to the surface and took a breath and told it, "You have to leave. No more hunting here."

I sensed it turning back on itself to face the fleet, to face me, but had no idea what it intended. Would this creature be the first to refuse my kenning? What power did I truly possess to stop it if it decided to ignore me?

It surfaced once again, an arrow's flight ahead of my boat—from which Leisuen was shouting and Murr was roaring and Eep was screeching, all of them presumably urging me to get back aboard. But I ignored them and focused on the eel even as it focused on me, for it had not breached with the intent to feed but rather to investigate the source of the new voice in its head.

I would never know how the Sixth Kenning translated my Nentian speech into something that animals could understand through either the air or water, but I would always feel awe when it worked for the first time on a new creature. The eel's huge yellow eyes, set close near the front of its head, appeared capable of both binocular vision and peripheral vision. It was a visual hunter that could see well in the depths and above the surface—hence the skill with which it employed its tentacles. It had two undulating antennae rising hornlike from the crown of its head, and these changed colors in the light, cycling through the cool end of the spectrum in blues, greens, and purples. I got the sense that it was curious, at least, and trying to decide whether to be annoyed or not.

"The people you just ate were friends of mine," I said, trying to lend my voice proper gravitas, which was undermined by my obvious struggles to tread water. "That's enough. I don't wish you any harm, but neither do I want my people to be at risk. Hunt elsewhere, please."

I was hoping for a sulky snort and an underwater exit, but that's not what I got. Instead, the cavern-jawed eel reared up out of the deep, fixed its glare on me, and opened its gaping maw to let loose with a sonic blast such as I'd never experienced before or since.

"Wow. Need an assist?" a voice said next to me in the water. It was a Brynt translator, bobbing along with Second Könstad Tallynd du Böll.

"Hmm? What do you mean?"

After a quick exchange with the tidal mariner, the translator said, "I'll lift you out of the water so you can do your own threat display."

"Oh. Sure, that sounds good."

I didn't know precisely what to expect, but in the next couple of seconds I was lifted and supported by a column of cold water that swirled around me and misted, leaving my torso and arms free to gesture. I was literally the size of a snack to the eel, but it had to know that water simply didn't *do* that, which hopefully meant I was impressive despite my tiny stature.

"We are capable of defending ourselves," I said. "If you attack again, you will die. That is not what I want, and hopefully it is not what you want either. You see that we have com-

plete control over water. We can therefore pull the water out
of your brain, killing you instantly, and you have no defense
against that. I have the ability to track you in the water now,
so I will know if you try to swim underneath us. Please leave
us alone and hunt elsewhere, and we will let you go in peace."

It remained defiant and still, gills flaring out to the side as
it glowered at me, and I worried that Tallynd would have to
make good on my threat. Such a magnificent creature should
not meet its end like that—it must be very old to have grown
so large and to have learned that ship hulls on the surface
could yield food. I imagined it could take on almost anything
in the ocean—maybe even a kraken, if it took a giant gulp of
the kraken's head before the tentacles tore it apart. Perhaps
this had been one of the creatures that Sedam had created in
an attempt to escape his island prison.

It roared once more in frustration before twisting around
and diving away from us. I confirmed that it was actually
swimming away before telling Tallynd that it was safe. She
controlled my descent and put me down right next to my
boat, where Leisuen hauled me aboard, and then Tallynd
pulled the water out of my clothes, drying me instantly.

Instead of joining us on deck, the second könstad did the
same trick, and the water lifted her and the translator above
the surface so she could talk to us easily. The translator relayed Tallynd's words flawlessly.

"I've heard that the eel took the zephyr. Is that true?"

"Yes. And his translator, Hondi Rett. What happened in
the back?"

"It started at the butcher boat, ate two whole oxen. Then
it grabbed a few sailors from a boat in the middle of the
fleet—I haven't heard names yet—before finishing off at the
front. First time I've ever seen a cavern-jawed eel. They're
smart."

"That was the first time I'd even heard of them," I said.

"None of the hulls are enchanted to protect against them, or we might not have had that problem. I feel terrible."

"It wasn't your fault. It was just doing what cavern-jawed eels do."

"Logically I understand. Emotionally I feel responsible. Because it didn't just happen on my watch, it happened *while* I watched."

"You're doing great, Abhi. We have lost zero boats while you were awake, and the eel surprised you, so you couldn't have prepared. You know better now, and I have all the faith that you will keep us safe."

"Are there any other huge predators in the ocean I should know about? My education on the plains was obviously deficient regarding sea creatures."

"You know about lion whales and bladefins?"

"Yes."

"How about leviathan crabs?"

"What? No."

"They're just giant crabs, and there are a couple of them living down near Möllerud. They can get to be the size of a ship. They eat the other huge animals when they die and snap up larger fish when they can."

"Do they attack boats?"

"I haven't heard of it. But theoretically they could. Those are the only other things that could threaten us besides krakens. And a profound dip in morale, I guess. With apologies, I think I need to go, because with the zephyr's passing, I'm the senior officer in the fleet. I need to take command and explain what happened and allow for proper mourning."

"Right. Yes. I'll join in that for sure."

She waved and then dropped herself and the translator back into the ocean before using her kenning to sleeve them through the water to the Seven-Year Ship. For my part, I dropped to the deck and got immediately piled upon by

Leisuen, Murr, and Eep. I needed that love and reassurance, because I didn't feel like a powerful plaguebringer or a great protector or anything else but a failure.

There are so many ways that the world can make us feel small, and only with love are we able to grow out of it.

TALLYND

Under Pressure

One evening, when my husband was alive and shortly after the birth of our second child, we sat wearily in front of a fire while the children slept, and I curled myself into his arms as woodsmoke curled up the chimney. He was in a contemplative mood, thinking past these times when we did nothing but feed the children and play with them.

"You'll be returning to work soon," he mused. "And we are finished with breeding."

"Breeding? Ugh."

He chuckled. "I know. That's a disgusting way to put it for some reason. Spawning?"

"Ew. That's not any better."

"You're right. But I've been wondering about something, Tallynd. Now that you will no longer take any leave for motherhood, will you seek a promotion?"

"A promotion? I'm already a tidal mariner and a gerstad. There's no danger of losing my job. Why would I want more than that?"

"Well, that's why I'm asking. Because there's more to be had."

"Like what?"

"You could be könstad someday, or maybe even the pelenaut."

"Ha! Pelenaut. No thank you. He works all the time. And he can because he doesn't have kids. Which is probably for the best."

"Why?"

"Because the children of leaders so frequently get neglected or become entitled monsters. Not always, mind—
I am sure Röllend would do his best to be a wonderful father.
But despite best intentions, it happens frequently enough
that I will never go there, the same way I will never take the
children for a hike in the Gravewood. It's not the kind of
thing you seek out if you want to keep them safe."

"Ah, I see. That's a good way of putting it. The risk is
greater than the reward."

"Exactly. Right now I have the ideal situation. I have a
fairly steady schedule, apart from the occasional night shifts,
plenty of personal autonomy, and excellent compensation.
Plus, you know." I patted his chest a couple of times. "An excellent husband and children. My ambitions don't extend
much further than that."

"Oh? But you do have ambitions?"

"Yes. I want to visit Kauria someday."

"That sounds good. Any particular reason?"

"You're going to laugh, because it's silly."

"I like silliness, though. Deliver it unto me, my love."

"There's a tourist trap down there called Mugg's Chowder
House. They sell coffee mugs with the owner's likeness on it,
so it's a Mugg's mug mug."

"Yes! I have seen people with those!"

"I want one. If you go to Kauria, you have to come back
with one or nobody believes you went."

"Ah ha ha! That is an excellent ambition. I will make it
mine also. Someday, Tallynd, we will go there."

We never got to go. And now I had a position—and
responsibilities—that far exceeded my ambitions. First I became second könstad, and now, abruptly, I'm leader of the
allied fleet against the Bone Giants. Considering how dangerous it is out here—even with Abhinava Khose's protection—
I have to wonder if I am spending my last days far from

home, never to return. Like many Brynt parents, I worry that my children may never see adulthood. In order to give them their best chance at it, I must accept the leadership I never wanted and excel at it—and there is no time to bemoan my fate. Because to fail at this position would be to fail my boys, and I simply will not allow myself to do that.

Once I returned to the Seven-Year Ship, I asked the Rael-ech bard to broadcast my voice and inform the fleet that Zephyr Bernaud Goss had perished in the eel attack and I was assuming command. As such, I needed certain officers to visit the Seven-Year Ship for a command meeting. Orders would follow, but the fleet was to maintain course for now and not worry about further attacks; the plaguebringer would pro-tect against eels as well going forward.

Soon afterward, I was poring over a map of the island na-tions in a packed cabin with Fintan, Gondel Vedd, and a smat-tering of Brynt, Raelech, Fornish, and Kaurian officers. Fintan and Scholar Vedd were serving as translators.

The map was one that Fintan had found in Lorson's atlas, and with Scholar Vedd's help he had written down transla-tions of the text. On one portion of the map, there was an illustration of a cavern-jawed eel and a warning to beware. Unfortunate that Abhi had never seen the map when he'd spent so much time on the road with Fintan. There were also several other maps of the individual islands, with more de-tailed indications of topographical features.

"Does anyone know where our present course is taking us?" I asked. I had not been party to the zephyr's plans but had rather been content to support whatever he ordered. A Kaurian commander pointed to the northernmost island, Brda, and declared that we were headed for a spot somewhere along its middle since that was, in theory, the closest to us.

"We're heading there simply because it's the closest? What strategic significance does it have for us?"

"I believe the zephyr planned to scout for targets once we confirmed visual sight of land."

"Hmm. There don't appear to be any cities along that coast."

"That was why he felt it safe to approach that way and conduct scouting operations."

"Ah, I see the reasoning there, thank you. But our objective is not to conduct scouting operations. It is to destroy the Eculan fleet and degrade Ecula's ability to attack us. Heading to a coast with no strategic objective is therefore a problem, to my way of thinking. Look here," I said, pointing to the map of the island with ranges and hills drawn upon it. "It appears mountainous, with no protected bays or any obvious location for shipbuilding. And once we reveal ourselves, if we are not in a position to strike anything, they will have a chance to warn their navies and armies and prepare for an attack. We will have lost the element of surprise. So my question is, where is their shipbuilding most likely concentrated?"

There were two prevailing theories: Sveto Selo, which Scholar Vedd said was their capital, or one of the cities on the island of Drvo, which appeared on the topographical maps to be the most heavily forested.

A Fornish greensleeve made the argument that Sveto Selo was the best target and the quickest path to victory, because as the seat of Eculan power, its surrender would bring a swift end to the conflict regardless of where the fleet was.

The Raelech temblor Priyit spoke up. "But to get to Sveto Selo, you have to pass through this strait, which has markings that may indicate defenses of some kind. They would be insane not to defend it. And once we fight past whatever that is, we would have to continue along a channel with multiple angles of attack, not to mention the very real possibility that we could have our retreat blocked from behind—especially if we're wrong about where their ships are."

"I think you both make excellent points. But look at

Drvo," I said, tapping a finger next to it. "It's covered in timber, if this individual map is accurate—"

"It should be," Scholar Vedd interrupted. "The word *drvo* actually means *timber* in their language. That is literally Timber Island."

"Excellent, thank you, Scholar. Drvo has a large protected bay on the western coast, with cities all around. One of them is far more likely to be the center of their shipbuilding, because otherwise you would have to transport timber across the bay—a costly exercise. I want to alter our course to approach this bay and scout there first. If there is no fleet, we dart back up to assault Sveto Selo, confident that we won't be boxed into the strait. If it *is* there, then we destroy it and prevent the invasion at the start. We can deal with the capital afterward."

The Kaurians were uncertain about this plan since it contradicted the zephyr's, but as the other officers nodded in agreement, they offered no objections.

"It is so ordered. Have navigators make adjustments. Thank you all, and may currents keep you safe." As they filed out, Scholar Vedd magically produced some cheese and wine and poured me a glass while I dabbed at the moisture on my forehead.

"That was masterful, Second Könstad," he said, and I reminded him that he could call me Tallynd while we were alone.

"Was it? I wouldn't know."

"Beyond doubt. You were remarkably cool under pressure."

"I absolutely was not. I was afraid I'd be challenged the entire time. My underclothes are completely soaked with sweat—which, to be clear, I can fix with my kenning, and I will. But I'll wait and do it in private, because if you saw any water being wicked away at this moment you might lose your appetite, knowing its origin."

"Ah ha ha! Well, then, Tallynd." He raised a glass. "May we all have the fortitude, when our time comes, to be gracefully terrified."

We clinked glasses and drank to that. In a war, there was little else to hope for beyond a graceful terror.

NARA

The Invincible Sense of Worry

It fascinates me when people say, *Don't worry!* like that is something you can actually do. If there is some kind of lever to pull in my brain to make that happen, I wish someone would show me where it's located. Maybe a Kaurian priest of the gale would have some useful instruction, some kind of insight to find peace.

In the Brynt faith, worry is a pernicious thing brought by the currents of life, and like all else—happiness, rage, grief, whatever—it is transitory. The thing to do is to swim with the current, not against it, and soon you will be awash in some other emotion—boredom or excitement or even that rarest and briefest of conditions, contentment. It's why we say to each other, *Currents keep you safe,* because we can reasonably wish safety to endure for many years when emotions like joy or conditions like prosperity can be so fleeting.

Except worry isn't easily ignored or dismissed the way other emotions are. It's like a huge obnoxious drunkard who refuses to shut up or leave. It resists all reason and is invincible to indifference. And I have been swimming in an ocean of worry since we launched, because the love of my life is on a different boat and if something threatens her—like, say, a hungry cavern-jawed eel—I won't be there to save her.

Not that she would appreciate the idea that she might need saving. The Mynstad du Möcher is supposed to be the person from whom you would need to be saved.

She has her own squadron of highly trained mariners, who have been engaging in joint training exercises with Raelechs under the command of Temblor Priyit, who fought the Bone Giants at Möllerud. The temblor freely admitted that they had a tremendous assist from a juggernaut and courier who got them into the city walls, but once in, they had to fight hand to hand, and the new tactics had proven effective. She taught the tactics to the mynstad, including the use of tall shields to counter the long reach of Eculan swords, and then she and her squad spread out to all the boats, teaching them the same.

The Raelechs had brought along all the shields they could so that the Brynt forces would have plenty, and because the mynstad's squad was elite and highly trained, they would be at the vanguard of any fighting, facing a horde of enemies that threw themselves at death and overwhelmed their foes by force of numbers. She would, therefore, be among the first targets of that overwhelming force. How could I not worry? With every hour we sailed closer to what might be an extremely violent and sudden separation, and when I thought of it my heartbeat sped up and I had trouble catching my breath.

I finally went to the Raelech bard and asked him if he knew of any priests of the gale in the fleet.

"Why, yes, I do. Are you . . . Nara, are you okay?"

"I will be. I think I just need to talk to the priest. Where is he?"

"On a ship called the *Shearwater*, about eight to ten boats to starboard of us. His name is Kindin Ladd, and I can tell you from personal experience that he's an excellent person to talk to if you're feeling . . . whatever. Not at peace."

"That's what I was hoping. Thanks."

"Tell him I said hello."

I gave the barest nod before turning and throwing myself off the deck into the ocean. The *Shearwater* wasn't difficult to find, and once I was granted permission to board, I wicked myself dry and asked for Kindin Ladd.

The man who eventually appeared before me was dressed in orange and brown robes, his hands clasped in front of him, and he wore an expression of polite curiosity.

"I'm Kindin Ladd. How may I help you?"

"I'm Gerstad Nara du Fesset. Fintan sent me. He said talking to you might help."

"Ah. Are you troubled by the same things he was?"

"I actually don't know what troubled him."

"Best to start at the beginning, then. Would you mind joining me on one side of the yardarm? It's a good place to talk and out of everyone's way."

"Sure."

We climbed up the mast and sat on either side of it on the yardarm, our feet dangling in the air.

"Tell me what's on your mind, Nara."

"I'm afraid I will lose my lifebond. She's going to be among the first fighters when we land, and I'm terrified that she'll fall in battle. I can't stop thinking about it and, well, I'm thinking about it now, and my chest tightens, and my throat constricts, and I want to cry all the time, and I don't know how to stop."

"I see. You are worried."

"Yes."

"Many people are right now, and they have reason to be, of course. But tell me, what does worrying accomplish?"

"Nothing. I have heard that before."

"So have I, but I am going to gently disagree with you. If worrying accomplished nothing, then we would not be so prone to do it. Our minds perceive some benefit to worrying, and we fall into it like an oubliette and get trapped there."

"Yes, that is what it feels like."

"Excellent."

"What?"

"I mean it is excellent that you are following my argument so far. Keeping in mind that we are trying to understand what worrying accomplishes, let us approach it from another angle. How much control do you feel you have over what will happen to your lifebond?"

"Absolutely none."

"Precisely. And what you want, more than anything, is to have some control, yes?"

"Yes."

"But since you can't have it, your mind tries to compensate with worry."

"What? How does that help?"

"It means you're doing something about a situation over which you have no control, even if that something is merely a continuous loop of anxiety. You are fundamentally incapable of doing nothing about a situation over which you have no control, so what you do is all you can: worry. The world compresses and shrinks down into this little ball of awfulness, and you gnaw on it as it gnaws on you, and all of that is your mind performing an action in an attempt to solve what is unsolvable."

"I . . . whoa." I gripped the mast a bit tighter, rocked by the revelation. "How do I deal with it, then?"

"The first step is what you are doing now: Recognize it. When you worry, your mind contracts and fixates and traps itself. To counteract this, you must identify it as reductive and negative and counter it by being expansive and positive."

"Okay, but . . . can you give me an example?"

"Certainly. One of the most expansive states of mind is curiosity. It is an openness to growth."

He stopped there when I thought he was going to explain more. "So whenever I worry, I should just . . . be curious about something instead?"

"Yes. Because you have complete control over your curiosity. And a lack of control, remember, is what initiates worry. Worry provides you with an inadequate and self-destructive sense of control. With curiosity, you have control and it's positive, and that is what you need."

"I don't understand. I'm worried about her right now. So I just start wondering about what lion whales do for fun and that takes care of it? How does that solve anything?"

"Well, you wouldn't be worried, for one thing. Here's how I approach it—because, yes, I get worried too. Whenever it happens, I stop and realize it, and then I ask myself this question: *What else could I be doing with my time right now that would be more productive than worrying?* Maybe you want to clean your home, or work in the garden, or something else—"

"Visit the old longarm who lives in the pelenaut's coral reef and tell her I saw a cavern-jawed eel today. I think she would be so impressed." I felt a tiny smile tug at the corner of my mouth.

"Aha! There, did you stop worrying for just a moment?"

"Yes. Just a moment."

"Good. It takes work, of course. You have to break yourself out of the habit of worry and give your mind a new habit. Because we can never control the future, the fear of that will always point us toward worry; but when that happens, we can always point ourselves in a more productive direction. With effort, you can control your present."

"Yeah. Yeah, okay." I nodded to emphasize that I finally understood, because focusing on the present had been part of my meditations by the reef, and these insights paired well with what I had already been practicing.

"So, Gerstad du Fesset. What do you think you'd like to do now, instead of worry?"

"I think . . . I'd like to just sit here for a while and breathe peace with a wise man. Fintan was right about you."

"Ah. That is kind. May I ask: Do you really speak to a longarm in the pelenaut's reef?"

"I do. She is very old and I think very lonely, so I tell myself that she enjoys my company."

"I have no doubt that she does. What would you tell her, if you could?"

"That she is beautiful and I think of her as a friend."

"That is wonderful. Imagine what else you would say, and when we return to Pelemyn, maybe take this Abhinava Khose with you. He can tell her for you."

I gasped because I had never thought of it, and tears welled in my eyes at the possibility.

"Kindin Ladd," I said, "when we get home you are getting the biggest gift basket I can find."

GONDEL

Pondering

The Seven-Year Ship was, in some ways, a curiously luxurious vessel for a ship designed to deliver rubes to a hungry and merciless god. Belowdecks was rubbish, to be sure—racks of bunks intended to serve as a flesh-delivery system—but topside and the cabin were fair to rather pleasant. There was even a viewing deck, which we did not recognize as such until someone with a drink realized what the odd squares and holes were intended to be. On the starboard side, just short of the prow, there were seven oddly thin planks sticking up out of the deck near the railing, only two feet high and two feet wide, with strange round divots to the right of them. These square planks lined up precisely with posts of the railing. The mariners were uniformly confused by their utility until one of them sat on the deck in front of them, poking their legs out between the posts and dangling their calves over the side, and saw that the divots functioned as decent cupholders for a mug. The square planks simulated the backs of chairs, and one could relax there as long as the seas weren't too rough.

On the sixth day at sea, while most of the crew was at supper, Maron and I slipped out there and sat together to watch the sun slide into the sea, kissing clouds with farewell beams of purples and pinks. It was beautiful—resplendent, really—and images of friends and family crowded my head because I wished they could be there to see it with me. And then I thought of how many people couldn't see a sunset of any kind anymore, and my head drooped down to my chest, and

I squeezed my eyes shut against a sudden flood that strained to break free and eventually did. Maron saw the tears falling down my cheek.

"What is it, my love?" he asked.

"I miss Ponder Tann."

"Ponder Tann? You mean the tempest you traveled with?"

"Yes. Mistral Kira sent him ahead to deliver a message to the Eculans, and we have heard nothing in return. We should have heard something by now. So I wonder what happened to him without . . . truly wondering."

"You mean . . . you think he's dead."

I sobbed once and wept freely. "Yes." Maron gripped my hand, providing support, but remained silent. He did not say it would be okay, because he knew it wouldn't be, and couldn't. But he would hold my hand while I grieved.

"I suppose I wonder exactly *how* he died, not *if* he died. When we parted, he said he was at peace with it, but what if he changed his mind at the end? Did he regret his choice in his final moments? Was his sacrifice worth it? Who had it benefited, beyond some abstract ideal he placed on a pedestal in his own mind? And what—what if he *wanted* to die, Maron, and I had the chance to say something to change his mind and didn't say what he needed to hear?"

He gripped my hand harder in response to let me know he had heard me, but he rarely offered an opinion at such times unless I asked for it. So I asked.

"What do you think?"

He didn't answer for a while, because he never replied quickly when I needed help. He would rather wait to say the right thing later than say the wrong thing at the behest of urgency. "I think too many beautiful people exit this world quietly when it should thunder in the skies, and the true calamity is that they do it without anyone noticing. But you noticed Ponder, and mourning him is testament to the fact that he lived well."

"He did. He was just *good*, Maron. I wish you could have met him. A truly good, selfless man devoted to Reinei and Kauria. His loss is a tragedy by any measure. And then I think of how many thousands of people have died over this, each of them their own exquisite tragedy. How much good has the world lost to the vanities and power games of terrible men? To exploitative, self-centered shits like Žalost? All those good people gone, entire nations moved to fight one another over the selfish desires of a selfish man—I have to ask, have we lost so many good people that the world has forfeited its chance to ever be good again?"

He took his time once more, because he liked to consider weighty matters before he took a breath to lift them. I appreciated that quality. I knew that whatever he said in reply would be careful and purposeful.

"I don't think we've forfeited anything, love," he said some while later. "If anything, we are on our way to the fight. Reinei may not smile upon it, but as the priests of the gale occasionally have cause to demonstrate, force must sometimes be redirected and counseled to a peace. I feel certain that we will have peace again. And Ponder Tann will forever be a good man."

I took many deep breaths to internalize this truth, until I finally breathed peace once more. And Maron never let go of my hand.

KOESHA

Land Ho!

In hindsight—a resource of which I am well supplied—it may not have been the wisest course of action to take a crew of pregnant women into war. Their due dates are still months away, but it's getting awkward on the ship already, and we are much more crowded than when we first sailed from Malath Ashmali, owing to some additional Brynt passengers. Simultaneous morning sickness from three to four women? That's a lot of horking overboard.

And we have one other very large guest.

Hollit Panevik wanted to hear everything about Olet Kanek that Fintan didn't share in his tales. She spoke Nentian as well as Brynt, so she functioned as our translator when we needed one for the Brynt passengers. But she peppered me with questions about Olet whenever possible. Did she tell jokes or laugh at anything? Could I give any examples of their government functioning for the people's benefit and not the benefit of the government? What happened when someone disagreed with her—or did anyone ever disagree with her? Did she order people around? Was she ever mean to anyone? On a scale from sunbathing rock chub to hearthfire, how power-mad was she? That last one confused me, since I had no frame of reference for either end of the scale. What in the southern winds was a rock chub? It all boiled down to Hollit's trouble believing Olet was truly trying to leave the government of Harthrad behind and try something new.

"I want it to be real!" she assured me. "I want it so much. But I haven't seen it, so it's difficult to trust the story on faith."

"That makes me wonder what you have seen. You and Olet seem to be of like mind regarding hearthfires. I know she really didn't like her father, who was one. But are they all like that?"

"Yes," she said immediately, then amended it. "I suppose I must make allowances, since I have not met them all personally. But the stories that Fintan told about Gorin Mogen and Winthir Kanek are in keeping with my experiences in Sardrik. Hearthfires are people who use violence or the threat of it to keep themselves in power once they have it."

"So they, what? Just set people on fire when they disagree with them?"

"Sometimes, just to remind everyone it could be done. But more often the hearthfire of Sardrik would smile at someone in the moment and pretend that no offense was taken but arrange for an 'accident' later. A pattern of accidents like that gets noticed, however, and eventually no one dares to disagree. It means hearthfires are not accountable to anyone, and it also means they get told everything is wonderful when it isn't. It's a terrible system of leadership."

"It sounds like they might be the source of our old stories about fire demons. They would burn their opposition within and without. Our people moved to the global north because they were in the global south. Do you have any old stories about us?"

"We do. In Thurik's teachings, there are stories of two tribes who followed the 'soft sibling' and moved away from the people of Hathrir. We always interepreted this to mean Reinei and that the tribes wound up in Kauria, but after meeting you and hearing about what you discovered on the Mistmaiden Isles, I realize that the Joabeians were the other tribe and the 'soft sibling' could also mean Shoawei."

"Except she—or they—are not so soft."

Hollit grinned at me. "No. Averse to conflict, perhaps, but not weak." Her smile faded. "I think the Hathrim tendency to equate a desire for peace with weakness is the root of our many failings. It is why Olet fascinates me so. A person with power who wishes for peace is rare."

"You are indeed rare," I told her, and she blushed, which I thought was adorable. "And so is Olet. You can imagine how surprising it is for us to meet fire demons after all this time and discover that they're friendly."

Shortly after that conversation, word came that a Kaurian cyclone, scouting ahead, had discovered land at the edge of his range. Tallynd du Böll ordered all cyclones, including me, to stop filling sails and to scout more thoroughly to find the Eculan fleet. She wanted us to slow our progress until we could pinpoint exactly where we wished to go. Specific instructions came by a note floated to me. I bundled up against the cold, figuring I would be flying fairly high, and went due south, in the direction I was instructed to fly. Other cyclones were going to scout on slightly different headings.

It was a half hour's flight before I saw the land, and my path would have me passing a coastal village—or more like a city—on my right. I'd seen the map of Ecula that Fintan had in Lorson's atlas, as well as old maps back home, and knew that on the western side Ecula didn't have many coastal cities. Their cities tended to dot the interior of their islands, no doubt to facilitate trade between them. On the outside coasts there was no one to trade with but krakens. Since we had altered our course to the southeast and I was flying due south, I'd be overlooking the island of Drvo, which meant in all likelihood that city was Kotao. If so, the land proceeded to the southwest and formed a peninsula, which meant I'd pass over it soon enough and encounter a large bay, and on the coastline of that bay—perhaps just to my left, or directly beneath my course—I'd encounter Zeleno Kej, one of two leading candidates for the location of the fleet.

Kotao looked like a fairly prosperous place—farms quilted into the land stretched away for many leagues along the peninsula, until dark-green brushes of forest swayed under the sun and wind. Nothing to indicate a military presence there; the boats I saw looked like fishing vessels.

When I spotted the bay to the south, I started looking for a fleet. There was nothing immediately visible, however. There were small fishing villages ringing the bay and there were fishermen plying their trade in the waters, and it occurred to me that from my vantage point it looked little different from Joabei. Here was no implacable enemy but rather some humble people making a living. I was grateful for the reminder that just because hurricanes form in the ocean, we should not assume the ocean loves hurricanes.

Zeleno Kej eventually grew in my vision, and it was a much larger city. Unlike Kotao, it had an obvious military presence; there were large rectangular buildings and parade grounds that could signify nothing but barracks. And there were soldiers down there, marching in formation, cubes of seven square like we had seen in the Northern Yawn.

The docks were much more extensive, and they had some ships that might be for military use among others that were clearly either fishing boats or pleasure craft, but there was nothing like an invasion fleet moored there. Wide roads leading to the east—which would be to the interior and therefore the capital—and south let me know that this was more of a trading hub and secondary fort than a primary port. There were certainly no shipyards.

I would have to continue south to scout the other theorized location, Riba Oči. I was flying over the waters of the bay as the land receded to my right, and I saw an unending patchwork of agriculture there, grains and fibers for the cities, but nothing in the way of cattle, I noticed, or other domesticated food animals. I spied a pair of oxen, but those were no doubt kept for work rather than meat.

Eventually the land curved back around to a point, as the map suggested it would, and when I saw that, I was grateful, for it meant I'd be able to make my assessment and turn back soon with news. News of where the fleet was not would be as important as where the fleet was, and other scouts might find it if I did not.

But I found it. Shoawei, did I find it.

Riba Oči possessed vast shipyards at the mouth of a river to the north and ranks and ranks of docks and moorings near the city a bit south of that. Nearly all of the slips were filled with troop carriers. This was clearly the staging area for the second invasion and most likely where the first invasion had been launched as well. Destroying this fleet and the shipyards would not only prevent their invasion but degrade their ability to rebuild anytime soon.

I checked for barracks too, and there were massive military compounds outside the town, large enough to house troops until it was time to launch. This was it. The target that the second könstad wanted. I circled around and headed north.

Riba Oči would get some closer looks before we attacked, but I had plenty to take back to the fleet now.

Did the people in Riba Oči truly support the invasion, I wondered? How many endorsed the attempted extermination of strangers across the ocean and how many just stayed silent because it's troublesome to say no to the large group of armed men on your doorstep?

When I returned to the Seven-Year Ship to report to the second könstad, I wasn't the only one with news. Another cyclone that had flown ahead on our present course to the southeast discovered that those strange hash marks along the straits on the map did not represent bridges or defensive fortifications but rather enormous moorings for underwater nets, which allowed the free passage of most creatures but would absolutely stop a kraken or cavern-jawed eel from entering. That meant that the Eculans had secured their interior waters and bays for the free passage of watercraft and large cargo barges.

"Can we sail over the nets?" the second könstad asked. "And if not, can we destroy them?"

"I was unable to tell from the surface. They'd need to be investigated underwater."

"Very well. We'll form a detail for that, because we'll have to confront it eventually and travel to their capital. For now, we need to set a course for Riba Oči."

HOLLIT

The Reluctant Arsonist

Thanks to some scouting on Koesha's part—and then a lot of
course corrections and many more scouting trips—we found
the Eculan fleet, and I found that much of my good humor
grown during the trip steamed away, hissing like raindrops
falling into fire. Because I knew that soon I would have to use
my kenning for destructive purposes. I'd made the decision
to do so already when I boarded the boat, but perhaps I'd
been hoping it would never become necessary. Wishful thinking along the lines of *Whoops, no fleet!* Or maybe the Eculans
would unconditionally surrender, and Thurik's flame wouldn't
need to burn anything. But word got passed along that we
would reach our target in the morning, and I received a visit
before dawn from none other than Second Könstad Tallynd
du Böll. She climbed up the side of the ship, wicked away all
the ocean water from her clothes, and looked absolutely perfect when she should have been a soaking, shivering mess.
The smile she flashed at me was even warmer than the light
from the firebowl.

"Hollit. Such a pleasure. I have been a quiet fan of yours
for some time."

"You have?"

"Yes. The Roasted Sunchuck used to be our favorite restaurant."

"Used to be?"

"I mean mine and my husband's, before he passed. I
haven't been back since, because it was our thing, you know?
Our visits are like a layer of fond memories, but they're aging

ones now, and I didn't want to spoon anything on top of them, if that makes sense."

"It makes perfect sense. I'm glad you have good memories of our restaurant. And I am a fan of yours, of course, for saving it and all of us. Thank you."

"Of course." She gestured to the firebowl. "May we sit and speak awhile?"

"Yes, yes. Please."

Even when seated, I still towered over her, and I thought it strange at first that I somehow felt like the short one. But then the strangeness melted away as I realized that some people have a presence larger than their physical beings.

There was no one else around except for the night watch. Most of the crew, including Koesha, were getting some bunk time. We kept our voices low.

"I want to thank you first for coming with us," she said, "and for what you'll be doing in a few hours. You'll be saving a whole lot of lives by preventing that fleet from setting sail. When I think of what we'd still have if we'd been able to stop the first one, I have to think of something else before I'm brought to tears."

"Yes. I'm in favor of lifesaving."

"Good. They have concentrated their fleet into a relatively small area to allow them to load up and launch together. There are ranks of docks—forty-nine of them, with twenty-one boats tied up at each. A bit over one thousand boats, all with canvas sails, all flammable. We are going to send you with some cyclones to set them on fire. We'll begin at the ends and allow the flames to push anyone who might be working on the boats or the docks time to escape them. But you will keep pushing. If they don't take the hint to run, you have to stick with it. We need to destroy every single boat."

Nodding, I said, "I understand. I promise it'll get done."

"Good. And then, after that, the forest."

"The forest? What forest?"

"They have enough raw material on the island of Drvo to build the fleet all over again. It's conceivable that they could do it in a year—we've seen how motivated they are. If we destroy their ability to make ships, we destroy their ability to attack us."

"But . . . that means destroying all the creatures who live there."

"Protecting our people is the issue here."

"Respectfully, Second Könstad, I think it is . . . *an* issue. One that is solved for at least a year by burning this particular fleet. If I need to return next year to burn a new one, I will."

The flames flickered and animated a stony expression, but I could bear those for a while. I waited.

"So if I were to order you to burn the forest . . . ?"

"I am not technically part of the Brynt military, so giving me an order would be difficult. But regardless, I would not do that. You can set fires without me, of course, and order cyclones to help spread them, but I will never participate in the razing of a forest."

"Hmm. Interesting." She leaned forward a little bit. "Clearly you have a moral objection here, and I would like to know more. Is it merely concern for the animals? Or something else?"

"The concern for the animals is real and not to be set aside, but . . . burning a forest feels deeply wrong to me. Understand that at this point I've lived in Brynlön for longer than I lived in Hathrir, but I grew up in Hathrir, and the reverence for wood there is without parallel. I mean old-growth, natural forests, the sort of wood you make heirloom furniture with or a door for your home, not the quick-grown stuff for fires. It's more valuable than gold or anything else. Even lives. That's because there are no longer any original forests in Hathrir, only managed timber farms and some wild places that have been allowed to regenerate slowly, because the forests were burned in old wars between hearthfires. Those

actions are considered war crimes now, and people still remember who burned what and hold grudges—there are me-
morials where forests used to stand. So, while I logically
understand your thinking, because of my background I
would consider burning a forest to be—"

"A war crime," the second könstand finished.

"Exactly. Even though neither you nor the Eculans may
consider it one. Forests are priceless and irreplaceable, and
robbing people of that is robbing their future. If you told the
Fornish that most Hathrim love forests, they'd laugh, because
it would seem like a joke to them. It's true that we don't think
of forests the way they think of the Canopy, but we do love
them. Timber raids on the Canopy are usually not undertaken for mere fuel. They're for hardwoods that we want for
tables and chairs and doors."

"The timber farms you mentioned, though—are they
priceless in the same way that forests are?"

"Close to it. But not irreplaceable."

"So what if we find timber farms? Would you be willing to
burn those?"

"Maybe. If they're really monocultures dedicated to building ships. I'd need proof, but I could be convinced."

"All right. We'll get Abhi and a greensleeve to check out
the forest and see what's there, and if it's a farm, we'll reconsider."

"I appreciate that. My feeling is that once you have the
fleet burned, they won't have a choice but to listen and rethink their plans."

"I'm glad we talked."

"I am as well. Thank you for taking on this burden, Tallynd. Cooking energizes me, but leading a kitchen staff drains
me like nothing else. I can only imagine what it must be like
to lead armies."

"So far it's been pleasant, as we've had no contact with the
enemy. That will change very soon, however. Thank you."

She rose gracefully from the firebowl, strode to the railing, and hurled herself into the ocean without a care for its cold or dark.

I could tell, however, that she cared very much about this mission's success. We were a large and strange coalition of talents, and she could have simply ordered me to burn down the forest and discovered too late that I would not do it. That might have caused problems elsewhere—others thinking that her orders didn't need to be followed. But she had a plan and wanted to minimize surprises, make sure everyone was ready to spark it up. She was thoughtful and methodical. We were lucky to have her leading us.

TALLYND

The Other Side of the Invasion

Dawn broke in a clear sky over Ecula, shining into our eyes and reflecting off our sails, and soon enough the alarm was raised. Small fishing villages rang bells and doubtless sent messengers to muster whatever response they could. We gave them more warning than they ever gave us, for all the good it would do them.

It felt intensely strange to be leading an invasion similar to the one I thwarted against Pelemyn. We did not come to wipe out the populace—we would never murder people in their sleep, slaughtering entire families as they did in our cities—but I was still in a position where I would have to issue orders that would ultimately kill people.

The convenient thing to do would be to imagine that all Eculans were evil. But I knew too well that there were plenty of people living on those islands who just wanted to raise their kids in peace and hope they were able to not only survive but thrive. I knew because I had been one of those parents in Brynlön when they came to our shores, thinking we, whom they had never met, were evil. The harder thing to do—the necessary thing—would be to exercise ruthlessness in achieving our goal, balanced with mercy where possible.

A predawn discussion with the Hathrim firelord Hollit Panevik had been instructive. I did not technically have the authority to order everyone around, but our shared interests in preventing a second invasion should avoid any issues until the actual mission was completed. After that, when we had to negotiate with the Eculan political leadership—if indeed they

consented to negotiate at all—things might get more difficult. Each country would have its own interests to look after,
and that might complicate things.

The Eculan navy scrambled a small force to meet us. It
was only a dozen boats—nowhere near enough—but they
were sacrifices and had to know it. Their mission was to delay
us for as long as possible, and my eyes squinted at the glare of
sunlight on the all-too-familiar bone armor that haunted my
nightmares. That was when I sent Gerstad Nara du Fesset
into the bay with Abhinava Khose. She would take care of the
plaguebringer in the water, since he was a less-than-proficient
swimmer, and he would take care of those ships . . . somehow. He assured me ahead of time that none would ever get
close enough to attempt a boarding, and we would therefore
be able to get near the docks so Hollit Panevik could do her
thing. Koesha and the Kaurian cyclones were on alert, ready
to divert any projectiles launched in our direction.

I was a little unclear on what Abhi intended to do. It felt
curiously like none of my business except for the most basic
question: "Will you be doing anything to incur a debt on your
life?"

"Oh, no."

I thought of one other query that was definitely my business: "Is there any way our fleet can be endangered by what
you're going to do?"

He shook his head vehemently. "I am going to keep firm
control."

I am not sure why I asked for nothing further, except that
it is borderline rude to ask how someone intends to use their
kenning, so I did not wish to give offense.

The Eculan ships grew closer and closer, and nothing
seemed to be happening. The stress built and built until I
wanted to say, *Nothing's happening,* simply to release some of
the tension, but Gondel Vedd was standing next to me and
gave my thoughts breath. Or something close enough.

"Uh?" he said uncertainly. We were very close to the vanguard and would therefore meet the brunt of any attack they could launch.

I quirked an eyebrow at him, just in case he wanted to say anything beyond the obvious, but then an absolutely thunderous eruption and crack of timbers demonstrated what Abhi had in mind.

He had found the leviathan crabs, and they in turn had found the Eculan boats. Enormous blue-green pincers burst from the surface underneath the boats amidships: They snapped shut and halved the watercraft, leaving a mess of blood and flotsam and some terrified swimmers who could conceivably survive if they swam for shore and nothing ate them—a prospect I judged unlikely.

Nothing but the pincers rose from the waves, but the bodies to which they were attached had to be truly gargantuan. They were probably mutated long ago by one of Sedam's metamorphs, or perhaps by Sedam himself, silently swelling in the bottom of the bay and always, always feeding. I saw one claw close around the pale bodies of four helpless Eculans, who screamed briefly before being dragged down into the deep, breakfast for a crustacean.

With all that blood in the water, Abhi wouldn't need to do anything at all to summon bladefins. The leviathans had eliminated their delaying tactics inside a minute, and we could sail through the wreckage unhindered.

Unhindered, that is, apart from the desperation of the survivors thrashing in the sea as we sailed past them. The cries of the Eculans, raw and ragged with fear, tore at my conscience. But I had considered these currents ahead of time and knew I must swim in them for a while. Those men had to die so that they could never cross the ocean to kill my boys—or any other Brynt—in the name of a petty god and his desire for a change of scenery.

I could see that it rather profoundly affected Gondel Vedd

and his husband—and perhaps all the Kaurians, since they were unused to contemplating violence, much less witnessing it. The scholar covered his mouth to stifle a sob and his eyes watered. His husband looked similarly distraught, and he threw an arm about Gondel's shoulders to reassure him.

"I'm sorry, Gondel," I said. "We will none of us be breathing peace today." I would have recommended he go to the cabin except that I would need him soon, along with the Raelech bard, to broadcast some warnings to the public. There were stages to our invasion informed by the extensive aerial scouting of Kaurian cyclones, and Gondel's ability to speak the Eculan language was a key part of my plan to save some lives.

The *Nentian Herald* was sailing off our starboard bow, with Koesha and Hollit and a Kaurian cyclone named Mardan Vess standing at the ready. I signaled them that it was time. Koesha gave the crew a warning, and they all held on to the railings or whatever they could before she and Mardan summoned winds sufficient to lift the three of them into the air.

For the record, it was quite something to witness a giant flying through the air—and something else again to hear that giant scream as she took off. I don't think Hollit was fully prepared for the sensation.

Once they got into position, hovering over the edge of the docks, Mardan was supposed to keep them in place, while Koesha was supposed to help Hollit spread her flames. As soon as the fire started pouring down out of the sky, igniting canvas and wood, that was the signal for Fintan to use his kenning to broadcast Gondel's voice to the city. The scholar sniffed once, wiped at his eyes, and delivered a speech he'd practiced beforehand, which he hoped would be intelligible to the Eculans.

"People of Ecula: We are the people across the ocean you attacked last year. Your fleets came in the night, and your soldiers murdered thousands of innocent people in their sleep.

You wiped out many of our cities. But not all. We, however, wiped out all of your armies.

"We are not here to kill you all, as you tried to do to us. We are only here to make sure you cannot attack us again. So we are burning your fleet now, and we will be destroying your barracks. We will not attack your city. Stay inside and do not resist and you will be safe. If you do resist, you will . . . not survive."

Because of that pause, I knew he'd changed his mind and said something else at the end, and I asked him about it. He was supposed to say, *you will be slain,* or something to that effect. He simply couldn't bring himself to issue the direct threat of violence.

But that was good enough. The Eculans heard and understood him, and that would hopefully prevent them from feeling they were backed into a corner and had to fight or die. We would never enter the city at all. Our targets—except for a final one—were purely military.

Using a spyglass that a Kaurian gave me, I observed the progress of Hollit's conflagration. She was spreading the flames quickly to the sails, and some figures were running away from them while a few others were running toward them, thinking they could help and then quickly realizing they could not. No one even approached with bows or crossbows for Mardan to defend against—they had not anticipated an airborne firelord over the docks, and by the time anyone could fetch archers, the flames would be pushing them back out of range anyway. That was satisfactory.

"Good," I said, collapsing the spyglass into a short brass tube. Our primary objective of burning their fleet was accomplished by the First, Second, Fourth, and Sixth Kennings working together. Our secondary objective, doubtless in progress somewhere behind me, would be achieved with the help of the Third and Fifth Kennings, under command of Temblor Priyit.

When I turned from the fire, I was expecting to see the same satisfaction that I felt written on others' faces. But what I saw instead were expressions of horror. I supposed that was to be expected of the Kaurians, but I didn't expect to see it so plainly on the Raelech bard's face. He looked for a moment like a little boy who'd had his lunch stolen by some fish head of a schoolyard bully.

Belatedly, I realized that the fire gouting from Hollit's outstretched hands probably reminded him of Gorin Mogen setting people on fire in Ghurana Nent. Or maybe it was Winthir Kanek and his fury, Pinter Stuken, setting Talala Fouz aflame. Or Olet Kanek charring Lorson the lifeleech to cinders. He had shared those stories with all of us at Pelemyn, and even though I could not see his face at the time, the fear in his voice had been unmistakable.

"She's not like the firelords you're thinking of," I told him. "She'd rather be cooking something delicious in her kitchen."

"I know that," Fintan said. "I mean, thanks—I know you're concerned. It's just . . . a terrifying kenning to me. When that power is directed at people—well, the screams and the smells tend to haunt you."

"I think the Brynts and the Raelechs all know what it is to be haunted at this point," I said. "My hope is that only the Eculans will be haunted after this."

DARYCK

The Bitter Feast

The Grynek Hunters were almost ashore by the time we heard Scholar Gondel Vedd's voice spit out an explanation, and then a warning, to the Bone Giants in their own cursed language. We and an entire brigade of allied forces under command of Temblor Priyit of the Raelechs dragged our landing craft onto a narrow beach just west of the city limits, rowed from the ships. It was a mixed force of Brynts, Raelechs, and Fornish.

I knew some were disappointed that the Raelechs had sent no juggernauts along on the invasion, but, honestly, we weren't going to suffer without one. We had three stonecutters, which could move just as much earth, three couriers—including the lifebond of the Raelech bard—and the temblor herself. While the vanguard of our fleet kept the Bone Giants' attention by torching all their ships in the bay, we quietly made landfall where no one could see us and sorted ourselves into ranks.

Brynts on the left, led by Mynstad du Möcher and her elite squad; Raelechs in the center, with the temblor up front; and Fornish on the right, mostly archers, with a few ranks of thornhands in the fore. I'd never seen them fight before and wasn't sure if I'd get to see them in action, since I was on the other side and presumably would have other things to worry about. But they looked incredibly deadly, with sharp, chitinous thorns starting out from their forearms and spines, and they had trained specifically to fight off Hathrim, opponents larger than the Bone Giants.

Aerial scouting had provided the location of the barracks on the southeastern edge of the city. The second könstad hadn't wanted us to enter the city at all but to circle around counterclockwise and come at the barracks from the south. It would take us through farmland and a few copses of timber and avoid civilians. I did not understand why we were taking pains to avoid innocent deaths when the Bone Giants made no such efforts to avoid ours. Had they not, in fact, come with the intent to slaughter us all? Why should we leave them with the ability to try again? Was this not an existential fight for our survival?

When I brought that up—privately, via a message sent to her on the wind—I got a reply back within minutes: *Letting them live is the only way I'll be able to live with myself. I understand your point very well, Gerstad, but we can win in the short term by destroying their military, and that will give us time to talk and remove their desire to attack us again in the long term.*

I deeply respected the second könstad—her character and love for Brynlön was and is indisputable—but I also deeply disagreed with her on this point. The Bone Giants had shown no interest in negotiation. What they did show was a desire to infiltrate our cities with wraith spies and then kill us all. When someone's default position is your death, the only possible thing you can negotiate is that they die first.

One step at a time, I supposed.

Our steps were going to be smoothed for us by the Raelech stonecutters, and it was truly a marvel to behold. Most cities tried to build defenses along roads and bridges, but with earth shapers in your party, new roads and bridges get built on the fly for your march, and you simply skirt those defenses. So one of the Raelech couriers moved ahead to scout the path and take out anyone who might raise the alarm about what we were doing, and the other two couriers escorted the stonecutters to blaze a nice even trail for a double-time march around to the fort. Crops, trees, barns—anything

in the way—were summarily flipped to one side, like opening
a book, and then we ran across a new road as if it were page
one.

We had moved a league and the fort was in sight across an
expansive field of bean plants before we encountered anything resembling resistance. A billowing cloud of smoke
from the burning fleet turned the sun red, and some of it was
getting in our lungs, making an already tiring journey more
difficult. Somebody back at the boats must have figured that
out—or maybe she figured it out on her own—because Koesha Gansu flew overhead and cleared it away from us. She
dropped down to report to the temblor, keeping time with us
for a stretch, then flew away again. Raelech couriers zipped in
after that to report sightings of approaching forces: The Eculans had finally figured out we were there, circling them to
the south. And then the couriers shuttled down the line, relaying battlefield commands. We were to stop and face left, as
the Bone Giants would be coming out of the city to the north
rather than from the barracks. Most of the barracks had already emptied in their attempt to save the fleet and defend
the city from an attack that wasn't coming from the direction
of the bay.

Functionally, these orders meant that the Brynts were
now the front line rather than the left side of a column—
a development that had not been unanticipated. That put us
on the right side of the front, with the Mynstad du Möcher
briefly on the right flank. The Raelech and Fornish columns
moved forward down the new-made road a bit, extending the
line and reinforcing that flank, and the Raelechs stepped up a
bit too. That put Temblor Priyit to the right of the myn-
stand's squad, forming a new flank, and it meant that we
were backed up by archers now.

We saw defenders begin to emerge from the trees surrounding the city, a large but undisciplined mob of bone-
clacking giants. They had swords but no shields, and once

they advanced somewhat but were still outside reliable bow-shot, they paused to form ranks before charging. Their forces were probably equal to ours in terms of numbers, and the young rapid Lörry du Bört was breathing a bit hard by my left shoulder.

"Kraken cocks," he whispered, looking at the towering figures preparing to attack.

"Don't worry. You keep that bigass shield up and just rip the water out of any giant coming at you." Our new myns-tad, Söla du Högyn, was on his left, and she reassured him too. It reminded me that my former rapid, Sören du Hyller, and Mynstad Luren should be standing with us, but one way or another, the brothers of the bastards facing us took them too early.

"It's finally time to get some of ours back," I said, loud enough for anyone nearby. "Just a mug full of revenge, but I'll drink it up and order another. Come on, then!"

That elicited a roar around me, and it was echoed across the field by the Bone Giants as someone on that side gave the order to charge.

"Ha *haah*! Yes!" I shouted, and similarly aggressive battle cries billowed up from our side.

While the Bone Giants charged, the Fornish archers poured arrows into them to thin the ranks, and the stonecut-ters came back in the company of the couriers and started messing with the ground in front of the advancing army. The soil—already somewhat treacherous because of the bean plants and raised rows—bucked and sank unexpectedly be-neath their feet, causing many of them to trip as they ran. When they went down, they tripped up several others behind them, and sometimes these accidents resulted in wounds from the swords they carried or even proved fatal, but, most important, their charge was slowed and its effectiveness dimmed.

They met us, therefore, not in a unified front but in spots, with uncertain reinforcement at their back; their typical tactics of throwing overwhelming forces at a problem were not going to work when they couldn't apply the pressure they needed.

They did, however, outnumber us—my initial estimate of even numbers had been too generous to us. Had it been a literally level battlefield, their advantage might have won out. But the Raelechs made sure it was never level for more than a few seconds at a time.

Finally, they reached me. The one I thought was going to first meet my spear instead got his brains scrambled by Lörry du Bört, so I shoved my spear through the guts of the giant behind him, raising my shield as I did so, the tall, hardened edge proof against the stroke he tried to rain down on my head as he died. I pushed with the shield as I yanked the spear back, scraping him off with a satisfying gurgle of death to meet the charge of the next, and, soon after that, the next and the next and the next. It was glorious for about six or seven kills. I felt justified and victorious. But then, for some reason I can't explain, it began to pall. Maybe it was the screaming that got to me. Maybe it was the fact that the faces of those charging us looked so young. These were not seasoned fighters but very young men, barely past the carefree days of boyhood.

To my right, the ruthless efficiency of the Mynstad du Möcher had created a pile of bodies, and the same was true in front of my part of the line and in front of the Raelechs as well. It was going to create a problem because the Bone Giants could climb over the bodies, using them as a step from which to launch themselves and attack from an even greater height than normal. The mynstad shouted this several times, until a Raelech courier came over to see what was needed— I think Temblor Priyit relayed the request. Once the courier understood, they redirected the efforts of the stonecutters to create a slope ahead of our lines, simultaneously dropping the land in front and raising the road underneath us a few inches, which effectively tripped up a whole wave at the point of contact and gave us the high ground. It allowed me to see that there was an end to the horde, if we could hold. The numbers of bodies charging us appeared finite, at least; there were some trampled beans in the space between the rear guard and the trees from which they emerged.

And then the thornhands attacked from the flank on some signal, moving right to left, and I caught only glimpses between my own engagements, but they were fearsome warriors. The thorns I'd seen earlier had grown and sharpened, and they fought in spin moves that presented their armored backs to their opponents. They took the odd hit as necessary, but then they pivoted and drove those thorns on their forearms into the Bone Giants from the side, tearing into their abdomens, spilling guts and spinning again to the next target, so fast that they whirled like spheres of death, utterly shredding people. And I began to wonder why killing the Bone Giants and seeing them killed didn't feel as good as I'd hoped.

Temblor Priyit ordered the archers to cease fire as the attackers thinned out. At first, I thought it was to protect the thornhands—and it may have at least partially been for that reason—but I soon realized it was also to protect the couriers, who were now joining the fray and quickly, efficiently dispatching giants from behind, moving fast and shattering a hip with their stone-lined clubs or knifing a kidney. Between the couriers, the thornhands, the stonecutters messing with the footing in front of our lines, and our shields and spears, the Bone Giants didn't stand a chance. It was over in another ten minutes. Thousands dead on their side, maybe a few dozen on ours. The bean field was watered in blood.

So there was a measure of the vengeance I had craved, but it didn't heal my pain or nourish my soul. I felt relief to still be alive, and I think that was a shared emotion up and down the line, but there was no great shout of joyous victory.

We re-formed our ranks, two couriers and stonecutters at the front, and continued on to the fort. One courier and stonecutter remained behind. The stonecutter would lift our fallen from the ground on a sort of moving platform of earth, which would flow beside them all the way to the beach, and they'd report what happened to the cyclone who waited there. The second könstad would hear about it shortly thereafter, and if she had any additional orders to give, they'd come to us by courier or cyclone. We still had our mission to complete.

The stonecutters raised earth all the way up to the lip of the fort's wall, so we were able to ascend the ramp. No one challenged us, and there was honestly nothing for us to do but rest. The Fornish archers rained fire arrows of Raelech crafting down onto the barracks, which they had brought for that purpose. Once the buildings were all burning—but still at a stage where they could be salvaged—a courier ran back to the boats to report that. A few minutes later, Scholar Vedd's voice boomed again throughout the city, thanks to the Raelech bard. I found out later that he told people their warriors had all been killed in a bean field to the south. They were to remain in their homes, let the fort burn, and we'd do nothing else. We had not come to kill them all but to illustrate what an incredibly bad idea it was to pick a fight with us ever again. Their leadership should be informed that we would cease all hostilities when we received their complete surrender. Until then, we would set their military and support facilities aflame.

No one came to put out the fire. The second könstad's strategy had clearly paid off in the short term, because we had destroyed their fleet and thousands of warriors who had prepared to invade us, with only minor losses in return. I don't know—maybe her approach would work? I don't think we met their full strength, and the element of surprise clearly worked in our favor, but we did have enormous advantages in battle.

Marching back to the boats past all those dead bodies, with blackwings already spiraling and croaking above them, we made no jokes, no boasts, no light chatter about weather or speculation about what we'd have for dinner. Gyrsön might have prepared something magnificent for such an occasion—I would not be surprised. For him as well as myself, this vengeance had long been anticipated. How disappointing to sit down to a meal long awaited and discover that it was bitter on the tongue, with nothing to savor.

The gods gave us six kennings to combat the seventh but no magical ability to heal our broken spirits.

HOLLIT

The Building Flame

The truly gut-clenching thing about being a firelord of the First Kenning is how remarkably easy it is to set things on fire. Even as I was repulsed by the destruction I was unleashing, I also heard, *Oh, pretty!* and *This is so cool!* flit in and out of my head, fighting for time with an omnipresent worry that I would hurt someone.

The flames spread even quicker than I thought they would, and because of that, my fears came true: Some people on the boats were caught and burned. Through a film of tears that sizzled away to steam on my cheeks as soon as they left my eyes, I saw ten people dive off boats into the water. I counted them all and did not look away, because I was responsible for putting their lives in jeopardy, despite it not being my intent. Some of them were on fire when they jumped. Only two of the ten resurfaced; maybe something under the water was taking advantage. Regardless, I had managed not to kill anyone in my whole life, and now I had killed eight in less than eight minutes, and it had been far, far too easy.

I wasn't taxed until the end, when all the boats and the docks were alight, because I had to make sure that the fire didn't spread to the city itself. The wind Koesha was creating floated some sparks and embers that way, and I had to put out dozens of small emergencies before they became large emergencies. There were also some folks out there with buckets trying to save at least one boat nearest the city, so I had to make that burn hotter and faster to make sure nothing was salvaged. None of them were hurt, apart from smoke inhalation, I supposed, and once the job was done and the city was safe, I was able to get my tears under control—until I returned to the deck of the Seven-Year Ship, that is, and saw Fintan's face.

He made brief contact then dropped his eyes, visibly afraid of me. People showered me with congratulations, saying that I'd done a great job, so many lives saved though I had clearly just killed some people, but that face . . . His face wrecked me.

"No, no, no," I said, then sobbed and broke into fresh tears. "I'm not like them, Fintan, I promise. I'm not Winthir Kanek. I don't ever want to be like them. Orden and I moved to Brynlön so I wouldn't have to be. We don't want power. All we want is our restaurant. Please don't look at me like that."

When he glanced back at me, he sniffled and blinked at some tears, then attempted a smile. "I know, Hollit. I'm sorry. It's simply impossible for me not to relive the worst days of my life when I see fire like that. You did what was necessary and no more, and our countries will be safe from invasion now. You deserve nothing but gratitude from all of us. I'll be getting you an obscenely large gift basket as soon as we are back in Pelemyn."

We both laughed at that, because the Brynt custom was endearing. I took a few deep breaths and was able to calm myself. I gave a report to the second könstad, and then she had Koesha return me to the *Nentian Herald,* since I took up way too much room on the deck of the Seven-Year Ship. Koesha flew off after that to get an update on the progress of the army and then maybe do something about the smoke, which was drifting in their direction. Inside of an hour, I was asked back to the Seven-Year Ship for a new assignment. The battle had been won, a rout of their garrisoned forces, but an additional target had been identified.

"We've located a lumber mill and the shipyards that are

clearly producing everything needed to build the fleet," the second könstad said. "We need you to torch those as well, and that will serve instead of burning their forests. They're just a little way up the coast, at the mouth of a river."

"Are there people inside?"

"Perhaps inside the mill. The shipyards are open to the air, and anyone there can easily escape any fires you set."

"That's fine, then, but I want the people out of the mill first."

"We'll do our best. We're sending a team along with you—this might be an opportunity to gather some intelligence, so we need to take it."

"Intelligence at a lumber mill?"

"Only the most basic kind. We need to know where to go next, and we're hoping that the people inside the mill would be willing to tell us where we can find the leaders of their society. Someone who can negotiate. Our only clue about where to go came from the zealot who died seeking the Seventh Kenning. So: Burn the shipyard. Burn the mill when it's clear. Defend yourself if necessary. Are you okay with that?"

I was, but I didn't look forward to flying again. That was fair-to-middling terrifying, and I didn't know how cyclones could stand it. But it turned out that this was going to be a slightly different situation, since there would be more of us and we had a longer distance to travel. The mill and shipyards were far enough away that they probably never heard Gondel's voice making his announcements in their language. If they hadn't looked outside and seen the smoke—which was blowing away from them—they might not even know anything had happened, unless someone had specifically come to tell them.

We were bundled into two landing craft—Mynstad du Möcher with a few of her elite unit and a couple of Fornish thornhands in one boat, with Fintan, Gondel Vedd, Koesha, and myself in the other. The second könstad and Gerstad Nara du Fesset dove into the bay and then used their kenning to speed us along in the water, a very pleasant ride that must have been close to a league. The military boat landed first on the side of the river where the lumber mill sat; the shipyards were on the other bank.

The mynstad and her squad spread themselves, shields up, while we disembarked. This was an effort to protect not me but the scholar and the bard—though there thankfully seemed few physical threats at first. I saw some tall pale people in the shipyards, and I requested that Fintan broadcast Gondel so that he could tell everyone to evacuate before I set the facilities on fire.

He was going to say something like, *The shipyards and lumber mill are about to be set aflame. Leave now,* and just repeat that until people figured out that it was actually happening. Once he got going, Koesha lifted me into the sky with winds, and I screamed only a tiny bit this time. As I hovered over the river, I began to rain fire down on the shipyards. That got folks moving and believing that the strange voice they heard was telling them the truth, and that was good. No one got trapped this time, and they all escaped. We had everything merrily ablaze in a few minutes, and they'd have to spend months just rebuilding the yards before they could start work on any more ships.

Even though I saw plenty of people facing our party outside the lumber mill, I wasn't sure that it was entirely evacuated, and I thought our side could maybe use a very tall person for intimidation purposes, so I asked Koesha to take us back down to our group. We landed well behind them, near the second könstad and the gerstad, who had hung back by the boats. They both gave me small wavy motions with their hands, palm down, a Brynt thing that indicated the currents were flowing well and I should keep going. The gerstad

smiled and joined us, but the second könstad remained behind. I tried to stomp menacingly toward the assembled
workers, braced on either side by women who were less than
half my height.

The Eculans weren't dressed in bone armor but rather in
wool tunics and breeches dyed in an assortment of reds, mustard yellows, and purples, and the vibrancy of those colors
indicated how new the clothes were. The tunics bore some
interesting patterns in the weave and . . . I kind of liked
them? I wondered if they could make a tunic like that in my
size, but it was probably not the time to ask.

There were both men and women present and a variety of
hair and eye colors, but no redheads. Every single one of
them carried a hammer or some other tool that wasn't meant
for battle but could do some damage in a pinch. They outnumbered our small party probably five to one, and their
raised voices indicated they were working up the courage to
attack.

That would be such a terrible decision. The two thornhands could probably take them all, and they had to realize
they weren't equipped for battle; they were counting on their
numbers to win and had already accepted that many of them
would die.

I needed to convince them that it was hopeless. So I did
my stompy thing, and their eyes moved toward me. Once I
had their attention and checked to make sure Koesha and
Nara weren't too close, I pulled up even with the Brynt soldiers and lit my arms and head on fire as a warning. You
could tell that the Eculans weren't used to looking up at anyone—or to people calmly setting themselves aflame.

Gondel Vedd took the opportunity to speak, with an assist
from Fintan so that everyone could hear him. Whatever he
said, it caused them first to look across the river—where I ha
obviously torched the shipyards, which they'd someh

missed—and then to look back at me, reassess, and put down their weapons. Once they did that, they eyed me expectantly.

"I told them that if they put down their weapons, they would not be harmed," Scholar Vedd said. "You should put out your fire now."

"Oh. Yeah, sure, I can do that."

GONDEL

Talk Fast

Thank Reinei, the Eculans decided to take a breath and choose peace instead of violence. When the workers began streaming out of the mill in search of the voice telling them to evacuate, they did not take kindly to our presence or the idea that we'd be burning down their place of employment, but they recognized that they were ill equipped to deal with us, except perhaps by force of numbers. That force grew and grew, and they were approaching the edge of a cliff where they'd have to jump when Hollit Panevik convinced them to back off.

"Thank you," I said in Eculan, my voice carrying to them thanks to Fintan. "Again I promise that we will offer you no violence if you offer us none. We represent a coalition of seven nations"—I almost said six but realized that Joabei was a seventh, and that number would resonate more with this crowd—"responding to the attack your country made on them. We are here to prevent the second invasion, and indeed we have already burned the fleet at Riba Oči. You can see the smoke rising in the distance. Burning the shipyard and the lumber mill will prevent you from replacing the fleet quickly, so it has to be done for our defense."

"You're from across the ocean? The source of the Fourth Kenning?" one man in the front spat. I couldn't be sure, but he acted like he was the foreman or the boss. Though no one else wore leather, he sported a leather belt across his purple tunic. He had grown a thin line of beard along his jaw, and a thinner line of whiskers arched over his upper lip. His fist were clenched, and veins stood out on his neck.

"I personally am from the source of the Second Kenning. Representatives of the Fourth Kenning are here with me, however."

"You shouldn't be here at all. What happened to the first invasion?"

"Your armies have been destroyed," I said, which wasn't technically true. We hadn't eliminated the army in the north, but Abhi had assured us that they wouldn't be a problem. "And we dismantled your spy networks." That, too, was stretching the truth, I supposed, though at this point any spies remaining would be sending messages to a man who no longer lived. "We also have the Seven-Year Ship."

"Where?" the man demanded.

"About a league away, near the burning fleet. It is now our flagship. And your god, Žalost, is imprisoned without hope of freedom. You are defeated."

"You lie!" He shouted that as if mere volume could make it true, spittle flying out of his mouth, and some grumbles of support from the others echoed this sentiment.

"I do not. The ship can be seen with your own eyes at Riba Oči—and of course I would expect you to verify this—along with the presence of our own fleet. A fleet that does not seek your lives but merely an assurance that there will be no more attacks. We would like to speak to your leader, the kraljic, to discuss this. Where may we find him?"

Several people started to speak, but the leader shouted over them. "I'm not telling you anything!" The spittle irrigated several of his coworkers. "Nobody tell them anything!"

"I see. I understand your feelings. But since this mill provides material to your naval shipyards, we have to burn it down. Could you at least tell us if this building is clear first so that no one gets hurt?"

"No! We tell you nothing. We give the enemy nothing!"

That showed a stunning lack of concern for others' lives. The man was clearly a problem, and he would likely have agitated for an attack if Hollit hadn't convinced them to disarm. He was still very dangerous, so I tried to rob his primary rhetorical tool of breath.

"The enemy?" I said. "Did you know that your armies came to our shores and killed innocent families while they slept? We could do the same—we could have barred the doors and set the building on fire with you still inside—but we are trying to keep you alive. If you are looking for villains, look in a mirror. We are simply looking for a leader to talk to, and we'll leave straightaway if you help us."

"You'll get no help from us!" the foreman shouted, but as he took a breath to shout some more, someone else spoke up a couple of rows back, a young woman with long straight brown hair tucked behind her ears. Her tunic had probably once been bright white with an intense red stripe at the neck and sleeves, but it had faded now to a dingy gray with a dull red collar, and it was overlarge on her bony frame.

"I can tell you where the kraljic is," she said. "He's in Sveto Selo."

"What? Who said that?" the foreman demanded, wheeling around. "Was it one of the new hires?" He stabbed an accusing finger at her. "Traitor! I knew you couldn't be trusted!"

I'm not sure if I understood every word she said after that, but I believe she may have suggested that he arrange an amorous encounter with an ox. The collective gasp that rose from the Eculans indicated that it was certainly rather rude. The foreman flinched as if she'd delivered a quick slap to his face, and then he reddened and purpled with rage.

"I'll kill you!" he growled, and he lunged toward her, which was exactly the wrong thing to say and do.

"No!" I said in Eculan, then switched to Brynt in desperation to save the one person who seemed willing to talk to us. "Nara, stop him!"

She didn't hesitate. She ripped the water—that is to say, all the blood—forcefully from his head. It exploded out of his left ear in a fountain as he dropped to the ground, manifestly dead in a spectacular fashion. The Eculans gave another collective gasp, but this one was shaded with horror. I was horrified as well—I hadn't thought through what would happen when I asked her to stop him. I had hoped she could do so nonlethally, but my request essentially killed him and lost Reinei's peace. I raised my voice in hopes of preventing further loss.

"I am so sorry, but any offer of violence will be met with your instant death. You are free to go, but if you feel, as we do, that the cult of Žalost must be overthrown if we are to live in peace, then remain here to talk some more."

A dishearteningly large number departed, two of them carrying away the body of the foreman. Only three Eculans remained, the young woman who'd spoken up among them. The other two were a stout-looking Eculan—the first I'd seen—with hair grown down like draperies in front of his eyes, and a young woman with blond hair. I told Fintan he could stop broadcasting me and I'd just speak unassisted.

"I am Gondel Vedd," I said to them. "What are your names?"

"I'm Fanje," the first young woman volunteered.

"Radič," the young man said. "Did you really burn the fleet? So we can't launch the invasion?"

"We did," I confirmed, and the three of them exchanged glances and smiled.

"That's wonderful," the blond woman said. "My name's Milenka. Are you still burning the mill? It would save us some work, because it was our job to find a way to destroy it."

"It was?"

"Yes. We are part of a rebel group called Šest. Others were supposed to attack the fleet, but you've done their job already, like you're going to do ours. So thanks."

"Doubly so from me," Radič said. "I was under orders to

join the invasion, and . . . I was not going to go. Now I can't,
so that's great."

"How many are in your group?" I asked. "If only three of
you out of nearly a hundred are willing to rebel . . ."

"Do not worry about them," Fanje said, waving her hand
dismissively at the workers who had departed. "Many of
them would like to throw off the cult, but it has too much
power over their lives—they are afraid for themselves but
also for their families. They need to see it can be defeated
before they join in. Right now they are simply trying to survive."

"As are we," I said. She waggled a finger at me.

"I want to be clear: I'm afraid for myself too, and for my
family. Because we'll all be dead within the next couple of
days unless you can stop the cult as you claim. The ones who
are still loyal to the cult will report us, and the svećenici will
come for us soon. So what's your plan?"

"Perhaps you can help us come up with one," I said. "Stopping the invasion was our primary goal, but we'd also like to
make sure we don't have to worry about another one later.
Perhaps we can negotiate a peace."

Milenka snorted, and Radič made a face as if he'd just bit-
ten into a sour apple. Fanje shook her head in pity.

"I can't help you with that. The kraljic is loyal to the
church, and the isposniks are fanatically devoted to destroying the source of the Fourth Kenning. So neither of them will
ever agree to a peace."

Sighing, I said, "Then I suppose we must make war until
you have new leadership."

Fanje grinned. "Now, *that* I can help you with."

"It is the only path to peace available to us. Much as we
despise violence, sometimes there is no other recourse. How
would you feel about joining us on our ship as an honored
guest?"

Her expression clouded. "A guest?"

"Certainly not a prisoner. If our intent was to imprison you, we would have no need to trick you. I am inviting you as a guest—an ally, if you wish—so that we may plan how best to achieve a change in Ecula's leadership with a minimum of bloodletting."

She looked to her friends, and they nodded.

"Get to Sveto Selo and tell Pavle that all the cells should activate now. The people from across the ocean have arrived, and the time for revolution has come. I'm going to guide the fleet there— Wait." She turned to me. "How many ships in your fleet?"

"More than three hundred. We have burned your fleet, the barracks at Riba Oči, and have killed all the soldiers defending it while leaving the city intact. Please confirm this if you wish. We have also burned the shipyard and, soon, this mill."

"Excellent." To Radič and Milenka, she said, "Let them know."

They gave one another hugs and smiles, and Radič and Milenka ran away about ten steps before Radič stopped and turned around.

"Hey. Can we watch? The burning, I mean?"

I chuckled. It surely wouldn't hurt if they witnessed our power firsthand. I told Hollit that it was time to set the building alight, and she stepped forward together with Koesha to direct a gout of fire at the mill until it caught and then spread all across the roof.

"Beautiful," Fanje said. She and her friends stood and watched for a while, chatting happily together, until they sobered somewhat. I overheard Fanje tell them to warn their families, as well as hers, to hide. They embraced again, this time in farewell, and once Radič and Milenka had left, Fanje turned to us. "I'm ready to go. Let's take down a cult."

FANJE
Opportunity Seized

Is it possible to perish from an excess of hope and fear? I feel as if I'm approaching that precipice. Because these strange short people have already accomplished everything that Šest had hoped for, but I worry about the consequences.

Radič won't have to join the invasion now, but once the other workers at the mill report us for staying behind—and they will definitely report us—the cult might kill him anyway, and his family too on the theory that they must be a nest of heretics. They will find heretics wherever they can, because someone has to be blamed for the loss of the fleet.

Which means that my family will also be targeted, as will Milenka's. If we are to have a shot at surviving now, we must throw our lives into openly defying and defeating the cult; there is no more chance of secrecy, no possibility to escape their wrath by keeping our heads down and hoping to be left alone.

The old man with dark-brown skin and white hair at his temples speaks our language with a strange accent, and sometimes he leaves out words or doesn't conjugate properly, but he's understandable, and I like him because he has mustard on his tunic and he also doesn't want to kill us all. No one else can speak our tongue—they all have their own, these people from across the sea. I recognize the Joabeian woman because I have at least heard of them before and saw illustrations of them in school. But the others are all new to me, and my mind is such a soup of chunky ingredients right now. A carrot of fascination for their varied appearances, especially the people with thorns growing out of their bodies. A bite of delicious, hopeful mutton that some of them might want to be friends. A sour wedge of cabbage that says, *Of course they'll never be your friends, because your people killed theirs by the thousands. They are here to use you and then discard you.*

Well, I'll be using them too, so I suppose it's only fair.

The old man, Gondel Vedd, introduces me to the others. Nara du Fesset is blessed with the Fourth Kenning, and it was she who pulled the blood out of the foreman's head. Her skin is a lighter brown than Gondel's, as are all the soldiers standing behind shields. One of the soldiers is perhaps the most stunningly beautiful person I have ever seen in my life, and she is married to Nara.

The giantess is a Hathrim, some of whom live in the islands that comprise Bačiiš. Her name is Hollit, and it doesn't look like she enjoys burning things down, which seems counterintuitive. She has pale skin like us except a bit pinker. The people from Forn also have pale skin, but they're even shorter than the rest and much spikier, because of the Fifth Kenning.

There's a man named Fintan, with black wavy hair and a large nose; he wears a gold band around his arm with three semiprecious stones set in it. He can say *hello* and *welcome,* simple words like that, but not much else. Supposedly he is a bard of the Third Kenning and it was his blessing that allowed him to project Gondel's voice.

I'm led to some landing craft and introduced to an older woman named Tallynd du Böll, who looks like she's in her fifties. She has some graying hair at her temples, but the rest is black tight curls. I have no idea what her title means, but Gondel explains that she's the leader of the fleet, so that's clear enough.

We pile into the boats, and then Nara and Tallynd just walk into the sea before using their kenning to propel us at impressive speed across the surface of the water. I take the opportunity to ask how they crossed the ocean.

"There is a man with us blessed by the Sixth Kenning. He can speak to any animal and ask them to help him or stop doing something he doesn't like, such as eating people. So far, they haven't disobeyed him."

"Oh! He can control krakens?"

"He doesn't like the word *control,* but yes. It's how we crossed the ocean safely."

"Wow. Those bones are going to season the stew well."

Gondel blinks and asks me to explain. "I understand the literal words you said, but that sounded like an idiom I've never heard before."

"Oh! A cooking metaphor. We let bones stew for a long time, and it makes everything taste better later. So I meant that information will give me ideas after a while."

He nods his understanding, and then a voice from overboard—Tallynd's—asks him something to relay to me.

"There were only a few thousand soldiers at the barracks," Gondel says. "That couldn't have been the main invasion force, correct?"

"That's right. Most of them are probably arriving next week. The majority are stationed in Sveto Selo right now. Did you . . . kill all the soldiers at Riba Oči?"

"We did, yes. But the city remains."

I had trouble imagining what it would take to accomplish that, but soon we came into view of the fleet and I was better able to understand. Hundreds of ships, most all of them bigger than ours, floating in the bay while our fleet and the docks burned. Gondel got into a conversation with Tallynd, and I was left to just take it all in—this enormous force that came in response to the cult's invasion the previous year. The isposniks had sworn they'd be all wiped out, but they weren't, and then the isposniks swore that the people across the ocean could never make the crossing to strike back, and here they were.

The Seven-Year Ship is an impressive boat, even more

grand than illustrations I'd seen, large enough to house the proper number of seekers and then some. I get some hostile glares from the crew, and I try to keep my face pleasant to communicate that I am friendly. But there's a lot of anger on plain display, and if I weren't boarding with the aegis of Tallynd, I think I would be feeding the fishes in no time.

I'm taken into the cabin, which is crowded with so many people in it, but there's a decent map of Ecula spread out on a table. I'm invited to sit behind the table with Gondel Vedd and Fintan while the others stand—Tallynd, the Joabeian woman, and a leader of the Raelechs named Priyit. She has a band on her right arm like Fintan does, but hers has different stones in it. That probably means something, but I don't know what. There's also another Raelech in there with a band on her arm, and I'm told she's a courier named Numa. I'm not told why a courier would be included in this meeting when so many others are left out, like Nara and the beautiful soldier woman and the giant lady and the spiky Fornish folks.

Well, no—the giant lady wouldn't fit in here, and the spiky ones might stab someone by accident the next time the ship hit a swell, so that makes sense.

Tallynd takes in the seating situation and asks Priyit to switch places with Gondel; for some reason she doesn't want him sitting right next to me. I think maybe she's worried I might try something, and she confirms that the next time she speaks and it's translated through Gondel.

"Just to be clear, Fanje, we want to trust you but don't trust you yet. If you attempt anything violent, I will pull the water out of your brain the same way Nara did to the mill foreman."

"I understand. I will move very slowly." I place my hands on the table and then intertwine my fingers. "But to be clear as well, I want you to win and win quickly. If you don't, all my friends and family will be killed by the cult. So I hope you are ready to do more than talk."

The conversation oozes and undulates like a slug, because Gondel has to translate everything I say into Brynt and then the courier, Numa, translates that into another language, Raelech, for Priyit's benefit. Then Tallynd or someone responds and Gondel translates for me while Numa translates that into Raelech as well. I was asked to be as accurate as possible when a Brynt historian named Dervan gave me a diary and asked me to write everything down, but I think I'll just pretend in my account that we are all speaking the same language, since it's so frustrating.

"How do we destroy the cult?" Tallynd asks.

I carefully move one hand to the map and point. "The isposniks are all at the Cloister in Sveto Selo on the island of Vlast, and the kraljic and the military are housed in the Citadel there. You need to destroy them both to have a chance."

We take a small break to define terms, as they don't know much about the cult's workings. Isposniks are the ascetic leaders of the cult, about as attractive and thoughtful of others as a yawning asshole, while the svećenici are priests who basically enforce their decrees; the bearded monks—they had seen a few of them in Brynlön—integrate with the military.

"So the church is involved in the military? What does the kraljic do, then?"

"The kraljic has been our secular leader throughout history, but since the cult came to power, he does nothing without the approval of the cult. He's still the leader, but it's really the church that's in charge. Which means that an isposnik named Draško is the one who's really making all the decisions."

"What was Ecula like before the cult took hold?" Tallynd asks. It's a huge question.

"Some of that is lost forever, because the people who are still alive to tell us are dying out, and the histories from that time are being rewritten while old texts are being destroyed."

"Do you know what your religion used to be?"

"Yes. I've read some old scrolls, and the old temple still stands in the capital, though it's been twisted to pay tribute to Žalost now. The old faith focused on all the gods, including the mother and father. It preached loving the beauty of what you beheld rather than pining for what you did not—probably because our islands have very different resources, and it was easy to long for something that someone else had. We have all these proverbs based around it, like *Do not scoff at what others would cherish,* or *Your mundane cheese is another's delicacy,* and that last one evolved into an idiom, where people say, *I have my mundane cheese,* when they mean they are content with their simple life."

I have to pause while this is translated, and once they nod, Tallynd asks how that old faith interacted with the government.

"Back then, not at all. Except that the government tried to reduce shortages through trade so people would be more content. There used to be bridges between the islands, built by the Omeshan earth shapers, and roads maintained by them. We traded our goods to them for those services because they made all else possible. We on Drvo would get goats from Žitnica or sheep from Brda. And everyone would get lumber and kafa beans from us, wild berries, lots of oils and seeds from the forest, while the guilds concentrated in Vlast made finished goods for us, like clothing and so on. As far as I can tell, we used to be good neighbors and trading partners with Omesh and even Joabei. But now the bridges are all fallen into the straits, the roads are terrible, and everyone hates us and we are told to hate them back."

Tallynd leans forward and taps the map. "What about this other nation, Bačiiš?"

"They are a mixed people who have access to the First Kenning."

"Fire demons," the Joabeian chimes in. Her name is Koesha Gansu. I'm not really sure if I can get to the marrow of her meaning. Who are the demons she's talking about?

"Well, that country is a bit of a salad. There are Joabeians who live there, and Omeshans, and Hathrim, like the woman who burned down the mill. And a fleet of Eculan refugees fled there when the cult first came to power, because they correctly predicted that things were going to get bad. They came back once, about fifty years ago—or their descendants did—to see what had become of Ecula. This was during the season when the krakens had receded, and they told everyone they met that Bačiiš was a wonderful and welcoming land. They were asking about starting up annual trade—my father heard about this because they were interested in kafa beans. But no sooner had people become interested than the trade delegation disappeared. Ships, crew—all gone. Not so much as a goodbye. Because that is how the cult takes care of things. We haven't heard from Bačiiš since then—or if we have, I don't personally know about it."

"What would you trade?" Gondel asks. "That was a question that merchants from my country wanted to ask."

"Brdan wool, most likely. The Omeshans and Joabeians love it." My eyes flick over to Koesha during the translation, and she nods to confirm this. "Besides the wool itself, we have an indigo dye for it that's not found anywhere except on the island of Slivovi. And kafa beans seem popular, if my family's good fortunes are any indication."

Tallynd redirects the conversation to military matters. "So there used to be bridges at the straits, and now there are only nets to keep out krakens and bladefins?"

"That's correct."

"So if we were to breach the nets here in the western strait between Drvo and Brda, allowing krakens to enter into Eel Bay, that would effectively cut off Drvo and Žitnica from the northern islands, but Clamshell Bay and Otter Bay would still be protected?"

"Yes. Oh, my, I hadn't thought about that."

"So the southern islands could still fish and trade between themselves in protected waters, and the same for the northern islands. But trade between the north and south—and the movement of troops—would be cut off until things are resolved to our satisfaction."

"I think so, yes."

"Good. What kind of military resources do Brda and Slivovi have?"

"Almost none. There are garrisons like the one here at Riba Oči scattered about, and they might get sent to reinforce Sveto Selo, but they're not going to prevent you from getting to the capital."

"Naval forces?"

"Sveto Selo has a huge port and plenty of boats. Lots of them are merchant and fishing vessels, but there are military craft too."

"How many?"

"A few dozen, perhaps? Nothing like the fleet at Riba Oči. But different ships—they're designed to fight other ships, not to carry troops."

"Okay. We'll scout those out. Would all trade cease if we make Eel Bay impassable? Would people in the north or the south starve?"

"They'd suffer from a lack of variety, perhaps, but they wouldn't starve. It might get worse if it were to go on for a long time, I don't know. But, no, there'd be plenty of trade in the north and the south. I think the south would suffer more because they wouldn't have access to all the goods that Sveto Selo produces."

"We'll try to be quick in everyone's interest, then, and preserve as much of your city as we can. We'd rather be friends going forward than enemies."

"That's a lovely sentiment," I tell her, "but, unfortunately, the death cult doesn't want friends. They want Eculans to rule everywhere."

"Everywhere? Why didn't they start with Omesh, then, since it's much closer?"

"They were sold on the idea that taking control of the Third and Fourth Kennings together in the west would allow them to sweep all others aside. Omesh would fall after the first two countries, and then Joabei. I'm not sure where they would have progressed from there."

Gondel catches Tallynd's eye. "If they had captured Pelemyn and let no one jump into Bryn's Lung, that would have freed Žalost."

"What? Freed Žalost? Are you speaking metaphorically?"

And then I am told the most remarkable tale—that the cult originated with the god of the Seventh Kenning and an Eculan lifeleech, and together they had launched a long-term plan to free him from his exile. Since he was imprisoned by his brother, the sea god, and isolated by the krakens controlled by his sister, he needed the Fourth Kenning to be weakened and the source of the krakens destroyed. To accomplish that, he wrote *Zanata Sedam* with the lifeleech to weaponize my culture and aim it at Brynlön. We'd been manipulated for his own ends. While I couldn't dispute the facts, I bristled a little at the implication that we were a nation of fools.

"You all have your own religions too, right—presumably the holy texts authored by the siblings of Žalost? And therefore your cultures are designed to benefit them and whatever ends they seek?"

"That's a valid point," Gondel admits immediately, before translating it for the others. They chew on that bone, make some grudging head bobs, and then Tallynd speaks for them.

"We might quibble and say that our faiths and societies were designed to protect us from Žalost, but, regardless, I think we can agree: All of our cultures have been manipulated by the gods. Or later, by elites who claimed that their will was god's will. Perhaps we can resolve this so that we can stop fighting and figure out who we want to be without gods pitting us against one another. Tell me, Fanje, under what conditions might your kraljic surrender?"

I think about it for a few moments, but it's as fruitless as a kupina bush in winter. "I can't imagine a scenario in which he would. He's obsessed with his own power."

"I feared as much. Fine. How can we remove him and his power structure without wiping out the whole city?"

That is an excellent question. "I suppose that would be possible, but it's going to be difficult. The Citadel is a vital target from a practical standpoint—the kraljic lives there, as does much of the military leadership. But even if you take that out, you still have the cult to worry about, because they will just install a new secular leader they can control. The Cloister of Žalost is where you'll find the isposniks—and if you get rid of them, that will either shake people's faith in the cult because it demonstrates they're not invincible, or it will make them worse because they'll call the isposniks martyrs."

"Perhaps we can control the messaging," Tallynd says, looking to Fintan, and he nods. "Where are the Citadel and Cloister located?"

"They're both on the west side of the city, and my people are mostly on the east side. I could show you in more detail if I had a map. I don't suppose you have a city map of Sveto Selo?"

They all shake their heads when Gondel translates, but then Fintan speaks up instead of Tallynd.

"I can make one. Have a cyclone fly me over the city. I'll memorize it and draw a map."

Tallynd orders it immediately and my jaw drops. I remember hearing that some people blessed with the Third Kenning have perfect memories, but I've never thought about how that might be applied in war.

"Leaping ahead, then," Tallynd says. "Let us suppose that
the Citadel and Cloister are successfully destroyed. Your organization would have freedom to take power—and maybe
others would as well. What would happen then? What would
your people do with a chance to lead?"

"First, I don't know of any organization other than ours—
but that doesn't mean they don't exist. As for us, I'm not privy
to all the plans of leadership, except that the death cult would
be banned and we'd focus on reopening trade with Omesh so
we can get those bridges rebuilt."

"I know you said the bridges fell into the sea, but how?"

I shrug. "They got old and crumbled away—some of
them before I was born. The stone is still sitting at the bottom
of the ocean. The death cult doesn't pay attention to roads
and bridges. Their entire strategy has been to build temples,
stamp out the old faith, and store war matériel. Whenever a
bridge crumbled, the isposniks said it was Žalost's will, and
that was the end of it. We just moved to using ships for all
commerce between the islands. Which gave the cultists more
control, because everyone can walk but not everyone can get
on a ship."

"And your ship hulls are stained with kraken blood, aren't
they?"

"Yes."

"How did you get so much kraken blood?"

"They send out a boat into kraken-infested waters—which
means any direction, I guess. It's full of cultists willing to risk
their lives for the cause. They carry harpoons tied to winches
onshore—and more cultists wait there. When the kraken tentacles rise up to crush the boats, they shoot their harpoons
into the tentacles. As long as three hit, they can usually reel
the kraken into shore and slay it with a ballista strike. The
blood from one kraken can protect up to twenty boats.
Plus—I hate to admit it—I had it one time, and kraken meat

is delicious. I mean, it's chewy, and you have to work at it, but it's more interesting than porridge."

"Okay, that's enough to move on. Fintan and Koesha, get on the map detail please. Once we have that, we can start planning an assault, Temblor Priyit. I want two more Kaurian cyclones scouting their warships. In the meantime, we need to get the fleet turned around and moving in that direction. We've done all we can here."

They tell me they'd like me to stay on but offer to return me to shore if I wish, and it's an unexpected moral dilemma. If I do return, I might be able to warn my family that the cult will be coming for them soon—in case Radič and Milenka don't do it for me for whatever reason. But warning them might do me no good at all: They might turn me in themselves and beg for mercy. It's a more likely outcome than them deciding to abandon the farm to seizure by the cult. There's no way for me to know where their loyalties truly lie. If I don't return, they might all be dead tomorrow or else screaming and spitting up blood in a torture cell somewhere. But I also might be able to help this allied group of nations topple a poisonous government that would sacrifice us all so long as they can continue to rule. Damn the death cult and all their minions.

I feel, in the end, that I must put everyone's families above my own. Perhaps that makes me a monster. Perhaps I'll live to regret it and hate myself for the rest of my days, whether I get seven or seven thousand of them.

Looking up at Tallynd with tears welling in my eyes, I say, "I want to stay and help."

FINTAN

The Spy in the Sky

When I first came to Pelemyn, I was held in deep suspicion by the pelenaut's lung, Föstyr du Bertrum. A bard's abilities made me a suspected spy at minimum, an assassin at worst. The mariner bodyguards surrounding the pelenaut almost gutted me. But spying had never been my mission, except in the most passive sense. I had always been intended as an ambassador of goodwill between allies that had suffered tremendous losses against a common enemy.

And in truth I'd never wanted to be a spy. But the prospect of an aerial scout of an enemy capital city sounded exciting.

But first we had to leave Riba Oči with a few choice words, using Gondel Vedd to deliver a message that the second könstad wished them to hear. She wanted to emphasize again that we had struck only military targets and tried to save lives wherever possible, and she also warned them that they would soon be cut off from the northern islands, so they should make arrangements to get what supplies they could now.

"Why tell them ahead of time?" Temblor Priyit asked. "Word's going to spread to the capital before we can get there."

"I hope it will," Tallynd said. "There's going to be a certain amount of chaos and fear, which will work in our favor. They will also try to rally what defenses they have in Eel Bay and call in reinforcements to the capital. We want them concentrated in one spot so that we can defeat them all and not have to deal with an extended campaign to crush their outposts on the islands."

"I doubt it will be such favorable conditions as here," the temblor replied. "We are going to have to fight through streets to reach the targets, and they will outnumber us. Typically the attackers need to have superior numbers."

"I am hoping that our kennings can compensate for our disadvantage in numbers. I will want to consult you and the Mynstad du Möcher on tactics once we have a map."

"Anything I should be looking for in particular, Temblor Priyit?" I asked.

"Yes. If the Citadel or Cloister can be approached with a minimum of street fighting, as we did here at Riba Oči, I'd like to know that. And if we must fight through the streets, how narrow are they, how many of the buildings are multistory, and are there any parks where we can take advantage of the open space?"

"Got it."

"And we want to know if you see any naval defenses and some likely places where we can establish a beachhead," the second könstad added.

We all took a break to eat, because we were quite frankly exhausted and Koesha needed to replenish her strength before flying again; there was also much to do to get the fleet turned around and sailing out of the bay. But the leaders were clear they wanted this scouting to happen today, to allow time for me to create a map and for them to study it and plan their strategy.

While Tallynd went above with Temblor Priyit to engage in the crafting and receiving of numerous messages, checking in on Abhi and others, I was left in the cabin of the Seven-Year Ship with Gondel Vedd, my lifebond, Numa, and the Eculan woman named Fanje.

Numa and I were mostly listening and trying to absorb as much of the Eculan language as possible; looking ahead, the alliance would need more than a single speaker of the language, and even if we did not wind up returning to the country, we could teach others back home if we learned enough.

Fanje was very curious about the food we ate and our Jereh bands and everything—and we, of course, were curious about her. She told us that we needed to try a beverage called kafa—similar to tea in that it was an infusion of plant material in hot water, but quite different in that they were a specific kind of dried and roasted beans rather than leaves. We told her that she needed to try the Good Shit.

Distilled spirits weren't really popular or well known in Ecula, it turned out; they had their ales and wines but few potent potables beyond a clear liquor distilled from sad potatoes.

Her family was into growing kafa beans, and she started to talk about her farm but trailed off in the middle of a sentence, her eyes seeing something that wasn't there. Numa recognized what was happening before I did.

"Ask if her family is safe, Gondel," she said. And when he did, her eyes filled with tears, and she sobbed and shook her head. It was her belief that the cult would find out she helped us today and her family would pay the price as early as this evening, and if not then, first thing in the morning.

"We might be able to do something about that," I said. "Are they far away? Would they come with us if we sent some cyclones there to pick them up?"

"No. They would never leave the farm. If they abandon it, the cult will seize it and sell it to someone else. They'd rather die. And they probably will."

"Is there nothing we can do?"

She looked desolate. "I told Radič and Milenka to warn them, so if they do, my family can make their own decisions. Maybe if they hide for a few days, the cult will be too busy with other things to rob them of their land. The best way to help is just . . . win."

"That's the plan. We're grateful for your help. We'll need more of it when we return."

Koesha picked me up when we were still trying to navigate our way out of the bay. She had an interesting tubular pack at her left hip, the strap slung diagonally across her torso. It appeared to be made of lava-dragon hide, and I kind of wanted one. She noticed me looking and thought I was interested in the contents rather than the pack itself.

"Hollit insisted on making us some refreshment since this could be a longer trip and I'll need a break. I don't even know what's in here, but she says it's a meal for two, drinks included."

Having had the privilege of spending some time on the *Nentian Herald*, I frowned and said, "Can she even fit in the galley of your ship?"

"No, she made it on the deck. We brought her the ingredients and a cutting board, and magic happened. Ready?"

"Yes."

"Okay. Once we get there, let me know with arm motions if you need to see something closer or see something again. We'll figure it out." And then she gave me a pair of goggles to wear, which was a good call.

I tried to be nonchalant about flying. For about, oh, twenty seconds, until we were well away from the fleet and they couldn't hear me, I was super nonchalant. And then, I guess, I was . . . chalant. Very chalant. I whooped and hollered, and Koesha laughed at me.

I smiled for about three leagues, until I got a bug in my teeth. Koesha laughed at me again, and I kept my mouth closed but kept smiling with my lips locked tight after that, because it was wonderful to fly, to skim over the tops of trees and startle birds and see people point at us in alarm and wonder as we sliced through the air above them.

We were flying almost due east, on a heading that would supposedly take us straight to Sveto Selo. The fleet would have to sail north and then navigate the straits to get there, a process that would take days, but it was a much quicker trip as the zephyr flies.

Once we got to Eel Bay, the canvas of sails lit by the afternoon sun directed our attention to their shipping—some of them merchant vessels, many of them trawlers with their nets, but nothing I could see that was obviously military in design. It illustrated that there was plenty of activity in the bay but nothing that would threaten us.

The city of Sveto Selo itself was another story. It looked tremendously threatening, simply by being larger than any city I'd seen before. The ports extended all along its front, and there were indeed some boats there that looked like they could fight, but it was a bustling place of commerce, of comings and goings. Ferries played a huge part in that, shipping people and livestock and other goods to the southern islands. Maybe they were shipping to Brda and Slivovi too, though I thought it might be simpler and cheaper to send things overland and just take ferries at the straits.

The city walls were comparable to any that might exist in our nations, but the sprawl of buildings outside them dwarfed anything I had ever seen. It meant that even if we could flank them on one side and approach the west walls near the Citadel and Cloister, we'd face a fight through the streets no matter what. And since the Eculans were tall, they built tall—even their single-story buildings would provide an effective height from which to rain missiles down on us, and there were few single-story affairs. They liked to build up, space being at a premium on the island. Most were two or three stories high, and within the city walls were several towering structures.

The Citadel and Cloister were unmistakable. The Citadel had its own walls and towers and was surrounded by a moat. The Cloister was secured in the northwest corner, on grounds guarded by an interior wall with only one gate. A grueling battle in the streets looked unavoidable, no matter how we approached it, but perhaps the military minds would have a better grasp of what I was seeing and how to exploit it. I just had to give them the most accurate intelligence possible. Koesha flew me in circles around the city several times to make sure I could take it all in. There were a few small parks here and there but nothing that screamed to me of a strategic advantage, except for perhaps the gentle grassy slope that led up to the old temple of all the gods, on the eastern side of the city. That wouldn't help us achieve our goals in the west, however.

I gestured that we should fly over the outskirts of the city so that I could memorize those layouts too; there was no telling where the military minds might choose to attack. Off to the western side of the city—but curiously outside the walls and beyond some rather disheveled housing and tradecraft sites—there was a river flowing into the bay. It was clearly navigable, since there were ships in it, and that might prove to be open to an amphibious operation.

Once beyond the sprawl of the city's outskirts, the farmland and pastures finally began. White and off-white dots on green carpet hinted at sheep and goats, and I signaled to Koesha that we should go down to one of those spots and rest. She nodded enthusiastically at the idea, her face somewhat strained, and wafted us down to a lonely tree spreading its canopy over a hill. The leaves whooshed and waved at our approach, and some very light-tan creatures scattered before us—they were sheep, not goats as I'd thought, though they were a different kind than I'd ever seen.

The rams had four horns that grew in front of the ears, and instead of curling around behind their heads in a sort of nautilus shape, the top two splayed up and out like antennae, pointing forward slightly, and the bottom two curved forward like sideburns running down a man's jaw. They looked incredibly dangerous, but the rams showed no signs of wishing to charge. There were no shepherds visible, and no one raised an alarm about our arrival. We had time to take a break and would have ample warning of anyone's approach.

"How are you holding up?" I asked her. She was clutching her side like she had a stitch there.

"That was . . . a lot. It's been a long day and I've relied on my kenning quite a bit. It started with Hollit this morning, you know. So I'm feeling it."

"I'm sorry. If it makes you feel any better, I have everything I need. I can make a detailed map when we return."

"That does help a little," she agreed, then looked down at her cylindrical tote made of lava-dragon hide. "I'm curious about what Hollit made for us. Plus I'm very hungry."

"Yeah, that would be gems."

"Pardon me?"

I had strayed into vernacular and apologized with a shrug and a wry grin. "Raelech slang that probably doesn't make a lot of sense when translated into Nentian."

We took another look around before sitting down in the cool grass: all clear. Koesha sighed in satisfaction and flicked a little metal tag that dangled from a dark stripe of metal circling the end of the bag. "Have you ever seen these? Zippers. Hathrim invention. Hollit told me they make them where she's from in Sardrik."

I gasped and then said, "Gasp!" aloud for emphasis. Koesha pulled on the metal tag, and it made a pleasant ripping noise as it released the teeth, unsealing the tote, which turned out to be insulated and packed with ice and six cloth-wrapped glass jars with metal screw-top lids. Two of the jars contained liquid, and the other four contained food.

"Hollit calls this a 'jar lunch,' and normally it serves one Hathrim. But it's also perfect for two tiny people like us. So what do we have here?"

It turned out to be Mistmaiden Ale in the jars from the Siren's Call in Pelemyn, and the main course was raw black-mack fillets twisted into artful rosettes, with ginger root sliced so thin it was translucent, accompanied by a cold salad of pickled veggies. So simple and refreshing—and entirely unheated. A silent, delicious reminder from Hollit that she was first a chef and secondarily blessed with the First Kenning. I was sorry for making her feel bad earlier, even though it wasn't a conscious thing on my part. It behooved me to be more mindful of my demeanor so that I did not hurt feelings unintentionally.

The sheep, seeing that we had no intentions of eating them or their grass, decided that we could safely be ignored and went back to grazing. A soft wind whispered in the leaves above us, shaking a few loose, and Koesha stared at them as they fell in twirling patterns to the ground.

"That's us," she said, pointing. "Leaves on the wind. All falling beautifully, tragically, to our deaths, each a unique journey to the same end. And what a journey for us, eh? I would not have thought I would be in Ecula, eating black-mack prepared by a fire demon, with a Raelech, on a hilltop that has never known war. I did not even know Raelechs existed until that day we met."

"It's been quite a journey, I agree," I said around a mouthful. "But if you don't mind me saying, you should probably not call Hollit a fire demon. I have met people who qualify—Winthir Kanek's fury, Pinter Stuken, filled out the cloak of that name well. But Hollit is not a demon of any kind."

She chewed for a while, thinking it over. Eventually she said, "That is true. And Olet isn't a demon either. I haven't been thoughtful. It's difficult to let go of what you're taught when you're young. But I should make that effort now that I know better."

"Aye."

"It's why Shoawei encourages exploration and travel. There is nothing like it to show you how narrow your scope was before. If you stay at home, you are never challenged. Difficult to grow."

"I agree. Do you think these sheep are the ones that produce the wool you like so much? I have my doubts."

"Me too. It looks too coarse to me."

"When we were flying, these were the off-white ones, and from a distance I thought they were goats. But I saw some others that looked bright white nearby. Maybe just over the hill?"

"Okay. We can go look. But we should probably start back after that. I mean, after . . . you know. I pee."

"Right."

She cocked an eyebrow at me. "Don't you have to?"

"Oh, goddess, yes. Especially now that you said something."

Koesha laughed. "We might be written about in histories someday," she said, "but no one will write down how inconvenient it is to pee far from home."

"I think that may be a large part of how legends are made. In most stories, no one does anything but bleed."

"Too true."

After we had finished our jar lunch and returned the containers to the lava-dragon tote, we wandered in different directions to empty our bladders, then met again to seek out the other kind of sheep we'd seen from above. A pleasant walk led us over the hill to a slope dotted with them. They were significantly different.

Their horns curled back from their heads like the sort of sheep I was used to seeing, but their wool—oh, my. It was incredibly dense and floofy. I studied a ram for a while as he studied us, and Koesha asked me if I was playing some kind of dominance game.

"No, no. Just memorizing. I want to get it right."

"Get what right?"

"These are two new species of sheep to us. Which means Abhi's never seen them before. He's going to love hearing about them."

"Aw, that's nice to think of him. Ready?"

"If you are. Rested enough?"

"As good as I'm going to be. A straight push shouldn't be too bad. It's the circling that wears me out."

We flew west, squinting against the sun settling into the sea, and I worried that we wouldn't get back before dark. If we couldn't see the fleet, what would we do? What if we overshot and wound up flying over the ocean until Koesha became too exhausted to use her kenning anymore and we just dropped into the abyss and crabs ate us and . . .

It's disturbing how easily my mind can conjure disasters now.

My apprehension grew as the sun slid lower and lower and we hadn't reached the fleet yet. I wasn't sure how much we'd be able to see during full dark—the moon wasn't full, and the sky was partly cloudy and would obscure what dim illumination the stars could provide.

But fire smoke soon told us we were getting close to the bay, and we flew over Riba Oči as the sun was a red half-coin on the horizon, and we rounded the tip of the peninsula at dusk. Koesha banked north, and we saw the white sails of the fleet in another couple of minutes. We landed on the Seven-Year Ship as darkness fell, and Koesha collapsed. It had been a taxing day for her, but she'd lost days or months, not years. And it was worth it. Or would be.

"The short version is, we can't avoid fighting in the city, but I can't make a decent map to show you on the ship," I told the second könstad. "If you can arrange a detail to take a stonecutter, Dervan, and me to shore at dawn, we'll get it finished by noon."

"Why a stonecutter?" she asked.

"To make us a quick writing table and chairs."

So it was arranged. Nara du Fesset took us to a beach of the peninsula in a landing craft at dawn, and a stonecutter molded a rough table and chairs for us to work on. Nara and

the stonecutter stood guard while we worked companionably, Dervan on his history and me on my map. My fingers
began to ache after a while from clutching the pen so tightly
to avoid mistakes, but I kept at it.

Dervan looked over as I leaned back and sighed, finished
with the majority of it. There was space at the top of the
page to fill, but I had plans for that.

"Clams and tentacles, Fintan, why are you going into such
detail? Is that the outline of every building?"

"Partially so that our military minds can craft the best
strategy possible. But mostly it's for you, Dervan. For history.
And the sheep are for Abhi."

"What sheep?"

I pointed to the room I'd left at the top of the page. "I'm
about to draw them now."

"Oh."

"I was talking to Fanje last night, to try to make sense of
something, and found her answers somewhat depressing."

"How so?"

"Well, from what we saw in the air, Sveto Selo is an impressive city. They might have had help from Omesh for
some of their infrastructure decades ago, but everything's
been built without the help of kennings for a long time now.
They are maximizing everything they have, and their land is
still beautiful outside the city. They have well-developed industry and trade, enough raw materials to make whatever
they need. So I asked her about the leather situation."

"The leather situation? I'm not sure what you mean."

"Maybe Raelechs are predisposed to look for it, since we
wear a lot of it. The Eculans have plenty of sheep and goats
and oxen, but none of their warriors wore any leather—not
even belts. And when we went to the lumber mill yesterday,
only one guy out of a hundred people had a leather belt.
Their armies wear fibers and bones, nothing else. I asked her
why."

"And?"

"She said that sheep and goatskin were useless as armor, but they're good for fancy clothes and other uses—and every single scrap of it is consumed by the rich and the clergy."

"Oh. So the people who invaded—"

"Were poor. Yes. Their bone armor is mostly made from sheep and goats."

"So if leather is an indicator of status in Ecula," Dervan mused, "the kraljic and the isposniks will probably be draped in it."

"No doubt."

Dervan gestured to the armor I was wearing. "You'd probably be considered very high class here, then."

"I suppose so. But I wouldn't want to be. Isn't it galling? This idea that the rich in Ecula hoard goods for themselves and instead of sharing and helping their fellows, they blame us, who live across the ocean, for every trial that the less fortunate face?"

"It is the nature of the rich to point fingers elsewhere when it is they who have shat in the well we all drink from," Dervan said.

I smiled at my Brynt friend. "A sentiment that Hanima Bhandury would agree with, no doubt."

"And Rölly. After that episode with the rich guy stealing food off the supply ships and listening to what Tamhan Khatri has done in Ghurana Nent, he's been considering the problem."

"The problem of rich people?"

"They're demonstrably destructive. So it's now part of his flow studies. I imagine we'll learn more soon. Have you heard any more about Hanima Bhandury and the rest? Maybe what happened to Suraji, the spider queen?"

"No," I replied, leaning forward and dipping my pen into the inkpot before beginning my first sketch of an Eculan sheep. "I've shared all I know. But I imagine we'll hear plenty from Ghurana Nent once their elections are held. I hope that Tamhan and Hanima will influence their politics—and everyone's—for a long time. I would like to live in a world where power is used only for moral, compassionate reasons."

"And our collective powers: Do you think we are using them morally right now?"

"It's a good question. I think the second könstad wants to preserve as many lives as she can while eliminating the threat to Brynlön. That's about as compassionate as she can be at the moment. Maybe they'll be willing to talk if we remove their leadership."

"I hear you. A peaceful solution is always preferable, but some fish heads will respond to nothing else but a spear to the brain—gravemaws and cultists occupying the top of that list."

Snorting, I said, "Let's hope Fanje is right and the support for the cult isn't as wide and deep as it seems."

As I sketched the sheep at the top of the page, I felt what I hoped was a modest amount of pride. I was not simply telling a story anymore but contributing to it. This map was going to help.

An Aerial Reference Map of

Sveto Selo

by Fintan, Master Bard of the Poet Goddess Kaelin

Mountain Sheep—
Bred for wool but
also meat, mostly
on hills of Brda

Behold my floof

Do not try to
milk me. It
will not go
well for
either of us.
I'm a ram,
kids

Lowland Sheep—
Prized for its milk
and cheese; wool
is of lower quality

Goat Market

The Woolens

Cloister

Featherdown

Hammerside

Citadel

Temple Hill

Inkpit

Fishskinning

Baitbucket

Black River

Cheese Wheel

North

Eel Bay

Map by Kevin Hearne

TALLYND

The Tentacles of the Kraken

When Gerstad du Fesset brought Fintan and Dervan back from their cartography project, I let Koesha know and she joined us for a command meeting in the cabin of the Seven-Year Ship. The bard grinned madly as he and Dervan scooched behind the table with Fanje, who sat across from Gondel Vedd, and then Fintan proudly presented his map of Sveto Selo, drawn from memory. Fanje was not the only one to widen her eyes.

There were sheep. One was extraordinarily fluffy and said, *Behold my floof.* But there was also an outline of every building within the city walls and outside it too—plus sketches of the Citadel, Cloister, and old temple.

"You utter fish head," I said. "Why did you go into such detail?"

Fintan shot a knowing grin at Dervan and replied, "For history. We could probably do with some labels, though. Perhaps our Eculan guest can help with names of neighborhoods, or even the names of these sheep."

Fanje told us first that the floofy one, the source of all the fine wool, was a mountain sheep that was native to Brda but could now also be found on Vlast, as they obviously had. The one with the four horns was a lowland sheep originally hailing from Slivovi; its wool was coarser, more affordable, and therefore worn by the majority of people, but it was also the source of a lot of cheese.

Once past that frivolous trivia, she gave us some actual intelligence. She skimmed her long index finger over portions of the map.

"Featherdown," she said, "the western half of the city, is where all the money and power are concentrated. Hammerside, to the east, is where the working people are, and they won't give you much trouble, unless of course they happen to be fanatic cultists. Most of them are more concerned with paying the bills."

The areas nearest the extensive port were divided into unappetizing districts called Fishskinning and Baitbucket. Outside the walls were districts named after the primary goods traded there: Goat Market, Cheese Wheel, the Woolens. Inkpit was of particular interest.

"This area is a terrible place to live. It's between the stench of the docks, where the gulls concentrate because of all the fish guts, and the nasty river water, which is undrinkable and full of shit by the time it gets there. So it smells, the houses are fire traps, and fire happens periodically because they are also doing volatile chemical stuff in that area. The air is terrible. The people are not particularly loyal to the cult—they are barely surviving, and they won't fight. That might make it seem like an ideal place to attack. But you have to watch out for the ballista towers. They have some kind of new shot that goes, uh . . . *pkkhh*." She splayed her fingers to indicate an explosion. "Starts out like the size of a melon, but when it hits it sprays little pieces of metal everywhere. Shreds people."

"You've seen them use this?" Gerstad du Fesset said.

"No, but I've seen the aftermath. They used it a few months ago to control a riot. It's made from something they mine on Slivovi. We haven't been able to figure out what it is yet. So start with the towers."

She pointed to the small circular bulges that periodically interrupted the thick black line of the city wall.

"They will put archers on the walls too, and they might just torch the district to slow you down. They've done it before—about five years ago they once shot incendiary rounds into buildings and set the district on fire."

"Why?" I asked.

Fanje shrugged. "There were several theories about their motives at the time, but in my opinion, they simply don't care if poor people die. Because the irrefutable fact is that they're assholes."

"So they do have archers."

"Yes. For defense. They don't tend to use them offensively, the reasoning being they consider it to be a lot of gear and food for limited utility."

"We didn't run into any archers at Riba Oči," Temblor Priyit pointed out.

"They didn't think it needed defending. Those guys were going to be the vanguard of the second invasion. But trust me, they have archers at Sveto Selo. And the bulk of the invasion force is there, because it's easier to feed and house and train them there than at Riba Oči."

"How many fighters?"

"Fifty thousand at least. They were going to conscript another fifty thousand and send them over with a sword in their hand and no training. The idea was to overwhelm the source of the Fourth Kenning, no matter what, because they sent ten thousand last time and it didn't work. They figured there would be no way Pelemyn could defend against a hundred thousand, even with the Fourth Kenning."

Bryn preserve us, no, we could not. It had taken all my effort just to dispatch the nearly one hundred boats they'd sent before. If I'd had to confront a thousand? It couldn't be done. Rölly and the other tidal mariners stationed at Pelemyn wouldn't be enough either against those kinds of numbers. Thank all the gods we'd prevented the invasion for the short term. But if they could muster that many fighters, we needed to do something about that, or they'd simply launch as soon as they could build more boats.

"Where are they?" I asked.

Fanje tapped the map. "Mostly in the Citadel, but lots of

them are being housed in individual homes because there isn't room for them all there. And there are more in the Cloister."

Temblor Priyit traced her finger along the length of the walls. "Is the ground salted underneath the walls?"

"No. Maybe?" Fanje's eyebrows knit together in confusion. "I don't know. Why?"

"To prevent the Third Kenning from undermining them. One of your armies was destroyed in open ground by a Raelech juggernaut. He effectively had the land swallow them up, simply buried them alive."

"Oh, I see—so the salt prevents them from moving the earth underneath the walls. Okay, yeah, it probably is salted. They wouldn't want to be vulnerable to Omesh."

I pointed to Fintan's illustration of the Citadel. "But there's an actual moat full of water surrounding the Citadel?"

"Aye," Fintan confirmed. "And the walls are stone."

Requiring more details, I pressed him. "So I presume there's a gate. What does that look like?"

"I confess I didn't examine it closely. I was flying high above it. Fanje might know."

Once she had the question relayed to her, Fanje nodded once. "There are large wooden gates with huge pulleys to operate them because they're so heavy."

"Are the doors mounted on hinges?"

"No, they're on rails. Two of them—one that slides across left to right, another right to left."

"Are they full of holes through which to fire arrows?"

"Solid. If you're worried about arrows, they'll come from above the gate. There's this platform for archers that's shielded so they can stand there and fire down without having to worry too much about return fire."

"So there are no holes in the wall either?"

"No."

"Very well. I think I have the beginnings of a plan, and I'll count on Temblor Priyit and others to craft details on top of the base. Fintan and Gondel, apologies in advance, I'll need you to translate a lot for our friends. Here's the plan."

I laid it out for them, leaving plenty of room on the back end for the temblor and other military leaders to improvise and adapt according to conditions, and Fanje had some suggestions about positioning in Eel Bay. Tweaks aside, it was agreed upon, and all we had to do then was keep scouting ahead of execution—well, that, and I had to confirm with Abhi that what I had in mind was even possible.

That turned out to be a longer and more difficult conversation than I anticipated, and in order to get him to agree, I had to ferry Fanje and Gondel Vedd over there so she could explain the Eculan procedures for hunting krakens and then making a stain for their hulls out of the blood. Once Abhi was satisfied, there was plenty of other work to do in anticipation of our arrival. I addressed the fleet in general, thanks to Fintan, but needed to send specific instructions to numerous leaders.

Around noon of the next day, we needed to address the large net across the strait that protected the bay from krakens. Kaurian cyclones flew Raelech stonecutters and a squad of guards to either side, where seven massive stone pylons sunk deep into the earth tethered the net and kept the tension strong. The top of the net was actually a tremendously dense braid of thick ropes anchored to those pylons, the redundancy a bulwark against failure. And understanding that these nets were the foundation of their safety and prosperity, the Eculans had stationed guards at the pylons. But they were bored and wholly unprepared for the excitement of having the Grynek Hunters drop down out of the sky on one side of the strait and the Mynstad du Möcher's elite unit drop down on the other. We didn't attack them: Our forces were just there to protect the stonecutters as they coolly dissolved the pylons, releasing the tension in the ropes. I think the primary conflict was a lot of shouting that we didn't understand.

Once the tethers were free, I ordered all available rapids to the area to drag the top of the net down, hastening what would otherwise have happened naturally. The bottom of the net was weighted, but the remainder of it could conceivably remain suspended in the strait for long enough to cause trouble. We wanted the passage free as soon as possible.

I let Abhi know immediately once I heard that the strait was clear. That was his cue to send in the krakens. He'd found two nearby, and he sent them ahead of us to clear the route with very specific instructions: They were to attack only boats stained with kraken blood, specifically targeting what they would have otherwise ignored, because those boats were the ones the Eculans wanted to be able to sail anywhere. Since the Eculans wanted their kraken-hunting boats to be attacked, those were not painted, but their naval boats were all stained. Thus the krakens would attack only those ships that were threats to us, leaving all their merchant and civilian fleet alone.

Those civilian boats might wind up getting used against us when the Eculans realized they had no other options, but at least it would allow us to navigate the straits without getting tied up in a naval battle.

There were lighthouses and small defensive forts along the straits that we had to take to prevent them firing upon us or raising the alarm—not that they weren't already alarmed by our attack on Riba Oči. We simply did not wish their leaders to know how close we were. The mynstad's squad or the Grynek Hunters took care of them for us on a rotating basis. But we weren't going to make it all the way to Sveto Selo in a day and the cyclones needed rest, so we spent the night anchored, out of sight, and Abhi had the krakens guard our fleet before and behind. I went to visit him before getting some sleep, and he said that they'd destroyed more than one

but less than ten ships with kraken-blood hulls—the creatures hadn't realized we'd want numbers and didn't pay attention to how many they'd smashed into driftwood.

When dawn broke, it struggled against a gray sky. That
was fitting, I supposed: No sun should shine on what we
would do. Part of me knew full well that we needed to balance the scales that Žalost—or Sedam—had tilted danger-
ously askew; at least, we did if we wished to have a secure
future. But at that moment I really didn't want to be the
weight that pushed it down in our favor. Viewed from outside, it was something that absolutely needed to happen, except that for it to happen I had to make the decision to act, to
open a sluice and let the force of water do its work, and
whether it was vengeance or justice didn't matter, because
either way it was death.

There was water below us and water above. Water without and water within. Water spilling from my eyes when I
thought of my boys. And more when I thought of my husband, who warned me years ago that the peace we used to
enjoy would have to be paid for one day.

We had been paying for it since the day the Bone Giants
invaded, but we'd pay much more today, and so would they.

Gerstad Nara du Fesset joined me at the railing with a cup
of tea cooling in her palms. She didn't say anything at first,
just stood in companionable silence, looking out over the
bow with me, her face grim in my peripheral vision.

Eventually she muttered, "Today is going to be sewage."

"Agreed. I hope we'll be here to remark upon the day tomorrow."

She had no reply for that.

"Nara, in case—"

"No," she cut me off. "None of that. Pardon me, Tallynd,
for speaking to you as a friend and not an officer right now.
You're going to do what needs to be done and live. That is
all."

I closed my eyes, took a deep breath, and exhaled. "I feel like we're caught in a whirlpool as deep as the abyss and there's no escape for any of us."

"We'll go to the bottom together and swim out from there."

"You're right. There's no choice but to see how deep this goes. Thank you. Give the order to get the fleet moving. If we have to paddle through sewage today, best to get it over with."

Fintan broadcast the order soon enough, and then the anchors were pulled up and sails billowed as the cyclones got us moving again. I checked in with Ahbi and his friend, Leisuen, to make sure they were awake and alert. I shouldn't have worried: The poor boy hardly slept. They both gave me a distant thumbs-up.

A Kaurian ship called the *Shearwater* sailed next to us, and a few cyclones began to ferry items from the cabin of the Seven-Year Ship to the *Shearwater*'s cabin. All of the maps and gear, everything of value, was transferred over there, because it would soon be our new flagship. I could have picked any of a number of Kaurian ships to do the job, but I liked the name.

Once Sveto Selo hove into view, I could appreciate what Fintan had expressed: It was large and sprawled far outside the walls. The ballista towers looked dangerous.

The bulk of the fleet dropped anchor at the river while we sailed ahead with the Seven-Year Ship, the *Nentian Herald*, and the *Shearwater*, plus Abhi's small boat.

Once in front of the city, a flurry of landing craft shuttled most of the crew off our ship and onto the *Shearwater*, including Fanje, and brought Abhi, Koesha, and Hollit Panevik to the Seven-Year Ship. Fintan and Gondel Vedd were already aboard with me, so there were only six of us remaining, plus Nara, before she dove into the space between the ships and started manipulating the water to move the ships around, in a way that would be impossible without a kenning. It was a precise pivot in tandem so that we faced the myriad docks of Sveto Selo, the width of a ship between us.

The docks were lined with Eculan soldiers and spectators. There were more pale faces staring at us from roofs and windows in the city—hundreds, maybe thousands of them—and more from the decks of ships.

Once our ships were in position and Nara surfaced in front of us, with a wave signal that we were good and she'd keep us in place, I told Abhi it was time. He dove overboard gracelessly and flailed to the surface, whereupon Nara seized him with her kenning and made sure the water supported him.

"Thanks," he gasped, one of the few Brynt words he knew.

"Okay?" I shouted down to him. Thumbs up. I turned to Gondel Vedd and Fintan. "Showtime, gentlemen."

Gondel's voice being broadcast to Sveto Selo and all its surroundings—we were fairly certain Fintan's full range would reach everyone—was the signal for the ships in the rear of the fleet to start filling up landing craft and rowing toward the river and the Inkpit district.

The scholar repeated some of the things he'd said at Riba Oči—introducing us in broad terms and listing the crimes of the unprovoked Eculan invasion. He mentioned that all their armies had been destroyed overseas, as had their entire fleet at Riba Oči and their shipyards and lumber mill. The second invasion wouldn't happen—in fact, it was they who were being invaded.

Abhi was waiting for a very specific cue, and Gondel looked down at him and waved to make sure he didn't miss it: the Eculan word for *kraken*.

"There are now krakens in Eel Bay, cutting you off from the southern islands. They are under our full control. If you look at the first two ships directly facing you now, you'll see a demonstration of that. The ship on your right is the Seven-

Year Ship your faithful went searching for. I know many of you recognize it from the last time it was here. It took the seventy-seven and seven faithful to Žalost, and he turned them all to wraiths—he hasn't blessed anyone in many years. He told us this himself and spoke to us at length. But by withholding the Seven-Year Ship from you, your leaders were able to use that as an excuse to launch an unprovoked attack on us. And in so doing, the Sixth Kenning was finally revealed. Our plaguebringer can command the animals of the world to obey his will. Behold."

And what they beheld was a kraken surfacing between our ships, slowly, magnificently, horrifically. We could hear the exclamations from the city travel across the water. They are not handsome creatures, bulbous and black as the abyss with orange and yellow eyes. And Abhi was elevated atop a tentacle, the end of it curled around like a pedestal so that he stood upon it with his legs spread for stability. His feet were surreptitiously held in place by suckers; there was no way he could topple over. To add a bit of flash, I pulled out the water from his clothes and hair in all directions, so that he shimmered briefly and his long hair poufed around his head rather than hanging like damp moss from his skull.

Distant rumblings of astonishment from the city could be heard at this spectacle, and Gondel continued.

"The krakens now know that all hulls stained with kraken blood are to be immediately destroyed. We have, in fact, destroyed your naval defenses, if you were not already aware. And there is more to come."

At this point, we all needed to contribute to the spectacle— the sort of thing no one had ever seen before—to make it clear that we were not going to be defeated by the same old tactic of overwhelming force.

Another enormous tentacle rose from the water, curled and flattened, and waited amidships for me to step onto it. Once my feet were in place, it shifted slightly, I felt suction

against my boots, and then I was moved steadily away from
the ship until I hovered next to Abhi near the other ship. This
process was repeated for Koesha, who admirably showed no
fear of it considering her past with krakens, then for Gondel
and Fintan. Hollit was last, but because she was so large and
required more support, each foot was balanced on a tentacle.
So six people on seven tentacles were held aloft above a krak-
en's head. I wished I could have seen it from the Eculans'
point of view, because it probably looked awesome.

"Six kennings are here to confront the evil of the seventh.
Against our combined powers you have no hope of victory.
Yet we are not here to slaughter everyone, as you tried to do
to us. Surrender and reject the lies of Žalost. Return to the
old faith, or whatever faith you wish, and we can be friends.
But one way or another, the cult of Žalost ends today. And it
begins with the burning of the Seven-Year Ship."

Gondel nodded to Hollit, giving her a cue, and she lit her
left arm on fire before using it to direct a gout of flames at the
Seven-Year Ship. Nara gently pulled the ship away once it
caught, and it was left to smoke and burn until it sank.

The scholar continued after an appropriate pause for people to take in what Hollit was doing. Fanje had coached him
on some of it. "I know many of you despise the cult. You remember the days before it came to power and replaced a life
of contentment with one of grievance. You want to live without fear again, without constant harassment by the watch or
worry about being reported to svećenici. Today is the day.
Fight the cult with us, or at least stay out of the way as we
take them down.

"To the kraljic and the isposniks: You have a half hour
from now to deliver your complete surrender. Otherwise
you will die today. We hope you will choose wisely and preserve many lives. Very shortly, we will deliver a small taste of
what will happen if you do not. We regret the violence to
come and wish the cult leaders had not brought us to this

place. Regardless, once the cult of Žalost is defeated, we look forward to being friends with a free Ecula."

Abhi had the kraken deliver us one by one to the deck of the *Shearwater*, whereupon the creature sank from sight, presumably to get out from under the impending wreckage of the Seven-Year Ship.

Someone handed Hollit a bow and a quiver of Raelech-made fire arrows. The heads were like the puffy seedpods of cattails, cylindrical and red-brown, a pasty and flammable substance that, once alight, would continue to burn until the fuel was spent, even in water.

Koesha Gansu sailed aloft, high above our ship and out of bowshot range, and signaled to Hollit that she was ready. The giantess nocked a fire arrow, aimed it vaguely upward, and pulled back on the string. She used her kenning to ignite the arrow, then let it fly.

Once the arrow was in the air, Koesha took over. Summoning a tight gust of wind, she guided the arrow precisely to the nearest ballista tower, which would otherwise be used against us very shortly. The arrow sank home into the wood of the ballista, whereupon Hollit reached out and encouraged those flames to spread and grow hotter. From a distance, the nest of that tower blossomed like a cheerful springtime flower, almost celebratory, but it was a violent demonstration of our power that everyone in the city could see. They needed to know we were not simply talking about the first six kennings but were willing and able to use them.

There were six more of those ballista towers along the western wall, which would be able to fire when we made our approach, so we would have to take them all out. We were going to land in the Inkpit district and along the riverbank to approach the Citadel from that direction. The landing craft were already on their way, because even if the Eculans surrendered—which we doubted very much—we would still have to remove the kraljic and isposniks from power. They needed to answer for their crimes.

Hollit and Koesha methodically took out the towers, while some boats full of Bone Giants made the foolish decision to approach us in civilian craft, swords at the ready. Since they were the sort we'd asked the kraken to leave alone, Abhi had to modify his orders to direct that those particular vessels needed to be destroyed. Koesha returned to the deck to wait out the remainder of the half hour. Gondel periodically reminded the Eculans that they had a certain number of minutes remaining to surrender. We just wanted to make it very clear that they had a choice, even though we knew what they would choose. Kaurian scouts were already reporting the deployment of forces to meet us on the west side, with archers lining the tops of the walls. They didn't try to put out the ballista fires, but since the flames wouldn't spread from the towers, they were contained losses.

The half hour passed, and Gondel announced that we'd be removing the kraljic and isposniks from power shortly. But we'd need the Inkpit cleared of civilians first, so everyone in that district had to evacuate immediately. This was greeted by jeers and defiant roars—which was fine. Hollit started a fire on the rooftops nearest the bay and then pushed it just a few streets over, so that people got the message to leave now. As soon as Kaurian cyclones confirmed that people were streaming out of the district and into the city, Hollit snuffed the flames. Temblor Priyit and the combined allied forces would land and make battlefield decisions from there. I was waiting for a different report and assumed it would come later, but it came very quickly as the Kaurian cyclone Mardan Vess swooped down to say, "They've closed the Citadel gates, Second Könstad."

"So soon? Has it been emptied?"

"No. If anything, it's filled up. They're preparing for a battle once we breach the outer walls. Protecting their kraljic."

The Citadel had impressive defenses—its own towers and battlements—and there were huge dormitories on one side and no doubt extensive underground facilities as well. There was a large central courtyard that functioned as a parade ground or training area, much like our facilities in Pelemyn. But what interested me were the windows in the dorms facing the courtyard: There were quite a lot of them, with only thin panes of glass to protect against rain. Reconnaissance by Kaurian cyclones revealed that the top floor was given over to offices—most likely for the kraljic and his official cronies and military leaders—while the lower levels were all dormitory-style rooms with multiple bunks in each to house soldiers.

"Inform your friends, then. It's time to do the windows."

"Aye, Second Könstad," she said, then flew off. Apart from scouting, the Kaurians would do this much in the way of war: They'd fire arrows at glass panes and break them. No one targeted. Any harm done to an individual would be completely accidental. And anyone inside would have a chance to escape what would come next, so technically the Kaurians were doing nothing more than target practice.

Except I was going to do my best to ensure that the chances to escape were very slim.

Once I saw the cyclones converge above the docks and fire toward the Citadel, using their kenning to guide the arrows unerringly to their targets, I nodded to Koesha.

"Let's go."

She summoned winds and abruptly I was airborne, and it was only partially the pressure of the wind on my face that made tears stream from my eyes. It was mostly the knowledge that I was about to do something that would trigger a severe debt from my kenning; my organs quailed from the anticipated pain.

Whether the debt would be more than I could pay I wouldn't learn until afterward. Physically I was already in my fifties; how much life did I have to sacrifice and remain alive?

These might be the last moments of my time.

Koesha flew us high over the city. Some arrows were launched our way, but they never got close—she made sure of that.

Looking down into the bowl of the Citadel, I saw that it was filled with soldiers, and the walls teemed with archers, bristling with challenge and determined to defend their leader—which was the same thing we would do. Some of those young men were devoted to the cult, some were conscripts, but all of them were the great hopes of their mothers, and I felt that deeply. But they were also the means by which evil men clung to power—men who would order them to kill us all if they could. So to remove those men from power, and to save as many lives on our side as possible, I had no choice.

The wide moat surrounding the Citadel, green with algae, contained more than enough water to fill up that courtyard, and they had clearly not thought about the possibility. The chances of a tidal mariner coming to the Citadel, after all, had been very low until they attacked us.

I pulled the water from all four directions and directed it to the center, the force of it sweeping everyone off the walls to tumble into an enormous cauldron, the incredible weight of all that water crashing down upon the soldiers inside. As it fell in, the deluge would necessarily push out from there and bowl the soldiers over, propelling them into the interior walls. If they did not perish from impact, they'd have to be very good swimmers to avoid drowning as the water continued to pour in and fill the Citadel. The thick gates were letting some of it out underneath, but they were holding. And the water kept coming. It rose to the top of the bowl, and I made sure to push plenty of it through those top windows, where the kraljic's offices might be. Let him be drowned in his place of power. Even if I missed him—there was a corner tower on the northeast side that rose above the rest, and he might be in there—he'd have no one to give orders to. Dumping the

moat on top of the Citadel would either kill him or neutralize him, and everyone nearby who saw it happen would
know that.

Of course, the kraljic might be taking shelter elsewhere.
But he'd be able to command next to nothing, wherever he
was. I had just taken out a third of his forces and most of his
command structure.

I did not even know his name and had purposely never
asked Fanje for it, though she had to know what it was. He
had callously ordered our deaths a year ago, caring nothing
about our names, so I did not want to write his name down
in history. He should be washed away forever, his bones
picked over by crabs, his legacy a silent failure. I would grieve
the people he goaded into war, but not him.

If I lived.

Satisfied that I had done all I could, the Citadel not so
much a fortress as a churning bowl of green soup with pale
bodies floating in it, I stopped channeling the force of my
kenning and faced the consequences.

The toll of years was more severe than anything I'd experienced before. However many years it was, *that* many years
of skin cells exploded off my body, a literal cloud of dust that
abandoned me, and it took all my hair with it, leaving me
cold and causing Koesha to cough before it was blown away
in her winds. But my skin wasn't the only organ that abruptly
aged. Everything else did too—piercing lances in my eyes as
the light faded from them, a drill through my kidneys, a
clutching tightness in my chest, a convulsing of my muscles,
and a horrifying loosening of my bowels that I was helpless
to stop.

I was helpless to do anything, in fact, but scream for a few
seconds before it ended.

NARA DU FESSET

No Victory in Death

I watched it all happen from the water—Tallynd, I mean, and her epic feat of dry direction. That she was even capable of it boggled my mind; I could never move that much water all at once.

She had undertaken the task knowing it could mean her death, especially since Culland du Raffert had demonstrated the sort of penalty incurred when moving such masses of water at Göfyrd. But he had pulled an entire bay into the city walls there, and this was pulling a moat into a building, however large.

It was a risky move but one she felt she had to take. Fornish greensleeves couldn't take out the Citadel, and we had no juggernauts or furies or tempests, so it was down to either her or Abhi, and she couldn't bring herself to ask Abhi to do that. He'd done so much already, and we needed him for the return trip home, because the krakens would still be patrolling the ocean no matter what. He was therefore ordered back to his smaller boat with Leisuen, protecting the fleet.

I cried out when I thought she was lost, because she convulsed and there was some kind of cloudy explosion around her that looked like she was dissolving. But, no, she remained, in obvious pain from a severe kenning debt. She passed out in midair, now bent and frail, and Koesha carefully cradled her in her arms and flew her back to the *Shearwater*. I hastily sleeved myself over there and climbed aboard, reaching the deck almost at the same time as Koesha and Tallynd.

The second könstad looked near death and was unconscious until they landed, whereupon she jerked back to life with a shuddering, ragged gasp that was a prelude to a keening wail of agony. Her eyes were clouded, and her hair had fallen out. Her beautiful brown skin had gone dull and paper thin, wrinkled and spotted with age, and her hands curled into arthritic claws; I doubted she could fend off an attack from a tadpole.

"Tallynd! Tallynd. You did it. Just hold on and rest. We'll get you home."

She couldn't reply. She could do nothing but wheeze, struggling against the waves of pain crashing inside her, all her body in crisis. She was still partially cradled against Koesha, who had knelt on the deck to let Tallynd rest there.

Koesha shook her head and said something to Tallynd in Joabeian, which meant no one aboard could understand it, not even Scholar Vedd. Then, while supporting Tallynd's head and neck in her left arm, she took the old woman's withered hand in her right, clutched it, and shut her eyes hard and said something else.

I didn't understand what was happening until a few seconds later, when Tallynd's breathing improved with a deep lungful and her eyes began to clear. At the same time, Koesha was clenching her teeth and sucking wind hard and exhaling between breaths, almost like she was in labor.

Tallynd figured it out at the same time I did: Koesha was using the Seventh Kenning. Sedam had made her a balm, and now she was sacrificing her own life for a woman she'd just met a few weeks ago.

"What? Koesha, no! Stop!" Tallynd said. "That's enough! Stop!"

Koesha let go and screamed, rolling over onto her side and curling up with what looked like severe abdominal cramps. A significant audience had gathered by that time, demanding explanations and offering help, and Fintan knelt down next to Koesha, and asked her something in Nentian. She took a few more quick breaths before grunting out a reply, which he translated for the rest of us.

"Ten years," the bard announced.

"She gave me . . . ten years?" Tallynd said. She was still much older-looking than before she left the ship, but she seemed alert and was propping herself up now.

Koesha muttered some more and Fintan translated. "She also healed you at the same time. So the net result is that you are older than you were, but you're healthy for that age."

Tears began leaking out of Tallynd's eyes, and she crawled over to Koesha. "There are no words to express how grateful I am. Time is so precious. Thank you, Koesha. Please tell her, Fintan."

He did, and Koesha nodded and then pushed herself upright with a groan. I helped Tallynd to her feet while Fintan helped Koesha, and then they embraced and cried. Koesha said something that Fintan translated for us.

"You had to do what you did. And so did I."

They both cried harder after that.

Koesha did look older, some lines cut deeper into her face, some shadows underneath her eyes, some loosening of the skin underneath her jaw. But she mostly looked exhausted, and Tallynd told her to go rest, she was done. The zephyr nodded weakly when Fintan translated, and she was led to the cabin. But our second könstad returned her attention to the invasion, because it was proceeding in earnest.

"We've done most all we can. There will be no easy resolution now. Even with the Citadel drowned, we are still outnumbered, and we must fight and win."

"Must we?" Gondel Vedd asked. "Can we not lay siege until they surrender?"

The second könstad regarded him kindly, knowing it wasn't a challenge so much as a genuine question from a pacifist.

"They will never be so weak as now. And they must always, always believe that we will not hesitate to destroy them if they strike at us. We are still trying to minimize civilian deaths, Gondel—and a siege always hits civilians harder. No, a decisive victory here will prevent months of attrition."

The old man nodded his understanding, resigned to sadness.

A noise from the shore and a shadow in the sky drew our attention. The Eculans had loosed a volley of arrows at our forces landing on the rubbish-strewn beaches of the Inkpit district. I waited for them to be blown off course by a cyclone, but they fell true, and many of our people were cut down as a result.

"We need cyclones out there!" Tallynd shouted, back to command. "Where are the Kaurians? Koesha can't do everything! They don't have to hurt anyone, just stop those arrows from killing us!"

But the volleys ceased. Bone-clad figures were already rushing the beach, trying to prevent us from establishing ourselves. My chest tightened with the realization that Mynstad du Möcher would have been among the first to land. She might have already been hit by that volley.

"Permission to join the fight, Second Könstad?" I asked.

"Granted," she said. "Return safely, Gerstad."

A couple of steps and I was diving overboard, then sleeving myself through the bay to the beach. Halfway there, I realized I had no weapons besides a glass dagger and no plan beyond finding my lifebond and fighting by her side, protecting her as best as I could.

When I hit the beach, it was already littered with bodies. Many were Eculan, but there was no shortage of allied bodies either, mowed down as they were getting off the boats. I picked up a shield and a sword from someone who wouldn't be needing them anymore and hauled myself across the sand into the Inkpit, keeping the shield up so that I could peer over it but otherwise hiding the whole of my body. Our forces had pushed forward into the grimy, hard-packed streets, the tops of the buildings still smoking from Hollit's flushing fire. They were basic, uneven shacks cobbled together from scraps and leavings of other carpentry, with gaps at the joints and some dangerous nails sticking out here and there.

It was only a block until I caught up with the rear guard, though more soldiers were still landing behind me. The vanguard was probably two or three blocks ahead of me, and that's where the mynstad would be.

Now that the Eculan forces had been pressed back, arrows were climbing into the sky again and falling toward the beach and our position, trying to thin out our army. I raised my shield over my head, but nothing fell onto it, nor onto those of any neighbors. I risked a peek up and saw that a Kaurian cyclone was now hovering overhead, blowing those long-range volleys away with gusts of wind.

That was a relief, but I soon realized the more-deadly shots were coming from atop the buildings ahead, from which there was a shorter distance to travel and the cyclones couldn't target and blow them away in time. So I started in with my own ranged attacks even as I tried to inch past others to find the mynstad. Every time I spied an Eculan archer, either on a building or the more distant city walls, I pulled the water in his skull out through his ear. Other rapids were in the throng doing the same thing—in one case I saw an archer I was about to target crumple before I could take him.

But there were so *many* of them. For each one we snuffed, another took his place, and our forces were crowded into kill zones, valleys of death between buildings. I raised my shield just in time to deflect an arrow aimed at my head—a flicker from a window in my peripheral vision had saved me. I slew the culprit and started scanning windows too.

As Fanje had promised, the air in the Inkpit was already terrible from a multitude of olfactory evils, but we kept making it worse with the coppery tang of blood and the sour stench of sweat and fear. The cacophony of men and women alternately yelling in killing rages and wailing as they were cut down was the music of slaughter. And every second of taking that in made me more and more worried about Mynstad du Möcher, who was near the front.

And fuck Kindin Ladd and his advice—gently and respectfully—for that shit did *not* work in a battle. I was practically weeping with worry.

I was still going to give him a huge gift basket if we lived, though, because it had worked until now. But at that moment I needed nothing so much as to stay alive and to know that my love was alive.

Yet I couldn't press forward. The bodies were too packed ahead of me, and I had too much work to do—the archers needed taking down. So I kept at it, grinding my teeth and keeping my shield up.

Whatever was happening up front, we were making progress. It was slow but steady: We were advancing, and my work and the work of other rapids was taking a terrible toll on their archers.

As I had to start stepping over bodies, though, I noted that many were Eculan but too many were ours as well. Brynt and Raelech and Fornish bodies. The Fornish were thornhands who'd made their sacrificial transformation—planting themselves and becoming a living lance that shot out, seeking flesh, until the last dregs of their life's energy was spent. Their particular blessing was intended to take out heavily armored Hathrim firelords, who might otherwise wreak untold havoc on Fornish troops, but against the Bone Giants massed together in close quarters they were incredibly deadly, because the Eculan armor was next to nothing. One of the thornhands managed to impale nine Bone Giants with his death—I counted, because I had to step over the line of them bursting with elongated thorns, like chunks of meat on skewers to be grilled. There was an arrow embedded in the trunk of the plant, so it wasn't too difficult to figure out what had happened: He'd been shot and realized it was the end, so he sacrificed himself and took out as many as he could.

We couldn't continue to sustain losses like that and hope to win. Though maybe it seemed to be worse than it was and we were doing fantastically well—I didn't know. There could be other fronts, or flanks, doing far better. I wasn't truly privy to the strategy but rather was part of the mob, simply trying to contribute. And get to the mynstad.

Our progress ground to a halt for a while, and that worried me further still—there might have been a counterattack, our lines broken, my love slain. I kept picking off archers from a distance and eventually saw no more.

A few thunderous impact noises reached my ears, but I didn't see any evidence of explosions. I wasn't sure what had caused them or if they represented a threat. But we began to move again, closer to the walls, and I kept turning brains into gelatin whenever an archer showed up in my line of sight. We were headed toward the southernmost gate, and once we arrived, I could deduce what had caused those noises: Temblor Priyit. She had simply used her incredible strength to bash her way through their gates with her shield, the metal prevailing against the wood. Once through, we were very close to the Citadel.

We were on a main artery of the city, with Featherdown on our left and Fishskinning on our right. It was very clearly a border between districts, since the houses in Featherdown were far more grand than the ones in Fishskinning.

Of more importance to me was that the richer houses had landscaping and therefore room to escape the streets and run around the throng in front of me in an attempt to get closer to the mynstad.

I churned past ranks of Brynts—many of them looking askance at me and wondering what was the hurry—until I hit the Citadel grounds. The moat, such as it was, provided an opportunity.

Tallynd's earlier efforts had emptied it, but the refilling had begun as water leaked out from underneath the double doors of the Citadel during our attack. There was only a small skim of water in the bottom now, perhaps an inch or two deep, but it would serve.

There was just enough of a slope on the side to be navigable, and I half-slid, half-stumbled down it, soldiers openly wondering what I was doing now.

I showed them.

There's little call for it besides showing off, but it's possible for rapids and tidal mariners to stand or even travel on the surface of the water, surfing along as the water supports your feet. Sleeving yourself fully submerged is much faster and takes less energy. But since I couldn't submerge and surfing the shallows was faster than running, I made rare practical use of the ability as soon as I hit the bottom of the moat. Halfway across, I reached the land bridge that led to the gate, and I had the water push me up the incline, scoot me across the bridge, and drop me down the other side into the second half of the moat. I repeated the surf until I was cresting the other side, and I gained plenty of ground that way. The front of our forces was in sight—but the Mynstad du Möcher, specifically, was not.

I did catch a glimpse of Gerstad Daryck du Löngren, however, marching with his unit, the Grynek Hunters. He was laden with a shield, a spear, and a heavy pack on his back in addition to his armor. I labored to catch up and eventually got his attention. He chucked a chin at me and scooched over a tiny bit so I could run alongside—we were crossing a main artery road that trailed north right after the Citadel, but it would narrow again as the buildings resumed. As I passed through, a Raelech courier—Numa—arrived with a stonecutter, who tested the ground. It wasn't salted, so he raised a wall out of the ground at the end of the street, which effectively prevented the Eculans from sending a force into our flank as we continued to pass.

"What's the plan?"

"The next main road to the left leads directly to the Cloister. That's where we're going. The kraljic might be dead, but word is there's another big nest of them guarding the, uh . . . whatever they're called."

"Isposniks?"

"Yeah. So the job's only half done. And the blessings we have to work with at this point are a Raelech temblor, three couriers, three stonecutters, some thornhands and greensleeves, and you and my guy Lörry."

"Lörry?"

A young man to our right saluted in motion. "Gerstad du Fesset."

"Oh, was it you helping out with the archers?"

"Yes, Gerstad."

"Well done."

Daryck flicked a finger forward. "You know the rest of my crew? Mynstad du Högyn's in front of us."

A heavily muscled woman turned her head and peered over her shoulder upon hearing her name.

"Welcome, Gerstad. Your lifebond is a legend."

"Thanks. Speaking of Mynstad du Möcher, have you seen her?" I asked Daryck.

The corner of his mouth quirked up. "Your love is alive and holding the center of the front line with Temblor Priyit."

That was a few ranks in front of us and I couldn't get there, but tension drained out of my muscles anyway just to know she was close by.

"Can we let her know I'm here?"

"Absolutely not," he said. "She'll be worried about you."

"Well, that's why I've come. I'm worried about her."

He gave a short bark of laughter. "I cannot imagine anyone defeating her so long as she sees them coming. Nara, let me give you some unsolicited counsel: Don't let her see you. If she knows you're here, she'll be worried to the point of distraction. You don't want that. Distraction can get you killed in a battle like this."

And then, of course, because we were distracted, we didn't see the Bone Giants coming in time to do anything about them. They fell upon us from the rooftops of the buildings to the left, a cry of defiance followed by the crunch of impact. We'd expected the appearance of archers but not headlong dives into our ranks. They were suicidal leaps and they had to know it, but they leapt anyway, and since we were tightly packed in formation, they couldn't miss hitting at least one person on the way down. More often, though, whoever they hit wound up taking out someone else as well, which disrupted the lines and our progress and created some space for the next waves to fall without contact and maybe take a few swings, if they didn't break an ankle or a leg in the fall.

One of the first to be taken down was the young rapid, Lörry du Bört. The Bone Giant who fell on him basically crushed his skull, the sword unable to penetrate the armor of the helmet but doing such blunt-force damage that it killed him anyway. The giant's body, meanwhile, fell on top of Daryck, bearing him to the ground, and his feet clipped my shoulder but didn't knock me over entirely. I turned his brain into a bloody soup so he couldn't do any more damage, but Daryck would have to get out from under him on his own. There were more coming, tumbling off the roof like migrating rodents that didn't know well enough to stop at the edge of a cliff.

Mynstad du Högyn raised her shield over her head and braced in time as a Bone Giant fell onto it. She grunted, rotated her shoulder, and redirected him to the ground, where she speared him. Daryck was struggling to get up, but I had to keep my eyes on the sky after that. I liquefied brains as quickly as I could, but there were too many of them to keep up with. Plenty were able to leap down to sow death and chaos in our ranks and meet their own fate. But what I thought was an improvised ambush soon proved to be a planned attack, for several poles were lowered from the roofs to allow warriors to slide down them. The initial suicidal attacks were intended to create room for these poles, which would funnel a whole lot more soldiers this way.

Why were they doing this? Why not simply attack via the roads?

We'd blocked the nearest one by the Citadel, so that might be part of it. But as I'd crossed it, there hadn't seemed to be any attack incoming. Maybe there was one coming along the next main road we wished to take—the one leading to the Cloister? Our front lines, currently facing this new threat, would have their backs turned and get flanked if they sent a force down that street. Someone among the Eculans still had a mind for tactics.

I was thinking I needed to fall back away from the drop zone even as Mynstad du Högyn and Daryck shouted the same. They covered my retreat to the other side of the road, then they stepped back with me as we regrouped to face this new threat. I mentioned the possibility of our vanguard being flanked, but Daryck didn't think it was our problem.

"I'm sure they've already thought of it. We need to find a solution to this river of whale shit pouring down on us."

Some Fornish archers had already taken the initiative and started shooting arrows into the Bone Giants as they skylined themselves on the rooftops. The attacks were all coming from the Featherdown side of the street—nothing from Fishskinning. The archers were helping, but it wasn't enough to stop them. We'd be in close combat soon, and they'd have that area secure to keep bringing in more.

"They have to be bringing people over on a bridge between buildings. We should ask the Fornish to take care of it—a couple of thornhands could mess them up."

Someone else was thinking along the same lines. Numa, the courier, appeared and asked me to concentrate my efforts on clearing out anyone approaching the pole nearest the front. I got on that and watched a response form. Archer fire was also concentrated there so that between us, the Bone Giants couldn't get anyone down that pole. Spore bombs were lobbed onto the rooftop as well, and once they exploded, the numbers on that roof dwindled significantly.

The Bone Giants were having some success in pouring down the buildings to our rear, extending back to the intersection, but the one nearest us was stanched for the moment. A greensleeve I'd never met but whom I later learned was named Ven Hap ben Lor performed an extraordinary act of acrobatics, getting a running boost from the cupped hands of a thornhand and then leaping toward the building. Shoots with barbs on them extended from the silverbark on his outstretched right forearm, hooked onto the lip of the building, and then pulled him up as they retracted, so he could grab on with his fingers and hoist himself the rest of the way. Once on the roof, he quickly lobbed a couple more spore bombs—to which he and the thornhands would be immune—and held that position while the thornhands shimmied up the pole. We noticed that no more Bone Giants fell from that building after that. Something would need to be done to counter their gains to our rear, but we at least were no longer being plagued. Which was a good thing, as the main force we thought would be coming to meet us along the road from the Cloister now turned the corner. The stonecutters were right behind Temblor Priyit—I could see her turn and shout at them, and Mynstad du Möcher should be there too, but I couldn't see her over the heads or between the bodies of others.

Working together, the stonecutters employed their kenning to raise a quick earthen wall out of the street, about half a length high, and simply shoved it toward the oncoming horde. Those in the front who were supremely athletic were able to hurdle it, but some weren't, and those two ranks back didn't understand what was happening until they were bowled over—either backward, thereby knocking over more, or forward, to fall over the low wall. Either way, the charge was broken. And the stonecutters weren't done.

The temblor wanted to press on to that intersection, so the stonecutters raised another earthen wall together, this one a full length high so the Bone Giants wouldn't be able to jump over it. Climb over it? Sure! But those who did would find themselves almost alone against our army, and their primary advantage of numbers was erased. This allowed us to push forward the extra block, and the stonecutters moved that wall across the intersection to block off any reinforcement from the dockside garrison. The stonecutters were worn out by the effort and clearly in pain afterward, a fairly serious debt incurred with their kenning. Raising walls was kind of their thing and they were good at it, but raising them quickly and making them move—mobility being a quality rarely associated with walls—was apparently juggernaut-level juice.

They were sent to the back with a courier escort, done for the day, while I was tucked into the center of the column, near the front but frustratingly behind just enough ranks that I was still unable to see my lifebond.

The Fornish were swarming up the pole the Eculans had lowered, and they pushed out from there, taking over rooftops to our rear and holding the line so that our left flank was protected from aerial assault.

But it was strange that we saw almost nothing from the right. It was like the Fishskinning district had no soldiers or members of a city watch or anything—which had to be untrue. So why weren't we getting attacked from that direction?

I asked Daryck, "Why aren't we seeing anything from the right?"

A corner of his mouth lifted. "They never planned for us getting past the Citadel. They thought they could hold us there and then bring these forces around to flank us. Instead, their flanking army is all they have left."

It was still plenty of army. We turned the corner and looked up the slight incline of the road leading to the Cloister, and all we saw were bone-clad warriors packed into the streets. Uncounted thousands of them, with the advantage of reach, and we'd have to fight our way through them all. Perhaps my shoulders drooped or something, because Daryck tried to encourage me.

"Don't worry, we have thousands too. And kennings," he said. But then he squinted at something down the road and chucked his chin at the interior walls surrounding the Cloister. There was a single gate and significant defenses. "Those ballista towers are going to be a problem, though, if we don't do something about them soon. I hope someone's on top of it, or large chunks of us are going to get ground into sausage."

A call went up for a rotation, and Daryck echoed it so the order would be passed down. The front line was going to come back for a rest, and we were going to move up a rank or possibly all the way, depending on whether gaps needed to be filled.

"You shouldn't go up," Daryck said. "You should rotate back and keep using your kenning."

"I admit that I'm not trained well for front-line fighting," I allowed, "but why go back? Why not simply stay here?"

"Because Mynstad du Möcher is going to rotate back for a breather, and as previously discussed, she might see you. It's best for her sake if she doesn't. She needs a clear head to fight well. She's a key piece of this battle and so are you. Trust a veteran on this, please. If I could order you to do it I would—that's how strongly I feel about it."

"Okay. I understand. I'll do it. And you stay alive."

"I'll do my best."

The rotation began. Daryck and Mynstad du Högyn pressed forward to form the new second rank, the former second rank became the front, and the front rank slid back two ranks to be number three and take a rest. I caught a glimpse of my love sliding back and I immediately turned, ordering the mariner behind me to switch places with me, and then I did it again, moving back two more ranks. That should keep me safely out of the mynstad's sight, and I would still be able to contribute there—and do so knowing that, at least for a little while, she was out of harm's way.

Archers began to appear again on the rooftops to the left, and I grimly resumed directing the water in their skulls to move forcibly elsewhere. The Fornish had not secured our left flank now that we'd turned north; they were still working on securing the left flank for the troops moving behind us from west to east. The clashing of swords and shields and the screams of the dying were louder than anything I'd experienced before. The enormity of it—the swelling sum of endings born from so many beginnings—wrung tears from my eyes.

Eighteen or twenty years ago, or whensoever these Eculan boys were born, their mothers did not cradle them in their arms and think that someday a woman from across the Peles Ocean would arrive to rip the water out of their brains. And my mother never considered as I gurgled happily in my crib that someday I would grow up to become a ruthless killer for my country. Yet while all our mothers dreamt dreams of peace and prosperity for their sweet babies, the Wraith and his network of spies were working in conjunction with Lorson, the isposniks, and the god of the Seventh Kenning to bring us to this point, where we were killing one another because they'd engineered an entire culture to be immune to reason, to hate vast swaths of people that they'd never met.

May every wretched fish head who dreams of power instead of love or art or poetry meet an early death and leave life to the rest of us who would rather celebrate others than ourselves. I realize that sentiment is not very kind and reeks of bitterness, but I think we have all been twisted from our gentler natures by these odious lampreys who drain us and give nothing but grief. They rob entire generations of the chance to be their best selves.

The Fornish, I noticed, began to make a push along the rooftops, not only securing us from attack from above but moving some of their own archers up so that they could fire down onto the Eculans. Within a few minutes, they had done such a good job of clearing the edges that I had no more targets. I got to rest, which might not have been the best thing for me, since I immediately began to worry about when the next rotation would be called and whether the Mynstad du Möcher would move to the front again.

Further worries heaped on top of that some minutes later when our progress forced me to step over the body of Mynstad Söla du Högyn. She had obviously advanced to the front line, filling in a space from some other mariner who'd most likely been cut down moments before, and it was likely that Daryck du Löngren had stepped up as well. She'd been an extremely capable fighter, which made me worry for Daryck and everyone else, but especially for my love.

I cast about, trying to see if Daryck's body was also among the fallen nearby, but didn't see him. That didn't mean he was safe—my field of vision was limited. But perhaps he was still fighting.

A new rotation was called and I leapt up as it began, trying to spot my lifebond. I spied her rotating to the front. But Gerstad du Löngren rotated back, bloodied and breathing heavily, his shield battered, and I took the opportunity to move up next to him.

"Are you all right, Gerstad?"

"Yes, just winded. Mynstad du Högyn fell, though."

"Yes, I saw that we passed her."

"She took down three before they double-teamed her and got a sword over the shield. This is a terrible day. Even if we win, there is nothing good about it."

"But it's manageable? We're clearly still advancing."

"Aye, because that temblor is unstoppable. Not sure we'd be advancing otherwise. And those ballista towers are going to start unloading on us soon. The temblor is pissing vinegar about it, shouted at all the couriers to make something happen. She said those need to be taken out now."

"They do indeed. That Eculan girl who gave us all the intel told us they fire some kind of round shot, melon-sized, that disintegrates on impact and sends small pieces of iron everywhere."

"So a single shot could take out . . . ?"

"Dozens. Wound even more."

"Fuck me with a jellyfish. So that's why you started with them before we landed. Say, can you maybe target the people in the towers from here?"

I squinted at them and shook my head. "No, the nest is entirely in shadow. I can't distinguish anything, and I'm not sure I could manage such a distance anyway."

"Hmm." Daryck turned his head to assess the forces on the roof. "We have a group of Fornish archers up there now. You see that huddle?"

There was a group of Fornish with quivers and bows standing together on a rooftop with their backs turned toward us, bent over something.

"Yes. What are they doing?"

A red glow suddenly illuminated them and flickered between their bodies.

Daryck grinned. "Lighting a fire arrow. Finally!"

More were lit from the first, then methodically shot in the general direction of the tower on the left. Their courses visibly changed in air, which meant that a cyclone was directing their flight, but when they struck the target, nothing especially brilliant happened, because Hollit Panevik wasn't there to spread the flames and clear out the operators. The arrows would work eventually, of course, and render the mechanism inoperable, but that meant they might decide to risk a long-range shot while they could.

Almost as soon as I thought this, the tower on the right fired. The cyclones were unready for it, and I'm not sure what influence they would have been able to exert over the flight of something so heavy traveling at high velocity anyway, so the shot flew true, whistling overhead and landing behind us, perhaps seven or eight ranks back. The impact was a *whump* immediately followed by a chorus of cries as it flattened dozens, as Daryck predicted, and a plume of dust rose in the center of a corona of bloodspray.

The two of us cursed and wondered how long it would take them to reload. I hopped up to do a quick survey over some heads and saw that wounded were being pulled aside and the hole in the ranks was already being filled as our infantry stepped forward into the void. But that wouldn't do much good if we couldn't do something about that ballista.

The one on the left was now visibly aflame and still hadn't fired, but the right one remained operational, the first arrows only now slicing through the air to sink into the weapon.

"What in the abyss is in their shot?" Daryck wondered aloud. "And why didn't they use that in the invasion?"

With a tiny shrug, I replied, "It was unnecessary, if you think about it. They were able to destroy our cities without it. But the briefing I heard was that the shot is a fairly new invention, based on something volatile they mine on the island of Slivovi."

We watched the right tower intently as the battle continued. A few more fire arrows slid through the air toward it, but
they managed to launch another shot in our direction. The
whistle overhead was slightly louder this time, and Daryck
shouted and sidestepped to get behind me, spreading his
arms wide.

The thump of impact could be felt this time, and cries of
pain rang out, including a startled grunt from Daryck as he
slammed into me and bore me to the ground. I lost all my
wind and wheezed a lungful of dust.

"Nara," he coughed. "Are you okay?" He rolled off me,
onto his back. There were bodies all around us; the front
couple of lines were still holding, but they needed reinforcement badly now, and soldiers were rushing to fill in the gap,
stepping over us as best as they could. I rose and knelt over
Daryck, taking deep gulps of air, trying to take up less space
so they could flow around.

"Yes, you knocked the wind out of me, but I'm okay.
What about you?"

"Not so much," he said, his face tight and sweating. "That
one got me."

"What? I don't— Where?"

"Several places in my back. Those iron pieces you talked
about."

"They got through your armor? And your pack?"

"Yes. The metal punched right through. Not through me,
though, so that's good."

"No, no, that means it's still in there."

A flicker of humor on his face interrupted the grimace of
pain. "Oh, I'm well aware."

The seriousness of his injuries became clear as something
warm and wet touched my fingers in the street. It was his
blood. It was spreading from underneath him on either side.

"You saved my life, Daryck," I said, realizing what he'd
done. "Thank you."

"Bah. I had to," he replied, and coughed softly and groaned. "Mynstad du Möcher would have killed me if I let you get hurt."

"You ridiculous fish head. Come on, let's get you out of the road and patch you up." The army continued to march around us, advancing against the Eculans, but no more shots came from the tower.

"No, Nara, don't bother." An involuntary splutter brought blood to his lips, and he gasped. "It punctured a lung. I can feel it filling—I'm drowning on dry land. Just make sure I return to the sea with my brothers and sisters."

"Stop talking like that. I can try to stop the blood flowing into your lungs, just give me a second."

"No. Listen. I have to tell you something."

"What?"

"Bitterness and gall is always a trap," he gurgled over a wet, labored breath. "You might think for a while that it's trapped inside you, that you're in control and holding the keys, but even if that's true, at some point it changes—it flips—and you're trapped inside the bitterness. And I can see now that I've been imprisoned by it. The door is open now, mocking me. But it's too late. I can't walk out." He clutched me urgently, his breath hitching, his head shaking back and forth in tiny movements.

"You can walk out, Daryck. You can. I'll help you. We'll get these wounds stitched and you'll heal up. We'll find your hygienist, Vera du Göslyn; she has to be near here somewhere."

"No. She fell, outside the walls, to an arrow."

"Then we'll get some other hygienist."

"No. I never should have taken a step . . . down the road of blood," he said. "Because you see what waits at the end of it. I have killed many Eculans now, but I am not satisfied, or proud, or fulfilled. I am emptier than when I began. I should have stayed in Brynlön and rebuilt Grynek. I should have written more cock sonnets—"

"More? Didn't you write the definitive work? One hundred sixty-eight of them?"

"Well, maybe . . . I have one more in my pack. If it's not ruined. In my diary. Will you make sure Dervan gets it?"

"You will give it to him yourself."

He ignored this and said, "I should have written a companion work about balls. Two of them." I laughed and he did too, but he immediately started coughing up blood in earnest, and that chased away my amusement.

"What I mean is . . . I should have defeated destruction with creation. I should have rebuilt my city and rebuilt my life. Instead, I destroyed myself."

He grasped my shoulder desperately, his eyes widening, his entire bulk shaking with the effort to squeeze out just a couple more words, lips quivering. "*Live*, Nara—"

And then he was gone.

KOESHA

Not This Time

Tallynd may have felt invigorated, but I felt drained and wanted nothing so much as a nap while the battle raged. I wanted to announce that I felt like dry crumbs of windblown shit but feared that it would be beneath my dignity, and no one had time to worry about me anyway. I simply staggered down to an empty bunk on the *Shearwater* rather than return to the *Nentian Herald*. But while I was drifting in and out of a fugue state prior to taking a nap, footsteps on the ladder roused me. It was Tallynd—moving slowly, gingerly, as an old woman would—coming belowdecks to ask me for one more thing that hopefully wouldn't be too taxing. A translator followed her.

"We need you to guide arrows to the ballista towers surrounding the Cloister," she said. "Our forces are approaching, and we need those removed."

"The Kaurian cyclones are still unable to do this?"

"They politely refuse to do anything so obviously violent. They are keeping arrows from falling on our troops and providing me some good reconnaissance, at least. On the eastern side of the city, and to a lesser extent the south near the docks, the Eculans are fighting amongst themselves."

I grunted at that. Good to know that Fanje had been correct and there was significant resistance to the cult. "Will Hollit be shooting the arrows?"

"No. We have some Fornish archers ready with Raelech fire arrows. They're on the rooftops on the left flank of our forces, protecting a greensleeve named Ven Hap ben Lor. Meet with him and he'll coordinate with you."

"Does he speak Nentian?"

"Yes. I'm told they're using a lot of spore bombs up there, so make sure you don't breathe any in."

"I'll clear the air around me. Once the ballistas are out, then what? We just take the Cloister?"

"Basically. The leaders of the church need to be captured or killed, especially a leader that our Eculan friend calls Draško. He's an isposnik—the primary one, who is functionally the true leader of the nation, since the kraljic does whatever he says. He's the one that ordered the first invasion and planned the second."

"What does he look like?"

"We have no idea. She's never seen him. He'll probably be wearing leather, however, as that is a status thing here."

"Maybe he will be considerate and occupy a ballista tower when the fire arrows arrive."

"Ha! If only he would be so helpful."

"He probably smells bad and sounds evil."

Tallynd smiled briefly and then reconsidered. "He's probably very charismatic. He'd have to be."

I didn't want to move. But then I imagined that our fighters didn't want to face a ballista either, so I should stop feeling sorry for myself and do the job that needed to be done.

"Okay. Okay. I'll blow out of here." I groaned and pushed myself up, securing my Bora to my waist again. "Buy me a drink later?"

"Absolutely. I'll buy you a keg."

The air above the city was incredibly turbulent because there were so many cyclones hovering above it now, pushing and pulling air around. My flight, therefore, was far less smooth than I would have wished, and my exhaustion didn't help much. It occurred to me that I'd have tremendous difficulty getting the arrows to their target when the Kaurians were doing their best to alter the paths of any arrows in the vicinity.

I'd missed a lot of the battle's progress and scanned quickly from above to find my target.

Our allied army was clearly visible. A packed throughfare full of fighters streamed in from the Inkpit gate, strung past the drowned Citadel, and turned north. It was advancing slowly in fits and starts toward the Cloister.

There were two surprises, despite my briefing: First, there were no attacks on our right flank. Nothing coming from Fishskinning or Hammerside, because those areas were churning with rebels fighting against the cult. And on the left flank, the Eculans had tried to use their flat roofs and densely packed buildings to attack our army from above, but the Fornish had taken it upon themselves to deny them the high ground. Apparently, they were accustomed to living far aboveground and had no fear of heights, so they were ideally suited for such a mission.

A squad of thornhands spun and dealt death in sync on one rooftop, looking like a deadly spined snake from above, undulating and spraying blood as it moved. Behind the line of the snake, a circular pod of four protected a fifth in their center, lurking near the edge of a building, farthest away from the fighting. I imagined that was the greensleeve. If not, they could at least direct me to wherever he was, so I dove and slipped through currents, plowed through updrafts, until I came down on the roof somewhat awkwardly in front of them, hands raised to indicate that I was friendly. Ben Lor, a sandy-haired and bearded fellow in a green vest, immediately thanked me for coming and said his thornhands had the arrows we needed.

Lighting them with flint was a bit of a trial and took longer than any of us wanted, but once we got one going, we used it to light the others. Without Hollit's help to spread the flames and make the nests immediately deadly, it also took a while to make sure the ballistas were out of commission—too long, in fact, because one was able to fire a couple of rounds into our forces that had advanced into range, opening great wounds in the streets and splashing blood and bodies about. But we kept pouring arrows in there, the work of five minutes that seemed much longer, and eventually that threat was neutralized.

At that point I could have technically retired to the *Shearwater*, my mission complete, but I knew I would not. The allies of Sedam could be defeated soon, and I wanted to witness it, perhaps even help if I could figure out how.

Thanks to the efforts of the Raelech stonecutters throwing up a couple of walls and the Fornish protecting the rooftops, the Eculans were confined to fighting us head-on, a tremendous feat in a city where we theoretically should have faced threats from every direction.

They had plenty of numbers, their ranks even more closely packed than our own along the street leading to the Cloister, yet we still gained ground one slippery, bloody length at a time.

"How are we making progress like that?" I asked ben Lor.

"Temblor Priyit and a Brynt mynstad are chewing them up."

"How?"

"The temblor has a thick outsized shield that no one but she can even lift. She used it to shatter the Inkpit gate in three blows. Now she's using it to bash whoever's in front of her—they are propelled backward, knocking down several at a time, and the mynstad is efficiently cleaning up and protecting her left side."

I remembered seeing this mynstad—she had an unforgettable face. "Does the mynstad have a kenning?"

"No, but word is that there's a rapid in the ranks near the front too, who's been helping out quite a bit."

"How does the mynstad not tire?"

"I'm sure she does. I've seen them rotate out and take breaks. Priyit creates some space, and the tired front rank turns sideways and steps back as the rank behind turns sideways and steps forward."

"So many leaves," I murmured, watching the battle continue.

"Sorry, what's that?"

"Oh. Just an observation. We are like leaves falling in an autumn·gale."

"I guess so. I want to hang on to the tree a bit longer, though."

"Me too. Be safe, ben Lor. I'm going to see what else can be done."

He wished me well, and I sprinted forward until I could leap off the roof and be caught by an updraft that carried me high above the fighting, behind the front lines and over the walls that surrounded the Cloister.

I am not sure what I expected to see there, but a brightly colored parade of men emerging from the building and striding toward the gates was not it. They stood out because they were covered head to toe in leather, the soft and supple kind and dyed in deep, rich colors that contrasted starkly with the white bone armor the soldiers wore. They were like the bright dab of a paintbrush on a blank canvas—red, purple, yellow, green, and a teal or maybe turquoise.

Checking first to make sure that no archers were targeting me from the walls, I descended ten lengths or so to get a closer look.

These were not young men like the soldiers. They were visibly older, as evidenced by their gray hair and braided beards, and did not appear to be in fighting shape, though they all carried the same swords. A substantial number of beard monks followed in their wake, younger and looking a bit more capable of battle. The soldiers parted before them all and bowed, demonstrating their obeisance. This was submission to authority, and that, together with the leather I'd been told to watch for, meant that I was looking at the isposniks. But which one was Draško? Was he even among them, or was he still in the Cloister and had merely sent out these lesser isposniks to deal with our justice? There was no way for me to tell. From my perspective, they were all receiving an equal share of adulation and worship.

I maintained my position above them as they moved, sensing that something important was about to happen. They began to infiltrate the ranks of their soldiers, which rippled and flowed to let them pass. I had no idea why they thought they'd do any better against our allied forces than their regular troops. Perhaps it was a mental game to motivate their side, to give them hope. It would be crushed once they met the temblor, who held the center of our front line. Now that I was looking at it from the Eculan perspective, the Brynt forces were to the right of the temblor and the Raelech forces were to the left. The Fornish had all migrated to the rooftops and were busy advancing there. Perhaps the Eculans realized that they needed to try something new, because we had countered their defenses and were advancing despite our losses.

Having the chance to watch the temblor in action, I could see what a tremendous advantage she gave us. The oversized shield she carried and bashed into the Eculans either broke their bones or outright killed them, and regardless of whether they survived, they were propelled forcefully into the ranks behind them, preventing them from mounting any serious assault on the center of the line. Some tried to time a rush at her immediately following a shield bash, only to find her sword waiting and the spears of the soldiers on her flanks defending her.

Too late, I realized that this was not a mission to boost morale but a mission to take out Temblor Priyit, who they rightly saw as the key to our attack.

Once the collection of monks and clerics got to the front, they charged in and got whacked backward by Priyit's shield.

But a second rush darted in quickly, not necessarily to strike but to fall onto the swords and spears waiting for them, including the temblor's.

They screamed as they died but held on to the weapons as long as they could, fouling them and preventing their removal, as the old man dressed in turquoise moved in and reached a rail-thin arm around the shield to grab Temblor Priyit's sword arm. The Raelechs don't wear armor on their arms at all, owing to the Jereh band that's always on their right biceps. Once his bony fingers dug into her flesh, the temblor immediately froze, except for some quivering that rapidly gave way to convulsions. Still the turquoise man held on. She threw her head back to scream, and then he got a spear in his guts, run completely through by the Mynstad du Möcher from his right side, or Priyit's left.

This abrupt change in his bodily integrity did not seem to bother him, though he did grab hold of the spear shaft so that the mynstad couldn't yank it out. Temblor Priyit sank to her knees, her strength drained away by the turquoise man, who was clearly a lifeleech. I had seen this horror before.

But we had no Olet Kanek here to burn the man down, no tidal mariner to rip the water out of his head. Ben Lor said there was a rapid somewhere in the army, but who knew if they were in position to see this happening? And the couriers, who might be able to do something, were obviously elsewhere at the moment.

Killing the temblor could turn the tide in their favor. The mynstad would be next, except that she saw that trying to hold on to the spear or yank it out was useless. She let go, drew a sword at her side, and fought off two different Eculans who tried to press their temporary advantage.

Isposnik Draško—for this lifeleech must be Sedam's key man in the country—took another spear to the torso from the soldier on Priyit's right while the temblor withered and died. He absolutely did not care about this additional ventilation of his body. He could back off, remove the spears, and regenerate while the Eculans rallied and pushed back, given new breath by their cult leader demonstrating the power of the Seventh Kenning.

"No," I said. "Not this time."

I drew my Bora, summoned a very tight funnel of wind, and pushed it with all the speed I could muster down toward the lifeleech. He was remaining fairly still, having drained Temblor Priyit completely and now latched on to the second soldier who'd speared him. My sword crunched through his skull just behind the top of the head and penetrated to the hilt, the blade emerging from the top of his mouth and spilling teeth and blood and brains as it shaved his chin. He spasmed once, let go of the soldier, and dropped dead, his kenning unable to rebuild a brain practically sliced in half.

I had learned a little something from my encounter with Lorson, when both my Bora and Buran had pierced his body and had as much effect as those spears: Go for the head.

His sudden demise affected the Eculans at the front, who stopped fighting when our forces decidedly did not, and as a result they were dispatched to an early end. The rest of the isposniks and bearded monks fell in short order, none of them really fighters but fanatical enough to give their side hope that they could win through some belief in Žalost's will. Draško's fall robbed them of all that, and with their demise the faith of the Eculans was finally shaken. Their cult leaders were mowed down, their Citadel deluged and drowned, and they had no hope now of defeating the invaders with six kennings at their disposal. Fear spread visibly through the ranks, and the Eculans either surrendered or outright fled, abandoning the fight altogether.

The Cloister was ours for the taking, the battle all but won.

I swooped down to the fallen body of Draško, making sure before I landed that everyone saw me and recognized me as an ally. Mynstad du Möcher was there, letting our forces flow around and ahead, recognizing as I did that the life-leech's body could still serve a purpose.

She said something in Brynt and gestured at my sword embedded in his skull. The tone suggested it was a question, perhaps wondering if I was responsible, so I nodded and bent to retrieve it, flashing her a quick smile. I spoke in Joabeian to her since she wouldn't understand me anyway in Nentian, but hopefully some of the general sentiment would be conveyed by my tone.

"Today we have foiled the plans of Vo Lai the White Demon. He is not defeated himself and I am not sure he can be, but at least this abomination of a being can no longer hurt anyone."

I removed my sword and flicked blood from the blade, wiping it completely clean on Draško's turquoise leather after that. The mynstad nodded her approval before removing her spear and the other soldier's too. Said soldier was still alive but kneeling down, breathing heavily, next to the withered corpse of Temblor Priyit. He accepted the return of his spear, but I doubted he would be getting up to fight again soon. I didn't know how much of his life Draško drained, but he couldn't be feeling very well right then.

The cry of a woman's voice caused both the mynstad and me to turn. Gerstad Nara du Fesset appeared out of the throng and threw herself at the mynstad, who opened her arms to accept a fierce embrace. They kissed each other deeply and I realized they were bonded, which made me happy for them both. To survive a battle like this together was a victory of its own.

A courier arrived, belatedly, to discover that the temblor had fallen. That meant that either Nara or I would be the new battlefield commander, and I immediately deferred to her. I had no forces under my command, and everything I said would need to be translated. Nara's first order to me, relayed by the courier, was to fly back to the *Shearwater* and inform Tallynd that Draško was dead, along with much of his cult leadership. The Cloister should fall soon, and she needed guidance on what to do when it happened. She was still giving orders as I left.

Tallynd took the news immediately to Fanje and Gondel Vedd. Together they crafted a quick announcement and Fintan broadcast Gondel's voice:

"The kraljic is dead. Isposnik Draško and the cult leadership are dead. Lay down your arms now, surrender, and let Šest negotiate a new and peaceful relationship with us. Leaders of Šest—Pavle, if possible—approach us unarmed and ask to see Gerstad Nara du Fesset to arrange negotiations with a translator. We regret the loss of life and do not want anyone else to die. We will leave your country as soon as we have assurances from a new government that no more attacks will be launched against our shores."

Further instructions were broadcast to our allied forces in Brynt, Raelech, and Fornish, to secure the Cloister but leave everything inside untouched once personnel were removed—records were to be preserved, and we didn't want them destroyed by the cult. We were to make no more inroads into the city but rather defend the corridor to the Cloister until further notice. Stonecutters were to raise temporary barriers at every intersection, effectively halving the city, and we wanted archers on the walls and guards at every gate.

None of these things, however, required my aid. Tallynd asked if she could give me a hug, and I accepted it gratefully. But I was even more grateful for her dismissal, which allowed me to return to the *Nentian Herald* to get some much-needed rest.

FANJE

The Old Temple Is New

I don't get to witness any of the battle except for what can be seen from the harbor aboard the *Shearwater,* and most of that is plumes of black smoke from the burning ballista towers and cyclones flying in the air above buildings. But after repeated pleas for confirmation that Draško is really dead, beyond all doubt, and emphatic reassurance from the Joabeian woman, Koesha Gansu, that he truly is, everyone gets to witness me dance for joy.

"The death cult is dead!" I shout and whoop as I spin and flail my arms about, and no one but the old man, Gondel Vedd, understands me, but that is okay. I am sure the celebration is being repeated throughout the city of Sveto Selo, in private if not publicly.

Because true believers still exist, and I suppose it's not quite dead yet. Its limbs will twitch for a while, but I don't think it's going to get back up. And the other islands have no idea, and they probably won't believe it at first. It will be weeks, maybe months, before it's real to the entire nation.

Pavle arrives on the ship in the company of Kaurian cyclones about two hours after the announcement, together with a woman I've never met before. She's older than anyone else I've met in Šest, perhaps in her forties, and wears a purple cloak over her tunic but no leather anywhere, which means I might be able to trust her someday. Dark waves of hair fall down to her collarbone, and some bags under her eyes indicate she hasn't slept well recently. Pavle introduces her as Nebesa, the secret leader of Šest and possibly the new leader of Ecula, if she successfully wins election as kraljic.

She beams at me. "So you're the reason these people knew what to do?" she says, and I protest that I was only part of it.

"If so, you were a vital part. Most of the city is untouched and the cult is demolished."

"They're really dead?"

She nods and smiles in triumph. "All the isposniks, the beard monks, and the military leadership. There may be some fanatics left who will cause us some trouble, but they won't control our lives anymore. I think most people are going to be fine worshipping the six again, or nothing at all."

"That is wonderful news."

"So tell me who is most important here before they tell me, in case it's different."

"The woman who destroyed the Citadel. She's a tidal mariner and has the authority to negotiate on behalf of the Brynt government, which is good because they're the ones who have the Fourth Kenning that the cult was trying so hard to destroy. They suffered the most. If you can satisfy them, the other nations represented here can hardly complain."

"Good. And your relationship with them?"

"It's excellent. I've told them no lies, so they have reason to trust me."

"That pleases me. Would you be willing to sit in on our negotiations?"

"Me?"

"Why not you? It would be good to have someone they trust involved. And you might make an ideal ambassador for us."

My jaw drops. "An ambassador?"

Nebesa laughs at my expression. "A bit much for the daughter of a kafa farmer, eh? Well, I think you might have a better idea of what our country needs than some pampered, leather-bound groin meat from Featherdown. So think about it, for all our sakes."

At that point, Tallynd du Böll emerges from the cabin and introductions are made. A small table is brought out onto the deck; its legs unfold on hinges and then lock in place with brackets so that it doesn't move with the undulations of the hull in the bay. We sit on stools that likewise have folding legs but no brackets—we have to keep them in place ourselves and hope we don't tumble over. Since we are anchored in the bay and it's fairly calm, this is no trouble.

Gondel Vedd is introduced as translator, and Fintan is there as well and the historian Dervan du Alöbar who asked me to write this down, and there is a tiny dark-haired woman named Kel Fes Jin of the Black Jaguar Clan, a Fornish diplomat brought over from another ship. Neither she nor Fintan can speak for their country's leadership, and Gondel Vedd cannot speak for Kauria, but each can report faithfully what is negotiated with Brynlön and advise their leaders to ratify it or else suggest modifications specific to their wishes later.

"Thank you for coming," Tallynd says. "I suppose I must first ask if there are other groups with whom we should negotiate. Do you have the power, in other words, to speak for your people?"

"We don't have it yet," Nebesa admits. "The respected title of office is kraljic, and I must stand for election to earn it. However, with your help, I feel certain I can win that office. There are no other parties besides Šest that I know of—as you might imagine, the cult ruthlessly eliminated rivals. We have been a secret society for many years."

"But some other parties may emerge."

"That is true."

"What help would you require to win this office?"

"Roads and bridges. Visible rebuilding efforts. A clear, tangible improvement in our lives as a result of cooperation with your people rather than enmity."

Tallynd looks to Fintan. "I think we can provide that, if our Raelech allies are agreeable."

"I feel certain that I can convince the stonecutters to rebuild a single bridge between this island and one other as an act of goodwill—you choose which one. But anything beyond that will need to be negotiated in trade."

Nebesa does not even need to think about it. "The old bridge between here and Drvo. So many of our raw materials and foods come from there. Our internal economies would immediately improve without having to ship everything across the bay."

"Fine," Tallynd says. "We will ask our Raelech friends to get started on that. We will also remove the kraken from the bay and restore the net in the strait so your shipping can resume in safety. But let us speak of what we need from you."

"Yes."

Tallynd ticks off points on her fingers. "A complete purge of the cult. A peace treaty between our nations with nonaggression as its foundation. The welcoming of diplomats from all nations, and the establishment of Eculan embassies in our lands. A trade agreement between our nations. And we are going to tear down the Citadel and the Cloister."

That last item surprises everyone. "Why tear them down?" Nebesa asks, but I can see that all are curious for the answer.

"They are symbols of cult power, of a regime that made Ecula enemies of the world. You may remove whatever you wish from the sites before their destruction. In place of the Cloister, at no cost to you, we will build embassies for our nations, symbolizing Ecula's new peaceful relationship with the world. In place of the Citadel, we will help build whatever you like so long as it bears no military function. A new seat of power for the kraljic and Šest government offices, called whatever you like except the Citadel. That building, however, will need to be purchased from the Raelech stonecutters in trade."

"Understood. Is that all?"

"Almost. As we said, peace is our primary goal. But we would like to request that you ban the hunting of krakens."

"How will we cross the oceans to trade, then?"

"The same way we did: with hulls enchanted by the Sixth Kenning. Our plaguebringer will enchant some hulls for you to allow for trade. The price of that is a total ban on kraken hunting."

"Done," Nebesa says.

Kel Fes Jin speaks up. "What about reparations?"

That question sparks a spirited debate on the other side of the table, which Gondel Vedd does not fully translate for us, but he does get around to summarizing.

The Fornish want reparations for their cost in sending troops overseas, and Fintan is fairly certain the Raelech Triune Council would want this as well, plus reparations for the loss of an entire city, and Gondel supposes Kauria would also like to be reimbursed for sending their navy. But Tallynd takes a much different view.

"You will all have access to a new large market for your goods and services. That will pay your costs back and then some. You will also have guarantees of security from a formerly hostile nation. I recognize that honor requires some sort of reparations, but if they are punitive and onerous, then you will only foster more of the same resentments that led to war in the first place. It is better for everyone's long-term security if Ecula immediately sees the benefits of living together in peace. And if Brynlön can bear such generous terms when we have lost so much, I feel certain that Rael and Forn and Kauria can as well."

Talks of reparations and trade opportunities continue for some while, with some haggling here and there, but eventually we arrive at a place where Nebesa and Tallynd feel satisfied, and if the other parties aren't entirely satisfied, they're at least able to accept it. They craft a plan to get Nebesa and Šest formally in power, after which the treaties will be drafted and the armies of the six nations will return home, and a new world can begin. The plan has plenty of details, but foremost among them is using Kaurian cyclones to fly Gondel Vedd and Fintan to all the cities of Ecula, where they will announce the regime change and the election to be held in a mere six weeks.

Nebesa begins first, however, by addressing Sveto Selo, with Fintan's help. She announces an end to hostilities, the banning of the cult of Žalost, and the negotiation of a peace treaty with the six nations. She calls for an election and invites other candidates to run for the many offices now left vacant since the Citadel has been drowned. She declares with pride that there will soon be a bridge between Vlast and Drvo, and in coming years there will be bridges between all the islands, and people will walk in freedom once more. And speaking of freedom, she proclaims that all prisoners in the dungeons of the cult are to be released.

"So many years and lives have been wasted on grievance with the six nations of the west, when we could have spent them growing and living together as friends. I know it will be hard for many of you to let go of the hate you've been fed. But you can see in the skies now what comes from eating such poison, and it will come to you also if you do not walk away from those bones. Let us walk together in peace instead and experience the many riches such a life brings."

I leave the ship with Nebesa and Pavle after that to get to work in the city. We're assigned an honor guard of Fornish thornhands to protect us wherever we go until we can be sure the cultists are eradicated.

All the members of Šest are called to clear out the Citadel's documents and treasures. Many of these will help pay for reparations, but the documents detailing where the wealth of the cult is concentrated are more important than the trinkets.

We take up temporary offices in a warehouse in Fishskinning, and then the Raelech stonecutters tear down the Cloister, crumbling the stone with their kenning and repurposing it to build new embassies for Rael, Brynlön, and Kauria, each according to their preferred architectural styles. They leave space for Hathrir, Ghurana Nent, Joabei, Bačiiš, and Omesh to build their embassies later, while the Fornish grow their own with the help of a greensleeve who had the proper seeds and acorns with him.

Fintan joins Nebesa the day after that at the old temple, where she begins by telling the people they can worship anyone they like from now on except Žalost, or even worship no one at all. She invites priests of all faiths to set up services in the temple, which will honor the six children of Teldwen and Kalaad. She reads from a scroll of the old Eculan faith that survived the cult's purges, and then a Kaurian priest of the gale speaks for a while about Reinei, followed by Fintan, who shares passages from the scrolls of Raena, Dinae, and Kaelin.

Nebesa and Pavle both want me to commit to being part of the new government after that, especially since they want candidates they can trust to run against some leather-bound men that they can't, but I tell them I need to see to my family first. Because I don't know what happened to them or if they're even still alive. Milenka showed up in Sveto Selo and told me that Radič went to warn my family, but she hasn't heard from him since they parted. That's worrisome, so Nebesa gives me leave to go check and hope for good news, and I return to the *Shearwater* to ask for a favor. Could a cyclone fly me to Drvo? They immediately assign me Mardan Vess, and together we fly south to my family's kafa farm.

Returning home is such a stew of hope and fear, boiling angrily at me to appreciate it or loathe it. I wonder what I shall see: parents relieved that I'm alive and welcoming me home, a chorus of accusations casting me away like broth gone bad, or nothing but a field of ashes? The potential for joy or horror is nearly without bounds, because I'd made the decision to put all families above my own.

The hope surges to the fore as I see that the farm is intact and there are no obvious signs of cultists in control of things. Insects hum and thrive, birds chirp, and it seems that all is well.

When we land, I call out to the house, burst into the kitchen, and meet the icy glares of my parents. The hope wilts in my heart, seeing their expressions.

"Mother! Father! I'm so glad you're well!"

They make no reply, unless a low grumble from my father counts. Their faces harden.

"What's wrong? The war is over. The cult is no more. We're safe."

"Safe?" Father says. "I think we're the opposite of safe here."

"Why? What happened?"

A tear runs down Mother's cheek, and she sniffs but otherwise makes no sound. Father answers.

"Your friend Radič came here, saying that you'd joined the invaders." He chucks his chin at the Kaurian cyclone. "I see it's true. And because of that, he said we should run and hide, because the cult might come after us."

"And did they?"

"Not yet. Perhaps they will soon, because I do not think they are no more, as you say. But your brother objected to the use of the word *cult*. He accused Radič of being a traitor and a heretic and of turning you into one as well. He attacked Radič."

"What? No," I say, recalling that Radič hasn't been heard from yet. "Is he okay?"

"Who?"

"Radič."

Father's eyes widen and his nostrils flare. "Why do you ask about him? Why do you not ask about your brother?"

"Is my brother okay?"

"No, he is not! He's dead! And so is your friend Radič! They killed each other, and it's because of you."

"They're both dead?"

"That's what I said!"

It strikes me dumb, because I never considered this outcome. Except that my suspicions about my brother being a fanatic follower of Žalost have proved to be true. He was never kind to me or anyone, so I don't feel any grief over his passing, as I know I should. But Radič—much more a brother to me, and whom I loved as a brother—for him I shed tears. Especially since I sent him to what turned out to be his doom. His family will never forgive me.

And neither will mine, apparently.

"Get your things and go," Father says, and gestures briefly at Mother. "We've already discussed it. We can't have you around here, reminding us every day of what we've lost."

That spurs my mouth to work again. "Wouldn't you be reminded every day anyway? Why can't I stay?"

"Because I don't want to look at you!" Father rages, his face purpling. "Go make your way elsewhere. Go with these foreigners, since you betrayed us for them!"

I appeal to Mother, who often gives me honey to cut through the heat.

"Can you spare me no shred of understanding or forgiveness?" I ask.

She shakes her head, wipes briefly at her cheeks, and crosses her arms beneath her chest. "Perhaps in time, Fanje, we will find a welcome for you again. For now it is lost."

Gods, it hurts so much. I knew there would be consequences but made my choices anyway, without a care for the pain, because it was in the future. But now that it's present, I'm unsure how it can be borne, and I stand there, shattered.

"I will go, then," I say through sobs when I'm able. "I will miss you and love you. And hope that someday you will feel the same." Turning to Mardan Vess, I ask her in awkward hand signals if she'll wait while I gather a few belongings. She nods and indicates that she'll be outside.

In my room, half blinded by tears, I cram as many clothing items as I can into a bag along with a toothbrush and a comb and a pitiful purse of coins I've been able to save over the years. There are no keepsakes, no memories I wish to take with me. But I do leave Father with a piece of news.

"I've negotiated the sale of our kafa beans to the Fornish. It's a whole new market, and they'll be back for more. The demand will be enormous. They'll eventually grow their own, but imported Eculan kafa will be a luxury good forever. So I hope you'll prosper."

"Who are the Fornish?"

"People from across the ocean who possess the Fifth Kenning. I hope you'll be well. Goodbye."

"Goodbye," Father says with finality, and neither he nor my mother looks open to a farewell embrace, so I don't even attempt one. Crying openly, just an absolute mess of a person, I leave my home perhaps forever and ask Mardan to fly me away from there.

I tell Nebesa when I return that I will accept her offer to be Ecula's ambassador to Brynlön. Having lost everything tying me to my country, I might as well do as Father says and make my way elsewhere with these foreigners.

HOLLIT

A Drink Aflame

After I burned the Eculan fleet, their shipyards, the lumber mill, and the Seven-Year Ship, there was little for me to do during the invasion. I had no significant armor beyond lava-dragon hide, and I would have been an easy and obvious target if I tried to enter the city, so I remained on the *Nentian Herald* once I got transferred over there and hoped I could find some way to be useful and nondestructive. Once the fighting ended and it became clear that we were trying to foster goodwill going forward with the Eculans, I volunteered to enchant firebowls until it was time to leave. Soon after the first batch, I had more orders than I could handle, which at first surprised me but then made a lot of sense.

Firebowls have long been a popular alternative to candles in the six nations and a staple of the Hathrim economy—every hearthfire has firelords working on them, because they're a steady source of income. People like having more light and heat that not only lasts longer than candles but can often be presented in an attractive bowl without all the mess of wax—go figure. But Ecula had never had access to fire-bowls, because the Hathrim never traded with them. I'd stumbled into a virgin market.

I was able to trade twelve of them for some Hathrim-sized cloaks and tunics made of Brdan wool, both for me and as a gift for Orden. I thought he'd like the Eculan dyes and patterns as much as I did. But the orders kept coming, and I realized I basically had a new business on my hands, which would keep Orden and me afloat financially until Pelemyn's food supply and economy improved enough for us to reopen the Roasted Sunchuck.

But primarily I was grateful that I was able to use the First Kenning in a way that was productive rather than destructive.

Like many of us—Tallynd du Böll and others—I feared I'd been irrevocably changed for the worse by this journey. I didn't think I'd strained myself to the point where I incurred a debt from my kenning, but I felt as if I must have the lines of a murderer etched on my face now, some telltale sign that I'd taken lives instead of nourishing them.

I was counseled to think of all the lives I'd saved by torching that fleet. Lives on both sides—tens of thousands of Eculan conscripts who wanted no part of the war would be able to stay home and thrive now, in addition to the Brynt lives that would be saved. But I couldn't see those saved lives in my mind. The eight deaths, however, were seared in my memory.

Would Orden still care for me after this? Someone who had used the First Kenning to kill? It was exactly the sort of thing we'd spent our entire lives avoiding. He might forgive it since they were not targeted, and my actions did prevent the second invasion. But how long until he decided that a haunted woman woken by nightmares—yes, they'd already begun— was far too difficult to love?

Someone from the *Nentian Herald* blabbed about my troubles after a week of such nights—I guess I was waking others in addition to myself. I know someone talked, because an orange-robed priest of the gale named Kindin Ladd came over from the *Shearwater* to join me as I worked on filling a stack of orders. Priests of the gale don't make a habit of paying visits to the lavaborn while they're enchanting firebowls, so it was a visit urged on by persons unknown.

We both pretended for a while that it wasn't what it was. He patiently admired the bowl I was working on, an attractive hammered copper, and commented on what great progress the Raelechs were making with building a bridge across the strait for the Eculans and how pleasant it was to work with the new leadership of what was being called the Šest bloc, which was busily purging the other cities of cult loyalists and reallocating their resources from war matériel and army logistics into infrastructure and trade. Then he began his final approach.

"Still, quite a bit of violence to get us to this place. Many people—Kaurians especially—are having trouble with what they witnessed. Feelings of guilt, and loss, and so on. How are you feeling, Hollit? Are you sleeping well?"

I grunted. "You know I'm not or you wouldn't be here."

He smiled at me. "True enough. Your friends are concerned. They have arranged for you to talk to me in strictest privacy."

"On a boat?"

"Even so. Look around."

That was a strange enough request that I did. There were almost always crew members on deck, performing some kind of task or another, but curiously we had the entire fore to ourselves. I narrowed my eyes at him.

"It's a conspiracy."

He chuckled. "I suppose it is. But if so, it is the kindest sort of conspiracy, which comes from a place of love. You don't have to talk to me, of course. It might help, however, and it's difficult to fathom how it could hurt. Fintan has spoken to me, as have Nara du Fesset and many others, and I like to think I've helped them in some small way. They've told me that they feel better, at least, and I hope they wouldn't feel it necessary to lie about that."

"Hmm. What are you going to do? Tell me to breathe peace?"

"Ha! Very likely at some point. But that phrase is almost meaningless unless you know how to do it."

"How to breathe? Isn't that something we all do unconsciously?"

"Yes, exactly. And we want you to internalize the processes of rebalancing yourself so that you can restore peace unconsciously as well. The phrase becomes a mantra that helps your mind reset and rest. It's widely misinterpreted as something that Kaurians just say. Sometimes, perhaps it is. But there's also a serious origin to the phrase."

"What's that?"

"It varies from person to person. Because we are all troubled by different things, and so the path we must each walk to peace is unique to ourselves."

"So what troubles you, Kindin Ladd, and how did you walk yourself back to peace?"

I expected a vague evasion, a redirection to me, but he surprised me.

"Like you, I hurt someone. I felt guilty about it and had nightmares. On rare occasions, when I've had a stressful day or I've had to use my blessing, they return. These kinds of feelings, you see, can never be fully fixed. They are part of who we are now; they're embedded in our minds, like grit that builds up in gears, reducing their efficiency and sometimes bringing them to a grinding halt. And so they must be cleaned and maintained to preserve good working order, if you'll allow me the metaphor."

"I'll allow it. Who did you hurt?"

"A young man in Linlauen who had stolen a blackmack from a fishmonger. I was a young priest, eager and inexperienced, and I took things too far."

"How do you mean? I suppose I don't understand your blessing."

"Raelech couriers have tremendous speed, but in practical terms they jog at a sustainable pace. They do, however, get winded after a while, whereas I do not. I can run at top speed—which is not particularly fast in comparison to the athletically gifted—and never tire."

"That's it? You just never run out of breath?"

"It's a tremendous advantage if you know how to fight. Because everyone else always gets tired eventually."

"Oh. And you know how to fight?"

"I am very skilled. We train to immobilize our opponents and do no lasting harm."

"But you did in this case?"

"Aye. I chased the thief down, intending to immobilize him, and I did—but it was permanent. When I bore him to the ground, he landed awkwardly and I accidentally paralyzed him, and he remains so to this day. He was simply hungry, and the punishment he received far exceeded the crime. I had not restored peace that day."

"What had you intended to do with him?"

"Return the blackmack to the fishmonger if it was still edible, compensate the fishmonger if not, and deliver the young man to Reinei's temple, where he could be counseled and given aid and never need to steal his food again. Instead, I robbed him of an enormous amount of potential, harmed my own reputation and that of every priest of the gale, and I live with that guilt every day. It is not the same as your situation, I know, but I think I understand much of what you're feeling."

"Yes, I imagine you do. So how do you live with it?"

"First, recognize that the past cannot be changed, because time is oppressively linear. We both did something that was destructive to others, and it haunts us. Our pasts reverberate and echo in our present and future, so the second thing you must do is choose whether those echoes will bring further destruction or instead be creative."

"What do you mean?"

He gestured to my firebowl. "What you're doing now is creative. But you could, in response to your recent trauma, become self-destructive or even habitually violent. The latter is not in your nature."

"No. Very much not."

"Even so. The former is still a danger. Guilt and regrets can eat away at you like acid if you do not do something to counter them."

"So what do you do?"

"I do this work right here. I remember that boy because of course I can never forget him, but then I reaffirm, daily, that I will do better and help people, and I do. It doesn't remove my guilt, but it does allow me to live with it and feel that since that day I have been a better person. Which, in the end, is all we can do, yes?"

"I . . . don't know?"

"Come around to the conclusion in your own good time. I have studied it for a long while now and assure you it's correct. I can be sorry about what I did to that boy, and I can help people. Those are positive outcomes for me and for everyone else. The alternatives are unpleasant. So I think you have much to ponder, and the journey will be long, but you will learn to appreciate it in time. You feel sorry for what you did. You are helping Eculans with these firebowls, and when your restaurant reopens in Pelemyn, you'll help Brynts remember how sweet and savory life can be."

"So just . . . live my life? That seems inadequate."

"It is not simply living as if nothing happened. I'm very conscious of what I did and regret it every day. There's a seething mass of self-loathing within me—"

"Yes!" I interrupted, perhaps a bit too loudly, because that was something I felt too. And still feel.

"Indeed, you know what I mean. So. That self-loathing is going to gnaw at you. And it can sour your disposition, make you reclusive, antisocial—you might come to believe that others must loathe you as you do yourself, and therefore you could lash out at them and ruin relationships you cherish, which would of course only make things worse in your head. Doing something to be a better person is your shelter against that storm inside. It will rage, but you have the power to calm it. Every day, you can either do something to help others or remind yourself that you already did. Over time—and it *will* take time, I don't want to suggest that any of this is easy— you will be able to say that you helped and you're going to help some more. You were better and will continue to be better. And that is how you will learn to breathe peace. You do the work—and it *is* work—every day."

Grunting to let him know I heard all that and was thinking about it, I bent to my firebowl and finished the enchantment. I ignited the oxygen in the air, and a small fire, suitable for illumination, blazed forth along its interior surface, no higher than the thickness of a toenail. It could continue like that for months, with no fuel other than ambient air. Add fuel and it would burn brighter and hotter and consume that fuel more efficiently than a normal fire.

"Ah, that's lovely," the priest said.

"Thank you."

"My parents used to buy small firebowls made of colored glass, though I am unsure of their provenance. They used them to set moods in different rooms."

"They may have been from Sardrik or Haradok. They tend to focus on glass more than metals there. We use orange ones in our restaurant. Stimulates the appetite."

"I remember. I look forward to eating there again someday."

"We'll look forward to having you. I appreciate your counsel, Kindin. You've given me much to think about, and I believe it'll help."

"It's been my pleasure, Hollit."

It *was* helpful. Minimally, at first, because I didn't see how I would ever balance my ledger. But I did get a full night's

sleep after a couple more rough ones, had a few more eve-
nings of terror, and then some blissful slumbers after that.
The intervals between the nightmares kept getting longer,
and by the time we set sail for home, I was able to go to sleep
without expectations of waking myself and everyone else on
the *Nentian Herald*. It still happened sometimes, but everyone
recognized that I'd gotten better and hoped I'd continue to
improve.

I'm not sure I can definitively say what had the most effect; perhaps I'd worked myself to exhaustion, or perhaps
rationalizations and time wore down the sharp edges of my
trauma, or maybe the priest of the gale really did know what
he was talking about and I was learning to breathe peace.
Regardless, I thought my struggles with it were worth noting
for the history being compiled by Dervan du Alöbar, because
it might help others someday dealing with similar woes.

When we finally arrived back in Pelemyn to much fanfare
and celebration—thanks to the Raelech bard broadcasting
our imminent appearance—my heart dropped somewhat: I
didn't see Orden towering over the cheering crowd, a smile
gleaming through his beard. It actually gave me cause to
worry. Had he taken the opportunity of my absence to exit?

Muttering thanks to well-wishers and excusing myself, I
hurried to our home outside the city walls to the southwest,
a large wooden structure that would be considered unspeak-
ably rich in Hathrir but was fairly nondescript—except for its
height—in Brynlön.

Orden wasn't there, and my throat tightened and my vision blurred, my fears growing. Where could he be? Shopping, perhaps? I dismissed the possibility, because if he'd been
in the city, he would have surely heard of the fleet's arrival
and come to see me. He might be out in the countryside,
hunting. That was the most likely answer, I thought, because

his things were still in the house. He hadn't packed up and left.

It was utterly impossible for me to sit and wait for him to come home. I had to find him. Maybe he was at the restaurant for some reason? Cleaning it, perhaps. I suppose it was plausible that it could even be open, if he'd hired an interim chef to offer a limited menu, and that meant they'd be preparing to reopen regularly soon. I decided I would check there first and then resort to wandering the city, shouting, *Has anybody seen a giant?*

Back I went into the city. Excitement was on the faces of everyone I passed, but I must have looked unhappy and therefore uninformed, since several people shouted up at my face that the fleet had returned victorious and the second invasion wouldn't be happening.

A sign hanging on the door to our restaurant said CLOSED, and a flyer posted on the door said that we would be closed until further notice. But the glow of orange firebowls could be seen through the windows to the side. Someone was in there.

I tromped around back, entered the kitchen, and called out, "Orden? Orden!"

"Yes! In here!" he replied from the dining room, and I had to stop and take a breath in relief—and also to make sure I had plenty of air to fire questions at him as I plowed through the swinging doors of the kitchen to find him standing behind the bar.

"What are you doing here? I've been looking all over for you. Don't tell me you hadn't heard we returned when the Raelech bard announced it for all to hear!"

"I did hear, I did indeed. Welcome home, Hollit. I came here because, when we first met, I was behind the bar, and we began to forge a bond that day that has lasted a dozen years. You had a problem to solve, and I made you drinks and listened and together we figured it out. I thought this journey—

the purpose of it, and what would be required of you—would burden you with a new set of problems, so I wanted to face them here, together, in a place we built, where we can reforge our bond and make it even stronger."

I wanted to be angry, but he was just dropping gallons of water on my fire. "You couldn't have left a note at home?" was all I managed.

"I'm sorry. I was in the city when I heard you were coming in, and I didn't think I'd have time to run home and back here. Please, come sit, and let's talk. I've created a new drink for your homecoming."

The bar in the Roasted Sunchuck was built at two levels: half of it to accommodate Brynt-sized customers, and half of it above their heads to accommodate me and provide Orden an adequate working space. Making tiny drinks for tiny people was actually challenging for him, so we often sold "drinks for two," which were normal sized for us, but packaged and sold to our customers as larger shareable drinks with straws. Some part of them would often be on fire, because that was the fun of ordering drinks from the lavaborn.

I leaned over the bar, and he met me halfway for a kiss. It was a perfect melding of my memories to reality: his beard smelling of cedar and pine from the oil he used, his lips soft and tasting faintly of whiskey and peaches.

"Mmm," he said. "I missed you so much."

"And I missed you."

"I want to hear everything. The good and the bad."

"There's plenty of both."

"Okay. Sit, and I will make you Hollit's Homecoming Hooch."

I laughed at the sweet silliness of the name. He started to craft it and narrated what he was doing as he went, pouring ingredients into a shaker filled with ice.

"It's a celebration of the six nations. It begins with two shots of the Good Shit from Rael, then one shot each of Hathrim emberfruit liqueur, Panevik's Potent Pontish black-tea syrup from Forn, and lemon juice. Shake with ice and strain into a Hathrim crystal coupe. Then we sprinkle in some Kaurian blood-orange bitters to surf on top like blooms of lava and set that spent half of lemon to float in there with a sugar cube nestled into the middle of it. Then we drizzle that sugar with a few drops of emberfruit juice, spark it for a wee merry blaze, and garnish with a sprig of Nentian mint. There we go."

"Wow. Whoa, hold on: There's nothing Brynt in this drink?"

"Of course there is. There's me, and since you are part of my life, there's you. For are we not Brynt ourselves now? And won't we be Brynt from now on? This is far more of a home for us than Hathrir ever was."

Well. A rather large buildup of emotions wanted to erupt at that, but I feared it wouldn't stop for a while, and I needed to try this amazing drink he made for me first. So I sipped it, declared it delicious, and thanked him, and he got to smile in satisfaction for a half second before I tried to laugh and cry and howl at the same time and he looked properly alarmed.

Everything tumbled out then, what I'd done and what others had done, my nightmares and fears and more, and he listened like the kind man and professional he was while the city of Pelemyn celebrated without us. When I finally wound down and said I was finished and wanted to hear him talk instead, he made us both fresh drinks in crystal goblets and held his poised near mine to chime in accord.

"Life brings us dark hours sometimes. But you, my love, are the light that ends all my darkness, as I hope I am yours. You have nothing to fear now. I am so happy you are home."

I sniffled and smiled through a sob. "Me too. I won't ever be leaving again."

GONDEL

Reinei's Peace

The translation workload after the fall of the cult was exhausting and endless, but as it served to fashion a lasting peace between our six nations and Ecula, I could not think of anything more important to do. Not that I desired anything else, except sleep. It was tremendously gratifying to facilitate that process, and it would have been sufficient in itself, a validation of all my years of study.

But I was very richly rewarded with books. Actual books that taught the Eculan language, from basic texts to advanced linguistics, and even a dictionary and a selection of their favorite works of literature. And Fanje, the young Eculan woman who had helped us earlier and returned to Pelemyn with us as an appointed ambassador of their new government, spent the journey to Brynlön helping me refine my pronunciation and coaching me on finer points of conjugation and syntax that I had never fully understood, even as she reminded me of things I'd forgotten due to the trauma of an attempted possession.

I also received two very generous welcomes as a hero: one in Pelemyn, and another some weeks later, when we returned to Kauria with the fleet.

We were sent off from Pelemyn with yet another impossible cargo hold of gift baskets filled with mustards and cheeses. And I reflected that since my lifelong pursuit of discovering what happened during the Rift was now largely answered—Sedam's story having been confirmed in many of its essentials by Abhinava Khose's visit with Raena in the

Northern Yawn—I would need to redirect my energies elsewhere. Many adjustments would need to be made. I was looking forward to seeing how the church would react to the news about Reinei having another aspect, as Shoawei in the north, and furthermore possessing no gender. I suspected that they would accept it and keep going, as many of the Kaurians in the fleet had already done. The god we worshipped and looked to for guidance and moral clarity still existed, after all; a change in pronouns and some layers of nuance did not alter a whit of Reinei's core message, and Kindin Ladd, priest of the gale, agreed with that assessment. He was finally returning home after years of service at the embassy in Pelemyn.

He did wonder aloud if these revelations might change the number of people seeking a blessing—not just in Kauria but at all the other sites. Would seekers want to throw themselves into the Tempest of Reinei, for example, knowing that they would either be blessed using the life energy of other seekers or else become energy used to bless others?

"That, to my mind," he said as we leaned on the port railing of the *Shearwater* together, "is far more important than Reinei's gender."

"I suppose it depends on whether one feels the nature of the sacrifice has been changed," said Maron, who stood on my right. "Or perhaps whether the nature of the death has changed. When one dies without a sacrifice—at home from disease or old age, or an accident in the street—does one's spirit experience a different fate than during a seeking? I think that is the question that all faiths must answer. Perhaps some will calculate that the sacrifice benefits others either way— their lives will serve Kauria one way or another. But some, I am sure, will be dissuaded by the perception that they're being eaten by a god."

That did seem to be the crux of the issue, and Kindin Ladd and I both made appreciative noises. I was experiencing this pleasant feeling of being proud of my husband's intelligence, and then Kindin Ladd brought up the matter of whether Kauria might have any wraith spies in our cities. My eyes flew open in alarm at that, but before I could say anything, Maron snorted.

"Who cares? I'd rather have spies than dickskin mites."

Ah, well. I was still proud of him but would have to ignore the occasional side dish of embarrassment he served up. He did his best to ignore my many faults, so it would be petty of me to criticize his method of maintaining a proper perspective.

Kindin Ladd startled me, though, by bobbing his head up and down. "You know what? Me too. I mean, how bad could spies really be, at this point?"

"Not that bad, in comparison," Maron said.

"Not at all," the priest agreed.

Teela Parr, the mistral's chamberlain, greeted us at the docks in Linlauen with a smile that did not quite reach her eyes.

"Scholar Vedd. Welcome. The mistral would like an immediate audience. I see your husband is with you, so I hope we won't have a repeat of what happened last time you came home?"

"No. Today you can rely upon my good behavior."

Her eyes trailed down my tunic, searching for stains. When she found none, she said with some surprise, "You're looking well kempt."

"For a limited time, yes. I've made a special effort."

"Very impressive."

Mistral Kira was dressed in layers of flowing oranges and violets, her headdress a towering torus. The court dandies, with their high fashion and effulgent riches oozing from their pores, looked upon me with something other than condescension and contempt this time. I am not sure what it was, because frankly I had never been regarded favorably before.

But the mistral lauded me as a triumph of Reinei, a Kaurian whose contributions to the allied forces helped restore peace to a war-torn world. Then she led a round of applause for me and it just kept going and going, because no one would stop before the mistral did. It was the sort of applause scholars never receive, and I simply nodded and smiled nervously at everyone, because I didn't know what else to do. The mistral eventually stopped clapping and mercifully waved everyone silent.

Then she informed me that I would be nationally celebrated and there would be parades and fêtes and things, which I think she intended to be welcome news but which terrified me because it meant I'd need to continue to dress well.

"That's all unnecessary," I began, to which she replied, "Nonsense!" So I admitted instead that it was all very kind.

"Tell me, Scholar—we owe you so much—what boon would you have of me that is in my power to grant?"

I considered for a few seconds and then said, "Come with Maron and me to Mugg's Chowder House." That set off a hubbub of scandalized murmuring among the courtiers. Even their perfume smelled outraged.

"I beg your pardon?" I had clearly not asked for anything she was expecting. Maybe she thought I'd want a bedroom set of carved silverbark or something.

"Let's have a mug of chowder and a mug of beer. And there we will drink to my brother, and to Ponder Tann, and to Zephyr Bernaud Goss and Hondi Rett, and everyone who purchased this peace we all breathe at the cost of their own lives."

"Yes," the Mistral Kira said. "Yes, I would happily do that."

"Right now."

"Oh—right now?" She shot a glance at Teela Parr, perhaps realizing this would interfere with whatever else she had scheduled that day, and the chamberlain's eyes widened in panic as she shook her head, advising against it.

"Yes," I said. "Honoring them first seems the proper thing to do."

"It does, yes indeed. You teach me well, Scholar. Very well. Let's go." The chamberlain visibly sagged in defeat as the mistral descended from her dais and the hubbub grew. The mistral was just leaving to get a beer? In a mug? And not any-place civilized but down at the docks, where the air smelled of fish and unwashed tourists? What should they do? What was the protocol? What about her schedule? Was this even allowed?

To her immense credit, the mistral appeared to be every bit as amused by the courtiers' confusion as I was.

She took my hand and led me to one of the guarded doors behind her throne. She leaned over just the tiniest bit and whispered out the side of her mouth, "I really missed you. I love how you get them so upset."

"It's remarkably easy. You just have to act like a normal person with empathy."

Mistral Kira tittered, her eyes glinting. "I would keep you around if your talents wouldn't be utterly wasted. I could use some more normality."

"There's plenty of it to be found outside the palace grounds. I highly recommend seeking it out."

"Perhaps I will. Or perhaps I'll simply retire and not run for this office again, leave all these elitist snobs to be someone else's problem." Once behind the door, she barked orders for a carriage for immediate departure, then looked back at Maron, who was a step behind, and beckoned him to her other side, where she took his hand as well. We continued down the hallway toward some destination to be revealed. "Come, gentlemen. Some of the snooty folk will try to fol-low us, but the faster we get there, the longer we will have to speak alone. Or now, in fact, might be best, if you wish to discuss anything in particular. Once we get there, there will be quite a bit of distraction, I imagine, and this might be the best chance we have for some privacy. A mug raised to heroes can't be all you want, can it?"

"Oh. Well, I confess that there might be one other thing."

The mistral's mouth tugged upward at the corner as her eyes slid sideways.

"Mm-hmm. I knew it. Let's hear it."

I opened my mouth to speak, but Teela Parr interrupted from behind.

"Mistral, we don't have enough security in place at the docks to guarantee any peace."

"Are we a peaceful nation or not?"

"We are, but—"

"If I'm threatened, Teela, I'll fly away. Benefits of being a cyclone. Problem solved. Grab some windguards and some priests of the gale if it makes you feel better. We'll be fine."

"Yes, Mistral. What about your appointments with the city ministers this afternoon?"

"Cancel them all."

Maron was looking at her with awe, and she caught it.

"What is it?" she asked.

"Mistral, while being fully committed and in love with my husband, I am deeply smitten with you right now. If you cancel anything else, I may swoon."

She laughed, such delightful music.

I could feel Teela's eyes burning into the back of my neck. Once again, I had made her life difficult, and once again it had something to do with Mugg's Chowder House. She would probably avoid the place forever after this, and it occurred to me that might not be so bad.

We exited the labyrinthine halls into a courtyard just as a carriage clopped up to our position; a windguard smartly stepped down from the back and opened the door for us. Maron and I bundled ourselves into one side while the mistral and her chamberlain took the other. Teela Parr looked thoroughly disgusted and the mistral noticed, thoroughly amused. I suppose if one's life is scheduled so completely, there must be an exquisite satisfaction to finding excuses to shred the schedule.

As we got under way to Mugg's Chowder House, the mistral said, "Now, what else is it you wished to discuss?"

I handed over the proposed treaty between Ecula and Kauria. "That's a nonaggression pact and trade agreement with Ecula, written in both Eculan and Kaurian. Of course you will need to review it and perhaps make changes to some details, but regardless of how long ratification takes, we are assured of two things: peace and commerce. Kaurian merchants will soon have access to a vast new market, which will no doubt please many of your courtiers."

The mistral hummed in pleasure. "Very much so. The gleam of avarice in their eyes when they hear of this will be so bright, I may have to shield my vision, lest it be damaged."

I barely managed to stifle a laugh at this, but Maron did not bother trying and he chuckled heartily.

"Since trade is to begin soon, I would like your blessing and perhaps your aid in forming the Eculan language department at Linlauen University. It's my belief that Kaurian merchants can secure an economic advantage over other countries if we are able to communicate effectively."

"Yes! Absolutely." Mistral Kira turned to her chamberlain. "Teela, I want the university president standing before me first thing in the morning. Whatever he has scheduled will need to be rescheduled."

"Yes, Mistral."

"Whoo. Oh, my. I feel dizzy," Maron said, and he clutched his forehead.

"You do? Are you all right?" I asked.

"I think I'm getting drunk on the mistral's power, it's so

intoxicating. She's canceling *other* people's appointments now! It's too much!"

"Gah. You rogue." I punched him playfully in the arm as the mistral laughed musically at his joke. "You had me worried."

"You are both treasures," Mistral Kira said, and waggled the treaty in her hand. "Thank you for this, Gondel. We'll begin our review after we have honored those who purchased our peace."

We arrived at Mugg's Chowder House in high spirits, and Mugg was so incredibly happy to have the mistral visit his establishment that he could not stop smiling. He tried at first to offer her something fancy, hollering for a wine list and talking of crab and lobster in butter and things of that nature, but she waved him silent. It had the effect of silencing the entire restaurant, however, which may or may not have been her intention. She took advantage of it regardless and spoke up, projecting her voice so that all could hear.

"I have come, good friends, at the request of Scholar Vedd—our national hero who has just returned in triumph from the Giant Wars—for a mug of chowder and a mug of beer. We want to raise our mugs to honor the brave Kaurians who did not return, but whose sacrifice brought us the peace we breathe in this moment. So please, let me buy a round for everyone, so that all those who wish to participate may do so. We'll drink when everyone is served."

Mugg could not move quickly enough among the general cheer. He served Mistral Kira, Maron, and me with his own hands and thanked me profusely for bringing the mistral to his restaurant. Her presence was already attracting a host of new fancy customers, who looked bewildered to be in such a humble house of ale.

Eventually the beers were all in hand, and we had chowder too, and the mistral called for silence and got it. Then she asked me to name the names. I began with my brother, who took Ponder Tann and me to discover what was happening in Brynlön and set us on the journey of discovery. And then I spoke of Ponder, "who told me at that bar, right over there, that he was flying to Ecula to seek a peace, though he may not return," and he never did. And then I told them of Zephyr Bernaud Goss and Hondi Rett, slain by a cavern-jawed eel in the Peles Ocean but who set the operational standards for the fleet that proved to be so effective.

And of course there were uncounted others I could not name. Brynlön and Rael and Forn lost many thousands of people, while Kauria lost only four. We certainly had Reinei to thank for our peace, but we had our allies to thank as well.

"Let us be forever grateful to them all," I said, and we drank to their memories and breathed peace together.

The mistral then took the opportunity to speak of what I had done—how my scholarship and translation efforts proved crucial in the war and resulted in a peace treaty and a new trading partner in Ecula. She announced there would be a parade to honor me next week, and it was all quite embarrassing, which Maron enjoyed particularly, but thankfully it ended after an excruciating minute and I felt certain I would be able to disappear into anonymous scholarly life soon. People would not be seeking me out in the library to secure my autograph.

But while conversation swirled around us, the mistral asked Maron what he would be doing now that we were home and I'd be very busy soon with a new language department and a large number of students.

"Oh, I'm going to take advantage of Gondel's famous name."

"You are?" I asked.

"Mm-hmm." He nodded, a mischievous look in his eye. "We have so much mustard now—a full cargo hold or more from this trip, plus everything we brought home earlier—that we can start selling it."

"You mean like a side business?"

"No, as the start-up for a long-term business. We're going to put *Gondel's Imported Brynt Mustard* on every jar we have in storage and sell them while we build an actual mustard-production business."

"Oh. What will the labels say then?"

"They'll say *Gondel's Homemade Mustard,* of course."

"I like this plan," Mistral Kira said. "You must send me a jar when it's ready. I will suffer no other mustards to adorn my cheeses."

"I will do so, Mistral, as surely as seagulls will circle the fishmonger."

"You're going to turn me into the Mustard Man of Kauria, then?" I asked.

"I expect so, but that title will be a distant third behind *Maron's husband* and *the hero of the Giant Wars.*"

"Hold on: I'll be primarily known as Maron's husband?"

Maron smiled at me. "Well, it's how I think of you, my love."

"Ha ha! As you should."

KOESHA

The Navigator's Return

It took no small effort to persuade Haesha and the others that I really, really needed to sail back to Blight before we went home to Joabei. Because I was the only one who could tell Sedam—or Vo Lai—that his plans had been foiled and have a half-decent expectation of surviving. And it needed to be done, because while the war might be over, the true threat—the architect of it all, whose selfishness had pitted nations against one another and led to hundreds of thousands of deaths—remained untouched and undeterred from trying something else.

We had the wraith cloaks in the hold and a bunch of unspun Eculan wool besides, half of it dyed that exquisite indigo from the island of Slivovi, and half undyed. Both our fame and riches were assured when we got home, and we were so close. Haesha pointed out correctly that we had pregnant women getting closer to their due dates and that we had already escaped death so narrowly so many times that it would be foolish to flirt with it again. But I couldn't go home without fulfilling my promise to let Sedam know what happened, not least because I truly wished to see how he reacted, but also because it behooved us to prepare ourselves for what he might do next.

We anchored off the east coast of Blight, never approaching the dock, and I told Haesha to give me a day before sailing home without me. I fastened a wraith cloak about my neck and gave her a stern warning: "Do not, under any circumstances, come ashore to look for me. If I don't return in a day, I'm dead."

Haesha had already argued with me and it had been settled days before, so she only nodded, said, "Aye, Zephyr," then requested permission for a hug.

As we embraced, I whispered, "I intend to come back, but if I don't, you are the finest of friends and I wish you long life."

I grasped the sides of her head and used my kenning as a balm to heal her scars from the pine shrikes. Haesha felt the change, gasped, and put her fingers to her face, feeling the smooth skin there.

"What did you do?"

I smiled through the pain that effort required and kissed her briefly on the forehead. "Just being a balm." I likewise healed the scars on Leisuen, even regenerating the lost cartilage from her ear, then summoned wind to fly me to the kenning site and landed in front of the throned god. The grass between the paving stones, I noted, had grown somewhat unruly. But as before, there were no wraiths in this area; they preferred to keep their distance from Sedam, no matter what state he was in.

I took a closer look at him; his stonelike skin was of a slightly different hue than the marble statues of his siblings. A faint rose blush to it, perhaps. He had obviously sunk into his dormant state while he waited for events to play out. I wanted to put an end to that waiting.

Removing the wraith cloak, I spoke to him in Joabeian. "Sedam, it is Koesha Gansu, and I have come to you with news. Please wake so I can tell you what happened." I repeated variations of this for perhaps a half hour, keeping a nervous eye on the surrounding forest. If any wraiths decided to risk coming for me, I wanted some warning.

The rose blush of the marble eventually deepened, and the eyes cleared and focused on me. The stone cracked and then smoothed again as it transformed to skin, and the lips finally moved.

"Koesha. Welcome. I see you have used your powers as a balm. You look significantly older than the last time I saw you. What news?"

"First, let me remind you of your promise to do me no harm."

He smiled indulgently. "I need no reminder. I wouldn't think of it. But that's an inauspicious beginning. Have you come to deliver bad news?"

"When I left, you spoke of events in motion that you could not stop and that had an even chance of succeeding."

"Yes, I remember."

"While I don't know precisely which events you had in mind, I believe your schemes have come to naught. Your army in the north is destroyed and will not be bothering the krakens. And the second invasion from Ecula will never happen. The fleet is burned, your cult is outlawed, and a new government rules there now. Isposnik Draško is dead by my own hand, and the kraljic slain."

He clutched at his throne, visibly seethed for a few seconds, then calmed himself with an effort before grinding out in a tight voice, "How is this possible?"

"An alliance of the nations and people blessed by your siblings. All six kennings against the seventh."

"*Six* kennings?"

"Yes." I pointed to the last statue on my right. "Your sister finally blessed someone. A young Nentian man who calls himself a plaguebringer. He can speak to any animal, including a kraken, and they obey him. That allowed us to cross the ocean with our fleet. He walks around with a bloodcat."

Sedam's face reddened and he bellowed at the sky in frustrated rage. Then he slumped back on his throne, defeated. "I did not think she would ever bless anyone. She played a much longer game than I did. So all is lost."

"For you, perhaps. Your siblings are still determined to keep you here. For the rest of the world, I believe they would say all is won. Ecula will rejoin the nations as a trading partner."

He covered his eyes with his hands. "So much work ruined. I should have made that last fool a harvester of souls. He might have tipped the scales in my favor, had he been there."

"Perhaps."

Sedam abruptly sat up, eyes boring into mine. "And you say you played a crucial role in this defeat. Where did you kill Draško? Was he at the temple?"

"If you mean the temple of all gods, then no. He was at the Cloister."

"And how did you do it? Your kenning should not have threatened him."

"A sword through his head that he never saw coming."

"Ah. I suppose that would work. And did you burn all of Sveto Selo down with the fleet there?"

"No, the city stands, except for the Citadel and the Cloister. But the fleet was at Riba Oči in Drvo."

He slumped again, since I had passed his tests. "So it's true. You were really there."

"Yes."

He sighed. "A result far short of what I hoped, but much as I feared. Outmaneuvered again by my siblings, so my exile shall carry on. I am so tired. And . . . defeated." He fell silent and looked around despondently. I dared not disturb the air with my breath. Eventually he continued, his voice moribund. "I cannot bear to think of enduring this isolation for centuries more, with no allies left and no hope of escape. Perhaps it is best to give you the final victory you crave and give myself an end to this torture."

"What do you mean?"

"I'll make it clear shortly."

He rose from his throne, standing on the dais, and spread his arms out from his sides. He looked to his left and then his right, spoke in a language I did not recognize, and beckoned to the trees with outstretched fingers.

And then the wraiths that had been absent from the temple grounds came to visit.

All of them.

They streamed past me, moving backward, as though pulled against their will. And I realized that they *were* being summoned against their will—summoned to Sedam—and they fought to escape like people fighting to stand against a hurricane. Then they were consumed, as he absorbed them one by one and glowed with their collected power. By the time the last one had been sucked into him, he was nearly too bright to look at, and I had to squint against the glare. But he exhaled slowly, and the light dimmed.

"There," he said. "This island is no longer plagued by wraiths. A boon given freely to all. And for you, to show my gratitude for bringing me this news, I return all the years you have sacrificed thus far, and then some."

His arm outstretched to me, and I felt my body firming up, my skin tightening, the vigor of youth returning.

I didn't know what to say, so stunned by what I had witnessed that the breath of Shoawei escaped me.

"Much better. You look to be the paragon of health and vitality. And if I can beg a boon from you, I hope you will not consider it an imposition."

I snorted in disbelief. "What boon could I possibly grant a god?"

"You have already seen how I prefer to escape boredom and wait out the years, correct? I slow down my body's rhythms and needs and grow a skin not unlike stone." I nodded, and he continued, "But you perceived that it's not quite stone, if you looked closely?"

"Yes."

"Good. So you will know the difference this time. I am going to leave this world by transforming myself fully to stone—a metamorphosis that requires tremendous energy. I ask only that you let it be known."

I blinked at him a few times. "Known to whom?"

"To whomever you meet. But primarily to my siblings. They have stunted the growth of this world to keep me in exile, and it's time for them to give everyone their freedom."

"How would I let them know? I can't speak to them as I speak to you."

"They will hear it at the kenning sites if people shout it long enough and loud enough. Though I'm not sure about the sixth. How did she make that work?"

"The source changes every few weeks among different groups of animals who attack the seeker. Bloodcats, monkeys, spiders, whatever."

"Clever. Might be dangerous to inform her, then, but I hope it can be done. They should know of my passing."

"Very well . . . I will do that, if you, uh, you know. Actually do that."

"I will do it now, since waiting accomplishes nothing. I have waited a very long time already and thought of such an exit on numerous occasions. But I wish to thank you, Koesha, for keeping your word. You have proven to be a formidable adversary but also the closest thing to a friend I have met in centuries. There are much worse ways to go than a pleasant conversation with a remarkable person."

I didn't know what to say. Was he simply being polite, or was he trying to flatter me for some reason? What reason could he have if he was about to commit suicide? I merely nodded once, and he returned it. Then he sat back on his throne, arms resting on either side, and spoke again in that old language. He glowed briefly, then his mouth closed and his face arranged itself into an expression of peace. He paled even more than was customary, and his clothing likewise lost all color as it transformed into marble along with his whole body, rewriting the very codes of flesh and fiber and transforming to something other. The entire process took less than a minute, and I stood still, watching him, for a full minute afterward. Was this real? Had that just happened?

I crept closer, comparing the tone of his marble to that of the actual marble of his siblings' statues, and saw that it matched. I stepped up to the dais and snapped my fingers in front of his blank eyes. I tickled underneath his jaw. Tugged on the solid protrusions of his braided beard. I climbed up onto the chair, standing on his thighs, and delivered a swift but ineffective kick to his stone groin. Not a single reaction. He either possessed tremendous restraint or he really had chosen to become stone.

"No way," I breathed, and since it was uttered without thinking, the breath of Shoawei speaking through me, it deserved some thought. Why did I not believe the evidence of my own eyes—and the evidence of my touch? He both appeared and felt like marble. What else could he be?

A sneaky, conniving anus of a man, that's what. The kind who farts silently and blames someone else for the stink.

The kind who manipulates an entire civilization with lies so that it attacks others. The kind who sheds not a single tear for the deaths of uncounted thousands just so long as he gets what he wants: freedom from consequences. I did not believe he would suddenly accept them now.

And the rest of us were not free from the consequences of his past behavior, so neither should he be free of them. It was because of him that krakens cursed the oceans. It was because of him that my sister died, and all her crew and countless crews before her, and a third of my crew as well. Though I had to admit that it was also because of him that I was blessed, as were so many others, if his stories of the Rift were true.

He'd had too much power over this world, even in exile

and forgotten for so long. I did not think he would willingly
give it up or exit gracefully for everyone's benefit; he was the
sort to stay alive out of spite. Someone accustomed to long-
term scheming would never make such an abrupt decision,
no matter how much he protested that he'd thought about it
for ages. I was certain this had to be a trick, because he was
Vo Lai the White Demon and not to be trusted. But I was
unsure what to do with my certainty.

I descended to the courtyard stones, somewhat nervous
because I worried that the wraiths hadn't all been expunged.
There could be some lingering at the perimeter of the island.
It would be best to confirm their absence, so I picked up the
cloak from where I'd dropped it and resettled it over my
shoulders.

My eyes fell on the temple opposite Sedam's throne. What
was inside? I'd never taken a look. It was time.

Once I stepped over the threshold, I discovered that the
shrine and relics and candles I expected were not there, nor
any altar or priceless paintings or art of any kind. It was nothing more than a fancy toolshed, meant to appear sublime but
housing the mundane. It contained everything one would
obviously need to maintain the temple grounds, as well as
some other items whose intended purpose was not so obvious. There was a stack of split logs for firewood, but I had
seen no firepit. There were tools for outdoor work and fine
finishing tools for carpentry but no evidence of why they
might be needed. Perhaps there was more on the island that
I had yet to discover, hidden beneath the canopy of trees. A
garden, perhaps, or even a dwelling of some kind, if Sedam
felt like being present for a while.

My gaze rested for a time on a particular tool without reg-
istering what it was or why my eyes wouldn't move on. Some
distant flurry deep in my mind stirred and whispered of possibilities, of the many paths a leaf might take as it falls to the

ground, of the often vast differences between our plans and their executions. But that uncertainty, applied to me, applied to everyone else as well. I seized the tool with both hands and lugged it out of the temple, leaning to one side with its weight, then realized it would be easier to simply drag it behind me. My plan, in the end, was pretty simple.

Was it rash? Ill-conceived? Perhaps. But he had fooled us all for so long. If history wished to call me rash and unthinking, I'd prefer that to being called a gull.

With some spirited grunting and no little effort, I clambered up onto the new statue of Sedam with my prize. Balancing precariously with my feet planted once again on his thighs, I stood over him and lifted the tool over my head. Calling to Shoawei for help, I summoned a bit of wind to give me some extra velocity as I brought the sledgehammer down with all my strength and then some onto the crown of Sedam's head. A large chunk of his forehead shattered into pieces, leaving a sizable, ragged dent, but it certainly felt like stone upon impact and broke apart like stone, none of the crunching of bone.

Except that the statue jerked and *moved* afterward. It even produced a grinding, inchoate cry of surprised pain.

Sedam was still alive! He'd been trying to trick me after all, and if he got any words out, maybe he'd rip my soul from my body and eat it like he did all those wraiths.

Horrified and furious and needing most urgently to end him, I struck again and again, all the while screaming, "Die, Vo Lai!" until my voice cracked and I went hoarse, wheezing past ravaged vocal cords.

After the seventh strike, he finally stopped moving. His head was essentially rubble, and even if he managed to return to flesh after that, he'd have no head. But in the very center of the ruin, there was a spot of color: It was blood. The very core of him was still flesh. Was that because I'd interrupted the transformation before it was complete, or was it his plan all along?

The former was possible, I supposed—who knew how much time such magic took to work. But the latter, I thought, was more in keeping with the character of a conniving anus. All that power he absorbed from the island's wraiths—power he'd purposely saved for a very long time, judging by their numbers—couldn't have been necessary to transform him to stone. But it would be necessary to transform him back. Or—since he had said metamorphosis was a one-way street—transform him into something entirely other. Something that wasn't exactly Sedam, something that maybe his siblings would miss. When caterpillars spun their cocoons, they dissolved into goo inside before re-forming as butterflies or moths. This stone exterior might be his cocoon.

That made much more sense to me. The way he'd led me on and suggested that I tell everyone what happened here betrayed his design. The very fact that he'd stored up wraiths for literal decades, only to consume them now, meant that he had planned something like this a long time ago. If someone like me—a reliable sort who worshipped a different god—reported he was dead, then maybe the krakens wouldn't patrol the oceans anymore. Everyone would let their guard down, and he'd be able to escape. And it would be my fault.

There was no way I'd let him use me like that.

I went back to work, with the same determination if not the same level of frenzy as before, because all that energy he'd inhaled was still in there, and if it was capable of healing him, of regrowing a head or transforming him into something else, I needed to destroy it. The people of Teldwen needed to be free of him. No more sisters lost to the deep. No more brothers lost to war.

His arms had risen somewhat and moved inward to grab at me, and I was trapped in an incomplete embrace, which I discovered when I tried to back up and got poked. But once I struck the arms off, I was able to focus solely on the torso. The pool of blood thickened and widened the farther down I went, and it bubbled too. The heart was still pumping, albeit weakly. That needed to stop.

I kept going, even though my arms felt like noodles. I toyed with the idea of bringing some sailors in to help me but dismissed it. This was a job I needed to do. It wouldn't pay for the lives of my lost crew or my sister, but at least it would prevent anyone else from losing their loved ones because of this despicable god.

Two more strikes and the beating heart was exposed, pulsating in a hollowed-out cavity of solid marble. It had a small shimmer around it, like an ethereal protective shield. Which I supposed made sense, or else the impacts from my strikes would have already damaged it. Just to make sure, I swung at the heart, and the hammer bounced off it with such force that it was torn from my hands and clattered to the pavestones below. But I had my answer regarding his intentions.

There would not be a shield around the heart if he intended to exit the world. He had planned to come back somehow, no doubt about it, and swim away while no one was looking.

I drew my Bora—forged in likeness of the sword that was supposed to defeat Vo Lai the White Demon so long ago but never did—and pointed it at the heart. I hesitated for a moment: Could I even pierce that shield? And if so, what would happen when I tore a hole in a vessel that contained so much stored energy? Would it destroy me?

It didn't matter, I realized. All that mattered was making sure that it was destroyed and that the seventh son of Kalaad and Teldwen could never scheme against humanity again.

I wept, realizing I might well die. "Shoawei, forgive me my countless bad decisions. Maesi, I am so sorry I never found you. May my crew and family forgive me my pride and stubbornness and innumerable faults. May they never forget that I loved them."

Then, certain that I was doing the right thing, I plunged the tip of the Bora into the heart with a quick stab, feeling it slice through the shield and sink into the flesh, and let go of the hilt.

As I feared and expected, the heart exploded.

But most of the energy shot straight up through the rent I'd created and engulfed my sword, and the rest of it crumbled the stone surrounding the heart, reducing the statue's torso to pebbles, more than a few of which knocked me back off the statue and perforated my chest and the arm I threw up in front of my face. They didn't penetrate to any fatal depth—but my uniform was shredded and my cloak torn up. The well-spun wool prevented anything from penetrating to my skin, though, so I only had injuries down my center, where the cloak didn't cover completely.

Moaning, I sat up and picked rocks out of my chest and forearm, the wounds bleeding freely. Could I use my blessing as a balm to heal myself, if not restore my own youth? Yes. I aged a little, but the bleeding stopped, the skin closed.

Struggling to my feet, I examined the remains of Vo Lai the White Demon. The legs below the knee were still intact, but they had no blood coursing through them. I'd obliterated everything that could bring him back—though I'd make utterly sure of that.

My Bora was a twisted, blackened snake of metal, practically slag. If I hadn't withdrawn my hand, no doubt it would have been melted off. I would keep the sword as a souvenir, but it needed time to cool before I touched it. Good enough: I gathered winds to return me to the *Nentian Herald*.

After explaining, I brought a cloaked squad of sailors back with me—no wraiths seen—and we dumped every single piece of Sedam's stone remains that we could into the wheelbarrow and took them out to the ship. We even broke down the remains of the legs, leaving only an empty throne and six untouched statues.

Once the *Herald* was loaded up, with everything stowed, I finally gave the order everyone had been waiting for: "First Mate Haesha."

"Aye, Zephyr?"

"Set a course for Joabei. Take us home."

The general cheer was loud and sustained, and it swelled again as I filled the sails with the breath of Shoawei. Our faces soon hurt from smiling so much. That is a rare pain but one that I relish.

I dropped bloody marble pieces of Sedam—our ancient adversary, Vo Lai the White Demon—into the ocean at intervals as we sailed, scattering him into the abyss.

Once we cruised upon the open ocean, where we knew there simply had to be krakens roiling in the deep, and we were no longer under the protection of a larger fleet, I spotted signs of worry among the crew. What if Abhi's enchantment on our hull failed? And even if it didn't—well, there was plenty of guilt to go around, the sort that survivors feel when tragedy strikes people they know. We would be facing the families of the lost crew members soon, seeing their crushed expressions and hearing their howls of grief. They would ask the same question I asked myself: Why had I lived when others had died? They deserved to be here every bit as much as I did. And I know many people in Brynlön and Rael must ask themselves that question too. It never goes away, that guilt, and it lurks like a longarm in a coral cave, ready to emerge and strike when least expected.

"There's no satisfactory answer to your question," I called in Joabeian, which left out the Nentians among us, but it was appropriate in this case. The crew turned their faces to me. "I mean the one you're asking about why you're still here. I will tell you this: You must live in such a way that you discover the answer yourself. For my part, I am following clues. I am here to love and protect you. I am here to complete, with your help, a historic journey that so many of our sisters were never able to accomplish. I am here to witness and celebrate a new generation," I said, gesturing to those who were pregnant. "But that is not the fullness of why I am here. I will need to discover that each and every day. And those days will always contain a measure of mourning, and another of regret, but also a measure of pride and a measure of hope, and, if we are fortunate, a measure of more discovery. And so I order you now to do what we must all do until we die: Carry on."

I whispered a soft but earnest prayer to Shoawei when I tossed the last piece of her—or their—little brother into the sea. Perhaps they would not be able to hear it, now that I knew they were bound to specific places in the world. But it was deeply felt nevertheless.

And our faces hurt from smiling again when we spotted Joabei on the horizon. We were not expected, but a small crowd had gathered anyway by the time we docked, because we had come from the deep waters without krakens consuming us and our ship didn't look precisely Joabeian.

I'd prepared the crew for this: We did not immediately disembark. We lined the rails instead, with our Nentian partners in plain view and the painted name of the *Nentian Herald* facing the quay. Because this was history—the first crew to circumnavigate the globe—and we wanted as many people as possible to witness the moment so they could tell their friends and family that they were there when we docked.

Our hold full of Eculan cloaks and wool would fetch us a pretty sum, but the true prize—the indisputable truth that we had been around the world—was the Nentian husbands.

Joabei comprises only two islands, the northern one being inhospitable and unable to sustain life except seasonally. As such, we have strictly limited our population to ensure that all those who live do not have to starve. Women earn the right to bear children by serving the nation somehow, and exploration is the only guarantee of earning that right. It is the most dangerous and most esteemed activity to our people. We have all indisputably earned children.

To others—Omeshans, for example, and certainly Eculans—our restrictions make no sense. But the Omeshans live on bountiful islands, and the Eculans reproduced so far past the ability of their land to support them that they wound up becoming starveling people who fought for more land, ribs showing through their skin so that the Brynts called them Bone Giants—or maybe the bone armor they wore had something to do with that nickname, now that I think of it. They earned it either way.

I was pressed with suitors after my return but distrusted them all, since it was so clearly a result of my fame and newfound fortune. We sold our cargo for an enormous sum; the cloaks, enchanted by a now-dead god halfway around the world, fetched even more than we thought. It was enough to purchase additional ships. Haesha, Leisuen, and I started a new trading company and were immediately flooded with merchants eager to trade with Brynlön and Rael.

I captained the *Nentian Herald,* Haesha captained *Maesi's Legacy,* and Leisuen captained a ship she named the *Plaguebringer,* after the young man who'd saved our lives twice and made it all possible. Using the trick we learned during the counterattack on Ecula, they sailed their ships in tight formation with mine so that the enchantment on the *Herald*'s hull would protect their ships as well.

Our trading would no doubt prove to be immensely profitable, but that was not so important to me as another errand when we reached port in Pelemyn to formally begin our mercantile relationship with Brynlön. Before I could attend to base matters of goods and coin, I needed to visit the pelenaut and inform him of what had transpired on Blight, that the Mistmaiden Isles were now clear of wraiths, and that Joabei would like to settle an island or two—along with anyone else who wished—if he would be agreeable. I handed over letters from our leader, introduced a woman who would be our ambassador to Brynlön, and delivered this account to the historian Dervan du Alöbar. Then I visited the Raelech embassy, there to engage a courier or, if not, their speediest conveyance to a courier in Rael who could find Abhi, wherever he was in the world, and this is what I sent:

My dearest friend and brother in my heart,

Žalost—or Sedam, or Vo Lai—is absolutely dead. I returned to Blight, destroyed him with a sledgehammer and my sword, and have personally scattered his dismembered remains in the Peles Ocean. You can inform the kraken in the north, she can lift the curse, and then all nations can sail freely at last and become a united world.

I would expect you and the old kraken to verify first. But to prove that this is me and not some trick, here is something between us that never got shared by the bard, and therefore is unknown: One night in Malath Ashmali, you were getting drunk with Haesha, Leisuen, and me on the beach by the howling tube. Despite your warning that you were not attracted to women, Haesha tried to kiss you, and you fell backward over your bloodcat to avoid it and then staggered away into the dark. She was monumentally embarrassed by her poor judgment, and we still tease her about that. And we all still adore you. Haesha and Leisuen send their love with mine.

Let the world know when it is done?

Forever yours,
Koesha Gansu

I hoped I would see that dear boy again, and if I did, I would most certainly require another hug from him. But if circumstances never allow it, I shall count myself blessed to have known him for an all-too-brief span in the sunshine of my life. I am forever a leaf on the wind of Shoawei, and they have sent me to so many unexpected places.

ABHINAVA

Homecoming

The demands on my time during the invasion were such that I never got to write in the journal that Dervan gave me. I was sleep-deprived and stressed out in both directions, and Murr and Eep were annoyed at having to spend so much time on a boat. We did get some shore leave after the Eculans surrendered, and my friends went hunting in the woods on Drvo and that replenished us somewhat. The krakens willingly left Eel Bay at my request, and Tallynd du Böll detailed some people to repair the net, reestablishing safe shipping between the islands. She allowed me to enchant the hull of a single Eculan merchant ship after extracting a promise that its first trip would be to Pelemyn and would bring a full complement of embassy staff as well as trade goods. The idea was that it would return to Ecula with diplomats from Brynlön as well as other nations. I also took the opportunity to update enchantments on a few of our boats, like the *Nentian Herald,* to include cavern-jawed eels.

Once back in Pelemyn, I spent days catching up on sleep and trying to conceive of a future that wasn't plagued by our imminent destruction, but it wasn't long until I informed the pelenaut that I was ready to accept contracts as a member of the beast callers clave. Weeks of work poured in, all contracts for hull enchantments—Brynt and Raelech and Kaurian ships, and one Fornish ship as well—to get transoceanic trade well and truly started. I charged a handsome fee for each, but it wasn't the sort of work that filled me with pride or wonder or even a sense of contentment with my blessing. It was merely profitable employment, and the gleam of the gold began to pall when I was so very bored.

Eventually I realized that I didn't have to do it any longer than I wished to. I was free to follow my heart, and it had always been in Khul Bashab. I'd missed some of Fintan's initial tales because I'd been elsewhere while he was entertaining the masses in Pelemyn, but since I'd arrived in time to hear the one about Melishev Lohmet's death, it should finally be safe for me to go home.

Some evils must absolutely be fought, but others can simply be outlived.

So I made my insincere apologies and told my friends Murr and Eep that it was time at last to return to the plains of Ghurana Nent. Eep squawked excitedly and flew in circles, and Murr was so overjoyed that he ran circles around me three times before flopping down, rolling over, and presenting his belly. I gasped.

"Does this mean what I think it means?" I asked him. "You're finally going to let me give you a belly rub?"

He squirmed but nodded, and I collapsed to my knees and immediately went at it with both hands.

"Murrrrrrrrrrrr," he said, his red eyes closing in pleasure.

"See? I *told* you it was a good thing. You denied yourself this the whole time. We could have been doing this for *months.*"

"Murrrrrrrrrrrrr," he replied. I wasn't sure if that was any different from the first time but decided to count it as validation.

My building excitement at being alone with my friends for a pleasant journey through the wilds was crushed by the news that I would have no choice but to trail a caravan of gift baskets behind me. Foremost among them was a personal gift from Nara du Fesset. She had taken me to the pelenaut's reef and introduced me to an old longarm who lived there, and I was able to relay her words of love and friendship to the creature, who could not respond verbally but changed colors and wiggled its tentacles happily. Nara could not stop weeping and smiling at the same time when we returned to the surface, and to thank me she gave me a beautifully preserved nautilus shell gilded at the section edges with gold.

"It will remind you of the beauties of the ocean while you're out there on the plains," she explained. "They will always be here for you when you feel like visiting."

The pelenaut was also sending a rather large contingent of hygienists with me, since I could provide them safe passage across the Poet's Range, and it was time for Brynlön to pay back the generosity of nations who'd supported them in their time of need. Many of the hygienists were deployed in Rael, so my train decreased in size as I went, and more peeled off for cities in Ghurana Nent, leaving me at Ar Balesh to travel wheresoever they needed from there by boat along the river. The exceptions were one being sent to Malath Ashmali and another that came with me all the way to Khul Bashab; the latter took a particular horrified delight in counting all the ways she would have died without me there to protect her from the animals of the plains. She got up to fifty-seven, but I privately thought she'd missed a few, like the skull wasps that would have paralyzed her long enough to wriggle into her ear, chew through her eardrum, and lay eggs in her head. She'd have been able to walk around for a few weeks after that until the eggs hatched and the grubs ate her brain.

We came to Khul Bashab from the north, so we needed to cross the river to enter, but I noticed differences right away. There were people walking around *outside* the walls, and they weren't hunters or gatherers of any kind. It looked like a group of children—it was!—being taught outdoors under the supervision of a couple of adults.

"Wow," I said.

"What is it?" the hygienist asked.

"Kids walking around without fear. I've . . . never seen that before. In my country, I mean."

The list of things I'd never seen before only grew from there. Khul Bashab was a very different city from the one I'd left.

We took a ferry across the river, and I stopped at the dockside gates of my own accord, expecting to be accosted and to account for myself and be searched and told my animals couldn't enter and so on. But the guards were smiling at each other, chatting amiably about something, and paid attention to me only because I'd stopped in front of them. One quirked an eyebrow.

"Can I help you, young man?"

"Help me? I, uh." The request was so strange I couldn't process it. I pointed a finger at the city through the gates. "Can I just go in?"

"Of course," the guard said.

"You don't need my name or anything?"

The guard shrugged. "Not unless you think we need it for some reason. Are you visiting from another city?"

"Well, no, but . . . my companion is." I introduced the hygienist and explained that she'd need to be introduced to the city minister.

"Oh! Welcome!" the guard said to her. "If you'll come with me, I'll take you right there."

We said our farewells and I walked through the gates after them, somewhat dazed, with Murr and Eep on mild alert because they could sense my confusion.

The streets were clean. People were smiling. No one looked miserable or homeless. There were, in fact, no beggars.

I had heard in advance that this was the new normal, of course, but it was still a shock to see the evidence of it in person. The district in which I was standing used to be incredibly poor, with drafty hovels providing the meanest possible shelter to those who dwelled there. The hovels were all gone, replaced with new construction. The new housing wasn't fancy by any means, but it was solid and safe, and there were flower boxes hanging from the windows with bees buzzing among them. I stood there, agape, until someone politely asked if I could move because my cargo wagons, pulled by horses who naturally followed me, were blocking the road. I apologized and resumed walking. I supposed I'd need to figure out where to go, since I had no home there any longer. Stables, I figured, would be the first order of business, so that I could then move about freely and find a money exchanger to turn my Brynt coin into Nentian currency. Temporary lodging for myself would be next, and then I could inquire about any new regulations regarding construction of homes outside the walls.

People grinned at me as they passed and made no comment about Murr at my side or Eep on my shoulder. They simply assumed I was a beast caller and accepted that. The stable master, however, did finally say something, but only by way of making friendly conversation.

"Beast caller, eh?" he said. He was a lean but muscled fellow who kept his hair pulled back.

"Yes."

"Affinity for bloodcats? Haven't seen that one yet. It's remarkable that your horses get along with it so well."

"Yes, I suppose it is." Eep agreed with a chirp, and the man saw her for the first time.

"Hold on. You have a bloodcat *and* a stalk hawk?"

"Yes. This is Murr and Eep."

The stable master's eyes widened. "Wait. Are you Abhinava Khose?"

"I am."

"Kalaad's sky-blue balls! What are you doing here?"

"Why? Is it not safe?"

"No—I mean, yes, it's safe. I simply can't believe you're stabling your horses with me by yourself."

"I don't follow. Is someone supposed to be with me?"

"Well, I guess not—I don't know. It's just unexpected. I never thought you'd walk in here like this."

"I'm so confused. You obviously know me somehow— have we met before?"

"Everyone has heard of you! You discovered the Sixth Kenning! Khul Bashab owes you such a debt of gratitude— the entire country does! Was Murr one of the bloodcats that blessed Hanima Bhandury?"

"I don't think he personally participated in her blessing, but it was his pride that did it, and he was one of the blood-cats that blessed me."

"This is such an honor. Thank you for coming here. Your horses and wagons will be stabled free of charge, of course."

"What? No, don't be ridiculous. You deserve to be paid for your labor."

"But I want to make it my gift to you."

"I can't accept it. If you want to give me a gift, I'd be grateful for directions to an inn that accepts animals."

"All inns accept animals now."

"Oh. Then perhaps directions to an inn with an excellent vegetarian menu?"

"They likewise all offer vegetarian meals. No one wants to seem inhospitable to beast callers. But I have heard that the Ruby Hummingbird is particularly good."

He gave me directions to a money exchanger after that, and I promised I'd be back once I figured out where I could move my things.

"No hurry! Take your time!"

I had a rather heavy sack of coin to haul to the exchanger but felt utterly safe doing so. Not only because Murr would seriously ruin the day of anyone who tried to attack me, but because the baseline of housing and food security the city clearly enjoyed meant there were no desperate people looking for marks.

Once the sack of coin was converted, I took my Nentian money to a bank to open an account, and it was there that some breathless members of the city watch caught up with me.

"Plaguebringer? We heard you were in town and have been looking for you," one said.

"*Abhi* is fine. Is something wrong?"

"No, no, we come to issue an invitation. Minister Khatri is delighted that you've returned and would like to see you at your earliest convenience."

"He would? Okay, I'll be able to go with you after I finish up here."

I tried not to show any of my elation at this news and hoped my voice didn't reveal how excited I was. They waited for me outside and then escorted me to a building I'd never seen before. I was expecting to be taken to the Tower of Kalaad or the old viceroy's sky room, but instead there was a new structure where the viceroy's place used to be. It appeared to be six-sided, and there was a lot of stone in the construction—I suspected a Raelech stonecutter had been involved.

"What's this, then?" I asked the man who had turned out to be the head of the watch, Commander Dhawan.

"This is the new ministry building. It holds the offices for the city minister as well as offices for clave and ward council members. There are also several meeting and assembly rooms and an office for myself. Best of all is the small park in the center."

"There's a park?"

"Yes. The offices are built like a hexagon around the park, which is open to the air and has a wide range of trees and shrubs growing in it. There's even a very small grove of nughobe trees."

"A nughobe grove? Truly?"

Murr's ears perked up when he heard me say that.

"Naturally. It's supposed to commemorate where the Sixth Kenning was discovered. That's why it's called Khose Park."

I stopped, slack-jawed, and shook my head slowly. "I don't deserve that. There was nothing heroic about getting blessed."

Commander Dhawan waved my objection away. "It doesn't matter. You were heroic afterward. You put us on the path that led us here today. We are all better off because of you."

"I suspect Tamhan and Hanima had much more to do with that than I did."

"They'll get their recognition too. But Khose Park is a place where people and animals can relax. Your bloodcat and stalk hawk should be safe and welcome there. They're not supposed to eat any other animals or be eaten in turn. All animal companions of beast callers are supposed to follow those rules inside the city walls."

"Good to know, thanks." I relayed this information to Murr and Eep and promised they'd be able to hunt outside the city again soon. They were utterly okay with it as we stepped through a public archway that led into the park, the tufted tops and sprawling limbs of three nughobe trees plainly visible. Murr and Eep made joyful noises and hurried over to take proper naps in the branches. There were some other animals there as well, which were initially alarmed by their arrival, but I spoke to them all, introduced them to Murr and Eep, and announced that they would behave themselves and that I appreciated all of them being there.

Dhawan led me through an arched doorway into the minister's wing of the building—one side of the hexagon, basically.

"There are wings for the clave and the ward council member offices, another wing entirely devoted to meeting and assembly rooms, and the remaining wings are government offices like the Ministry for Human Dignity, employment affairs, public health, and even my offices for the city watch."

"What's the Ministry for Human Dignity?"

"Housing. No one sleeps unhoused anymore. We make sure of it. It's the foundation for our prosperity."

"That's amazing."

Dhawan threaded his way through hallways and some open office spaces, exchanging greetings with a few people who nodded and smiled at him, until he stopped at one desk by a window that looked out onto the courtyard. Or . . . Khose Park? I could tell that was going to be difficult for me to say out loud to other people. How would I ever do that without sounding epically pompous?

The man at the desk was older and looked like he'd had a rough life. One arm was withered and immobile, either to disease or an old injury; one eye was covered by a patch. Few teeth remained in his head. But that didn't prevent him from smiling at us and greeting us warmly.

"Commander Dhawan. Here to see the minister?"

"Yes, please. We don't have an appointment, but I've brought the plaguebringer, as requested."

"Oh, wonderful, yes, he's been expecting you." To me he said, "You're Abhinava Khose?"

"I am, and I'm pleased to meet you under this sky. What's your name?"

"Pallav Madukhar, the minister's assistant. Welcome home. It's an honor. We are all so grateful to you."

"I'm very happy to be back."

"I'll take you straight in, since he's cleared his schedule for you."

"He did? He didn't have to do that."

Pallav chuckled as he rose from his chair. "He most certainly did. If word got out that he kept you waiting, someone would use it against him in the next election."

Sentences like that made it sound like I was an incredibly important person rather than someone who'd literally stumbled into a blessing one day.

Tamhan's office did not appear to be especially grand from the outside, and the inside was minimalist and spare, largely populated by books. His desk was made of stained nughobe, the rich grains reminding me of wind blowing across the plains, and it was piled high with stacks of documents, which he immediately dismissed and came around once we entered the room. His desk was placed far back in the space, near the windows facing the park, which I imagined gave Dhawan fits as head of security but which I knew Tamhan would have insisted upon. Nearer the door we'd entered was a small polished nughobe table, just large enough to support a pot of Nentian herbs like our native mint and rosemary, and four chairs surrounding it for easy conversation, all next to more windows facing the park. No ostentatious art on the walls, because the space was basically windows on one wall and books on all the others. Some of the shelves left space for smaller potted plants or the occasional display of what was clearly a political gift from some country or other, which I bet he rotated depending on who was visiting.

"Abhi!" he cried, delight on his face. I hoped mine looked similar, because I felt delight in seeing him but also abject terror—he looked even more handsome than my memories, and I was afraid the longing would show on my face. He wore whites and yellows, hues that spoke of softness and power at the same time and absolute brilliance.

"Minister Khatri!" I replied as he approached. His eyes flicked briefly to Dhawan and Madukhar behind me.

"Thank you, Pallav, and Commander Dhawan. I'm very grateful." They made polite noises and closed the door.

Recalling that we shook hands the last time we saw each other, I offered mine again. He saw this and spread his arms wide.

"No, my friend. It has been so long, I would rather embrace you, if you will allow it."

So much for me to navigate in a split second. An embrace? Yes! But only because it's been so long? And because we are friends? Did he embrace a lot of people, or was I special? And Kalaad's thunderous ass, I hadn't had a chance to bathe yet!

"Of course," is what I said, "but I've been traveling all day and probably smell frightful."

"Ah, never mind that! You are welcome no matter how you smell."

And then he was in my arms, no mere polite hug but the genuine embrace of two people who had missed each other, and while I cannot speak for myself, he smelled wonderful. Lavender and mint in his hair, which fell down his back and my hand touched, silky and soft.

I am not sure how long such hugs are supposed to last, but it was good for me and would have been better if it kept going, because it felt like he should always be there in my arms. But he pulled away, gripped me by the shoulders, and beamed.

"I am so happy you're here," he said, eyes shining.

"Me too. It's incredible, what you've done. It's nothing like the city I left behind. You've made all your ideas a reality."

"Most of them," he allowed. "There is still a lot of work to do. But we are definitely in a better place. And we have you to thank for it."

"No. I did nothing."

"Nonsense. You stood on top of a hill and pushed a boulder down at the monarchy. All of our work, all of our momentum, was made possible by you. Come, sit. This is where I spend most of my days, talking to council members and diplomats and the like. I hate being behind the desk. So isolating."

We took the two chairs next to the windows and just sort of grinned at each other for a while. I felt a bit dizzy and realized after a few seconds that I should probably say something, but couldn't think what.

"Sorry, I'm just overwhelmed that you're actually here," Tamhan said, breaking the silence. "It's been so long."

"I can hardly believe it either. I'm overwhelmed that *you're* here. That there's no viceroy. That you're in charge and it shows."

"I've had a lot of help. We have so much catching up to do, and I want you to relax and enjoy it. We shouldn't be interrupted unless there's some emergency, and thankfully those are rare now."

"Good. I've heard some of what happened—you defeated the king's army, exiled the viceroy, and he later plotted a coup in Talala Fouz but got killed by a face jumper sent by Suraji the spider queen."

"Yes."

"What happened to her, by the way?"

"I think she's in Forn now, working with the White Gossamer Clan and those giant spiders they have that produce a lot of silk. Doing very well for herself."

"Has she been exiled, or maybe ejected from the beast callers clave?"

"No, the new king pardoned her, and I think the clave's vote wound up being in her favor, but it was a close enough thing that she didn't feel welcome. She still has a business here that imports silks, but we unfortunately do not have her services for pest control and the like. The Fornish are very happy she's with them."

"So this new king—"

"King Kalaad the Last!"

"Right. He's really giving it up?"

"He is. But he'll be our first national minister for sure. Hanima and Adithi are behind him, all the river cities love the guy, and we love him here too. It's just Batana Mar Din and Hashan Khek who'd rather see someone else."

"Oh, yeah. I imagine. What's going on with the other Senesh brother?"

"He should be on his way out but is clinging to power however he can. The king informed him—and all the viceroys—that he must hold elections and institute what are being called the Khul Bashab Reforms."

"That's amazing. They're really the Tamhan Khatri Reforms."

"Influenced greatly by yourself and Hanima—I'm fine with them being named after the city. It gives the city a point of pride to be the birthplace of our new government. But Viceroy Senesh likes being in power and doesn't want to lose it. So he is standing for election as city minister against a raft of opponents, because he has to, but there are indications that he will try to rig the election in his favor—and against Naren Khusharas as national minister."

"What's being done about that?"

Tamhan gave me a sly grin. "Many things. Surreptitiously. Mostly a nonstop propaganda war against him. We constantly have people in the city posting flyers that speak out against him or promote our excellent way of life here, and they get torn down almost as fast as they're put up, but the message is getting through. And we are placing people in his city watch and other positions, and a few beast callers have moved in just in case they're needed if he does something outrageous. He might still win—perhaps even honestly. But we won't stop promoting the reforms there. If he wins city minister but continues to rule as he did as a viceroy, the people will eventually realize that he's the problem. But if he wins city minister and actually governs the way he's supposed to, lifting up the least of us, well, we still win."

"What about Hashan Khek and that city Gorin Mogen started, Baghra Khek?"

"They'll be holding elections too. I think Baghra Khek will be an interesting place to live—from what I understand, a lot of Fornish will be living there soon, and there's some debate on citizenship and voting rights."

"What debate? If you live somewhere, you should have a say in the government, shouldn't you?"

"That's my position as well. The objections surround claims that they're short-term or even seasonal residents and involve scenarios where they might tip the scales for their favored candidates in an election but then leave afterward. There's no evidence of this yet, of course, but that's where the discourse is."

"What about Malath Ashmali?"

"That's another interesting case! The king has issued a carve-out for them and they are not subject to the Khul Bashab Reforms. The justification is that they have already jettisoned the monarchy there and have their own system of government in place that, so far as we know, serves the people well. I'd like to hear more about it from you, because eventually we are going to have to reconcile the systems or decide to keep them separate, which would mean treating Malath Ashmali as its own political state. So we are essentially letting that bloodcat run through the grove and see if it comes back to bite us—oh! I'm sorry. Does that expression offend you now?"

"No, but I won't be repeating it around Murr."

"That sounds wise. Anyway, I'm very curious about what they're doing there and wonder if they might have some ideas we can borrow."

"Will I be able to vote in the national election?"

"Absolutely. We'll get you registered when you settle on which ward you're going to live in. Elections are run by the wards, and I can fill you in on who's running for the national positions. Do you have any ideas about where you want to live?"

"Sort of. I mean, I have a lot of ideas and have been wanting to share them with you."

"Please do."

"I suppose I don't particularly care where in the city I live at the moment, because it will only be temporary."

A line formed between Tamhan's brows as he knitted them together. "Temporary? You mean you're not here to stay?"

"I'll stay for a little while, but . . . I don't want to be here forever, and there's a reason why."

"Okay," he said, and waited patiently for me to explain.

"During my travels, I saw how cities were shaped by the kennings present there. Raelech cities, Tamhan—they're incredible. Beautiful stone and clay buildings and mosaics wherever you go, impeccably paved roads, literally rock-solid places to live. And in Brynlön, the buildings are not so stunning, but they think about water in everything they do. There are waves in their structures—nothing is truly square. But anything you drink there, from water to wine, is the finest quality, because it's been purified and balanced and filtered and everything. They lost a lot of their farmers in the invasion, of course, but their methods are brilliant, and they'll bounce back quickly because of it. And you hear water wherever you go, splashing in fountains, whispering in sluices. They are cities, in other words, built to reflect their kennings and to incorporate those kennings into their lives. So you probably see where I'm going with this: Nentian cities have, until this point, been built to keep out animals—the exact opposite of what a Nentian city should be now. My dream is to live in a new Nentian city that's been thoughtfully designed to reflect the Sixth Kenning."

"We've made a lot of changes in that direction," he said.

"I know you have." I gestured to the window. "This park is great, and animals are welcome in the streets, and inns have vegetarian menus—that's all wonderful. But I can't live inside walls anymore, Tamhan. They have to go. They isolate us and perpetuate this idea that we survive alone instead of together."

"I hear what you're saying, Abhi, but I don't see how we can survive without them. The beast callers keep control in the cities, but go outside unsupervised and it's no different from before."

"You don't have enchantments?"

"What? No. I wasn't aware that was a thing."

"Oh. Maybe I'm the only one who can do it. That would be a good thing to find out."

"I agree. What can you do?"

"I can enchant a stake, put it in the ground, and it will repel any animals I wish for a decent radius. Surround an area with enough stakes and you have an invisible wall. So, starting from there, we can rethink what Nentian cities look like."

"These stakes remain enchanted in perpetuity?"

"I don't know, since I haven't been around that long."

"Good point. Well, I am very excited about the general idea of rethinking our cities, Abhi, but the details will make all the difference. Would you be open to chairing a committee on this, where we bring in experts from different claves and gather lots of suggestions to make this purposeful? You can also work on converting our current cities to more animal-friendly spaces while designing a new site."

That was fine with me.

We spoke happily about Tamhan's plans for redevelopment, his frequent but not total success at converting old monarchist systems to clave-republic systems, and his plans for many improvements and refinements. Time slid past and he ordered food for us, then he asked me to share some of my adventures. It was late afternoon when he suggested that we visit Khamen Chorous, one of his favorite ministers, to discover a suitable home for me.

"I don't require anything fancy," I said. "Something modest. I will most likely be there only to sleep."

"No one would begrudge you a palace here," he said. "But we can find you something modest. I have a small place as well."

"Where is that? Perhaps I could live somewhere nearby—or someplace near the ministry building, if I am going to be spending a lot of time there."

"I think we can find something suitable."

I checked on my friends, and Murr was content to remain and nap in the nughobe trees, but Eep wanted to come along and see the city. So we left the ministry building after that, together with Commander Dhawan and Khamen Chorous, the Minister for Human Dignity, to seek out a place for me to live. I thought at first anyplace would do but then quickly realized that wouldn't be the case; Murr and Eep would have preferences—the primary one being a spot well above the ground—and that suggested a place with rooftop access.

Khamen Chorous had very few teeth but smiled hugely nevertheless. "Ah, something up high. I think I know of a place. A recent confiscation."

"Confiscation?"

"Yes, from a weaver of fine tunics. Well, to be truthful, he wove nothing but misery. He owned a tunic mill, which mostly made clothes for wealthy people, but he refused to reorganize his business and share profits with his employees. Instead of remaining the owner and enjoying a double share, he closed his business and fired everyone, thinking he would simply leave with all the profits and burden us with a set of unemployed people. We gave him the chance to do the right thing and continue to prosper, but he passed on the opportunity. So we seized all his assets, including his home and his mill, and sent him down the river on a raft with the equivalent of what he paid a weaver for a year. Sold the mill to the employees and it's owned as a cooperative now, doing fantastically well. But we haven't been able to do much with the home."

"Why? What's wrong with it?"

"Stairs." Minister Khamen Chorous punctuated his disdain for stairs with a fart worthy of a thunder yak but kept speaking as if he hadn't just polluted the air with pungent gases. Eep squawked in outrage and flapped one of her wings desperately in an attempt to wave them away. "It's a tower, essentially, with room on top of room, nothing adjacent. The kitchen is on the bottom floor, and above that is a conversation room; next is a bathroom, which is quite large, but it's the only one in the structure. Above that is a library or study, and then two bedrooms, each on its own floor, and finally a covered rooftop terrace with a charming view. It's centrally located, each room is wonderful—I've seen them—but the stairs are a pain for older folk like me. Maybe not so much for you."

"Hmm. It sounds promising."

"I hope you'll like it. We've found it impractical to locate a family here."

From the outside, it looked like nothing special, just a tower of varnished wood planks with some planter boxes outside the windows. Inside the entrance, there was a foyer with space to hang coats and remove boots before ascending the stairs, and a wide double door led to the kitchen on the right. It was elaborate and huge, with a root cellar and wine cellar and another room for aging and curing meats. Khamen pointed out a dumbwaiter on one side, for sending trays of food up and dirty dishes down.

"It's the one thing that makes living here possible, or else you'd be going up and down all the time. But it does mean you'd be employing someone to work here."

Next we headed upstairs to the conversation room, which reminded me of the Raelech space—plenty of seating, some paintings, and some shelving on the walls for displaying pieces worthy of discussion. Might be a good place for Nara's chambered nautilus shell.

The reminder of Raelech luxuries only deepened when I saw the bathroom. There were several tubs and showers, and it appeared to be a space designed to be shared. All of the plumbing ran through the wall where the dumbwaiter was.

I liked the study best—all shelves, except for a broad window with a reading ledge; a single desk occupied the middle of the room.

"You kept all his books?" I asked.

"Yes. All his assets."

The bedrooms were fine, not decorated to my taste, but that didn't really matter. I was anxious to see the terrace.

As soon as we hit the open air, Eep trilled in relief. The terrace was covered by an elevated roof supported by posts on the four corners, and from the edges hung planters of decorative flowers, largely dead now. There were planters along two sides as well, also currently bereft but intended to raise herbs and vegetables for the kitchen. Several sets of outdoor furniture suggested that the former owner entertained here often.

The western side afforded an unobstructed view of the Tower of Kalaad—now called the Tower of Compassion—and the new ministry building. Our elevation allowed us to see into the middle of the hexagon and view the treetops of the small nughobe grove.

Pointing, I said, "Eep, look—Murr is taking a nap down there. You can visit the other animals anytime you like and come back up here whenever you want."

"Eep?"

I wished I could understand her, but that sounded like a question. "I'm thinking about living here. And you're welcome to live here too if you want, or you can live somewhere else that you like better. I thought you might like this terrace because you have a good view and room to fly. What do you think? Do you like it?"

"Eep." She bobbed her head up and down.

"Good." I turned to Tamhan and Khamen. "So how much?"

"It's yours, Plaguebringer," Khamen said.

"Nonsense. If you confiscated his assets to compensate the people he took advantage of for years, you have to get something in exchange. Let me pay a fair market value for the property, and then you use the money to build more housing for people who need it. Or provide reparations to the employees he exploited—or both."

Khamen looked at Tamhan. "Did you tell him to say that?"

Tamhan smiled. "No, he's naturally like that."

"Good one, then."

We made arrangements for purchase and to move my things from the stable, as well as hire a cleaning company to scour everything and bring new sets of linens for the bedrooms. Eep left my shoulder and started exploring her new aeric, deciding where she'd most like to perch. Tamhan also requested that his chef come to the tower and use the kitchen to make us dinner, and Khamen Chorous departed, promising to find me a chef of my own soon.

"Do I really need a chef?"

Tamhan shrugged. "It's the only way this tower works. Don't think of it as an excess; you'll be employing someone, you'll be able to afford it, and their work will allow you to do yours. You'll want a very good one. I imagine visiting the home of the plaguebringer is going to be a great honor. You'll be expected to have parties and the like."

"Parties? I'm no good at parties."

Tamhan reassured me. "Small ones that are either held up here or in your conversation room. And they'll be working parties, meeting clave and ward council members. They'll all want to say they've met you, and they'll be the ones that can help make your ideas of a new Nentian lifestyle a reality. I can help you arrange things at first, until you get accustomed to it."

"Oh, good. That's a relief."

Tamhan laughed, and I asked him why.

"I just think it's amusing that you speak to gravemaws and krakens and cavern-jawed eels but are terrified of parties."

"Well . . . humans are dangerous."

"Fair enough. It's a relief to me that you're home safe. We worried about you a lot."

"Likewise. I had no idea you'd be able to launch a revolution."

Tamhan shrugged again. "It just sort of arrived one day, thanks to Hanima and Adithi, and we had to jump in and make sure it didn't become chaos. Now I'm riding bareback on an ebon-armored rhino and hoping I don't fall off. Which reminds me: I can't do this often."

"Do what?"

"Take a day off to be with you. As much as I want that, I can't. There are too many demands on my time."

"Oh, that's okay. I imagine that I'll have plenty of demands on my time too."

"You absolutely will. In fact, I wanted to suggest that you let me assign a social secretary to you for a while. You're going to be flooded with invitations, and rather than going to them, they should come to you. Let your secretary invite small parties each night, until we get everyone in government through to see you. I'll attend as many of these events as I can, and that way . . . well, I can see you more often."

"That's really all I want," I blurted out.

"What? To see me?"

"Yes." I ducked my head. "I could see the world, Tamhan. See the whole thing and never fear for my life. That was my plan, in fact. But I came back because . . . you're here."

"Oh." He looked stricken.

It wasn't rejection, but it wasn't encouragement either. It might just be filler until I made myself clear. But to do that, I'd need to be actually courageous. It doesn't require bravery to talk to dangerous animals when you know your kenning will prevent them from hurting you. Talking to Tamhan about my feelings, however, was terrifying. But the only way to move on—in joy or sorrow—was to reveal my feelings to a clear sky.

"Tamhan, I'm sakhret. And I've had a crush on you for a very long time. Since we first met, years ago."

"Oh."

"I completely understand if you're not interested. I just thought you should know that . . . I have always thought you were wonderful."

"This is . . . unexpected," he said, and I might have died a little bit. "You see, I was trying to work up the courage all afternoon to tell you the same thing."

"What? You have a crush on me?"

"Yes! Everyone keeps asking me why I'm not in a relationship, a nice handsome minister like me, and the reason is, I've been waiting for someone in particular."

"But why didn't you tell me?"

"Why didn't you tell *me*?"

"I just did!"

"We have wasted enough time, Abhi, don't you think? Come here."

We folded into each other, and now there was no polite distance, no wondering if the hug meant something more, because we knew very well what it meant. It was the home we'd always wanted but never had. But I still worried that I might smell terrible. Apparently, that was not on Tamhan's mind.

"May I kiss you?" he asked.

"Yes."

His lips were soft and warm and—most important—his.

When we broke apart, we rested our foreheads against each other and smiled in the blissful realization that our feelings were requited. Tamhan chuckled softly.

"What is it?"

"When you sent that message from the Raelech courier, Hanima heard my reply spoken aloud and told me on the spot that love is the best. She tends to think everything is the best, which is in a strict sense impossible, but I think that particular time—maybe just that one time—she was right."

With a full heart, smiling at him, I said, "I could not agree more."

PEN

The Fourth Tree

Spring is so very fulsome and fine. Even in a strange land, far to the north where the sunlight is weaker, it is a wonder to see sprouts climbing out of soil, hear the industrious hum and buzz of insect wings, the mating calls of birds, and inhale the pollen that foretells fruit some months hence. My silver-bark exulted in the sun, and after making my farewells to friends in Talala Fouz, I basked on the riverboats that took me upriver to Ghuli Rakhan.

There was a sense of optimism among my fellow travelers, for Naren Khusharas had taken on the title of King Kalaad the Last and had announced elections to be held at the local and national level, transitioning the whole of Ghurana Nent to a government and economy modeled on what were being called the Khul Bashab Reforms, together with a formal recognition of the beast callers clave. This good news, coupled with the unfolding of spring, resulted in smiles blooming more frequently than I had noticed before.

I joined a trade caravan heading to Malath Ashmali from Ghuli Rakhan, and we spent nights in very nice waystations built the prior year by a Raelech stonecutter. I lost a bit of sunlight in the canopy of the Gravewood, but having a canopy of any kind again was good for my spirit, and I was reveling in the discovery of new plants and trees. I felt the joy of learning twofold, once for its own sake and another for imagining I was Sprout, who could show Sage a thing or two. It was pleasant to think perhaps I could become a sage in my elder years.

It was obvious from the start that Malath Ashmali was not a typical Nentian city: There were no walls. But there were plenty of stone dwellings, erected by the resident Raelech stonecutter to house the Nentian citizens, and taller wooden lodges for the Hathrim, who thought wooden structures to be the very height of wealth and luxury. The city's boundaries were protected from large predators by wooden stakes enchanted by none other than the plaguebringer Abhinava Khose, who had played an important part in the Battle of the Godsteeth, where my cousin Nel had died. I liked the idea that he had also come all this way to escape the shadow of that event, to attempt to craft a different society with others of like mind.

Olet Kanek, the Hathrim firelord who was the elected executive of the city, was nearly three times my height, and I worried that the ancient enmity between our people would be a thicket of thorns between us. But she was wholly unlike any giant I'd ever met. When I was brought to the city's main lodge and introduced, she smiled, got down on one knee so that she was merely twice my height, and bowed her head in respect.

"I believe I speak for everyone when I say we are so happy you decided to join us," she said. "You are the first Fornish person to visit, and to have a greensleeve is an honor beyond our dreams." She introduced me to an assemblage of smiling people, who were all very welcoming. They were the town council of Malath Ashmali, made up of Nentians and Hathrim, plus three Raelechs: a newly arrived ambassador, the master stonecutter Curragh, and a master courier named Tuala.

"Tell us, what brings you here?" Olet asked. "Exploring opportunities for your clan, perhaps?"

The answer was, *A talking acorn in my pocket,* but I didn't say that. Better to start with smaller truths.

"Certainly I come to scout for Canopy and clan, but once

I get myself oriented, I might decide to stay, if that's . . . allowed?"

The giantess snorted, her eyebrows climbing up her forehead. "Oh, it's definitely allowed. I'd say it's encouraged! We would like nothing more. We already have land set aside for a Fornish embassy and can set aside some more for you as needed. Simply advise us on what might be required for your clan or personal use, and we will come to an arrangement."

"That is most kind. Perhaps I can assist your farmers with plantings, and if sufficient glass can be found, I might be able to start a greenhouse and supply the community with a variety of fruits, greens, and vegetables year-round."

"That would fulfill not only our desires but a great need. Building a greenhouse was already on our list of projects to complete this year, and to have a greensleeve supervising will only ensure its success. I will craft the glass myself to your specifications."

My needs were few, beyond the glass for a greenhouse and a stonecutter's services to drill a well. Ambassador Ken had gifted me with a boiler and a pump system that I'd brought along as cargo on boats and later on one of the wagons, but everything else I would grow from seeds, including the bamboo that we preferred to use for our pipes.

I did have one question: "How would you feel in general about more Fornish coming to live here? I mean not just a few blessed; I mean settlers."

Olet shrugged. "All are welcome, so long as they agree to live by our laws. Brynt, Kaurian, Raelech, Fornish. We have plenty of work to be done, and we need labor. Why do you ask? Do you think our little village in the cold north would appeal to many Fornish?"

Smiling, I said, "It might, once I grow a tea treehouse and some other Fornish amenities."

It was too soon to mention the Fourth Tree. For one thing, I didn't know if this was the proper place for it. But wherever it wound up growing, a significant number of Fornish would want to be nearby. There was a reason our three largest cities surrounded the First, Second, and Third Trees.

They eventually gave me into the care of Curragh. The stonecutter would show me the land set aside for an embassy, some parcels that I might use for my personal home, in addition to some space for greenhouses and a proposed area where I might accelerate the growth of timber for fuel, which would be preferable to cutting down older growth.

Once I chose a place for my home, at the far southwestern border of the city, protected by Abhinava's stakes, Curragh consulted with me on the placement of a well and then began his work immediately so that I'd be able to get my pump and boiler running.

I got to work too, encouraging a tall and stout crimson pine tree to grow and change to become my residence. I'd decided to pioneer a new Fornish architecture with a native species, because silverbarks were not native or well adapted to the climate. I worried, in fact, that the Fourth Tree would not do so well in the cold. But perhaps the consciousness living in the acorn in my pocket had thought of that already.

A crimson pine, I mused, would likewise do well for the tea treehouse. It had a reddish bark and reproduced with bright-red berries that became seeds after passing through the digestive systems of birds and squirrels. And that bark might serve well not only as an exterior wall but as insulating material when chipped and filled into the space between the interior and exterior walls—a necessity for the colder weather. I'd been thinking quite a bit on the journey up how I'd have to build; the open plans of the Canopy wouldn't work here. Treehouses would need shelter from the elements but also from flying and arboreal predators. I'd been warned specifically that meat squirrels and pine shrikes could still reach me aboveground, so I'd need to have an enclosed space and think about light and air circulation. I left spaces for windows that would tighten against panes when completed, but for now I grew a lattice of branches that would keep out critters while letting in light and air.

Days passed while I got to know the citizens better and learned more of their current diet and what it lacked, and especially what they'd need during the long winters. It allowed me to present a plan to Olet and the council for not just one but many greenhouses.

But what I didn't hear, though I listened carefully, was anything from the acorn in my pocket, and it made me wonder if I would need to move on. My feeling about the people in this place—entirely justified and even better than I'd hoped—may simply not have any bearing on the needs of the Fourth Tree.

I asked, after another week, if someone might accompany me to the west, outside the protected boundaries, where we might be attacked. Everything I'd experienced so far, including the trail up to the city, had been protected, but I wanted to experience the forest with its normal complement of creatures—a risk, for sure, but perhaps not so dangerous with an escort. There might be noticeable differences in the plant life outside the protected zone, and if so, I wanted to observe them. Tuala and Olet agreed to go with me, as long as it was only an hour's time away from the work we had to do.

The differences turned out to be subtle—a slightly springier feel to the moss, a smidge more robustness to the trees and undergrowth—but I had feared that there would be something, and over time it would only become more pronounced. Abhi's enchantment was protecting the citizens from being eaten, but it was also keeping out some creature—or maybe many creatures—that were vital to the health of the forest. Crafting those enchantments should be a thing that he worked on in consultation with a greensleeve who knew the area, or he would prevent access to pollinators and symbiotic creatures and so on.

"Speaking long-term," I said, "you won't be able to keep your animal enchantments as is and not affect the health of the plant life within city limits. I understand that they're keeping everyone safe, but there will be negative consequences over time."

"Like what?"

"Your plants may not reproduce properly; food may lack nutritional value or taste worse—I'm not sure yet. It's something to be studied. I'm simply alerting you to an issue that will need to be addressed eventually. In the short term, it means I don't want any greenhouse inside those enchantments. I will devise some more-traditional defenses against pests and larger predators."

"What about large herbivores who might either see or smell the vegetables you grow in a greenhouse and decide to smash their way in and eat them all?"

"That's something I need to worry about?"

"Yes. They exist. Bone-collared dreadmoose and more."

"Good to know. We should definitely make defensive plans for the greenhouses—but all-natural ones."

We came to a grassy knoll overlooking the ocean—we'd gained some significant elevation—and paused to note that it was a high point, the land sloping away in either direction. Peering over the side, I saw that there was no way down, no beach, just waves crashing into the cliff face below us.

Something squirmed against my side. I thought at first I was under attack from some creature, but, clapping my hands to my abdomen, I quickly realized it was coming from my vest pocket. The one with the acorn in it.

I slipped in my hand, and as soon as my palm closed around the acorn, the Fourth Tree spoke.

I like this place.

Here? I asked, because it didn't seem the magical sort of spot that the Third Tree had chosen in Pont. There was a nice view of the Northern Yawn, and some wildflowers were sprouting in the turf, but a tree would hardly care about that.

Yes. Here. If you would spend some of yourself to help me grow quickly, I would be honored by your sacrifice.

Of course. The honor would be mine. But it's very cold here in the winters—freezing temperatures for months, and the snow, once it falls, doesn't melt until right about now. Will you be able to weather that?

Yes. I am not going to be a standard silverbark tree. I will be something new: a silverbark fir, able to thrive in cold temperatures and all elevations. My berries will nourish both human and animal.

Berries?

Yes. They will spread and germinate more quickly, and you can help. Plant them along the route you took to the north. Others will take them farther along the Huntress Range and across the Godsteeth until, years hence, I will be connected via root systems to the Canopy. And on that day, Pen, you will join the sway again, and I will tell them of what you have done. You and your cousin Nel have given so much for the Canopy.

Fresh petals, that was the sort of thing to make a pair of eyes well up. And then flood shortly thereafter, because the enormity of it shook my knees. Ben Min would be a name as revered as ben Sah in the White Gossamer Clan, and in all of Forn, because we both served the Canopy first, though in completely different ways.

Tuala and Olet noticed and asked me what was wrong.

"Nothing is wrong. Except that I have a surprise for you, and I'm uncertain if you'll like it."

"What is it?" Olet said.

"I'm to plant the Fourth Tree."

Tuala's jaw dropped. "A sentient tree? Like the others in Forn?"

"Sentient, but not like the others. It will be called a silverbark fir. We'll be able to plant many of them—non-sentient ones—and eat the berries, and I have no doubt we'll probably be able to grow some for fuel."

Olet leapt ahead quickly to the consequence. "Is that why you asked me if we'd welcome a lot of Fornish? Because they'll come to be near the Fourth Tree?"

"Yes."

"Well, I'm not sure I do like it. We didn't come up here to have another hearthfire, and we didn't come up here to have another viceroy or a Triune Council, and we absolutely did not come up here to turn the Gravewood into another Canopy with clan politics and exclusionism and telling us what we can and cannot harvest. You can't refuse entry to anyone or make the rules—this isn't Forn."

"I know all that."

"Then what is this? Are you taking a page from Gorin Mogen's book? Colonize by settling somewhere outside your borders and build defenses, then dare the Nentians to dislodge you?"

"No, no—absolutely not."

"If you think you're going to flood us with immigrants and change our constitution with a bunch of Fornish seats you vote into the council with your new majority, that's not going to happen either. We have safeguards against the majority stomping on minority groups, and I'll make sure we reexamine those and strengthen them before your clansmen get here."

"Olet, please—none of that is our intention."

"Then what is your intention?"

The acorn had digested all of her suspicions through me and responded, which I relayed.

"The Fourth Tree, like you, sees a chance here to try living differently, with all peoples and all manner of the blessed welcome. She wishes to participate, not dominate. And . . . she wants more of the Fornish to live outside the Canopy. There is security and comfort there but stagnation also. This is a place where risks will be taken, failures absorbed, and victories celebrated together, rather than in our old tribes and allegiances."

When I stopped talking, Olet simply stared at me and the forest quieted, even the birds deciding they'd like to hear what happened next. Her fists clenched, and I worried that her clothes would begin to steam. But her voice was perfectly calm when she next spoke.

"Why did you wait to surprise me with this? Why not announce your intention before the whole council when you arrived?"

"Because I did not know until we came to this precise spot that the Fourth Tree wanted to be planted here. My instructions were to head north of the Canopy, and eventually I'd know when it was time. Once it informed me—you saw when it happened—I didn't hold back; you were the first to know. And I'm surprised too, by the way, that it won't be a silverbark but instead an evergreen, which will provide a new food source and timber for fuel."

Olet grunted. "And that's all it wants? To help?"

"Well . . . it also wants to not be chopped down or set on fire. And free access to the creatures of the Gravewood. No enchanted stakes surrounding it, in other words. An easement, which should be easy enough since we are currently well outside the city boundaries."

Again, the giantess leapt ahead. "And I imagine once the city begins to expand, only Fornish will be able to live near the borders of this easement, and only certain businesses will be allowed to operate?"

"I can't imagine an objection to anyone living on the borders. The only objection I can imagine for businesses would be ones that emit pollutants that might affect the health of the tree—and, yes, the Fourth Tree confirms that. All are welcome to live nearby. The Fourth Tree wishes to stress again that this is not an effort to re-create the Canopy here."

"You've given me much to think on. And the council as well. I cannot say how they will react to this or whether they will agree to anything at all, and they will doubtless wish to question you themselves. But we are outside the city limits and we have no authority here, so do what you will, with the understanding that there is also no protection here. If you'll excuse me, I think my walk in the woods is finished."

She turned to leave, and Tuala called, "You're going back alone?"

"I dare *anything* to try to attack me now," Olet replied over her shoulder, and kept walking.

"Don't let me keep you," I said to Tuala. "I'll be okay."

"Oh, no, I want to witness, if that's all right. Seems like the sort of thing you don't want to miss if you have the chance. Because you're going to accelerate its growth, yes?"

"I am."

"Well, I'm fairly sure I'm never going to get another chance to watch a sentient tree get born, or grown, or whatever—especially a kind of tree that no one's ever seen before—so I really don't want to miss it."

"Ha! Yes." Recalling that Raelech couriers spoke all the languages, I switched to Fornish. "Bright sun to you, Tuala."

"Bright sun, Pen Yas ben Min," she replied in kind, not missing a beat. "Have you . . . forgive me, but have you heard about recent revelations from the Mistmaiden Isles? The story about the Rift, and how the sons and daughters of Teldwen changed themselves and bestowed certain blessings on their favored people?"

"No."

"Well, the sixth child, the goddess we call the Huntress Raena—the one that I worship—has inhabited the body of a kraken living pretty much right off the coast here."

"What?" I laughed in disbelief, because she had to be joking.

"It's true. We saw her emerge from the icepack over the

winter and speak to the plaguebringer. Her elder siblings all merged themselves with certain natural features to become the sources of the kennings. Most significant here is that the fifth child, whom we know as the Poet Goddess Kaelin, wrote her scrolls in our capital of Killae, but eventually returned to Forn and became the First Tree."

"Stop teasing me."

"I'm not. She split herself into three, and now . . . four. I bet she likes it here because it's close to her sister."

"Are you being serious?"

"Completely. I can tell you the whole story as I heard it. But there's a faster way to prove it to you. The acorn is communicating with you somehow, isn't it? That was the impression I got from the way you spoke to Olet. So ask. Did she once walk the earth as a daughter of Teldwen?"

As I slipped my hand back into my pocket, the answer was in my head before I could even ask.

Yes. I am a daughter of Teldwen. And I have come to be near my sister. My roots will delve into this earth and deep underneath the ocean bed. Eventually one will find my sister, she will twine her tentacle around my root, and we will speak.

I cried again, because what else could I do? Tuala asked if she was right and I nodded, unable to speak until I'd taken a few deep breaths.

"This is a little bit more than I expected," I admitted.

Carefully, I brought the acorn out of my pocket and showed it to Tuala. It shone somewhat in the sun, small facets of the acorn's crown catching the light and winking.

"That's the prettiest acorn I've ever seen."

"It had better be. It's a goddess."

Smiling, I squatted and placed the acorn on the ground but kept my fingers in contact so I'd be able to hear it speak.

Here? I asked.

Not so close to the cliff. Say twenty paces south and five paces west, and then we will see.

I picked it up and moved the prescribed number of paces away, then performed another spot check. That wasn't quite right either, so there was another adjustment, then two more, until, on the fifth try, the acorn pronounced itself satisfied.

"Okay," I said to Tuala, "situate yourself wherever you like, but give me maybe three lengths of space here."

She backed off, smiling, and squatted down, ready to bear witness. Using my fingers to dig down into the turf, uprooting some grasses in the process, I placed the acorn in the shallow depression I'd made. Flicking some dirt over the top of it was an act of modesty more than anything a culturist would consider a proper planting, but it was sufficient to begin.

When a greensleeve accelerates the growth of a large plant, there is a point at which doing so will begin to take its toll on the greensleeve's life. It is the same for all the kennings, and indeed that is what killed my cousin Nel as much as Gorin Mogen's rain of fire: She accelerated the growth of the roots she used to tear him apart so quickly that the kenning demanded her life in return, and she is a silverbark now in Forn, growing in the White Gossamer lands. But growing a tea treehouse, for example, can be done over the course of a day or more, so that the energy expended is not so great. And accelerating the growth of smaller things, like vines or mushrooms, takes so little effort that there's no need for caution.

But the Fourth Tree needed to grow big very fast— decades of growth in mere minutes—so that no one could simply stomp on it or snap it easily as a sapling. It needed deep roots and a thick trunk and significant natural defenses, because, apart from humans, there were the larger animals of the Gravewood, which might try stripping its bark or something. And it needed to bear reproducing fruit right away rather than years hence.

All of which meant I'd need to push this growth much

faster than that of a treehouse but hopefully not so far that I wound up paying the ultimate price.

I knew from Mak Fin ben Fos and others that it was possible to grow a tea treehouse in a day without debt, and then it could be endlessly encouraged, expanded, modified over time after that. A thirty-six-year-old tree in twelve hours. But the Fourth Tree needed perhaps six decades of growth, and I was going to try to fit all of that into the space of an hour—a year per minute.

At first I felt nothing as the sapling rose through the turf, little more than a twig as it grew down every bit as much as it grew up. The debt began around fifteen minutes—or fifteen years—into the process. I got a headache, which began as a soft general pressure but soon grew into a stabbing needle between my eyes. Sweat prickled on my forehead, and soon I was dripping everywhere, clothing soaked, even though it wasn't that hot outside. The internal pains began after that: sharp lances in my guts, my chest, the involuntary twitching and spasming of muscles suddenly cramping. I breathed heavily and did my best to bear it all without any audible cries of pain, but I'll admit that I whimpered once or twice.

"It's okay," Tuala said. "Don't hold back on my account. Make whatever noise you need to. This is both wonderful and difficult to watch. Wonderful because of the tree—it's growing and shedding needles so fast! But difficult because I can see that it's rough on you."

She was right on both counts: Each minute thickened the trunk and sent branches questing toward the light, and needles sprouted and browned and fell for many minutes until finally some berries showed up, ripened to the color of rubies, and dropped in a bunch in between us.

Tuala gasped. "Can we eat those? The first fruit from a silverbark fir?"

I nodded and made a grabby motion with my fingers, unable to speak. She wordlessly picked up the bunch and thrust them into my outstretched hands. I immediately crammed them into my mouth and bit down, desperate for anything to replenish me. The sweetest juices flooded my mouth, quenching with just a hint of tartness to delight the tongue, and it gave me some quick energy.

"Have some," I wheezed at Tuala, "but keep giving me more."

She collected berries as they fell and piled them in front of me within easy reach, and she moaned in pleasure as she took the first bite of her own.

"These are going to be very popular," she said, but then busied herself with tending to my needs, feeding me more, until the Fourth Tree spoke in my head.

Enough, the voice said, slightly deeper and richer than when she was an acorn. *Thank you, Pen Yas ben Min. I will be forever grateful, and you will be forever celebrated.*

You are welcome. The berries are delicious, by the way.

I am glad to hear it.

Withdrawing my shoots from the earth, I crawled away from the trunk on shaky limbs, feeling drained and aching everywhere. I rolled over after only half a length and curled in on myself, moaning.

"Pen! Is it over?"

"It's over."

"Are you all right?"

"I think I will be. My body needs to stabilize and find a new normal. And I need sun. Can you maybe help me out of the shade?" The Fourth Tree towered over us now, and we were on a carpet of needles shed by the growth process.

"Can you get up?"

"No. Just drag me. You can do it. I'm tiny." I held up my hands over my head, and she grabbed them by the wrists and pulled.

She grunted a little bit and I did too, though we both did it for different reasons. Soon she had me in full sun just outside the shade of the Fourth Tree's canopy, and the sunlight on my silverbark and skin was immediately bracing.

"Ah! So much better. Thank you."

She dropped my hands and then knelt down next to me.

"You've lost so much life, Pen," Tuala said, her face a mask of worry, eyes tracing lines on my face that weren't there before.

"But I have gained too," I replied. "The Fourth Tree is my legacy, and it's one that will literally nourish generations to come. I would have spent my time trying to nourish others anyway, so I've lost no time at all if you think about it."

"Huh. I think about lost time a lot," Tuala admitted. "I wasted so much of mine. Or—like you—none at all, depending on how I decide to look at it. At least I know where I want to spend it now: here, as much as possible."

"I want to be here too," I said, and pushed myself into a sitting position, now that I had the strength to do so. I placed my hands on the ground behind me, locked my elbows, and leaned my head far back, looking up to the needles of the Fourth Tree. My legs splayed out straight in front of me. "But more specifically, I want to enjoy this light at the moment."

Tuala laughed and mimicked my pose. "I can't imagine what it must be like to derive some of your energy from the sun. I bet that feels good."

"So good. Yes. This new place in the world is my home now, and the shade and sun I live in will be my own. Here I will grow and bloom."

"I'm glad you are here."

"Thank you. I'm glad you are here too. Are you familiar with the Fornish poet Nat Huf ben Zon?"

"I've heard of him and have read a couple of passages from *Leafsong,* but I've never had occasion to read the whole thing. Why?"

"I'm reminded of the end, when Sage is on his deathbed,

and Sprout is desolate and convinced that life will never be so fine again without the wisdom of Sage to call upon. There will simply be a void that can never be filled. And Sage takes Sprout's hand and shakes his head. *Life is full of withering and culling and the calamities of hardship,* he says, *yet there is no fairer blossom than the possibilities of new friendship.* Then he makes Sprout promise to enlarge her circle of acquaintance and to continue to grow until it is her time to return to the earth. It's the last lesson he gives."

"That's wonderful. And I think what he said is true. Obviously, I need to read more of his work. A fresh perspective is always welcome." Tuala let her elbows buckle so that she could lie flat and stare up at the sky. "Like this. I hardly ever look at things this way. This is lovely."

"Indeed it is."

I laid back in the grass with my new Raelech friend, my head in the shade, my silverbark in the sun, and basked in the light of a bright and winsome world.

FINTAN

The Tale of Ages

There's no party like a you-just-won-a-war party. There's the euphoria and impromptu singing, of course, but there's also sex and vomiting in the streets and a general inability to get any sleep at night. This state of affairs lasted in Pelemyn for weeks.

I kept my own revels down to just a couple of days, then threw myself into working with Dervan to complete what was to be a history of the Giant Wars. I was writing every bit as much as he was, recopying the whole thing into the Rael-ech language, including his additions, which I found interesting considering how much he (and the Brynts in general) mistrusted me and the Triune Council at first. But I thought it would be good for Raelechs to see how we are viewed through a Brynt's eyes, and how trust must be earned, and how suspicion might still endure because of the betrayals of others.

I also thought his additions and personal dramas were excellent counterparts to my stories, because Dervan wasn't alone in wrestling with his grief. And stories are collaborative by their nature: They do not exist in a vacuum but are rather born of their place and time and audience every bit as much as they come from the storyteller. Pelemyn's people deserved to have their own piece of the narrative.

Eimear told me that some of the bards back in Rael were surprised I'd allow my tales to be written down, but that was shortsighted, in my opinion. It was precisely the sort of thinking that may have led to the histories of the Rift being lost to us. No, this age of upheaval should be documented thoroughly—and not just by Dervan and myself but by many others. There would be plenty of writings on what this council or that leader did—the pelenaut would probably have entire books dedicated to sifting through his leadership—but I was proud that our narrative largely steered away from them and elevated others who had to make decisions that were every bit as important, if not more so. Leaders do not always appear in our lives with titles already attached but reveal themselves under pressure.

I suspected that there might be some diplomatic kerfuffle over the fact that Brynlön had sent a rapid to steal a council member's personal records, but since that had been ordered by a wraith who'd been directing their spying for years, I had little worry that it would come to anything serious.

The courier named Tuala arrived from Malath Ashmali to deliver unto Dervan the tale of Pen Yas ben Min and announce the planting of the Fourth Tree, but also to give me a deadline to return home: None other than Numa would be coming to pick me up soon. But before I returned to Rael, where I would be able to profitably retell the tales of the Giant Wars for the rest of my life and maybe even earn a smidgen of respect from my parents, there were endless farewells to make, many of them tearful, and many gift baskets to accept, all of them generous beyond words.

I saved a few farewells in particular for last. Numa joined me in midafternoon the day before departure, tired from a long run, and told me she'd spend the night but we'd leave at dawn. I could delay it no longer.

We took Dervan du Alöbar to the Roasted Sunchuck, which had recently reopened. Hollit Panevik was overwhelmed by our appearance—she came out of the kitchen as soon as her hostess informed her of our arrival—and she began weeping as she spoke.

"I'm so happy you're here! I was worried you'd never want to see me again."

"Oh, nonsense. I'm leaving in the morning, and I wanted to say goodbye and have a remarkable dining experience."

"Then you shall! You absolutely shall. Is it okay if Orden and I create your menu this evening? We'll send the food and drinks over in courses."

"That sounds like perfection."

And it was. I cannot say I will never eat better, because the future tends to defy such declarations, but I can say with all the certainty of a perfect memory that I had never eaten so well up to that point in my life. There were seven courses:

- Reef prawns cooked in lime acid with scorched mango salsa on a blue corn handcake
- Fireglazed sunchuck balls nestled in marshland kraut
- Naïve sardine with sea salt and sublimated lemon zest on a toasted acorn cracker
- Blistered ramp tapestry in a tormented plum reduction
- Charred swamp duck breast in a Möllerud spice rub, activated fig dip, frightened asparagus bathed in riverland pasture butter
- Thunder yak marrow with peaches on an uplifted rye plank
- Emberfruit sorbet, naughty goat cream, celebratory chocolate soil

And Orden thankfully did not ply us with seven alcoholic drinks, as we'd be unconscious if he did, but rather gave us three intended to last for two courses each, and a hot chocolate to go with dessert.

- Sparkling white wine, Kaurian orange bitters, Kaurian orange juice

- Culturist Gin from Forn, infused with 21 botanicals, Raelech meadowberries, Pelenaut's Tonic
- Aelinmech Rye (the Good Shit), smashed peaches, muddled mint, brown sugar syrup, splash of ginger beer

By the time we got to the final course, we were incapable of making sounds beyond soft groans and whines. We rolled our eyes in gustatory bliss and realized what a rare experience this was.

"I'm so glad we got to do this tonight," I finally told Dervan as I finished the last spoonful of emberfruit sorbet. "We have shared many meals together, of course, but never one like this. A glorious and fitting end to a literally historic relationship."

"An end?" he said.

"Well. It's possible we may meet again but unlikely, since I have little intention of traveling after this. I'd be delighted to maintain a correspondence, however, once the tunnel reopens."

"When will that be?"

I turned to Numa, lifting a brow in question. She would know the latest.

"They're making good progress. I'm told it'll be open in as little as a month, but more likely five or six weeks."

"Outstanding," Dervan said. "I'm sure merchants on both sides are eager to resume trade over land."

Numa chuckled. "*Eager* might be too generous a term. *Howling with impatience* might be more accurate on the Raelech side."

"Yes, that would apply here too," Dervan affirmed.

Once our server cleared away our last course, Hollit and Orden both came over to our table to visit.

"I hope you enjoyed it?" she asked.

"That was the best meal I've ever enjoyed. The standard

against which all other food and drink will be judged. And I'll remember it perfectly forever—Numa too, of course. And I will remember your good hearts, for it is you who have helped me overcome my troubled memories of Gorin Mogen and Winthir Kanek. I will always seek solace in your bright and joyous memories when the dark ones threaten to overwhelm me."

"Ah!" Hollit raised both her hands to her mouth, as if to stop any more sound from coming out. Her eyes welled, and I realized she'd wanted to hear the last part more than my praise of her culinary mastery. Orden, too, seemed affected, for he raised a hand to his heart.

"Will you forgive me for inadvertently hurting your feelings in Ecula?" I asked Hollit.

"Of course. I already forgave you before we returned."

"Thank you. I will tell everyone in Rael this is the finest food and drink in Brynlön and quite possibly the entire world."

The two of them bowed, which, owing to their stature, felt a little like watching a tree fall toward you and making no attempt to get out of the way. But they straightened up and thanked us and wished us all well. They then proceeded to check in with other tables as they returned to the bar and kitchen, respectively, and we left a giant pile of money on the table even though the server insisted it was all on the house.

Outside, in the darkness lit by the soft orange glow of firebowls enchanted by Hollit herself, it was my turn to get emotional.

"Dervan, how can I ever thank you enough? I know you didn't ask for this assignment—to be attached to me, a minder of sorts or even a counter to my assumed role as a spy. But I'm glad you were. Glad that we were able to untie knots of suspicion and twine together, if you will, to create a record of our times that will outlive us both."

"It's been the honor of my life," he said.

We embraced, and I said, "I do hope we meet again. But you will write to me, I hope? With the tunnel opening again soon, I imagine we'll have regular post."

"I promise I will. And thank you for bringing such a wonderful tale to life. It's the tale of this age, and perhaps many ages hence."

That was the kindest possible thing he could have said to me. But Dervan is a very kind man.

I have borne witness to unspeakable evils, the absolute worst that humanity has to offer. But I have also seen the best. Sharing such darkness and light is my calling as a bard of the Poet Goddess Kaelin, so that the careless might gain a measure of empathy and the despondent might gain a measure of hope. I hope we will all learn from our folly and do better, so that such a tragic war never happens again.

DERVAN

The Golden Age

The euphoria in Pelemyn lasted for weeks upon our return from Ecula, and by the time we collectively remembered that we had a nation to rebuild, it was already autumn. I spent much of those weeks working with Fintan on editing these volumes, adding in the last accounts from far-flung personages as they came in, and finalizing a chronological appendix of events for the historical record, since his tales had necessarily been told out of their actual sequence. We were able to have long discussions about our initial misunderstandings and distance, to decide together that my personal feelings and worries about Rael's motives should be left in and nothing should be sanitized, because trust always has to be built and that should be reflected. And after reviewing it, I noticed that neither of us had relished the assignment at first, but it grew on us, and we each earned a great friend because of it. But once our task was finished and the world's greatest bard returned to Rael, I was just about ready to wrap up my work for the pelenaut and look to the future.

The spying part of it—or my absolute bungling of it—remained horrific in my memory, but I had come to appreciate the history we'd compiled by the end. And I did keep everything in there—my own legion of mistakes and Rölly's too, because he made an excellent point the night we blew up at each other: People are messy. Histories that pretend otherwise cannot be trusted.

I was able to squeeze in a breakfast appointment with him in Barebranch. He arrived late, muttered a perfunctory greeting, and told me he'd be leaving early, then sat down and grabbed a roll, when there was a perfectly fine stack of toast waiting to be anointed with butter and preserves.

"What's kept you so busy?" I asked him, reaching for the good stuff.

"Remember I told you before the invasion that I wanted to start a Golden Age of Brynlön?"

"Yes, I think I remember that."

"Good, because I'm starting it now. Turns out, though, that creating ages like that are a lot of work, and if I don't do it all, then I won't get the fancy title for my legacy. We're not just rebuilding what was destroyed—we're founding two new cities."

"Two?"

"At least. Ghurana Nent has two new cities—that one Gorin Mogen started and then Malath Ashmali. They're probably going to have a Golden Age too, what with their fancy new kenning and new government. So we need two new cities at minimum. One's going to be a replacement for Grynek. We're going to turn Grynek into a memorial site, or maybe a historical park sort of thing, and build a new city some distance away but still nestled against the Poet's Range."

"Why?"

"Because it really was ruined, more than others. Hygienists tell me it's unsalvageable in the near term, which may as well be the long term. Something happened to the water table there."

"You mean it got polluted by the Gravewater?"

"No, something worse. They're still arguing about what happened, but the current theory is that it had something to do with the collapse of the tunnel—a shifting of earth that released something into the water table. Hygienists are telling me that they can clean it up, but it's going to take years. Problem is, we don't have years if we're going to resume regular trade through the new tunnel. It's impractical for anyone to live there anymore, and the Raelechs don't really want to build their new tunnel to Grynek anyway. At some point they'd probably run across the army they buried in the mountain, and that would be unpleasant. They're going to bend the tunnel to the south—the spot's all picked out—and the hygienists have said we'll have plenty of good water there from the table and a lot of clean runoff tributaries to the Gravewater. Should be finished in a month or so, and provided we're not blanketed in snow by then, they'll lay down some quick roads for us to connect the city to Tömerhil and Sturföd."

"What's this new city going to be called?"

"You're going to love this: It's Löngren. A tribute to Daryck."

"Oh, my. That's indeed lovely."

"Right? So a lot of my energy is going into the civil engineering for that city. Endless meetings about infrastructure. That's where my time goes now."

"What about the other city?"

"I've delegated authority to its quartermaster to deal with that."

"It already has a quartermaster?"

"Well, it's going to be called Tallynd, so who else would I assign for the duty besides the living legend herself?"

I nearly choked on my toast. "The second könstad is designing her own city? Where?"

"On the island of Böll in the Mistmaiden Isles—the one that she had initially called Bolt. She's been doing a whole bunch of scouting, making doubly sure all the islands are clear of wraiths, mapping fishing waters to create safe harvesting limits, things like that. And she's intentionally leaving spaces for Joabeians to move in and settle there, mixed among us. The hope is that it will become the primary trading destination for them, and it will leave room here and at Festwyf for our regular seagoing traffic."

"That's wonderful, but I'm astounded by Tallynd's change of heart."

Rölly frowned. "Change of heart?"

"Hmm. Perhaps you haven't read it yet, but in her first diary entry she wrote that she never wanted to be a leader because the children of leaders so often turn out poorly."

"Oh! Yes, I think I did read that. But I'm pretty sure her thinking has evolved on that issue. Or she's figured out how to make sure her kids stay humble."

"I'm sure she has. But have I missed something? Why hasn't any of this been announced yet?"

"It will be very soon. You don't call a nugget of coral a reef until it's had time to grow. Once this happens, we're hoping it will clear out Survivor Field entirely. Who wouldn't want a new chance at prosperity under the leadership of a national heroine? Pelemyn can return to itself again."

"Remarkable. Okay, I understand now why you're so busy and eating that fast."

He was shoveling eggs into his mouth. "Sorry. Fuel for the day. Wish I could enjoy it."

"So who's going to be quartermaster of Löngren?"

"That nice deadly woman who beat you up."

"What? The Mynstad du Möcher?"

"Indeed. Resigning her service here and taking on new service in Löngren."

"And Gerstad Nara du Fesset will be going with her?"

"Of course. Why would they not want to live in a city dedicated to the man who saved Nara's life? They're very excited and say it will be the jewel of the country soon. And you know how competitive the mynstad can be." His eyes trailed to the giant stack of papers that formed my manuscript, and he flicked at finger at it. "I think it's time I asked about that."

"It's the assignment you gave me: Keep a written record of the bard's tales and add whatever I want. It's our history of the Giant Wars, but I don't think that's a very good title. If you think about it, the wars were not so much about giants as they were about the kennings. So that's what I'm going to call it: *The Seven Kennings*. It's extremely close to being finished."

"What's left?"

"This conversation, mostly."

"Ah, I see. You know I've read large portions of it already, but I'll look forward to the finished edition. What will you do next, Court Scribe?"

I shrugged. "Something else entirely."

"You mean like a career change?"

"I never wanted to be a scribe, Rölly. Or a spy. We've spoken of this at length and sometimes at high volume. I'm an historian."

"I know, but I thought you could continue to do that for me. Record all this Golden Age stuff for me."

"Forgive me, but I can't. No more intrigue or politics for me. I'd like to teach again. But since the university here has no need of my services, I'll have to go elsewhere. Perhaps a kind word from you would secure me a position at Setyrön."

"Perhaps. But you don't want to start over again, do you? Be the newest faculty member?"

"Well, I don't see what choice I have."

"What if I told you that there's a position open for a dean of history and it's yours if you want it?"

"I'd assume you were playing with me like some fish head down by the docks."

"I'm not. But there's a catch."

"Of course there is."

"In addition to teaching, you'd have to develop and curate a national monument. It's a heady responsibility. And that was a pun you'll understand in a moment."

"What are you talking about?"

"You remember Meara, the Raelech stonecutter who rebuilt a large part of Göfyrd?"

"Of course."

"I've commissioned her to build Löngren University, the centerpiece of which will be an enormous tower with a certain silhouette, which I'm sure you can imagine."

"Oh, no—will it have white jets of water geysering from the top?"

"You catch on quickly. Only at scheduled intervals, though, because it will require a rapid to make it happen, but we're fairly certain it will encourage a lot of tourism. Everyone's going to want to see that tower, and the head of it will be a museum that houses the Daryck du Löngren collection of cock sonnets and a history of the service that the Grynek Hunters—formerly the Rapid Woodsmen—performed for our nation. We need all of their biographies and fates, not just Daryck's."

"I understand your pun now and condemn it as an atrocity. But the Grynek Hunters: I'm not sure I know what happened to them all—"

"Then you need to find out. Visit Gyrsön. He can tell you. He was with them the longest."

"The chef with the incredible sense of smell? Where is he now?"

"Back in Fornyd, engaged to the quartermaster, Farlen du Cannym."

"He is?"

"He followed through on his wish and cooked for her. The story is that the meal was so extraordinary she wanted to meet him, and their love developed quickly from there."

"That is fabulous. Good for both of them."

Rölly gulped down some tea. "So what do you say? Does that sound like a sweet job far away from the Wellspring?"

"It does. Thank you. I—I'm a bit overwhelmed. I didn't expect anything like this." Leaving the Wellspring hadn't been my goal so much as leaving Pelemyn in general, with all of its haunting memories of Sarena and reminders of what we'd lost. I had made as much peace with it as I could, yet I

A CURSE OF KRAKENS 681

felt it was time for me to find a new life elsewhere, as Elynea and her children had. It would be unfamiliar and challenging and not at all the same, a new chapter in my own history.

"Well, I expected you wouldn't want to stay here any longer, so I was hoping you'd help me out with this instead. Thank you, Dervan. And again, I'm so very sorry for what I did. But let me add that this offer is not made out of any guilt—you earned it and deserve it. The nation owes you a debt for the work you've done."

He really said that to me, so I guess I can include it even if it seems self-aggrandizing. He gulped down his tea and rose.

"I must get to it, my friend. But I'm glad we have this settled, even if everything isn't entirely settled between us."

I grunted as I rose too, hoping my knee would stay stable enough not to embarrass me.

"It's settled, Rölly. Look, we can't walk away from each other without a resolution, forever unsatisfied with an unfinished story. It's easy enough to fix. I won't forget, because that's impossible, but you are forgiven. We have been friends since childhood, and I hope we still are. And in case no one's told you in a while, you really are a good leader. I'm not sure Brynlön would have fared so well with anyone else in the Wellspring."

"Thank you for saying that."

I really did say it, unprompted, so I'm not fluffing up the pelenaut for political purposes in hindsight. I think his efforts to keep us all fed through the shortages quietly saved many lives, and his unseen labor to rebuild our nation would likewise prove to be quietly brilliant.

We embraced briefly, with a couple of fists pounded on the back. "Take your time at breakfast," Rölly said. "See Föstyr soon about who the president of the university is, because I don't know. Whoever it is will give you a budget and a salary and so on."

"Oh, okay. Where will my office be?"

My old friend grinned. "In the shaft, of course. Don't teachers always get the shaft? Whole thing will be faculty offices. But listen, there will be a steam-powered lift inside, like in the Steam Spire Loose Leaf Tea Emporium, so you won't have to constantly climb stairs with your bad knee."

"Magnificent."

"I can't wait to see it when it's all finished. I'll get there someday. Make sure Föstyr takes good care of that manuscript, all right? He's been working on setting up a new government print shop, and we want a copy of *The Seven Kennings* in every Brynt household. Currents keep you safe, Dervan."

And then he swept out of there, meetings to attend, an age to usher in with his will and charisma and the cooperation of a hopeful people.

I lingered over some happy toast, savoring the prospect of a productive future and maybe giggling over the fact that I was to have an office in the shaft of an enormous stone phallus.

The longshoreman attending me promised to inform the lung that I needed to see him regarding the manuscript and Löngren University, and I was left to hobble gingerly out of the palace, the flow of waters around me now whispering of fresh new challenges ahead. And indeed I think that same whisper would be heard soon by every Brynt, if it wasn't already.

For too long, we have bottled up our grief and drunk from it in small sips, or sometimes longer draughts, but never enough to exhaust our supply and call for something else. Now it is time to leave those bottles on the shelf—if we're unable to pour them out—and plunge ourselves into the springs of joy and contentment that have been there all this while, waiting for us to find them. Since we have escaped the whirlpools that kept us looking inward, we can all swim in gentler currents, each to our own happy end.

THE END

APPENDIX

The following sonnet was found in the diary of Gerstad Daryck du Löngren, leader of the Grynek Hunters, formerly known as the Rapid Woodsmen. He composed it while sailing from Pelemyn to Ecula on a Kaurian ship, shortly before his death in Sveto Selo. As such, it is the last cock sonnet he ever wrote and should be included in his enormous, swollen, turgid canon as Sonnet 169. May he dwell in peace forever at home in Bryn's blue sea.

169.

Though many times I have been chastised for
Impertinence and flippance and caprice,
More often I am fulsomely praised for
The serpentine contents of my codpiece.
It is a salve to my mind that among
My myriad faults, my consolation
Is that I'm spectacularly well hung
And it's the bulk of my reputation.
In the end I may regret my choices,
My exploits derive to detraction,
Yet still you shall hear high, winsome voices
Sing songs of me as a man of action.
For how could I live life sedentary
When I have a cock this legendary?

CHRONOLOGICAL TIMELINE
FOR THE SEVEN KENNINGS

It's a historian's duty to record dates for posterity, but in this case, I also had to set this in writing for my own sanity, once I realized how out of order Fintan was telling his tales and how much was being kept from me.

I should warn you in advance that if you are reading this prior to reading all of the tales, you are in for some spoilers. Best to leave it as a reference and enjoy the events as the bard presented them.

Beginning with the year 3041, on the left we have the actual calendar date on which something happened, followed by a brief summary of what that something was, and then, in parentheses, the "Day" on which the bard actually shared that event with us in Pelemyn (his 54-day performance began on Thaw 2 of 3042, almost a full year after the first events in Thaw of 3041). You will quickly see how much he jumped around. Keep in mind that Volume 1 comprises Days 1–19; Volume 2 contains Days 20–39; and Volume 3 spans Days 40–54, plus the recorded tales of various narrators going forward.

Part of the time-hopping was necessary, as Fintan did not arrive with all the pieces of the tale in place. He learned of many Brynt events once he arrived in Pelemyn, and of many events in Ghurana Nent and elsewhere as new information kept coming in. But some tales, by his own admission, were told out of order purposely for dramatic effect—such as Day 1, the events of which happen much later chronologically but were vitally important to us in Pelemyn. He chose to begin with the story most relevant to his audience. Occasionally I will annotate some events in italics.—*Dervan du Alöbar*

3041

THAW 17: Eruption of Mount Thayil (Day 2).

THAW 18: Kallindra du Paskre meets Motah on the Brynt coast (Day 2).

THAW 19: Nel Kit ben Sah sees giants heading north in the night while patrolling the Fornish coast (Day 3).

THAW 20: Saviič wrecks his boat near Linlauen, Kauria (alluded to on Day 3).

3042

BLOOM 1: Gorin Mogen lands in Ghurana Nent (Day 4). Nel Kit ben Sah convinces the sway that they must scout for giants fleeing the eruption in Harthrad (Day 4). Abhinava Khose starts his journal (Day 3).

BLOOM 2: Kallindra hears at the merchants clave of other strange encounters with tall pale people (Day 4). A mustard-stained Gondel Vedd is sent to the dungeon to meet Saviič (Day 3).

BLOOM 4: Viceroy Melishev Lohmet of Hashan Khek *(may he suffer eternal torment)* sends Chumat south to look for giants along the coast (Day 4).

BLOOM 5: Gorin Mogen names his illegal settlement Baghra Khek (Day 5).

BLOOM 6: Nel Kit ben Sah discovers Baghra Khek and confronts a patrol of houndsmen. Several Fornish folk die (including Yar Tup Min), as well as several Hathrim (Day 5).

BLOOM 7: Abhinava Khose loses his family to a khern stampede and discovers the Sixth Kenning (Day 5).

BLOOM 8: Abhi meets Murr (Day 6). Melishev Lohmet learns that Hathrim are indeed squatting on Nentian land, as he suspected. He takes a Hathrim, Korda, hostage, then orders his chamberlain, Dhingra, to sail south with a small grain shipment and scout Mogen's forces (Day 6).

BLOOM 9: Abhi meets Eep (Day 7).

BLOOM 11: Nel Kit ben Sah successfully scouts Baghra Khek with a group of grassgliders (Day 7).

BLOOM 12: Abhi returns to Khul Bashab (Day 8, first part of Abhi's tale). Gorin Mogen kills Dhingra and all his crew (Day 8).

BLOOM 14: Abhinava Khose, Tamhan Khatri, and many seekers leave Khul Bashab and head for the nughobe grove where the Sixth Kenning currently is (Day 8, middle of Abhi's tale).

BLOOM 15: Khul Bashab's cavalry kills Madhep. In response, Abhi summons a plague of insects and takes on the title of plaguebringer (Day 8, remainder of Abhi's tale).

BLOOM 18: Sudhi, Adithi, and Hanima are blessed with the Sixth Kenning (Day 10).

BLOOM 21: In Kauria, Gondel Vedd takes a break from his duties in the dungeon after many discoveries. Has a row with his husband, Maron (Day 9).

BLOOM 22: Abhi parts ways with Adithi, Sudhi, Hanima, and Tamhan outside Khul Bashab. He heads south with Murr and Eep, thinking he'll try his luck at Hashan Khek (Day 13).

BLOOM 25: Melishev Lohmet kills the giant hostage, Korda. Assigns his tactician, Ghuyedai, to take a force of conscripts to confront Gorin Mogen. They will travel with Fintan, Numa, and Tarrech (Day 8).

RAINFALL 5: Fintan watches Tactician Ghuyedai order two thousand conscripts to die by fire at Baghra Khek to trigger the Sovereignty Accords (Day 10).

RAINFALL 6: Melishev Lohmet hears from Numa that half his force has been wiped out. The Raelech juggernaut, Tarrech, will not help, however, without direct orders from the Triune Council. Lohmet formally requests aid from other nations to expel Gorin Mogen. He kills a healer who cannot help him with his disease (Day 10).

RAINFALL 7: Hanima and Adithi get a message from Khamen Chorous (Day 21).

RAINFALL 12: Hanima sees the first broadsides posted in Khul Bashab (Day 24, the first part; Fintan did not include a clear indication in his tale that she spent weeks in hiding with Adithi while Tamhan fomented rebellion).

FOALING 5: Hanima and Adithi meet Jahi after the city watch tramples through the riverbank area. They get Jahi out of there and into the city, where they begin their stealth program of housing the unhoused in empty buildings, coordinated by Khamen Chorous (Day 24, the remainder).

SUNLIGHT 15: Bhamet Senesh is getting frustrated. He offers a full year's salary to his city watch commander, Khatagar, if he can capture any of the blessed kids (Day 25).

BOUNTY 17: The Bone Giants invade, and most of our nation perishes in the night. Tidal mariner Tallynd du Böll saves Pelemyn and warns the quartermaster at Fornyd (Day 1).

BOUNTY 18: Hearing of Festwyf's destruction and the death of his family, as well as the approaching army of Bone Giants, Culland du Raffert heads south to Tömerhil (Day 11).

BOUNTY 20: Gondel Vedd learns of the invasion and is sent to Brynlön with his brother and Ponder Tann. He learns that the invaders are seeking the Seven-Year Ship and heads north to Setyrön (Day 11).

BOUNTY 22: Kallindra du Paskre meets Gondel Vedd and

Ponder Tann on the road. She shares her diary account
with Gondel (Day 12). In the west, Gorin Mogen attacks
and destroys remaining Nentian forces camped outside
Baghra Khek. Gorin sends Fintan, along with Jerin
Mogen and Olet Kanek, to Hashan Khek with a message
for Viceroy Melishev Lohmet: He's staying (Day 13).

BOUNTY 23: Tallynd du Böll kills a Bone Giant officer
outside Hillegöm and steals his documents (Day 13).

BOUNTY 25: Kallindra du Paskre's caravan is attacked by
Bone Giants (Day 15).

BOUNTY 28: Stonecutter Meara collapses the Granite Tunnel
(Day 14).

BOUNTY 29: Melishev Lohmet kills a tactician from Bhamet
Senesh in response to Senesh's cry for help against the
beast callers. He sends a letter in reply asking for help
against the Hathrim; perhaps the beast callers could be
sent (Day 15).

BOUNTY 30: Gondel Vedd finds the du Paskre wagon (Day
15).

HARVEST 1: Abhinava Khose, after spending a season alone
and learning about his powers, arrives in Hashan Khek
and meets the utter shitsnake Melishev Lohmet (Day 16).

HARVEST 2: Daryck du Löngren and the Rapid Woodsmen
return to Grynek to find that the city has been massacred
(Day 25). Culland du Raffert becomes a tidal mariner in
Pelemyn (Day 16).

HARVEST 3: The cleansing at Göfyrd. Meara, Tuala, Culland,
Gondel, and Ponder all meet (Day 17).

HARVEST 15: Abhi arrives at the foothills of the Godsteeth
and sends a hive of moss hornets at Jerin Mogen (Day
18). Some days earlier, Nel Kit ben Sah was named
Champion of Forn by the First Tree and leads a picked
force to the hills above Baghra Khek, which arrives on
this date (Day 18).

HARVEST 16: Battle of the Godsteeth. Abhi and Fintan flee with Melishev's journal, the indisputable source of his thoughts that the Nentians would like to deny (Day 19).

HARVEST 17: Captain Koesha Gansu, a zephyr (the equivalent of a cyclone), sails east from Joabei with her crew (Day 21).

HARVEST 18: Gondel Vedd, having arrived in Pelemyn a few days after the cleansing at Göfyrd and been given access to the documents that Tallynd confiscated, delivers an intelligence briefing in the Wellspring. There is a traitor named Vjeko in the city, as well as two additional Bone Giant armies: one in the Mistmaiden Isles, and another in the north (Day 19).

HARVEST 20: Gerstad Daryck du Löngren and the Grynek Hunters encounter Bone Giants at the northern coast. Gyrsön kicks one of them around for a while (Day 30).

BLOODMOON 3: Tallynd du Böll, scouting for the Bone Giant army that's supposedly somewhere in the Mistmaiden Isles, finds the Seven-Year Ship, in addition to a whole lot of wraiths on an island that she names Blight (Day 21). Meanwhile, in the west, Olet Kanek and the Hathrim refugees arrive in Talala Fouz. King Kalaad the Unaware sells them some food, gives permission to found a colony in the north, and sends them upriver to meet Viceroy Naren Khusharas (Day 20).

BLOODMOON 6: Abhi and Fintan arrive in Talala Fouz, shortly before Winthir Kanek. Kanek assassinates King Kalaad the Unaware, and then the entire city is burned by the fury Pinter Stuken. Abhi dispatches Kanek with a face jumper he names Cutie Pie, and then sends a Larik whale to take care of Stuken. The plaguebringer exits the burning city by taking a boat upriver with Fintan and the Raelech diplomats (Day 20).

BLOODMOON 7: In Rael, Tuala summons the juggernaut Tarrech to muster at Mell (Day 23).

BLOODMOON 9: Tallynd du Böll and Gerstad Nara du Fesset

steal the Seven-Year Ship after a close encounter with wraiths (Day 22).

BLOODMOON 10: Abhi meets Olet Kanek outside Talala Fouz, and she learns that her father is dead by his hand. But she allows Abhi to join her group headed upriver (Day 22).

BLOODMOON 13: Fornish ambassador Mai Bet Ken learns that Melishev Lohmet will take over as king of Ghurana Nent (Day 22).

BLOODMOON 15: Abhi, Fintan, and Olet meet Viceroy Naren Khusharas and get a ton of dried meat (Day 23). In Hashan Khek, Ambassador Mai Bet Ken demands the cashiering and imprisonment of Lieutenant Ranoush Mukhab.

BLOODMOON 17: Gondel Vedd, on his way home to Kauria, discovers the name of the Eculan god, Žalost (Day 23). Mak Fin ben Fos arrives in Hashan Khek to meet Mai Bet Ken (Day 28).

BLOODMOON 18: Tallynd du Böll, with the help of a couple of hygienists, discovers that the Eculans used a kraken-blood stain on the hulls of their ships, which allowed them to cross the oceans (Day 27).

BLOODMOON 21: Koesha lands on the west coast of Ghurana Nent; her landing party is attacked by pine shrikes and a gravemaw. They head north for fifteen days to see if they can find any trace of other explorers, planning to turn around after that (Day 23).

BLOODMOON 23: Abhi meets a nonbinary gravemaw named Rrurrgh. He asks Olet Kanek to teach him the secret of enchanting something with a kenning (Day 25).

BLOODMOON 27: Tuala, Tarrech, and Temblor Priyit lead a Raelech army against the Bone Giants at Möllerud and successfully defeat them, albeit at the cost of Tarrech's life (Day 26).

BLOODMOON 28: Gondel Vedd, back home and thrown into

some court intrigue, confirms with Saviič that the Bone
Giants will not attack Kauria, because the Seven-Year
Ship is elsewhere (Day 27). Meanwhile, Daryck du
Löngren and the Grynek Hunters find a huge Bone Giant
army camped on the northern shore of Brynlön (Day
33).

BLOODMOON 29: The Grynek Hunters kill forty-nine Bone
Giants with the help of a gravemaw. New intelligence is
collected from an officer (Day 35). Meanwhile, in Khul
Bashab, Captain Khatagar finds Sudhi and kills him in the
dungeon (Day 28).

BLOODMOON 30: Gondel Vedd and Elten Maff make a
significant breakthrough with Saviič regarding the Rift
(Day 30).

BLOODMOON 32: Hanima meets Mak Fin ben Fos and Jes
Dan Kuf in the new Red Pheasant Tea Treehouse in Khul
Bashab. She learns from them that Sudhi is dead (Day
28).

AMBER 4: Koesha is shipwrecked by a kraken in the
Northern Yawn and loses a third of her crew. She meets
Abhi, Fintan, and Olet as they are about to establish
Malath Ashmali (Day 29).

AMBER 5: Daryck du Löngren delivers intelligence to
Quartermaster Farlen du Cannym in Fornyd (Day 35).

AMBER 8: Olet realizes Abhi didn't kill just her father, he
killed Jerin Mogen too. Smoke and fire ensue (Day 30).

AMBER 9: Master Courier Tuala and Master Stonecutter
Curragh meet and begin their work building a road to
Malath Ashmali (Day 31).

AMBER 10: Revolution comes to Khul Bashab. The abuses of
the city watch spark revolt, and at the end of it, Viceroy
Bhamet Senesh is trapped in his tower and Tamhan
Khatri's confederates are in charge (Day 32).

AMBER 14: Lieutenant Mukhab is put in the dungeon in
Talala Fouz. Mai Bet Ken sends Mak Fin ben Fos back to

Khul Bashab to tell the rebels they have Forn's support, but first: a kiss (Day 33).

AMBER 17: Hanima expresses to Jahi for the first time that compassion is the only moral use of power, which becomes a founding principle of the new system of government being crafted by Tamhan Khatri (Day 34).

AMBER 18: Four new tidal mariners and twelve rapids are blessed in one day at Bryn's Lung in Pelemyn (Day 35).

AMBER 19: Mai Bet Ken is thrown in the dungeon by Melishev Lohmet; he collapses from illness (Day 36).

AMBER 23: Tactician Varman is soundly defeated outside the walls of Khul Bashab, but he vows to return with a bigger army (Day 38, first part, which is continued chronologically in the next month on Barebranch 2–3).

AMBER 27: The people of Malath Ashmali meet Lorson and learn the horror of the Seventh Kenning. Mirana La Mastik is slain (Day 37).

AMBER 28: While exploring and looting Lorson's house, Fintan discovers that Lorson was hundreds of years old and in contact with a traitor named Vjeko who plotted the Bone Giant invasion. He also finds an atlas of the world, including maps of Ecula, Omesh, Joabei, and Bačiiš (Day 37).

AMBER 29: Though her journey obviously began a few days prior, this is the date that Pen Yas ben Min meets with Mak Fin ben Fos in Batana Mar Din, and he joins her on the Red Pheasant ship heading up to Talala Fouz (Day 40).

AMBER 30–31: Gondel Vedd decides to return to Brynlön and take Maron and Saviič with him. He is worried about Ponder Tann traveling to Ecula, and he has dispatches to translate, originally secured by the Grynek Hunters from the Bone Giants in the north (Day 39).

BAREBRANCH 2: Hennedigha's army is harried in the night

by bats, ebon-armored rhinos, and thunder yaks (Day 38, middle bit).

BAREBRANCH 3: Bhamet Senesh officially removed as viceroy of Khul Bashab. The monarchist army, led by Hennedigha, is routed outside the walls of Khul Bashab. Senesh is sentenced to cabbage and exile. Khul Bashab is now independent and will be ruled by elected leaders. Doubtless to become a holiday in Khul Bashab, if not the entire country someday (Day 38, remainder).

BAREBRANCH 4: Pen Yas ben Min and Mak Fin ben Fos arrive in Talala Fouz and learn that Mai Bet Ken has been abducted. Pen frees Mai Bet Ken from the dungeon (Day 41).

BAREBRANCH 5: Daryck du Löngren requests permission to scout the shore north of Fornyd and receives it from Quartermaster Farlen du Cannym. He will set out with a new rapid and a new hygienist, plus others (Day 40). Meanwhile, Pen and Mak grow a whipthorn wall around the Fornish embassy in Talala Fouz. Pen has a rather important conversation with an acorn (Day 42).

BAREBRANCH 8: Daryck du Löngren finds a lodge on the north shore, hidden in the woods. There is a hostile inside that the rapid Lörry du Bört slays, only to find out that he was possessed by a wraith, and the wraith then attempts to possess Luren. The rapid drowns both Luren and the wraith, and then they discover that the lodge is full of documents in the Eculan language. The hostile was a spy, and there's a trail heading north. Daryck vows to follow it after reporting (Day 41).

BAREBRANCH 18: The Fornish embassy is strengthened by the arrival of a squad of thornhands under the leadership of Rin Fel ben Sek (Day 43).

BAREBRANCH 20: Gondel Vedd, aboard a ship sailing from Linlauen to Pelemyn, realizes in translating the papers he was given that there are spies in Fornyd. He asks to sail directly there rather than to Pelemyn, because the quartermaster must know as soon as possible. Also he's worried that any message he delivers in Pelemyn will be intercepted by spies on the way to Fornyd (Day 42).

BAREBRANCH 22: Daryck du Löngren and the Grynek Hunters arrive at an Eculan spy outpost and supply station on the coast of the Northern Yawn, having followed the trail all the way through the Gravewood. They are unable to make any of the wraith spies talk, but they take all the written intelligence they can find (Day 42).

BAREBRANCH 30: Hanima Bhandury comes to the painful conclusion that she must leave Khul Bashab (Day 43).

BAREBRANCH 32: Gondel Vedd arrives in Fornyd and is made welcome by Quartermaster Farlen du Cannym, who gives him plenty of documents to translate, courtesy of the Grynek Hunters (Day 43).

FROST 2: Abhi, Fintan, and Koesha bid farewell to Malath Ashmali and sail east with all the Joabeians and some Nentian folks on the *Nentian Herald,* an icebreaker craft with an enchanted hull that protects against krakens (Day 39).

FROST 3: Gondel Vedd learns from his translations that there are dead drops in Pelemyn, Setyrön, and Tömerhil, though he suspects he's learned this too late. He suggests that they attempt to capture a spy and let him speak to them in the language of the Bone Giants (Day 44).

FROST 4: The arrival of a Raelech bard and courier at the Fornish embassy in Talala Fouz allows Pen Yas ben Min to hear of Malath Ashmali, a new city in the north that sounds like an ideal place for her to visit as a possible site for the Fourth Tree (Day 44).

FROST 5: Koesha Gansu, Abhi, and Fintan are surprised to find a Bone Giant army encamped for winter on the northern shore. It turns out to be a whale of a tale (Day 44).

FROST 9: Abhi and others find the lodge that Daryck found a couple of weeks earlier, on Barebranch 22. On discovering that there's a path heading south, Abhi decides to leave the *Nentian Herald,* with his apologies, because it's just too cold and he needs to get Murr and Eep warm again. Fintan is torn but chooses to go with him. They befriend a bone-collared dreadmoose (Day 45).

FROST 17: Fintan and Abhi meet Gondel Vedd, Daryck du Löngren, and Farlen du Cannym. Fintan provides copies of the maps in Lorson's atlas to Farlen and begins to understand the scope of both what's happened and what's to come. Daryck is pleased to hear the Bone Giant army suffered many casualties. Gondel learns from Lorson's files that in the spring or summer of next year— just a few short months away—there will be another invasion. On Frost 24, Abhi and Fintan leave for Rael (Day 45).

FROST 31–32: Gerstad Nara du Fesset is sent by the pelenaut to get an intelligence update from Gondel Vedd, and the update is this: Some kind of special cloak on the Seven-Year Ship is the key to seeking the Seventh Kenning on Blight, one of the Mistmaiden Isles. Nara remembers finding that cloak in the hold of the Seven-Year Ship with Tallynd du Böll and Föstyr du Bertrum at Dead Man's Point but is not sure where it is now. Perhaps Föstyr has it? Best to go check. She departs the next day to Dead Man's Point, where they left the ship. It's still there, but there's another ship there too—the *Nentian Herald* (Day 46).

SNOWFALL 1: Captain Koesha Gansu had arrived the day before, on Frost 32, at Dead Man's Point after hugging the coast of Tentacle Peninsula. Koesha is given a tour of the Seven-Year Ship and spies an unusual and exquisite cloak hanging on a hook in the cabin. She asks to try it on. The Brynt mynstad gives permission, and once it's on her shoulders she doesn't want to take it off. She feels warm but protected somehow. She offers a trade, which the mynstad accepts: her short sword, a unique weapon to him. A few hours later one of the Brynt blessed arrives—Nara du Fesset—and there is much ado about that cloak (Day 46).

SNOWFALL 4: Second Könstad Tallynd du Böll travels with Nara du Fesset to Fornyd, and they catch up with Koesha heading upriver. When they get to Fornyd, they try to convince Koesha to give up the cloak because it's key to seeking the Seventh Kenning. Koesha refuses but offers to ally with them. She proposes that she fly over the island called Blight to see if she can find the source of the Seventh Kenning (Day 47).

SNOWFALL 10: Abhi and Fintan arrive in the capital of Rael, and Fintan introduces Abhi, Murr, and Eep to the Triune Council. Abhi sends messages to Tamhan Khatri and Hanima Bhandury in Khul Bashab and enjoys a remarkable lesson in Raelech hospitality (Day 47).

SNOWFALL 12: Hanima leaves Khul Bashab with Adithi, Jahi, Charvi, and Suraji the spider queen. Right before she departs, a Raelech courier arrives with messages from Abhi. Hanima leaves smiling and tells Tamhan that love is the best (Day 48).

SNOWFALL 18: Pen Yas ben Min and the Fornish are still under siege, and no one has come to deliver an apology for Mai's imprisonment, but they're made aware of a caravan leaving the capital for Brynlön; the hope is to somehow get to Pelemyn across the continent even though the Granite Tunnel is collapsed. It's led by a meat merchant named Subodh Ramala, and he's picking up some other guys in Ar Balesh. They're to trade, of course, but also to ask for a hygienist to save the life of King Kalaad the Unwell (Day 48).

SNOWFALL 22: Hanima and company arrive in Talala Fouz and are welcomed at the Fornish compound by Mak Fin ben Fos. But then, the next day—Snowfall 23—an army floats into town. It's the remnants of Hennedigha's army, led by Bhamet Senesh. He's come to take over and crown himself king, since he's accurately assessed Melishev's condition and military capability. Suraji the spider queen—acting outside Hanima's orders—sends Cutie Pie the face jumper to assassinate him, like Abhi killed Winthir Kanek, citing an old grievance against Senesh. The impending coup melts away. Melishev is safe—weak, but safe (Day 49).

SNOWFALL 31: Fintan is given an assignment by the Triune Council: Go to Pelemyn and announce that we are sending an army to counterattack Ecula before the second wave arrives. In the meantime, he will entertain Pelemyn as an ambassador of Raelech goodwill. Abhi says he'll follow later, since he is hiring himself out as protection for a Nentian caravan angling to traverse the Poet's Range (Day 49).

SNOWFALL 32: Pen Yas ben Min reports that Viceroy Naren Khusharas arrived in town with a force to repel Bhamet Senesh, only to discover that Senesh is dead and there's no need to defend the king. He'd responded to a week-old report. But, O, glorious news! Melishev Lohmet died of his illness on Snowfall 29, before any hygienist could arrive from Brynlön *(indeed, Rölly won't send a hygienist until Thaw 18)*. And Khusharas finds out that Melishev had named him as his successor. So, rather abruptly: He's king (Day 50).

THAW 1: Fintan and Numa arrive in the Wellspring of Pelemyn. *(And here's where things get really complicated, because events are still happening elsewhere that will be* *included in the last tales of the bard, but I'm also providing present-day events in Pelemyn, where we only discover what happens elsewhere as the bard reveals it. Going forward, I'll note the calendar date and the Day of the bard's tale. Pelemyn events will follow first and any events occurring elsewhere second, together with notes on what the pelenaut and others knew and when they knew it, contrasted with what they made public or revealed to me.)* On this day in Ghurana Nent, Hanima goes to visit the new king *(which Fintan won't learn about until Eimear arrives on Day 40)*. Khusharas agrees to be King Kalaad the Last and hold elections in six months to transition to a clave republic (shared with Pelemyn on Day 50).

THAW 2: Fintan begins his tale on top of the wall with Day 1 of Volume 1, which I have titled *A Plague of Giants.*

THAW 3: Day 2 of the tales. Elynea looks for a job, doesn't find one.

THAW 4: Day 3. Fintan brings up my late wife, Sarena, and my suspicions about his motives are elevated.

THAW 5: Day 4. I discover that my home has been robbed of most everything and Elynea is gone.

THAW 6: Day 5. Fintan and I eat in a fancy place, where Föstyr tells us that Nentians are trying to assassinate Fintan for his tales of Viceroy Melishev Lohmet. After the tale, Elynea formally moves out to live with an old friend who's now her employer.

THAW 7: Day 6. Fintan and I discuss loneliness and the members of the Triune Council.

THAW 8: Day 7. I inform the pelenaut that maybe Clodagh of the Triune Council is the one to worry about. The pelenaut commands me to start training with the rapier again because the threat from angry Nentians is real. I meet Mynstad du Möcher, get a rapier, and am intensely embarrassed.

THAW 9: Day 8. I have my first lesson with the mynstad and it goes much better, though I have issues with my knee. I share that the knee injury was from long ago, when I quite nearly got eaten by a gravemaw.

THAW 10: Day 9. Fintan and I meet Gerstad Nara du Fesset at High Tide Chowder House. Three mariners are slain, along with some fish heads and a Nentian mercenary. I am stabbed, though not fatally. Nara blames herself. That night, I am guarded by a priest of the gale, Kindin Ladd, and it's a good thing, since Garst du Wöllyr breaks in with a knife, looking to make me reveal Fintan's whereabouts. I'm appalled to find out that Garst is who Elynea was staying with—and that she left his place because he hit her son, Tamöd. Kindin and I leave to search for her in the dead of night.

THAW 11: Day 10. We don't find Elynea. Fintan has a nice night chatting with Tallynd du Böll, where he learns how she got her limp *(her adventure of Bounty 23, which he shares on Day 13).*

THAW 12: Day 11: I meet the Wraith—or Master Butternuts. He wants to know how Fintan knows about Melishev's inner musings and asks me to find out.

THAW 13: Day 12. I meet with Rölly and Tallynd at Tallynd's house while longshoremen remodel my house. The schools are going to reopen, but there will be food shortages in the coming weeks.

On this date, Abhinava Khose arrives in Tömerhil with the caravan of Nentian merchants, who will continue on to Pelemyn and meet us on Thaw 18. Abhi, however, leaves them there and travels back to Fornyd to allow Ohhwuh, the bone-collared dreadmoose, to return to the Gravewood. He takes his time at this, however, prolonging the time he gets to hang out with Ohhwuh, disappearing into the Brynt backcountry for eighteen days. He arrives in Fornyd on Bloom 10, when much else is going on (Day 51).

THAW 14: Day 13. Elynea and her kids come back to live with me. Fintan and I visit a cheese shop with very little cheese in it, an indicator that many dairy farmers have gone out of business—or been killed.

THAW 15: Day 14. The Nentian ambassador, Jasindur Torghala, is expelled. *(At this time, I'm unaware that Torghala was the one who poisoned my wife at the behest of Melishev Lohmet. Röllend is aware of that, however, and doesn't tell me what's going on.)* Fintan and I have lunch at the Roasted Sunchuck and meet Hollit and Orden Panevik, the Hathrim owners. Fintan has a bit of an episode when they show up at our table; he's shaking and sweating, remembering Gorin Mogen and other horrors.

THAW 16: Day 15. I learn from Mynstad du Möcher that Nara du Fesset is away on a special mission *(to Rael, we find out later; Röllend wanted intelligence on Clodagh, since I mentioned that she might be one to watch, and the Wraith sent Nara).*

THAW 17: Day 16. Elynea is apprenticed to a Fornish woodworker. I learn that I won't be getting my job back as a history professor. Fintan learns from a Kaurian priest of the gale—Kindin Ladd—about the practice of presence to deal with his trauma.

THAW 18: Day 17. I meet Elynea's new woodworking master, Bel Tes Wey. I hear from the mynstad that Nara has returned from her mission, albeit with a broken arm. Fintan practices presence at the Roasted Sunchuck and feels better. After the day's tale, we meet with the Nentian merchants, at which point Jahm Joumeloh Jeikhs chokes on a swamp duck and dies face down in a delicious sauce. Pelenaut Röllend learns that King Kalaad the Unaware is dead and Melishev Lohmet is now king, as of five months ago. *(Neither he nor anyone else in Brynlön is aware that Melishev is already fabulously dead and that Viceroy Naren Khusharas is trying to cobble together an elected*

*government, because what Rölly is dealing with are the
merchants who left Talala Fouz a month ago, on Snowfall 18,
when Melishev was still alive.)*

THAW 19: Day 18. Nothing of significance happens in
   Pelemyn, but Fintan sings about khernhide boots.

THAW 20: Day 19. The Wraith flat out lies and informs me
   that Clodagh may have poisoned my wife, Sarena. But he
   can't do anything about it now, except maybe arrange an
   accident later. When I meet with Fintan, his lifebond,
   Numa, is in town. She relays a threat from Clodagh
   about the stolen journal. I am supposed to communicate
   to Rölly that she wants it back and they'd better not use it
   against her.

THAW 21: Day 20. This marks the beginning of Volume 2,
   which I entitled *A Blight of Blackwings*. I wake up
   hungover and discover that Elynea and the kids have
   once again moved out.

3043

BLOOM 1: Day 21. Fintan and I have breakfast with the
   pelenaut at Tallynd du Böll's house, where she shares
   that there are nutritional deficiencies being suffered by
   the refugees and she's going to donate most all of her
   gift baskets. I volunteer at the refugee kitchen.

BLOOM 2: Day 22. Nara delivers a letter from Master
   Butternuts. It asks me to take a letter and drop it under a
   waste bin outside the walls but burn the instructions
   before I do so. Feeling indebted for the remodeling and
   so on, I follow through. After leaving the letter under the
   bin, I'm immediately arrested. *(Mariners have been
   watching the site since Frost, when Gondel Vedd revealed their
   locations based on translated intelligence Daryck du Löngren
   collected from the spy huts.)* In the dungeon, I'm

interviewed by the pelenaut himself, along with his lung, and they figure out together based on handwriting samples that the Wraith is the traitor Vjeko. The Wraith is in fact an actual wraith possessing a Brynt body, and he's 150 years old or so. And I'm told that Clodagh did *not* order the death of my wife, Sarena. *(But in reviewing this episode and comparing it to what I learned later, Rölly was flat out lying to me: He said they didn't know where Gondel was, but he knew very well that the scholar was in Fornyd, translating the raft of intelligence brought to him by the Grynek Hunters and Fintan. That's how they knew where the dead drops were, after all. And, again, he knew that Torghala had killed Sarena at the behest of Melishev Lohmet and could have told me right then, but he chose not to. They were keeping things from me and concealing their sources in case I was a traitor or, more likely, came into contact with traitors, which, of course, is exactly what happened once I was contacted by Nyssa du Valas.)*

BLOOM 3: Day 23. I'm interrogated in the morning for a few hours but released in the afternoon, along with Nara du Fesset, who had also undergone questioning. The Wraith and Approval Smile have been captured and imprisoned, but I am not to reveal their existence until the pelenaut approves it.

BLOOM 4: Day 24. While writing the tales the next day, I ask Fintan how he knew about Gondel Vedd's tale from the day before. Fintan reveals that Gondel Vedd is back in Fornyd and that is intel I can relay to Rölly *(though of course Rölly already knows this and Fintan knew that too. So both Fintan and Röllend were messing with me)*.

BLOOM 5: Day 25. Nara and I are taken to ask questions of the Wraith, who refuses to answer. Rölly assigns Nara to take the letter that the Wraith wanted delivered at the dead drop to Gondel Vedd in Fornyd to get a translation. *(The result of that was never shared with me, though I imagine*

the note was to inform Lorson that the network was
compromised. But this is where Nara essentially disappears for
most of the month, due to events that will play out there soon.
And this is also when Tallynd du Böll's crucial narrative
begins.) Tallynd takes her meeting with the pelenaut and
the könstad after I leave the palace, then goes to the
archives. She leaves Pelemyn on Bloom 6, arrives in
Fornyd on Bloom 7. She goes to Blight on Bloom 8 with
Koesha, Gondel Vedd, and the Eculan prisoner Saviič,
and arrives there on Bloom 10 (Day 51).

BLOOM 6: Day 26. I try and fail to get information out of
Fintan about events happening in the north with the
Bone Giants. Fintan insists he'll tell his tale in the order it
deserves and that he's not holding back any information
that will help us right this instant.

BLOOM 7: Day 27. Fintan asks me about Clodagh's journal
again, and I have no answer.

    Meanwhile, in Tömerhil, Gerstad Daryck du Löngren
and the Grynek Hunters have been staking out a dead
drop for a long while, and they finally catch an Eculan
spy (Day 53).

BLOOM 8: Day 28. While volunteering at the refugee
kitchen, I note that the food is pretty scarce. I ask Fintan
how the Bone Giants might have gotten hold of so much
kraken blood, but the bard has no idea. *(We won't learn*
that until we gain a new source of information in Ecula.)

BLOOM 9: Day 29. The refugee kitchen is out of food,
period. I fire off a note to Rölly. Inquiring at a chowder
house, I hear that part of every fisherman's catch must be
sold to the refugee kitchen at a discount. Well, that's not
happening. Fish heads are up to something. The law isn't
working as intended.

BLOOM 10: Day 30. Sardines made it to the refugee kitchen,
the discount law having been axed. I meet Fintan at the
dockside fishblade and Numa is there, waiting for me.

They press me on the issue of the journal. I back-channel and admit that so far as I know, Rölly plans to do nothing with it. I inquire about poison-making *(because I'm still trying to figure out who could have killed Sarena, even if it wasn't Clodagh).*

Meanwhile, on the isle of Blight, Koesha Gansu and Gondel Vedd have a historic and revelatory meeting with the god of the Seventh Kenning, Sedam. Saviič does not survive his seeking (Days 51 and 52).

BLOOM 11: Day 31. Thanks to Gondel's Day 30 tale regarding the Rift, there's lots of speculation on it and what the Seventh Kenning might be, etc. *(Of course, Fintan hasn't heard yet about the meeting the day before on Blight and what was learned there.)* I wonder if Nara has found Gondel Vedd in Fornyd yet *(and I'm astounded, upon review, of how clueless I was. Nara has known Gondel's whereabouts since Frost 31).*

BLOOM 12: Day 32. We eat at the Roasted Sunchuck and are told it will be closing soon, as many restaurants have, due to lack of supply. Food's running low.

Meanwhile, in Fornyd, Nara du Fesset brings the spy that Daryck caught, Henning du Ludvöll, into an interrogation room to meet Gondel Vedd, who has just returned from the isle of Blight with Koesha (while Tallynd returned to Pelemyn to report to the pelenaut). Henning attacks Gondel, and Nara kills him to protect the scholar. The wraith in du Ludvöll immediately attempts to possess Gondel, and Farlen du Cannym is called in to destroy it. She successfully purges the wraith, but the scholar is left in a coma. The vigil begins (Day 53).

BLOOM 13: Day 33. Rumor swirls through Pelemyn that the Raelech and Fornish armies are less than two weeks away. That would put it at . . . Bloom 25–27. Same with the Kaurian fleet.

BLOOM 14: Day 34. Lots of worry in the city about the Eculan army in the north. Tallynd du Böll *(who has recently returned from Blight)* reassures the people of Pelemyn that while terrible things indeed happened during the winter, and the bard would share them soon, there is no current threat. Göfyrd, Möllerud, Setyrön, Festwyf, Fornyd, and Tömerhil are all open for settlement with incentives to become farmers. There's a resettlement ministry up and running now.

BLOOM 15: Day 35. Riot at the dockside over a shipment of food. Mynstad du Möcher comes along to break it up. I ask her about Nara and get the reply that she's "out of town," which makes me wonder what is going on in Fornyd. *(The answer, of course, is that she's anxiously hoping Gondel Vedd wakes from his coma.)*

BLOOM 16: Day 36. Some additional shipments arrive; full bellies for a few days. But Fintan warns that criminals will adjust to new measures and the crime will resume soon. We warn Hollit and Orden to protect their restaurant supplies.

BLOOM 17: Day 37. Fintan slept so little the night before, plagued by nightmares, that he sleeps through his work session with me. He dreams peacefully of sheep.

BLOOM 18: Day 38. I get a gift basket from Rölly. Yesterday's tale about the death of Lorson made the Wraith and Approval Smile talk a bit, so I don't have to keep the Wraith's existence secret anymore, since Rölly announces it to everyone. Rölly tells me that Nara is alive but isn't back from Fornyd. Rölly tells everyone in Pelemyn that he doesn't know how messages were getting to Lorson. *(But of course he did know, thanks to the Grynek Hunters rolling up that operation and Gondel Vedd's translations. He was lying to preserve those sources of intel, because more spies might be listening, and he wanted them to believe the network was still active.)*

BLOOM 19: Day 39. While I'm working at the refugee kitchen, Dame Nyssa du Valas visits me and reveals that it was the Nentians who ordered my wife to be poisoned. Specifically, Melishev Lohmet ordered it while he was still a viceroy. Nyssa reported it to the lung, and for that, they expelled the Nentian ambassador, Jasindur Torghala. Which means that the lung and the pelenaut had both known for a long while who murdered my wife and they never told me. More than that: Rölly had sent a hygienist to Ghurana Nent who could possibly cure Melishev *(we had still not heard the joyful news that Melishev died on Snowfall 29)*.

BLOOM 20: Day 40. First day of Volume 3, which I've entitled *A Curse of Krakens*. I lose the day with the Raelech bard because another bard arrives—one I've not met before, named Eimear—and she brings news from Ghurana Nent along with fresh seeming spheres for Fintan. It's just as well. I feel so betrayed by everyone regarding the death of Sarena. Fintan begins with the tale of Pen Yas ben Min from Amber 29.

BLOOM 21: Day 41. After hearing about Pen Yas ben Min and her journey to Talala Fouz, I ask Fintan if he's heard about the fate of Melishev Lohmet, and he has, but he won't tell me, under orders from the pelenaut.

BLOOM 22: Day 42. In an attempt to work around the gag order Röllend placed on Fintan, I go to visit Kindin Ladd and arrange to interview Nentian citizens the next day.

  Meanwhile, in Fornyd, Gondel Vedd awakes after spending ten days comatose. He's lost some Brynt and Eculan language, owing to damage the wraith did (Day 54).

BLOOM 23: Day 43. Kindin Ladd informs me he's been gagged by the pelenaut as well. But he gives me the idea to start this chronological timeline and at least begin to figure out how badly I've been deceived.

BLOOM 24: Day 44. The slow-rolling famine arrives—we're pretty much out of food and I don't eat much—but it won't last terribly long, because we're informed the Raelech army is arriving the next day with supplies.

BLOOM 25: Day 45. The Raelech army arrives. Pelemyn finally hears about the Eculans' plans for a second invasion in the day's tales, which no doubt spurs the visit that I receive the next day.

BLOOM 26: Day 46. Dame Nyssa du Valas comes to visit me at the refugee kitchen again and asks what else I may have heard regarding the invasion. I'm utterly unaware of how suspicious that is, until mariners arrive and arrest her. She was a double agent. A spy for the Eculans, using me as a source of intelligence. And I didn't see it.

BLOOM 27: Day 47. The Fornish army arrives. I confirm that Nyssa du Valas at least worked at the Nentian embassy, as she'd claimed, so her story about the poisoning of Sarena was still plausible.

BLOOM 28: Day 48. I'm making more progress on this timeline and understanding the scope of the lies I've been told.

BLOOM 29: Day 49. The Kaurian fleet arrives, under leadership of Zephyr Bernaud Goss.

BLOOM 30: Day 50. Daryck, Nara, Abhi, Koesha, and Gondel Vedd all arrive in Pelemyn from Fornyd and huddle up with the bard, which will allow him to share all the forthcoming revelations about Sedam and so on. But after the day's tales, where I finally learn that Melishev is dead, Rölly shows up and tells me I had essentially been bait to catch spies from almost the beginning, and Nyssa du Valas took that bait. In response, I get really drunk on a bottle of the Good Shit.

BLOOM 31: Day 51. I recover from my hangover.

BLOOM 32: Day 52. A day of revelations: We hear about Sedam and his version of the origins of the Rift, which

Gondel and Koesha heard about on Bloom 10, so historians can argue which date was more important—the day the tree fell or the day we all heard it.

RAINFALL 1: Day 53. I choke down a Kraken Dawn and discuss the previous day's revelations with Fintan and how the world may or may not change as a result.

RAINFALL 2: Day 54. I meet Elynea and her kids by chance and am uplifted to hear they're doing well. I say goodbye to Chef du Rödal at the refugee kitchen on my last day, because I'm to leave with the fleet.

RAINFALL 4: The allied fleet departs for Ecula.

RAINFALL 13: An unfortunate encounter with a cavern-jawed eel. Zephyr Bernaud Goss is lost; Second Könstad Tallynd du Böll takes over leadership of the fleet.

RAINFALL 20: Allied forces destroy the Eculan fleet at Riba Oči and gain the assistance of Fanje, a member of Šest.

RAINFALL 23: Allied forces destroy the Citadel at Sveto Selo; Daryck du Löngren perishes while saving the life of Nara du Fesset; Koesha Gansu slays a lifeleech, the Cloister is captured, the isposniks leading the cult of Žalost all fall. Negotiations with Šest begin, and a new age of peace has a chance to take hold.

FOALING 17: Captain Koesha Gansu returns to Blight and confronts Sedam, though we do not learn this until months later, since she sails home afterward and summers in Joabei before revisiting Pelemyn in the autumn and sharing the news. I would argue that this date is the true end of an age and the beginning of a new one: It was the end of seven kennings and the beginning of six.

KAURIAN CALENDAR

Though Ghurana Nent insists on a different timekeeping system for their internal use, the six nations otherwise use the Kaurian calendar. It begins on the day of the spring equinox and ends on the last day of winter. It uses eight-day weeks: Ten months have four weeks, but months six and twelve have three, for a total of 368 days. A few days are usually subtracted from the last week of the year to ensure that the spring equinox falls on Bloom 1, which means in practical terms that Thaw is often only twenty-one to twenty-two days long. Bloodmoon 1 is usually the day after the autumn equinox.

The Giant Wars began in the winter of 3041 with the eruption of Mount Thayil and the destruction of Harthrad, followed closely by the du Paskre Encounter and the capture of Saviič in the east.

SPRING SEASON

Bloom (32)   Rainfall (32)   Foaling (32)   (96 days)

SUMMER SEASON

Sunlight (32)   Bounty (32)   Harvest (24)   (88 days)

APPENDIX

AUTUMN SEASON

Bloodmoon (32)   Amber (32)   Barebranch (32)   (96 days)

WINTER SEASON

Frost (32)   Snowfall (32)   Thaw (21)   (85 days)

DAYS OF THE WEEK

Kaurian Language

Deller, Soller, Tamiller, Keiller, Shaller, Feiller, Beiller, Reiller

Raelech Language

Delech, Solech, Tamech, Kelech, Shalech,
Felech, Belech, Ranech

ACKNOWLEDGMENTS

This trilogy was a labor of love—the reason I wanted to become a writer, in fact. The stories of folks who aren't world leaders or legendary warriors are rarely told, merely hinted at in phrases like "there was much suffering." Or, worse than that, their stories are ignored completely, their injuries, illnesses, and deaths tallied as mere statistics. And telling those stories from a first-person point of view—twenty-two different ones, all told—required a structure that I hadn't seen before. So I am deeply grateful to my editor, Tricia Narwani, for her keen sense of storytelling and patient feedback as I tried to write something new.

Likewise, I am grateful to the team at Del Rey—Scott Shannon, Keith Clayton, cover designer Regina Flath, copy editor Kathy Lord, page designer Caroline Cunningham, Bree Gary, David Moench, Ashleigh Heaton, and Tori Henson, who shepherded the book through many processes to get it into your hands.

Thanks to Alan O'Bryan for being a stalwart champion of the series from the very beginning and an excellent friend.

Speaking of excellent friends, super mega turbo thanks to Delilah S. Dawson and Chuck Wendig for keeping me sane through the pandemic and my years-long process of finishing this. They were both early adopters of the Seven Kennings, but more than that, their reassurance and encouragement during our frequent chats were key.

Daily good vibes also came from Kace Alexander and Jason Hough, who were always ready to deploy the brain lube.

Would it be weird to thank my camera? My trips outdoors to capture nature did much to keep me even-keeled when the anxieties of the world threatened to derail my progress. Maybe I should just thank the birds of the world for being so dang cute.

And I am very grateful to Mom, Kimberly, and Levi, for whom I would do anything. Love is the best.